CULTURES

Tina Bridges

authorHOUSE®

AuthorHouse™
1663 Liberty Drive
Bloomington, IN 47403
www.authorhouse.com
Phone: 1 (800) 839-8640

Published by AuthorHouse   08/23/2016

ISBN: 978-1-5246-0519-3 (sc)
ISBN: 978-1-5246-0520-9 (hc)
ISBN: 978-1-5246-0518-6 (e)

Print information available on the last page.

This book is printed on acid-free paper.

Dedication

To my dear friend Sonia who took the time from her busy schedule to help me with editing this book. I like to say thank you for wanting to see me succeed. Thank you for all you done. And I hope the journey was as good for you as well as my next reader. Thank You.

From the author to the reader.

This is my suggestion on how to read this book. I feel its best to end a chapter just before going to bed and when you awake in the morning its best to start the new chapter.

Good reading,

Reader

My oldest daughter say, "Mommy you're my role model."

My son said "I'm his' hero."

And my baby girl ... Well, I'm just her mommy.

Prologue

I don't know what to say about this. I don't even know why I haven't flipped the fuck out yet.

You know ... like flip out like the "twilight zone" or went psycho and started paying them back for what they done. (They know what they did). Trying to pretend like nothing happened. Acting as if I have a psychosis disease, walking around like I don't exist, telling everybody lies about me when asked "Where's Electra?"

Anyway I haven't gone over the deep end yet ... ... so I guess I've got to tell this story. I might as well.

Remember years ago that picture that came on TV? On, one of those late nights, back in the eighties? It was a TV show but it also asked a question. The question was "What Ever Happened to Mary Jane?" Just hearing that question and saying that to myself spooks the shit out of me. "What Ever Happened to Mary Jane?"

Shit!

Dam!

I could just hear the people saying what ever happened to her? Me? ... Electra? Man, I don't want to end up like her, (Mary Jane.) People asking that question about me, wondering ... what had ever happened to her? Pointing their finger and whispering that dreadful question about ME. Watching me with pity and wondering to themselves ... ... What happened?

Fuck that! Fuck that shit. I am not going out like that!

I'll tell you what happened to her. I should know because, because ... ... I'm her.

It's me, Electra. Wait ... but before I talk, I have to ask you something? Do you really want to know the truth? Are your ears willing to hear what I have to say? Are you going to let me tell my story?

Good. Then let's get started. Get comfortable because it's something else!

I am going to make everything right and set the record straight. I owe it to my kids and to you. You know what, I owe it to myself too. Yep! It's going to be hard to write it all down but if the good Lord wakes me up another day, then just maybe, I have the time … … … … … … … … … … …

So, here goes.

Chapter One

November 2008

In Brooklyn, New York City. Another year in the shelter, and yes, it is around the holiday time. I hate living here but I have nowhere else to live, shower, eat, shit or lay my head.

Happy Thanksgiving. Merry X-mas and-let's not forget, Happy New Year.

"Again Homeless."

"No family."

"No, love ones around me."

"No familiar faces of the good times of the life I had before."

"Nothing."

I had family and lots of close friends at one point in my life, but they are nowhere around. Instead, I'm here in the shelter with a bunch of losers. Dud-spud motherfuckers. All day eating fat ass bitches. I shouldn't really call these women out of their' name because like it or not, some of them became my chums, associates, and pals.

It is their faces I see when I wake up in the morning and when I go to bed at night. It is their faces I see on holidays, such as Mother's Day, Fourth of July ....and this is the season to be jolly.

Oh! Let me not forget how we bring in the New Year together. When it's my birthday, I'm with them... (Even though I do not mention what day it is). They are the ones I confide in when I am angry or when things go wrong. I see them when I eat breakfast, dinner, or going to, or from work. They are everywhere in my life.

Lord knows, I have seen my share of shelters. It is a revolving door to some of us, including me. When I'm outside taking care of my personal business. I occasionally bump into females I knew from previous shelters, just to find out that she too, is still in the shelter system.

It is sad when I hear news like that. What kind of life is that? Moving from one shelter to the next? Anyway, these girls aren't my family members, neither do they treat me like family but somehow, they became my family in a sense.

These females have taken the place of my bloodline family. Some of them sit in the seat where old girlfriends from Westbrook Project had sat.

One thing is for sure, no matter how many times I have come through those doors, I have seen familiar faces as well as unfamiliar faces. Their bearing is still the same. Their expressions are of sadness, loneliness, humanist lost, anger, feeling unloved and sick.

When I look at them I see pass their outer appearance. It like I could see a glimpse of their soul. What they are hiding. What they are not saying, or asking. They hide behind the façade of being a strong woman but some of them have been abused and are very hateful. Some of them are sick mentally, physically or both.

Lots of them are on some sort of medication. Some of them wear dirty-messy looking wigs on their heads. Some of them talk to themselves. Some do not talk at all. Some of them are bullies and behave like children, with their loud talking. Some girls only are followers.

Many have already given up on life by going along with the flow. They have given into circumstances and things such as drugs, alcohol and prostitution. They stop caring about their own appearance by gaining tons of weight. Most of them enter into the world of lesbianism and start losing their femininity. They are made to become weak by society and also, by the rejection of love-ones.

By their own choice they let go of their dreams and their hopes and start to fade away.....slow.....slowly....but surely. It is a pity to look at someone and notice her life is being sapped because of boredom. Thinking that they're living life only for any sort of handouts, such as food, clothes, loose change or a cigarette.

So far, in my experience of being homeless, I have come across women from all walks of life and lifestyles. These women, ethnic are from Korean, Mexicans, Black women from all heritage, Caucasian women from all heritage, Asian women from all heritage, Spanish women from all heritage, Chinese, Indian and Jewish. Some of the women are mothers, grandmothers, young adults and the elderly. The youngest females I have seen living in the shelter, was nineteen. The oldest female I've met so far, was seventy-eight.

I could tell ya one thing for sure, homelessness does not discriminate. Regardless of all of what I just said most of them are beautiful and smart. Some are extremely talented; from artisanship and to how they lived with little to nothing financially. Most of them are fighters, but due to the fact some had already given up on life. I do not see them as survivors.

Somehow along the way, we seem to have gotten lost, dumped and forgotten. Somehow we've lost our way along this path which we know as life. So long, I've been hanging on trying so very hard to fight and stay alive and not give up on my own life. Not give up on my dreams such as a loving marriage, a great job and a lifetime of friends. What good is a life if it's not shared, nourished, supported, loved and.....And lived?

I don't want to waste away like Mary Jane, and simply disappear. I don't want to stop believing in God as if He didn't exist. As if some really smart person made the bible up and added fake prophets.

At this point I am wondering what the resident women see, when they look at me? What kind of vibes am I giving off? I could hear them whispering, "She keeps coming back to the shelter herself. She's always well dressed. Mind her business….always on the go….yet, still she here with us, again."

Not getting off the subject.

Right now, I am reflecting on a conversation I had with my thirteen-year-old son, JB. The topic was about when I get my own place. In a slow and low tone, he said "Mom, right now, you live in a shelter and you look so very nice."

My son thinks I'm hot, and that's cute. However, I'm at the lowest point of my life. What JB doesn't know is, I'm trying to hang on, and I am getting a little discouraged.

I can't believe I've been living this way for so very long. It's not easy living in a shelter. There are just way to many rules…..**And** they change depending on the staff member who wants to enforce it. I jotted down a couple of the shelter rules I have come across.

Whenever any residents enter into the building, a security guard must hand-search you. All of your belonging must go through the scanner (ex) bags, suitcase, pocketbook, coats, hat, scarf etc. Everything has to go through the scanner. Then on top of that, security has to perform a physical hand-search on all items, and the resident as well.

In the shelter, we share sleeping quarters. I like to call them dorms. Nine - ten girls' sleeps in a dorm. We lay on cots. The only thing that separate the person sleeping next to you, is this twelve by seventeen locker, or in another shelter it can be half of a wall, and then again, there can be nothing at all, but just another bed.

The guards are the ones who turns the lights out by eleven pm, and the guards are the ones who turns the lights on at six am every day, except on Saturday and Sunday. Those are the only two days a resident could stay in her' bed without permission, and those are the only two days security do not enter the dorms, to turn on the lights.

During the week, Monday – Friday residents must be up and fully dressed ready to leave the dorms, by nine-am. No matter what the weather condition is. Nor does it matter if you have somewhere to go or not.

We sign for everything too. The staff employees serves our meals, three times a day. Every time you eat, you sign. We sign for laundry slots, and we also sign weekly for two small boxes of their detergent.

We sign for a care-kit package, which contain toiletries. We sign for our monthly supply of sanitary napkins and we sign weekly for our bed linens. We sign for special events, such as going to the movies or something as simple as a nature walk.

We sign the attendance sheet if we attended, or participate in a church service. We sign for our TV slots. We even have to sign in and out for charging our cell phone and picking up and receiving our mail. A resident has to sign her initials-when taking her dosages of medication.

We sign when our contrabands have been confiscated, and we sign when we take that contraband off the premises. We sign to use their computers, and, to borrow their library books. We sign for recreational activities, and most importantly, we sign nightly for our bed, which is anywhere between nine-thirty and ten-pm.

Put it like this, we sign for everything.

Every shelter has their own set of rules but one thing is for all shelters, and that rule applies to all the shelter systems, regardless as to who's running them.

How can I forget...... us grown women have a curfew we have to be in our dorms every night sitting on our beds by ten pm. That is the official bed check time. DHS, is the abbreviation for Department of Homeless Services. Every bed has got to be accounted for unless your caseworker has been given documented reason explaining why you are late.

If a resident is not on time to sign for her' bed, the staff has the right to strip that bed. Removing all linens from the bed. Clipping the locker and bagging up all personal items that's inside her' locker, as well as around her bed.

That resident who had lost her' bed has to wait for another bed. She has to stay inside the intake office to find out if her' bed is still available, but, has to wait until bed check is officially over and that could be any time after eleven pm but no later than eleven-thirty.

That client has to wait until the shift supervisor, also known as the ASW counts every bed. Depending on the outcome, more likely, she would be given a different dorm, with a different bed. **Then**.......she has to wait for her bagged items.

Sometimes if all the beds are accounted for, staff would have to ship/bus the resident out to another shelter just for a night ...and here's a tip from me to you; do get back early to that shelter because you have to have your name put on their list to retain the next available bed. The first intake/ client on the list, is the first intake/client to a bed.

We residents also have to get TB shoots every six months to a year. The reason for that is we live in a large close population of people. Its call the city shelter. There are woman from all over the world gathered together in this place. For your knowledge, there are family and private shelters too. Just to let you know, I also have lived in, family, domestic violence and private shelters, as well.

I've never started out living in shelters but to my surprise I ended up living in them.

Now at this point in my life, I am wondering what the shelter staff are thinking this time when they hear security on their walkie-talkies saying, "We have a Miss Electra Tami Jones downstairs for intake." I could just hear the intake employees saying to themselves, "She's back too? Again?

The intake staff replies, "Yeah! Let her up, she's one of ours."

Today I'm finding it difficult to keep living this way. How did I get lost...dumped...and forgotten? So I decided to write. Just in case I don't make it. How the **fuck** did I get like this? Man, my life damn sure didn't start out this way. To tell you the truth, at this moment right now, I feel afraid to look back on it.

....Why?

I notice my hands are trembling. Why is my heart aching? Why am I having these feelings?

Why do parts of me not want to go back ....back into my past? Then parts of me want to tell everything. I want to expose the torture, the hate and all the rage that I have inside.

I sometimes ask God for direction - in secret. I came to call on Him because I was told that he listens. That He knows all things. All you got to do is ask Him. For he is God of all Gods. That He and He alone made the heaven and the earth. He is the author and finisher of our faith. And He will reveal...........................All Truth.

I say... "I know that you are holy. For me to come in your presence I must become holy." So I say, "God forgive me for any wrong doings that I may have done. Have mercy on my soul, and hear my prayer."

Let me pray:

"Our Father which art in heaven. Hallowed be thy name. Thy kingdom come. Thy will be done on earth, as it is in heaven. Give us this day our daily bread. And forgive us our debts, as we forgive our debtors. And lead us not into temptations, but deliver us from evil. For thine is the kingdom, and the power, and the glory forever. Selah."

I say, "God forgive me for any wrong doings direct my path and clear my thoughts. And God as I write remove all the evil. Bring me out of darkness and into the light. Shine nothing but the truth forward. Help me to recall everything from beginning to end. For without you, I know that nothing can be done. I ask all this, in the name of Jesus Christ.

Amen."

Stop! Reader, now let's go back.... come go with me back......*back into time.*

Here I am seven years later waiting to push out my third and last child. I said, "Look Thomas my water broke it's time. I need to go to the hospital. Barf, Barf, Barf."

Feeling weak I said, "Oh I feel sick Thomas. I don't feel good."(Sounds of throwing up.) "Barf, Barf, Barf."

Thomas said "Alright Tami I'm going to take the kids downstairs to Shelby's."

My panty and pants were wet so I went into the bedroom to change. Oh I see my water broke. As I was changing I heard Thomas calling to Champagne. He said "Your mother's about ready to have the baby. Get ready to go downstairs to Shelby' house, and get a couple of pampers for JB while I get him, and his' bottle."

I was not about to leave out of the house with a big wet stain. I heard him say through the bedroom door "I'm leaving to go downstairs with the kids now. I'll be right back."

Listening, I heard our apartment door close. Damn, I'd just changed my clothes and I barfed again. Thoughts started going through my mind, (this is a first for me, spitting up so much.)

Thomas came back into the house, he asked me "Are you ready to leave?" I told him, "Just let me get my documents. I'm ready I said."

As we walked out of the door and reached to the first floor, I saw Shelby. She was standing by her door smiling. She too is pregnant. Shelby going on her sixth child with her' husband Wilbert. She is my closest friend in the building. Her marriage isn't a happy one though. She was always complaining how he's never home. How her husband had never made any money and how she is so sex starved.

Shelby is the saddest person I ever knew. Even though others on the block may view her as, she and Wilbert are having another baby. I know them so much better. She's such a dear to me but she still reminds me of: The little old lady who lives in a shoe, has so many children, she doesn't know what to do.

Anyway, knowing what I do know about her. I was still very shocked when she told me she was expecting again.

As Thomas and I hurried past her she said, "See ya Tami when you come home with your pretty bundle of joy." I looked at her while saying, "Um, I don't feel good." Shelby put a stupid look on her face and said, "You're not supposed to, you're having a baby."

Just at that moment Wilbert had poked his' head out from the door, and told Thomas "Drive safely," and said to me "I hope it's a fast delivery." There were quite a few people standing outside in front of our building as we passed them by. They said to us "Good luck!"

Thomas and I are the hippest couple in the building out of my so called group. I'm the youngest. Shelby and Wilbert, are about five to seven years older than me. Then Thomas, well he has me by ten years.

We arrived at the hospital and surprisingly, the pain wasn't intense like I've known it to be. Instead of unbearable pain I was sick as a dog. I felt so nauseated and weak with this delivery.

The doctor, he had checked my cervix opening. He said, "You need to walk around the halls of the hospital, because your cervix hasn't opened enough for you to deliver the baby."

We started walking through the corridors of the hospital, with me spitting up.

Now the pain is starting to kick in. I started moaning, "Thomas the pain!"

We went back into the delivery room. I walked in saying, "I'm ready" to the doctor. He began checking me, his hands hurting me so much. The doctor inserted an IV in my vein and attach the bag to a tall pole that had wheels on it.

Still.... he sent me back walking the hallways.

Once again walking down the hospital hallway as people were watching us. I'm so weak from all the vomiting. Thomas put one of his' arms around me and the other one in front of me for support as I slowly walked the corridor. "Ooh....Ooh - barf...barf – man," I said weakly as I wiped my mouth. This is really a first for me with all this vomiting.

Every pregnancy is different. I guess.

Walking...and walking. After a while I said, "Come on Thomas lets go back to see if it's time." This time they put me into one of their rooms. I'm so weak. Maybe because of all the vomiting I got dehydrated or this is just the way my labor is going with this baby. Thomas, he escorted me inside the room.

The nurse said to me as I laid down on the hospital bed, "You're having dry labor. If the baby doesn't come out soon it may become distress and we may have to take the baby. You might have to have a cesarean." Or she said something about receiving... a needle in my spine?

Weakly, **but** I immediately said "No. I want this birth to be a normal delivery just like with my other two children."

On that note, the nurse said, "You will be given some medicine to help along with the delivery, so just relax." While lying-in the room, that's when I thought, (maybe it's a girl)? Pain and more pain. Not to mention the drama of child birth.

Thomas said "Well it may be a while. I'll be right back."

He had to pick up the children from Shelby and drive them over to my' mother. Shelby already had enough on her hands. Now in her' last trimester close to her own due date, and taking care of her' demanding family. I couldn't impose on her anymore. Plus Thomas had something else he had to do but for the life of me, I can't remember what it was. I watched him exit the room.

The nurse comes back into the room. She attaches another small bag to the IV and adjusts the dripping dosages that flowing into my veins. At that moment right then and there I knew the baby was a girl. As I lay there looking at the bed rails along side of me I found my mind drifting on the delivery of my first born child, Champagne.

I gave birth to my first born seven years ago. Back then I was living in the projects which I grew up in, Westbrook. At that time I was with this guy name Tray. He is Champagne's biological father. Anyway, I lived in that apartment with my mother, step father, my sister Tonya and her' newborn baby girl, named Hope.

Reminiscing that night I went into labor with Champagne. We were all hanging out. Riding around in Desmond's car, (that's Tonya' boyfriend). Tray and I was in the back seat and for some reason or another we were arguing. Honestly, we had always argue and fought but I'll speak about that later.

Anyway we were arguing and I wanted out of the car immediately. Desmond pulled up in front of the projects. I got out of the car and Tray followed me. He was going on and on about some bullshit. I'm telling you that's why my baby Champagne came two weeks earlier than her due date...........Stress!

He talks from the car, to the elevator. He talked while we were riding in the elevator as we were passing the floors. He talked until we reached the twelfth floor. We got out of the elevator. He still going strong till we reach in front of my mother apartment door. Standing in front of the door I realized I left the house key in my purse and my purse in the back seat of Desmond car. I'm quite sure they drove off already because Desmond was speaking on picking up a bag of weed.

I knocked on the door.

Damn! My mother not home. Now I had to stay in the hallway until someone came home. Tray still talking all that bullshit, embarrassing me, because I know some of my neighbors are listening.

You know how it is in the project with all those noisy people.

I was wishing that he'd shut up.... shut Up.... Shut Up and that's when the pain hit me, pow- ya! It was strong and powerful.

I remember I put my arms around my stomach and laid on the floor. Tossing, turning and moaning. Tray stood there watching me and then he said rapidly "Yo, T get up, get up." He always spoke fast especially when he's on a rampage. Tray preferred calling me T, its short for my middle name, Tami. T & T. Tray and Tami.

Anyway, about twenty minutes later my next door neighbor opens up her' door. I guess she heard the commotion.

Miss Perking asked, "Electra are you alright?"

Laying there on the floor I said, "Yeah." I sat up from the floor with my back now leaning against my apartment door. I said, "I'm waiting for someone to come home. I left my house keys in Desmond' car. Hopefully he and Tonya be back shortly."

Knowing damn well they won't be. Both of them knew how Tray behaved when he's high. Desmond and Tonya enjoyed it when Tray made a damn fool of himself in front of other people with me by his' side, embarrassing both of us.

Miss Perking said, "Electra you don't look to well would you like for me to call EMS?"

I didn't want to look her in her face because I was so ashamed. I caught her rolling her eyes at Tray. I could tell she didn't approve of him. He such a piece of shit. Now I'm having his' child. He was such a loser.

I said, "No thanks, I'm just in a little pain that's all."

She said knowingly, "Well you look as if you could be going into labor." I said slowly, "Naw, I'm not due for another two weeks."

The pain hit me again. Tray wasn't saying shit. He pulls out a cigarette and started smoking it. I was pretending to be strong in front of her, like… you can go back inside. It's okay. I got this.

Miss. Perking knew me since I was a little girl. She'd been our next door neighbor for many years. She knew my mother and father very well before they split-up. She even knows when my stepfather entered into our lives.

Her daughter Paris and I attended the same elementary school. We were in the fourth, fifth and six grade together. We even attended the same Jr. High School.

Miss Perking insisting, "Listen Electra what harm can it be in getting checked out, right?"

Tray said in a fast tone "Yeah T, I don't see nothing wrong with that."

A woman's body is amazing. It's weird. The different stages we go through. The changes in our body - giving birth - you know the whole pregnancy thing. I was noticing in the mirror that morning how my neck got so dark. Even the line I never knew I had. The line that splits my stomach straight down the middle got dark.

Another pain hit me and this was a little stronger than the first. I remember saying, "Oh shit." I look up at Miss Perking, "Yeah go ahead and make the call." She closed her' door Tray bent down in front of me. He said slowly in a more concerning voice "Yo, T, yeah you should get off the floor. Come on stand up."

I told him, "Leave me. I feel comfortable right here." Miss Peking opens her door and said, "They'll be here shortly." Tray said "Thanks." Before I could tell her I appreciated it and thank you. She closed her' apartment door.

Tray finally shut the fuck up. I guess he realized he is about to become a father. His eyes were glistening from the weed he was smoking early. I heard the paramedics getting off the elevator. The paramedic asked me "Can you stand?" I said, "Yeah. I hope so."

They helped me off the floor and the four of us got into the elevator. When the elevator door opened for us to exit, another pain struck. I notice the pain was stronger than the last.

My first time going into labor and with this last sharp pain I couldn't move. I had to stand still and wait till the contraction passed. Once it passed I walked as quickly as I can. I walked out of the building moaning going towards the ambulance.

The paramedic drove Tray and I to Kings County Hospital. That year, that month it was baby boom season at the hospital. Kings County delivery room was so full that I couldn't even get a bed. They had me laying on a stretcher in the hallway, in the delivery-room area.

I remember hearing all different kinds of crying, screams, moaning, cursing coming from the ladies in the rooms, behind the walls. I recall others trying to calm down their love ones. It was very frightening to me. I watched the nurses and doctors walking quickly pass me, going from room to rooms.

I'm telling you it was so busy, not one staff member even acknowledged me. I was left all by myself. Finally a nurse showed up. She moved me to another room, it looks like an examination room. She said, "A doctor will be with you soon and she left."

Tray came beside me and grabbed my hand. He didn't know what to say he was just standing there saying nothing, doing nothing. The contractions are really getting strong that I couldn't really keep my cool. I asked him, "Tray can you go get the doctor."

The pain was getting so **intense** I yelled at him, "I want this baby out of me right **now**. Go and get the doctor!" He left in a hurry. I know he was glad to have an excuse to leave anyway because, he didn't come right back.

Oh man the pain is getting unbearable. The contraction had me to a point where I couldn't even speak. I was just curled up trying to catch my breath before the next contraction came. At this point, I wasn't even tossing and turning anymore. I was just curled up, looking at that big window, sweating, then …….I heard a voice….. Or did I?

"Electra, Electra," the voice is coming from behind me. It became louder as she walked into the room. I was in such pain I couldn't barely open my eyes. "Electra," she said. I slightly open my eye to see it was my mother. She was standing in front of me. Then I notice the bar attach to the hospital bed was pulled up. The nurse must've had done it before she left.

My mom said, "Hi, Electra it's me. Desmond drove me over here." My mother didn't say much either. She just stood over me looking at me.

I was in such pain. I was sweating so badly. I had sweated out my perm. I was curled up but my hand had to be out in front of me because she took my hand and my sweated hand just slip right out of her palm and dropped on the stretcher. Then she was gone.

The pain had gotten so severe that I wanted to jump out of that big window that's in front of my view but I couldn't. It was too high up, besides I couldn't get my ass off the stretcher if I wanted to.

I heard her voice over my head. In the back of me, where the door was. Mother was saying, "I'll be in the waiting room with Tray and Desmond." I knew exactly what that meant. I just couldn't focus on that right then. Anyway, that's my very first time looking so weak in front of my mother.

The pain is really intense, so for the doctor, I started screaming, "Doctor!"

"Doctor….Doctor! Doctor."

"Doctor…ouch …..Ooh this shit hurt," I said to myself.

I found myself cursing, "Fuck! I want this fucking baby out of me." I was saying other stuff too that I don't want to put down on paper.

It's my first experience. I really didn't know what to expect or how to act. I wish I had gone to one of those pregnancy classes about birth and delivery, but back then, things weren't so knowledgeable like it is now. So I started yelling like the others, but I was calling for the "Dooocttoooor! Doctor!" The pain is unbearable. I can't take it. Ooooh my God it hurts so bad, oooo.

Again I yelled "Doctor!" Then I started cursing at him for not coming to me. "#@&%!."

When the Doctor came to me, angrily he asked "Why are you making all this noise?"

I said in a whining voice, "It hurts, it hurts."

The Doctor asked me to open my legs. I remember I didn't want to. The black male doctor said "Come on you wasn't acting like this when you became pregnant were you?" He said loudly "Come on now there are a lot of women waiting on me so open, your, legs."

I started acting like a child whining about the pain. He became impatient with me he stood there and looked me dead in my eyes and said in a very stern but serious voice "Open your legs."

I did what the doctor said but I did it slowly, really not wanting to because of the pain.

I manage to open my legs. He quickly put a pair of gloves on. Then he put one hand on my bended knee. I felt his muscle strength as he spread my legs wider apart with no kind of gentleness as he checked my insides.

I started flicking my head from side to side bearing the pain. A nurse came by my side to comfort me. She started rubbing my hand to let me know she understands that it must hurt but this is something that had to be done. The nurse held my hand tightly for support as she watch what the Doctor was doing to me.

I could feel his rough hands inside of me-examining me, poking me, rubbing my inside. He burst my water bag because I felt warm liquid running out of me-wetting up the stretcher I laid on. He continues.....until I felt his' finger touch and scratch the top of my baby' head. Until this day Champagne has a small dent on her scalp. Too bad I was too young with problems and inexperience because I could have sued that Doctor, I think.

Anyway he asked the nurse to move me to a bed in another room. The nurse lined the stretcher I was laying on next to a bed. This room wasn't so bright. As a matter of fact, it was dim. The nurse said to me, "You have to move from the stretcher to the bed." As I was sliding from the stretcher to get on to the bed I got hit with another serious contraction.

By now I was learning how to deal with those contractions. I knew I couldn't move. I had to wait till it passed. The only problem, was they were coming much faster, stronger, and lasting longer.

Once I got on the bed. I told the nurse while moaning, "I want this baby out of me. It ... it hurts." I remember I was looking at her-in her face. She was a dark skinned black lady. A little on the chubby side. I wanted her to understand I meant business. I was so serious.

The nurse sat down at the bottom of my bed she said, "Open your legs," as if I was a child. She looked between my legs. She stood up, looked at me, and said, "Okay push."

The word push, echo inside my head. I heard her clearly. She wanted me to push.

I said the word again to myself. "Push!?"

I got frighten!

I was scared and the nurse knew it.

The nurse said, "**Push!**" as if to shock me back into reality. I thought to myself, "Oh shit. The time has come." Then for a quick second, I thought on how the pain must feel if I did pushed out this baby inside of me that made my stomach look so big.

I started thinking.......I know this is really going to hurt...... and I didn't want to push because of the pain I was already in.

Out of frustration and the stress of many patients, the busy nurse seems to be overwhelmed. She immediately started to move away from my bed. She said, "You don't want to have this baby," and she started walking away from me.

I was watching her back as she started disappearing farther out of the room. I didn't want her to leave so I pleaded, "No! Wait, don't leave me."

Yeah, I was scared. I knew it was going to really hurt because those contractions weren't no joke. I wanted this over with. The last thing I wanted was to feel another contraction so I open my legs and I said to myself, "**Fuck it**...push!"

But silly me, I didn't even know how to push. I gave a light push. The sounds of "uummh," came more from out of my mouth, than me actually trying to push the baby out of me.

When the nurse saw that, the nurse kept walking she didn't even look back. Not wanting her to leave me alone. I quickly moved in a pushing position.

"Wait nurse," I said......She wants me to push well then I'll give her a push. I put both of my hands on each bended knee and gave a hard push from within, as if I was constipated. "EEeemmmh!"

I felt a huge object from within. Slowly coming down my tiny birth canal path as it was tearing up my flesh in my insides. An unstoppable force, strong and steadily trying to free itself out pushing at full force. It felt like, as if an earthquake was going on inside of me-ripping me, tearing me up from the inside.............**Wow!** The act of giving birth!

The next pain that came.... Oh...my...goodness! From inside it felt like a heavy huge hard object, piercing, ripping up and opening my tiny birth canal. That pain! And that feeling, sent me to scream in degrees. First from soft to medium... To loud...Too louder.... Too loudest, all in one breathe. My scream was so long and so loud that a bunch of staff members came running to me.

All I saw were people on each side of my bed rolling me down the corridor as fast as they could as they went racing down the hospital hallway. I caught a glimpse of myself in a mirror that was on top of the hospital hallway wall. What I saw was my head moving from side to side in quick motion with my mouth wide open.

I looked possessed.

As I was being rapidly rolled down the hospital corridors I could still feel the baby slowly coming out, tearing me apart. I pictured the baby's head must be hanging out of me as I laid on the bed. I almost didn't feel human.

They rolled me into this well-lit room where I saw a strange bed. The bed had straps of some sort by the foot area. They quickly transfer me to that bed and tightly strapped each foot. One foot strap on the left and one foot strap on the right. Which made my legs spread wider apart.

The bed was in a reclining position, with metal shining rails on each side. I looked as if I was sitting and I can truly say, I was totally uncomfortable. This Doctor, he was a white man. He told me "**Stop pushing**!" I was stunned because I wasn't aware I was pushing. ......Maybe subconsciously... I was pushing, or the baby was just doing its own thing.

The Doctor warned me again "Stop pushing." He was in front of my open legs standing next to a big bright floor light that was directed on my vagina. The Doctor was holding a very long needle in his hand.

He said, "Listen to me! If you keep pushing, you could hurt the baby."

I notice there was a mirror down by my open legs. I looked and to my surprise.... I didn't see any sign of a baby.

Oh shit!

The baby is still inside of me. After that hard pushed I could've sworn at least the baby' head was out, or at least half way out.

The doctor calmed me and made me become focus and showed me how to be in control of the delivery.

He said, "You push when I tell you to push."

I got hit with another contraction.

He said "**Push!**"

I grab the bed rails and I push deep down within, with all my might, "EeemmmH!"

Again he said "Push," and I pushed, "Eemmmmh!" Then he told me to stop, "Breathe."

I don't know when Tray came into the delivery room but he was standing by my bedside with a pillow in his hands. He tried to put the pillow behind my back but I asked him not to because it just made me terribly uncomfortable.

Another contraction came. Dr. said "Push!" And I pushed, "Eemmmmh!" "Push again," he told me.

Holding on the bed rail I pushed again "EemmmmmmmmmmH!"

Tray became involved in our baby birthing because he left my bedside to watch our child come into this world. I wanted to see it too. I wanted to see how my vagina looks as the child passes out from me. I wanted to see my baby come into this world too - but from where I was sitting all I could see thru the small mirror was hair sticking out my vagina.

Another contraction hit me. Dr. said "Push!" and I pushed. "EeeemmmhH!"

The Dr. said, "The baby's head is out." He asked me not to push because he had to remove the umbilical cord from around the baby neck.

He continues "Push! The baby' shoulders are coming out," he said.

"They're out," he said. As he helps guide the rest of the baby' body from mine. I felt a bunch of warm slimy and gushy liquid coming out of me.

Wow........what an experience! And it's amazing how quickly the pain has stopped. I could breathe normal now. I'm exhausted and I'm glad it's over.

The Doctor took the baby over to a small table that was in the room. All of them were standing over my baby. I saw the doctor's hands moving doing something to my baby.

Their backs are turned to me. Everyone was quiet. I wanted to know what was going on. Could something be wrong with the baby?

Then I heard a baby cry. The nurse came to me with the child.

"It's a girl."

Tray left to go to the waiting room to tell my mother I had a girl. The nurse asked me, "Do you want to hold her?"

She brought my baby closer to me.

The infant was all wrinkled and had white stuff all over her body. She was crying. I didn't want to hold her because she hurt me so bad so instead I checked to make sure she had everything a baby supposed to have, like ten fingers and toes, two eyes and two ears. She looked more like her dad than she did me. The nurse took her away.

Maybe the old saying is true? You know the one people say when you are pregnant and if you dislike someone, the unborn child comes out looking more like that person.

The doctor came back to me and told me "You need to push."

I said, "**Again**? The baby is out!" "Yes the hard part is over but you need to push out the placenta," he said.

I gave three tiresome painless pushes and the placenta came out. It looks like a gigantic beef liver. The Doctor performed his examination on me and said "You will need three stitches and after two weeks they will fall out by themselves."

As he was stitching me, he joked, "You won't be back in here anytime soon pushing out another baby with the scream you let out."

The orderly came in the room with a clean bed for me to lie on. The Doctor put the chart at the foot of my bed as the orderly rolled me out from the delivery room. I was left in the hallway. I was told I needed to wait for a bed then I'll be taken upstairs.

Labor pain and the act of bringing a child into this world isn't a joke. I reached for my chart to see what the doctor wrote. He stamped spontaneous delivery.

There is an old saying I heard. I don't even know if it's true, but it goes like this, when a woman is giving birth every hair strand on her head is dead, except one. I guess if that one strand goes, well... you can finish the rest.

My mother is coming down the hallway with a smile on her' face. She said "I heard it's a girl." I looked at her. Happy the whole experience was over. My mom said laughing, "Electra we heard your scream all the way in the waiting area. It was so loud and long."

I said, "You did?" Well it had to be funny to her because I rarely made her laugh. My father is the one with the sense of humor.

Enough reminiscing the past. I'm still sitting up here waiting to delivery my third and last child.

I glance at the clock on the wall and realize, damn! It's almost twelve O'clock midnight and this baby ain't come yet.

I thought to myself -twelve O' clock (that's Tonya's Birthday).

I do not want my baby to be born on her' birthday. I could just see it now, every time I'm celebrating my baby birthday, I will always think of her. I didn't want that kind of memory for myself or that type of connection to my child.

I remember how I started rubbing my stomach and wishing - (come on baby, don't be born on her birthday) and precisely at that moment, I realize today is the date I was born. Then I started wishing (be born on the date I was born.)

Somehow I thought if the child be born on my date, he/she will be more like me and nothing like her.

I'm sure is sickly with this pregnancy - hooked up to an IV, was given medicine to help along with the delivery.

I tell you I feel so miserable and weak. I'm just plain old disgusted.

This time when the nurse came in to check up on me she started messing with the IV, she made the liquid drip much faster. Then my mind drifted on Thomas. Wondering, where is he? I'm thinking he should be back by now. Maybe he's in the waiting room, waiting for some news. **OH GOSH....** it's time!

I grab hold of both bed rails on each side and dealt with that excruciating pain.

I remember how I tried to literally detach the iron bed rail from the bed. My arms were shaking with such strength and power. Normally labor pain starts mildly. Then as it goes on, it intensifies - but the medication made my contraction more dreadful than the labor pain itself.

Now...this is where it gets strange. I can't remember anything else after that. I can't....... recall giving birth.

That's funny? Funny meaning strange. One thing I can tell you is ...I was right, the baby was a girl and she was born on the date I came into this world.

I named her Moet. At first, I was going to name her after me but then, it was a toss-up between naming her Moet, or calling her Baby Cham. Don't even ask me how or why I chose those names. I should have named her after me, you know, to keep the name in the family. I really wish I would have named her after me.

Looking up, as I looked around the shelter' dining room table-I sat up. Thinking and writing about my past bought up memories. Good memories about how both my daughters came into this world. Going back into time I sure did do a whole lot of writing. I put down the pen and paper as I laid my head upon the table.

Shortly after, Security Guard Mia Dowser, she tapping me on my shoulder "Electra, Electra are you alright?" she asked as I laid with my head on the shelter dining room table, still reminiscing what I had just written about.

Lifting my head up from the shelter dining-room table. I say, "Yeah I'm alright I was just deep in thoughts."

Mia Dowser the security guard said "I just announced that open studio is in progress on the fourth floor. Did you hear the announcement?"

"Naw. I was thinking about something. I didn't even hear you," I answered.

Security M. Dowser said "I know you like participating in activities because I always see you doing something. You are always joining in the shelter groups and doing stuff."

I just gave her a smile.

Then I said "I be bored. What else is there for me to do? Sit around all day twinkling my thumbs?"

Mia Dowser said "See I know you're not like that. That's why I tapped you on your shoulder. I said to myself, Electra not getting up going to a group? Let me go tap her to see if she's alright."

"Thanks. Good looking out. Simone supposed to be teaching me how to sew on the sewing machine," I said.

Mia said "Yeah she got some skills. Did you see that jacket she made for herself?"

"Maybe I did. Simone made some many outfits for herself," I said as I started gathering my belongings to go to the class.

M. Dowser said "Alright Electra I speak with you later." She turns walking towards the dining room door. She put her walkie-talkie to her mouth and say, "Attention to all guards. Announcement has been made in the dining-room and on the first floor, copy." From the other end I heard a guard say "Copy."

M. Dowser is American. I think she's in her' early twenties. Melan, dark-skin born Black American with permed hair. She's nice to me. Always allows me to enter into my dorm if I forget something and she always has something nice to say.

I made my way to the fourth floor.

The opening studio class was full and the radio was playing. I looked towards the sewing machine and Simone was already on one of the machines, sewing away.

As I walked into the class I looked around the room and Samantha was looking my way.

All cheerful and happy "Hi," I said to Samantha as she looked to see who else was entering into her' classroom. "Please sign in for me Electra," Sam said as she handed out materials to the clients. Speaking a little loudly I said "Sure, where is the signing sheet?" "Over there on the table," Samantha pointed.

There's only two sewing machines in the class. Samantha is the person in charge. To the participating residents, Samantha asked loudly from across the room "Can I get you anything? What are you going to do? Crochet? Make a pillow? Tell me what you need."

Walking over to Samantha I said "I don't know what else yet because Simone supposed to be teaching me how to sew." Samantha smiled and shook her' head for agreeing, yes of approval, saying, "You have a very good teacher."

Lots of girls here know how to sew on a sewing machine. Especially the Caribbean women. It seems like the majority of them know how to sew on a sewing machine and them doesn't need to work with a pattern to make an outfit either. I find a lot of the Caribbean women not willing to teach the Americans women their' skills. They like to sell and make money from their creations. Simone, she isn't like that. Maybe because she Black American like me. She doesn't mind helping somebody out if you ask.

It not like I want to become a professional seamstress. I just would like to learn the basic. Since I been coming to open studio I haven't seen much of the Spanish girls sewing on the sewing machine.

Anyway, I walk over to Simone who is now zzzzing away on the machine.

"Hello Simone," I said.

She looks at me and say "Hi," as she continually sewing fabrics together. With the loud noise coming from the machine and from the radio, audibly I said "You remember you told me to come to the next open studio class and you going to teach me how to sew." Looking at her I'm hoping she wouldn't go back on her word as I stood there.

Simone said "Yeah I remember and I'm glad to see you made it to the class. As she zzzzing away on the machine she asked "Have you ever sewed on a sewing machine before?"

"Nope. Never used a sewing machine in my life. I only know how to sew with a needle and thread and the only thing I ever did with that was sew a button or two on a blouse," I said.

"Oh," Simone said. I watch her as she continue sewing. Simone said, "It easy. You can accomplish anything if you put your mind to it. Let me finish with this piece I'm working on then I teach you the components of a sewing machine because you got to know what you working with before you use it."

"True," I said.

I couldn't wait to get started. As I stood over her, watching how she held her hands and guided the pattern. The sewing needle was moving up and down very quickly as her foot pressed on the foot pedal.

She was moving so quickly because just like with the computer, we, us residents are allow a certain amount of time on the machinery so that others can use the tools as well.

Looking around the room I saw some clients making hand sewed pillows for their' bed. Others were using art and craft needling. Some were crocheting while we all listen to the music sounds from off the radio.

When class was over. I went to my dorm-laying on my bed, looking up at the ceiling till I drifted off to sleep. I was awakening from the knocking sounds that were coming off from the dorm door, from security announcing, "Bed check ladies." I signed for my bed.

The lights were turn out at eleven o'clock.

Chapter Two

Urrrnnn...Urrnnnnnn... The sound is so loud. The fire alarm is going off in the building. I could hear the guard shouting in the hallway. "It's a fire drill everyone has to evacuate the building." Sounds of Urrrnnn....Urrnnnnnn.

"Not again!" I just came in and laid down. I was out walking around all day! I grumble getting off my bed. As I started opening up my combination lock so I can grab my belonging out from the locker-I call to Lacy. She is bed number three.

"Lacy didn't we just have a fire drill two days ago, at six o'clock in the morning," I asked frustrated.

"You know the staff here has no sense of education. They supposed to help us. Do they help us? No! So what could we do?" Lacy said as she walked out the door wearing her plastic grey jacket.

"Everybody must clear the dorms! Exit the floor. Fire drill, fire drill!" Here comes Fancy the security guard yelling "Fire drill....fire drill! Get up ladies everyone must exit the building," as she knocked and open up each door to the dorms on the fourth floor.

Sounds of Urrrnnn...Urrnnnnnn. Urrrnnn....Urrnnnnnn.

"Oh boy! Let me get my stuff so I could get out of here," I said.

The fire alarm is echoing throughout the building Urrrnnn...Urrnnnnnn. Urrrnnn...Urrnnnnnn.

My dorm is the Q dorm on the fourth floor at Bridge Net Women Shelter. Abbreviated BNWS.

I just recently got transfer to this dorm. I originally was in the A dorm on the first floor. I was told the A dorm would be an overnight bed. Not a permanent one because I wasn't sick enough.

"Electra, come on, move it now!" Fancy said harshly while glaring at me standing with one hand on her hip. I looked at her and just walked out of the dorm door.

That's one thing about being homeless you always carrying bags. If it's not in your hand, it on your shoulder-if it's not there it's on your back. Being homeless made me hate carrying even a pocketbook. I don't care if it's a designer pocketbook from DKNY, Banana Republic, Dior, Furla, or a purse from Marciano. It's just another bag to me.

I used to be a person that loved fashion. Damn this homelessness!

On the 4th floor I could hear and see all the girls exiting their' dorms. The elevator is always shut off when it's a fire drill. We all have to take the stairs, and there is only one staircase inside this shelter.

In Bridge Net stairwell there's one window for each floor. I'm stuck on the third floor because the elderly and the cripples are holding up the line.

I see that Fat Caribbean lady the one that carries all those big bags every day. She always standing on the corner with ten or more raggedy huge bags. She look like she could be from Haiti or Africa. Most of those women have unhealable, deeply cut scars in their' face and it's not like those keloid scars. You know the ones people may get from a blade cut while in prison. Those blade/razor scars, always seem to turn into a bubble shape form but her' scars look more like ritual marks.

As I'm slowly making it down the stairs, I glance out the window. I see Lacy already going across the street. I came to like her, meaning I may hold an honest conversation with her from time to time. Lacy is white, tall and way older than me. She's older than my mom.

I think she may be from England but she never tell me when I asks. She would say something like "Why you want to know?" Or she would politely change the subject.

Maybe she could be from London because she have exceptionally good taste and mannerism about herself. Anyway she reads a lot of books from that author Danielle Steel, and for her age she always on the go. Like me, never stay inside. I met her here, at Bridge Net, and overtime we develop somewhat of a friendship.

I got transfer to this shelter in January of two thousandth and five. From a shelter in Manhattan named Sixty-Eight Lexington but us girls called it Sixty-Eight Lex. That was my first single adult woman shelter I ever been in.

This line in the staircase is a constant slow move. I be downstairs soon. I just passed the second floor. It's where the intake office is located, the social service department, the medical room, the kitchen and, the kitchen slash/dining-room sitting area for us residents. There is only four dorms located on that floor. They are dorms A thru D.

Okay just one more flight.

A couple of security guards are posted standing on the bottom floor directing us girls to go across the street. Residents are never allowed to stand and stay in front of the building during a fire drill. Staff has to make sure everyone is out of the building before they let us back in. As for me I'm going to find something to eat...................Finally I'm out the door.

Everybody not home yet. Isn't that funny, I just called the shelter home. Before I used to always say the shelter. I been homeless for so long now I came to realizes it's not a shelter. It is my home.........thinking it softly, "For now."

This shelter holds about one hundred and sixty clients. The ladies that are awaiting across the street some of them are smoking cigarettes. Some are talking to each other and some are looking across the street waiting for the guard to say, "Time to go back in."

Anyway I'm out. I walked around the corner. I see True God, doing his hustle. I knew of True God since I was a teenager. He occasionally hung out with Dove (the first boyfriend I ever had).

"How you doing True," I would say.

"Electra whatz going on," he say.

"Nothing much," I reply as I keep it moving. We were never that sociable to each other. We just respected each other because we grew up in the same neighbor and Dove were both of our friend. Back then, True God remember me as a fly girl with potential. After a while True God went to jail, that's where he been for a while because whenever I asked Dove about him, Dove would always say, "He's lockup."

Eventually Dove and I broke up and many years has passed. I guess when True God seen me coming out of the women shelter he probably wanted to know...... what happened? Last time he saw me I was doing well and he probably thought Dove and I would have been married.

I don't think True God would have ever thought he would see me coming out from a woman shelter. Back then everybody, even I thought I would be successful in life, **And** family orientated. Back then, it seemed like I had the whole world in the palm of my hand. I was why too intelligent and fly, ready to conquer it all. Maybe even have it all. The American Dream that is. Going down the road towards that straight and perfect life, we all dream about.

But shit **happens** as you live life. In life it could happen to the best of us. I think that's how he chuck it up too, being that his' youth was spent behind bars. I guess his jail time is over with because I see him every day now. Never once, did either of us mention Dove name and never once did he ask me what happen? I caught him staring at me a couple of times out of curiosity but the discussion never arose.

The first shelter that I had ever entered, was a Domestic Violence shelter with me and my three kids, Year... December, of nineteen ninety-five.

The second time around for me living inside of a shelter, it was at Sixty-Eight Lexington Woman Shelter... Year Two thousandth and One...I think...it been so long I really forgot or you can say, I just lost count.

So what am I going to eat today? Which is always a good question when you homeless. It's like, it had become one of the greatest highlights of a homeless person day. Getting housing, well that's number one, which almost never comes fast enough. The majority homeless people, can do two years easily inside a shelter......Why hell! You got to be in the system nine months consecutively before an assigned caseworker can submit your housing package, and that's JUST putting the package in.

What am I going to eat today? Why is that a good question?

It becomes routine that's why. Until your housing comes though, the second best thing is food.

When it comes to food and being homeless, you are always eating on the run, in between appointments, outside, or in a hurry. Residents can eat the food inside the shelter. They give us three meals a day but you get sick and **tired** keep eating that tasteless type of food. Or, you can eat where ever you can monetarily afford. Welfare is now my only income.

I can bet you one thing, when it comes to restaurants and a homeless person' money, majority of the time you will find them eating inside a fast food joint, **And** mainly from the corner store-off of their' food stamp card. In Brooklyn and Harlem some people like to call the corner store the bodega. And, what's the highlight on the menu...It's called a sandwich.

I ate a cold sandwich every day for several years while living inside the shelter. It was eat that or eat the shelter food. Most of the times, I chose the sandwich because it taste way better to me. In Manhattan the corner store to me is, Duane Reade.

Shortly after the World Trade Disaster, the United States Government had cracked down on welfare recipients, meaning, we were no longer allowed to purchase any hot food with our food stamps. Remember back in the days, from the corner store, a person could order any hot sandwich, or have a turkey with Swiss on a roll made hot, or what about this one, order a butter roll hot and pay for it with your food stamps. Those were the good old days when a person on welfare could go to the Chinese restaurant and order whatever and how much they wanted. Then pay by using their' food stamps coupons but, since the crackdown with the Government, it is now the thing of the past.

For those who don't know what the word welfare means, well, its money the government gives to people who is unemployed. The social service department calls it, Public Assistance. Under another name most poor people call the word public assistance, welfare. But abbreviated, lots of people would say the word, PA.

Everyone PA. amount is calculated with two factors.

Fact # 1, deals with **cash money**.

For fact # 1, the government wants to know from the applying applicant, who all would be on their' budget and who is employed. Is the head of household or the applying applicant marry? Does the head of the household have any children and if so, how many? The total number of people on the budget determines or should I say, living in the household would determine the amount of cash the government would issue out, every two weeks.

The government only gives out two-hundred and fifteen dollars a month for rent. Since I don't pay any rent and there are no children on my budget, the cash benefit that I receive is twenty two dollars and fifty cents every two weeks and to add on to that, is when I go to the check cashing place, on my pickup day, the government now take out a service fee-of two dollars and fifty cents. So actually my cash is twenty bucks.

Fact # 2, deals with **Food Stamps**.

For fact # 2, depending how much money you receive monthly and how many people are on the budget, determines how much food stamps the government issues out for the applying applicant. My food stamps allowance is one-hundred and fifty dollars a month.

Looking ahead I saw the pizza parlor. Yelp, it will be pizza. I have decided. I enter and order two slices. One pizza plain and the other with sausage.... and a Pepsi. I'm going to sit in the pizza parlor and eat my food. I didn't want to eat inside the shelter because there are residents who always beg for outside purchase food.

As I sat there eating my pizza and looking out from the window, I saw a couple of girls who live inside the shelter, heading home. They all were lugging bags or at least had one bag on their' shoulder while camouflaging their clothes, personal papers and food in large Duane Reade shopping bags; pretending they have been out shopping.

Every Wednesday at eight pm, the church of Everlasting Faith Outreach Ministry comes to Bridge Net to bring spiritual awareness. I enjoy attending, it gives me positive hope in such a negative atmosphere. Plus it gives me something else to do then just laying or sitting on my bed. So on that note, I won't be walking around outside after I finish my pizza which that's something I do a lot of-walking around. Instead-once I'm finish eating, I'm going straight back to the shelter.

"Can you help me out with any change?" Ugina asks as she put the cup in my view. I just kept walking as if I didn't hear her. Ugina live in the shelter too. Every day she's out here begging. I see her all over the place in this area, with a cup begging for change. It became a full time job for her.

As I turned the corner, I notice Beverly, Country, and Valarie standing next to the entrance door to the shelter-smoking their' cigarettes. Those are some of the loud mouth troublemakers at Bridge Net.

As I was approaching and got closer I see Valerie, turns her head and say something to the girls she with. Valerie and Country both live inside my dorm.

"Excuse me," I said as I passed them to get to the shelter door. I tap on the glass part of the shelter entrance door. Security takes a look at me then buzzes the door, allowing for me to enter.

"Hi Michal," I said. I like him. He's our new young security guard. He is a Black American. Which is good because the majority security here are West Indian and Spanish. I like him because he does his job fairly well.....so far, and Michal doesn't play favoritism like some of the other guards here. From what I see and hear, he treats everyone with respect and then he goes home.

As I walk towards the machine. "Hello Miss. Jones," he reply. Michal presses a button to start the machine. I put my bags on the conveyer belt and watch it go inside the machine for scanning. While standing there I asked him, "Why did we have another fire drill back to back like that?" Puzzled he asked, "Didn't yall just have a fire drill a couple of days ago?"

"Yeah," I said.

Looking confuse himself, he shoved his shoulders and answered, "Don't know. Ask intake when you go up Miss Jones."

Teasing him I said, "You always so polite."

"Why I supposed to be a bad guy?" He asked while smiling. When my bags came out from the scanning machine, physically Michal started hand checking my bags. Once he finished.

I left my bags behind on the belt as he asks me to go walk through the magnetometer scanner. After walking thru, it buzzed. I now spread my arm and slightly separated my legs as I stood still while he now physically hand wand my body.

"You could call me by my first name Electra, you know. Every time you see me, you don't have to address me by Miss Jones, Michal," I hinted. Shyly, he said "Miss Jones would be just fine for me."

Once he had finished. I turned around to pick-up my bags from off the conveyor belt. I proceeded to the second door so he could buzz that door which allows me entrance into the shelter. Looking at him as I'm walking backwards towards the 2nd door, I said "Wellbeing you like saying Miss Jones all the time. You can have it your way then."

Once my back touches the door, he buzzes the 2nd door for entrance. Looking at him smiling. I said "Goodnight Michal." "Goodnight Miss Jones," he said with a smile.

I push the door and immediately started walking up the steps. The elevator is not too far from the staircase but, ever since I arrived at Bridge Net, I prefer taking the steps, maybe because the elevator was always slow and crowded.

I exit on the second floor to go to the intake office, to check if I have any mail. As I'm walking down the corridor towards the office-I smell food. Its dinner time. I could hear the residents' loud talking. It's coming from the residents who standing in line waiting to be served their dinner. I turns the corner and goes into the intake office and there is a line of females waiting to be assisted.

One girl is waiting in line for her curling iron. Another one, waiting to charge her' phone. One girl is putting her name on the trip sheet. A couple of females are standing waiting to pick up their' mail. Another resident is taking her' message off of the message board. One girl is drinking water from the water cooler.

Someone comes behind me smelling intoxicated saying she missing a bag of clothes that the staff had bagged up for her. A couple of new girls are sitting waiting for beds. Wow, I see.... I see Sunset lost her bed again!? Because she sitting down waiting too for another bed. The security guard at the large front desk has her hand full, issuing out medications and trying to help the other girls at the same time. Therefore the Shift Supervisor get up from behind her desk and start to help the guard out, in order to get the crowd out from the intake office.

"Who's next?" Shift Supervisor Lisa ask. The girls bum rush forward trying to be first. In a loud voice Lisa start saying... "Oh, no! Back up...back up or no one get serve. I'm only one person." Then out from the bathroom, walking thru the crowd of females, going to his designated area behind the desk, is her' partner, coworker Jefferson coming to her aid.

Mr. Jefferson saying, "If you guys got to act like this, we would close this office down!" Now he's standing there with both of his arms folded across his' chest causing everything and everyone to stop. Mr. Jefferson speaks, "Until you guys learn how to show us respect and not attack us, because we are not going to serve anybody and I do mean anybody under these conditions. Understand? Comprende?"

Shift Supervisor Lisa reply "That's right so how yall want it? Do you want your belongings? Well form a line and one at a time or yall all can leave!" She has both her hands leaning on the desk and her' face all twisted. That's her way of letting us know she means business.

I'm standing there thinking to myself (Talking about power control.) Out from the blue, Valarie enter the office with her loud mouth jumping in front of the line saying "I want my phone!"

Jefferson asks her, "Which phone is your?" Immediately I say "Oh that's not fair Jefferson! What happen to waiting your turn or you close down the office?"

Lisa backs him up by saying "Miss Jones she the only one here wanting to retrieve a phone." I say "So?! She has to wait in line like the rest of us."

Loudly Valerie say "Give... me... my Phone! Now I don't have time for this cramp!" Audibly displaying her' disappointment giggle-Valerie says "I feel sorry for you Lisa."

Now she pointing her finger at shift supervisor Lisa, while saying angrily, "They don't pay you enough money to deal with these client who lost their kids. Don't want to try and get their kids back."

While her saying all that Jefferson unplugging her' cell phone and now is allowing her to sign her signature in the cell phone log out book.

Valerie continues "Shit! I bet you her' kids don't want to be with her anyway. That's why she goes to church all the time because she knows ain't nobody else going to help her. She deserve everything she getting. What kind of mother leaves her kids?" She grabs her phone and turns around telling others to **move** out her way.

She walks pass me and didn't even look my way, and she **knew**! She better not have even touch me when she passed because honestly, we would have been **fighting**. I really don't like that girl. Where does she get her information from? I don't know her. I just came to that dorm and since I been there she always joking and like gossiping, making comments concerning me and my kids.

I said loudly to the other clients in the intake office "Did yall just see that? We all had to stay in line while she just walks in, get what she wants, and walks out while we all are still here waiting to be served."

Not one person said one word. Not even the security guard who supposed to keep law and order.

All I got to say is, "READER! WELCOME TO BRIDGE NET.

I finally moved up to the front. Jefferson asks, "How can I help you Electra?" I said "I wanna check to see if I have any mail." Quickly I starts scanning the mail sheet that's on top of the desk in front of me. Before I can finish Jefferson had covered the mail sheet with his' hand and says, "No you don't have mail." He looks up at the crowd and ask "Next?"

I was thinking that was quick as I walked away from the desk. I glance at the messenger board to see if my name was up there but I knew better. No one never calls me, even though I still like to hope anyway-or look normal like the rest of the girls as if I do receive calls from people on the outside.

I'm not going to go to the dining room just to see what they served for dinner or who's in there. I want to put down my bags. Leaving the intake office and once I'm in the hallway, I turn around the corner. I walked pass the elevator and open the door to the staircase, while proceeding up the steps.

As I walked up the steps. I glanced out the stairwell window and I look out into the shelter yard. I saw Brenda, Lenore, Maria, Short Stop and Daisy all sitting down smoking their' cigarettes.

Passing the third floor and by the way, on the 3rd floor are dorms E thru K. There's also a laundry room, our TV room, and another caseworker' office. I have one more flight of steps. Last step, I enter on the fourth floor. The first thing I see besides the elevator door is Officer Mac Dan on her' post. She sitting on the chair, next to the fourth floor laundry room.

On the 4th floor, besides the laundry room are dorms L thru R, the shelter library which this room is also use for meetings, as well, as for the shelter recreational activities and last, there is Bridge Net Administration office. It's where the Director, Clinical Director, Director of Security and their' receptionist work.

"Hello," I say to Officer Mac. Dan. "Hello Electra," she replied.

I continue walking down the hallway. Pass the library. Passing other dorms. Towards the Administration Office. Make a left turn. Pass a couple more dorms. Walked some more till I reached the Q dorm. Open the door to Valarie loudly talking on her' cell phone.

As I enter inside the room. Whomever she speaking to-she is telling the person, "She need to be a mother and get an apartment for herself and her' kids. If I had children I wouldn't leave them."

I'm ignoring her because number one, she didn't say my name. The last time I got physical with a resident I was ban out from the shelter system for 1 week. Only after serving several years inside Sixty-Eight Lex-that altercation I had, jeopardized my acceptance for NYCHA (New York City Housing Authority)-the projects. When I finally got called for an interview from NYCHA, at the interview I had no proof of residency. When I explained to the interviewer I was homeless and that I had gotten banned out from the shelter system because I got into a fight. The interviewer seen me as a threat.

He told me that NYCHA has changed their tenants' criteria for who gets accepted into the projects and who don't. That NYCHA had inputted new bylaws for their tenants to live by. He told me if anybody been in jail, coming home from jail, sell drugs or appear to be a threat, that put any of their tenants in harm-way, would no longer be accepted into New York City Housing Authority. Because, I had gotten banned out from the shelter system due to a fist fight I was seen as a treat therefore at the interview my application for New York City Housing Authority was denied. I was told by the interviewer, "People like me are no longer being accepted into the project. Goodbye."

So I learn to overlook and not be so sensitive to a lot of bullshit from dumb ass residents, besides number two, fuck that horse face fat ass looking bitch.

I goes to my area and starts to open up my locker. Inputting the numbers for my combination lock as it clicks open. Valerie is getting on my last nerves. She never mention my name when she speak. What she does is say thing like…
…"Go back to family court and get her' kids back, right? Then all she need to do is go to a family shelter." Or she say something like, "The only thing she eat is white rice and chicken from the Jamaican restaurant."

She always make me think about my children. True....my kids' father is Jamaican and true, I been in family court more than I want to remember and yes, my youngest daughter Moet always eating white rice and stew chicken from the Jamaican Restaurants.

I use to think when Valerie spoke, her conversation was coincidental to mine personal affairs, but now I realize that she is in my business. Why? Who is she and where does she come from?

Turning around to sit on my bed, I notice Lacy laying on her back with earplug in her ears reading another thick book. Sometimes I wish I could do that, tune out my surroundings by reading a book but for some strange reason I can't. Maybe it because I'm not a reader, or my mind is preoccupy with my thoughts, or plain and simple I'm just not comfortable.

Now Valerie in the bathroom running water with the door open talking on the phone about some guy she met. She really thinks this is her' very own apartment and there's nobody else in here but her. I laid back on my bed-I started thinking about the past, wondering where did I go wrong? The only thing I can recall with my last child birth is the excruciating pain I got after my labor was induced and that I tried to pull off the bed rails.

Why everything is so foggy with Moet delivery? Now, what I do know, is that I didn't have a cesarean, and I wasn't put to sleep. I had a normal delivery, meaning, I push her out.

Thinking and writing about my past.

I remember when my gynecologist Dr. Lehman told me I was expecting again. Dr. Lehman has been my gynecologisl since the age of nineteen. She helped me nurture, bringing in two, now going on three healthy kids into this world. After hearing the news I'm expecting again this time I had to ask her to take a seat. I express to her not wanting to give birth to anymore children.

I remember I told her "Dr. Lehman I don't want to have any more children. I'm having such a hard time trying to provide for the kids I already have. For me, it's a constant struggle. I feel like every time I get pregnant it holding me back from doing things that I want to do. Because being a parent it's a fulltime job and a big responsibility, with no pay."

Honesty, I believe she has known this about me (struggling) for quite a while. She seen me all these years I came to her for my yearly visit. She perform all my pap smears tests and help me conquer my frequent reoccurring yeast infections. She was the one who told me I was expecting my first child and provided me with excellent prenatal care.

Dr. Lehman took pride in her job. Ever since I known her, she was always so professional. After telling her how I really felt. I remember how she just gave me this long stern look sitting from behind her desk. Then she bent her head down and wrote something on paper. She hands it to me. She made an appointment for me to speak to someone in the clinic.

Dr. Lehman said to me "It's the clinic procedures for me to have you speak to someone first about not conceiving anymore children before I could issue the surgery to be done."

So, I met with a black man. He was Caribbean or African descent. He asked me, "Why would you want to do this? You still so young."

I corrected him. I said "I'm old enough to know I don't want any more children, beside I'm not that young. I'm twenty eight. I'm been on welfare for the last eight years. I don't have any money or money stash away. Public Assistant has been and is my only support financially in helping me with these children."

He asked me, "What about birth control?"

I told him "I tried them but still I got pregnant beside I didn't like how the pills made me feel. I was always nauseated."

Then he asked, "So why didn't you request for a different level of dosage?"

Getting annoyed. I said "It just didn't work. I kept forgetting to take them every day. I found myself constantly doubling the pill the next day. I really would prefer this way of prevention."

He tried to tell me some bullshit.

He said, "Look your kids are young.... true....I understand you wanting more for yourself out of life and not being able to do it right now. I know it's not easy raising kids but can't you put them in daycare and, what about your family support?"

I explain to him how I tried putting my oldest in daycare but there always was a waiting list and how I applied for a child voucher for the private daycares. Yet I never received one and when I did leave her with a babysitter, there was always something wrong when I came to pick the child up. As far as family, well, I'm on my own.

He said, "Ohm....What about the father of your children?" I told him, "My oldest child' father hasn't been in her life since she was six months. As for the father of these last two kids, what about him? He is not trying to help me with child care. He doesn't have any of his' family members coming over given me or him a break so that we can go out."

He asked, "Well isn't he supported? Doesn't he help you out financially? How do you think he feel about this sterilization? Have you spoken to him about your decision?"

I told the man who was asking me all these questions "If we were marry I would consult him but he is not my husband. And if he was so supported, why am I and my kids still on welfare? None of my monthly bills are in his' name. He's not taking responsibilities for anything. The government pays for me and my kids' medical bills. I receive food stamps for myself and the kids, so he's not even buying any major food for the house. As a matter of fact, he lives in my apartment with me."

The man said, "Come on you are a beautiful woman. What if down the road you were to get marry and your husband wants you to have his' child?"

That's where Donald Trump come in at. I'm known for throwing up his' name whenever it comes to a man cheating on you or in this case wanting another child.

I told him, "Well at this point, the only way I'm going to have another baby if the man is Donald Trump, meaning he has money. I will have a nanny if I needed to rest, or, wanted to go to work or even back to school. Everything wouldn't be solely on me. Besides a man like Donald Trump could help me reverse the procedure if he really wanted me to have his' baby."

I had continue by saying "It's a struggle for me every day since I had given birth to my first child. As a single parent I struggle every day to make my ends meet. Let me rephrase this. I sacrifice all my time and money for my children basis needs, like Birthdays, Holidays, Celebration, keeping clothes on their' back, shoes on their' feet and I'm doing this not for one child but now three. The only way I can make sure my kids have summer, winter and school clothes is through layaway. Thanks to Young World Department Store downtown Brooklyn."

"Shoot, I put my needs, my wants, on hold to raise my kids' right. I may don't have much but I keep my place clean. I don't get dress up and go out to nice places, example, like dinner. I cook every day. The kids are used to having a home cook meal because I can't afford restaurant food like McDonald or pizza parties. I don't have any kind of a sociable life. I don't have any or everyone running up inside my apartment like it's an open house. I don't smoke nor do I drink. I feel like I committed a crime. I gave birth, and I been locked up in the house ever since.... Like a criminal. I feel like someone throw away the key. Shit!" I said.

Shaking his head of comprehension, the man said, "I understand. So, tell me would you want this procedure temporary or permanent....Hold on. Before you answer if you decide temporary, you won't be able to conceive up till five years. Which, (putting on his' agreeable face) I think would be more suitable for you."

I told him, "Listen. (Like I know what I want.) I really, really don't want to have any more kids and I'm not as young as you trying to make it seem."

I paused.

"I just don't see my life going anywhere. Besides, I'm like a bunny rabbit. I have sex......I get pregnant. I already had a miscarriage and a couple of abortions. Look, if Thomas and I don't make it, and if down the road another man shall come into my life. He will already have kids of his' own and he wouldn't want any more kids either," I said.

He said, "Alright we've discuss why you want to have a sterilization but I would like for you to go home to speak with your children' father." I asked, "Why?"

I said "It's my life and my body. I want to sign the paper now."

The man said firmly, "No paper, will be signed until thirty days. That shall give you enough time to think thru your decision." Well ...I went home. Eventually I spoke to Thomas about the idea.

You know what he said! In his Jamaican accent. "Tami, supposes you meet a rich man and he wants more children. I don't tink that be a wise choice gal."

When the thirty days were up, you know I took my ass down there and signed that piece of paper.

Sounds, from a person knocking on the dorm door stops me from writing about the past. The knocking sounds sent me to look at my reality that I'm laying on my bed inside the shelter.

"Knock. Knock. "Is everyone dress?" The guard asks from outside the Q dorm door. The ladies in the dorm say, "Yes. Come in."

Security Guard Mac. Dan opens the door announcing to the room "Everlasting Faith Outreach Ministry is on site."

Man, reminiscing-I didn't realize it was eight O'clock. I get off my bed. Look into my locker and pull out my bible. Then I secure my locker. Before walking out the door, I scan my area for anything I might have left out.

Once out the door, I saw Billie coming out from her' dorm. Which is the P Dorm. She had a small bible in her' hand. I said, "How you doing Billie." She give me a smile then waits for me to catch up to her.

Billy asks me "Are you ready to sing tonight?" "Yeah" I said.

I asks, "Are you going to help me?"

Billy respond "I don't know all them gossip song like you do." I said "They easy, you just got to feel it in your soul."

As we walked and talk going down the corridor. There were a couple of ladies in the hallway holding an intimate private like conversation. I notice their behavior as we walked towards the library, heading towards the security guard who by now is sitting on her post.

Talking, looking towards Billy and I, Officer Mac. Dan said as she sat on her post which is by the laundry room, "I knew you were going to church Electra. I see you like keeping yourself busy. I wish some of these other girls were more like you so positive and uplifting."

Billy jumps in and say "Wouldn't it be nice if we can get them to come. The only thing most of them want to do is drink, smoke and beat each other up."

Billy is a mad cool white girl. She from the south. She remind me of sister solider ready to cut you up with a knife if she could do it and get away with it. She may be hard on the outside but really, she a sweet heart and she sure do love to worship the lord and sing praises.

Us approaching and now standing in front of the elevator, as Billie presses the button, she turn around and say to me "Meet you downstairs." She knows that I prefer to take the steps.

I knew I will beat the elevator downstairs. As I passed the intake office I quickly glance in. It was empty besides the same girls who were there before, waiting for an assigned bed. Oh sweat, begging ass Ugina there too. Her and Sunset always losses their' beds.

Soon as I passed the medical office just about to go inside the dining room, I bump into Sister Riley. She said "I'm glad to see you made it. Please come with me to the kitchen and help me bring in the cups and bowls."

When I first met the Everlasting Faith Outreach Ministry I introduce myself as Sister Jones and always address them as Sisters and Brothers even when they didn't do it themselves. As a child my parents didn't bring me up in church. After I had my children I became very spiritually incline. So therefore, when it comes to church, my vocabulary is, Sister and Brother. Instead of saying, "What's up," I say "Praise the Lord." I came to show and give respect because to me you got to have boundaries between the spirit world and the carnal world.

We brought the cups and bowls out to the dining-room. Heyyy, they had decorative gift bags all on a decorative table. Billie, she's over there helping set up the chairs. One thing I could say about Bridge Net is this shelter has several churches that enjoy helping us ladies out.

Hearing the gospel is nice, but I did forgot to mention one more thing. What us· girls loves the most, including me.....is that when the churches come here, they always come with food. I take it as a blessing. I spent my last couple of dollars buying the pizza for dinner. All I have left is a little bit of food stamps that gotz to last me for the rest of this month.

The decorative table had upon it; a sheet cake from BJ, eight, sixty-four ounces of assorted sodas, three, sixty-four ounces of different favored juices, a bag of ice, the big tube of munchies, several large bags of potatoes chips, cheez doodles and pretzels, and a box of individual wrap crème cookies.

I know some readers are saying where the food? Some shelters doesn't allow outsiders to bring in food. Bridge Net was one of them but us girls was always so......so THANKFUL for whatever anyone brought and gave to us. Lots of girls really don't have any money, especially the ones who aren't doing what they supposed to be doing.

Sometimes apparently for no reason at all you will hear females complaining that their' welfare and food stamps just got cut off-without any notice. Regular people who have an income doesn't know how that feel when out the blue your case just get cut off. And what all takes places in order to get a case active again. So it's always a treat and a blessing for us when anyone is kind.

All the participating clients are sitting down in chairs. While the sisters' stand by the table. Sister Riley asks, "Do anyone have a song on their' heart?"

Yes I do therefore I stand and start to sing, "With my hands lifted up_____ and my heart fill with praise_____ with a heart of Thanksgiv__ing__, I will bless thee O' Lord___." The ministry joins in singing "With my hands lifted up_____," more females' starts to come in. Some take a seat in the back and become spectators. Others, they come closer and join in with the singing by standing in agreement. "And my heart fill with praise_____ with a heart of Thanksgiv__ing__, I will bless thee o Lord___. I will bless thee O' Lord____. I will bless thee O' Lord___. With a heart of thanksgiving. I will bless thee O' Lord___."

The ministry start to sing .... "What a mighty God we ser__ve__.

I immediately join in and start singing "What a mighty God we serve___. Angels bow before him. Heaven and earth adore Him. What a mighty God we serve___. Jesus is the God we ser__ve__ Jesus is the God we serve__. Angels bow before him. Heaven and earth adore him. What a mighty God we serve__."

Some of the residents and church women are looking at me amaze to see that I'm so familiar with spiritual song. They become a little more involved themselves by clapping their' hands. More songs will be sung and before you know it theirs about twelve or fifteen participate of clients inside the dining-room.

After the singing Sister Riley asks one of the sisters, she brought with her to give us a scripture from the bible. They will preach verse St. John three: sixteen "For God so loved the world that he gave his only begotten Son that who so ever believeth in him should not perish, but have everlasting life."

Tonight according to how we came in they gave out the gifts bags until they ran out. The gift bags contain body shower gel and perfume body lotion. Once all the gifts bag were given out we form a line and receive soda or juice of our choice. A piece of cake and a plate of the goodies.

By the time the snack are about to be served that's when several more residents starts to show up. They enter the dining room and got in line and receive the snacks as well. This ministry knows how the women are because they have been coming here for a while. They never deny any resident from enjoying what they brought. Even if they didn't attend the service. The ministry share and share until it's all gone. As we sit and ate you would see some of the shelter females' fellowshipping with each other as well as with some of the members that came along with the church.

After a while, "Goodnight," they will say. Us residents, we all say "Goodnight," as well.

Majority of the residents that has participated had already left the area. Billie and I stays behind wiping off the tables, putting away left over cups and bowls, putting the chairs by tables and throwing out the empty soda bottles.

It's nine o'clock pm.

Employed shelter girls or the girls who been out all day taking care of their personal business are making their way into the dining-room to get their' reserved diner which the staff has held. Country, she stand on the chair to put the radio back on. The dining room radio always gets turned off when the church comes. Some females are just hanging out with their' friends before bed check.

I say to Billie "Goodnight." As I leave the dining room, standing in front of the kitchen there are four girls waiting in line, to sign up for a laundry slot. In all shelters, all residents have to sign the night before in order to do their laundry for the following day. At Bridge Net, the laundry book open every night at 9pm.

I head upstairs.

Once I'm upstairs in my dorm, I knock on the bathroom door, gets no answer. So I prepare myself to take a shower. At Bridge Net every dorm has a bathroom inside. I quickly remove my shoes and take off my clothes. I wrap the towel around me and take out my flip flop because I never take my shower barefoot. Out from my locker I get the bathroom tilex cleaner and a pair of plastic gloves so I can clean out the tub. Without delay I rush in the bathroom before someone beats me to it. I goes in the bathroom and locks the doors cause if you don't someone will walk right in on you.

I was just about almost finish taking my shower until I hear someone turning the doorknob but the person can't get in. Then I hear a knock at the door.

"Who is it," I asked from inside the bathroom.

"It's me, Country. Don't use up all the hot water Electra I want to take my shower too," she say. "I'm coming out right now," I replied.

Before I leave the bathroom I always check to make sure, I left it descent and in order. I always cleans the tub when I finished. Make sure no water on the floor and all my personal items are gone. From my experience, I found to always implement this tidiness as I walked out.

Valarie runs in the bathroom and start making noise saying "It stinks in here Country! Bring me my perfume sprayer on top of my locker. It smells like baby do-do in here."

She's a trip. I'm thinking, she watches me. She make stories up about my personal business. Valerie always starting. She such a bully and she has a problem. One day, I'm going to FUCK that BITCH up! Watch.

I could hear Security Mac. Dan is making her rounds on the fourth floor. Knocking on each door, announcing "Bed check ladies."

Laying on the bed. Underneath my covers, I thought about, I can recall every inch of my delivery with my first and second child. Out of my three children births, never once did I want to know the sex of the unborn child. I always wanted it to be a surprise. What a joy it was for me to wait and find out the sex of my newborn as if the sex of the child is my present. "It's a boy! No, it's' a girl!"

I kinda enjoyed the guessing game too. You know like looking at a pregnant woman stomach and because of the shape and height of the stomach you could tell if it's going to be a boy or a girl.

So, reader: On that note. *Let's go back, back into time. Back to the story.*

You see, when I had my son, yes, the belly was slightly different. Also the labor was different too. With my son everything was totally fast, referring to my labor.

My water broke in the house. We sent my oldest (who was four in a half year old) across the hall to Shelby. I remember Thomas was very excited. It's our first child together as a couple. Thomas drove me to the hospital, which was right down the street (actually we coulda walked).

We enter thru the emergency room and Thomas said, "She having a baby!"

I was immediately put in a wheel chair and rolled upstairs. We got off the elevator and went into a small examination room. Thomas helps me from the wheelchair on to the hospital bed. He also helps me remove my clothes and put on the hospital grown.

While I laid on the bed, I thought about that white Doctor. The one who help me delivery my first child. I thought about what he said, "How to focus and how to stay in control of the delivery." So I started practicing my breathing technique along with the contractions.

The nurse was like getting me prep for the big event. After she gave me the hospital grown. She said "I need certain information about you. Like your name, age, medical and coverage." Thomas had my bag and he pass her the required documents, as I performed the breathing techniques and I told her my name…and age.

She asked me "If it's a boy, would I want the hospital to circumcise him?" I told her "Yes." Then she gave me paper to sign like the hospital policy and a consented form for the circumcision.

Everything was going fast and accordingly, no waiting for anything at all. Even my contractions were getting stronger by the minute. I continue my breathing techniques and focusing on relaxing my body so that nature could take its course.

Thomas was sent to the hospital' delivery waiting room area and I was move to a comfortable clean and cozy hospital room. Within five minutes of being in the room I got the weirdest sensation. I felt pressure on….my butt hole?

There it goes again.....but with a harder thrust. "Ouch," I found myself saying, the sensation went away then within seconds it came back again.

"Ouch."

I couldn't believe it. It felt as if the baby was trying to get out through my butt hole. I couldn't believe with all that meat on my ass, that child, could find the middle of my butt hole from inside of me and try to push itself out. "Ouch!"

I started calling for the nurse, she came in within minutes. Like I said, everything was moving fast. No beating around the brush.

When she came into the room, I told her, "The baby trying to come out from my butt!"

She gave me a weird look. She told me "Lay there and relax I'm going to go get the Doctor and don't worry it will pass."

She left the room.

"Bull cramp!" That shit didn't pass. It got worst. It made me feel like I had to shit. That's when I knew it's a boy!

Signs of man, they just don't know what hole to enter, in this case, exit. "Oouch!"

You see, I'm a cusp born baby - meaning - my birthday date is the ending of one zodiac sign and the beginning of another. I like to look at it as having the best of both worlds. Anyway my children are cusp born people too, except the first child. She was supposed to be born on a cusp born date but she came two week early. I blame that on stress. I remember Dr. Lehman told me Champagne due date was the same date as Moet and mines.

Another observation I made on this child.......is his zodiac sign and that his zodiac sign Gemini is the more dominating sign because..........he was coming out the wrong way!

STOP! To the Reader: "Just a minute," I hear Shift Supervisor Lisa voice in the hallway. Security Mac. Dan knocks on the dorm door then quickly opening the door, saying "Bed check."

I stop writing because I have to sign for my bed. Shift Supervisor Lisa enters the dorm and begins making her' rounds to each bed in the Q dorm. I look at the time on the wall. The time reads 10:14 pm. Lisa comes to my bed with the rooster. I find my name and signs my signature on the line, for bed Q-10. Once the whole dorm completed Shift Supervisor Lisa and Security, Mac. Dan exit the Q dorm. They off to the next dorm to collect that dorm residents' of signatures.

Back to the story:

The Doctor came in the room. This Doctor was young. He was a young tall slim white boy. He was kind of cute.

I said, "Doc....the baby trying to come out through my butt."

The Doctor replied "Really." He checked me. He said, "You just about there."

I said "No Doctor, I got to push...Ouch!"

The young Dr. was standing there looking at me bewilder as if I can't be really ready to have this child. I said, "Doc I can't take it. The baby wants to come out...Ouch......the baby pushing out my butt hole....Oouch!"

The Dr. and the nurse who both were inside my room, both of them looking at me, wondering?

The Dr. said to the nurse "I don't think she ready but let's get the delivery room set." Both of them left to go to the delivery room.

The baby was pushing so hard against the inside of my butt hole it felt like a thin tough layer of butt hole skin was keeping the child inside.

Oh...my....Gosh! It felt like my butt hole was about to pop! Like my butt is chewing gum then trying to blow, a bubble... "Ouch."

The sensation keep going away than within seconds another thrust "Ooouch!"

The nurses came back I started saying, "I got to push, I got to push!" The nurse quickly took hold of my bed and rolled me, three doors down from my room. We enter into the delivery room.

The tall slim young white Dr. was standing there waiting for me. This deliver room was spotless, roomy and shiny.

There was a metal shiny narrow table in the middle of the floor and it didn't have any bars. I remember thinking that I could roll off the table.

Once on the table the Doctor wanted me to push.

But I couldn't do it lying on my back.

He found it to be a little funny, because I was saying, "Ooouch my butt, my butt!" The sensation keep going away then coming back with a harder thrust.

Have you ever seen that movie deep sea?

Remember how the shark was banging at that fence trying to get free before it blew up.

Well that how it felt!

I couldn't push out the baby laying down like that because if I push the baby, it felt like I would had want it to come out from my rear.

So I had no other choice but to do what felt best.

I turn completely on my side. The arm that was facing the ceiling I used that hand to grip and hold on to the table. I lean on the side of my back for support. With one legs open wide, I push down as if to deter the baby from the rear to my vagina.

I remember how the young Doctor was amazed at the way I position my body to push the child out. He stood there watching me as I was doing all the work.

As the Doctor watched, he said "I have never seen a baby being delivered in this position."

What a relief it was to feel that pressure slowly moving upwards towards my vagina from my butt hole.

Doc said "It's a boy!"

I said, "I have a boy? Oh wow! I have a boy... I have a son!"

Words couldn't express how I felt. One thing I always knew, whenever I did decide to have children, I wanted boys. Don't get me wrong, I love my daughters, wait, I adore my daughters and I wouldn't trade them for nothing in the world. Girls are so special in their' own way - but boys well, they're my favorite.

What I'm trying to say is if I had the chance to choose, I would have chosen more boys than girls. To me, I think boy child/kids/children/teenagers are the coolest. They are the cutest, handsomest little kids on this earth. They are so much fun to be around.

There so much you can do with them. So much I wanted to teach him as his' mother. Like when Valentine Day comes around he should do something special for that female he likes. It doesn't have to be big, it could be as sweet as giving a rose or one big chocolate Hershey kiss.

Not to be ashamed to pick up flowers on a special occasion. Tell him, "Its gentlemen like when he goes out to dinner, sometimes pull out the chair for his' female companion." Teach him how to do a respectable two step on a slow jam. I would enjoy educating him on different walks of life, from a female prospective. Read to him, as well as listen to him read to me. I think that is so sexy when a man reads to a woman.

I couldn't wait to tell him some secrets on what girls like. I want to watch him grow into a man that I am so very proud of. I want his' wife to tell me one day, "Thank you for bringing this wonderful man into this world."

I have the same love for my girls too. There are lots of things I want to instill into them too. But as a Black American woman, I don't see a lot of black men that I'm really proud of or even respect for that matter. Now I have a son who's going to become a black man that I could help cultivate his' mind, manners and actions.

My son he's my pride and joy. I had always wanted a son even way before I came to realize how Black Men has distraught my faith in them, so when the Doctor said "It's a boy," those words, really did set my heart on fire. I had always wanted a son.

Anyway I'm happy he's healthy and those are just some of the things I wanted to instill in him.

They rolled me out of the delivery room. At that moment, I was so ecstatically happy I forgot all about Thomas until the bed stop rolling and someone kissed me on my cheek.

When I turned my head to see, who kiss me? Thomas was all smiles. He said to me "Thank you for giving me a son."

I remember thinking why is he so happy? I mean he was really ecstatic too. He was so fill with joy. We both were. I was just laying on the bed thinking I have a son.....I have a Son....I HAVE A SON.

Well that's how it went down with the birth of my son Brandon. Its eleven pm security ajar the door and said "Lights out and turned off the lights."

"Speak to you tomorrow. Good night."

Chapter Three

The sound of her' voice woke me up, from out of my sleep. "Good morning," Abuja the security guard said. I open my eyes, to the very bright lights, that shines in my face. I immediately throw the covers over my head, as a way of blocking out the lights.

From underneath my covers I could hear Security Guard Abuja saying "Its six o'clock ladies, breakfast will be served downstairs."

Security Guard Abuja works the grave yard shift. Bridge Net has a twenty-four hour security system and their' work hours are divide up as the following. The first shift of guards starts eight am in the morning, until four pm that evening. The second shift begins at four pm until twelve midnight. Then it the grave yard shift, twelve am, until eight am in the morning.

As I laid in the bed with the covers over my head-I'm thinking, how I hate to get up so early in the morning, but I have to...because... I... am.... broke. The first day of next month is my pick up date, for my government allowance from public assistance. Abbreviated (PA). It's my government benefit allowance that consist of cash and food stamps. The little bit of food stamps that I have left for this month, I got to make it stretch till the end of this month, because it's bad when you walking around outside all day and you can't even buy yourself a soda.

Every day breakfast is served from six-thirty in the morning until seven-thirty sharp. While laying underneath my covers, it had brought back an old memory, of a trick I learned while living at Sixty-Eight Lexington Women Shelter. The trick I learned was how to live in a dorm...... for my eyes. When laying in the bed and let say, I'm not ready to leave the dorm but the lights are on, by placing a pillow, a piece

58

of the blanket or any article of heavy clothing like a sweater over my face, helps, while living in this kind of dormitory, because majority of the shelters.........their' dorm lights! Are eye blinding.

Reminiscing now, about the females from Sixty-Eight Lexington Women Shelter, I used to find it to be so funny, because around ten-fifty-nine pm you could hear those girls in my old dorm, shouting "Cut out them lights!" Eleven pm.....for all shelters, lights out. Way back then, the guards didn't turn out the lights in the dorms. Us females did it ourselves, anyway enough reminiscing time for me to get out of bed.

Here goes!

Quickly I pull the covers away from my head and just got up. My neighbor is gone. Whenever you hear me speak of my neighbor I'm referring to the person who sleeps next to me. Everyone else in the dorm I just consider them as my roommates.

My bed is Q ten. It's the first bed by the door on the right hand side. It also, is a corner bed, which I prefer. For starters, the only person lying next to me is my neighbor, on the other side of me, is a wall. For the other residents, who also have a corner bed, besides their neighbor, it could be a wall or a window that's on the other side of that resident. It all depends on what side of the room, that resident' bed is located, which determines if that resident would have a wall or a window. Also a corner bed offer you a little more privacy. You could use the door from your locker as a semi shell, in a way which helps block you somewhat, from being seen and looking at the other females who live in the dorm. Eleven pm all dorms lights get turned out so by having a corner bed, its attached locker-door, plays as a great shield for privacy, especially when I'm laying down while the room-lights are on-not wanting to look anyone in their face or have them just looking at me in my face, also the locker-door serve as a semi-shield in putting on and removing my clothes.

Did I mention to you the dorms are extremely large with extremely high ceiling? My bed, is also several feet away from the bathroom, which I like too. Once I had a bed next to the bathroom and my roommates were always walking in front of my bed, walking back and forth to the bathroom which after a while their actions, I did learn how to tune out.

Looking at the bathroom door I see no one standing there to go in. So I proceed to the bathroom. I knock on the door. There's no answer so I turn the doorknob but it's locked. I immediately starts pulling on the door knob thinking its jam. Then I heard the voice of Luting. The Chinese young girl saying "I'm in bath tub. Sorry, me unlock door."

Listening from the outside of the bathroom door I said, "That's alright. I wait till you come out." Then suddenly I just heard the bathroom door latch un-lock.

That one thing I don't like, is going inside the dorm bathroom when someone else is already in there. Even though we live in a shelter I feel like everyone do need some sort of privacy. It's not like our dorm bathroom is an open bathroom with several stalls and toilets. It's just one dam small toilet and one dam tub in there. I decided to go get breakfast instead.

Leaving my dorm. I turns the corner and as usual this early in the morning there no guard sitting on post. Just an empty chair by the laundry room door. You could never find a guard on post on the fourth floor early in the morning. Walking towards the elevator I see Rose wearing her white terry cloth bathrobe with matching slipper. She pressing for the elevator with a cigarette in her hand. She's going outside to the yard to smoke. There some other girls waiting too for the elevator but I don't know them.

"Good morning Rose," I said before I open the exit door to take the steps. Rose and I shared a dorm together. She allowed me to use her cell phone to call my kids a couple of times.

Reaching on the second floor, I see the line that's forming from the kitchen is around the corner. As I get closer, wow, the line, it's reaching all the way to the D dorm. It's Thursday. Every Thursday we have bacon egg and cheese. It's everyone favorite. The line is moving so slow. I get closer to the kitchen and I see why we are moving slow. Mrs. Alfre is serving.

As I approach the entrance to the kitchen, I hear an oldie but goody song from Motown playing. It sound like Smokey Robinson. I take the breakfast clip board and started turning the pages looking for the Q dorm. Once I reach the Q dorm page, next, I scan the sheet for my name which is by my bed number Q-10 and I sign.

Listening to Smokey Robinson sing as I inch up in the line. I'm the next one to be served. Mrs. Alfre, a small frame elderly Black American woman stands there with her apron on, hairnet neatly in placed with a utensil in her hand. She's the person who playing the music. She enjoys listening to her homemade music cassette tape that she made from off the radio. As I stand in front of her, firmly she says with a smile, "Good morning," while her listening, quietly jamming enjoying the sounds of her own homemade R and B cassette.

I don't feel like saying good morning because it's so early in the morning. I still have on my pajama. I didn't even brush my teeth yet because that Chinese girl was in the bathroom. That's why the line was moving so slow because Mrs. Alfre acting like her teaching us ladies' etiquette manners. Always wanting us to respond to her so lady like with a greeting. It's early in the morning and she wants us to have manner. It's like this every morning when she serve. You approach her, then she just stands there look at you then gently with a smile, she says, "Good morning" and she won't serve a resident until that resident respond back by saying "Good morning Mrs. Alfre." She won't serve any resident until she get her way.

I know how she is so I look her firmly in her face and say with no smile "Good morning Mrs. Alfre."

Slowly, and she smiling, Mrs. Alfre ask, "Would you like turkey or pork bacon?" I look at the selection through the plexi-glass and said "Turkey please." She asks "Would you like eggs?" I shake my head in a yes position. Lastly Mrs. Alfre ask, "Do you want a cup of grits?" I say, "Yes please." Moving away from Mrs. Alfre I move up to the next server.

She younger than Mrs. Alfre. This server she always seem to be bored. Giving and showing us residents a lack of enthusiasm emotion about her' job. You have to be the initiator with her. She just stand there and looks at you. I ask her "Can I have white bread and butter." She appears to be lazy too because she will always have our morning desert next to our two small container of juices so she won't have to move. I put my juice and desert on my tray continuing down the line.

It's security guard Abuja! She knows she belong upstairs on the fourth floor sitting down on her post but noooo she down here getting some free grub. That one thing you come to learn about the staff, they always eating our food.

She ask me "Do you want a tea bag?" I say "Yeah." Then she ask, "Regular sugar or sweet and low." I say "Let me get four sugars." I take two more steps and pick up one milk from the crate box. Once I finish with breakfast I head upstairs back to the dorm.

Most of the girls are up in the dorm because everybody has to be out of the dorm by nine am. I goes into the bathroom to brush my teeth and wash my face. I notice someone left their personal dirty looking soap and their underwear in the bathroom. Ugh, I hate when roommates' leave their personal items behind and me have to clean up after a grown ass women. Some of them are so fucking nasty. Over the years I have seen purposely left bloody pads in bathroom stalls, smear feces on bathroom walls and shower stalls. Smear feces on toilet seats, piss on the floor and globs of spit stuck sometime sliding down bathroom walls and shower stalls. No wonder some of these guys have no respect for a woman, because some women are just filthy.

I don't know how females can leave their clothes in the bathroom. Especially knowing you got to share this space with nine other females. Everything from coats, blouse, their wet jeans, hand-wash clothes-like their bra and panties has been left behind for all to see. It disguising because we all got to use this one bathroom.

Leave your stuff by your area for goodness sake. In my dorm there is ten of us, now just imagine all of us not caring and being angry with disrespectfulness because no one wants to live here. It will be a catastrophe. As a matter of fact, we have had several house meetings on this very same subject.

It's a filthy way of living. Bad enough the staff barely cleans properly. I don't want to catch no one germs or see what color their underwear is or knowing someone on their menstrual cycle. We, are, all, grown, ass, women-they supposed to act like it but lots of them **don't**.

I have my own problems too. I don't conduct myself like a slob. I could see if the person was truly a sick individual or handicap. Then the Residential Aide, abbreviated (RA) would have to assist that person with their' hygiene until that clients moves out. Why do some of them that have good health behave this way is beyond me?

When confronted......Get this, the ones that causing the filthy surroundings, the first thing coming out of their' mouth is, "This is a shelter!" In other words this is how you live while you in a shelter. That's **bullshit**, they just plain nasty. I'm homeless and the last thing I want to add on the list is filthiness.

Not trying to be funny or bias but the nastiest women I came across so far are those foreigners. You know people that come from other countries. It doesn't seem like anything is wrong with the majority of those women meaning like, they may not have a drug or alcohol problem. They just do nasty things like don't clean up behind their self. Leave their food behind on the tables, purposely put hair on the floor. They don't make their beds and they drop their unwanted garbage on the floor. They leave their dirty things behind in the bathroom. Their body dirt inside the tub. Now, hold on, I'm not saying everybody who come from other countries are nasty disgusting people. I have seen, some nasty Americans too, but mainly what I notice about the Americans, they are the ones getting high and all the time getting into fists fights. They have serious addictions problems or always running late and losing their' beds.

When I first enter into a women shelter, it was Sixty Eight Lexington and it was the worst. That shelter had two huge bathrooms which was on the 1st floor by the kitchen/dining-room area.

One enormous bathroom contained several showers stalls, which are next to each other. I had to take showers most of the times with seeing shit on the floor. Showering while seeing someone bloody smelly pad laying on the floor or, showering while seeing a use up-stinking tampon laying on the floor. In that shelter us girls lots of times was waiting on one line to use a particular shower stall because no woman wanted to use the dirty stall with shit or filth smear on the tile or, on the shower curtain.

How would you like taking a shower while looking at dried shit? Or looking at the one feces that laying on the floor in front of your view as you shower? Or making sure you stand in one spot so you won't touch the glob of spilt that's on the wall next to you as you showering in a narrow stall. Sometime a resident may be in a hurry because she have an appointment or may have to go to work and the resident don't have the time to wait, so she jumps inside the disguising narrow shower stall. Taking a shower quickly with both eyes close while standing in one spot avoiding the shit that on the floor, or, leaving the shower curtain open, whereas other residents who in line waiting to shower can see her naked body as she is showering. All because someone had smear a lot of shit on the shower curtain. Therefore that resident doesn't want to close the shower curtain. Now, that resident got to take a shower exposing her body for all other residents to see, simply because she don't want to close the shower curtain due from the shit that smeared on the inside of the shower curtain.

A lot of shelters comes with a large open shower room like that and some shelters' shower rooms doesn't have walls, for individual stalls. Sometimes it just a large open shower room with nothing but shower heads. Or, sometimes there's dull half cleaned looking shower stalls but with no shower curtains. Just because a shower stall may appeal to be cleaner than the other shower stalls, because of no visible filthiness. Mind you, everyone else is thinking the same way therefore we are all using that one appear to be clean shower stall. Do you know how many times I have smell another female piss while showering? I'm not going to lie, a couple of time I peed inside the shower then quickly tried to cover up my urine scent by using my fragrant shower gel but back to what I was speaking on; how clean is the appear clean shower stall if we all are using it?

I have seen staff members at Sixty Eight Lexington cleaning floors and bathroom stalls with a dirty mop and black dirty water. When I first arrived to 68 Lex, the staff was cleaning whenever and however they wanted to. A shelter is large and some shelter are way larger than others, so when the water and mop is dirty, I'm talking about, water looking like mud dirt, I seen employees mop with. Mainly because no one cared and no one spoke up about it. The residents didn't seem to care. The staff seemed to be overwhelm because 68 Lex was an armory; it resemble a castle. I have seen 68 Lexington staff clean with a mop so black it look like the mop should had be thrown out. I have seen employees moping with a pail filled with filthy mud black water. **Come on**! That so **disguising**. As if it was so hard to throw out the dirty water and re-fill the pail with clean deodorized water. Seeing and smelling the funk as you got to take a shower. Then looking at the dirty tools that were placed on the side in the corner from the employees-showing us females the tools they were using, it was so awful. Maybe that's one of the reasons Sixty Eight Lexington got closed down. That place was disgusted. I have seen it, live through it and I'm just sick of it.

That why I always take a shower with flip flops on. I don't care how clean the tub or shower stall may seem in any shelter. That's another reason why I always leave the bathroom spotless when I'm finishing using it. Making sure I got everything I came inside with, out, when I leave. Hoping that it rub off on others which it did work after the YEARS of being and living in this situation; I found out it does work. Not to mention also by reporting and speaking up to staff supervisor about the maintenance employees who may not think no one cares how he or she cleans.

Anyway, the security shift has change now. I hear Monique, the Spanish security guard is making her rounds on the fourth floor. Knocking and opening up doors to each dorm announcing "Ladies it eight o clock. Dorm must be clear out by nine."

Reminiscing again about Sixty-Eight Lexington Woman Shelter which is located in Manhattan. I never had a problem with leaving the dorm because I was never there. I just slept there. I didn't even eat there. I got to say it. It was one of the nastiness place I ever had to live but lets' not forget Catherine Street-Family Shelter. Besides the filth, that shelter had those big rats running around, ugh!!!! Literally many people was getting intoxicated so they can pass **the**

fuck out when they had to go inside for bed check. And I... kid... you... not! That shelter was in China-Town and it got closed down too.

After several years of me living there, Sixty-Eight Lexington got closed down too. Then I got transfer to Brooklyn. In two thousands and five to Bridge Net Woman Shelter. Now Bridge Net became my permanent/home shelter. I came to Bridge Net employed. Every morning I was out the door by six thirty am going off to work.

Sixty Eight Lex was my first adult shelter. I didn't know shelters were made differently. For starter at Bridge Net, the bathrooms are inside the dorms. So I shower every night before going to bed in fear that some mean spirited, spiteful, jealous female will go inside the bathroom, hold me up, making me late for work, causing me to loss my job and be stuck in this shit hell hole, on earth, of a so called shelter system; that's completely unorganized with constant ever changing rules by their idiotic dumb staff, or by their headquarters DHS, needing....wanting to improve the system. Therefore it like, DHS were changing their' rules like-month by month or every six months it seem.

At Bridge Net, every night I set the alarm clock from my cell phone. I had to use a flashlight in order to open my locker so not to awake my roommates-quietly as I got dress. Because no one is allowed to turn the lights on before six am, besides, females be grouchy if you making noise waking them up out from their sleep before those lights get turned on. Females were still sleeping in their' beds when I left out. On my salary I couldn't afford to pay the rent, light, gas and all the other necessities that come along with obtaining and keeping an apartment. I was thinking, I would be able to apply and, after a while get section eight like everybody else, but New York has changed.

Section eight program was going through transition even though section eight was still accepting and giving out applications. Then, the housing program of section eight got put on a freeze. Then.... DHS or was it the city/government who came up with other housing programs names that kept changing because those housing programs simply wasn't working out. Then, the city/government or DHS decided for low income housing, that the best working program, was section eight, therefore the name went back to section eight as it re-open.

Due to all the housing programs changes, at Bridge Net there were a couple of house meetings on this very topic. A lot of angry residents including myself, because now, we the homeless people were just sitting stuck inside this shelter system wondering which way to go for housing. Then shockingly, again, we find out section eight back on a freeze! And that last freeze for section eight lasted a good while.

When section eight finally re-open, people was placed into categories. Come to find out the category I was place in (general population) is dam near at the bottom of the list for housing placement. Then section eight went on a freeze again. So I got caught up in this shelter system with their many changes. To stay normal and not flip out, like start drinking, not caring anymore and just give up, I had to think about the positive side of this stressful situation.

My positive side is at least thank God, besides my good health I had a piece of a paying job. My little bit of a paycheck at one time did help me buy the things I needed to stay sane and out of trouble. I had money to take me and my kids out to a movie. Buy something to eat instead of that slop the shelter served. I had money to purchase body lotion and toiletries I liked. I notice the shelter body lotion isn't lubricated enough with moisture for my skin because after a while my skin became dry and ashy looking. Being homeless, but with some money, do make a **world** of a different. After serving one year and several months inside Bridge Net, all that was being offer for housing to us residents was an S.R.O. That type of housing program is the new way for homeless people to obtain suitable housing. It's an abbreviation for the word single room occupancy which mean, I get a private room with a key but I have to share the kitchen and bathroom, the common areas they call it.

At Bridge Net we had several heated house meetings on this topic too, because that's what all was being offered-a S.R.O for housing. I never thought I see the day when having my own bathroom would become a luxury. I never imagine that having a complete apartment would become a thing of the past. I couldn't believe the way the world for housing with me was changing. It got that bad for housing, that quit a few of the Americans females was actually waiting for Bridge Net ex Clinical Director to come outside from work to beat her ass, because us Americans girls wasn't used to hearing that we had to live in a **SRO?!?**

By this time, sadly I'm no longer working. I got fired. And after being in the shelter system for so long I was willing to take anything. So I got housing in the Bronx under the SRO program. Due to the fact from my personal data, which is on my file, I stated when asked the question from my caseworker, "Do I have children?" The answer is yes, so my caseworker was able to get housing placement for me in Temple Horizon a SRO, under the title-family reunification.

Temple Horizon this SRO old building have five floors. I lived on the third floor. I shared the floor with eight people, consisting of males and females but mainly males. I think a couple of those men tenants came out from jail. The building didn't come with maintenance either. So who do you think clean that one floor with long hallways consisting of two full bathrooms and a half, a full kitchen and tenants consisting of eight people? ....Me! Who do you think clean the common areas that we all had to share? I did. Before I cook. I had to clean because the common area on my floor was half way cleaned, dull-looking, and it seem to be unused. The stove was extremely dirty mainly from the people who lived there and over the years, they didn't clean the appliance. They were just using the appliances. It seemed like they never really cleaned up behind their self.

Tenants-even though we all lived inside the same building. We couldn't enter on another floor unless someone who lived on the floor, open up their floor front door for entry. Reason is every floor had a different key for their floor front door. In other words, every tenant had 3 keys; one key let tenants inside the building. Another key open the front door to the floor that tenant lived on and the last key open up the door to the tenant rented room.

Every floor seemed to have a different vibe too. On a lower floor all the tenants that shared that floor, shared everything and even cooked for each other. The tenants who shared that floor they didn't even lock their' apartment-room door. On another floor the tenants label their frozen food in their' kitchen freezer also on that same floor the tenants had separated their kitchen-cabinets, by inputting small pad locks on each cabinet for the tenants who lived on that floor. On my floor, all kitchen cabinets and fridge was empty. It seems like everybody on my floor mainly ate out, therefore our common area wasn't clean or seem to be lived in. On my floor our kitchen and especially the oven was dirty. Mainly because the people who did share the floor with me, when they did cook in, they just cooked on top of the stove. I also like to express every night when I made my dinner, I had to clean the top of the stove as well as the kitchen counters because I wasn't cooking my food on unclean surfaces nor did I leave any of my food in that refrigerator.

Before I shower, I had to clean the bathroom that I was using. To make that floor I lived on smell like an apartment even though I lived inside a room; I clean the entire floor, including wiping down the walls because I wanted my kids and whomever to come visit me and feel comfortable. It didn't feel right just too only clean my room because I had to come out from my room to cook, to use the bathroom and to go outside. Also each floor came with a small slop room where the floor mop and broom was kept. I cleaned that dirty, filthy room too and the mop and the industrial bucket because how could anyone clean up using dirty shit.

Dam! Clean, clean, clean just like the shelters but not just for my own room, now for an entire floor of nine other people who sharing the common areas. I'm such a clean person that I started making the maintenance employees who work inside the shelter look bad, but.........**Finally!** I was out of the shelter system.

Gone from Bridge Net about five or six months. Sadly, now I'm right back again because that SRO turned out to be a **disaster!** Before I got housed at that SRO, I did try to live at my grandmother' house but that didn't work out either. Due to my 1st cousins who had always lived there- they didn't want to see me live there so there was a lot of fist fights and extremely heated arguments' within the family that caused a lot of conflicts with our entire family.

Yep, the housing system has for New York had changed. The United States government weren't giving out apartments like they use too. It wasn't easy getting accepted in the project anymore either because now NYCHA had guidelines. It wasn't easy anymore getting a voucher from section eight to help assist a person like me with paying the costly rent, and, it's no longer easy obtaining residency for those newly built low income buildings-because it now became a thing of luck. Meaning, all low income applicants'-application, has got to go through the lottery system. Meaning, applications got to be handpicked, or, another word is selected. The applying applicant could only hope that his or her application get picked. Yep, times have gotten hard for a single adult who's on welfare with no children on their budget. And time has changed how poor people get housing. The housing system has changed.

The city wasn't catering to the single adults on welfare. They were concentrating on the people with children, individuals with aids/HIV, people that had domestic violent background, the elderly, protective witness and now, living inside the shelter, I am considered and label as general population, which is dam near at the bottom of the list-for help-to get housing!

Another problem homelessness people encounter and had to face was first of all the people in the projects weren't moving out either. They were passing down their' apartment to their children or to the next of kin which was another reason applicants, who's on the waiting list had to wait so long in order to be call for an apartment interview.

Now.......... being that I wasn't out from the shelter system, over 1 year, I had to come right back to Bridge Net after leaving Temple Horizon because, DHS said, it's my home shelter.

What is a home shelter?

The definition of a home shelter is whereas, Department of Homeless Services (DHS) has locked an individual into a particular shelter for residency-but before that individual was sent to that particular shelter, steps had to have been already in place-in order to make it official with DHS. Like; the individual has already been finger printed. Has already been given a permanent HRA number. Has already been given and, provided the results of a ppd, has already provided an attach photo along with other collected information like name, date of birth, age, and.... it been proven that the person doesn't have anywhere else to stay. Once that person, personal file has been completed the assigned caseworker now has to wait for a shelter to call saying there is an available bed in their establishment. Once, a shelter with an available bed has been place, DHS is saying; this is where that individual could be placed, until housing is found.

DHS is now recognizing that particular shelter, as the home shelter for that particular person. I'll give you an example, let say I'm tired of living in this shelter and I decided to leave. Several months later or even a couple of days later I decide to return to an assessment center or any other shelter, and say, "I'm homeless and have nowhere to go." The employed personnel would ask for my name. Next, input my name in the system and if I have ever been in a shelter before, then up pops my name and next to it will be the given HRA number I had already received also the shelter where I was placed as my home shelter. Now if I haven't been out from the shelter system longer than one year and is now seeking a place to stay, the employee of DHS automatically would send me back to my original shelter which is Bridge Net because it had already been determine it's my home shelter.

Now let say I been out the shelter system over 3 years and is seeking a place to stay. I then would have to start all over by going to an assessment center, or a drop off center, or an emergency center to wait for any shelter to say there is an available bed in their place for me, but I would still have the same HRA number that I was given. The HRA number' for a resident of DHS never change. I would always have that same HRA number.

Now what if a person has never been in the shelter system, but is homeless now needing a place to stay? That individual, may know of a homeless shelter in the neighborhood and decide to seek a bed. The shelter can't provide a bed to a walk-in. The person would be sent to start out at an assessment center, or a drop off center, or an emergency center. The new homeless person will be assigned a caseworker who would obtain his or her personal data. Then the person would start the process of being finger printed, given an HRA number and have their photo taken.

Approximately four to six weeks a person supposed to stay at any assessment center but I have heard that some females did stay longer. These assessments centers of DHS also have the same rules just like a regular shelter; everyone got to be in by ten pm and sign for their given temporary bed. Once everything is in order the assigned caseworker for that individual, or family-is waiting for a shelter of his or her needs; rather it's a family shelter or an adult shelter. Once a shelter calls the assessment center informing them, there is an available bed for that individual or family, then the client will be transfer to that shelter along with their permanent HRA number-making that shelter become the permanent residency. By calling it-the home shelter until you find or get housing.

Well, since I'm not working anymore this time around I really got to see a different side of the shelter..... And a different side of me being that I had nothing else to do.

Oh, oh! Let me start moving because I hear the walkie-talkie of...Security Monique enter the dorm. She has her pen and pad in her' hand saying "Ladies time to exit the dorm. It's pass nine o' clock." She put her walkie-talkie towards her' mouth and report "I'm in the Q dorm and there several ladies still inside the dorm."

From the loud walkie-talkie I could hear Shift Supervisor Wilks saying "Check for bed passes, copy. And whoever don't have one issue out an infraction."

Before too many girls were lying saying they work at night or they on bed rest, staying in the dorms stealing other people shit. Then you have those females who were hanging out getting drunk and high coming in late as overnighters unable to get up and leave out the dorm on time. Them residents was stealing people shit too so the shelter started having caseworkers and the medical department check out residents'-stories. If everything for that resident was found out to be true, a bed pass would be issued. The bed pass would contains the date it was issued.

The reason why it was issued, and to whom it was issued too, along with the expiration date of when the bed pass expire. All documented data are supposed to be place inside the residents' file.

Security Monique walks to bed number one. There no one there. Moving along to bed number two; that's Valerie bed. Valerie say to Monique "Don't you see me moving." Monique reply, "Hurry up." Bed number three. Lacy walks away from her' bed to exit the dorm. Security taps on the locker to bed number seven, sleeping beauty......I leaves the dorm.

Mad girls are in the hallway going their merry o way. Everybody, got a bag. Most of them stop by the 4th floor elevator. I open the 4th floor exit door and take the stairs. I stop on the second floor which really is the first floor to the shelter. The entrance into the building where security scan the residents is on the bottom floor which Bridge Net employees see as the first floor.

Once I'm on the 2nd floor I see the maintenance guys in their uniform. They are gather together standing by their' small office door talking among each other and occasionally glancing at the ladies as they passes by. Shack, Moby, Black, Langston and Maranda are the maintenance crew for this shelter. "Good morning people," I said as I'm just about to pass them. Shack shook his head in a what-up body language. Moby and Maranda they both said, "Good morning." Black just looked and Langston smiled but he looked puzzle.

They know me as a working resident and I know they heard I moved out. So I figure them questioning what happen? Why is she back again? What happen to her job? Because around this time of the day I was never here.

I walk pass the intake office, mad girls are in there. I'm walking straight to the dining-room. The radio is playing and it crowded, while standing there, looking around with my eyes I'm searching for a seat but it so pack I just walk towards the window to get out of the way from the girls that's still coming inside the dining area.

The shelter staff, they should open up the other side of the dining-room and let us girls go and sit over there too, that's where there are more tables and chairs. But it's the kitchen side and it's not open-up to us residents unless breakfast, lunch or dinner is being served.

That kitchen area, at this time is only being used for the RA who is issuing out residents' toiletries or clients picking up their supply of detergent. Mainly, the morning shift security and maintenance workers like to sit on that side, eating their' breakfast or having their' morning cup of coffee. After lunch, when that kitchen side is closed off again, you find security and maintenance in their sometimes eating their lunch. Once in a while you may find the intake office receptionist and morning shift supervisor in there joining security and maintenance. All the other staffs at Bridge Net eat behind their' desk or outside somewhere.

So many girls are coming/going. I found a seat at the table by the bathroom door. Bertha starts arranging her belonging so that I could fit in comfortably at the table. I looked her way and say "Thank you." She lay her head down on the table. I'm watching and feeling the energy of the women. They're going through their' pocketbook searching for appointed paper work, gathering their information and sorting out their documents to handle the many task they about to do. Like going to their WEP assignments, getting updated ppd shoot, going back to school or maybe, making their PA cases become active again, some looking and asking others for a cigarette to go outside to smoke.

"What is that disguising smell?" I question on.

The sounds of, "mmmum" is echoing in the air. Someone shitting in the dining room bathroom and it stunk up the entire area. Majority of the females are holding their' nose. Some have a piece of tissue or their' hat is covering their' face......... Oh my goodness, it starting to smell so bad that the odor starts to sneak through our covered nose. "Mmmum. Open up the window!" Sabricka said offensively while crocheting.

Oh...my.... God. The smell just lingering like what the **fuck**!

Some girls was eating and drinking too. They starting closing and covering up their food with their hand. Whoever she is, is still inside the bathroom. A Caribbean women named Dottie, sitting at the table started saying "Whoever in the batroom she needs a wash out!" Now all the other West Indian women starts nodding theirs heads in agreement.

Boxer shouted, "Yo, go get Maranda tell her to come and spray." Females started calling, "Maranda. Maranda, Maranda," they yelled.

Security guard Cammy come into the dining-room area. She immediately frowns her' face from the awful smell. Girls without delay speaking audible, still holding their' nose they saying "Go get Maranda she need to clean and spray out the bathroom."

With a frown on her face, Cammy walks over and knocks on the bathroom door asking, "Are you alright in there?"

The resident answered.

Short Stop recognize the voice and said to the angry crowd "Oh she on medication." Boxer said "So! Still got to come clean this mother fucker out."

Brenda is American she said, "When people on medication their' bowls does smell." Some of us looking like we just found out some new kind of information justifying the awful smell. Dottie stated behind Brenda, "Well she still need a wash out, mon."

At this point Cammy, the security guard comes back into the room with an aerosol can in her hand saying "Maranda busy," as she spray the area but the only thing is Cammy sprays so much that we all start to choke.

"Damn Cammy," I said.

"Hey yall told me to spray right," she said as she continue spraying. The resident comes out of the bathroom. Cammy hold the door open while frowning from the awful smell. Cammy now starts spraying inside the bathroom. It stinks and I'm choking. I can't take it. While holding my nose I get my things and I leave out from the dining-room.

At the next house meeting I'm going to make a suggestion can resident be allow to go to their dorm and shit.

From nine am until four pm the medium size dining room is the only place we are allowed to sit. It getting disgusting with everyone takings turns shitting in the dining-room bathroom, as we all sit there and smell their' different bowel movement. As I walked and walked, and walked around outside, I found myself in a familiar area. St Paul Park, in my old neighborhood. It's where I grow up at.

I sat there thinking about my childhood. My old address was fourteen hundred Daren't Street, apt twelve C. In a two bedroom apartment I lived there with my parents. Ed and Sylvia Jones and a younger sister name Tonya. My mother told me I was three years old when I moved here. The project consists of nine building, and some building went as high as the fourteen floor but the building I live in only goes to the thirteen floor. When a person steps out of the elevator the first apartment door anyone see, is twelve A, then twelve B. People will also notice the apartments on the floor goes around in a circle. All the way to apartment twelve J.

Our apartment was under the top floor in my building, and what a spectacular view we had of Manhattan. At night time the view was awesome. So many bright lights shining underneath the sky, moonlight and stars. As a child it was breathe taking seeing the different heights of the office buildings, looking at the Twin Towers, watching and distantly hearing the sounds of the Long Island Rail Road train go by on the train tracks.

To me we had the best view and best decorated apartment. My mother have good taste in decorating. She especially loves window treatment. My mother had a thing back then for drapes. I recall a gold and white set, it was beautiful. It came with a draw string and tassels. My mom was so creative that she made our window look much wider by allowing the fabric to cover the blank wall that was next to the window. We also had a blue and white set of drapes too. Thinking back, a picture of her was taking making a drink from the mini wagon bar, in her long off white night gown standing by the gold and white drapes. She would change the drapes in the living-room every six months, so that our living room would have a different appeal.

In our living room sat a beautiful royal blue fur pull out queen size couch. Two swivel identical beige fur roomy arm chairs. A large wooden floor model television. My parent had a small bar made out of gold chrome that contain two glass shelves. The top level had a place for holding upside down Martini glasses or wine goblets and a matching gold plated ice bucket. The bottom had space for their liquor of choice. The mini bar resemble a round wagon. It had one big wheel on each side.

Opposite from the living room window, we had eight large anti-gold beveled square mirrors on one side of the living room wall. With glass and gold chrome matching end tables, and a center piece. There was a mahogany wooden-glass curio that hold four glass shelves. The living room was completely carpeted. I don't recall any picture hanging on our wall but we did have photo album books filled with pictures. We were consider a middle class family. Back in those days, you know you was well off financially when your apartment had appliances. In our apartment we had a washer machine, dryer, and a deep freezer. My parents were into music. We had every album and forty-five there was.

We could see the view of Manhattan from the kitchen window, living room windows and both bedroom' windows. I remember thinking one day I could have a piece of that. I couldn't help but dream big looking at that beautiful scenery every night under the moonlight with all those beautiful stars twinkling in the dark blue sky. As a child, I remember whenever I shared my dreams with my parents. My dad and my mother use to always say, "Electra s start small you dreaming to big." I can now only say, it too bad that my parents' dreams are so small.

Anyway passed the living room, you enter a narrow hallway. On the left is where the bathroom at. Both bedrooms was on the right side of the narrow hallway. The first bedroom is where Tonya and I slept. One year for Christmas our parents brought us a green organ, it came with a matching seat and a song book.

Passing our bedroom, on the opposite side is a medium size two door closet. In front of that is where my mom and dad slept. My parent were extremely blessed. Both of them had great jobs. My father was an EMS driver and my mother a supervisor at the Telephone Company. Our family was highly blessed with four loving grandparents, two aunts from on my mother side of the family.

My dad is an only child. As a young girl one day while visiting Grandma-Grace, (she my dad' mother). I was looking through her' photo album-book. I came across a picture of a little girl. She looked to be nine year old. I ask Grandma-Grace, "Who is she?" Grandma-Grace told me it's her' daughter and that she died as a young child. Grandma-Grace told me her' name.

When I was growing up back then families were in categories. You had the rich, middle class and poor. We were differently borderline middle class family. Sometimes daddy use to take us with him to go pick my mother up from work. I remember she got off work at night because I recall looking out the window while driving on the highway, it will be getting dark. Tonya and I would be in the back seat as my dad drove on the Brooklyn Bridge. My father enjoyed singing and listening to that one song all the time whenever he took Tonya and I out for a drive. I'm not for sure if daddy had it playing from his' car cassette player or if it came on the radio. All I know, whenever he took us for a drive the song will come on and daddy start to sing. I like to remember it as the road song.

The Song is by Frankie....somebody. It's the early seventies and I'm young anywhere between the age of eight or ten. I been through so much shit. I can't remember the artist name but I can hear some of the lyrics and the melody in my head....it goes something like this...There I go there I go there I go, there__ I go____. Pretty baby you are the one who touch my control___ such a funny thing about whenever you see me__ you fill my heart ba-by with your ma-gic___ there's beauty all around you. .... Can go now if you want to, we're____ through_____.

Anyway driving on the Brooklyn Bridge to pick up my mom, he will make a right turn to exit off the bridge. We go around and around and around on this ramp and exit off. The building my mother work in wasn't too far from the bridge. The lights that came from that tall office building were so dreamy. I use to like watching my mother come out from the building. She so pretty and had such a nice figure not to fat or skinny just right. Sometimes when we arrive to pick her up, she already be waiting outside for us. Standing in front of that beautiful building all dressed up. She walked with such confidence and assertiveness looking so professional and attractive. My mom has such a beautiful smile. I'm going to be just like her one day pretty and successful. I contemplated as a child. We had a great family and we all seemed to be happy.

Our Christmas were wonderful. Our parents went all out for us. My sister and I really did believe in Santa Claus. We go to bed and wake up to the most marvelous toys. In my time as a child us kids we played with toys. We had all the dolls and board games. My dad was the one who was really into the toys because he use to get down on the floor and play with us.

I mean our Christmas were really beautiful. We got all kind of toys even boy toys. Like electronic remote control train set and car sets that ran on tracks. Plastic water pistol guns. Remember that silver toy guns that made a clicking noise when you pull the trigger. Roller skates and several baby dolls, the really good ones too. Back then the TV would advertise all the cool toys for the holiday and whatever one came on the television if we wanted it, we got it. Not once a year, every year our Christmas were totally spectacular.

Our parents was wonderful to us. We receive not only toys. We receive jewelry, fur jackets and lots of winter clothes. Sparkle perfume lotions, pajamas and let not forget pretty panties and girly hosieries. Those gifts I believe came from my mother she always cared about appearances.

I remember one year, besides the toys, we got bicycles. I had the purple bike with a white basket. Tonya had the pink bike with the white basket. I couldn't wait to ride my bike. I remember we begged my parents if we could ride our bikes in the hallway. When they gave us the okay, we shot out the door in our X- mass pajamas. Jumped on that bike, which was a wonderful moment us laughing and pressing our' bike horn learning how to ride our bicycles. Going around and around on the twelve floor. Nobody complain because back then kids behave like children especially during the holidays. The sound of children laughter was a good thing.

My father had both of his' parents involved in our lives even though they lived in separate apartments. His' mother (who we call Grandma-Grace) lives with DollarBill (that's Grandma-Grace' old man) they live in Harlem.

Christmas, growing up for me and my sister, Grandma-Grace brought us gifts like bath robes, pajamas and slippers. But her specialty was giving us money. I'm speaking bills, like fifty dollars or sixty dollars each which was exceptionally a lot of money back then for a kid. Occasionally she would surprises us with other gifts like a crochet handmade sweater/ coat. They were blue and white and the other one was red and white both came with their' matching hats. One time my Great Aunt went to California and Grandma-Grace had her to bring us back a set of silk Japanese pajamas. One set was a beautiful light blue and the other was a gorgeous white.

My father' father, we called him Grand-pop. He lives in Brooklyn-walking distance from us. Grand-pop lives with Miss Joyce. She had a lot of grandkids that she babysat for. Every year Grand-pop gave money to Miss Joyce to pick us up exceptional great Christmas gifts. Mainly they were a lot of electronic gifts being that he served in the military. It explain why he was so technical and serious I guess. He served as a Marine. Just to let you know my dad he served in the Navy. We are so American.

Our gifts from Grand-pop will range anywhere from a camera, hand pocket tape recorders, radios, walk men, walkie-talkies plus a bunch of other cool gadgets. If the gifts were battery operated they will supply us with the batteries too. It didn't matter how many gifts we received at one time, if it was battery operated, we were covered. Plus he gave us money as well.

One thing I could say is that Tonya and I never had to share our Christmas gifts. My father' parents, they both made sure we had our own presents. When anyone of our birthday came, we both received money, I'm taking bills. It's funny because even though if it was mine or her birthday they will still make sure the other one got some cash too. It just wasn't as much as the birthday girl.

Not to mention every holiday my dad drove us including my mother to his' mother house in Harlem where we sat and ate Christmas and Thanksgiving dinner. My parent had cooked holiday dinner for us at home too. It was just our family tradition how we spent the holidays.

Just putting it out there Grandma-Grace made the best homemade biscuits, best homemade potatoes salad, best homemade gravy.........and some **dam** good sweet potatoes pies. She always made enough of whole pies for us to take back with us home too.......Yum. Because my mother wasn't a baker.

Thinking about her now (Grandma-Grace) and her' style-her favorite drink was a cup of hot tea. Whenever I spent the night at her apartment I always woke up to the delicious aroma of cooking oatmeal. Every morning she made **the best** darn tasting oatmeal. In her' refrigerator, you will always see a cold liter bottle of Pepsi and on her dresser in the bedroom you find a blue container of Noxzema. Oh yeah and in her' bathroom you find plenty of different scented Avon bubble bath and Avon skin so soft.

During the holidays my dad would send me and my sister to Grand-pop house and there we would eat our holiday dinner as well. Miss Joyce was a good cook too. She would make everything too. The only different at their home is you would find some chitlins, which I rarely ate. Tonya enjoys eating that. Just to be polite, I eat like two spoonful with a touch of hot sauce because they loved it so much and I loved them so much. Grand-pop, his' sweet potatoes pies would be baked regularly and some would be baked with coconut flakes.

I believed him and Miss Joyce both took part in cooking, knowingly Miss Joyce did the most. Grand-pop favorite things for the holiday was making homemade sweet potatoes pies, his' homemade cold ice tea and homemade cold lemonades.....**Yum**. Another one of his' favorite thing to make-was is homemade corn liquor which I didn't taste until I became of age.

My father' parents never did remarried. Even through DollarBill and Miss Joyce were not my biology grandparents they sure did make us feel like they were and in my heart is where they stay.

As Grandparents.

Now my mother parents' are home owners. They have a two family house. They have three daughters. My mother is the middle child and she have a lot of cousins. This is where all my first cousins and seconds cousins and third cousins come in at.

My mother' father, us grand-kids, calls him Granddaddy. He a very creative person. He have lots of creative ways of making money. He had purchase different tools to maintain his' home. He had a hot dog chart once. I heard he even wanted to purchase an ice cream truck but none of his' daughter wanted to ride in it selling ice-cream cones. I never knew what kind of job he had and I never heard my mom mention what type of work her' dad do but Granddaddy is a real cool cat. He enjoys wearing hats. Anything from a straw hat to a cap or a hat with a brim. You find him sitting on his' porch with a little drink in his' hand trying to speak Spanish, but the only words he knows is-se ya manana.

He was a good grandfather. Kind in nature and he truly loved his family, all of us. Granddaddy couldn't spoil us like Grand-pop did, because unlike Grand-pop, Granddaddy had a lot of biology grandkids.

When the ice-cream truck came down the block granddaddy always stop it and got all of us an ice-cream cone. Meaning all his' grandkids. He got a kick out of counting us as we all went up to get our ice-cream. We grandkids, love him **very much**. He couldn't give us big bills like my father' parents but he gave us love and support and always a quarter or fifty cent to go to the corner store and buy whatever we wanted.

To me, his' favorite thing was family and money.

My mother', mother, we all call her Grandmamma. Her' daughters calls her Mam. I don't know why because her name is Yvette. Anyway she something else. She works but I don't think she pay any bills, Granddaddy take care of her.

At this time in my life, it's the early seventies. When life was good and decent, and people didn't have a lot of money but we had fun and love. They from the old school........ my grandparents-meaning the man is the head of the household, and he is the one who mainly supports. Granddaddy is the main provider for his' household.

Come to think about it, my' grandparents are the same. Grandma-Grace doesn't work. DollarBill take care of her and Grand-pop is the provider for Miss Joyce. I'm quite sure Grand-pop, he helps her with her extended family.... when asked. Wait I'm not trying to make is seem like the woman stayed in the house and did nothing, because my Grandmamma worked holding cleaning jobs. Then she worked in a hotel and I already told you my mom worked. Grandma-Grace use to work before she got sick. Now that I'm thinking about it, my father provided for my mother and us too. All I could say is those were the good old days, when men were men.

Anyway back to speaking about my Grandmamma. She loves money. When we were young she enjoyed giving card games; selling food and beverages to the players. On every table Grandmamma made sure she got her cut. There was always a cup sitting on the table for the house. And the house was her. To get her' money it's like pulling teeth. Trust me, she bite your hand with her' gums before you take her' money. She's a tough cookie and a little spoil.

It comical looking back now on those days. My Grandmamma, reminds me of Grand-pop. They both act like a king and queen sitting on their' throne. While

Granddaddy and Grandma-Grace are both sweet and kind in nature. Both loves to give and express love. Not to mention they outwardly shows and express their love for their' family-deeply.

Anyway both my mother' parents.....their favorite thing is **Money**. They love to gamble... and they love their' daughters. What you find in their home is a number slip, the big red number sheet and my aunt Melody three children. All four grandparents are quiet people meaning neither of them did a lot of entertaining in the house.

My aunts, are Lynette and Melody, they are my mother sisters. Lynette has three children starting from the oldest, their names are Coon, Sheryl and Lee Keisha

My aunt Melody has all boys. They are slightly younger than their five older 1st cousins. Their names are Tie, Skyler and Malik.

So in order, starting from the oldest to the youngest as first cousins, we have Coon, Sheryl, Electra, Lee Keisha, Tonya. Now we all are close in age like a year apart from each other. So we hung out together, played and danced together. Tie, Skyler and Malik, are way younger than us but they were always around just downstairs with my mother' parents.

As children my mom took me and my sister to her' parent's house a lot. As children we spent a lot of time over there in that old house. Too me Grandmamma and Granddaddy sure did a lot for their' grown daughters. My aunt Lynette had a hard time as a single parent raising her' three young children so she moved in her' parents two family home. She occupy the four bedroom apartment upstairs, in my grandparents' house. It where my sister and I spent many of nights with our cousins.

My Aunt Melody had her own place but because of her not working and constantly not paying her bills because she choose to get high and party all the time. Not taking care of her' maternal responsibilities therefore her kids practically lived downstairs on my grandparents.

Don't get the wrong idea, my aunt Melody love her' boys. She just didn't sacrifice her wants, her needs and her time to do the right thing by them. She a tad bit spoil too and maybe, she look at it like-my boys with my family because we were more like brothers and sisters to each other anyway. My grandparents supplied all Melody' children needs. They were the one who made sure her kids had school clothes and their school supplies. My grandparents made sure they had food to eat. They were also the ones who made sure Melody' kids had somewhat of a holiday; meaning holidays home cook meals and their personal celebrations, like birthdays.

My mom pitch in, I'm quite sure, but mainly my aunt Lynette helped also in supporting and aiding in aunt Melody's kids. I witness my aunt Lynette helping out with Melody's kids. She was able to do more because she lived in the same house with them, just upstairs. Knowing her younger sister Melody were missing in action when her' kids were hungry. So Aunt Lynette supported them too with plenty of prepared meals.

My mother two sisters weren't as fortunate as her. My mom, she married. And has a great job; not depending on her' parents for anything. She has, obtain as well as maintain a fabulous apartment. My mom parents didn't have to take care of me and my sister because we were already being taking care of by our own parents. My grandparent didn't worry much about their middle daughter Sylvia because my mother, she totally independent and didn't show any signs of being a burden to her' parents. When my mom' birthday came around, my aunt Lynette used to always say, "I don't know what to get her because she already has everything." As a child I always question that sentence within myself. I hinted a taste of envy. I didn't feed into it because I was young and I adore my family. I consider myself to be very fortunate, because I was. I remember when we all got together, as the family, we sing that song by Sister Sledge "We are family. I got all my sisters with me." As children in that old house, we all ran up and down those stairs, sliding down the banister, enjoying my Aunt Lynette barbecues, going to the corner store for our grandparents, singing and lots of dancing and playing games. We completed the picture of a loving family. We had so much fun and love towards one another. I truly do miss those days.

Growing up my sister and I had one more aunt. Her name is Bee. Really she is my dad cousin who spent time with him, when his' sister was sick then later passed away. Aunt Bee played with him as a child after dad loss his' sister. Tonya and I grew up thinking Aunt Bee was our aunt on my dad side. We grew up calling her and respecting her as, Aunt Bee and her treating us as if we were her nieces. As you can see my parents were truly blessed and highly supported by their' family. There is nothing in the world their' parents' wouldn't have done for either one of them.......... **oh sweat**, it lunch time!

I ran out the park and I saw the B118 bus coming up Union Place. When I got on the bus I said to the bus driver, "You know that women shelter up the block on Broadway?" The bus driver said "Yeah I seen it." I showed my Bridge Net photo id and said "Well that's where I'm living right now and I don't really have the money to ride the bus. Its lunch time, can I please get a ride."

The driving wave his' hand as if to say come in have a seat and I sat down. Standing at the entrance of Bridge Net I knocked on the glass part of the door. Security guard Mia Dowser smiled and buzzes the door for me to come in.

I put my bags on the black conveyor belt, as I watch it goes through the scanning machine. M. Dowser said "Hello Electra." I say "How you doing." Once my bags came out from the machine Mia Dowser hand-check my bags. I asked her can she move quickly because I wanted to catch lunch. I proceeded and walk through the metal magnetometer detector and it buzzes. M. Dowser walks over towards me with the hand scanner as more girls' taps on the glass window wanting to enter.

Mia Dowser turns and press a button behind the chair for the entrance door to become unlocked, allowing the girls to enter. Now she performing on me her physical hand checks with the hand scanner. Once she finish. I turns around to go to the second door for entrance into the shelter. As I start walking I see other ladies are putting their' belongings on top of the conveyer belt. I'm standing by the second door awaiting to hear the buzz............M. Dowser has unlocked the door for me to enter. I proceeded up the steps.

Once I got to the second floor, I bump into my caseworker Miss. Taylor. When she saw me she said "Electra I need to meet with you tomorrow. I will leave you a reminder notice." I told her "Alright," as I quickly brush by trying to catch lunch before the door closes.

I made it, just in time. I got the kitchen roster, turning the pages looking for the Q dorm. Quickly I find my name and sign. We having sandwiches. Bridge Net always serve wrap-up sandwiches for lunch. What's left are pile up on the kitchen plexi-glass top. Us residents we have a choice of having the sandwich on white bread or wheat. All the food we eat at Bridge Net is cater from an outside vendor. They not tasty like the sandwiches you get at the corner store but never the less it still a sandwich.

Gloria the RA asks me "Do you want one or two sandwiches." I said "Two." Then Gloria asks me "White or wheat?" I said "One of each." Gloria ask me "Would you like a salad?" I told her, "Yeah." Their salad are just a bunch of lettuce in a small foam bowl. It comes with two small packaging of salad dressing. I moved down the line. Then RA Houser hands me two packs of small cookies and two half way frozen small juices with napkins.

During lunch time both side of the dining room are open making it easier to find a seat. Most of the ladies prefer to eat on the side where the music is. That the side I prefer anyway because I love music. The radio station is on ninety-eight point seven kiss. Someone donated the compact two dual radio cd /cassette player. The radio is a good thing because it breaks the silence in the air. Before us residents just sat in here quietly, doing whatever, which really meant nothing at all.

I'm finish eating my sandwiches so now I'm looking around in the dining room. You will find a couple of female crocheting. Other girls are absorb in their own thoughts. Some ladies reading a book to pass the time and others maybe sleeping with their' head laying down on top of the tables. When lunch is over, there not much to do especially when you broke. We ladies have to find something to do from nine am until four pm every day. Residents are not allow to enter their' dorm until four pm and that becomes boring too because all that's in a dorm, are beds/cots whatever you want to call those things we sleep on. So the girls sit and eat all day. That's why they so fat, they always munching on something. As for me, I just can't sit in that dining room all day glazing out the window, but, as I sit in the dining area I started getting absorb into my own thoughts. Seeing all these people including myself, wondering......... how did so many people get lost and forgotten?

When I was sitting in the park reminiscing about my past with my family, now as I looked around the room, I'm starting to wonder where these females', family are. Then I wonder, well **hell**, where is my family? Then it hit me there are different types of homeless people. The homeless people who got burned out of their' homes and lost everything, as a result from a fire. It would be kind of understandable why that person lives in a shelter. Then people who became homeless because they lost their' apartment and maybe even their kids due to their years of drugs addictions. Being unable to cope and deal with real life issues sober. Addictions is a disease. It's understandable why these people became homeless. They need help with their sobriety. Showing clear signs of inability to live responsible and independently sober. Maybe with therapy it can help that person take a deeper and honest look in the mirror asking their self that question of ....why...what happen in your life? That's causing you to behave in such manner?

Or what about the people who's coming home after being incarcerate/lock up or ageing out of foster care? Maybe they have no family and nowhere to go, and no money, or simply, there isn't any room for that individual to live in their' family home or can't stay with their' family member due to a violation in the lease, which also will be understandable; why he or she live inside of a shelter.

Then you have the people who sneak into the country and don't want to go back to where they came from. If you look at it they made their' own self become homeless. To me those girls are the ones that give the shelter a bad name with their stealing and filthy behavior. Now they live in America, the land of opportunity as they say. They take America for granted. Example taking companies toilet tissue, taking the shelter linen and their' cleaning supplies all because they feel look at what all this country have. To me that's one of the reason we are in this predicament now, this depression; people stealing any and everything that's not nail down. Then it's those who are in domestic violence relationships and those who had lost their jobs. So they enter into the shelter system seeing the place as a form of safe haven residency which is understandable.

This group of people well I don't see them as being truly homeless. They just want their' own apartment. These people really just sleep here. When the morning come they off at family house resting, bathing, cooking or watching TV. Some of them still have their' own bedroom and closet space for storing their possessions'. These are the people who quite often don't care about what happens inside the shelter. For example: like why staff haven't issue out the clean linen on the scheduled day? Or why maintenance hasn't clean up a dorm? They don't care about the bathroom being clutter with other' belongings because they wash their' bodies elsewhere. The only thing they care about is, housing. These people doesn't care when they hear staff have stolen a resident' belonging. Just as long as it not theirs. These also are the people who don't appreciate or help support and up kept the few activities the shelter does provides. Unless they heard the shelter is given out something of value. They don't care about house meeting. What someone donated and if we the resident got it. Participating and keeping the activities going, helping to prevent boredom. Their favorite line to say is, "Girl I don't care. I just want my housing." Or I have heard them say "I'm not here for that, I'm just here for my housing." One thing I can say about those clients is they do have their family supporting them in their time of endeavors. Assisting them and helping make their load a little easier to bare. Which make a big world of a different when you homeless.

Now, let take a look at one of the biggest problems I found out since being out of work and having to stay here all day. Is, why does security and the staff plays favoritism among the residents?

Then there are just homeless people. The ones who really don't have family support. I mean we all came from somewhere but plenty of homeless people really doesn't have their' family supporting them. The true homeless person after lunch, may just lay their head down on the table instead of facing the humiliation of that again she have to sit on a park' bench for an excessive long period. The true homeless person take tremendous long walks. Another thing they do or where you may find them is, in the library, sitting there for hours. When it's really bad, people find them sleeping on the train. The true homeless individual doesn't have any money mainly due to no refrigeration. The true homeless individual can't purchase $5.00 worth of luncheon meat and buy a loaf of bread, because where could it be stored? The true homeless person could purchase a sixty-four ounce soda but the downside to that will be carrying it around till it gone. Then don't forget after a while the soda my get hot. Then the person have to purchase a cup of ice and that cost money too. Now, in some shelter large beverage aren't allowed anymore-including water. So a true homeless person spend money wastefully especially when there is no family support. A true homeless person spends every holiday in the shelter and eats in soup kitchen. A true homeless persons like myself cares about the shelters rules, their changes and conditions because it does affect me being that I really do live here and I'm truly am this' homeless person.

One more thing I like to say before I close this chapter is, I hate being homeless but I am. In every negative situation I'm learning to always try to find something positive. So I say, I'm just glad I'm homeless in New York, in America, because I hear in other countries when you are homeless you actually sleep in the streets. In other countries when you homeless there is no one helping you out with food so once again I say, I'm so glad I'm homeless in America; where I can get something to eat, apply for food stamps and not starve or sell my ass, degrading myself. Once again I say, I'm so glad I'm homeless in America because I have no family support and literally I would be sitting in the street. So thank God I'm homeless in America having a place call a shelter to stay in. Somewhere I can sleep halfway like a human being, wash my clothes and wash my ass. While sitting at the table looking at so many faces of girls, especially black girls, once again I say, I'm so glad....... and that's the positive side of me living inside a shelter.

Chapter Four

Samantha enters the dining-room area. Security guard Cammy walks in behind her. Cammy walk straight to where the radio at. She stops and now she asking one of the old ladies for their' walking cane using the cane Cammy reaches up, she finds the volume button then she turns the radio completely down. Us girls know there's an announcement about to be made.

The director of recreational, Samantha makes an announcement, "On the third floor at three o'clock I will be having a yoga class. All are invited." Then she walks out with a bunch of rattling keys in her hand.

Security adjust the volume back on the radio and exit the area. When I lived in Manhattan at Sixty-Eight Lex I did a lot of walking around and window shopping. Occasionally I came across and read messages concerning yoga? I notice lots of white people are really into it. I used to see them going in or coming out of varies buildings with their' yoga outfits on while carrying a rolled up mat in their' hand. Yoga classes, some of them are expensive.

Being it is being offer to us here for free, and I don't have anything else to do. I decided to give it a try. I got up, took my bags and left out from the dining-room.

Once I'm in the hallway, I see the maintenance worker for the second floor, Maranda. She's popping in and out from one dorm to the next making sure the dorms are cleared of residents so she can clean. While her company industrial mop and bucket stood on the side of the wall. Maranda, her' mop clean as fresh snow with clear water smelling fresh and deodorized.

As I continue walking down the hall, I look into the second floor caseworkers' office. I saw Sunset sitting down speaking with a caseworker. As I continue walking, now coming up upon the intake office I could hear the office' telephone ringing. When I got closer to the intake office I glanced in. I saw Michelle, the intake office' receptionist sorting out the residents' mail.

I turned the hallway corner and open the stairwell door. I'm heading up the steps leading to the third floor. When I open up the door the first person I saw was Security Guard Watts. She sitting on her' post. Station by the third floor laundry room, talking on her cell phone. That guard, she always on her' phone holding a conversation.

Making the right turn in the hallway, as I passed the guard. Looking straight ahead I could see the closed door to the third floor caseworkers' office. All of a sudden, the door opened and I heard and saw resident Celeste angrily telling someone who is behind the office door, "I don't want to live in an SRO! I don't want to share a kitchen and bathroom with no one. I want my own place."

She started walking my way until Mrs. Porter the caseworkers' supervisor came out from behind the door saying, "Celeste, dar-ling, you can't keep turning down suitable housing. You will get transfer to Next Step-dear. Can you at least think it over?"

"I don't want to live in the fuckin Bronx and I'm not sharing shit! I'm tired of sharing," Celeste said as tears started rolling down her' face.

Tim came out from the office walking towards Mrs. Porter and Celeste. He's a caseworker and he must be Celeste's caseworker.

Tim, he looks generally concern as he watches the tears roll down Celeste face. He's standing there with both his hands inside his pants pocket, not knowing how to console Celeste.

Mrs. Porter said, "Celeste if I could, I give you an apartment overlooking the ocean but I can't. The interview is set for ten in the morning."

Displaying her authority position she now turns towards Tim. Mrs. Porter asked "Her interview is ten or ten thirty?" "Supposedly," Tim said, "It ten o'clock sharp."

I heard Mrs. Porter say just before I was about to enter into the room "Celeste please don't mess this up for yourself. My hands are tied there's nothing I can do after this point."

Decision making time for Celeste and Celeste is piss the fuck off! Angrily Celeste said "Excuse me!" as she angrily brushes pass me. "Dam!" I said as I watched her exit from off the floor.

Just as I was about to turn the door knob. I saw maintenance worker Shack coming out from the G dorm with his' mop and bucket. Audible I said "Whatz up Shack."

While he pulls his' industrial mop and bucket towards the next dorm. Shack turns his head look in my direction and said, "Electra."

I walk toward him and asked, "Can I get a sponge and a bottle of soap scrum so I can clean out the tub in my dorm Shack?"

Surprisingly.... Shack said .... "I just put a spray bottle yesterday in your dorm?" I said "Well it wasn't any in the bathroom earlier. Somebody must have stolen it."

Finding out this news, slowly, he said, in an uncertainly tone .... "I'll see what I can do." I just stood there as if I really needed that soap scrum to clean out the tub so I can take a shower. Then he said, "Meet me on the fourth floor at four-o'clock." Smiling I said "Thanks."

I walk into the room where Samantha is holding her' yoga class. I'm hearing meditating music? This room is really our TV room. Maintenance had mopped and cleared out most of the room sitting chairs. Samantha had placed, and they looked brand new, a couple of yoga mats on the floor. The mats were position several feet away from each other on the floor while the meditating music softly plays in the background.

"Welcome, welcome," she had said. As a couple of ladies came in behind me. It's Bertha and Thomasina.

Samantha said, "Please sign the attendance sheet. Listen guys this is a new class I'm starting, if you want you could go to your dorm to get a loose pair of clothing because we are going to be doing a lot of stretching and twisting."

I said "I'm good," as I signed the attendance sheet. I took off my sneakers. Then I went and stood on one of those blue yoga mats.

Thomasina said, "I'm fine but I'm not going to be doing too much bending because my back is hurting." I asked her "What happen to your back?" Thomasina said, "I woke up feeling like this, this morning."

"It is probably that cheap mattress we sleep on," Bertha said. "Yeah I can relate because I had slept on a couple of the shelter' bad mattresses myself," I said.

Overhearing our conversation Sam said "Class, I don't want you to force yourself if you are in any pain. Yoga does require stretching and breathing skills that are healthy and promote strength as well as balance. So do listen to how your body feels. As, we get into it your mind may tell you, you could go farther, but I'm saying in yoga listen to your body and not your mind. Okay guys."

We all shook our head in agreement by letting Samantha know we understood what all she just said.

In a concerning voice Samantha said, "In yoga what we do on one side of the body we must practice on the opposite side of the body. This is done for total wellness for completion of total healing. If your body says that's the farthest it could go comfortably, do listen."

Some older ladies came in to watch.

Sam started out by saying, "With both feet planted firmly on the floor let start rotating our shoulders by moving them backward. Slowly feeling our shoulders opening and stretching the upper part of your back with each precise movement. Concentrating and focusing on lifting and rotating of the shoulder blades. Guiding them both in steady movements as we breathe. Let inhale.......and exhale......."

This is easy I thought. I look around and I saw Bertha and Thomasina both moving their' shoulders.

Samantha said, "Now let move our shoulder blade forward, but slowly. Always concentrating on releasing any tension."

We girls did exactly what she instructed.

Samantha said, "Inhale deeply as you rotate on the lift ladies, and exhale as you guide your shoulder forward. Do you notice how it's opening your rib cage? Now let stretch our shoulder blades backward, slowly, with the upper movement of our arms, as if we are trying to open our hearts, rotating with precise movement for total wellness of energy, as we move this section of the body backward."

All I know is it felt so good!

Samantha then asked us to have a seat on one of the yoga mat. She came to each one of us and handed us each a rolled up yoga mat to sit on for extra cushion. Samantha announce, "It's sometimes better for beginners to use to sit on rather than sitting on the flat surface."

Next she sat in front of us demonstrating what she wanted us to do. She said "Gently put both of your arms to your side." And we did.

She continue, "Now with your left arm place for stability on the floor. Raise your right arm towards the ceiling. Now bend your right arm and place your fingers behind your neck. While keeping the right elbow pointed towards the ceiling, it's allowing your heart and ribcage to open up the good energy. Now for 5 minutes lel start to massage our neck to ease the tension anyone might be carrying in the neck area. As we inhale.......and exhale......."

We did the same for the opposite side of the body.

Sam continue, "Now with both arms place at our side I like for us to inhale as you gently move the neck slowly, towards the left. Ladies let exhale slowly, as you go to the right."

Us girls we were saying, "Oh that feels good."

I said "I could feel my bodies releasing some of my tension in that area and inputting positive energy as I breathe."

Samantha continues, "Now with both arms still at your side, extend both legs stretching and stretching those legs outward. Keeping your arm at your side for balance. Now, spread your legs as far as it can go without causing any pain."

Samantha asked, "Do you feel the stretch in your inner thigh area and quadriceps?" We all said, "Yeah."

She continue, "Now let's twist towards the right. Placing your right hand slightly behind you. Facing towards the right, inhale, now exhale while bringing your left arm over and placing your left hand behind your right knee."

"Oh yeah! This stretch feel so good," we were saying. Bertha said "I can feel the stretch in my back too."

"Good," Samantha said "Now let do the same for our opposite side. We did as we slowly untwist and came back to the center.

Sam now asked us slowly to "Inhale.......then exhale........ Next she had us to remove the rolled up mats from underneath us. While still sitting, she instructed, this is for balance, "Fold your legs and start to rock from side to side with your hands placed on both knees."

Sam spoke as she rocked, "Left, right, and left, right." While rocking Bertha fell on her side because she rocked a little too hard.

Sam continue, "While keeping your legs folded and now with both hands at your side I want you to walk only your pelvis bones towards your folded legs. Then lift your pelvis bones as you walk back."

For me it felt awkward and it was a little complicated too.

Then she asks us to stand as she said "Breathe. Class, release your finger by opening and closing them. Now shake both arms and don't forget to breathe."

"Let start to stretch the finger again by opening and closing them," she expressed.

Sam said "Now it's time for us to implant a warrior one position. Ladies while standing straight let take our right leg and step forward. Comfortable and with caution take your left leg and line it directly behind you. Please making sure that you maintain your balance with this movement. Now, bend your right knee while pressing forward. You should be feeling the stretch in your lower left calves and holding the position with balance. We are now ready for warrior two position. Extend both arms outward while holding them up for strength and balance. As we inhale....... exhale......."

We did. Then we did the same for the opposite side.

Then we sat back on the floor but this time Sam said, "Lay on your back. Guys, find a focus point while looking at the ceiling. I want you to do what feel comfortable with your arms. Either have your arms placed at your side, or rest the forearm bend upwards toward the ear. I want you to feel in your neck, the curve. Noticing how your upper backs rest on the mat and how your lower back is curved. That's the way your spine is shape. Now let inhale....... exhale....... Finding that spot on the ceiling, concentrating on breathing. Allowing the body to calm down and release any tension. Just let it go as you deeply breathe... inhale....... exhale......."

Once that was over we were asked to sit up.

While sitting on the floor in an Indian style with our legs crossed. Samantha had us put our hands in a sphere shape. Then she asked us to shape our invisible sphere with positivism.

She said, "This sphere is you. It is the grace in you. The strength in you. The love in you and everything about you. Acknowledging your sphere and feeling everything that's inside of you. Your accomplishments. Your entire being. This sphere is everything that you are inputting good health and wellness into yourself. Acknowledge it."

Then she brought both her hands together pressing the thumbs to the middle of her chest and said the word, "Namaste," which means, honoring the grace, in all living beings.

That was really cool. I was able to keep up with Samantha. I really enjoyed myself.

It took away the boredom. Took me away from my issues. I didn't think about where I was at. I just concentrated on balancing and feeling my body relieve some of the tension I carried.

Time now is four o'clock. The dorms are open. I'm going upstairs to the fourth floor to my dorm.

When I was coming out from the exit on to the fourth floor. I saw Michal the security guard sitting on his' post next to the laundry room.

"What up Michal?" I said. Michal asked, "Did you ever find out why yall had that second fire drill back to back?" I told him "I forget to ask because Valerie came in with her big mouth talking about me and my kids that day. I truly gotten side track. Plus the office was packed too. I truly forgot."

Michal question, "Aren't yall in the same room?" "Yeah," I answered as I had started to walk away from him going down the hall to my dorm.

"Electra, I don't want to come in there. So I hope you are on your best behavior," he said.

I turned around and look at him I quickly said, "Me!? She's the one who always starting." I turned my face back around proceeding down the hall.

His voice became a little louder as he spoke. "So you have to be the bigger person," he suggested. So I can see his face again. I turned back around this time while walking backwards heading towards my dorm and said, "Sometimes that's easier said than done."

When I enter into the dorm there is only one resident I see-she my next door neighbor, Q nine.

She always so quiet. She doesn't talk to anyone in the room. She never leaves the dorm for any activities. She always lay in her bed with all her clothes on while wearing those cheap black sun shades on her' face. She only wears dark colors-dark tights with a long dark skirt or, a dark color dress. She lay there in silent. Her' legs are crossed at the feet and quietly she lays for hours.

Anyway it feel good to be home. I start peeling off my clothes. I open up my locker put on my house coat and flip flops. Walking to the bathroom. I didn't hear the water running, it doesn't sound as if anyone is in there. I knock first. I waited a couple of seconds. Then I knocked again.

"Good," I say as I open the door checking to make sure it empty.

I goes back to my area hurrying getting my stuff. I rush into the bathroom locks the door, and realize.... I got to clean out the tub! I gotta go get the soap scrub from Shack. With my bathrobe on. I goes back out into the hallway. Before I make that turn. Looking around the corner I shout down the hallway "Michal is maintenance on the floor?"

Before Michal could answer I heard Shack' deep voice loudly said, "What you asking about me for woman."

Quickly I said "Hold up! I'll be right there." Hurrying back into my room to lock my locker because things go quickly up in this place. I'm walking down the hallway in my bathrobe and slippers. Shack hands me the bathroom cleaner.

Coming out from the bathroom the dorm is quiet. Lacy enter into the room as she goes to her' area. I'm lying on my bed with nothing to do so, I start pondering how come I can't remember Moet delivery. So now, I'm really begins to focus on it, searching the steps in my brain.

On that note reader: Let go back, way back.... *back into the story.*

I'm was lying on the hospital bed....... it's a blank. .... Hum. I can't feel or visualize the pushing.

I remember I did get my tubes tied. It just wasn't right after I had given birth which came as a surprise to me because I figure my tubes would be getting tied right after I gave birth to my baby. Moet was born before twelve am. I remember, I had the surgery early in the morning, maybe around six am?

After the performed surgery, my anesthesia had worn off and slowly I was coming into focus.

I'm lying on my side as I open up my eyes, and in my eyes' view, I saw a nurse. She was dressed in all white.

I'm coming more into focus and becoming more aware of my surrounding. I'm watching her. She doing something over there, on a table across the room. Her back is towards me.

I'm trying to get her attention but that's when I realize, I couldn't speak due to this abnormal pain I was in.

In a low painful whisper I said, "Nurse," but she couldn't hear me.

So again, in a low painful voice I said, "Nurse."

She was so involved in what she was doing and I was in such pain. I couldn't hardly make my voice audible. When she turn around I was in her' eye view. She notice that my eyes were open and I think she saw my lips moving. She start walking towards me.

I couldn't make my voice become audible. I couldn't even move. My eyes watch her as she came closer, closer. She came by my side and bent her body slightly down to hear what I was saying. She asked me, "Can I help you?"

The only words that were able to come out from my mouth-lowly, was, "Pain.....pain....pain." She stood up and said "I go get something for you."

At that point I thought to myself what the **hell** did I go and do? I'm wondering. Why I couldn't speak? I couldn't raise my voice, I couldn't move. The pain that was kicking me in my **ass**......it was unspeakable!

The nurse came back with this long pointy ass shiny needle. Attached to it was a tube of liquid. As she was standing there squirting some of the fluid out from the needle I whisper, "Where am I?"

She told me, "You're in the recovery room," then she looked at me and said, "This is going to hurt a little." She moved my hospital grown over and started rubbing my hip bone with an alcohol pad.

It looked like it was going to hurt.

So I started turning my arm to expose where I normally get poked in my vein as I looked at the needle. It was so shinning, pointy and long. Whispering painfully hoping that she can hear me I started saying "My arm, my arm." Thinking I could take the shot better in the vein.

The nurse said "Nope it got to be in the hip." I was in no position to argue. So I just laid there helplessly. She jabbed me. I let out an "Ouch!" I went out like a light.

This time I woke up in the same room they brought me to after I had given birth. There were four other ladies in the room too, lying in their' beds.

Visiting time was approaching.

The ladies were preparing their selves for their' visitors by washing their faces and brushing their' teeth. One lady was already done. She was sitting on her bed with her' bed top raised up, just waiting for her' visitor.

OH MY GOSH! This pain is horrible it hurts so badly.

People/visitors started coming in with balloons reading it a girl/boy. Some had flowers. Most of the visitors brought something to eat and drink. Everyone in the room had a visitor except for me. This was the worst feeling that I have ever had after giving birth. I was completely miserable. My stomach was totally cramped. The only thing I was able to move was my head, my eyeballs and my lips.

I couldn't move that much without every part of my body aching. It hurts to breathe, to cough. Dam I can't move. I couldn't even sit up. Normally around this time after pushing out my child I be so grateful the whole deliver thing is over.

I must looked pitiful because pretty soon everybody in the room started staring in my direction. I heard them whispering among each other "I wonder what happen to her?" One of the visitors came to my bedside and asked me, "Are you alright?"

I said, "I'm just in pain." She asked me, "Did you have a cesarean?" I told her, "No. I'll just gotten my tubes tied." She put a sorry look on her face for me as she asked, "Can I do anything for you?" "Yes. Can you go get the nurse? I need another shot for the pain," I told her.

The visitor left the room. She came back to me and said, "The nurse will be here soon." She left my side and went to the group of people she was with. I heard them asking her in low voices "What happen to her?" "She had a tubal ligation," the lady told them.

My first visitor have arrived. It was Shelby.

"Hi Tami," she said as she came through the door. Shelby definitely is a housewife who doesn't get the chance to get out much. Her voice always sounds so happy and in such a high pitch. I guess it come from being around her kids all the time and all day.

I could tell Shelby was just happy to be out of the house, even if she is just going to the hospital. She had a card in her hand with two balloons. One balloon said it a girl and the other read, congratulation.

In a low voice I said "Thank you." She put the card and the balloons on the table next to me as she said, "Thomas told us you had a girl. Did you name her yet?" I said, "Yep. I named her Moet."

She sat in the chair and said, "Moet? Tami what up with you naming your kids after alcoholic beverages? Champagne, Brandon, Moet...you don't even drink."

Stop! Reader for the record, we call Brandon, JB, back to the story:

I said "I know. It's a Jones thing. I just like how it sounds. My Grandma-Grace named my father Eddie but she called him Honeydew and her daughter, she named Peaches. Maybe subconsciously when my grandmother named her children. She wanted her kids to know that they are loved and how pleased she is with them. They are her' sweeties. Maybe that's why she gave them sweet names."

"Shoot, when I was younger my dad sometimes called me sugar, and maybe I like things that simulate me or things that gives me a buzz," I said painfully.

"My mother told me, that my Grandma-Grace (who is my father' mother) named me. I don't see the comparison. Eddie/Electra only that both our names begin with the letter E," I answered.

"Oh man! I'm in so much pain right now. Shelby could you go see if you see the nurse and ask her how much longer it would be before she come to the room and give me my shot," I asked.

In her usual high pitch voice, rapidly Shelby asked, "Tami, what's the matter with you? Why are you in so much pain? You supposed to be recuperating, not looking like you in hell."

Knowingly....that I already told Shelby.... and she supposed to know. I said, "I told you I was getting my tubes tied remember."

She asked with a questionable face, "And it making you feel and look like this...Umm.....I don't think I want to go on with mines now." I giggle, "Oh please Shelby don't make me laugh." She said, "Dam. That's some shit! It hurt to laugh?!"

I just nodded my head.

"I want to know why you're in so much pain?" she asked as she wondered.

Then she asked, "When you signed up for this did anyone tell you to expect pain afterwards?" I said "Naw, but out of concern I want to know why I'm in pain too?"

Shelby asked, "Do Thomas know you're in this type of pain?" "I haven't seen him since I had the baby," I said.

Shelby starts to leave my bed side saying "I'm going to see Moet, and I tell the nurse about you."

I said, "Tell her I'm in a lot of pain that my stomach is cramp and I can't move."

Shortly after Shelby left the room-the nurse enters into the room. She picks up my chart.

I asked her "Can I get another shot for the pain."

The nurse put my chart down and tells me "No. The doctor is on the floor making his rounds. I'll send him to you."

I ask her, "What can I do in the meantime?" The nurse suggested I drink a warm ginger ale soda.

Shelby came back inside the room. She said, "Moet is cute. I see both of you in her but she looks more like Thomas. Is Champagne father light skin or dark skin?" I replied, "Dark skin, why you asked?"

Shelby said, "Because all three of your children have your complexion. You must have strong genes Electra."

Security guard Michal is standing outside our dorm' door. He saying "Lights out ladies, its eleven o'clock."

I could tell this must be his first time ever working inside a female shelter because he so shy or do he have a lot of respect for females because he never opens the dorm door.

I said loudly, "Everybody is dress. You can open the door."

Then he crack open the door, peeps his head in and say "Lights out ladies," and turned out the lights. I get into my covers and turn over to go to sleep and as I laid in my bed.........I am thinking, how blessed my mom and dad are.

Goodnight.

Chapter Five

"It 6:00 ladies, breakfast will be served downstairs," Abuja the security guard announce as she clicks on the lights.

As I lay there underneath the covers I could tell that some of my roommates are getting up. I hear the sounds of their' lockers being open while hearing them search for their' belonging to start off their day. I open my eyes to take a peep out from underneath my covers just to see who's all up inside the dorm. After taking a good look I turned over, but, just before I threw the covers back over my head-I got a glance of my next door neighbor.

She laying down in her' bed on her back. She fully dressed this early in the morning with dark sun shades on her face. She facing towards the ceiling with both her arms laying perfectly still at her side and, NOT SAYING A WORD. I'm thinking *she is so fucking weird*.

Underneath my covers, I laid there thinking..........yep, before I started writing this book at one point I really didn't have any recognition of my childhood. I use to tell Billy, who I consider as one of my girlfriends at the shelter-how I don't have any memories of my past. I remember things like my children and how I became homeless but nothing of my childhood, and I'm really starting to wonder why?

So I started asking God to help me.

To tell you the truth, I never even had time to think about my past. I was so busy taking care of so many things like trying to get housing, going back and forth to family court, and dealing with various issues which were related to my children. When I had my apt-I was busy raising the children and trying to turn my apt into a home, and it never dawn on me, that I have forgotten my past?

109

Besides me telling yall about my living arrangement which is living here inside a shelter. My search, or story is beginning with the birth of my daughter Moet, and it's so weird how I can't remember and describe the birthing of Moet. I could see and feel the other two kids' deliveries so well.

Many times while attending various churches, lots of people saw me praying and seriously calling and wanting to speak to God. I'm quite sure that many people, even my own children, thought to their selves-"Yeah, she's asking God to help her not be homeless."

True... I was doing that as well, but there was more going on inside of me. Something spiritually. So I started asking God, to help me.....I was scared.

I feel like I'm fighting and every time I go one way I had to turn around and go another way.

I wanted answers but I didn't know what questions to ask. Nobody humanly could help me, and if anyone wanted to, maybe they didn't know how.

I'm by myself in this fight and to top it off, what had made it so bad, was that I didn't even know that I was........ fighting? .... Hmm. The fight of good and evil. A spiritual warfare. That what it's called. I learned this after attending many churches. Anyway what had-happened to me, all those years from childhood, until now my adulthood?

All I can recall precisely is the present. The right here and now but not my past. I mean, I'm so busy living in shelters trying to get my life together. Before that I was trying to make a steady foundation for me and my kids and yet...... ....I was never able to do that.

........Why?

I know I told yall about how I was raise and I described my family the best way possible but seriously, those memories was totally forgotten about until I started wanting to write this book.

"Uhmm?" That is odd I'm thinking.

When the many different ministries came to those various shelters where I lived. I always attended. I attended because something was wrong, like something is off and I came to really believe in the spirit of God, and all the magic and wisdom and healing it brings. I learned how to respect God because in some weird way the spirit was helping me. Guiding me.

I was completely unaware of all the unlocked doors I haven't open. All the locked doors to discover the truth about myself. It's awaiting for me to find out in this spiritual warfare. That I didn't even know......... EXISTED?

It kind of scary you know. The spirit of power leading you, guiding you to places of the unknown world. Making you see the truth and deception the naked eye can't see. But in the spirit world you could see and then you start to believe. You start to have faith even through you can't.......see it. It sound so weird, but I think I'm on to something.

I removed the covers from my face and see my neighbor has left the dorm. As I'm lying in the bed I notice we have a new roommate. She just come for the hospital because I see her hospital name tag is still around her' wrist.

She in bed number one, of the Q-dorm. Oooo, she has a deep cut on her' foot. It must be painful because every time she dabs the water from the basin on her foot she flinches. Next to her is bed, Q-two; Valerie. She laying down in her bed talking on her' cell phone. To me Valerie look like she could be in her late twenties. She an American Black.

Then there Lacy bed, Q-three. She sleeps with so much stuff underneath her' mattress. I can't understand how she gets a good night sleep laying with all that stuff underneath her like that. Where she lay her head, it is lifted up, as if she has one of those mechanical remote that can raise the head of the mattress. It looks like that due to all the stuff hiding underneath her mattress. Every day before she leaves the dorm she toggle with her bed in order to keep all that stuff neatly tied down so it won't fall out on the floor.

To hide all the junk underneath her bed she added a bed sham trying to make her bed appeal to be more cushion and homier then our flat mattress. Anyway Lacy she white; she older than my mother with no family.

Next to Lacy is aka Pepsi. Her real name is Maggie; she forty. Pepsi been locked up and speaks real fast. She has a speech impairment. Due to its because-she deaf. Even though she deaf, Pepsi has a great skill, she could read lips, and she fuckin good at it too. She's a former crack head; with short hair, short and skinny. Pepsi is American Black with no family. Pepsi bed is number four in the Q-dorm.

Bed Q-five is a Dominican girl. She looks to be about the age of twenty-four. She fascinated with scent always saying to me, "Mommy smell this" and she stares at me all the time.

On my side, where I sleep, the bed starting from the window, is bed Q six. Another Spanish girl but I think she is Puerto Rican or Dominican. She look to be around the age of twenty-three thru twenty-five. I believe she knows how to speak English she just prefer to speak in Spanish.

Next to her, is bed Q-seven. Aka Country. I never really got to know her real name. Anyway she's a Black American too, who like to smoke weed. Always getting a new boyfriend. She looks to be about twenty-five.

After Country comes Luting. Bed number eight, inside the Q dorm. Luting is Chinese who take baths with skin so soft by Avon. I know that scent anywhere, my Grandma-Grace loved that stuff. Anyway out of all my years living in a shelter, Luting is the only person I ever knew that sat in the tub and actually takes baths.

Bed Q-nine is my quiet neighbor. She looks to be in her early forties.

Then there's me, bed Q-ten. Age I won't say.

Getting out of bed, I goes to the bathroom to brush my teeth and wash my face but the door is locked. I knock on the door and I hear the young Chinese girl saying, "Come in." Outside standing behind the door loudly I said, "No thanks I wait till you come out."

She opens the door with nothing on but a wrap towel, and say, "You got to pee-pee. Come in. It's okay. I'm going to take a bath. I close shower curtain." Then she goes back inside the bathroom. Quickly I stop her by saying "No, wait. Would you mind if I go in before you take your bath? All I have to do is brush my teeth and wash my face." She said, "Okay." The next thing I know Luting come running out of the bathroom with the towel wrap around her body going to her' bed.

Once I get inside the bathroom, I smell the skin so soft. She had a lot of toiletries in a basket and the tub was fill with water. I thought to myself as I quickly peed. I can't believe her going to take a bath in that tub. When I reach for the toilet tissue there was none. Dam! So I drip dried then I wash my face and quickly brush my teeth.

I came out and started getting dress. I decide I'm going to Jose for breakfast. I have a taste for bacon, egg and cheese on a butter roll.

Jose owns the grocery store across the street from the shelter. He allow us girls to purchase the hot food with our food stamps. Knowing he not suppose too, but he does anyway, knowing, we have little cash but much more money in food stamps.

Security Guard Dumez enters the dorm, "Ladies dorms must be clear out by nine." She announce as she stood by the door. Then she exit.

The security guard shift has changed.

Lacy said to me "I'm going to Let Give Thanks Ministry for breakfast. Have you ever been there?" I tell her "No." Then I asked, "Whatz Lets Give Thanks Ministry?" She said, "It's the big soup kitchen up the block. They serve breakfast and lunch every day Monday thru Friday."

Pepsi said, "S. Ged thanks rigt, it up the block rigt." Lacy said "Yes." Then turning her face in my direction while sticking out her tongue in disguised because Pepsi completely naked while moisturizing her body.

Pepsi ask me, "Are ou going there?" As she bend her naked butt in the air putting lotion on her legs. "Nope. I'm going to Jose," I said.

Valarie get out her bed and bangs on the bathroom door saying, "Can you hurry up in there? There other people in this room who would like to use the bathroom."

Luting telling Valerie to come inside.

Valerie said, "I need to take a shower what the fuck I'm going to do. Hop inside the tub with you in there? Hurry the **fuck up**." Valerie goes back to her area picks up her cell phone and start saying to someone who on the other line, "Every day this chick taking these long ass baths. Shit like how dirty is her ass?"

You could hear Luting behind the door saying, "Me soon come out. Okay. Me soon come out."

See that why I like to take my shower in the evening. So I won't have to deal with the bathroom drama in the morning. I just happen to look by the window and I see that Dominican girl looking at me smiling and shaking her head saying, "Craz-zy." Now she looking at Valerie. She pointing her finger behind Valerie back. She doesn't want Valerie to see her talking about her saying, "Crazy right."

I walks towards the door. I walks out the door and say at full volume, "Everybody, have a good day."

Joining the crowd in the hallway. I pass security guard Dumez because her back is to us residents because she staring out the window on the fourth floor.

I went across the street to Jose and order my sandwich and a cup of coffee light and sweet. I saw Ugina outside standing on the corner with her pants all baggy with a cup in her hand begging for a cigarette. Coming back to the shelter I found a seat in the dining room and started to write.

For me it started December 25, 1995. It the first time I ever became homeless. That is the day my journey began. It also was a day of great courage. The day I decide to leave my safety net and step out into a world of the unknown. It took guts because it wasn't only me going to this unknown never heard of before place. I'm traveling also with my three very small kids.

So, when the cops made the suggestion for me and the kids to go to a shelter in the summer of 1995, I literally had to ask the officer, "What is a shelter?" I tell you what though, it was the sadist day of my life.

STOP! Reader, before I take you any further, let me take you back, *way* back, *back into time* of how I came to that point in the summer, of *the year of 1995*.

I'm speaking about a time in my life when I was living at Westbrook Projects. On the twelfth floor. Sharing the two bedroom apartment with Tonya, (my sister) Desmond (Tonya' boyfriend) and their' baby girl, name Hope.

At this time in my life I have only one child, my oldest daughter.

Me and Tray had split and I was raising Champagne, our' daughter as a single parent on welfare. I was having a lot of problems living with my sister and her' boyfriend. Lots of times I would escape the madness by hanging out next door with Patricia Conwell. She, as well as her' family, was well aware of the difficulty I faced inside my apt. It was a constant ongoing battle in apt Twelve-C.

Patricia have a seven year old daughter. They live in her' parents' apartment twelve E along with her' younger siblings and a niece. So... she too needed her own space. Both of us discuss, contemplated and marvel at the idea about how wonderful it would be to have our very own apartment. Our very own space.

It had to be Patricia who came across the ad in the newspaper regarding apartment rentals because I had no idea how to move out from the projects. I was young and my parents didn't teach Tonya and me how to live in the adult world. Since it was Patricia newspaper I asked her would she mine if I jot down the address so that I can try out for the apartment too.

Surprisingly, an application was mailed out to me. I filled it out. I also stressed on the application the reason why I applied and needed my very own place. I was having big problems sharing the apartment with Tonya and Desmond. They help made my life a miserable hell and I wanted out from them mother fuckers.

When you have problem some people say you suppose to pray. At this time in my life no one was telling me to pray. I didn't know nothing about no praying. I didn't know anything about church because my mom and dad didn't raise us up in the church. Growing up in their households, they never even played church music.

The closest my sister Tonya and I came going to church was when we were children and this old woman named Mother Keeips used to take a group of us from the project to her' church.

The group consisted of me and my sister, my best friend' (Fran) and Karen Roach from the eleven floor. Then eventually Mrs. Collins, who is my mother best friend her' two daughters-Salt and Pepper started going with us.

Mother Keeips was a very spiritual lady. She took us to Washington Temples Unified Congregation of Christ. She was like an usher or mother in the church. Anyway she was way older than both my parents. She wore all white and a veil on top of her head. I can't remember how it came about us going with her to her' church. At this time in my life I was so very young, like maybe in the fifth or sixth grade.

We rode on the forty-two bus. The church inside was large and red. It's completely carpeted....red. The church has long pews that were red just like the carpet. The red pews are cushioned for your butt and your back. The walls are beige with very high ceilings. Where the pastor preach, behind him is the choir. The organ player is on the left side of the pastor. That entire area too is carpeted with the color red.

Lots of times Mother Keeips had to do her service inside the church and us kids be sitting in those big pews dress up all by ourselves, and every time during the church service we all start to fall asleep. Our heads would start to nod to the left or to the right and we be bouncing our heads back up again trying not to fall asleep, but I will catch myself before I fell completely asleep. I would look at my friends, and my sister, their' heads will be nodding off bouncing left to right until each one of them has fallen completely asleep.

Surprisingly, I stay awake for the service because I found it to be amusing. How the preacher voice will change, and the organ player will hit a note, as the preacher spoke, "God__... then he takes a deep breath. He__...then he takes that deep long breath again.......... Alive!"

I watch how the ladies and men will shake at the sound of knowing he is alive. I found it to be amazing. I also enjoyed the choir, listening to the sounds of church music, but the best part of all to me was when we got to go down stairs because the church has a kitchen down there, with lots of different cakes to choose from.... Yum. They had pies too. Their dessert will be wrapped individually on small white paper plates, which, I would slowly walk, and examine all the dessert slices sizes. Trying to decide which one am I'm going to pick?

Looking at the chocolate cake or the Lemon, yum. What about the homemade upside down pineapple cake or the German chocolate cake? Maybe I take the strawberry on top of strawberry or the vanilla on vanilla cake...yum, yum, yum, yum, yummy so many choices to choose from, but I can only have one.

So depending on what favor my taste buds had a taste for, bet you, I be pointing out for the largest slice.

They serve diner too that we can order. I would order a fried chicken sandwich, but my main reason coming downstairs really was for getting a slice of cake. I was in heaven in that kitchen because my mother wasn't a Betty Crocker type of mother. She didn't bake. She more of a meat eater.

Anyway all our' parents always gave us enough money to buy a dinner after the service. We even had money to put into the church collection when the silver big round tray came down the pew.

My life has been so hard. I question myself repeatedly. Whatever did I do to deserve this? Who did I hurt? So I remember when I use to go to church with Mother Keeips and when the silver collection tray came down the long pew I use to put in a quarter, and take out a dollar in change, and continue passing down the silver tray.

After a while Mother Keeips, she sometime stayed for the night service and us girl had to go home by ourselves. The church wasn't far from the project so instead of taking the bus we choose to walk. This way we could stop by Cousin Pearl Laci candy store using our bus fare money to buy our goodies on the way home.

One day in the candy store my mother girlfriend (Mrs. Collins) her' daughter Pepper asked me, "Electra how come you always have so much money to buy candy after church?" I believe I ignore her and I didn't answer her right away, I think, I like changed the subject.

By walking home again it allowed us to go to Cousin Pearl Laci store. If they didn't have enough money to buy what is was they wanted. I would say, "Go ahead I help pay for it."

Remember back then, candy was cheap, a penny, and 5 cents to 10 cents. With a quarter you can buy a lot. Anyway Pepper she put me on the spot again and asked, "Electra where are you getting the money from to buy all of us candy?"

Now all eyes were on me.

Even my sister Tonya said, "Yeah, where are you getting the money because we had the same amount and all my money is gone. So how come you still have money?"

My best friend wanted to know the answer too because quietly she was just looking at me. So, I confess. I told them, "You know when the silver tray come down the aisle with the money in it." They all said, "Yeah."

Pepper said, "You talking about the one for collection right." I said, "Yeah. So when the tray comes to me I put in my quarter and take out a dollar." Then Pepper said, "Oooo! I telling what you did. I going to tell you mother." My sister and Salt was looking at me like you did what! Then my best friend Fran said, "Yeah Electra, don't do that anymore it's not nice."

So now when we all went to church all eyes were on me when the big silver tray came to me. When I put the quarter in, before I pass the tray, I would look up. I had no other choice but to look their way because they all were watching me. They all watched me very carefully, making sure, I drop my quarter and that I didn't pick up any change.

Mother Keeips took us to church especially on Easter Sunday. When I was growing up Easter was a big holiday for us kids. It was the day everybody got a brand new outfit and, an Easter basket filled with Easter candy and decorated colorful Easter eggs.

My parents used to go all out for me and Tonya. Onetime my parents brought us a short white fur shawl that had a long string and attach to it was a big white fury ball. We used that long string to fasten the hood from the jacket to our' heads. We would wear shining Easter shoes-black one year. White the next year. Our parents brought us white gloves and cute little pocket books that matches the color of our shoes and we would wear those pretty girly dresses with girly fancy stocking, or ribbon, or lace -ankle socks. Mommy would takes us to the beauty parlor so we can get our hair press and curled. Sometime we have ribbons in our hair along with the curls or fancy barrettes. We celebrated Easter like that every year as children. It was like our Black American tradition.

For us children, Easter was a special day for us. We all came outside seeing who had on what. It was the way of life, for us back then. Us kids knew the routine we got formally dressed up for Easter. Back then, all the parents behaved the same way. At least the majority of the parents did. That's the era I grew up in.

Anyway like I said this was so many, many, many years ago. We were in public school at this time and mysteriously Mother Keeips died and we never went to church anymore.

My parents and we kids didn't attend any funeral service held for Mother Keeips. The only service or respect I can remember attending vaguely, was a visited inside her' apartment and her one and only son was there, and I believe I said, "I'm sorry to hear about your mother." I think I told him, "She used to take us to church."

Anyway my sister Tonya has changed over the years and she had become very mean towards me. It after she got with Desmond. She changed a lot towards me. I wanted to get away from both of them. They was causing such a derangement in my life, and I had a child to take care of. I needed to move away from them in order to have a piece of mind. I wasn't happy at all. I spoke or I simply just wished to move away from them.

I was very uncomfortable. I knew nothing about raising a baby. I just went on instinct. I knew nothing about the real world. The adult world and how as an adult to make things happen.

Life; I learned as I went along.

Every day I got up and every day I dealt with my pitiful shit of a life. I didn't complain; looking back on it now. I thought that I could make it all better, eventually. I guess I was so numb and overwhelmed with misery and grief, that

I couldn't put it in words. I got up and did the best that I could every day.

To my surprise I received a letter in the mail from Asbury Management asking me to come downtown for an interview. The letter also stated that I bring legal documents for everyone who would be living with me inside the household; plus to bring in a budget letter from welfare in order to prove my income.

I couldn't believe it! I read the letter over and over again. I would be going downtown and I have to bring these documents along. I'm thinking that's a good sign? Maybe now I would get the chance to live my own life the way that I would best see fit. I would build a stable home for me and my daughter.

When me and my baby got downtown, I was anxiously anticipated, what would happen next? I couldn't wait to go, **And** see what this was all about, and how will it affect my future as I had sat in the waiting area, patiently, for someone to call my name.

"Miss Electra Jones," a black slim lady said as she held the door opened. "Yes," I said.

"Follow me," she answered. I followed her to her' desk. She said to me, "Have a seat."

I sat down while not saying a word. This moment was so crucial. I was waiting for her to say something.

Finally she had said, "We have a one bedroom apartment in Brooklyn on the first floor. The building is under the section eight program, meaning that the government pays the majority of your rent. Are you interested?"

I just couldn't believe that this was happening! I was thinking to myself, I'm getting my very own apartment?! I said, "Yes."

"Light and gas is not included. Would that be a problem for you," she wanted to know. I said, "Right now being that I share my apartment with my sister I'm not receiving the full amount of my welfare allowance. So when I move out on my own my budget should go up. So the answer to your question is, I shall be able to pay it."

She smiled at me and said, "Good."

Then she asked me questions like, "Did you bring your budget letter? Can you supply me social security cards for everyone who will live inside the apartment. How many people would be living in the apartment?" I said, "Just me and my daughter." As she started writing on paper.

I couldn't take the suspense anymore. I asked, "So where at in Brooklyn is this one bedroom apartment?" The lady said, "1578 Union Blvd. Are you familiar with the area?" I said, "I know where Union Blvd is."

The nice lady said-while looking up from her paper, "On the corner of Quincy," as if she trying to help me pin point the location. I immediately said, "Oh yeah I know where it's at."

The lady then pointed out to me that one of the owners would be paying me a house visit very soon. Something about he like to see how his' tenant live in their' own environment before issuing out the key.

At this point in my life, I was really at a loss for words. I couldn't believe that this was really happening. Walking while pushing my baby in her stroller I was smiling all the way home.

Patricia had applied for this same apartment too I believe. I mean we didn't go to the mailbox together, while dropping off the application, but, both of us knew about the ad. I was the one who had gotten back the response and the apartment. She wondered why I had gotten the call back and she didn't especially, being her child was much older than mine and her' apartment was way more crowded. She was the only one who knew that I had applied for an apartment and she was the only one who knew that I have gotten a response.

Anyway I remembered being so happy that I couldn't wait to see the area that I would be moving too. I wanted to see the building. So one day while I was outside with my daughter in her stroller I walked and walked until I found the building. I had scanned it quickly and then I kept on going wanting not to be noticed.

I was like...... oh sweat, it down the street from the project.

In the meantime Tonya had been in the hospital. She about to give birth.

I was in my bedroom in the projects and Desmond had knocked on my bed room door. I said, "**What!**" without moving. He said "Listen to the radio. Your cousin has died," and he left the house.

I'm like what is he talking about? I turned on the radio and I heard that my cousin had been shot and killed.

The radio was just repeating his' name over and over ..."Has died. Been shot and killed."

I couldn't believe that. I said out loud "Oh no! How the fuck did that happen?" Then I questioned....... wondering to myself, "What was he doing over there in that area?"

Next I heard knocking sounds coming from my apartment front door. "Knock, knock, knock, and knock"

I had left my bedroom while carrying my daughter Champagne in my arm. Not wanting to miss what was being said therefore I had put the radio on inside the living room before I answered the door. With the radio volume turned up I look through the door peephole.

I see a strange black man wearing a beige trench coat and a brim hat.

I asked, "Who is it?"

He replied "I'm looking for Electra Jones." I put the lash on the door. Then I ajar the door while peeking out. I said, "That me, how can I help you?"

He said "Hello I'm Mr. Jacobson. I'm here for the second part of the interview for 1578 Union Blvd."

"Oh yeah. Just a minute," I said. I closed the door to remove the door lash as I open up my apt door and said,

"Hi. Come in." The news on the radio was playing loudly in the background as Mr. Jacobson walked in. I offer him a seat at the table. He was looking around at the apartment.

I asked him, "Could you give me a minute. That's my cousin they speaking about on the radio and I want to hear what's being said."

We both sat in the living room, while listening to the announcement of his' death.

Mr. Jacobson said "As I was driving here I heard it on my car radio." Then he said to me "I'm sorry to hear that about your family."

Sad and still confuse, while I'm thinking to myself, damn that's **fuck up**!

Looking at Mr. Jacobson I said spellbound like, "Thank you."

Mr. Jacobson said "Well, I see your place is well kept. There is no need for me to stay any longer. Let's go to the apartment and if you like it, it's yours. The place it about twenty-five minutes away from here. Not far at all and it shouldn't take long, so let get out of here so you can go and be with your family. How long will it take for you to meet me there?"

Being that I already went over there. I knew exactly where the building was at. I said, "I should meet your there in twenty-five minutes. Just let me get my baby dress and grab her diaper bag," as I walked Mr. Jacobson to the apartment door.

I couldn't believe that this was happening! I was about to have my own place. I was ecstatic but hearing my cousin's name again on the radio. Had brought sadness on my joy. I started getting my baby dress to leave and go meet Mr. Jacobson as I listened to the shocking, unbelievable news on the radio.

By the time I had gotten there Mr. Jacobson was standing in front of the building with his briefcase in his' hand. We both walked together up to the building's entrance.

Mr. Jacobson had taken out a set of keys and open the building's heavy metal door.

He opened up the door to apt 1cb and we both went in. I immediately fell in love with the apartment, it felt like home to me. Mr. Jacobson watched me go through everything. I went into the bathroom. I checked out the closets and the kitchen cabinets. I loved that I had so many windows in my spacious living room. The apartment came with wooden floors and ample closet space. This is perfect I thought.

I guess Mr. Jacobson appreciated my sense of enthusiasm because the very next thing I knew he was telling me about another empty one-bedroom apt in the building around the corner, located on the third floor. Me being caught up in the moment of looking at this apartment. I was eager to see how the other apt looked, so we went around the corner and took the elevator to the third floor.

When we got in front of the apartment door. Mr. Jacobson opens up door. He's relishing by my emotions and my facial expression especially after seeing my reaction after viewing apt 1cb. He seems pleased that his office has pick a good candidate for a tenant.

When I went inside the second apt. I didn't like it. The first thing that I had noticed was those big windows which were covered by that ugly silver gate. Ugh, was the first thought that had come to my mind. That apartment made me feel caged in. I immediately looked at Mr. Jacobson who was already looking at me. I told him, "I prefer the apartment in the other building."

Mr. Jacobson smiled and said "Not a problem," and handed me a set of keys. Once we gotten downstairs Mr. Jacobson departed. I was hype!!! As I had taken my baby who was in her pretty purple stroller to our very own apartment!

I had my keys, going around the corner to 1578. The building itself is a six story brick. It sat on the corner of Union Blvd and Quincy and has held approximately, seventy-two tenants. Once inside the building you notice two set of staircases; one on the left and the other on the right. My apt 1cb was on the left hand side where the elevator was at; but you have to pass the elevator, walk up a small set of stairs. Make a left turn, take a couple more step and voila!

No more elevators for me.

After living on the twelve floor all those years and walking up and down those steps whenever the elevator was broken, it was a pleasure just to come into the building and walk straight into my apartment.

The 2nd reason that I had chosen apt 1cb is that I like the cut of the apartment. When I opened the apartment door, I would be standing inside the hallway facing two huge closets, with sliding doors. Behind the apt door to the left is my small L shaped bedroom. To the right of the apartment door is the bathroom, which is in front of the closets. Walking pass the closets and bathroom make a short left then a quick right; the apartment opens up to a gigantic well lit room.

Security guard Fancy turns down the volume on the radio and makes an announcement, "Ladies open studio is going on upstairs." She put the volume back on the radio. She leaves the dining area while saying on her' walkie-talkie, "Announcement has been made in the dining area, copy." I needed to take a stretch so I decided to attend the class.

A lot of us clients enjoy open studio. It held from 2 thru 3:30 on the fourth floor every Friday. Samantha have everything out for us girls to utilize at this time. We can sew and make things like a pillow or jewelry, paint and make conversation.

When I got inside of the classroom I looked for the signing sheet. I sign the attendance sheet for open studio and signed the computer sheet for computer number one. Bridge Net only has two-old computers. Which looks like they could had been donated. All residents are only allowed thirty minutes on each computer. Reason so, that others residents could get the opportunity to use the machinery as well.

Quickly I sat down and started typing. As I began typing I heard Dottie, Brenda Sabricka, Liz and Tasha enter into the room. I got to say, this is how I spent my days in this shelter. Participating in their' activities. It helped me pass the time and it's doing something positive that keeps me mentally sane. I started typing.

So, Reader: On that note let's go *back into the story.*

Not only was there enough room for a complete living room set. I had space for a kitchen set and the matching china cabinet. Across from the dining room area is my medium size narrow kitchen that is filled with wooden cabinets on top of the wall as well as the bottom.

Oh my goodness the windows were plentiful and huge with attach ledges that you can sit on. I could view the entire front of the building. In my dining room area there is only one window that gives the view of the side of the building which is going towards the building entrance door.

It perfect, just right for Champagne and I. Airy. Spacious. Lots of sun light. A great place to make a home. I really lucked out.

My father lived 6 block behind me. My mother lives twelve blocks in front of me. My sister live eight blocks on the left of me and Grand pop and Miss Joyce they five blocks away from me. My other grandparents and cousins on my mom side was 2 bus rides away. Anyway I didn't move in right away because I had no gas or electricity. I had to open an account. In the projects we don't pay for light or gas. So this was something new for me. After I had gotten the keys, Champagne and I rode on the bus going to my grandparents' house to find out more about Skyler unexpected death.

When we got off the bus, walking to the house. I wasn't expecting to see everybody who was somebody there....

and there was also people, who was nobody there. Some people were already organizing rallies for neighborhoods marches. All of these people, were coming over to my grandparent's home asking to set up interviews, donating money, sending cards of sympathy and wanting the family to appeal on talk shows.

Suddenly distant family members started popping up. Family I haven't seen in a while and there were some people that I didn't even know, but were saying "Hi cousin."

Wow...........our quiet family was now the attention of the world.

Overnight we become the news and the gossip on people's tongues. There were so many people upstairs, downstairs, coming from around the corner and coming out from cars. The telephone was constantly ringing. It was crazy. All of this going on and my sister was in the hospital about ready to give birth.

My cousins Coon, Sheryl and Lee Keisha were upstairs with their' mother. Aunt Lynette was handling the numerous people that were in her' apt. My two younger cousins, Tie and Malik were downstairs in my grandparents' apartment. They were consoling each other for comfort, since it their' loving brother that they had just lost. When I had gone back outside on the porch, I had seen their' mother, my aunt Melody.

I ran towards her but as I gotten closer I saw she was deep in agony. I have never seen my aunt so sad. She was mourning a loving lost. She loved her children even though she wasn't the perfect mother. My heart had went out to her. I was hurting too, in all of this crazy madness.

Our family, all of us was heartbroken and shocked at his unexpected, young death. My aunt Melody was completely overwhelmed, gone in grief that she wasn't even with us.

Wait a minute..........You think that's something!

To top it all off, Aunt Melody, the love of her' life, and the father of her' three sons, suddenly appeared out of

nowhere! Knocks on her' door and come back into her life. After all these many fuckin years!? He just knocks on her door, then her' son, the next day got shot and killed for no reason at all. I don't think Skyler gotten the chance to meet his' father before he died or did he pass away at the same time, that the missing in action father reappeared. I forgot exactly how it all went down. Anyway, all I know is it was too close for comfort.

Stop! To the reader-I got to point this out.

Reuniting with a very long, lost uncle who we all adore as children. Even though they were never married we kids always saw him as uncle _____. She was crazy about him. She loved him so very much. They used to watch us, as children. All we know as children was Aunt Melody was madly in love with _____. So therefore we were too, referring to us four girls, Sheryl, Me, Lee Keisha, and Tonya, he was our fine uncle _____.

Back then Aunt Melody was living in the two front rooms which were located downstairs in her parents' home. So as children when uncle _____ came by to visit Melody, us four girls used to run to answer the door to let him in. Saying, "Uncle _____ here. Uncle _____ is here," laughing and giggling because he was truly very handsome.

Then we all as children used to sit there while watching him and making googoley eyes at him, showing our express of......oh he is so fine. He knew that we adored him so he would say things like "I wish I had a tall glass of water." Sending us four girls who were knocking each other over to be the first to get him the glass of water. "I'll get it," one of us would say. "No. I'll get it," the other one would say, and before you know it all four of us showed up with glasses of water saying, "Here uncle_____. No, here take mine uncle_____. Here uncle_____, my water is colder than her so take mine uncle_____. No uncle_____, I got here first," and my Aunt be sitting there shaking her head at her four nieces making a fuse over her' man. He got a kick out of us. Then he take the water from each one of us while saying, "Thank you and thank you and thank you and thank you." Giving us all a kiss on the cheek sending us girls ballistic with joy. Even though Coon is a boy he loved him too.

Aunt Melody loved him. Maybe that's why we loved him too cause we loved our aunt Melody. Like I said, we were a loving, caring family. One day he left and it broke my aunt heart. Leaving her behind with three very small children that she never really took care of. Melody never been the same after that. Maybe it explain why she behaves the way she do? But there is no excuse for neglect or maybe there was, when it comes to matters of the heart.

I didn't get the chance to tell my family my good news that day about me getting an apartment. It just wasn't the right time.

Samantha, the recreational director tapped me on my shoulder while saying, "Electra your time is up. There is someone else waiting to use the computer. Could you press print? You can go to the social service office on the third floor and pick up your printed copies."

Once I got inside of the office I asked the first caseworker I saw.

"Hello Tim, I printed some paper from open studio to your printer. May I get my printed copies?" Tim said "Stay right here I'll get them for you."

Miss Taylor my caseworker, had heard my voice and had come from behind her cubical. She said, "Electra when you are finished can you come over to my area?"

Once I gotten my printed copies I went over to see Miss Taylor. She said, "Electra I'm glad that you had come down here. Have a seat. I was about to leave a memo on the board for you, requesting that you are to meet with me."

I said, "You told me that I was going to receive something from security from you last night but I didn't."

Miss Taylor had said, "I'm sorry. I rush out of here last night. That why I'm glad I see you now. Listen I need an updated ppd for your' file. Therefore I'm going to make an appointment for you to see medical."

Looking at her I said, "I have my own doctor. I prefer going there."

Miss Taylor said, "Okay. That's not a problem. Bring in the result so that I can put it in your file."

I asked Miss Taylor, "Could you put me in for carfare? I would go first thing on Monday morning."

"Yes I put it in the carfare book tonight before I go home," Miss. Taylor had replied.

I went back upstairs to open studio and quite a few girl was still up there. The music was playing. They were doing all sorts of stuff. I see Samantha brought snacks out for the group. She had cookies and juice on the table. A fresh pot of coffee brewing and hot water for tea.

I walk over to the area and started to make me a cup of coffee for myself. "Electra open studio will be closing in twenty minutes so if you like I can help assist you with any material you may need." she said.

"Okay, being I still have time I like to start on a collage. I like to have something else to look at in my dorm beside the walls," I said.

Samantha told me, "I'll get a folder to hold your pieces in, and you would be able to put the collage together the next time we have open studio."

I got a couple of magazines of interest. A pair of scissor and started cutting.

"Ladies you have five more minute before closing so please start cleaning up your area," Samantha asked.

Just before open studio closed Samantha made an announcement, "Yarn for crocheting would only be issue out now on Sunday at five thirty. Open studio is now closed."

We girls started exiting the room. I'm on the fourth floor already so I just snuck into my dorm. When I got into the dorm I saw the new girl in bed number one, she has a bed pass. She was soaking her foot in a small basin of water. "Is anyone in the bathroom?" I asked her.

She said, "No." I quickly took off my clothes to take my shower before other starts to make it into the dorm.

When I came out of the bathroom she, bed number one, was sitting quietly on her' bed. I said, "Hello my name is Electra." I'm, "Marcell." "What happen to your foot?" I ask. "I fell," she said.

Country came in talking on her cell phone, as her walked to her bed I heard her say, "Meet me downstairs in an hour and bring a Dutch too... a vanilla one. I have some good weed, okay Kevin.....Kevin......Kevin you hear me talking to you?"

As I put on my pajamas I noticed I had a dormitory inspection sheet laying on my bed. It states that my living area was found incompliance with fire safety standards and DHS rules and regulations. Thank you for your cooperation and consideration of others. Your privileges are available!!! I have a check in the box that say area is in compliance.

As I sat on my bed thinking, I went back to the story about my cousin's death.

My cousin's funeral arrangement was taking place. I still was living inside Westbrook Projects. I haven't officially moved out yet.

Nobody was in the house just me and Champagne. I already had my clothes out for the funeral. I pack Champagne diaper bag and had her dressed. To keep her quiet and staying still on the couch I gave her a bottle while I'll take a quick shower. I went into the bathroom. Took a quick shower and the strangest thing happen when I was about to come out from the bathroom.

I was naked and I had the towel wrapped around me. I open the bathroom door, just to find this enormous white bird looking right at me as I was about to come out from the bathroom. Shocked! I stood by the bathroom door. Because it startles me.

Then **I gasp**, because the bird was standing facing my direction just watching me with his' beady black eyes. I said, "Oh shit what kind of bird is that?"

I watch the bird before stepping out from the bathroom. I never saw a bird like that before. I'm just use to only seeing pigeons, **and**, I never saw a bird stand on our living room window ledge.

Oh sweat!

This huge bird was trying to come inside the house and his eye was **glued** on me. Thank God for the projects management to install those window guards. Because the bird was twitching his head from side to side staring at me diligently, trying to get inside the apartment. Twitching his' head watching me with one black beady eye then switching to the other beady eye.

Then the bird started poking his head towards me, just watching me. I gasped, "Oh shit! **What the fuck.**" I started to close the bathroom door as I stood there with a towel wrap around my nude body but then I thought on, my baby! She sitting on the couch!

I made a quick move to the left and I froze when I noticed the bird has step with me. Following me with his' beady eyes. It was just watching me and poking his' head trying to get inside the house. Following each of my steps with its beady black eye ball while twitching his' head from one side to the next. Piercing me with his' dark eyes.

I want to run out of the house! So I move to the right. The bird moved it feel to the right too. Still with his' eye connecting to mines. I wanted to slam the door and go back inside the bathroom but I couldn't, I knew my baby was out there!

So I got up enough guts and dotting into the living room.

He was a stubborn bird he wouldn't move. He was insisting trying to come inside the house. I was so scared.

I just watch the bird as I quickly got dress to run out of the house and go to the funeral.

"Oh my God what kind of bird is this?" I was saying to myself because every time I moved, it walk a step, or following me with those eyes. Then a thought came to my head, is that my cousin Skyler? He came by to tell me bye. Then the bird just flew away-just like that.

I was to frighten to go by the window to see which direction it flew in the sky. I was still moving quickly to get out of the house. That was a little too much for me, but while I was pressing for the elevator, I thought to myself again, was, that, Skyler? In a bird form telling me goodbye?

When I got to my grandparents for the funeral everything was fuck up. Uncle _____, he was there preaching about this white boy killing his' son. My aunt, well she devastated plus dealing now with her long lost love and all the many people coming to her sending their' condoles, telling her what to do, what to say and how to act.

She in too much pain. Melody not with us right now.

My cousins who lived upstairs Coon, Sheryl and Lee Keisha acting like they are the cousins of the year. They taking over **EVERYTING**, calling all the shots. Inviting who they want to attend what function and handling the press.

My sister she still in the hospital.

My younger male cousins they moaning the loss of their' brother. They holding on to each other for comfort and seeing their' mother disappearing in her' pain. Now watching their' absentee father who they only heard about all these years, suddenly appear in their lives. Standing in his' rightful position leading the pack.

My cousins Coon, Sheryl and Lee Keisha all of a sudden had their distant cousins on their biological father side coming into the picture claiming now they all are family. My cousins treating them better than they are treating me. Telling them how there was a rainbow over the house earlier that day of the funeral as I sat there listening like I'm a friend or a bystander.

My mother she running around driving people here and there. She claiming them just using her as the chauffeur. My dad is on the scene but he is in the background watching while my cousins Coon, Sheryl and Lee Keisha allow their' absentee father to sit in the seat where my dad should be sitting. My dad he felt left out too because after all he was always there for them when their' father wasn't around just like **Uncle _____.**

We couldn't or at least I didn't get the chance to give Skyler his proper grieving respect with just the family cause there was always way too many people in the house. So I grieved alone at night time when I laid in my bed.

Even through people turned his' killing into a black and white hate crime. We lost someone who we truly loved. He was young, honest, good-looking and a descent aspiring American Black male human being with potential.

I got push out that why nobody in the public eye realize he was my cousin. Only very close friends to the family and my childhood friends, knew I was related to Skyler.

I wanted to tell them, my family, that Skyler came to tell me bye and still no one knows that I will be moving out of Westbrook Projects soon and...........little did I know this family..... I grew up with, sharing holidays with, laughing with, singing and dancing with, played with and shared so much joy, love, and weekends with, that I will no longer be.....a, part, of, their, lives.

Well, the lights and gas for my new apartment are on now. The rent has been paid for the month. So on that note inside my bedroom which will no longer be mines I started putting my personal belonging into a shopping cart. I'm ready to move into my very own place.

While I was in my room packing, "Electra," I heard Desmond calling me from his' and Tonya back bedroom. "Electra...Electra." I really don't like him. The only reason why I responded to his voice was because I thought he had more news about my sister. Tonya who is still in the hospital with her now newborn twins........or maybe he had news for me about Tyson. Around this time in my life I started thinking about having more of a relationship with this guy named Tyson. He who has always been just a good guy friend in my eyes.

So when I reached their' bedroom. I got the shock of my life. There Desmond was in the bed, buttass naked with a hard on, asking me, "Do you think I have a good body?"

Me!?!?

I always knew that mother fucker was a dog. My sister deserved so much better than him. Not showing any alarm or fear. I didn't want to give him any satisfaction of a response. I took a deep breath and very calmly told him, "Today I'll be moving out."

The look on his' face suddenly became puzzled.

"As a matter of fact I'm packing as we speak," I told him.

Then he started to stroking his' erect penis with his hands asking me again "Electra do you think I have a good body?"

I totally ignored the question, instead I said, "The problems you and my sister are having, yall could no longer blame or use me. Now both of you will be force to deal with each other and work it out for yourself."

Now, what he is doing, is he take a pillow and cover his penis area and sat up on the bed in an Indian style manner. The words that proceed out of his mouth were "You know Electra that why I like you. You so wise I really admire your smartness."

My eyebrows went up a little bit. I did a quick smirk and I said, "Thanks." Then I just walked away. I went into my room got my baby and my shopping cart with my packed belongings. Locked my bedroom door and quietly left the apt without saying or telling him goodbye.

Chapter Six

Man, you shoulda have seen me. I guess I was a sight to see. There I was pulling my shopping cart full of my belongings with one hand while pushing Champagne in her large purple stroller with the other hand. Going to my new apartment, 1cb.

Walking through the projects curves, heading down blocks, passing one after another, just taking my time walking, going straight to my brand new building.

It was a sunny day, which was kind of odd because normally in late fall it starts getting cold where as you will need a coat. It seem like Mother Nature for some apparently reason was being kind to us all because I recall the seasons wasn't acting like how they were suppose too.

I'm wearing a brown suede jacket. I remember being so glad that it wasn't cold because I couldn't afford a coat. Less than, within a month, my daughter Champagne she will be two years old. I recalled being proud-like I had achieved something because I have gotten us our very own place before she had turned two. Over and over I watched so many Black Americans young people have children, and they are still living in their' mother apartment-raising their' children.

So walking down the blocks even though I kinda looked funny pulling one end and pushing the other-I felt as if I had accomplish a major accomplishment. I got my own apartment all by myself. Outside of the projects, and I'm, head of household, while, single handedly raising my daughter... and you know, something about it felt so right, but something also felt so wrong. I felt like I overcame a situation or an obstacle where I wasn't supposed to win.

Anyway when I final reached Union Blvd there were a lots of people who were outside that lived on that block.

As I walked down the street looking at the people. I said to myself, what a small little block. As I continue walking I also thought... I'm just a few blocks away from the project and how convenient it will be for me to go back and forth.

I was also thinking, how I will not be hanging out with anybody on this block. Coming from the project I know firsthand how noisy people who don't want nothing out of life can be. And the rule of thumb is-the less low life niggers knows, the better your life will be.

I also thought on how I will be visiting my sister, nieces and nephew. I guess a small part of me would be showing off a little bit. That single handily I beat the odds. I left the projects. I visualize my sister coming over to my house hanging out with me and her' kids playing with my daughter. I figure now that I had my own place Desmond wouldn't be so involved in our relationship. How my cousins will be coming over too, visiting me. Us girls going out partying and doing mature things.

When I reached the building the janitor of the building was in the hallway in his' blue uniform leaned up against the wall smoking a cigarette. I said, "Hello."

"Hello," he said back.

It felt good just walking into my apartment without going inside an elevator. It was a new feeling and I liked it. I open the door and walked into this big empty living room.

Without taking off my jacket and leaving my daughter strapped inside her stroller quickly I started taking everything out of the push cart and putting it on the floor because I knew I had to go back to the project getting the rest of my belongings.

I was so excited I couldn't believe this had actually happened. I did it all by myself. I was so very proud.

Tray because of his' drug addiction had destroyed and sold the majority of my things so I didn't have that much. Leaving everything on the floor, I left right back out to go get some more of my stuff.

Pushing Champagne. Pulling an empty folded shopping cart walking up Union Blvd while looking at my new neighborhood and my new neighbors. When I got back to the projects Desmond wasn't in the house. If he was there, he was quietly in his' room.

That last stunt being naked on the bed and all, it really proved to me how much he is a low life bastard and eventually Tonya would come to see that for herself. Since she will be here alone with him. Now she can't use me as the excuse for her' misguided anger anymore. Now she would be able to face the truth about Desmond and realize what a piece of shit he really is.

Even through Tonya was stupid for Desmond and allow him to bully her. I didn't hate my sister. I hated Desmond.

Since he moved in I hated the petty arguments and the confusion my sister and I went through every day in that apartment. Tonya watching me, competing and comparing every fuckin thing. She needs her own space to grow as well as I needed my space too. We both need the space to live the way each of us see fit and happily, so we can raise our own family. There's an old saying, two women can't share the same kitchen.

I'm hoping now with some space between us my sister and I could rekindle our relationship without so much interference from Desmond.

I got more of my stuff out from my room. Putting the items in the shopping cart. Leaving out, walking back to my new apartment the same way I did before. Pushing Champagne with one hand while pulling the shopping cart full of stuff with the other. Walking the same path. Dropping off items and leaving right back out until I have gotten everything out that I could carry. It took a couple of trips but I got it done.

Tray, he just appeared out of nowhere.

I figure Desmond ran and somehow got in touch with Tray. Telling him; "Yo, she moving." But, honestly, occasionally that's what Tray did. Tray had always came back around checking up on us. Popping in and out of mine and Champagne life. Anyway he was right on time this time because I did need help with one more thing. It was taking down and moving the enormous wooden crib/bed he bought for Champagne.

Because of Tray's constant use of drugs we often fought. We break up. We get back together. For some odd reason I did wanted us to get married. Mainly, just because I am carrying his' child, and also in addition to, how I was raised-with a marry-mother and father. I was so young and naïve and totally inexperience to life.

I did wanted the relationship to work especially now that I have given birth to his' daughter. He even gave me an engagement ring. That he wand-up taking back. Pond it, so he can go and get high. Anyway just to let yall know, Tray' proposal wasn't like a thought out one. It was more like, "Here T." Maybe it's because he knew deep down inside I wanted to be married when I brought a child into this world.

First he selling the crack now he smoking crack. Throwing my good clothes he brought me with the drug money out from the twelve floor project window. All in a get high rage, embarrassing me one to many fuckin times.

Stealing my shit and not caring about the baby shit. Like what all she needs. Always taking back the jewelry he brought me. Crying when he fucked up the money. I never forget how he cried like a bitch that day, after all the drug hustling and sacrificing and saving we did. Me, thinking finally, we have a little nest egg put away. Just to find out all the money was gone.

I got to say, I never saw a man cry like that. I should have realized at some point he wasn't a responsible man but I was so naive to this adult world plus I was trying to hang on to my version of the American dream-relating to, how I expected to raise my family. One thing for sure, I realize he went too far and I couldn't take it anymore. No, it's not that

I couldn't take it anymore, I simply didn't want to deal with his bullshit. This crap of a shit that supposed to be what he calls a relationship?

What kind of life is this shit! Enough is enough. He had a bad habit constantly getting high, creating drama after drama, way too much embarrassment and disappointment. I deserve more and I wanted more. He wanted nothing out of life and his actions showed it. There so much I lost being with him. But I was glad when he came by.... to help me move on that day.

As we both walked carrying Champagne' crib/bed to my new apartment. I could see Tray thinking, hoping maybe him and I could have another chance at this relationship. Being that it will be just us. Meaning him, me and our' baby (Champagne) with no added interferences from Tonya or Desmond.

There was times when Tray tried to put down the weed but here come Desmond and Tonya bringing him a joint to smoke, enticing him.

Anyway, when Tray enter into my new apartment he looked around impress to see I had a nice place for myself and our' daughter. Tray was well aware of the turmoil that went on with me in that apartment.

He knew he was wrong for the way he had treated me and I guessed I chump his face achieving the impossible on my own. Getting myself out from a stressful situation and taking exceptional good care of our' daughter with me on such a low financial budget. That I didn't take the punk way out of my responsibility, like him, as a way to escape parenthood.

He want me to give him another chance but he keep stuttering so bad he couldn't really get the words to come out of his' mouth.

"Tami so, so what so what about us trying, you know, trying to make a go at it again? I know I mess up. I'm going to get another job, as, as a matter of fact I have some things line up," Tray said.

While he was trying to say what he wanted to say I looked at him with pity. I honestly felt sorry for him. He needed help. Tray had a problem and it was bringing us both down. I had just enough strength to take care of me and my daughter. The fighting and arguing. All the lies and stealing-I felt Champagne deserve to have a good life and living with him, she and I wouldn't have that. I tried and tried so many times already.

So I told him, "Tray, Champagne deserve to be happy and I don't want you to keep coming back and forth disappointing her. Making her promises you know you won't keep. So if you can't be a father to her then I don't want you to keep coming back here playing with her' head and her' emotions."

Stop! Security knocking on the door. Knock, Knock "Dinner time ladies," the guard said from behind the door. Once I finish eating my food I goes back to my dorm. It's quiet because majority of the girls in my dorm are out on weekend passes.

To get a weekend pass you have to be doing everything you supposed to do. Like have no fractions meaning your area is found satisfactory and you leave the dorm on time. You comply with the shelter rules, for example; your file are up to date with recent ppd shots, medical and psyche evaluation. That you do meet with your caseworker every two weeks, and you're not a curfew violator. Meaning you in the shelter every night and by your bed ten o'clock pm.

The Dominican girl just came out from the shower. She walking quickly to her' area. She's preparing herself to go out as she lavish her body with scented body lotion. She sprays perfume. In her' Dominican accent she ask me, "Mommy you going out tonight?"

I said, "Nope."

"Why, you don't want to go out?" she asked.

I said, "I don't have anywhere to go and I don't have any money."

"I'm going to the Bronx. I have a late pass until two am. Mommy I can't stay here I go loco," she said.

The only people in the dorm beside me was the new girl who soaking her feet. Lacy who is lying on her bed reading a book with ear plugs in both her' ears and my neighbor who is lying down on her bed with no covers on her, but fully dress curl up like a baby.

To the reader, that is reading this book. Before we go any farther I like to introduce myself. Sorry I have to go back and forth to different period of my life in order to make you best understand. So on that note let me stop and introduce myself to you. Then I can finish what I started.

"Hi. First of all I just want to say I'm a Black American born female. You already know my name is Electra Tami Jones. I'm 42 years old. Born with sandy brown hair. First born child of Mr. and Mrs. Jones. Raise in Westbrook Projects along with one sister. I think I'm fairly attractive but lot of people tells me I'm very attractive.

I took my complexion from Grand pop, a high yellow very serious no joking military kind of fellow. My complexion is the lightest in my immediate family. Being that my grandparents on my father side has Cherokee Indian in them-I kind of red boned with a nice grade of hair.

God has bless me with a youthful appearance. My breast s are small but perky. I have somewhat of a flat stomach. My legs are shapely attracted. My figure, well I'm tall and medium built with no hips. I have no scars or tattoos on my skin. I'm told I have a great smile and a great ass.

When I was a child I sweated on my nose and because of that I was told that I would have a temper. Then again I was told also that I would have a temper due to my complexion being a red bone. Now that's my outer appearance.

On the inside I love being in any type of water. Being that I don't have a pool I love taking long baths. I can be very quiet at times and easy going. I respect and love my privacy. I love cooking up sumptuous meals and great deserts. I love celebrating the Holidays. I'm totally an animal lover and an activist if I have to be. I have three of the world most wonderful kids. My oldest daughter name is Champagne, she is four year older than my son Brandon. We like to call him JB. He is a year and a half older than Moet, who is my baby.

....Wait ...I could just hear some of the readers saying, why didn't she introduce herself as an African American woman?

Because I am an American, there's nothing African about me. I know and heard stories from other black people about our ancestors being from Africa but my momma, daddy or grandparents or even my great, grandparent never told me any African stories or that we had come from Africa. And I knew and had visited my Grandmamma' mother way before she died.

Plus there isn't anyone in Africa inviting me to come over and stay. If I was to purchase a plane ticket for me to go to Africa ....trust me, I be paying for my room/board and my food too.

Remember the famous line by James Brown, "Say it loud. I'm black and proud."

At one point we were announce as color folks. In a negative sense I heard we were call niggers. Now some people want a title, African American. I don't have a problem with using the word Black only. I know who I am. I am a Black American female born in Brooklyn come from Bed-Stuy do or die know as Bedford-Stuyvesant and proud of it."

Okay, now that's out the way I like to get back to the story. Let's go *back to the story*.

I finally got my own place but I had no money. For some apparent reason welfare hasn't changed my budget. I'm still sharing my case with my sister. I have this big L shape apartment with all these gorgeous big windows that I simply adore but I'm broke as hell. I can't even fix it up. The only thing that came through for me from welfare was my moving and furniture allowances.

I use that money to help purchase this beautiful brass twin bed that I plan on giving to Champagne when she turn five. In the meantime I will sleep on the bed.

The bedroom resemble a small L shape only a twin mattress could fit on one side of the wall. On the other side Tray and I put Champagne's bed. The smart investment paid off in buying that expensive crib that converts into a bed. The wooden crib detachable three drawers came in very handy because I didn't have any money to purchase bedroom furniture. Instead I purchase kitchen supplies, like a T-fal pot and pans set, shower curtains and cleaning products.

After cleaning up and settling in I went back to the project to visit my sister but nothing has changed with her. She still wouldn't allow me and Champagne to be a part of her' life or her children' life. She would always find an excuse why she didn't want any company or she would say things like, "I'm busy with the twins."

I offer to help her but she always said, "No," and closed her' apt door.

One time when I went by her' house again trying to hang out and be sociable she said, "Electra that guy came by here looking for you again."

"What guy?" I asked. With a smirk like smile she answered "Kerchief." "When did he come over here," I asked. Desmond interfere and said "He came over here quite a few times looking for you."

Tonya asked, "What shall I tell him if he knocks on the door looking for you again?"

I said, "Tell him that I move and you don't know where I moved to."

She knew I didn't like him and I didn't want to be bothered. Tonya snapped, "Why should I lie for you? Why won't you tell him yourself?"

Trying to make her understand I said, "Because I already told him not to come over here and I'm shock to hear that he still coming by."

"Well he has been coming over here a lot since you left," she added.

I had to point it out to her. I said, "Okay, when or if he does come back around tell him I moved and that I don't live here anymore. So there is no need for him to knock on your' door."

To tell you the truth that was one of the best conversations I had with her since I left. I asked her if she wanted to come by the apartment. She always found an excuse not to visit. It has gotten to the point, I see she didn't want to have a relationship with me. So I learned to accept her decision even through it did hurt me.

Instead of concentrating on her and mine relationship, when I came by this time I would ask Tonya, "Can I bring the kids to my house?"

I wanted to get to know my nieces and nephew.

She said, "Desmond don't want them to go to your house." This is all I have heard, since my niece-Hope, been born. When we had shared our' parents apartment, the little bit of time that Hope and my daughter had played together, Desmond had always accused me of being irresponsible.

When he found out his child spent any time with me he would angrily ask Tonya "Where did this scratch come from?"

....Or he would enter the apartment and he would see Hope fall while playing with Champagne and I'll be sitting on the couch. He would say "You stupid bitch my daughter fell and you didn't even pick her up. Tonya..... Tonya that why I don't want Hope with this unfit bitch."

Before I had my own child, one day I had taken Hope to the store and he drove up on me all fast. He jumped out the car and **he snatched!** Not picked her up I literally mean snatched Hope out from my arms, away from me, and said to me "Give me my daughter. Don't you ever touch my fuckin daughter again! Unfit bitch."

I don't get it! Why he had to snatch her out my arms like that and **drive off!** I wouldn't hurt his' daughter. I loved Hope the 1st day Tonya brought her home from the hospital and placed her basin in between both of our twin beds in our bedroom that we shared. She's, my, niece! What is his fuckin problem? So Desmond wouldn't allow it. Therefore Tonya wouldn't allow it. Then Tonya will say things like, "I don't want to hear his' mouth. No, the answer is no Electra."

A part of me is very mad at Tonya for not letting me get to know her' children. What the **fuck happened** to, my, sister! You can choose your friends but you can't choose your family. Like it or not but their' children are my family too. They are my only nieces and nephew. I use to plead with her, "Okay. For the children sake let them play together so they can get to know one another."

Hope has my daughter by seven month. Desmond was just being cruel. Why is he being so mean and nasty?

Champagne don't have any other family besides me and my family. She was lonely. She needed playmates. I wanted her to get to know her' cousins. The only other family Champagne have is Tray very old grandfather, Mr. Stevenson and his' girlfriend, Shirley. They are the ones who occasionally watch her for me when I need a break. But it was okay for Desmond to take Hope downstairs to his' mother apt to hang out alone with his' sisters. We all live in the same building, his-family lives on a lower floor in the projects. Tonya and Desmond's children are allow to get to know his' family.

I was so angry at my sister and especially at Desmond for treating us-me and Champagne like an outcast. Their children are our family too. I'm their only aunt on their mother side. I have spoken several times to my sister about this situation but it always gotten nowhere.

I even spoke about her behavior to my parents, several times. By the time Hope was born, our parents had split-up. They were living in different households but they were still both of our parents.

I went to my mother and spoke on this issue and my mother always said, "Electra those are his' kids," and she will leave it like that which boggle my brain with her' nonchalant attitude between her' only two daughters. What does she mean his kids? She doesn't care about my feeling as if I'm a piece of shit who doesn't deserve to have any kind of involvement. She's fine with the situation of seeing me be left out.

........Why......?

Why not say something about it? Why not speak up on this situation?

I go to my father's house and mention it to my father and he would say "That's your one and only sister, what happened between yall?" Then repeatedly hearing me speak on the concerning issue again about Tonya behavior towards me, out from his' frustration my dad would say "Electra...... Electra how many times are you going to keep talking about the same thing?"

Eventually I got tired of knocking on her' door wanting and trying to have a relationship with her. I got tired of seeing the repeatedly closed door being put in my face and hearing the word. "No."

She is my only sister and I love her so much. I remember the first time how I felt when my sister started behaving so mean towards me. She put a mark on my heart. That feeling is intangible. It a deep aching feeling and I felt it penetrate.... going deeper, penetrating....... until she cut my heart without her even using a knife.

We never had a fight. We used to be best of friends and sisters. All I can say is it really hurt and I could tell you I know that scar is still imprinted on my heart till this very day.

After feeling how that cut feels on my heart, I made a vow to myself never to allow Tonya or anyone to hurt me as deeply as she did when she implanted that mark on my heart. I have always been a very good sister to her. Many years has passed and I healed from some of those old wounds but that scar of betrayal she left on my heart-it will never heal properly. I know it there for life. I got the message loud and clear. Her actions, well it does hurt but no more scar will be embedded on my heart. I simply won't allow it because it hurt so badly.

Anyway I got tired of hearing her constant rejection and I finally said the word....... Goodbye.

My family has changed.

What could I do when I done all I can. I reached out repeatedly and always got put down, left out, wasn't invited. I sometime walked by Westbrook Project and occasionally I would see someone who would tell me "I saw your mother driving your sister and her' kids food shopping."

Or a person would say, "Your mother is watching your sister's kids."

While outside and always I'm struggling since I had my daughter Champagne, sometime I occasionally seen and had even bumped into my own mother and sister together with her' children in the back seat, riding in my mother car.

I heard from lots of different people the same sentences. "I saw your mother and Tonya together......she was babysitting the kids......she has taking them food shopping, or your mother at-or.... just left from the projects after visiting your sister Tonya."

Why I'm bickering about it, because my mother has always help Tonya from day one. Ever since Tonya brought Hope home from the hospital. Yes, now Tonya has the twins to take care of and my mother is helping aiding her with her many errands which is nice but it was painful and unfair to me and my daughter who she doesn't help out. With me who learning from outsiders how close they are and how much my mother is doing for Tonya and her' kids since I left the projects. Even before I had left the project my mom had helped Tonya a great deal.

Or I would hear from the many people that lives in the projects who saw them all the time together say to me, "I asked your mother or I asked your sister about you," especially they knew I wasn't around them, and I guess, out of genuine concern or maybe even curiosity. They are wondering what going on with us or what happened?

I didn't know how to respond to it because I didn't understand it myself. All I know was I had a baby to support. I have no money to decorate my empty apartment. My mom and my sister treated my very wrong but I couldn't concentrate on that because I could have lost my mind worry about..........why?

Yes to me, it was very unfair how my mother didn't show me and Champagne the same kind of love and support she given to my sister Tonya and her' children. Unfairness too from my mother towards Desmond, as well-like why she showed and respect him so much knowing he help in aiding too our family destruction.

Yes it was so unfair that my mom didn't help me when I had ask her many times to watch Champagne so I can find a job or go back to school. Or it would had been nice my mother just sitting with me in the apartment, with me, doing nothing and her helping me out around the house. The many times I just needed a break when I lived in the projects to relax or hang out, like the other young girls my age are doing. Going to parties and hanging out with friends/family. Or just going to a discotheque letting my hair down like girls my age.

And yes my mother is so very wrong when she allow Desmond to come into our family, in her' house and do stupid mischief as she still support him and accept him, and treat him like he is a royal prince who bestowed good fortune to her' daughter Tonya.... by the way, who is the head of her' household.

Which all seem like bullshit to me. It been this way since Hope was born. Like what happen to us supporting each other in the family? So what could I do? I had to go on with my life.

As for my father he used the oldest trick in the book. He cop out by doing drugs and when I would bring it to his' attention he would say things like "**What**, he did that?" Or say, "I didn't know that was going on**?** Or why didn't you tell me."

Every day Champagne woke up she needed her bottle. She needed to be fed. She needed to go to the park. She needed to be held. She needed someone to be there for her because no one else was there, but me.... and it been like this since day one. Now I have my own apartment and I was hoping things between Tonya and I change.

So I couldn't flip the fuck out on my parents **and say "WHY ARE YOU TREATING ME LIKE THIS**!!" You don't love me anymore? You don't care about me anymore? Maybe I would had snap and lost my fuckin mind.

I had to deal with my struggle all alone. Then the disappointment of the realization pain of what they call-being the BLACK SHEEP OF THE FAMILY. How and when the fuck did I become the black sheep of the family. Why is my family acting so nonchalant seeing me get kick out!

Dam!

This is whatz happening and this is just what it is. Beside what being shown to me and whatz is occurring I had to have a mindset of what's more important, the here and now or learning how to survive in all this emotional madness.

I chose learning to survive in all of this bizarre emotional madness!

It's Friday night. Security came in and turn off the lights. Goodnight.

Chapter Seven

Thank goodness that it's the weekend. Saturday morning. It's the only time security doesn't turn on the dorm lights. It's always so quiet when the weekend comes around. This is when the staff, as well as other residents could tell who has family and friends and who don't.

In the shelter I had went through my stages with the weekends. At first I couldn't wait for the weekend to come around because residents had the option to stay inside their' dorm all day if they liked. Doing whatever it was that pleases them as long as it didn't interfere with the other girls, who were living inside the dorm.

Mainly everyone would just be sleeping anyway. It's a lot of work that brings on negative stress being homeless. You always carrying a bag. You always got to eat out. You have no privacy. You always got to leave early from where you sleep.... for 7 to 8 hours daily. It like you have a job but you don't. If you're not working you either walking around or sitting around for lengthy amount of hours a day. So therefore when the weekend rolls around you just exhausted from being exhausted.

Another good thing when the weekend rolls around is that, not one single dorm lights would be on. The lights to the dorm don't come on until a resident had decided to put it on and it's only to see something they searching for if they couldn't find it. The sunlight coming through the dorms' enormous windows is efficient enough lights for us girls.

Then after a while at Bridge Net, for me the weekend became depressing and embarrassing. Mainly from me always watching other girls come back on Sunday with their' home cook dinners wrapped up in plastic bags or food storage containers, and hearing the females say, "My mother cook." Or listening to others say, "My sister or brother made me dinner." Or "We gave my niece a birthday party," made me feel as if I didn't have anyone who truly loves me.

I'm going to Jose to order breakfast with a cup of coffee. Once I got back inside the dining room I saw there was a small line formed of females who were waiting to use the microwave. From the store I also brought a package of microwavable popcorn that I wanted to pop and sneak upstairs to my dorm. Sneaking food up to the dorm is real easy all you got to do is carry a tote bag and cover the top of the tote bag with a jacket or sweater.

Oh no, this is so disguising!

I don't understand how these grown ass women put their' food inside the microwave when its messed up like this. Bridge Net has the nastiness microwave I ever seen. People spill their' food and leave a mess inside. Soups and coffee has been blown-up in the microwave, and have been left inside. Sometimes you would find the black stains-left in the microwave, from burnt-up popcorn. Sometimes you even see the brunt popcorn itself. So therefore, when you open up the microwave door you would find everything inside that has been splatter and blown-up on its walls, forming different colors and stains, that's accumulating smells. Gross!

What make the microwave also so polluted and sickening is that the clients will nuke their' eatable foods on top of the leftover mess, uncovered, and they do this on a regular basis. Uugh.

I'm not going to even lie, sometimes but not often, only like when I'm in a hurry. I too had even put in a cup of coffee but not food, and I had nuke it when the microwave was in this kind of condition. I just made sure that the lid was tightly closed because plain and simple, you get tired of cleaning the dam microwave all the time when I need to use it.

Being homeless, lots of time a person be tired and stressed out just from living inside a shelter. You got to clean the table before you sit down. You got to flush the toilet behind another person that used it before you came inside of the bathroom. You got to wash your hand frequently because you've been outside walking all day, then to only find out there no paper towels to dry them on.

Imagine feeling like this, drained, exhausted, broke, tired and bored because there nothing else to do but to wait until you get suitable housing. You walk around all day because you don't have money to do anything. Or a person would just sit in the dining room smelling other people bowel movements, while just glazing looking out from the shelter dining-room window...... but, only if you that lucky client, to get the seat by the window. Then, you always got to be home by 10 pm. I'm asleep by 11 pm every night. Every day a homeless person got to be up and fully dressed to leave out from the dorm by 9 am. Then the homeless person has to sit around or either walk around waiting till 4 pm-just to re-enter their dorm. And when you reach the dorm the person would be just sitting on their bed, all evening waiting till the lights get cut out while looking at everyone else bags and unmade cots. That's enough for anyone routine boredom to slightly turn into a form of mental illness, like depression. To me, living like this long enough can cause anyone to develop a lack of vitality, meaning a loss of energy or liveliness.

Have you ever notice homeless people just sit glazing or picking their face or skin because their boredom and poverty has done develop into some form of a mental illness? To me that so sad, and, it's not a laughing matter. The homeless person come back to the shelter after being out all day or sitting in the dining room all day. She has the option of letting it stay as is, or to clean up behind someone else mess. Something she didn't do. If she need to use the bathroom, she got to clean the toilet seat. Or when she got to take a shower, she got to clean the tub and sometimes the tiles on the wall. Or, sometimes she got to clean the garbage can that's inside the bathroom because it smells like dried blood from thrown-out bloody tampons, as well, as the bathroom floor because someone peed on it. I done did so much cleaning. Really, sometimes a homeless person don't have the energy to keep cleaning all the time.

If a resident doesn't clean the area, like so many of the girls do, then what are, the, result? You overlook the filth and go as is. I can't do that because I care about my health therefore my only solution is to clean before I use it. Clean, clean, clean, clean, CLEAN! Damn so I'm tired of fuckin cleaning!

When I got back to my dorm there was only my roommate Marcell, who nursing her' foot back to health. Lacy was gone, she out every day walking around doing what it is she do. The only reason I'm in, is because I have a new project, writing this book. I became an early riser too thanks to the sound of security's voice waking me up at six am every day. So what if it is the weekend? Once I'm up, I'm up. I just can't go back to sleep unless I'm extremely tired or sick.

So, reader: Let's go *back into the story.*

So now I had nothing else to do but concentrate on Champagne and my apartment. Making it a steady and stable home for us. After the constant rejections from Tonya. I had learned how to stay in my own surroundings. I started learning the stores in my new area. Started recognizing new faces. Now I'm speaking to people who lives inside the building.

Having my own place was great but it was hard because my budget was still the same. I'm still receiving the same amount of money as if I was still sharing the apartment inside the project with my sister Tonya. So I had to go to the welfare office to speak with a caseworker concerning my PA allowance.

The worker that had handle the case assured me that it would be taking care of, and had, sent me on my way. I waited two weeks just to find out that nothing has changed. I found myself repeatedly going down to social services, questioning, "What's going on with my budget?" Finally, I had to request and apply for a fair hearing. Waiting for a fair hearing takes time. I was getting sixty-eight dollars and fifty cents every two weeks.

Every month I had to cash in some of my food stamps in order to make my ends meet. Out from my PA cash allowance I had to pay for the light and gas and not to mention keeping up with the toiletries in order to maintain a clean household. Also keeping good hygiene for both me and my baby. I was left with no spending money.

After going to the laundromat which became expensive. Back in the projects, we had a washing machine and a dryer that my mother had left inside the apartment when she had moved out. Lots of time Tonya washing using the machine for her' family. After I left Desmond throw out the old machine and brought in a new washing machine so Tonya could honestly say, "It not my washing machine." If I now needed to use it.

All my extra cash was going towards paying my light and gas bill. Lots of time I had to wash my baby clothes in the tub....... underneath the faucet running water. When washing the clothes with my hand got to be a bit too much. I started adding the baby deft detergent and soaking her' clothes in the tub. I would rinse them out by hand. Then I air dry the clothes in the house on a folded clothesline that I had purchase from one of those discount stores on Main Street. All in an attempt to help me have some money for functioning with our daily needs on such a low budget. In order words, I'm robbing Peter to pay Paul.

Mine you, separately I had washed her' clothes and now, my clothes by hand. I washed our clothes by hand so much that it had gotten to be a bit too much because I started getting callouses. Then, I remembered that segment on the I Love Lucy show. Remember the scene when Lucy was making wine by stepping on grapes. Well, that's what I started to do. Instead of scrubbing the clothes with my hands. I rolled up my pants or sometime I just had on my bra and panties. I would step into the tub with my clean feet. Stepping and rubbing the clothes together. After a while I stop to let the clothes just soak inside the detergent water. Repeat the process of stepping and rubbing again. Next I would have wrung the clothes out underneath running water, removing the clothing. Re-wash the tub. Fill the tub up with clean water allowing the clothes to soak again for the rinse. Then I will squeeze out individually each piece of clothes again underneath running water. Lastly, I hang-dry on my store bought clothesline that I purchased from the discount store on Main Street.

With nothing else to do and not much money, to keep myself busy I debug the apartment from roaches. I clean and wash periodically the kitchen wooden cabinets with Murphy Oil polish. Washed and clean the floors, fridge and oven often. Kept all the closets in the house organized. So at the end of the day all I had was a big clean empty apartment.

I cooked in. We didn't eat fast food since we couldn't afford it. I had bought dishes, bowls, silverwares and a pitcher so that I could make Kool-Aid. This stuff adds up quickly. Therefore, my money was always gone.

Instead of buying pampers, I had even tried to save money by buying diapers. You know, the ones that are made out of cloth and you have to use safety pins to hold it together. They are washable and reusable. Anything to help me function on such a low budget. I needed everything; a broom, a mop and a bucket. You name it. I needed it.

Inside my apt I hear a loud buzzer go off.

It's my intercom.

I go to the unit to press the talk button. I asked, "Who is it?" "It's me your mother." I buzzed her in. I'm so excited because it's my first visitor. I'm hype, all because I hear the knocking sounds coming upon my apt door. I go to open up the door.

"Hi mom," I said.

She comes in looking unbelieved but also impressed that I had gotten my own apartment.

I was so excited! I immediately wanted to show her around. "This is my bedroom," as I open up the door to the small room. My mother looks in like okay.

Then she herself has gone to one of the hallway closet's and said, "Oh they sliding doors." She looks inside the bathroom. I'm behind her so proud. I say, "You got to see my living room." Leading her to the living room. "Wow. What a huge living room, and the kitchen is cute. You have a lot of cabinets," my mother said.

"Yeah I know," I said while shaking my head in agreement.

I sat on one of the window ledges and said, "I don't have any furniture yet but I'm working on it." Champagne was happy to see her too she started making noise like to get her' attention. I guess she too was happy to see someone else beside me and that we had a visitor in our new apartment.

My mother picked her up and asked, "Do you like your new place? Oh Electra, she looked as if she has gained some weight."

Knowing I haven't done anything different since I left the project. I said, "She do?"

So my mother tells me…. "Roland my next door neighbor asked me if I know anybody that could use a couch. He's buying a new sofa."

I asked, "How much do he want for it?"

My mother said, "I think he's asking for one hundred dollars."

"I don't have that kind of money right now," I answered. My living room windows had cheap see through window shades because I had noticed people were looking at me as I had sat on the window ledge. So I got up and took a squat on the floor as we continue having our conversation.

My mother said, "I'll buy it for you. Take it as my house gift to you."

I asked "What color is it." My mother kind of frown her face and said "What does it matter? You don't have anything in your apartment." I said, "I know. I just wanted to know the color that all."

Then it like she started thinking about it. Mommy said, "It's a print. That has flowers on it and I think it is *red* or burgundy. If I get the couch do you have anyone who can come pick it up?"

"Nope," I said. She put a disgusted expression on her' face and shook her head.

"How did you find out about this place," she asked. "I answered an ad in the paper," I responded. Out from curiosity she asks "Which paper?"

"I forgot," I said.

I felt I didn't have to answer all her questions because she wasn't helping me when I was back inside the projects anyway. And besides, I'm much happier here in this empty place then I was when I was in the projects. So in my book what did it matter which or what paper I answered the ad. She told me she getting me the couch and that's nice of her so I wanted to change the subject. I figure, let's talk about this.

I asked, "How your sister Melody?"

"I don't know. I haven't heard from her. I guess she alright," my mother responded.

Then I said "Yeah that was messed up the way Lee Keisha, Sheryl and Coon had kicked me out and didn't include me when they were going to different events on issues dealing with Skyler's death."

Immediately my mother said, "So you see they had me as a chauffeur running all over the place."

I said, "Yeah I notice you were moving around a lot. They act as if they were his' only cousins going places, get invited... Immediately my mother stops me.

She said, "I didn't come over here to hear talk about why they did what they did."

Then my mother got all righteous and said, "I'm his' aunt and they treated their' father' girlfriend Shirley (she talking about Coon, Sheryl and Lee Keisha) better than me. Even Dave said they were out of order the way they handle things." David is my mother boyfriend.

Going more into the topic, wanting to justify what our family did by us gossiping. My mother said, "Tonya even said that wasn't right the way they treated you. But what can I do about it. Nothing!"

Not wanting to talk anymore about what happen quickly my mother said, "Look, let me get out of here." She started walking towards the door. I got up. Pick up Champagne and walked my mother to the building lobby as I watched her exit from the building.

Very soon afterwards my mother she re-visited. She, Dave and their' next door neighbor Roland had brought the couch over to me. While Dave and Roland were trying to get the couch inside the apartment. I took my mother into the kitchen showing her the new kitchen tiles I brought to lay on the floor.

She said to me, "Why won't you ask Dave to put it down for you?" So after the guys sat the couch in the living room. Mommy paid Roland and he left, and Dave laid the tiles on the kitchen floor.

The weather had dropped and it started getting cold. All I had was that suede light brown jacket. Champagne had everything she needed for the winter. I didn't know how I was going to get a coat to keep me warm because all my money was already accounted for. People were already staring at me, knowing I must be cold in that light suede jacket. Mother Nature has been kind to me for several years since I became pregnant. It seems like she has known I was having financial difficulties because buy the time I had to buy a coat, it was late in the winter season and the coats would already be on sale.

Winter coming early this year because its late fall and everyone was wearing a coat. I figure I just won't come outside or hibernate like a bear, but I really won't be able to do that because I still had to go outside to pay my bills, pick-up WIC checks and do grocery shopping.

I started getting a little depress.

I didn't have shit. I was dirt poor.

It was a normal day just like every other day, boring. I went to bed like I normally do and the telephone rang. Sounds of ranging-rang, rang, and rang. "Hello," I said. Slow, in her county voice she said, "How you doing." "……. Grandma-Grace? Grandma-Grace! Hiiii! Oh I missed you so much. So much has happened! So much I need to tell you...I had a little girl! I named her." I **stopped!**

……. "**Wait?!** How could I be talking to you? When you... dead." I said.

Suddenly realizing, I thought to myself, oh shit! I don't have a phone. Suddenly I became very acute of my surrounding by saying and thinking within myself......I'm lying on the twin bed in the bedroom. My eyes are closed and I'm lying on my side with my hand to my, *ear?* As if I am holding a telephone? And on the *other end*, I'm talking to my dead grand*mother?*

Without moving or opening my eyes and a little scared. Cautiously-I said, "Grandma-Grace please don't be here when I open my eyes because if I open my eyes and I see you standing here. I'm going to have a heart attack. Then who's going to take care of my baby? My baby doesn't have anybody else to take care of her but just me."

Although I waited two minutes in silent and I didn't change nothing. I left my hand up by my ear with my fist closed as if I was holding something. I waited before I open my eyes and I'm going to tell you, I actually peeped. My hand was still at my ear with my fist closed as if I was holding on to a telephone.

When I opened up my eyes what I seen, was totally darkness. Slowly, I moved my hand from my ear. I was trembling a little as I turned my head, slowly, while looking around the room.

Slowly as my head turns completely around in darkness with the only hint of light that was coming in the bedroom, from the tiny gated window. Now I wanted to look at the bottom of my bed where my feet at but my thoughts really went a little too far. I pictured or I thought about my Grandma-Grace being like Linda Blair from the exorcist. That she would be dress in a dingy off white grown while sitting at the foot of my bed with her body towards the door but her head was completely turned around while looking me in my face and saying, "How you doing."

But thanks be to God she wasn't and what the FUCK was that?

Once I realize no one else was in the room. I looked at Champagne, who was laying in her bed. She was sound asleep. I sat up saying and thinking what the **fuck** was that? My heart was racing. I was spooked, but it was so real. But something else had taken place because in that brief happy conversation Grandma-Grace, was showing me something.

As I was speaking to her and was so very happy to hear her voice. I saw the pictures. So I got the hell out from the bed. In darkness, I started to walk, while wondering and thinking, how did I hear her voice? Then I started rehashing the visions of pictures of what I had seen as I walked slowly thinking in the dark while going towards the bathroom.

The last thing I saw was me and Dove together with his arm around me standing by a banister. We both were smiling and there were some kids standing on each side of us. Some of the kids seem to be running behind us. It looked like were posing for a family portrait. Or was it a photo shoot of how things were supposed *to be?*

I had felt the happiness and warmth inside as I walked into the bathroom remembering the photo. We both looked happy and those kids looked like they were our children?

When I got inside the bathroom I looked in the mirror and I had a tear rolling down my right cheek. I touch it with my index finger to make sure it was real. I'm crying? As I was looking at myself in the mirror, touching and catching the few tears as it ran out my right eye.

Dove?

I haven't thought about him in years as I watch myself in the mirror. Then I thought about Grandma-Grace, when she called me on the telephone. How her voice sound. How I was feeling so sad before I laid down and how the sound of her voice had made me come alive with joy and happiness.

I saw her face. She was looking at me with such love and admiration in her eyes, through those brown glasses that she had worn something. She loved me so much and I loved her so much. She leading me, as we step up on the bus and took a seat. She was just looking at me while smiling at me. Others was sitting on the bus too they knew my grandmother loved me because they were smiling too.

I left the bathroom and started walking towards the couch that's in my living room. Walking down the hallway in total darkness, except from the light coming from the bathroom. I sat on the couch holding myself, remembering her face and the love I felted as my heart starts to calm down. I was still holding on to her spirit, wanting to rehash everything in my brain, from the time I said, "Hello."

We were on the bus then quickly next we were in her' apartment. I remembered, feeling good being and seeing her old familiar surroundings. We were very close my Grandma-Grace and I. Then I saw the room where I had spent many nights. Now both of us were standing by that old room heavy door, that's always ajar.

Now we both -standing inside the room. The heavy room door is semi closed. Behind the door was a strong long nail. It served as a hook for her small collection of clothes. Standing there I watch Grandma-Grace hand move pass a couple of garments, until she reached and showed me the coat. The tweed coat. I saw the coat all by itself, shinning like a star.

Then I saw the vision of Dove and me. I wanted to tell her that I was having such a hard time right now, before, I realized she's dead. Then I got frighten and I remember I didn't want to feel her presence or see her face. I told her to go away.

As I sat upon the coach holding myself in my living room. The only light is coming from one window. The window the lead towards the entrance of the building. Its rays of light that is piercing through the window shades from outside. Now I'm staring toward the hallway-into the dim darkness.

I'm still amazed at what had just taken place. Then my imagination has gotten the best of me again as I had sat there, on the couch, with the rays of the street light piercing through my window. While looking toward the hallway into the dim darkness. I thought, while turning away from the dark hallway Grandma-Grace was going to come floating towards me in a dingy nightgown. But she didn't.

I felt, maybe she knew, she spook me.

Maybe I shouldn't have been scared because maybe she wanted to tell me more. I always felt something wasn't right but I just couldn't put my finger on it. Maybe I should have just went along with it.........Naww. That outer body experience really did spook the shit out of me. Then I thought well maybe she come back and this time I be ready to handle her spirit much better.

I don't believe in ghost but I'm started to question spirits. The dead spirits. Could it be possible when someone passes away their spirit are still around us? I sat on the couch as an unbeliever at what just happen but it really did happen. Then I took another look towards the dim hallway thinking............ I hope she don't come down here floating.

Here I am sitting on the couch, it like three am in the morning.........Then I gets this fantastic idea! I'm going to Harlem to see if that coat is still there.

So at this time in the morning being I was up I put running water in a large pan and stuck it into the oven. Leaving the oven door open. I turned on the oven because for some odd reason I wasn't getting any heat in my apartment. At least by the time Champagne and I get up, the place would be nice and warm.

When we got up, Champagne and I got on the A train going to Harlem. I felt weird because I hadn't ridden this route to Harlem since Grandma-Grace died. As I sat on the train I had wanted to feel those same old feelings I used to get whenever I knew I was about to visit Grandma-Grace, but I didn't. Even getting off the train by the Polar Ground Projects, everything looked different. It looked dull and gloomy. I got excited as I started approaching her old building. I didn't know what to expect, even if DollarBill still lived there.

Passing old stores and buildings, wanting to rehash and capture the past. While my child sits in her stroller I wanted to express to her the joy I had inside, making the announcement, "This is where Grandma-Grace, your great grandmother used to live. And if she was alive how much love she would have poured on you." Champagne was too young for me to express the joy I had inside of me. She was just sitting there sucking on her' bottle enjoying the new scenery.

I got in front of the old run down building. Walked up those stairs. Got in front of her old door, took a breath and I knocked on the door. I was thinking I could really use that coat because it was cold outside. Looking around hoping to see if I saw any old faces. If someone remember me coming over here so many times before she died. This is the only apt I ever knew her to have. She lived here in this apt for a very long time. I remember thinking it sure would be nice to see her open that door again. Life has changed so much for me since she died.

"Who is it?" I heard DollarBill ask from behind the old door. Happy, and sad, because I knew Grandma-Grace didn't live here anymore but happy to hear his voice I said, "It's me DollarBill. Electra."

I could hear him unlocking the many door' locks, and the police bar lock. The door open immediately DollarBill was so happy to see me. He said "Couz! Come on in!"

DollarBill open the door and he takes the small blue folded stroller I had from me. I travel with that stroller because the purple stroller is strong and way too heavy to lug up and down steps and buses when I'm traveling far. It's more of a luxury stroller because it has more room for her to sit and plus, I could hold my grocery bags at the bottom of it.

When I got inside the apartment I was surprised to see that it was so dusty. DollarBill had left the apartment the same way it was when Grandma-Grace was alive. He didn't move a thing. It looked like spider webs were forming on the picture frames. I had guessed this was his way of holding on to her' memories. Anyway DollarBill was glad to see me but he was still heartbroken saying to me "Couz I miss her so much. Nothing the same since Gracie been gone." As we walked toward the kitchen he got the tea kettle and put running water into it, remembering how we (Grandma-Grace) always sat down to a cup of hot tea. I looked into the bedroom that's next to the kitchen everything was the same except it was dusty.

DollarBill said to me "Couz you cut your hair. You look like a boy! Why did you go and do that, couzz?"

So much has happened to me since the last time he seen me. There were so much disappointments going on in my life I didn't want to come over here being the barrier of bad news. I just didn't say anything especially seeing that he didn't look too well himself. I tried to put on a front and I said, "DollarBill this is a haircut. It called the high and low style."

He sat down gave me a good look and he said "You look like a boy." He didn't approve. So I ask him, "Have anyone been over here to see you?" DollarBill shook his' head indicating no.

I started feeling kind of bad for not checking up on him after Grandma-Grace had passed. Lord knows, I had my own shit that I was going through. I asked, "Have you heard from my father?"

He said "He called. Said he be coming by and Honeydew told me he was coming to get Gracie belongings. I waited in this house all day. You know Honeydew **never showed up**!" I just put my head down because I never heard DollarBill upset with my dad. Then I looked in the kitchen corner and seen the same old glue trap that caught any mice that may had wonder inside their apartment.

Sadly, but again DollarBill expressed and said to me "I miss her. The apartment isn't the same without her here."

As I sat at the table I agreed because my life isn't the same neither. DollarBill said "I didn't think I would miss her so much. I really Gracie." Seeing him thinking of her. I did the same. I admitted out loud, "I miss her too DollarBill."

Reminiscing now about her. I told DollarBill "I remember one-day Grandma-Grace ask me. Electra when I died will you miss me?" At the time I was thinking what a dumb question. "**Of course I will**," I said to her, but I didn't really know how it had felt to miss anyone before, until now, because no one I knew hasn't died before."

DollarBill really did look lost without her, when I had looked up at him. I felt bad and I wondered if Grandma-Grace was mad at me for not checking up on him because after all, he was like family too. After she died I never came back around or call DollarBill to even say hello because I was so busy with bullshit after bullshit till I had completely forgotten about DollarBill.

Looking at me he could tell I have change as well because I saw his facial expression as he watches me with my child. DollarBill asked me "So how your mother?" I told him, "Since she moved out with Dave I don't see her so much." I didn't want to let him know how mean she and Tonya became towards me.

Then he asks me about my sister. I said, "She alright." Then he looked at my baby.

To break the silent that's now in the air and the ugliness of the bad treatment I received from my mom and sister, and his stares of questioning of what's going on with me. I told him "Grandma-Grace came by to visit me last night."

It perked him up a little bit. He started chuckling. He said "Oh yeah couz. She didn't come by to see you couz." I said "Yes she did. She showed me the coat in the room." I told him, "She said I could have it."

Looking like he starting to believe me. DollarBill knew we were close and he knew I wouldn't lie on her. So he said "She did?"

Getting up from the table I said, "Yeah, this one right here."

We walk into their spare bedroom by that old heavy door that's always ajar. The bedroom I spent many nights in. DollarBill helped close the heavy door because it doesn't close all the way. I started moving the article of clothing behind the door just like how I saw her did it last night. I started passing her' clothes until I came across the coat. "Ooh. It's so beautiful!" I said.

I tried to remove it from the wall but it was stuck on that big nail, so DollarBill helped. He removed it from off the nail and gave it to me.

"Ooh its heavy too," I said as I held the coat. Wow, the beige tweed coat it had a cape attached to it and at the bottom of the cape it was trim in fur.

DollarBill was standing next to me watching me. I was thinking I'm going to look funny in this roaring fifty or early sixty coat. I tried it on. It a little snug in the arms but it fits. Looking at DollarBill I asked "DollarBill would you mind if I take the coat?"

He said "You could have anything you want. I don't know why your father never came and got the stuff. He keeps saying he coming-but Honeydew never shows up. One day he told me he was coming to clear out Gracie belongings." DollarBill started chuckling again. He said "I waited all day for Honeydew to show but he never showed up. I was so mad."

Once he said I could have whatever I wanted. I got open. I took off the coat and started looking to see what else she got that I like. I went to her' bedroom and looked through the drawer everything still nicely folded because of her illness she sent everything to the cleaners. Grandma-Grace didn't do laundry. All of her bed linen included her pillow cases went to the cleaners. Everything she sent to the cleaner will come back deeply pressed and nicely folded. Wrap up in brown paper and tied with twig like rope. Grandma-Grace is differently old school and back in those days' people took pride in any work of their craftsmanship's.

All of her nightgowns and housecoat were so nicely creased. I was kind of shock to find everything still in the house. Then I came across her photo album book. I couldn't carry too much stuff, with my baby and all. So I took a blouse or two and the photo album book. I wanted to have a picture of her inside my apartment, and I wore the coat out of the house.

Even though people stared at me when I walked down the block and when I got home. Because it was such a fancy coat. I didn't mind. I sure was warm and I said softly, "Thank you Grandma-Grace."

When I went to visit my father, bringing him a plate of food like I always do. I had on the coat. Upset he said "Why did you go and get that coat out from my mother's house!" I told him, "I was cold and I needed a coat."

Daddy asked me "What else did you take from her' house?" I told him, "The photo album book."

Boy! Was he mad at me but it was too late I already had the stuff. He said "Electra you buy yourself a coat and bring my mother coat back to me." I tried reasoning with him. I had asked him why, and, I believe I told him how I came about the coat.

He was seriously angry "Electra, do you hear me. I want the coat back. Do you hear me and bring me the photo album book."

There was a picture of my grandmother that I wanted to get restored. I remembered when I priced it. It was going to cost me a good penny to restore the picture. I was going to save up the money because I wanted to have a picture of her inside my house.

Back then, it did sadden me to hear how my dad was behaving about the situation. Now all of these many years have passed as I am sitting down writing this book. I'm puzzled? Why did my father behave so ugly towards me for her' possessions after she had already passed away?

A very long time ago when I was a teenager, maybe 19 or 18 or was it 17 or 16? I remember Grandma-Grace had given me a necklace that belonged to her. She sat me down and handed me her necklace of white pearls. She said, "Electra, I want you to have this in case I'm not around. It's for when you get married. I want you to wear these pearls. When the time comes for you to be married, you are supposed to have something borrowed. Something blue. Something old and something new. I want you to wear these pearls for something old. That way I be there with you on that special day."

To the reader, I want you to know that I really did forget a lot of this stuff and now that I'm writing the book, it's bringing out all of these old emotions and memories and surely, some of them are bringing me to tears.

Back to the story.

I remembered I went to my mother' apartment and I told her I had a dream about Grandma-Grace. Anyway not knowing I would return so soon back at my mother's door. When I went into her kitchen, my mother had a small picture of Grandma-Grace that I have never seen before. She had it in a tiny frame, sitting on the counter next to a burning candle.

When I question my mother, "What this about?" She didn't want to talk instead she waved her' hand in the air like it was no room for discussion. I remember being very curious about it because it looked so fuckin abnormal and weird. Anyway my mother tells me, "Isaac came by the apartment visiting Dave and while he was here Electra he asked me and Dave how you doing? I told him you have your own place and he wanted your address."

I said, "Mommy, I know you didn't give out my address without my permission."

"I didn't. I know how you are. So I took his telephone number and I told him I will give it to you the next time I see you. I put it up in the room. Let me go get it," she said

As I sat there in her living room waiting I darted my eyes into the kitchen while looking at the picture and at the burning candle. Wait.... I remembered that picture, that was taking a long time ago when Grandma-Grace used to visit us in the projects. When Tonya and I were very small children.

My mother came back with his' telephone number. I asked "Mom can I call him from your phone?"

She said, "Just a minute." My mother went and picked up the house phone then she hands me the phone saying, "I was checking to see if Dave was using the phone." I dialed the number and Isaac picks up.

I said, "Hello Isaac."

"Bambi?" he said before I got a chance to say another word. I hate that I told him people called me Bambi in high school.

"Yeah it me. How" "Oooo wow. I been asking for you. How have you been," he asked all perky and cheery. "Alright," I responded. "Bambi, you never will believe it. I won a pair of Stephanie Mill concert tickets and I wonder, well I'm hoping you go with me to see the show?" Isaac asked.

Out of curiosity I asked, "How did you win the tickets?" Because he always winning stuff. I could tell over the phone he was still soaking up his' moment of glory, and can't actually believe it happen to him again.

He said "I was the one hundredth caller on the radio station. "O," I said. Sounding so happy he won Isaac said "So tell me you go, Bambi."

He appeared to be interested in me but he wasn't my type. He's older than me and he smiles a lot when he talks. He has a boyish polite mannerism about himself. I just didn't find him to be sexually appealing. Quite often in my mid-teens he had visited Dave inside the apartment when we all lived in the projects. Much later he found out that I loved music. He told me he used to be a DJ and that he has an awesome music collection. I visited his place briefly and together that's when him and I made me some great music tapes.

Enthused he asked "Bambi so you going right?" "Ohm I," …. "Bambi," he said "This is **Stephanie Mills. A live concert!** Come on what wrong with having a little fun and what better way to celebrate, now that you have your own place?"

I gave him my new address and everything was set. After I hung up the phone I told my mother, "He asked to take me out to see Stephanie Mills." My mother said "Oh, that's nice. Stephanie Mills she made a lot of songs."

I said, "Yeah she sure did. Everybody knows that song Feel the fire...and mom, remember that song called Home and what about I found love under new management."

My mother said, "Yeah I remember that song feel the fire. I have some of her records." Then I said, "And what about the other song she made, I need the comfort of a man."

Changing the subject mommy said, "I hope you and Champagne coming over for Thanksgiving Dinner. Dave and I just order this bad pot set. I saw it being advertise on TV. We paid a lot of money for this set. I can't wait to try it out. It supposed to drain the fat from the meats and also help retain its own juices."

Stop! Reader: Isn't it funny because I'm starting to notice when I do something my mother does it too and I must point it out, that since I been writing, I'm realizing this and I'm starting to see a pattern with her imitating me or copying me.... hum? Let's go back to the story. I said "I know a good pot set can be expensive cause the T -Fal set I brought from Macy Department store I got on sale. The original price was a little over one hundred dollars."

My mother said "Yeah I saw that set you got. That set you have is nice but the one I order, it's something else, because it lids serves as a pressure cooker and the material is non scratch able that why I'm paying so much money."

I said, "Well I can't wait to taste the food and see for myself how good this pot set is. Do you need me to help you prepare anything?"

My mother said, "Maybe if I need help you can cut up the greens and help cut up the onions and peppers." "Alright no problem," I said.

Getting up from the table my mother said, "Let me get back to cleaning up this house I'll speak to you later Electra."

Champagne and I left. While I was walking down the street. I was thinking, if it was Tonya with her' kids, my mother would have drove them home.

My apartment is coming along slowly. Finally, the fair hearing of welfare got my budget corrected. I got all the back money back that welfare owed me. With the back money I purchase a high power am/fm cute little compact dual cassette/three CD player.

I had a professional photographer come to my home and take pictures of my daughter. After I passed pictures out to my immediate family, I still had some many left over pictures, so I left them in the folder they came in.

My cousins Sheryl and Lee Keisha their' girlfriend she was in need of an apartment. I refer her to Asbury Management and she had gotten an apartment in the building around the corner. Anyway when I went to visit her she gave me the last kitten from her litter as a thank you gift for helping her.

Tonight is the night I be going to see Stephanie Mills live. I was in my living room listening to one of the cassettes tape Isaac just mailed me on my brand new system. When I heard someone knocking at my door. I was excited cause it been a while since I been out like an adult. You know what I mean, without my daughter. Feeling good, I check out my place before I open the door. I told pebbles who is my cat, be on your best behavior. I immediately goes to the door and open it because I knew I'm expecting Isaac, but instead I got a big surprise. It's not Isaac, it was Kerchief the guy who I didn't want to know where I lived.

There I was standing at the door dressed up and in shocked. I ask him, "What are you doing here?"

"Hi. How are you doing Electra? I was in the neighborhood and I took a chance hoping you be home. Sooo here I am," he replied.

Still in shock, looking in his face I asked, "How did you find out where I live?"

He said "You forgot? You told me you were getting the apartment before."

I didn't want to make a scene or show disgust at him appearing at my door uninvited. I just moved here. I didn't want to behave like a bad tenant and start yelling and cursing the motherfucker out like, I know I could do. I figure Desmond had to be the one who told him where I lived. So I said, "You caught me at a bad time. I'm about to go out." And soon as I said that Isaac turn around the hallway corner coming to my door.

He walks up on us and say "Hello." I said, "Hello. Come on in," as I moved to the side to let him inside my apartment.

Looking back at Kerchief I said, "Yeah you caught," .... Kerchief jumps in and say "I see you going out. I don't want to hold you up. I just came by to say hello and I speak to you another time. Have a good night Electra." He walks off.

I closed the door and goes inside the living room where Isaac is sitting down on the couch rubbing pebbles the house cat. "Bambi you didn't tell me you have a cat," he said.

"I had her for a while now," I replied.

"Did I interrupt something?" he asked. "Naw. I believe Desmond gave out my address when I already ask him not to." was all I said.

Isaac said "Wow he's a real character. That's not good and he had no right doing that. One day someone going to hurt that guy and you know what, he would have nobody to blame but his self."

I said with attitude "Desmond is the one person who name I don't like to bring out of my mouth. Furthermore, hold a topic on. So, Isaac," .... "Yeah Bambi," he said all quick and cheery, eager to hear the next word coming out from my mouth just because I called out his name.

Getting excited I said "So let get out of here and go see," I shouted "Stephanie Mills!"

Time flies when I'm writing. Its lunch time in the shelter. I'm feeling hungry so I get up to go get lunch. There are only two people inside the dorm with me. My neighbor and Marcell, and both of them are lying on their' beds, in their own world just like me.

Exiting my dorm. I turns the corner and I see Security Guard Dumez. She making her rounds on the fourth floor, announcing, "Lunch time."

I exit out from the building. Turn the corner walking straight, I see True God leaning up against a building door, "How you doing True?" I say as I walked pass him. "Electra," True God holler back.

Walking towards Dunkin Donut I see Ugina is holding open Dunkin Donut door with a cup in her hand, asking the people as they enter and exit the establishment, "Could you help me out with some change so I could buy me a cup of coffee?"

When I got inside Sub-Subs delicious supermarket. I'm deciding what it is I'm going to eat for lunch. I'm tired of eating chicken. So I walk over to the frozen food department and pick up a frozen Salisbury Steak TV dinner. A bag of UTZ sour cream and onion potato chips and a root beer soda. Goes to the cashier and check out. She hands me the receipt and I see that was the end of my food stamps for this month.

I go back to the shelter, tap on the glass part of the door, Security Guard Watts buzz the door for me to enter. She pressed the button on the machine for my items to go through the scanner. Next she hands wands me and allow me to go upstairs without physically checking my grocery bag but she had announced I have food as she continue with her conversation on her' cell phone.

She is the only guard who doesn't pressure clients with the rules and regulations. The only thing she cares about is talking on her' cell phone.

When I entered the dining room I finds a seat. I put my items down to hold the seat and then go inside the kitchen asking the RA for a clean cloth with soap because I needed to wipe out the microwave. I took my frozen TV dinner out from its packaging. Nuke it. Then went back to my seat and start to eat my food.

The radio in the dining room is on z one hundredth. While eating and listening to the music on the radio. I happened to look towards the microwave and I saw Marcell removing her basin from the microwave. The one she soaks her cut up foot in. "Ugh!" I said.

Then she quietly limped away carrying the basin with a towel. I'm thinking that is Gross! I saw her soaking and rubbing her deeply cut foot in that basin. The women in the shelter are so space out, or depress that no one besides me notice that shit. Well I tell you what? I'm not going to be using that microwave anymore.

As I listened to the music I started thinking; I was in my dorm lying on my bed writing all morning so I guess I can sit down here in the dining room telling the rest of the story.

So Reader: *Let's go back into the story.*

Well today is Thanksgiving. I heading over to my mother' apartment. As I proceed into the building' small hallway. I saw a girl I think I know? If, it's her we attended the same high school. I asked, "Sheryl Ann is that you?"

She always been very quiet and I do believe she saw me first. Turning at the sound of her name, she gives me a quiet, "Hi." I noticed her is pregnant. Come to think of it I remembered her being pregnant back in high school too. Trying to be friendly and make conversation. I said, "Happy Thanksgiving and how have you been? It's been a long time since we have seen one another."

Sheryl Ann acted as if she really didn't want to be friendly. So I continued, "So Sheryl Ann this will be your second child, right?" She said, "No it's my fourth child." Shocked at the answer I said, "Wow! Hum well, I'm having Thanksgiving dinner with family. My mom recently moved into this building so what are you doing over here in this area?"

Not sounding too happy she said, "I live upstairs with my mother."

Shock again at her answer I said, "Wow what a small world." Then I wondered is this where she been living since high school?

Sheryl Ann said, "I'm waiting for her and my kids now." Then a lady opens the front door to the building and some kids came into the vestibule saying "Mommy." I heard Sheryl Ann' mother tell her to go to the car and get some of the grocery bags. Then I got hit with another, "Wow," because I didn't realize Sheryl Ann was Caribbean. I assumed she was a Black American like me because she doesn't have an accent in her' speech.

Once again I said, "Happy Holidays and nice seeing you again."

I enter through the building second door. Heading towards my mother apartment which her' apartment too, is now located on the first floor. No more elevators for her either. Mommy has a two-bedroom apartment. The apartment came with two separate living room. The living room closest to the kitchen she turned into a dining room. It where we will have our Thanksgiving dinner.

I and Champagne were the first to arrive and it is where we are sitting. By the way, I did call my mother asking her what day she wanted me to come by and help with the preparation for the meal instead she told me she didn't need my help that Dave was helping her. Anyway, shortly after, my sister Tonya arrived with her children' and Desmond.

I could hear my mother and Dave making a fuse over them at the door. They were helping them come inside the apartment because Tonya just given birth to a set of fraternal twins. They are the first twins in our family.

Everyone now is coming down the hall, to where Champagne and I are sitting. I offer to help Tonya with the babies but Desmond told my sister "I don't want that nasty bitch touching my children." I said, "You a bitch you nasty slut." Then he goes on talking saying how bumme I looked. Trying and wanting to insult me in front of everyone. Then he and I immediately get into this vehement argument.

My mother rolls her eyes, like not again as she puts away their' coats.

While Tonya is sitting in the chair, Desmond turns to her very bossy saying "You better not let her even breathe on my children. Tonya you hear me. For all I care she can have a disease."

My sister sat at the table rocking back and forward with both babies in her' arms.

As we sat at the table I told my sister, "You are so wrong for letting him boss you around like that."

My mother standing there while shrugging her shoulder and looking at me like there was nothing she could do. Dave he standing on the side where some bottles of liquor is at. He making his self a drink.

Then I say to my sister, "Why do you allow him to talk to me like that and you say and do nothing? Never ever Tonya did I ever allow any of my friends or boyfriends to disrespect you. Never!"

Stop! To the reader: Put yourself in my shoes. I low would anyone feel if your one and only sister or sibling, did this type of alienation with her kids to you and also allow her' children father to talk to you in this manner and treat you this way? It always so easy when everyone in the family tells me "Let it go," but, it hurts. Those children are my family too. Nobody in my family say anything to Desmond about him bad mouthing me. So I'm always feeling like I have to defend myself around him.

I'm hurt and I'm angry. Turning towards my mother, I say, "Why don't you get involve or say something for once while we are all here. I want you to stop standing by like you are encouraging his' behavior. Say something!"

My mother making disappointing sounds of, "Um," standing there shaking her head from left to right, while disappointedly saying, "Not again. I don't want my neighbors hearing this on the holiday." I'm sitting there thinking what the hell is wrong with our mother.

Tonya sitting there rocking, not saying nothing so I say to my sister, "I can't be around Hope now I can't have nothing to do with the twins. What is the matter with you?"

Even Desmond himself made a statement once. "If I tell Tonya to run through fire with gasoline draws on, she will."

I was so angry and it's the Holidays my favorite time of the year too. I just blunted it out, "That's why when you were in the hospital giving birth Desmond came on to me **butt ass naked** with a hard on, laying on your' bed."

Everyone was totally quiet.

No one saw that coming not even me because at first I was never going to tell her that but he so dam disrespectful towards me. Can't hang around my nieces and nephew. I totally dislike Desmond, and besides it's the truth, because he did. I just don't understand how my family sit by and says nothing.

While pouring a drink, now standing next to Dave, Desmond said "You know you want me to fuck your nasty ass. You flat chested bitch. Who want to fuck you when I have this," pointing at Tonya' titties. He said "Look at her' breast and look at yours." My mother said, "I'm not cooking next year."

Dave took Desmond to the other living room in the back. Shortly Desmond left to go be with his' family for the holiday.

My mother said, "This is the last year I'm cooking. Yall have your own family now. This is the last time anybody will embarrass me so my neighbor could hear this on the holidays."

Then upset Dave had come inside the living room saying in his West Indian accent "Sylvia, I don't want no more cooking going on in this house."

You see how loud and clear they can say all their words and Desmond not around to hear it. I'm sitting here listening, and they making me feel as if I'm the culprit who messed up the holiday. Anyway, since my mother been with Dave she has never made, or had another Thanksgiving dinner inside her home. Not to this very day and my daughter Champagne is twenty-three years old.

And I'm tired of my family pretending Desmond not a piece of shit. Not only does he disrespect Tonya but he disrespects us too, with his cheating ways for everyone to see. He doesn't care. He has no shame. Everybody caught him cheating on Tonya. I caught him a couple of times. My mother even caught him. One of my dad' closest friend caught him and when he saw it he told my dad "Eddie I seen Desmond riding in his' car with another female."

All of our girlfriends from the projects seen him. One day when I came outside, someone in the project came running up to me saying "You know I saw Desmond cheating on your sister."

Just a couple of months before Tonya deliver her twins, a crazy girl had come from the Bronx wanting to fight her. While putting up slander graffiti on the project walls about Tonya. I happened to came outside, people pointing the girl out to me saying "That the girl who making all the noise wanting to fight your sister."

I went up to the girl and said, "Can you please not touch my sister while she pregnant. Cause if you hit my sister while she carrying my nieces or nephews I going to have to jump the fuck in and I don't want to fight you because of

Desmond. I hate Desmond! So, if you are so much in love with Desmond and you want to fight my sister for him wait till she conceives which should be in a couple of months. That way it's a fair fight and I won't have a gotdamn thing to do with it."

Days after that horrible Thanksgiving, in the wee hours of the night. I woke up inside my freezing apartment again. There were sounds of breathing hard, "huuum......huuuum." As I lay inside the semi dark bedroom it only light coming from the small iron gated fence in window. I could hear me taking deep fast long breaths, "huuum......huuuum". As I was coming slowly into full consciousness I could hear and feel my heart beating loudly, rapidly, "bombombom. Bombombom. Huuum," as I breathe. I just came out from a night mare or a vision.

I was in a graveyard, all by myself. I'm young. A child in my nightgown and barefoot. Sitting by myself.

My bedroom is dark and ice cold. I'm shaking; not because of the coldness coming from inside my bedroom. I'm shaking from what had just taken place. I look like I was seven or eight years old. I don't have on any shoe. I'm bored as I played in the dirt.

It was so weird because at first my eyes were watching this little girl, who is me. My eyes were looking quietly at myself, as a child playing in the dirt. This is where it gets weird. Then somehow I'm inside of the little girl who was really me because my eyes were now looking at, my little hands. With my hands I'm tapping the dirt forming the mountain.

I'm not alone. I sense he's watching me as I played in the dirt. I know he's there. He's always there. I look up and see, he's sitting over there, not too far away from me. Watching me as I look down and watch my hands pat little dirt mountains.

I think he loves me. He not human, he's a man creature. I don't see any tombstones but I know it's a graveyard. I been here before with him. I'm walking back and forth just picking up dirt and carrying the dirt to the dirt mountain I'm building. I'm bored that why I get up and walk to another area to pick up the dirt and place it, pat it on my dirt mountain.

I'm in my own little world not paying him any attention. I'm just patting the dirt. I sense him and I/we talk to each other from time to time. I'm not afraid of him even though he not attractive. He's hideous. He has horns. He's dark, very strong and he's abnormal big.

He doesn't have a color meaning like black or white. He like a shadow that's dark but he not a shadow because I have touch him before. This whole place is dark. It like a moonlight dark. There nobody else around, it just him and I.

He very powerful and victorious when he wants to be. He like a gate keeper or is he the devil? Well I'm not sure but he allowed me to come out and play. It his place/world. I don't know how I had gotten there if he took me there or if I was place there. It's weird, it like I sense I'm company for him or is it each other? He always let me out and play but I'm bored and he knows it.

Stop! To the reader: This psychosomatic or clairvoyant experience had happened so long ago. So much has taken place since this time in my life. That I can't see him to describe him like I use too because now his' **being** is far away.

Let's go back to the story.

So as I was saying, he always let me out and play but I'm bored and he knows it.

Chapter Eight

All of a sudden out of nowhere Grandma-Grace appeared!

It was weird because now, I'm not young anymore. I'm me and I'm running. I can't see me running but I know that I'm running because I can feel the adrenaline flowing through my veins as I ran. **I'm panicking**.....because I don't know what direction to go. It just an open space under moonlight darkness and dirt underneath my bare feet. There's no street signs, no light posts or roads.

Grandma-Grace is showing me the way how to get out of this place. She not running with me. She just appear strategically around me as I'm running.....and she points out, as I run in the directions her pointing to. I'm running **so very fast**, at top speed. I running so fast.

Grandma-Grace she have friends with her who is helping her to help me or are they looking out for something for her?

I can't really get a good look at them because they not as close to me as she is. But I could tell they are males and females even though I just can't see their' faces so clearly. They are in a distance and I'm running so fast.

Then all of a sudden the car appeared! I could see it as I'm running so fast towards it!!

It's in the middle of a dim road.

I'm running so quickly towards the car and it's ready to go!!! It's a 4 door Oldsmobile. The car it's in a wide open space. We all on dirt, even the car. The people are on the side like standbys but in a distance. I can't see their' actual faces but they are people, human beings.

The car is in front of me; away from the people. It like the biggest visualize object I could see. Grandma-Grace and me are the closest people to the car. I'm already inside the car **and I didn't even open the car door!**

I'm not driving because my eyes is pressed up against the back seat window looking at the people and I must be on my knees because I'm looking at what I'm about to leave behind.

I sense he knows I'm escaping. If he wanted to he could have stop me, I believe, but I'm not for sure because, maybe, he knows too, that I didn't belong there. The car took off!!! Leaving Grandma-Grace and the people behind in that place as I watched. My face is pressed against the back seat window.

The car is driving so very fast.

Now I'm behind the wheel as an adult. I'm driving. I want to get away from that place. I'm no longer a little girl. I'm an adult and I'm speeding. The car is going super-duper fast. Grandma-Grace pops here and there pointing helping me find my way out.

It was so intense. It felt so real. The car speeding off leaving them all behind as the people and Grandma-Grace are very happy watching me leave as I watched them fad away, they fading away in my view mirror. Then I woke up in my bedroom.

My apartment is so cold.

My heart is pounding like I was running very fast "huuum, huuum," as I listen to me breathe. It felt so real like it was more than just a dream.

To the reader: This was so very long ago when this had happen to me. I don't remember if it happen before or after I got Grandma-Grace coat? I think it happen before I got her' coat because I would have thought the coat was jinx and I wouldn't had wanted it. So I believe it had to happen before I gotten the coat. I think.

What I do know, is after I left Westbrook Projects these dreams about Grandma-Grace had started. When I was living in the projects, and after she died, I didn't have much memory of her, really none and I don't know why that is. Especially being we were so dam close. Was it because her death it was too painful? Or, did I chuck it up as; she's dead and gone; let her rest; why hold on to her' memories. Or could it be, because I was experiencing such a tremendous hardship I couldn't believe it was my life so fucked up like this. That just surviving in it, and coping, has taken all the energy that I had. Therefore I had no time to recall Grandma-Grace.

I loved all four of my grandparents but Grandma-Grace and I were extremely close. After she died maybe I didn't get the chance to mourn her properly? Looking back on it now I don't think I mourn her at all. She was the first person in our family who I known to die. Like I said my parents didn't talk or teach us anything after childhood. They didn't talk about important issues in life such as death, babies, people, life ambitions or even marriage. The only thing my dad said "No babies till after high school and get a city job." And it's not like he repeatedly said it either. When they separate it like they just left and in a way we (meaning Tonya and I) were on our own. We just lived inside the apt with my mother. When Grandma-Grace died I was 8 months pregnant approaching 9. I remember I didn't want to get to upset when I saw her body in the coffin. It was like I was at the funeral but I wasn't. It was a very sad day but I remember thinking it had to come to this. Maybe mainly because she was a healthy sick person. If you understand what I'm trying to say. I didn't mourn her I just let her go. Plus, going thru my life experiences, such as having a baby and becoming a single parent, along with issues that I didn't anticipate for my life; like struggling all alone and being on the welfare line this serous state of poverty.

Finally, I have gotten my very own apartment. Now I'm completely on my own, and in the worst kind of way. By now my parents not actively in my life anymore. Desmond giving me no contact with my only nieces and nephew which caused much conflicts between my sister and me. She is a sister who had abandoned me, when I had needed her the most, especially since she knew I wasn't acting like myself being all alone with none of the family and familiar friends that once had help me filled my life. What a fucked up way to end up after being and growing up with all this wonderful family and fantastic friends. Me still holding on to yesterday when my life was good. I didn't want to face what was staring me dead in the face, which was, without a warning how did I become the family outcast?

I see, and could say this now, but back then when this was all new to me, it was so devastating what I was going through, handling and dealing with life's complex issues did occupy my time and thoughts just to stay alive and not go off on the deep end.

I'm waking up in a freezing apartment again. With all those big huge windows each one of them must have a draft because it is freezing in this apartment. Where is the heat? I got up with my blanket wrap around me. Touching the radiator, it was ice cold. Again I had to turn on the oven. This time I left the oven door open. Then I put water in a large pot and set it on top of the stove with a high light underneath it.

Soon the large pot of water will start to boil and my place should be warm soon. So many times the janitor of the building came and bled the pipes so I can get heat but nothing happen. I watched him let all the water come busting out from under the radiator and still nothing had happened.

Once my apartment got warm I got dressed went over to my cousin's house wanting to hang out. My girl cousins Sheryl and Lee Keisha didn't have any kids. Both of them had attained good jobs after high school. They were busy working on their' nine to five job and on the weekends they were going to parties and hanging out with their friends.

They didn't have any time for me nor did they make the time. I couldn't keep up with them, I had no money, even though Mr. Stevenson (Tray's grandfather) and his girlfriend

Shirley had occasionally babysat so I can hang out. My cousins they were doing their own thing. Living their' lives. They never even once visit or came to my apartment to hang out.

I had a best friend (Fran). We were best friend since the second grade. We did everything together. I thought that one day I be her baby' godmother and that she would be mine! Because that's how it was when I was growing up. Good girlfriends, they became their' best friend baby' godmother. We were the best of friends' dam near twelve years or more. Friends... way before I met my first boyfriend Dove.

Then one day out the blue my best friend came to me crying and saying she could no longer be my friend. It broke my heart. It devastated me so much that I couldn't even speak.

Maybe two or three years after that, while still living inside the projects. I was about to go to the corner store. Tonya and I were inside our apartment. Tonya said, "I heard Fran she getting married today. Look Electra, there she is getting out from the car."

Rushing to the window because this was shocking news to me. Both Tonya and I, we were looking out from our twelve floor, living room window. Unbelievable but sure enough I saw with my own eyes, my so called best friend coming out from a fancy car. Quite a few people from the projects were gathering around waiting for her to come out from the car. We lived in the projects for so long, I guess too, they were congratulating her. My 1st impression as I looked out of the window was......she got married? Wow! As I watched her from the window she looked so happy and excited. I felt joy for her as I watched her looking completely overwhelmed.

Within seconds as I watch them all from my living room window, reality hit me.

Fran got marry! And didn't tell me or even invited me? As I watched...... a deep sadness overcame me. And I said to myself Fran just got married and I'm not there for the celebration.

Stop! To the reader: I'm crying right now. I just like to say remembering your past is a good thing and that my tears right now are both of joy and sadness. I so glad that I'm writing this book and bringing out things that obviously had an impact on my life. Now since I'm writing I have the time to express them.

So I had continue watching for the next person to get out from the car. I thought I get to see the groom but instead I got the surprise of my life. It was Salt coming out from the car. She is her bridesmaid or maid of honor. Both of them were coming out from the car going to her wedding reception. Tonya told me it was being held in Westbrook Projects Community Center.

I always thought I'll be standing in Salt shoe for Fran on that special day. As well as I always thought she be my' kid godmother and I would be her' kid godmother. Remember that old saying. I thought like Nelly, and everybody knows Nelly thought shit was jelly.

Well, hell she didn't even tell me she was getting married. What kind of best friend she turned out to be not to invite me to her wedding. Even though after she dropped that bombshell on me "we can't be friends," surely I figure after all we meant to each other back in the days, she could have at least invited me to the wedding.

You know what, years later after I left the projects, many people had said to me "People change Electra." My mother and sister told me the same thing too; people change. Whenever I pointed out an individual action, so many people used that phrase; people change. I can understand that people do change as they age. For instance, first they don't eat eggs but as they age, they change and like how it taste therefore now the person eat eggs. Or as people go thru life, they use to be a meat eater but now the individual is a vegetarian. Or you were marry to someone and you got a divorce, but what I can never understand is how a person is friends with someone for decades and then just stop being their friend without a fight. Without an argument. Without an explanation. My ex-friend (Fran) she was the best girlfriend anyone would ever want to have. Even though we don't hang out like we use too I'm more than stun that I wasn't invited to her wedding. I didn't do a crime that serious that I couldn't at least had been invited to her wedding. Now I'm questioning, all those years were she truly my friend? Well to me, the answer is No!

As for my girlfriend Patricia who too I hung out with for many years. Her' family felt like, family-because I was always in their home around them. Anyway she stayed in her parents' apartment in the Projects never wanting to visit. Could it be she was envious that I got accepted with the apartment and she didn't? Or could it be she never really truly was my friend just like Fran. These 2 girls I hung out with them for decades and I see them are very good at impersonating- a true friend.

Anyway I found myself by myself. Everybody that I was accustom being around seemed to want to break ties from the relationship I had with them and now went their own separate ways. They all seem to have the same attitude, like this is my life with my own family. Now Electra you go live your life with your own family, who is Champagne. Even though I wanted to still hang around with them all, but, like I said, nobody wanted to hang out with me. So I accepted it. I had no other choice.

I took it as, well we are all growing up and everybody doing their own thing which seemed kind of stupid to me after being in someone life for such, so many years. So I didn't look back mainly due from my pride and in reality....... I'm not such a needy individual as they trying to make it seem.

Loneliness did play a part in my life. So when Kerchief came by for the 2nd time I did welcome his company even though I didn't appreciate someone giving out my address without my permission.

How I met this guy, Patricia begged me to go with her on a blind date when I was living in the Project. I was in college at the time; with no kids. Patricia went on how the guy she were seeing at the time had another friend and she didn't want to go out by herself with both guys. Actually I was in the midst of studying when she knock on my door.

So I caved in, went against my responsibilities as a college student, and went on this blind date. Kerchief, we became sociable to each other. While speaking to him I found out he was in prison. I had never dated or even went out with anyone from prison. And it's not because I'm bias either. It just that he was the first person I actually dated from the joint.

Kerchief had serve time and knowing me I had to ask him what he did in order for him to go to jail. I know he didn't commit murder or anything outrages because I wouldn't had let him befriended me.

Kerchief was a polite, very well mannered, American light skin looking brother with a very nice medium built muscular body.

I tested out the water with him and had dated him briefly. The only thing he was offering me was a somewhat friendship with sex. We didn't go out to places. With him money wasn't even the issue. I found him to be boring, his' conversation became mindless. After a while I realize we didn't have much in common. Kerchief wasn't fulfilling me so I started leaning away from him. Then he left a letter underneath my door in the projects and that really became a turn off. I found his action to be unorthodox and also a little disturbing. My mother had found the letter and she said to me, "Electra I found this letter underneath the door with your name on it."

Dumbfounded I say, "For me! This letter is for me?" As she hands the letter to me, my mother was like, "It has your name on it." Kerchief letter wasn't a love letter. It was a 5 or 8 pages long letter, front and back about how he saw me which I through was insulting and senseless. All because I felt he wasn't my type and I didn't want to be with him. After I read that letter it really became a complete turn off. So I stop dating him and, even seeing him. He had stop coming by for a while. I done had a baby and everything. Then out the blue here he is trying to come back into my life which didn't happen. That why I was shock when my sister told me again he came back around. Now here he is, at my brand new apartment front door, knocking.

Not wanting to cause a scene or attention to myself in my new place and not having anything to do. Not having any friends or family around. Not fully aware of the danger of life. I figure what the heck he found me, he came by. It's not good not sharing my life with no one so maybe I miss something, because after all he did go out his way to find me again and to come visit me.

We even made out in my place but I still found him to be boring. For me, he wasn't bringing anything stimulating to the table. Instead he be sitting quietly on the couch. We not going out anywhere. After a while I found myself finding excuses for him to leave my apartment.

Loud sounds in the shelter of Urrrnnn…Urrnnnnnn. Oh shit it a fire drill. Urrrnnn….Urrnnnnnnn. Sounds of Urrrnnn…. Urrnnnnnn echoes the building. Getting up from the table gathering my belonging ready to evacuate the building. Security rushes inside the dining-room announcing "Ladies it a fire drill! You got to leave the building!"

Gathering my stuff. Making my way towards the dining-room door. I hear the security guard knocking loudly on the dorms door located on the second floor, "Fire drills ladies! Get up and get out! Fire drill, fire drill."

I throw my empty bottle of root beer soda in the garbage can. Rushing to beat the crowd because I didn't want to get caught standing in the stairwell trying to exit from the building. Once I'm outside I go across the street and take a seat on the curb.

I'm watching the females pile out from the building. The security guards is directing everyone to go across the street.

Girls always do the same thing when it's a fire drill. Some smoke cigarettes. Others going to Jose to get a cup of coffee. Some girls are standing up in their robes cause today is Saturday meaning, all dorms are open.

I'm sitting down on the street curb as I see and hear the fire trucks comes rushing down the street, blowing their loud horns. Now they were turning the corner. To me this is the best part of a fire drill; watching those cute men in uniform make their way off the truck.

Yo, firemen are sexy!!!

I started shouted loudly from the curb, "You can come rescue me any day. Come pick me up." Making loud kissing noise, "XOXOXOOOO" at them. The fire department seem to hire the cutest looking guys. They are macho men. Don't you think so? They ready to run into a burning building, risking their' own life to save a life. Yo, that takes guts. Nothing but much admiration I have for them, and police officer too. I just don't throw kissing sounds at cops, not that I don't think them sexy. I just don't want to get a ticket. Anyway, I continue making loud kissing sounds at the firemen. They are so sexy!

I see Marcell made it out the building limping. Looking around I see my next door neighbor. Wow, I didn't know she smoked a pipe. She's standing with her dark sunshades on. I wonder, why she never take off those shades.

This fire drill was a quick one. Mainly because not many girls are inside the building, since it's the weekend. The firemen were loading back on the truck driving away with their hard hats on. When up close on them you can smell the scent of smoke.

The security guards are signaling for us girls showing that it's okay for us girls to come back inside. There always a crowd of females rushing to get back into the building. I went back to my same seat in the dining-room, sat down to continue writing.

Reader: Back *to the story.*

Then one day Kerchief came back around when I wasn't home because some of the neighbors in my building came up to me saying, "Hi, that guy was looking for you. He was in front of the building all day and he had a dog with him."

I remembered being stunned with hearing the new that he had waited for me a lengthy amount of time. Lately he has been coming to my apartment with this really huge dog. I started becoming wary and question myself why is he acting like this?

One time I went out just to come back to find Kerchief done tied that dam dog to my doorknob. I just turned around and walked away while pushing my daughter in her' large purple stroller. I shouldn't had to turn around and walk away from my own apartment but I did.

Like I said I didn't know much about life situations and how to deal with obnoxious people. I was young. I didn't even know people like him exist. I came from a beautiful home. Had a baby by a guy who was hooked on weed. Then started smoking crack.

I had problems with my sibling' boyfriend, his' issues with control. Then having a step father who made me feel uncomfortable in my own home. I went out on my own obtain my own place to live. Then hear comes this guy uninvited now he's becoming a nuisance.

Young and inexperienced coming from a descent upbringing. Without seeing cops involved in my family life. I didn't even think about it. I should have called the cops on him when I saw the dog tied to my door. Instead I just walk away.

Having so many fights with Tray and heated arguments with Desmond, moving from place to place at such an early age, not wanting to cause a scene in my brand new place, wanting a place to feel like home. Tired of arguing, I simply turned around and walked away thinking when I come back the dog will be gone.

When I came back home later on that night the dog was gone. Then one day coming home I saw Kerchief passed out drunk laying on top of a car in front of my building. I didn't even try to wake him up. I just walked in the building as if I didn't know him.

Days later putting my child to bed. Then tidying up my place like I normally do. I was up listening to music. Enjoying my quiet time. My radio was on low. Someone knocking at my door. Who can that be at this time of night, I ponder.

Going to the door I asked, "Who is it?" "Kerchief," he said. I partially opened the door. "Hi Electra I was in the neighborhood and I was thinking about you so I came by to visit. I brought some food over if you don't mind cooking it." Lifting up out the bag and showing me a small box of Caroline rice. I mean the really small box of Caroline rice. Then he showed me a package of frankfurter. I realize I had to put a stop to this.

"Can I come in." he asked. I allowed him into my apartment. He walked ahead of me removing the trivial food items from the bag. I sat on the arm of the couch and lit a cigarette. I started out by saying, "I appreciate the attention and you wanting to be friends and all, but this has got to stop. You coming over here every day…. And it's late on top of that."

Kerchief said "I thought you needed the company." "Well not every day Kerchief. You come to my apartment like it's yours. Like you live here and you don't," I expressed.

"Electra I never said I live here. Now is that the kind of thanks I get for checking up on you?" he asked.

"Naw Kerchief, it just that it's my apartment and you coming over here every day. Not giving me my space, and tying your dog to the **doorknob!** Don't you think that's going a little too far?" I said.

"I can't help it that you're a lesbian," he said. "A lesbian, o come on now, just because I ask you not to come by every day," I said.

"Yeah you know you a fuckin lesbian," he said. "Kerchief stop saying that! I'm not a lesbian and you know it." "People told me you were a lesbian and I see they are right about you," he said insulting. Then he started mumbling to himself.

I couldn't make out what he was saying. Then I heard him say lowly "Bitch…..you lesbian bitch."

Becoming insulted I said, "First of all Kerchief this is my place and I never asked you for anything. You can't get mad at me for asking you not to come over here every day."

"Yeah you know you a fuckin lesbian," he said. "Kerchief I'm not a lesbian and stop saying that! You just mad because of what I'm saying to you." I said to him. "You bitch," he said loudly. "You just can't keep coming over here like you pay rent, I'm sorry," I said.

Then he started mumbling again. What the fuck is he saying? I heard him repeatedly say "Bitch…..you lesbian bitch." Ooh he is going too far with this. I said, "Kerchief I appreciate if you leave please."

As I sat on the arm of the couch, smoking my cigarette. I'm waiting for him to leave my apartment. Kerchief got up from the couch and pick up his jacket with his right hand……. something told me he was about to hit me……. I saw his right hand put and laid the jacket on his left arm then that when I got punch in my face so hard.

That… that sucker punch flip me from off the arm of my couch. The blow sent me flying so fast, I didn't know where my cigarette went. I was laid out on the couch with my face, facing the ceiling.

I didn't have any time to think because the next thing I know Kerchief had me pin down. Holding me down brutally with his knee directly on my neck as his body nailed me down to the couch and he savagely punching me with both fists at point range blows to my face.

The only thing I saw with each blow to my face was colors, bright sharp blinding colors,...red!....white!.... white!....black!...red. I said, "Jesus! Then I got a glance of his' face. He was in a rage, eyes disoriented mumbling underneath his' breath.

I started screaming, "Kerchief...Kerchief," as if I was trying to snap him out of it! But I didn't.

He starting saying "I'll show you. I'll show you." I was trying to get up but I couldn't since he had me nailed down to the couch. Punching me with his balled up fists. I saw sharp white colors with each blow. Then I saw colors. I couldn't move....so I started yelling his name,

"K E R C H I E F!"

I couldn't believe he was doing this to me. There was nothing in my view to grab to fight with.

Maybe because I didn't have shit.

He had me pinned down like they do on a wrestling match as he reach for the volume on the radio. In between the colors I got a glance of him moving the volumes bar all the way up, to the top, and, those little speakers played very loud.

He didn't want anyone to hear me scream. Pretending I was up playing loud music. I watch him fumbling trying to unzip his' pants. While holding me down, I started fighting. He tried to unzip his' pants but I was fighting so hard, he was having trouble unzipping his' pants and holding me down at the same time.

STOP! To the reader: I would just like to say I and Tray fought but Tray never fought me like he was fighting a man.

And I just want to say to AKA Slam, if you ever read this book thanks for all the time we played fight cause it really came in handy. Thank you. Back to the story.

Kerchief he was very strong I couldn't get him off of me. I saw him starting again to unzip his pants, "oh no, he trying to rape me." I looked at the nearest window closest to me in my living room. "I jump out that window before I let him rape me," I was thinking.

I heard people voices outside. Normally there's small groups of people who stands in front of my building. I tried to scream for help but the music it was so loud that I could barely hear my self-screaming out his name. Hoping him snap to his senses, before he do something both of us will regret but he was in a trance.

So I started praying to God. I closed my eyes as I laid still pinned to the couch and focused on the spirit of God, "Could you help me right now, I need you Jesus. Jesus!" I yelled.

Then I got this amazing strength. I knocked him so hard he fell into the couch. I didn't even feel my body being lifted up from the couch as I started running. I was running so fast I didn't even feel my feet touching the floor.

Kerchief he was right behind me. Grabbing and pulling at my shirt but he couldn't get a good grip to hold me. It like, I was floating in the air, zipping through my L shape apartment. He was running so fast that he was tripping, trying to keep up with me as I ran down the hallway.

While running looking ahead. I saw two doors. One door that led to my small bedroom where my daughter was at sleeping, and a picture of that small window, that's completely gated came to my mind. Then my apt door that leads out to the hallway.

Stop! To the reader: I thank God for growing up in the projects playing all those games I did as a child, because remembrance came into play. I remember how when we played childish hallway games and when I wanted to slow the other person down from catching me how I would closed the exit door so that person would have to stop. Twist to turn the doorknob in order to continue with the chase.

As I ran, I choose the door to get out of the apartment. But then a panic attack occurred! Because the only problem was the door had TWO LOCKS! I didn't have a minute to lose or I'm dead.

As I ran towards the door, I prayed and said, "Jesus be with me," as I put both hands on the door. One hand went on the top lock and the other on the bottom lock and mind you.....they both unlocked in different directions, as I ajar the door just enough for **me** to escape.

Due to Kerchief behavior and especially that nigger made me run out of my own apartment. When I squeeze out from the door as I turned my body I saw all, his eight ugly fingers grab a hold of the door to stop the door from closing. With both my hands now on the doorknob. Quickly I put one foot up against the wall and I **PULLED!** I pulled the door so hard with all my strength slamming and smashing the door on all his eight ugly fingers! I was hoping his' fingers had pop off his' **HANDS**, and I know that shit was painful as I jetted down the hallway.

I had a little lead on that motherfucker now.

Time for remembrance.

I can upon the stairs, I remember as a child how I skip stairs to be the first to hit the bottom. It amazing how my brain works when I fight or when I'm mad or when I want to win or when I have to SURVIVE!

My body automatically went into position as I leaned up on the wall and my legs and feet started to skip those stairs. Then how I leap from the last couple of steps to get that extra lead. I landed on both feet like a cat; running at top speed. I busted out the building entrance door by banging my shoulder against the door, to slam that bitch wide open. I was gone!

Thank be to God. For having me obtain an apartment whereas the 56th precinct is station at the corner, which was the very first time I ever thought about seeking real physical help for myself. Me, going inside a precinct? This is my 1st ever! Even though I'm an American with a lot of personality and charisma living in the United States, I never had a reason to go into the precinct or to call a cop!

I know I must sound lame, but honestly, my folks didn't teach us to call a police officer when in trouble. Maybe because they were just good people and they worked for their earnings. Besides back then there wasn't commercials on TV, or talk shows telling you to call 911 or a police officers for help.

I'm a good and decent person that came from family that didn't have police officers coming in and out of our home. The only officer I remember seeing and being up close to was Officer Pine. He was the police officer that patrolled the project grounds a long, long, long time ago. He was bald headed a Black American and he use to walk through the projects making sure us kids rode our bikes in the designated areas. I recall Mr. Pine, walking thru Westbrook projects as a mean of safety. He had made sure there wasn't any trouble taking place. I told you the times has changed. Anyway we had knew him well as children. "Good morning Mr. Pine," we all use to say.

We as children went outside by ourselves and played. Our parents didn't monitor us the way these parents watch their children today. I even seen parents who have like a leash on their kids or I see parents, simply holding their children hand. Showing others their child can't even walk down the street by their selves. It wasn't like that when I was growing up. Growing up we played as children by ourselves. No parents were around. My mother didn't even walk Tonya and I to our public school nor did I recall seeing any other parents because back then it was just us kids. Us kids walking home from school with our awards, book bag, school friends or holding our siblings hand while the crossing guard assist crossing us cross the street. Us children having fun acting like the kids we were. Maybe that's why we were so creative because we actually played with other kids to have fun. And our parents were with other parents doing the adult stuff not carrying us around or holding our hands till the age of 7. The times has really changed. Also back in my days we didn't run to the cops. When in trouble we went to friends or family. Back then cops were for the really, really bad people. Not like how it is now cops arresting people for really dumb shit. Like I already said, the times has changed.

So this is my first time running for help for a cop. I notice the precinct which is on the corner, when I was scanning my new area as I walked up and down the street. I can't believe I left my baby in the house because this fool tried to rape me.

So I ran to get the cops but I stopped when I saw an old familiar face of a guy who lives in my neighborhood. We went to elementary school together and I haven't seen him in such a long time.

"Ronny is that you," I said. "Electra is that you?" He asked. He came closer.

I had to be looking all flushed after getting punched repeatedly in my face. Now dam near running down the street. My face complexion must be really rosy.

I said, "Where you been?" Ronny said "I just came home. What's wrong with you? Is everything okay?" I told him as I'm looking behind me but not seeing Kerchief, "This guy was attacking me! I ran out ot the house and I left my baby inside the apartment!"

Ronny asked "Where do you live?" I pointed up the block and he said "Come on I go with you."

So he and I ran back down the block just to find my couch was on fire!

Remember the cigarette? I had it in my hand when he punched me in the face. Well it flew underneath one of the pillows on the couch. However my baby was fine. She was still sleeping in the bedroom but my cat, (Pebbles) was on top of the cabinet in the kitchen which I had never seen Pebbles way up there before.

Anyway there was no signs of Kerchief. We had put the small fire out from the sofa and opened up the windows.

Some time has passed and still no signs of Kerchief.

One day I went to the grocery store. I left Champagne in the house by herself because I wanted to walk to the store by myself, besides she was such a good baby. I said to her, "Here's your bottle and I want you to stay on the couch. I be right back. I'm going to the store."

The corner store is around the corner from the building. I just needed to run to the store. I wanted to go to the store by myself and come right back. Besides she wasn't dress and I didn't feel like getting her dress just to go to the store.

As I was coming back from the store about to turn the corner I saw Kerchief across the street from my apartment building. He had his dog with him on a leash. I see the fire truck is in front of my building! I immediately panicked and ran inside the building.

Coming up the small section of steps, I turned the hallway corner, "Noooo," I said loudly," as the fire man stop and turned his' head before he hatched my apartment door with his' ax. I asked, "What are you doing!?"

"We gotten a call about there a fire in this apartment," the fire man had said.

I'm thinking that dam quick. Calmly because I knew I left my child in there by herself, and the apartment was a little junkie, from not having any money, plus Champagne's cheap fitti diaper was in need of a change. Anybody whoever had brought cheap pamper knows when a cheap pamper get spoil it looks so nasty. I didn't want the white fire men to get the wrong impression of me and take my child away from me thinking that I was an unfit parent. So I said, "Please I have the key. Let me open the door so I can prove to you there is no fire in my apartment." As I was unlocking the door I said, "I just ran out to the store and there isn't any way a fire could have started this fast."

So I cracked open the door saying, "I don't smell smoke. Someone must had sent in a crank call."

Once they hadn't smell any smoke or seen anything out of the ordinary they left the building.

Oooo that was a close call. I'm thinking I bet Kerchief did that. He call the fire department on me hoping they would take away my child. So I cleaned up but my place but still it looked like a poor house. No pictures on the walls. Cheap shades at the bare windows. The only thing in the enormous living room was a couch. Even my wooden floors looked dull and gloomy. The apartment was just an existence because I haven't turned it into a home like atmosphere.

Eventually Kerchief he did come back around. This time he left a card underneath my door of a character going home, traveling with a suitcase.

Now I'm thinking Kerchief becoming a real fuckin problem, so I went back to the project but this time I went looking for some guys I knew. One day while riding in the elevator before I left the project I had seen Soda-Pop. He had a gun in his' pocket.

I said, "Soda-Pop what you got a gun for?"

You see, we all grew up together. Playing with each other. We went to school together so when I saw the gun. I ask him, "What you doing with a gun?"

He said "Where you been?" With his lip turned up looking all hard and gangsterish, "Everybody's got a gun."

I said, "Everybody doesn't have a gun because I don't have one." Soda-Pop lean against the elevator wall and replied "Electra, you better go get one, cause you the only one I know who doesn't have one."

So that's what I'm going to the project for. To get a gun. But, I didn't want to go to the people in my building because I didn't want anybody to know that I was planning on shooting and killing Kerchief.

I'm always so very nice and quiet. I don't bother a soul. Nobody would ever suspect me of killing him. He is invading my home, and my privacy. He violated me by hitting and beating on me like that for no reason. All because I didn't want him coming to my house every day, with his' cheap ass self. Now he tried to have my child remove from me after all I had sacrificed to raise her properly. After all the hard work I'm doing as a single parent.

I just wanted to turn my apartment into a place where Champagne and I can say, it our home but he is stopping me from doing that with his' bullshit. I already had it plan how I was going to kill him. It going to be so easy and sweet.

Seduction! It's going to be so sweet. I'll teach him about putting his fuckin hands on me and making me run out and leave my baby in the fuckin house with the couch on fire!

So I went to the project. But I went to the people I only knew. Like my quiet schoolmates I always spoken to. My family nor the girls that I hung out with, when I lived inside the project they don't know everyone I'm cool with. I was always a very private, observant and independent person anyway. Totally book smart. Smartest out from my family, close friends and just friends. I'm way smarter than all of them. I was always in the top classes for my grade and I always received some kind of award of recognition, so therefore I do have shy and quiet book smart friends too.

These people are the people I've always spoken to on the down low. Some of them were former classmates or kids/people who I had competed against in one way or another. I have this A+ personality that everyone tends to be attractive too. My grandparents, my elementary school teachers, some high school teachers, friends of the family always told my parents, "She's going to be somebody; she's special."

I'm capable of succeeding or wining anything if I put my mind to it. A beauty contest, intelligence at board games, creativity of ideas, a dare devil characteristic and I'm outgoing yet totally quiet, but murder? I never thought about killing anybody before until I met Desmond.

He brought out a side in me I didn't even know I had with all his constant cruelty behavior towards me, not allowing me to have any contact with my extended family, speaking to me degradingly and interfering with the relationship between me and my sister until he destroyed it! No one outwardly never treated me so mean. I started hating him. I hated him so much at one point I couldn't even say his name without literally gagging almost to the point of splitting up. I remember my Aunt Bee saying, "That's not good you must really hate him."

Then one day something had happened to me.

When I use to go to sleep, I started having nightmares of killing his' family as a result of payback. I had the gun in my hand and I shot his' sisters. Repeatedly I shot them. Repeatedly I had the same nightmare of how I shot his' sister. I always shot and killed the youngest one. At point range with a pistol, without blinking an eye.

Desmond he was making me sick. Now I got away from all that madness. Finally having a peace of mind, now here comes this mother fucker Kerchief with his' bullshit. Making me remember those feeling of how it feel to be a killer! How it feel to hold your prey at point range with the trigger pointed in their face. It gotta give you some satisfaction when the individual kept fucking, and FUCKING and **FUCKING** with you!

You've got to have somewhat of a madness in you to become a killer. Someone or something taking you over to the breaking point of wanting to taste your enemy's blood!

So I saw Bernard and said, "How you doing Bernard?" "Hey. It's been a long time so what up Electra," he said, while looking pleased to see me. I said, "Same o same o. It's good seeing you as a matter of fact I glad we bump into each other."

Bernard smiled as he replied "Electra it always a pleasure to see you."

We always said hello to one another. I think he liked me but for sure, I know Bernard respects me. I knew him for years, as he walked ahead I ran up to him. He was a little stunned to see me standing at his side. He started smiling.

I said, "Sooo, Bernard I need a flavor."

He looked shocked that I'm asking him for a favor.

I said, "Between me and you, right?" Bernard said smiling "Between me and you. Electra, what's the favor?" I said lowly, "I need a gun."

Bernard stopped walking.

Lowly he asked "You need a gun?" "Yeah," I said.

As we stood outside making eye contact. He looked me up and down. I was so serious because I rarely went over the edge and Bernard had seen in me that I meant business.

He gave me a quiet stare and said "Electra you need a gun?"

"Yeah," I said.

Then I told him, "Someone violated me and I need a gun for my own protection." He looked at me kind of impress that I wanted to take care of myself, in such a manner. I could tell Bernard was shocked to see that quiet little me will go as far as pulling the trigger.

But Bernard he's smart and quiet too. He said "You not going to shoot anybody, Electra."

Thinking quickly not letting him become aware that I was planning on killing Kerchief. Taking Kerchief under the boardwalk in Coney Island to make whoopee while fuckin him I was going to shoot him with a silencer.

I said, "Who said I wanted to shoot somebody? I just want a gun for protection. So tell me where can I get a gun?"

Seeing that I'm for real and really wanted to get my hands on a gun. Bernard he still in shocked at my request. Finally he said, "No! No Electra I don't know where to get a gun." So I said, "Let me borrow yours." Bernard gave me a double take look.

Stop! Wait reader do yall know what a double take look is? Well it is a look that you give someone twice. You look at the person, then you move your head or your eyes quickly, and the second look at the person is more intense, than the first.

After his double take look, and a wondering stare.

Bernard said "Naawww, Electra I'm not giving you my gun. And I'm not telling you where to get a gun from either. I just don't want to see you get hurt."

Now he wants to play big brother with me, because everyone knew I am the oldest in my family, and that I didn't have any brothers.

Then he asked me "**Where's your man?!**" As if let my man handle it. What if a girl needed protection from her' man, I thought to myself.

Then I said, "Well you right Bernard, just because everyone else has a gun why should I want one? I mean, I made it this far without a gun. Why should I want to start now? Looking like the smart good girl he sat next to in class. I just didn't want him to know the real deal, because I'm going to kill Kerchief.

"See you later," I said looking all sweet and innocent, like he knows me to be. While I was in the projects I decided to see Patricia since she is the one who brought Kerchief into my life.

When I got to her place she was sitting on the couch with her family. I told her, "Kerchief kept coming around to my apartment and do you know that nigger he beat me up!"

Patricia said, "Electra you know he came out from a mental hospital." SHOCKED I said, "A mental hospital!" She was sitting there with her family all around her. I said, "I didn't know he came out from a mental hospital." "I told you he was in a psyche ward," Patricia said.

At that moment I wanted to jump on Patricia but I was quite sure her family would have jump in and I would have been out numbered. So I said, "Naw you never mention no psyche ward because I would have never gone out with him."

I went home really upset. Finding out that Patricia who supposed to be my dear friend had set me up on a blind date with a nut. All these years she must have really hated me.

Finding out the new news about Kerchief. I really wanted the gun now. It was the perfect way for me to get back the peace I had already made for myself.

Looking at my daughter. I had also thought about my daughter wellbeing and who is the love of my life. Not wanting her to be left out in this world alone so instead of sitting around allowing this nut to play games with my emotions making me do something I regret. I left my apartment. I went too stayed with my dad for a little while.

And........that's when I met...........Thomas.

To the reader: It's late now. I'm tired and it's bed check. I'm going upstairs. I'll speak with you later.

Goodnight.

Chapter Nine

"Good morning ladies, it's six o'clock. Breakfast will be served downstairs," security Abuja announced to the Q dorm. Shortly after this announcement my sleeping is now being disturbed because I hear clunking sounds. It sounds as if it's coming from someone who tapping on top of a locker. I turn over from facing the wall to see what is going on inside my dorm.

I see security guard Abuja is standing over someone's bed in the back. She tapping on the client' locker saying, "It's time to wake up. Hello."

The person not moving due to her still sleeping. From the guard, the loud tapping sounds started hitting upon the locker again "clunk. Clunk! Clunk! Clunk! Clunk," were echoing loudly inside the room "Clunk! Clunk! Clunk! Hel lo! You need to get up and go downstairs," Abuja projected.

I see the person's feet starts to move while laying still underneath the cover.

The guard said, "This bed was given to you as an overnighter. You have to get up and go downstairs." "Alright," a voice said, "I'm getting up."

I don't know what establishment enforces this regulation for what I'm about to say. If it's Bridge Net rule or DHS rules. Because when I lived at other shelters, clients with the permission to stay out from the shelter wasn't happening.

Whenever a resident sleeps out over the weekend, is because, she went to see her caseworker and had asked for either a weekend pass, late pass or an overnight pass. The caseworker writes out the pass. The client then tape the pass to the front of her locker. When that resident uses her privilege to stay out from the shelter overnight, if needed a bed, Bridge Net would use that resident' bed for any homeless person to sleep on, who is seeking shelter. The shelter who has-giving out a bed to a homeless person in this type of situation, DHS and the shelter refer to this emergency placement of a bed, as an overnighter.

In New York City, anybody, who is homeless and seeking shelter is not supposed to be turned away out into the streets. If this shelter was full with no available beds. The intake office would have to bus the homeless person out to another shelter that has an available empty bed as an overnighter.

All overnighters (a homeless person without a permanent bed) must be up, dressed and out of the dorm by 6 am sharp. The reason for that is, that homeless person need to go back to the intake office and have their name put on a list for a permanent bed. Another reason why the overnighter has to leave the dorm so early, is because, the shelter staff (RA) has to strip the overnighter bed of its linen.

That why when most residents take their' pass, they would put their' bed linens inside their' locker, not wanting anyone to sleep on top of their' sheets. The resident she remove everything from off the top of her locker and around her bed. Providing it all can fit inside her locker. Majority of residents who spend the night out would lock everything up because #1, theft. #2, just in case the resident not back on time, the resident knows she would lose her bed and that the RA (residential staff) would have to strip the bed as well as her entire area including clipping her locker and bagging and tagging up all her' possessions.

Then sometimes you have residents who purposely lose their bed just wanting to change their dorm. And these residents just leave their area looking as is. Knowing RA going to tag and bag up their possessions'.

Majority of the time, it becomes a headache when the Residential Aide staff (RA) bags and tags up clients' personal belongings, mainly because it's a process for getting your belongings back. The client that took the pass and has lost her bed now she has to wait inside the intake office till bed count is officially over to be given a new bed. Then she has to wait to receive her bagged and tagged items. Providing, she get everything back because the staff do steals too.

Inside the intake office they have plastic gloves and tilex if a resident chose to use these items to clean the area she would be going to. When she gets assigned another bed, in another dorm the client has to lug all those bags to her assigned room. Remove her items and input her possession back into a locker. Most of the time she have to clean by wiping down the locker before inputting her possession and that's only if she a clean person. Some of the ladies in this shelter do wipe their lockers clean before inputting their items. Then she has to wipe down her plastic mattress and bed rail and that too, only if she has good hygiene about herself and do care what she laying on. Then put her bed linens on the mattress. In the shelter you do have a lot of girls who don't give a hoot how they sleep if their area is clean and those are the girls who live out of their many bags. And if a person does lose their bed and get assigned another bed, majority of the time it's those girls' lockers you find that you got to clean because the inside of their locker sinks.

Anyway, today is Sunday I normally goes to church and use this day for seeing my kids. Since I'm writing this book. I am going to stay in, skip church and trying to see the children for today. As I look out from the covers, my neighbor she so quiet. She always looks the same. She always in a long dark skirt, wearing dark color tight and her' arms are always covered. Then those black sun shades are always on her face but this time, she also has on earplugs.

Oooh let me get up and do what I got to do. I pull the covers from my head and I look around the room. Oh! No! I see Ugina sleeping in Luting's bed and I see another new face. A black girl sleeping in Country's bed. Which one of the girls was the guard talking to this morning? Please let the overnighter be Ugina, please. I heard she steals and she stinks.

Looking around the room, I notice the bathroom door is crack open. Slipping on my slippers I walk towards the bathroom door. I open the door. It's empty. I goes in and start to pee, reach for the toilet tissue and there isn't any. Shit! I hate when that happens. So I press the dispenser for some paper towel. I can't believe it! That's empty too. We just had a full roll and there not a lot of girls in the dorm. Where the stuff going? I hate when I got to drip dry.

I'm putting on my robes to make it downstairs for breakfast. I see Marcell getting up. So I ask her, "Are you going downstairs for breakfast?" She say, "Yes." Then she flinches as she move her injured foot.

For breakfast they served us pancakes and sausages, two small frozen juices; with tea or coffee. This shelter is always exceptionally quite on Sunday. Mainly, because lots of females goes to church and for the other residents that are here, they sleeping in late because it's still the weekend.

When I got back upstairs to the dorm I overheard Ugina asking Marcell, "What happen to your foot?" Marcell said, "I fell." Ugina said, "It looks painful," then she asks, "Do you smoke cigarettes?" Marcell said, "No." Ugina just walked out and left the room. That Ugina for you, talking to you just to get something from you.

Now it was just me and Marcell inside the room. I said to Marcell, "Marcell, you know that's not cool putting your basin inside of the microwave. People heat up their' food and beverages inside there."

Marcell act as if she didn't hear me. Quietly, she continue in getting herself dress but I know she heard me and she knows what I'm telling is right.

Sitting on my bed I went back into my past. Reader; Let's go back *into the story.*

After the ordeal with Kerchief me and my baby left our' apartment. I went to my dad. I just stayed inside his' apartment cleaning. One day taking my child to the park which is across the street from my dad' large apartment building. As we got inside the park I was shocked! I saw Kerchief. He was sitting on one of the benches inside the park!

Immediately I had turned around. I went upstairs and said, "Dad you know that guy I told you about. The one that beat me up!" My dad said "What about him?" I said all fast, "He's down stairs sitting in the park." "The one that beat you up Electra?" he asked. All shocked, surprised and upset I said, "Yeah dad. He's downstairs. He downstairs sitting in the park!"

My dad grab his' baseball bat. I'm thinking to myself (yeah. I'm jumping in this mother fucker.) I don't know why, but I always felt like, me and somebody was going to kick some one **ASS**. I use to think it was going to be me and Tonya fucking Desmond up.

I remembered when Tonya and I was sharing the apartment together after my mother has left. I went up to Tonya saying, "Why won't you stand up for yourself. He keeps disrespecting you. Tell Desmond off. Listen, I got your back if he starts to hit you. I'm going to jump in and together we are going to beat the shit out of him."

Tonya was just looking at me. She know he deserved to get his' ass kicked. My sister knew I was so fuckin serious too. I told Tonya, "When he comes through the door let's just jump him," but Tonya didn't go through with it. She punk out. I remember I was so disappointed at her for doing that.

Anyway my father along with me and my baby we are all going downstairs to the park. I love both of my parents but my mother often kicked me out from the house as a young teenager, and my dad always took me in, whenever I knocked on his' door. No matter what time it was. Because of that, in a way, I grew a special kind of love for my dad. Seeing my dad walking with that baseball bat I think I'm just going to blank out and kill Kerchief. He better not touch my dad.

When we cross the street going toward the park. I saw Kerchief. He still sitting inside the park. When we got inside the park my dad asked "Do you see him Electra?"

I said, "Yeah dad I see him." Daddy asked "Where he at?" I pointed, and said, "He's over there sitting on the bench."

My dad and I walked up on him as he sat on the bench listening to a small radio. My dad asked "You put your hands on my daughter?" All nonshala he turned his' face towards us and said "No sir. I've never seen her before. I don't know her," and he turned his head away from us, continue listening to his radio.

My dad looked at me and said "Electra he said he don't know you." I whisper, "He's lying." Looking at him as he sat there listening to his radio, not acknowledging us. Daddy said "Well if she tells me one more time that you put your hands on her I'm going to come looking for you." My dad nod his' head toward me, signaling for us to leave.

As we walked away I said, "Dad he's lying that's Kerchief!" My father said "Electra what am I'm supposed to do? Walk up to a strange man and start beating him with my bat?" I thought in my mind, "yeah."

Daddy had said "He said, he didn't know you. Are you sure that is the guy?" "Dad I'm not lying. That's the guy," I said. My father asked me, "Did you tell him you were coming over here?" I said "No." My father asked "So how did he find out the address to where you are?"

"That's a good question dad. I think Desmond gave him your address and my address to my new apartment," I said.

Daddy shook his' head in frustrations as we walking out from the park. "You think.... you think. You think, if we ask Desmond that, he could lie too," daddy said.

Periodically I checked on my apartment, feeding Pebbles our house cat. While over there one day my mother came to the apartment telling me, "Electra Tonya in the hospital."

I asked, "What happened to her?" My mother didn't want to go into detail but she seemed to be sad and concerned. She wanted me to go to the hospital and see her but I didn't want to go. Especially after the way she been treating me. I didn't want to be bothered.

After a day or two passed then my father got on my case too, saying "Electra, that's your one and only sister. Go see her in the hospital."

The way my parents was acting like Tonya was really sick. Like she might not make it. My mom had pleaded with me to go see her. Genuinely out of concern I did went to visit my sister in the hospital. She was lying in the bed and I saw something move in her legs. The skin on her legs looked like they were bubbling rapidly but then the movement had stopped.

I felt sorry for her. I had tried to talk about something other than her being sick because I know she hates it. She used to be sickly all the time when she was much younger. I think my sister probably thought she wasn't going to make it because she gave me an apology.

Tonya said, "Electra I'm sorry for telling Kerchief where you live. I didn't know he was going to beat you up like that."

I was so shocked. I couldn't believe she was the one who had told him where I lived.

She was too sick for me to start yelling at her but that didn't matter now. I wanted her to concentrate on getting well. So far I made it through Kerchief bullying. I didn't even think at the time to ask her did she also give Kerchief daddy's address. I just wanted to see Tonya get better. It was nice to hear the apology and how he got the information because he really did hurt me. Just to think I always thought Desmond did it........I betcha on the down low Desmond saw Kerchief outside and told him where I lived too.

After two or three weeks of me staying inside my dad house. My dad said "Electra take this money and go see a movie." I said, "That's alright dad. I'm fine." "Take the money and get out of the house and leave the baby. I'll watch her," he said. **That's a 1st**. My dad has never watch my daughter for me. Nor did I know of him to watch any of Tonya Kids. I got the message, loud and clear. My dad order me out the house so I got dress and left out.

Instead I stop by the project. I walk yet upon another surprise of being left out by my family. I bumped into my cousins who were having a celebration for an individual on their dad's side who they now viewed as their close family members. Discovering not only was I left out from their celebration. I finds out the job I created for myself when Skyler had unfortunately passed away, that, that family member on their dad side had gotten the job.

1st of all, it was a job that I created and marketed for myself by asking a famous known individual who had attended most of the rallies for Skyler. Now I'm finding out that the family member on their dad side got my job. That was a double whammy hurt. I was pissed.

Now walking back to my dad, angrily because of all what I just found out. Feeling like I'm never going to get out of this situation of poverty. I'm about 23 years old. Knocking on my dad' apartment door I didn't get an answer. Not knowing if my dad high or if the baby sleeping. So I went outside to call the apartment. Still no answer. Where can he be?

I didn't want to knock too long or hard, just in case he left Champagne in there alone. While he went to go pick up his' get high. Around this time in my life my dad had a serious cocaine habit. While standing in the hallway, I listened to his apt' door to hear if I heard any sounds or movement? All of a sudden I had to pee. So I went outside to find the nearest bathroom.

My dad lives across Eastern Parkway, in Brooklyn. It's were a lot of the Caribbean People migrated and settle. In this area there are a lot of grocery store, small business, Chinese vegetable stands and liquors store run by the Caribbean's. As I started walking down the hill I came across Caribbean businesses that didn't have public bathroom.

Oh my goodness I had to go really bad.

As I continue walking down the street, up ahead I saw a spot named Tiny Tim-Tim. I saw people coming in and out. I didn't see a bouncer standing at the door. It didn't look like you had to pay to get in so I walked in.

Went up to the bar and asked the bartender, "Can you point me in the direction to the bathroom?" The bartender said "Walk straight make the first left."

Oh boy did I had to use the bathroom. As I peed listening to the music. I realize it's a little hangout spot for the people in the area. The bar/club was playing loud Caribbean music.

Once I finish using the bathroom I exit the little night club. Walking back up the block going to my dad. I'm thinking, if he went out he should be back by now. My dad never walks anywhere. He drive everywhere. Even to the corner store. "Yo girl. Hey.....you hear me calling you........ wait." I heard this guy with a heavy accent making all this noise behind me.

I continue walking. "Mon come here......hey you girl," he shouted. I don't know why but I turned my head looking behind me to see why or who he's calling.

"Hey you pretty girl," the dark skin low haircut guy said. As he pointing his' finger my way. I turned around to see who it was in front of me him talking to. As I continue walking. He giggles "Yeah mon." Shouting he said "Hey pretty girl you in the blue jeans."

I have on blue jeans. Is he speaking to me? So I looked back again and this time he started waving his' hand for me to come to him but I turned my head and kept walking. Knowing, I don't know him.

Stunned. He caught up to me saying, "Hey slow down. Why are you leaving the par tee?"

I looked at him and he was smiling. He had on mad bulky flashy jewelry. A beige linen short sleeve shirt with matching pants and shining shoes. He looked kind of nice.

"Don't you want to come back to the par tee girl," he ask me as we both continue walking up the hill.

He has a deep accent I notice.

He took his hand and touch my hand firmly for me to stop walking. When I stopped walking to look down where he was touching me at I notice three bulky gold rings on that hand. One ring had a stone. His' rings started from his middle finger going towards his pinky finger. "Slow down the par tee this way. It's no-ting up that way," he said while leaning on the side with his' other hand indexed finger slightly under his nose while looking me up and down. He said "I love for you to come back to the par tee with me."

I said, "I'm going up the block to my father house. I just stop in the bar to use the bathroom," as I pulled back my hand from his. "Where does your father live?" he asked. I ask him, "Where the accent from?" While making his accent deeper he said "You don't know a Jamaican when you hear one girl." I said, "Jamaican." "Yeah mon, I'm a Jamaican," he said.

I said, "My father lives up the block. I got to make sure everything alright. I left my baby in his' care and when I knocked on his' door I got no answer." "A nice looking lady like you shouldn't be walking by yourself, eehey. Let me walk with you to check on your father. Then, you come back to the par tee?" he asked.

Not showing much interest of going back to the party. I said, "I don't know."

I turned around and started walking up the block. He asked "How old is your child?" "She two and a half, soon be three," I said as I had allowed him to walk with me together as we going up the hill to my dad.

When I got to the door. I knocked again, still no answer. He asked me "So what are you going to do? Stay here in this hallway by yourself and wait till your father come home?"

I didn't respond because I was thinking.

Sounding so convincing. He said "I'm quite sure him and your baby are okay. Why won't you come back to the par tee with me and we come back here later to check on them. Making sure everything okay, eehey."

I'm considering it while he was just smiling, looking like he was in the mood to party.

The long hallway in this large building was cold, empty and deserted. Looking at my situation, me standing here inside this cold lonely deserted hallway or going to hang out with him at this night club. I thought about it again. Finally, I said, "Alright." So we left.

He asked "What's your name?" I told him, "Tami." I been going by that name for a while now. Since I been with Tray. I'm still young and exploring, guess I'm being silly. Anyway lots of Black American people have aka names. AKA names abbreviation for altering known as, whoever you want to be. I think it hip and cool given yourself an aka name. So my aka name is my middle name…it something different.

"My name is Thomas," he said.

When we got back into the night club. He pulled out a knot of money from his pants pocket and placed a crisp fifty-dollar bill on the counter telling the bartender "Start me a tab."

That was impressive, I thought. Being I'm not a drinker I asked, "What are you drinking?" Thomas said "Me not a drinker but so you won't drink alone me take a Heineken, mon."

I said, "Fine. I like a Heineken too."

When the bartender came with two Heineken. Thomas went to take both of the bottles but I said to the bartender, "I take that one."

Thomas giggle saying "What you think me going to do put something in your drink?" I said, "You never know."

The music was playing it was sounding alright the lyric was saying murder she wrote.....murder she wrote. Then the next record went to them bow..... them bow... them bow .... them bow throw up your hands if you know you can bow. Them bow.... them bow...them bow.

The beat was loud and nice.

Thomas started moving his body, he said "Come Tami let go on the dance floor," before I said a word he done grab my hand and we were in the middle of the dance floor.

I shouted, "I don't know how to dance to this kind of music." As we were in the middle of the dance floor. He said loudly "What," as he danced "Me can't hear ya," as he moves closer toward me.

The music was loud and pumping saying....... wind up them body and bow.... them bow...them bow...them bow...... The music, I like it! The beat makes you wanna dance. Thomas said loudly "Come Tami move your bodtee girl." Speaking loudly, I said, "I don't know how to dance to this kind of music."

Thomas was moving his body. He was very impressive. Thomas had no shame. He wasn't shy at all on the dance floor. I was bouncing from side to side like nothing special. I look around me and I saw the ladies moving their hip and the guys were very close up on them. So Thomas came up on me putting his hands on my hips moving me. "Wan your bodtee like this," he said as he started helping me along.

The music was fuckin pumping! As I looked around on the dance floor. I tried imitating their movement. Loudly he said, "This is reggae dancing, wan your bodtee girl." The music lyrics now saying..... Feeling hot hot hot. I saw other people getting fancy with their dance style.

The mc got on the microphone speaking loudly saying "Reggae muffin people in the houseee!"

The crowd went berserk! Pointing their index finger up in the air. Resembling as if they were pulling a trigger of a gun saying "bhoop, bhoop, bhoop!"

I saw guys tapping their foot to the music. Swinging their body to the song. There dancing is different from American dancing. I was starting to have a good time. I love dancing and Thomas can dance! He was moving his body, waning it up and down. I think he was showing off, but he really knew how to dance reggae style. Everybody in there was killing it!

They notice I didn't know quite how to wan. I look like I was trying to hula-hoop. Going around and around without the Caribbean rhythm. So it looked like the crowd started showing off on me, by throwing their hand up and waning their' bodies to the rhythm of the music.

After like three or four songs done went by, I couldn't let Thomas freak me out on the dance floor. He was dogging me on the dance floor. So I started waning my way. My style and just feeling the beat going to the rhythm. Now Thomas was the one being impress.

Thomas came up on my body closely starting waning his body on mine.

I only close dance to slow song (we Americans call it grinding and we do it on slow jams.) But these people were close dancing to every song, even fast songs. After a while to me it became dirty dancing.

I was a little shy. I'm not accustom to the close dancing, as a way of dancing. Anyway him and I dance every song but, just not so close. I like to dance and I like to get wild but within good taste of course. We really was having a great time. After a while we both were sweating.

Thomas seem to be enjoying my company. Loudly he offers "Tami come get another drink girl." "I haven't finish the first one yet," I said loudly. So we dance and dance and dance till we both became hot and sexy. We dance till the break of dawn.

I had a great time before I knew it the night club has closed. Thomas wanted me to hang out with him some more so we took a cab to Church Avenue.

I was so skinny probably a size five/six. I found out his age. He has me by ten years. He was quite older than me but you couldn't tell on the dance floor. He told me he have three daughters back in Jamaica that he has to support which I totally agreed and admire because I know the difficulties of a single mother.

Being that I am one.

He told me that his' children mother had moved on being that he been in New York for a lengthy amount of time. When we got to his place. I was surprise to see his' living arrangement. He share his two bedroom apartment with a woman. I questioned, "Who is she?" Thomas said "She's my roommate but I be looking for another place to live." His bedroom was in the back behind the kitchen. Most guys I knew live with their' mother or have their' own place. He the first man and person I ever came across having a roommate?

Anyway that waning dancing, all that rubbing and dubbing made both of us become hot and bothered. So when we got to his bedroom we started making out.

Because of my skinniness Thomas thought he was hurting me but we couldn't quite get into it because the woman, his' roommate she came into the kitchen and started banging on the pots and pans.

I asked Thomas "Why is she acting like that if she just a roommate?" Thomas said "Don't mind her she cooking in there she soon be gone."

So we started back making out but the lady was out of control. She was behaving like a jealous woman. Loud sounds of "pitter-patter, crash, and clatter," came from the kitchen. It became very distracting. Thomas said, "Let me go see what the problem is."

As I sat and waited for Thomas, I started thinking. Well he did introduce me to her when we came into the apartment so she can't be his' girlfriend. He not wearing a wedding band....Thomas came back into the bedroom. He put on his reggae music from the enormous radio box that's sitting on top of the dresser. So we started back making out while she banged on her pots and pans in the kitchen "crash, clatter and pitter-patter." Thomas whisper "She soon stop, Tami."

After we finish I came into the kitchen with Thomas. He wanted to make me something to eat. After we finish eating he took me to my dad apt in a cab. He offer can he pick me up for dinner and I accepted.

Thomas came to my dad's house quite often to pick up Champagne and I. Taking us out to breakfast or to dinner. My dad didn't care that much for Thomas. He said, "Ooh no Electra, he not the one for you."

I asked, "Why you say that dad?" My father said "I just don't care for those kind of people." I figure my dad felt that way because when he left my mother and us in the project after a while my mother met this man name Dave. She brought him home to live with us who also is a West Indian man.

"Pamper yourself ladies. Pamper yourself, in the fourth floor library," security Dumez announced inside the dorm. Her voice bringing me out from my past now looking around in the dorm, at the presence. Everyone seem to be sleeping. So I got up throw on my sweats and walk down the hallway to the class.

When I reach the room Samantha had the station 107.5 playing on the radio. She had multi-colors of nail polish together in a white medium sized plastic container. Several nail polish remover in the center of the table. A couple packs of cotton balls. Lineup, she had a variety of facial mask and shrubs as well, and a variety of body lotion. About seven face mirrors that sat on a stand, toenails clippers and small wooden fingernail emery boards. Being that I couldn't afford a real manicure and pedicure. This is second best.

The shelter had viewed the metal finger nail file, nail polish remover and mirror as contraband items. Even the small nail clipper that contain that small nail file is seen as a threat and is not allow in the shelter.

Samantha supposed to monitor us as we client get to use this stuff.

I gather the nail polish colors I wanted which were bright red and white. As I painted my finger nails red, with the white nail polish I made poker dots. I did the same pattern for my toes. While living in the shelter I found I like making poker dots on my nails. Who would have figure? I did it so much that other residents started imitating the design.

Inside this recreation room we have a bathroom for washing our hands after using the paint or chalk. Tiffany come into the class after taking her shower and starts lavishing scented body lotion all over her entire body. More girls come in to do a facial and polish their' nails and toes. Some residents like Evelyn and Bertha copy my poker dot design. Samantha pass around the attendance sheet. Once I finish I leave the class heading back to my dorm.

When I enter the dorm I continue writing my story.

Thomas took to my daughter right away. He inquire about Champagne biology father wanting to know why he wasn't in this beautiful little girl life and mine too for that matter. I keep it short telling him he had a drug problem and that right now I don't know where he's at.

Lot of guys in my neighborhood didn't have jobs. They were hustlers. A small amount were in college. Lots are in jail. Or been to jail and those that were in jail couldn't find descent paying jobs when they came home. Plain and simple lots of the Black American men in the neighborhood just didn't collect a paycheck.

Thomas he didn't drink. Nor do he smoke weed or do drugs and I like that about him. He's not a drug dealer either. Instead he's a hardworking man that earns an honest paycheck at the end of the week.

After a while I finally told Thomas I had my own apartment. He didn't believe me. He said "No, stop. Don't tell lie Tami."

I said, "Thomas, I'm not lying to you. I could prove it." Thomas said "Eehey?" Looking at me like he starting to believe me. I said, "Come on. I'll take you over there." Which was a few blocks away from where my dad lived.

I lived on the other side of Eastern Parkway. Where mainly the neighborhood are filled with Black Americans, like myself. When I open the door to my apartment Thomas was in shock. My place had an awful smell of bad cat litter. I allowed my cousin Coon to stay there. I had call myself trying to fool Kerchief making him think I moved again.

Talking out loud I said, "Who told Coon to bring in this black cat causing the apartment to smell like stinking cat litter!"

Walking in thru the door with now both cats following us. Thomas asked me "Why you not living here?" I told him, "Tonya my sister gave out my address to this guy named Kerchief. He won't leave me alone and he keeps coming over here uninvited so I left to stay with my dad for a while."

I didn't tell Thomas everything like him wanting to rape me or beating me up.

Thomas asked "Kerchief. Where is he now?" I said, "I don't know," as I open up the windows to air out the apartment from the smelly cats. Thomas asked "Do you know where to find him?" I said, "Yes. He work as a barber."

As Thomas spoke and listened, he had his right index finger pressed up against his nostril, underneath his nose as he stood leaning on the side. We were standing very close to each other as if he was whispering. He was very serious. He said slowly "Listen Tami." With his left hand he grab my wrist to let me know he serious. He said "When we get to his' job. I want you to bring him outside, eehey." And he squeeze my wrist a little tighter. He continue "But don't tell him I'm with you...eehey. Just bring him outside so I could see how he look."

Once we got to Kerchief job. Thomas stop and waited for me, peeping from around the corner. I went into the barber shop. Kerchief had a guy sitting in the chair. He was shocked when he had seen me. I walked inside the barber shop. I said, "Hi Kerchief. Can I speak to you for a minute?" Kerchief said "Sure Electra." "Can you step outside because I have something privately to say to you," I replied.

Kerchief had followed me outside and we stood in front of the shop. I did just like Thomas said I brought him out of the shop and I started making small talk. I was turning and moving from side to side, letting Thomas have a good look, of his' entire body. That the last time I ever seen Kerchief.

When Thomas officially moved in. One day he walked into the house carrying an empty barrel. I asked, "Thomas what that?" He said "Tami me picknee back in thee yard need some tings."

That Jamaican slang, picknee meaning children and the word yard, means home. I didn't make a fuse about it because I saw it as being very admirable. A black man taking care of his responsibilities. Knowing how it feel to raise a child single handedly and being the primary support for my daughter.

Mad at my cousin Coon for bringing this black cat to my apartment. I had fleas inside the apartment now. I didn't have any more money to spare for the vet because I just recently paid to have Pebbles neutered. Me not knowing she was a boy cat until he sprayed onto my couch.

Thomas insisted on me getting rid of Pebbles, saying he didn't want to live inside the apartment with the cats. I couldn't throw Pebbles out in the street so I made Coon take Pebbles to live with him since he had no right bringing that black cat inside my apartment and giving Pebbles fleas.

Coon said "I'll take both the cats." He did that because sometimes they had a rat or two up inside the house.

Thomas and I really seemed to be hitting it off. I met one of his brothers named Rude Boy. He a mechanic. Rude Boy came to the apartment often visiting us and he too fell in love with my daughter. Every time Rude Boy visit he said "Champagne."

By now Champagne and I was settle back into our apartment. Thomas got up in the morning and went to work. Being Thomas was helping me, by paying the light and gas bill I had a little extra money to do things with for my daughter and myself.

I went to the laundry-mat. Purchase items for the house; mainly more cookware and bathroom supplies. I did the food shopping in the area, cooked and prepared food for us daily while Thomas was at work.

Briefly Thomas and I hung around and partied with a few of his' close Jamaican girlfriends that lives around the corner from me on Union Place. Shortly after, one of the girls had moved away and started a family of her' own. There seem to be somewhat of a slight attraction going on or probably he was just a flirt. I felt Thomas may had liked her. Or did they just like each other?

They were all friends before I came into the picture. Every night Thomas came home and he stayed with me. Therefore in my mind maybe they were only just friends. I don't know if Thomas was trying to get me jealous or if he wanted me to become jealous. Anyway she moved but Annie and her' family still lives on Union Place to this very same day.

I cleared up a lot of Thomas myths he heard about Americans, like, we were a lazy set of people, that we don't want to work, that the women only wash their' panties in the sink, that we don't know how to cook or clean. Thomas came to see none of that stuff was true with me, instead he seemed pleased with the way I conducted myself. How

I took care of the house and my child. He loves my cooking and it seems he like everything about me.

I had a new girlfriend who I meet, and befriended in the building. Her name is Shelby. Besides, us living on the same floor, and on the same side of the building. We were the same in a sense. Starting out with our families and supporting the men in our lives. Taking care of the home and handling our young children. Shelby and Wilbert are married raising their' many children.

Surprise Thomas purchase a huge used motorcycle. It was a vehicle for taking him back and forward to work. Just because I had this enormous empty living room, he use to bring that motorcycle inside the apartment every day because he didn't want anyone to steal it.

I remember telling him, "Thomas I could smell the gas from the motorcycle. Can't we get sick from the smell?" "No mon it okay Tami the smell soon go away," he said. I use to crack all the windows anyway. I really didn't want the motorcycle inside the apartment.

When Thomas got paid he came through the door with items he brought to put inside the barrel. He insisted on making sure his girls had their school supplies and that his mother was well taking care of. He brought so many notebooks like compositions notebooks, five pocket spiral notebooks and plenty of folders. He purchase several packages of loose leaf papers; writing pens of different styles, glue, scissors, rulers, pencil sharpeners any and everything his girls would need for school. Then he came through the door with several pair of shoes throwing them too inside the barrel.

Thomas just came home with all the merchandises telling me "Tami this stuff would be shared among my kids and my mother."

He purchase hair grease, body lotions and sent tremendous amount of can good products. Bags of all-purpose flour and sugar. Multiple cans of sardines, mackerels and large cans of cooking virgin olive oil. Thomas made sure they didn't go hungry. He made sure they had ample amount of food, school supplies and toiletries. When the large barrel was full he shipped the barrel and the motorcycle off to Jamaica. I asked, "Why did you send the motorcycle?" Thomas said "It's easier to get around when he's in Jamaica."

That the year I wanted Champagne Christmas theme to be the ultimate dollhouse. I bought her a playschool table with matching four chairs. A fisher price kitchen with the make believe burner that lit up when she turns the knob. Inside the fisher price cabinets I purchased toy pots and pans. For the top of the table I purchase children dishes, a tea kettle set, an easy bake oven and lots of Christmas music. Besides her Christmas clothes and winter coat for the finale touch, I bought her a crib that had hush little baby doll laying underneath a real baby blanket I had purchase.

Thomas and I drove in a rental to every Toys R US; everywhere trying to find that doll-hush little baby. I remember Thomas saying "Tami I don't believe you want me to drive you all the way to New Jersey for a doll." He did, and that's where we found her. I mean the doll. It's Christmas! The holiday is special beside I wanted Champagne to experience Christmas the way I did as a child, magical with anticipation. I paid very good money for that doll.

That year when Champagne went inside the large empty living room, it was filled with Christmas music, a beautiful decorated Christmas tree, toys, and my added special touch of fresh baked goodies.

Thomas and I marvel as she went to each area but when she got to the doll laying inside the crib. She pick the baby doll up, we were so quiet. I said, "Champagne remove the baby pacifier," and when she did the baby doll lips and cheeks starting moving, making the sounds of a crying newborn saying "wag...wag...wag." While holding the doll Champagne took a good look at the doll then she'd threw! Not drop, she'd threw the doll on the floor. It was so funny. Thomas and I burst out hysterically laughing.

Suddenly there was sounds of knocking, someone knocking at our apt door, "Knock, knock and knock." I asked, "Thomas are you expecting someone?"

Thomas goes to the door. I heard Thomas asks "Who is it?" I'm wondering who Thomas was speaking to because he didn't come right back into the living room. "Tami," Thomas said, as I turned my head looking in Thomas direction. He's came back into the living room and from the hallway, in walked Tray with him...........I was stunned!

Tray had one present gift wrapped. Carrying it in his' arm. Thomas said "Champagne' father brought her a Christmas gift." I was so shocked! The Christmas music was playing. Champagne didn't even know who he was. She was playing with her pots and pans set. The only thing Thomas had on were his red nylon boxer shorts. I was sitting on the couch.

Stop! To the reader: Wait, I would just like to say Thomas always just worn boxer shorts when he was inside the house with no undershirt, slippers or socks on as if he on the island and for his age he has a nice body. Anyway I'm planning on buying him a house robe but back to the story.

Tray spoke saying "Merry Christmas Tami, I brought," then he looked around at the many gifts she had. Then he looked at the one gift he had in his' hand and said "I brought her a Christmas gift. It's not much. It's a doll I saw and I wanted her to have it." I pointed and said, "There she is."

Tray came and sat down on the couch. He called to Champagne. She looked his way but then she continue playing. Tray got up and pick her up and sat her on the couch saying "I brought you a gift. Do you want to open it?" Then he help her open the gift. It was a doll. I finally had something to say I said, "Tray this is Thomas. Thomas this is Champagne's father, Tray."

Thomas went to him and offered a hand shake. Tray stood up from the couch and shook Thomas hand. Tray sat down and started playing with Champagne and the doll. Giving Tray some privacy with his daughter I stood up and went into the kitchen. I'm standing there watching, thinking how much they look alike, besides it was an awkward situation, Tray, Thomas and I. Knowing Tray is her father, I didn't want to disrespect Tray by not allowing him to see his daughter in front of Thomas, even though I moved on.

Tray, when he did pay attention to Champagne, he was always gentle when it came to Champagne. He was saying "Look how big you got."

She really is an adorable child.

After a couple of moments has went by, I asked Tray, "How is your grandfather Mr. Stevenson and Shirley?" "He alright Tami," he said as he watch and played with his' daughter.

After Tray stop playing with Champagne he said "My grandfather bought her a Christmas gift. He told me to tell you, him and Shirley would like to see her for the holidays."

I said, "Tell him I would bring her by for a visit." Thomas intervene and said "That's good you came by to see your daughter. She needs her' father in her life."

I offered, "Would you like something to eat or drink Tray?" "Naw that alright. How your' sister and Desmond?" he asked. I said, "I don't know." "Same o same o, huh," he said. "Yep. Same o same o," I answered.

Thomas asked "So what kind of work are you doing?"

Tray said proudly "I got my vendor license. I'm selling hat/scarves and other things. I have a spot in lower Manhattan."

As I listen. I thought quietly to myself, "That job seem perfect for him because Tray is a hustler to his heart." Showing off Thomas said "Well come over here and I buy some things from you."

I sat next to Champagne and I saw Tray looking at us as we both were sitting upon the couch. Tray said "I didn't come to stay long. I don't want to hold yall up T. Enjoy your Christmas," and he kiss his daughter turned around walking toward the door.

Still a little stun I said softly, "Bye." Thomas walked him to the door talking about "Whatever man you bring I'll buy from you."

To the reader: Just to clear things up. I bought my daughter stuff that year. Thomas drove me around. Not trying to be disrespectful or have anyone think Thomas had made her Christmas that year.

Anyway, much earlier, Thomas already told me that he would be going back home for the Christmas holidays. He told me that he wanted to purchase some land to started building a house in Jamaica for his kids comfort and a lot of his money he made here in America went on buying expensive machinery and material in helping him build his home in Jamaica. This time he sent not one, but two barrels home filled with so much stuff. I counted fifty-two bars of soap, unlimited amounts of body lotions, dish detergents, much seasonings, cleaning products, can goods, clothes and Christmas games for the kids. He brought watches, earrings, and underclothes, bags of sugar, flour, hair accessories, paper towels and toilet tissues. There was so much of stuff Thomas was shipping. I think I just named a few.

Thomas said the merchandise in Jamaica cost so much. That one dollar bill of American money was like thirty dollars compared to the Jamaican dollar bill. That's why he preferred to buy here and to ship the stuff over........It's cheaper. He wrapped the clothes he brought around the machinery as a way of hiding it, and, for cushion, while burying the tools under, in between all the nonperishable merchandises. Something he said about custom. Getting the stuff pass custom?

When Thomas went shopping for his three teenage daughters, he never included me. He just came home with the items. Never once did he say "Tami lets go shopping for my kids. Or what do you think they would like?" Thomas just came home and put the many items inside the barrel.

The barrels is so very heavy that he need a dolly in order to lift each barrel. Anyway the barrels were already out of the house before Christmas day. Thomas had already shipped them off, being he wanted the barrels to reach Jamaica by the time he got there.

That's the Christmas Thomas went to Jamaica like the Black Santa Claus.

When Thomas came back from Jamaica that Christmas. He came back empty handed. Meaning he just came back with his self, no suitcase, no clothes and no souvenir for us.

I asked Thomas, "Where all your nice clothes that you pack in the suitcase before you left. And, where is the suitcase? Thomas said "Some people back in the yard needed some clothes so I gave it to them. I don't have any clothes so mon me didn't need the suitcase."

You know, I just knew Thomas was going to come back home with a souvenir from Jamaica for me and Champagne. I was looking forward to seeing what he would bring back from Jamaica for us. Being that he left out from the apartment with so much stuff, taking home to them. After all, I think I had help made the trip with all those gifts possible. By me not pressuring him to concentrate only on us. I'm not a selfish person. Thomas family back home, he wanted to make sure they were alright and that they had a great Christmas but at least, I'm thinking he could had bought us something back from his country.

After a while the company or firm that Thomas worked for didn't have any more work for him. I think they went out of business. He was force to look for work elsewhere in the construction business.

Finding new work was slow for Thomas.

He started finding odd jobs, but nothing steady or permanent. He work for two months. Then the job was over and he be right back searching for work again.

He left the house early every morning in his' work clothes. A pair of dingy blue jeans, thermal beige construction boots, a hard hat and his heavy dingy dusty work jacket. Carrying his construction bag that consist of measuring tapes, hammer, other tools and a bunch of old nails.

I maintain my daughter and the apartment, by making sure the lights and electricity stayed on. Preparing home cooked meals and having enough food for whoever Thomas brought home with him for dinner. Keeping a tidy home with charming characteristic and a pleasant atmosphere was my job.

By now Thomas had brought a bike. He's traveling from one construction site to the next. Riding in varies neighborhoods hoping to find work. Sometimes he came home for lunch just to leave right back out. He was very persisted and diligent in looking for work for his self.

That's the first time I ever saw a grown man ride a ten speed bike looking for work. On top of that, he's riding the bike in the cold weather too. He looked a little funny to me riding a bike in cold weather going from construction site to the next asking for work but I guess it beats walking.

By now Thomas brought a full body beige thermal to keep him warm as he'd pursuit his' quest in finding work. I had to give him much credit though, for him as a man looking for honest work. He went up and beyond and I respected him a lot for that because most guys in the neighborhood wasn't that diligent.

A lot of the people on the block respect us because we gave the appearance of a really cool couple working together trying to achieve something. The young guys who often hung out in front of the building always said "hello," to him. They gave us a lot of respect, as well as the people that lived in the building too.

When Thomas came home, he always went straight to the bathroom and took a shower. I go in the kitchen warming up dinner for us all to sit down and eat. One evening as we sat and ate dinner at the table. Thomas said "Tami I'm going to join the collision because it's hard getting put on a construction site if you're not in the union. Mon, me head hurts. So much problems trying to get work. I'm tired. I went all over and I got no ting."

I said, "Don't worry Thomas. I quite sure you find something." "Yeah mon, I seen this guy I know named Conroy. He with the collision located in Brownsville. He going to come pick me up tomorrow and we going to ride the bus with the collision. You see me, I'm not like them pussy boys who don't have a trade mon, me is an experienced and skillful tradesman…eehey."

I asked, "Thomas, so how can the collision help you?" "Listen Tami, me going to ride with tim in the morning… eehey, me got to pay dues and attend weekly meetings and they going to fight for me to get put on a construction site…. eehey. Then me going to work really hard showing the white man me can do the work…eehey."

I asked, "So how you going to pay the dues and you don't have any money?" "Nooo. No. No Tami, when they get me on a job site…eehey then me going to start to pay the dues after I get a paycheck. Me not going to pay dues and they won't help me get a job…. no sir. Once me start working then I would pay dues Tami."

"O I understand," I said "Okay Thomas that sound like a plan. You shouldn't worry so much. I quite sure everything would work out just fine for you. Ohm Thomas I'm going inside the kitchen would you like some more food to eat? If so I get it, if you want."

Then my curiosity got the best of me so I asked, "Most of them boys that ride the bus don't have skills?" Thomas said "They mostly sweepers or demolition guys, but me can do sheet rock and plumbing mon, so it should be easy to place me."

Listening I said, "Being you have skills I don't want you to worry. Everything will be just fine."

The next day early in the morning, I heard someone knocking on the apartment door. I asked, "Who is it?" "Conroy mon," the person said.

I kind of shouted, "Thomas….. Conroy at the door." "Let him in Tami," Thomas said. When I open the door I said, "Good morning. He's in the living room eating breakfast."

As I lead Conroy toward the living room. Thomas jumps up from the table and say "Hey mon. Me ready man, have a seat I'm just about finish my breakfast."

Thomas introduce us. I asked, "Would you like to have some food to eat Conroy?" Conroy said "Thanks Tami me belly full already. Tami looks like a nice girl man." Thomas said "Eehey."

Thomas got up and goes to the closet and put on his work body thermal and grab his construction bag. He came back inside the living room saying "Let go mon. Tami me soon come." I walk them both to the door and locked it.

After Thomas left out for work, later on in the day I went to Shelby's house like I normally do.

When Valentine day came around and Thomas came into the house empty handed I got very upset with him. He didn't understand why I was so mad with him. I explain to him, "That Valentine's Day represent Love. It a day we Americans celebrate and recognizes the ones we care about. Most men brings home flowers or jewelry to the women in their' lives."

Later on he came in the house with some flowers but I threw it at him because the day was over and it didn't feel as good receiving the flowers behind an argument. Plus I shouldn't have to tell Thomas what to do on Valentine's Day, American or not. He could see all the advertising that going on.

After a while I became pregnant with Thomas child. I wouldn't have mind being marry to Thomas even though, I wasn't marry I decide to have the baby anyway. To tell you the truth I had my second baby for Champagne's sake. I know that may sound stupid having a baby for another baby, but Champagne was lonely.

Tonya had completely cut not just me out of her life but my baby too. I grew up with all this family and here it is Champagne only had me. I didn't want me to be her only universe. She needed a sibling. Just in case if anything happen to me, I would feel good knowing they have each other. She deserves to have a family. Family members sharing her life with way more than just me.

A part of me didn't want any more children while another part of me did. The part of me that did want more children was the part of me that pictured the American dream.

My version of the American dream was so simple; a big old house, a picket fence, backyard with a grill pit, a supportive husband, not to mention a husband I'm madly in love with; a bunch of kids running around about four thru six. Me as a loving wife and mother that would go through any links for my family, to ensure their care and wellbeing. Besides providing a stable home, making sure my family had moral and values with us celebrating all holidays while throwing lots of parties, gathering, with close friends and family.

I never was a person who focus on a lot of money or keeping up with the Joneses. I focus more on family happiness, comfort and creating a better environment for myself as well as for those around me. Something as simple as that, was all I had ever wanted.

The part of me that didn't want another child was the reality of what it takes being a parent. Having a child is a serious responsibility. All the sacrifices, money and time that goes into raising and taking care of a child. It's not easy. To tell you the truth, I never thought I would be a single parent. I always picture myself being marry while raising my family and living inside a big house.

I never forget that moment after I had given birth to Champagne. It was feeding time in the hospital. The nurse roll her to me in a bassinet. She was all wrap up and sleeping then she started to cry. The nurse came to me showing me properly how to pick her up and how to hold her in my arm so that her head is supported. That's when it hit me as I was feeding her.

I realized that she was going to be with me till death do one of us part. And it was my responsibility to take care of her. Tray wasn't even there the day when I was leaving the hospital to bring her home. It was Mr. Stevenson (Tray' grandfather) who was with me on that day.

I started noticing Thomas is set in his ways. When I had morning sickness and when he brought me breakfast in bed, it had to be Jamaican food. I enjoyed eating Jamaican food. I even learn how to prepare and cook some of the Caribbean dishes but sometimes I wanted a bacon and eggs sandwich. Or pancakes with sausages. In the kitchen Thomas rarely cook but when he did he enjoyed making Porridge and fish soup.

I couldn't get him to cook me an American meal. He would say "No mon this is better." I found it to be a little selfish on his' part. Like, why couldn't he bend? You know, like compromise for me, because I feel after all that I had did and done and is doing for him-like some of the things I didn't want to do.

Anyway after Thomas left for work while cleaning the apartment listening to music I heard someone knocking at my door. I goes to the door and asks, "Who is it?" "Adrianne," she said. "Who," I said again not recognizing the voice.

"My name is Adrianne. I believe I have something that belongs to you," she said. Something for me I thought? Out of curiosity I opened up the door.

"Are you Electra T Jones she asked?" I said, "Yes. How can I help you?" Standing in front of my door is this light brown skin black, woman with hair that was longer than mine.

I look younger for my age but she appeared in age to be slightly younger than me, believe it or not but there was something about her I pick up on but I quickly dismayed it when she said, "I believe this belongs to you," as she had stuck her hand out with an envelope.

I look down at what she had pointing in my direction and saw my name written on the standard size envelope. She said, "It was in my mailbox," as she held the letter out, waiting for me to take the piece of mail. "Oh thank you," I said.

As I took the mail, out loud I questioned, "I wonder how they mixed up our mail?" She said, "We have the same last name." I looked at her. I said, "Ooh," as she had stood in front of the door.

Then she said, "I picture you be an older woman."

I recalled I just looked at her as if to say, where did that come from? From a name....I don't get it. Again I said, "Okay thank you," now wanting to close my door but she said, "I live on the second floor above your apartment on the right," as she pointed toward the door diagonally from mine. At this point I smiled not knowing what else to say. Then she extended out her hand saying, "Hi, my name is Adrianne."

Feeling slightly awkward I smile and said, "Adrianne it's nice meeting you. Bye," as I close my door.

The following day I goes over to visit my grandparents (my mother' parents.) By now sadly both my dad parents had passed. I occasionally brought them a plate of food that I cooked. Or I would bake them a cake. I'm the baker in the family. I did the same for my dad too always bringing him a home cook meal. Since he eats out so much at fast food restaurants.

That's all I was able to give was a home cook meal and spend some time with the people I love. I enjoyed cooking for them anyway. While inside my grandparents' house I goes upstairs to visit Coon and check on Pebbles. Coon said to me "When are you going to come get your cat. I can't afford to keep feeding both cats."

I said, "You got a lot of nerves after you gave my cat fleas. Who told you to bring that black cat in my house?" He said "I was doing you a favor because you didn't want that guy coming around."

I said, "**So.** No one told you to put fleas on my cat." Coon said "You better come get him or I'm throwing the cat out in the street." Immediately I went downstairs to my grandparents and I spoke to granddaddy, who by now was completely blind, and was living in the front part of the house downstairs. Grandmamma unfortunately by this time had went cripple. She was confined to a wheel chair.

I asked "Granddaddy could you do me a favor?" He said "What is it Electra?" I asked, "Can you keep Pebbles my cat? I had the cat until Coon made him get fleas. Now Thomas doesn't want the cat living inside the apartment with us. I don't want Coon to throw the cat out to the street because he doesn't want the cat living with him any more upstairs."

Granddaddy said "Yeah Electra you can let the cat stay down here. I don't mind as long as he moves out my way because I don't want to step on him when I walk through the house."

I said, "Granddaddy cats are real smart. The cat probably sense you disable because lots of times you walking while touching on the walls. Then sometimes you walking while tapping the floor with a cane."

Lots of time granddaddy just walk through the house touching the walls. He knows his' house very well. The only reason I use the word, disable is because granddaddy had a very hard time dealing with his' blindness. I believe he still hates that he went blind. So knowing it a sore spot for him I chose the word disable instead of saying that awful word he hates, blind.

I'm very independent. I don't ask my parents or my grandparents for anything. This the second time ever in my life asking granddaddy for anything. The first time I ever ask him for something was when I applied for college. So eager anticipating going to college. I was sadden when I got the news my financial aid came back too late for me to attend classes for that semester. I told my grandfather what happened and, I actually stutter when I ask him can I borrow the money. Without any hesitation granddaddy ask me "How much do you need." Him wanting to hear that I'm succeeding in life.

Anyway after he said it was alright for Pebbles to stay he suggested that I go to the back room to let Grandmamma know about Pebbles which she didn't have a problem with either knowing occasionally, she had dealt with seeing or hearing a rat inside the house.

Chapter Ten

Coming in the house from work. Thomas brought yet another barrel inside the house. I remember being a little alarmed. "Another barrel?" I said to Thomas.

"My father need some underclothes. He's an old man and he need someone to take care of him, eehey," he said.

Thomas had about ten packs of fruit of the loom cotton white tee shirts and ten packs of cotton white briefs. He throw them inside the large barrel.

Stop! To the reader: Have you ever seen these large brown, study cardboard paper looking barrels? They hold extremely a lot of stuff. They are so big and tall, that, if anyone have to ship this type of barrel, the person writes the forwarding address on the barrel itself. A pen won't do. It's best to use a black magic marker because the person handwriting shows much better when using a marker. Thomas said it goes on a weighing machine and that determined the cost. It make sense because how else can you price it, in order to ship it? I never went with Thomas when he shipped the barrels off but I should have.

Any way going back to the story.

Thomas put the barrel right back in the same spot, inside the living room. In the corner that's by the window. I begin noticing a pattern with Thomas and these barrels. He was shipping a barrel to Jamaica like every three or four months. Back then, there wasn't any large supermarkets, like Costco or BJ; where as a person can purchase food or personal items in bulks. There was just regular supermarkets; like Pathmark, Food Town and Fine and Fare, so I seeing Thomas sending this amount of food and toiletries, it was overwhelming. Around this time I think Pathmark was about or has just turn into a 24 hour supermarket. Thomas even came home with a brand new whirlpool refrigerator, sitting the fridge in between our living room and dining room. He wanted me to use it, saying it will cost him less money to bring the fridge into his' country because it had been used. I didn't use it, because I was getting a little teed off because every time I turn around another large barrel coming inside the house and he got to fill it up. Taking away his' money again that he could have used to help me prosper. He was doing more for them then he was for us! I'm the one doing all the sacrificing for a better tomorrow. While having nothing and creating something from nothing, keeping our home up and running and cozy. All he kept telling me "Tami your day soon come."

Even though me and Champagne still didn't have much in our apartment to brag about, but, our home was filled with love, and holiday's celebrations. As a family we sat down and ate dinner together every night which is something I treasure but that's not all I wanted.

Thomas and I were truly happy together. Helping him take care of his family back home, made him happy and content. So I was happy and content, but I still expected me as well as our relationship to progress. Maybe at 1st I didn't say much because as a single parent raising a child, it was very difficult on me. So watching him support his' family I didn't mind because I was thinking from a woman's point of view. That he was not supposed to just walk away from his responsibilities'. I thought it was admirable but he is getting a little out of hand with this because he doing it too much! I started thinking and asking him .... "What about us?" Thomas always say "Tami your day soon come." Then the next thing I know he running up to me hugging me wanting me to calm down and relax.

While Thomas was gone during the day riding the collision bus, getting jobs here and there. I kept myself busy cooking and cleaning up the apartment, attending WIC appointments, going to the corner store or our' neighborhood supermarket, purchasing food and our supply of milk and cereal from the WIC vouchers, keeping my prenatal care appointments and Champagne's doctor visits. Going to the welfare office adding my unborn baby to my public assistance case and also putting in my request for my pregnancy allowance and my 2nd furniture allowance allotment. Then going downtown to my management building, requesting and doing the procedures, for a larger apartment, taking Champagne out to be among other children, having his' meals ready when he came home, keeping our clothes folded and clean, even though I didn't get paid for what I was contributing, it still was work. Housework, handling children, maintaining the home, turning our apt into a home with celebrations, which consist of preparation of planning and decorating and supporting your man needs, is serious work. So I work hard too.

I went next door to Shelby. Us going outside like always, we stood in front of our building having a conversation as we watch our young children run and played. While standing outside in front of the building Adrianne came downstairs with her' three kids.

She came up to me striking a conversation and not wanting to seem impolite to Shelby. I introduce Shelby to Adrianne and from that day on Adrianne started hanging out with us.

Sometimes we all be standing outside and Thomas, he would pull up in the car with Conroy. Both of them are coming home from work. Shelby's children and Champagne would run up to the car as Thomas getting out from the car. All the kids saying "Hi Thomas," as he say to all the kids "Hello." Then Thomas would pick up Champagne tossing her up in the air as a form of greeting her. Conroy yells to me from the car "Hello Tami." Then he say to Thomas "See you tomorrow," as I watch them both ball one of their hands into a fist then tap each other knuckles before Conroy drives off.

Not often, but occasionally Shelby will come to my house listening to music giving herself small breaks from her husband and kids. Keeping me company when Thomas at work inside my apt. Adrianne came downstairs too but being her a single parent she would have her three kids with her. I didn't mind the company sometimes. Actually I enjoyed it. We just be talking enjoying each other company as the kids played. Taking us away from our mundane activities' like housework, raising children and cooking. We be listening to the reggae tape I made or sometimes we sat and listen to the music tapes Isaac and I made.

One day while visiting me inside my apartment Adrianne ask, "Tami what that?" I told her, "It's a barrel. Thomas use it to ship things to Jamaica."

Shelby said, "Oh that what that is Tami. I saw Thomas struggling trying to get that out of the building a couple of times. I know he does construction work, but seeing him with that I didn't know what that was for. So he goes to Jamaica and he ship stuff over there too. In that?"

"Yep," I said.

I hear my apartment door is opening.

Thomas hears us ladies in the living room with the music playing and he enter the living room. Everyone says their hellos. Shelby say, "Alright Tami I speak with you later. I got to go home and figure out what to cook. I said to Shelby, "I cooked my dinner early. Only thing I got to do is heat and serve."

Shelby said, "If I don't get out of here my family will be heating and serving for their self at the corner store or going to the Chinese restaurant." We both laughed as I walked her to the door. With the music still playing, I goes into the kitchen starting getting our food ready for our slt down super.

Thomas makes his way back to the front, comes into the kitchen as him and I are talking briefly about our day. Both of us goes into the living room. Adrianne and I are engaging lightly in our conversation until I make the comment on how late it getting. So Adrianne softly calls her kids to come to the front. She telling them they are about ready to leave. Once all the kids came out from the back-I walk Adrianne to the door. I say to her, "I speak with your later. Have a good night Adrianne." "Goodnight Tami," Adrianne replied as she asks her kids not to run up the steps.

After a while Thomas and I our relationship turned into building. We needed a larger place because our baby will be coming soon. Thomas brought us a used car. Therefore we started doing our food shopping anytime we wanted too at the 24 hour Pathmark in Brownsville, where my grandparents live.

Now I watch Thomas load and shipped that barrel and refrigerator off for the Easter holiday.

One night Thomas and I was awaken by running water. When we got up and went into the hallway tremendous amount of water was running from the ceiling. The water has destroyed a small section of the ceiling in our hallway. I'm going to have to go to Asbury Management and put in a request for repairs.

The next day when I goes over to Shelby house. She having cake and ice-cream for her baby son Kent. It's his' birthday. Someone knocking at Shelby door. "Just a minute," as Shelby walks to her door. Looking thru the peephole, Shelby opens the door.

"Hi Shelby," Adrianne said as she walks in with her three children. And as soon as her kids enter the apartment they dash off, running to play with the other kids who's already inside the house.

"Hi Tami," Adrianne say. "Hi Adrianne," I said as she takes a seat.

Adrianne asked, "Did yall hear all that fighting that went on last night?"

Both Shelby and I said, "What fighting?" Adrianne said, "I didn't come out my door. I think it was those brothers on the third floor. What is her name? She about my height...

always wearing long skirt? Sometime I see she has her hair wrap up like a Muslim."

Shelby say, "Oh you talking about Miss Butts?" "Is that her name?" Adrianne asks.

Shelby said, "She the only one I know who wear the Muslim attire and they always fighting up there. She keeps a house full of people. I told my son Wilbert Jr, I don't want him going up there because there's always something going on."

As I listen I said, "Well I have to go downtown. I need repairs done cause last night someone had a serious leak and it destroyed the ceiling in my hallway." "For real," Shelby said. Adrianne said, "I wonder where the leak could have come from?"

I said, "I don't know but it a bad one. Yall wanna come over and see it." Both of them looking curious to see how bad it is so Shelby yelled to her husband, "Wilbert! I'm going next door to Tami for a minute. Watch all the kids, we be right back."

When I open the door to my apartment Shelby and Adrianne both say, "Wow." Shelby looks around the area and said, "Tami, it messed up this side of the wall too."

"Yep," I said. Locking the door as we all go back to Shelby.

When the time came, everybody sung happy birthday to Kent. Then we ate ice-cream and cake.

When I got downtown, I seen Asbury office has change. The lady who initially gave me my first interview is now sitting at the first cubical. I walked in saying, "Good afternoon."

The lady looks at me and say, "Hi. And how are you doing?"

Smiling I say, "I'm Miss Jones. Remember, you interviewed me when I first got my apartment with this management."

She looks at me saying, "I remember you. How have you been and how can I help you?"

I told the nice lady, "Someone had a bad leak on the upper floor in the building. It damage the ceiling and a part of the wall inside my apartment hallway. I need to have it repaired."

She said, "I put the repair in for you right now. Other than that is everything else alright?"

I told her, "I'm expecting and I had already requested for a larger apartment."

She asked me, "In the same building?"

I told her, "When I came down here before requesting a larger place. The person that was at the front desk only took my name-telling me that I would be placed on a waiting list. But the question never came up about which building I prefer? If I have a choice I would appreciate a larger apartment in the same building."

Smiling the nice lady said, "Once the baby is put on your budget and you provide me with a birth certificate. You could be considered for a larger apartment Ms. Jones. Then, I see what I can do about getting you inside the same building."

When Thomas came home I told him, "I went to the management office today and they will be sending someone to repair the ceiling. The lady from the management department told me once the baby is born and I provide management with the birth certificate hopefully management will be able to get me a larger place inside this building."

Thomas said "Oh that good. Um-hum, that be really good mon."

Thomas was so occupy with work and bringing in money while I was occupied with family and making a home which to me was a good combination.

Officer Dumez opens the Q dorm door and announce, "Ladies, Over Comers Tabernacle is on site."

Wow times flies when you busy. I did a lot of writing this weekend. So I'm going to stop for now because I like this ministry. Putting away my notes. I grab my bible. Locked my locker and walk out from my dorm.

Walking in the hallway towards the security post I see the same group of ladies holding their conversation, as I'm about to pass them this time I spoke. They were shocked that I spoke that neither one of them said a word back. So I looked at them again and said, "Hello."

One of the female quietly said, "Hello." I noticed she has an accent from the Caribbean descent.

When I got downstairs they were already in worship singing "we shall o ver come__. We shall o ver come__. We shall o ver come! Some_ day__ ___ __. O' ooh deep__ in my heart__. I___ do be lieve. That, we shall o ver come some __day__. Black and white to ge_, ther. Black and white to ge_, ther. Black and white to gether some __day__ __ ___. O' ooh deep__ in my heart__. I___ do be lieve, that, we shall overcome some day."

While in the sprit he said loudly "Yes we shall overcome. With faith believing we shall overcome. This won't last forever! Ladies this homelessness won't last forever, you will, overcome. Just believe and have faith because all things are possible with God. Man will fail you but God is a delivera to all who calls upon him."

Then they started singing "Who report shall you believe. We shall believe the report of the Lord. Come on now! Who report! Shall you believe? We shall believe the report of the Lord. His report said I'm am heal. His report said I'm am fill. His reported said, I am free. His report **say what?** Victory__ __ee. Come on now! Who report shall you believe. I shall believe the report of the Lord. Come on now! Who report shall you believe. We shall believe the report of the Lord. His report say I'm am free, his reported say **what**? Victory___ ___ee!!"

Then we went into "What a mighty God we serve____ what a mighty God we serve___ angels bow before him, heaven and earth adore him. What a mighty God we serve_____. Jesus is the God we serve_____ Jesus is the God we serve_____ angels bow before him, heaven and earth adore him. What a mighty God we serve_____

Larry asked "Do any body in here know Jesus? I tell you, Jesus is. Then they started singing. "He a way maker. Yes he is__ he may not come when you want him but he be there on time. He a way maker yes he is__. He on time, my God is on time. He's on time, my God is right on time. He's a way maker yes he is___.

Larry started preaching "I'm here to tell you that **God** is a delivera! He a healer! He's your lawyer. He can be everybody everything and anything if you just let him in. He will make a way when there isss no way.

So many of the homeless ladies were starting to become a believer.

Larry continue "He's and **conquer!** Have you ever been in trouble and you needed a friend. Well I'm here to tell you Jesus **is that friend**. Just call on his mighty name and he be there on time cause he is a way maker. Yes he is! Who in here need the Lord to come into their life and be delivered! Who in here has committed a sin and want **forgiveness**! **Who**, need a friend? Who want knowledge? Who need healing in the mind or the body? Who needs **Anny thing?!!"**

To the reader: Ain't nothing like a Holy Ghost party. Quickly back to the story.

I say "Call upon the name of my Jehovah and he **hears** all things. **See** all things. **Knows** all things. Jesus is the only way."

The girl was rail up saying, "I need Jesus. Yes, I need Jesus." Billy was there to with both her hands lifted in the air moving from side to side enjoying the present of the lord saying, "Yes lord. Yes lord. I need you. I need you."

I lifted up my hands too saying, "Yes lord. Yes lord I need you."

They started singing "Every hour I need thee__ touch! Me now my Sa vi or I come__ to need thee_."

Larry read from the book of John. Jesus is the way the truth and the light and only through him can you be saved and see **God**. A lady from the ministry step forward asking, "Who need prayer?"

A lot of girls got in line, so did I. When it came time for him-Larry to pray for me he ask "What is it you need?" I said, "I want to be free."

He put his hand on my head and said "God you know her needs. You know her desires. I ask right now in the name of **Jesus**, Lose **it!** And it is **done** in the name of Jesus Christ of Narsareth.

Everybody really enjoyed the service and I bet you a lot of souls got saved that night. We all mingle and drunk juice and shared cookies. Before they left. Larry turn around standing by the dining room door he said "I want yall all to know that Jesus love each and every one of you. May the grace of God be with each and every one of you every day, have a good night ladies."

Sometime you just need to hear that. Going thru this type of hardship. It's giving me positive hope that everything going to be alright. Keeping me holding on at this low and confusing point in my life, giving me strength to hang on. I could hear God whispering in me to "Hang on. Just hang on. I know you tired but just hang on. Weather through your storm. Good days are coming."

On that note I sat down before going back upstairs to my dorm. I'm feeling good. I see everyone is making it back home. Coming in from their' weekend pass.

The RA started giving out the reserved left over trays from dinner. I wasn't hungry. Maybe I got filled at the service from the spirit of the Lord.

Lot of the ladies are hanging out waiting for bed check. Some girls stood on the laundry line signing up for slots to wash for the next day.

By the time I reached inside the dorm, I was feeling so much better spiritually. Lacy she was lying on her bed with her legs resting on the fake head board she made for herself, while reading her book. When she saw me enter the dorm. She took one earplug away from her ear and asked me, "What you so happy about?"

I said, "I had a nice time. It was a very nice service held downstairs by the Over Comer Tabernacle Ministry."

With the rolled of her tongue Lacy pronounce, "Really?"

I said "For real. It really was a good service and a nice turn out of girls showed up. Next time when they here you should come down in the dining-room and participate."

"**Me!** Come to that shit you got to be fuckin kidding. HA HA HA HA," she said. Then she plug back up her ear and stretch out on top of her bed to continue reading her book.

Lacy has a wired sense of humor she like to curse and imitate black people. I don't know why? All I can say, really she harmless, but seeing this white lady reading all those books, you wouldn't think she act like that but she does. Her favorite author is Danielle Steel. She read all her books, and you know what I do believe Lacy she really do cares for me because I'm the only one she actually hold a conversation with inside the this dorm. I never seen her speak to any other resident either while eating, dinner or lunch.

"**Yeah bitch**, I said it," she said.

"Oh gosh!" As I just sat down its Valerie, she just walks in talking on her cell phone, going to her area. Talking as she put her belongings inside the locker.

Shift Supervisor Pam and security guard Dumez enter the dorm. Security says, "Bed check ladies."

Shift supervisor Pam goes to every bed. Getting, collecting everyone signatures for the office bed roster for the Q-dorm. Once she finish quietly she says, "Goodnight ladies," as her exit the dorm.

I did so much writing today. I'm retiring early tonight. I gets inside my cover and turn over facing the wall to go to sleep. I could hear my roommates' starting to preparing them self for bed. As I lay there I'm thinking, if I hold on to

Gods words and keep my faith maybe I would have the chance to live and enjoy the rest of my life....... but dam, at such this late age.

After a while security Dumez come back to the dorm, she asks, "Ladies is it alright to turn the lights off?"

Everyone in their' bed. No one said a word. Security standing by the door, after three second has passed she turn out the lights while saying, "Goodnight ladies."

Chapter Eleven

Monday morning and I woke up before the security guard had turned on the lights to the dorm. I'm thinking…. I wonder what time it is as I laid in my bed facing towards the wall. Soon as I'm turning over, I catch a glimpse of the forearm and hand of security guard Rowena (another African guard) as she just reaches in and clicks on the lights to the dorm.

Oh it got to be 6:00. So I look at the clock on the wall. The time reads 6:10. With the bright lights shinny in my face I'm thinking it's too early to get up for breakfast so throwing the covers back over my face, I laid down for a couple more minutes before I exactly got up to have breakfast.

Coming back inside the dorm after having breakfast, the shelter had served us waffles and sausages. Sitting on my bed, looking at my weird neighbor, thinking, one day I'm going to strike a conversation with her. I goes to the bathroom and turn the doorknob, it locked. Knocking on the bathroom door while saying, "Hello, is anybody in there?"

In her Chinese accent I hear Luting say, "You wanna come in, I'm in shower. I unlock door come in." The bathroom door made a clicking sound.

Talking loudly from outside the bathroom door with my mouth close-up on the bathroom door. I said, "Luting that alright really I could wait till you come out."

"**Well,** I, **Can't!** …..Hurry up Bitch! As Valerie came and bang on the bathroom door. Valerie saying, "Shit! I leave out you in the dam bathtub. Come back your ass still in the dam tub. Bitch I got to go to work and you better not had used up all the hot water either, cause me and you going to fight!"

As I'm standing there waiting to go inside the bathroom. I started thinking. I kinda understand how Valerie feel because I use to work. Anyway, I'm glad to see Luting didn't lose her bed. So Ugina was the overnighter.

Quickly Luting scurries out from the bathroom in a wrap towel smelling like skin so soft. As I proceeds to go into the bathroom Valerie quickly brushed up on me trying to get inside the bathroom. Holding the door and guarding the bathroom entrance with my elbow I say "**I'm next!**"

Valerie pushes to go inside the bathroom and I brush up against her saying, "I'm **next**, I said." Quickly closing and locking the door. Valerie bang on the bathroom door and shouted "Bitch!" I'm saying from inside of the bathroom, "You a bitch, **Bitch**!" But I understand how she feels so I quickly peed and came out from the bathroom.

When I come out from the bathroom, I start to get dress. Pepsi said, "Heyy ou, Q ten." I look her way she came walking into my area asking me, "Do ou wanna piece of chicken? I made it O er at my man Hous."

I look down and saw Pepsi have several pieces of fried chicken legs in aluminum foil. I told her, "I just got finish eating, maybe later."

Pepsi said, "I'm gO ing downstairs to heat it up in the micOwave. I save ou a piece. I said, "I definitely don't want none now."

Smiling Pepsi asked, "Why ou say it ike that." I said, "Because you see her right there." She asked "Ouu ou talking bout?" I pointed to Marcell as she just dab her sick foot with the wash cloth. Moving closer to me Pepsi said, "Wat about er?" I said, "I saw hcr putting her basin in the microwave heating up the water."

Pepsi asks with a questionable face, "The une she soak er foot in?" "Yep," I said. Pepsi mouth open putting a disgusted look upon her face and said "Ugggh, dat a dirt e bitch!" I shook my head in agreement, saying "Yes she sure is."

When Pepsi walked back to her area she stop by Marcell bed and said loud, "Ou a dirt e bitch!"

Marcell looked up from her foot and said in her African accent all slowly and clear, "Excuse me what did you say?"

Due to Pepsi being deaf she has a speech impairment. Pepsi said again, "Ou a dirt e bitch, I wat to warm up my chicKen in the micOwave and you put that basin in the micOwave to wrm the water for Yaw sick foot! Ou a dirt y bitch."

Valerie stop talking on her cell phone and said, "I better not get sick! Are you stupid putting that nasty infectious thing in the microwave and other people has to use it?"

Marcell acting like there is nothing wrong with what she did. She said, "Maggie, can you move away from my bed, please." Then all hell broke out. "Who ou calling **Maggie**? Who ou calling **Maggie**. I told ou my name is **Pepsi**. Nobody calls me Maggie. Call me Maggie again **bitch**."

Pepsi is all rail up like she ready to fight. "No un call me Maggie...call me Maggie again I step on yaw O-her foot and ou won't b able to **alk bitch**!"

African Security Guard Rowena comes running into the room, "Can you please lower your voice. You disturbing other clients." Small Pepsi goes closer to Marcell face and say while shoving her, "Gid head call me Maggie, **gid** head, gid head do it, do it!"

Marcell turn to the guard looking for help saying slowly and politely in her African dialect, "I don't know what wrong with her. Please I don't want no trouble."

The African guard tries to talk to Pepsi. In her African dialect, security guard Rowena saying, "Can you go to your own area? Miss. **Please**... go to your area."

Pepsi ignore the guard. Saying to Marcell "I don't ike that name no un calls me Maggie." Security Rowena see she can't control the situation. She radio for back up saying, "Hello. Mr. Berry."

"Go for Mr. Berry," he said. "Can you come to the Q dorm? The client is acting out of control. I need help," Rowena said. From the walkie-talkie we heard Mr. Berry quickly say "I'm in route."

Pepsi is still ranting and raging, "**Don't no un call me Maggie**." She goes into the bathroom and we all can hear the shower curtain erupting. The African guard goes to Marcell she asks "What happen? Are you hurt? Did she hit you?" Marcell says quietly, "I didn't do anything to her." Valerie jumps in and say, "You didn't do anything you just a **nasty Bitch**." The guard said, "Please refrain from name calling."

Mr. Berry knocks rapidly on the Q-dorm door announcing "Man on. Can I come in?" Suddenly Pepsi run out the bathroom going towards Marcell saying "**Call me Maggie again.** I kill **ou bitch**." Mr. Berry run into the dorm as he yells "**Pepsi!** You don't want to do that." Pepsi breathing very heavily. Mr. Berry shout, "**Pepsi. Look at me**. Look at **me** Pepsi. Listen I want you to calm down right now or I have to call NYPD and I know…. you don't want that."

Pepsi is staring angrily at Marcell.

Carefully, Mr. Berry walks and stands in front of Pepsi, blocking her angry stares from Marcell saying "Talk to me Pepsi do you hear me, talk to me." After he got Pepsi to quiet down he asked "What happen?"

Valerie says, "Mr. Berry that a nasty Bitch!" Pointing at Marcell who's limping towards the bathroom. Mr. Berry said "No, name calling." Valerie say, "She put her infectious basin in the microwave and we all got to use it Mr. Berry."

Mr. Berry asks "Who did what?" Valcric points her finger while she said, "Her right there put her basin that she soaks her disgusting foot in, inside the microwave and we all got to use it."

Mr. Berry asked "Who are you talking about?" At the same time Me, Valerie and Pepsi said together pointing with attitude, "**Her!**" Mr. Berry he looked to see who we were pointing too. Then he said surprisingly "Marcell?"

Us three said, "Yes, Marcell." I said, "Look at her foot." Mr. Berry looked at her foot and was shock to see the swollen slash and asked "Did you put your basin inside the microwave Marcell?"

She didn't say a word while standing next to the bathroom door. I said, "Yeah, I saw her. She did it on Saturday during lunch time." Mr. Berry asked "Did you wipe the microwave out afterward?" We all looked at each other because we all felt that was a dumb question. Anyway back to the story.

A couple of seconds went by still without her not saying a sound. I said, "No! She just walked away, and I'm not using the microwave no more."

Shamefully, Mr. Berry said "Marcell. I'm surprised to hear you did something like that. Don't you know other residents uses the microwave? And your action could make other people sick?"

As we all watched and now listening to Mr. Berry. He said "If you need the water to be hot I suggested you use the foam cups and heat water that way. Then pour the hot water inside the basin. This way we all get to respect one another. Okay Marcell."

Marcell shook her head as a way of comprehending.

Busted and disgusted. Finally, now she looked a little embarrass for her careless action.

Mr. Berry said "I don't want to hear you did that again but I would let security know no basins are allowed inside the microwave. And if I hear of you doing that again I'll make sure you only allowed to soak your foot inside the intake office. And, I will take the basin away from you if you can't act like a responsible adult."

I asked, "What if she pour the same dirty water back inside the foam cups and nuke that again?" Mr. Berry asked, "Miss Jones can I handle this?"

Looking at Marcell. Mr. Berry said "Marcell, once the water cools off and if you need to reheat the water again use fresh water please."

Then he turned to Pepsi and said "**You** cannot threaten to kill anybody. You could go to jail for that. All that for this?" "She called me Mag gie," Pepsi said.

"So I think Maggie is a beautiful name. Now do I have to change your room because I don't want to hear you up here trying to kill somebody because they called you Maggie," Mr. Berry said. "My name iz Pepsi," Pepsi said.

Mr. Berry said "Why don't you go get your name change legally since you don't like that name cause from time to time someone will call you by that name."

Pepsi said, "When I get my s s i check I'm put aWay somum e money. Dat a go od idea." Mr. Berry said "Alright be good ladies," he and the guard left the dorm.

Shortly after I exit the dorm. I goes to the intake office to pick up my metro cards because I'm going to my primarily care doctor to get me an updated ppd shot. When I lived in Manhattan at Sixty-Eight Lex. I had to go to the health clinic all the way on Ninth Street.

When I reach the intake office and I walked toward Mr. Berry. Standing behind the desk he asks "How can I help you Miss Jones?" I said, "I need my metro cards."

Mr. Berry walks over to the area where all the large notebooks are kept. He scans the books then he pulls out the large metro cards notebook. Coming back in front of the desk, standing in front of me he searching down the sheet for my name. Once he found it. He hands me the book to sign for two, two dollar metro cards.

My doctor office wasn't too far from Bridge Net Women Shelter; even though it is a nice little walk-so instead of using the metro card, I walked. I get to my clinic and have my doctor implant the ppd shoot. I was told to come back in two days for the reading. Every time I visit the clinic and because of my medical coverage I'm entitle to a metro card so I ask the receptionist at the clinic for my four-dollar metro card.

Just before I leave the clinic. I decided to make an appointment for the dentist.

Walking back to the shelter I get this great idea. I'm going to hustle off and sell my metro cards. I can sell the cards and have eight dollars in my pocket. I know it ain't much but it's something. At least I have a little chump change in my pockets until my next pick up date of Public Assistance.

Public Assistance only give me twenty-two dollars and fifty cents every two-weeks. Walking, ahead I see Eastbrunwick train station. It's one of the busiest stations in Brooklyn. I should be able to sell them fast down there.

When I get to Eastbrunwick station I stands by one of the vendor machines. When I see the people come down in the train station. I start the hustle of trying to sell off my metro cards. I say, "Excuse me Miss, do you need a four dollar metro card?" "No," the lady answered as she walks pass me. As a group of people come down the steps I asks, "Do anyone need a four dollar or single ride metro card?" The people keep walking going on though towards the turnstiles.

I see a gentlemen going over to the vendor machine. I walk over to him and say to him, "Excuse me sir, do you need a four-dollar metro card?" The guy said "No, I need a single ride." I said, "Well I have a single ride metro card. Could you buy the card from me?" The guy looks as if he didn't trust that the card could be good. Wanting to make the sell-quickly I said "I don't need the extra card. I'm trying to buy me a cup of coffee."

The guy asked "How do I know if it's any good?"

I thought quickly as I looked at the metro card vendor machines.

Finally I said "I'll show you it a good card." I press card information on the vendor machine and inserted the card.

It read two dollars. Once the guy saw the card was good he brought it.

I go back over to my original spot. Standing by the steps I asks, "Do anybody need a metro card?" Another guy asks "How much you selling it for?" I say, "I have a four dollar metro card and a single ride." He asks "For how much?" I said "Two dollars and four dollars."

The guy said "I buy the four dollar card for three dollars." I said "Naw I bought the card early for four dollars. I want four dollars for the card. I'm trying to get me something to eat." So he brought the card for four dollars. I told him, "Thanks."

Standing by the vendor machine I saw two girls getting ready to purchase a metro card.

I went up to them and asked "Do anyone of you need to purchase a metro card?" The young ladies looked at me. One of them said, "I need a single ride." I said, "I have a single ride and it's good too." Quickly I press the card information on the vender machine and inserted the card. The vendor machine read two dollars. The dark skin girls hands me two dollars.

Now I had eight dollars in my pockets. As I walked home I bought a ninety nine cent bag of chips, a fifty cent bag of pretzel and an orange fifty cent, C and C soda.

Once I reached the shelter, security guard Monique is at the front door post. She see me and buzz me in. I put my belongings on the belt to be scan. As my belonging goes through the scanner, security guard Monique hand check my bags of snacks. After I proceed pass the magnetometer, she hand wands me.

Monique buzzes the second door for clearance into the shelter and announce on her' walkie- talkie, "Miss Jones coming in with snacks, copy." The guard on the first floor said "Copy." As I pass the intake office I seen shift supervisor Mrs. Wilkes sitting behind her desk talking on the office telephone. Receptionist Elaine looks my direction as she answer the office ringing telephone.

I proceed to the dining room cause I got to play it off being Security Monique announce I have a bag of snacks. I wanted to go to my dorm and get my yarn just in case if I get tired of writing I have something else to do. So I find myself a seat and open up the bag of chips and the soda.

Sunset come over and ask me, "Can I have some potatoes chips?" I say to her, "Open your hands." Cause I hate when people put their' hand inside my bag of chips. You never know where their' hands been if they clean or dirty. I starts to pour some chips into her hand.

Then Smith come over and ask me, "Can I have a little chips please." I say, "Smith open your hands and I pour some chips in her hands as well. I ask Smith, "What you going to do in the next ten minutes?" Smith say "Nothing," and she goes back to the table and sit down and starts to rock back and forth in her seat as she eats her chips.

I ask Smith, "Can you watch my stuff? I need to go to my dorm and get my yarn." She say "Go ahead I watch it." I arrange my soda and chip to hide underneath my stuff in my bag so that the guards think I already ate up all the snacks because no food is allowed upstairs in the dorms.

When I exit the stairwell on the fourth floor I see Security guard Marsha standing by the laundry room. I say to her," I just need to go to the dorm and pick something up." She give me a nod of approval to proceed pass her.

I see the maintenance workers Shack and Black on the floor cleaning dorms. When I open the Q dorm door I was shock seeing the Spanish girl buttoning up her bra getting ready to leave the dorm. She looked well rested. I ask her, "Are you sick?" She say, "No." I goes to my locker to unlock my combination lock and gets the yarn. Out of curiosity I just had to ask her because I don't think she employed. So I ask, "Do you have a bed pass?" She says, "No."

Wow I was stun to see she didn't have a bed pass. She don't work and it's almost twelve o clock and she still inside the dorm.

I went to the cafeteria to have lunch. The shelter served us those dry, cold sandwiches again. Security Guard Fancy enter the dining room and announce, "Art therapy is going on. On the fourth floor in the library ladies."

After I had eaten my lunch. I attended the class.

When I reached the fourth floor. I see Security Guard Watts was now on the fourth floor. She sitting on the chair by the Laundry room, talking on her' cell phone. This is my first art therapy class. When I walked inside the room, there on the table I saw some canvas, a stack of color papers and color pencils. Different color paint in plastic bottles and a container of paint brushes. There also were palettes for us residents to input the paint in. In front of each seat, was a foam cup half way filled with water, and newspapers that served as tablemats for the participating resident.

Samantha announce, "Please guys sign in and find a seat." Samantha had vanilla and chocolate crème cookies on the side table where the radio at. She also had a pot of coffee brewing and hot water for tea or hot chocolate. As girls came in, we all took a napkin and grab some cookies. Then found a seat. Then we went back and got our choice of beverage. While listening to the music from ninety-eight point seven kiss us girls talk quietly among ourselves as we drunk our beverage and ate our cookies.

Sam waited to see if anymore clients will come in. Then she went to the guard posted outside the door and said, "When I close the door no one else will be allowed to come inside the group." A few more ladies have entered inside the room.

Samantha turns down the radio and said, "I want yall to get a palette and choose your paint of colors or choose your color pencils. Then I'd like to know what type of material you want to put your painting on."

I decide to use the color pencils and I wanted the color paper-pale beige.

Sam said, "Choose the size of paint brush yall like to work with. Guys, do yall see the cup of water that's in front of you. It can be used to dab off the paint so that you can apply a different shade of paint. Please listen up, after you guys have dab your brushes in the cup of water yall can use the newspaper, it will help to wash off the paint from the brush so that you can apply a different color of paint. Another thing....... please listen up people. Please paint on top of the newspaper so that the table underneath don't get destroy."

After the girls got their' supplies, they sat and started to draw. Making the announcement Sam said, "Listen up guys. No one else will be allowed to come inside the room once I close the door. I think it wouldn't be fair for late comers to hold up our small group because I would like each of you to share your artwork with the group, but that's only if you like too."

Sam turned off the radio then she went to the guard as she nodded her head. Then she closed the door. Walking back to us from the closed door. Sam said "everyone is to be respected and everyone gets a chance to explain their' artwork. But most importantly, what is shared here, stay inside this room. I don't want the group gossiping what they heard to other residents outside this group because some artwork can be personal and, if they wanted to come they should be here. If I find out anyone has violated the rules of art therapy that individual would not be allowed to participate in future art therapy groups."

We girls had enough time to finish our artwork. Samantha asked, "Who is finish?" As she collects the finished pieces and tape them on a wall for all of us to view and see.

Samantha asks, "Who like to go first?" No one said anything. Then Samantha said, "I'll pick a picture." She pick the picture of colors. She asked, "Who made this beautiful portrait?" Jessica said, "It mine." "Tell us about your art work," Sam suggested.

Jessica said, "I'm not in a good mood. I feel depress because this is my first time living in a homeless shelter and I don't like it." Sam asked, "Is that why you didn't put your name on your picture?" Jessica said, "No, I just passed it in." Her painting contains color of purple, black and brown. It's intangible with no definition.

We all clapped, and Samantha said, "Thanks for sharing. Who next?"

I raise my hand. Sam asks, "Which picture is your Electra?" I said, "The one title 'So Full of Love.' I made a picture of a large heart that had an array of bright dotted colors. Some colors were dark but the painting contain mostly brighter colors. The large heart had a small crack going down toward the middle.

Sam said, "Tell us about your art work."

I said, "I drew a picture of a heart because I'm always a person who love to give and express joy. That why I have lots of colorful dots inside my heart because I have no discrimination." Sam asked, "Why is there a crocked small line towards the center?" I said, "Ooh…. The heart is strong and it's very giving but it also can be touch. The crocked line is when someone I loved very much had hurt me. The pain, it hurt me to my heart, and left a scar…. and that's all I have to say." Everyone clapped and Sam said, "Thanks for sharing."

Sam asked, "Who picture is this one?" Ellen said, "It mine picture." She drew a picture of a woman and a child. Sam asks, "Can you tell us about your artwork?" Ellen is a much older resident. She said, "It's a picture of my mother taking me to the park. When I was young my mother always took me to the park and pushed me in the swings. My mother has passed. I was thinking about her because today is her' birthday." Sam asked, "Do you remember how old you were in the picture?" Ellen said, "I was nine I tink." Ellen is

Caribbean. Sam said, "Thanks for sharing." We all clapped our hands.

The last picture was of a mother with four children. Bertha said, "It me and my four children going out on Mother Day. My children are in foster care and this is the day we all had on the same colors going to the movie on Mother Day." Sam asked, "What made your wear the same colors?" Bertha said, "I thought it would be a fun thing to do as a family, and we took a picture too on that day."

We all clapped and Sam said, "Thanks for sharing."

Samantha said, "If yall like I will make a folder for all of you. This way you would have all the pictures you made in the class. I'm look forward to seeing each and every one of you at the next art therapy group. Have a good day ladies. Art therapy is now over."

When four o'clock came we were allowed upstairs to the dorms. When I enter the dorm I put my painting on top of my locker, leaning it up against the wall. Next, I got my belonging to take a shower. When I came out from the bathroom I was taking back a little by my neighbor. All of a sudden, she had a red heart placed on top of her locker. "Wow," I said to myself.

I lay across my bed thinking about Thomas and me. So, on that note Reader: Let go *back into the story*.

Thomas had accumulated a name for his self in the construction business. All his' hard work has paid off. When he showed up on the sites, most bosses already knew him from seeing his face around. It became easier for him to find work. He's very good at what he does. Thomas could help build any building blindfold, after he had taken his' measurements.

One day Thomas came home saying "Tami, let's go shopping for the baby." After getting dress we all walked out the building together. Walking from the building entrance going towards the car. I saw Adrianne and Shelby standing outside in the front of the building with their' children. As we approach them closer. I said, "How you doing Shelby. Hi Adrianne."

Shelby turned around and say in her high pitch friendly voice, "Hi Tami, hi Thomas… Hiii! Champagne." My building consists of a lot of single women on welfare raising their' children. So when Thomas came home from work, he/we, really stood out. The block is small. All the mother brought their' children outside to play in front of the building as we stand or sat watching our kids run and play. All six of my two girlfriends' kids starting saying "Hi Tami…..hi Tami….Tami," those kids love me. Adrianne turns her head in our direction look at all of us and smiled.

As we pass them I heard in a low voice, Adrianne said, "Hello Thomas."

Thomas got into our car and unlocked it for me and Champagne to enter. I sat my daughter in the back seat and closed the door. "Tami you going food shopping?" Shelby asked. I said, "No. We going shopping for the baby." Shelby said, "That sound like fun, see you later." I got into the car and we drove off.

Thomas said "Tami lets drive to your' mother and drop Champagne off." "Okay we can try it and see what she say," I said. Thomas found a parking spot in front of my mother' building. As we walked into the apartment, I heard "Surprise!" Thomas was smiling and laughing at me as he was pulling my fat ass to the living room next to the kitchen.

When I got to the living room, all excited, I saw my cousins Sheryl and Lee Keisha. I saw my sister Tonya and they were taking pictures of me. My mother had rented a baby chair. I sat in the chair taking more pictures. Then Thomas and I sat in the chair taking pictures. Then they took a family picture of us; me, Thomas and Champagne; all together sitting in the rented baby chair.

Looking forward to the party (I'm thinking, let's get the party started) I looked around saying, "Where everybody at?" By now Thomas has left me with my family. They were busy setting up the table of ornaments so I asked again "Where my friends? Mom did you invite Fran and Patricia? Are they coming?"

I was looking forward to seeing them. Surely I thought they would have come, especially with me not seeing them in such a long time. Nobody saying anything.

I asked "What about Penelope or Sandra?" My mother said, "I don't know how to get in contact with those people from the Projects. I don't go over there no more." I said, "Well Tonya could have gotten in touch with them."

Tonya said, "I had Fran phone number but I lost it." I asked my sister, "Do Patricia still live in the Projects?" Tonya said, "Of course. Where do you think she going?" I asked, "She didn't want to come to my baby shower?" My sister said, "She went down south with her family."

"Well at least yall could have invited Shelby and the girls I hang out with in my new area," I pointed out. My mother said, "I don't have their' numbers." I said, "Thomas could have given it to you. I have their' telephone numbers in my address book."

Getting annoyed my mother said "Electra we just throw this together in a spare moment. I didn't think about invite those people. I don't want all those people in my apartment anyway." "Does my father and Melody know your was giving me this baby shower?" I question.

By this time, sadly, my aunt Lynette had passed away too. Just Lee Keisha and Coon is living upstairs in my grandparents' private home. So we sat at the table as I open up my gifts and they made me a baby hat to wear from my gifts wrapping paper. They staple several pieces of the gifts wrapping paper to a white paper plate. For the hat to stay on top of my head they took the gift decorated ribbons and staple it on both sides of the paper plate so that I can tie it underneath my neck.

It wasn't fun like I anticipated. I didn't have a good time, we talk about my life, like what's going on. Lee Keisha said,

"Electra I didn't think you would have any more children."
Mommy said, "Yeah it took you a long time to have another
baby." Sheryl asked me, "Where did you meet Thomas?"

I said, "At a Jamaican night club." Lee Keisha asked me,
"Do you know how to wan?" "Yeah," I said. Tonya ask, "Do
yall party a lot?" I said, "We used to but I don't go out with
Thomas like I used to. Thomas still goes out and party on
Saturday nights with his' friends. Those Caribbean people
love to dress up and party. They party all the time."

Tonya asked me, "Did you make that curry chicken yall
had for Thanksgiving? I said "No. Thomas did." Tonya said,
"Well I'm going to ask Thomas to tell me how he made that
curry chicken because that shit was slamming!"

I was disappointed I thought they could have thrown a
much better party than that. It was cheesy but I'm kind of
grateful cause that was the only baby shower I ever had.
Compare to the one my mother gave for Tonya-**she** had a
knock out one! A baby shower of all baby showers. I have
not seen anyone who had a baby shower like hers yet.
Tonya didn't have to buy not one thing way pass Hope-
turning 9 months old. Not even a box of pampers. She had
one hell of a fly baby shower.

When Thomas came back to pick me and Champagne
up he wonder why I wasn't overly enthusiastic. He just
loaded everything inside the car and when we got home
and he saw the gifts, he understood why.

P.S. Reader, they could have even invited some of
Thomas's people. Anyway back to the story.

Well I had a healthy baby boy. I named him Brandon
but we call him JB. Champagne would be starting school
soon. While Thomas was at work I went to Young World
and started laying away her' school clothes off my PA
allowances. As usual we had a barrel in the house. Thomas
started to stock up on school supplies and other things for
his' family back home.

When it got close to the time Thomas normally came home from work I went by the window to see if I see him coming in or if the car was park out in front of the building. I didn't see him or the car but I notice Adrianne standing outside. She standing on the side of the building by herself without her' children. At first I didn't pay any attention to it. So I went back to doing what it was I was doing, until Thomas he finally came home.

There's knocking sounds coming from our apartment door. "Who is it," I asked. "Adrianne," she said. I open up the door, "What's up Adrianne."

"Hi, Tami can you tell me how to cook that fish dinner yall had the other night," she asked. I said, "Oh, I didn't cook that meal. Thomas did. That was a Jamaican dish?"

"Can I ask him how to cook it and what ingredients should I buy?" Adrianne asked.

I didn't see anything wrong with that cause a lot of Americans don't know how to cook Caribbean dishes. So I said, "Come in."

When we got inside the living room I said, "Thomas Adrianne wanna know how to cook that fish you made for us on Sunday." Adrianne said, "Hi Thomas. I'm going to the fish market and I wanted to know how to prepare the dish you made the other night."

"It called stewfish," Thomas said. Adrianne said, "Stew... fish? Is there a certain type of fish I should buy or any fish can make stew... fish?" Thomas said "You need to buy red snapper, mon." ".... Red Snapper," she repeated.

Then she asked, "Is there a certain way I should have them clean the Red Snapper?" Thomas said "Mon tell them to clean the fish and have them to leave the head on. Go buy some lime, eehey, and scrub the fish. Wash it good with the lime. Put it in the pot with some seasoning, add some pimentos seed, tomatoes and butter. Then stew it down mon." Adrianne stood there for a moment as if she putting a list in her head of what all Thomas just said. Then she left out.

About a half an hour later she knocking back at the door.

I answered the door. Adrianne asked, "Can yall come upstairs to my apartment I like to know if I'm doing it right." So Thomas and I went upstairs to her' apartment. Adrianne stood next to the pot that's cooking on the stove in the kitchen. I stood at the entrance of the kitchen as Thomas walk next to Adrianne and the cooking pot. She open up the lid to the pot and look at Thomas waiting for his' approval.

You know when you cooking and when you remove the lid from the pot if it don't smell good, nine times out of ten it won't taste good. It didn't smell like a Caribbean dish. Thomas said "Add some ketchup mon." Adrianne started acting really dense saying, "This much Thomas?"

Thomas said "Pour it mon." Then Adrianne asked, "Is that enough or shall I pour more?" Thomas said "That's good. Let it cook."

Then she asked, "Is the fire underneath the pan to high?" Thomas said "Lower it and let it simmer." Then Adrianne started acting dense again "This much Thomas or this much."

Thomas looked at me shaking his head as Adrianne asked the stupidest questions, like is she really that slow. I watch him as he reach for the knob on the stove and put the fire under the pot to the right setting.

As I watched them, something inside of me said something else is going on here. Then I remember how lately I been seeing Adrianne outside around the same time Thomas come home. Then I said ......naw maybe I making too much of it. I watch them quietly though. Questioning myself have he been untrue?

As Thomas and I walk back downstairs to the apartment I felt a little complex.

After having the baby. Seeing Thomas leave out for work I started watching Body Electric. It a morning program that came on every day, during the week for exercising. I wanted to get back into shape so I started working out inside the house with body electric. I lost the baby fat in no time. Going shopping on Main Street I notice a brand new meat market in the neighborhood. So I, Shelby and Adrianne we started going to that meat market. The black guy in the butcher store wanted to get to know Adrianne.

I remember this guy, every time he saw either one of us meaning me or Shelby, he always wanted us to give Adrianne a message from him. He thought she was fine. I remember Shelby and me encouraging Adrianne to give him a chance but she wasn't interested. We even pointed out he has a job. Adrianne said, "He's too young for me."

To me, he seem descent and he was around our age. Adrianne just didn't find him interested and I remember me and Shelby use to always wonder, why?

Thomas surprised me and came home with a whirlpool washing machine. I was so happy I had my very own washing machine and it was so convenience with me having the baby and all. I was so thrill I brought a cover to go over it making sure it stays clean and scratch free.

Then again, I notice Adrianne waiting outside by herself around the time Thomas is supposedly be on his way coming home. So when Thomas came into the house. I ask, "Thomas did you see Adrianne outside before you came in?" He said "No mon," and went into the bathroom to take his shower.

When he came out from the shower I ask, "Is there something going on between you and Adrianne I should know about?" Thomas said "No mon."

Because of this *knobbing feeling* I was picking up on. I asked Thomas, "Do you think Adrianne is interested in you?" He said "No," and I let it go.

Champagne finally started public school. I'm so excited for her. I had started this homemade scrap book that I plan on giving to her for her eighteenth birthday. I had the scrap book made by a women who does arts and crafts. It's an album book, cover with lilac material that has lilac lace all around it; a lilac ribbon that ties it shut. In front of this scrap book sat a picture frame for me to insert a picture of her. In the scrap book I had a beautiful medium color picture of me and Tray. We were sitting in a park in Manhattan and someone had taken the picture for us.

Tray always had a sense of fashion. He just took me shopping and brought me some expensive maternity clothes. I just had to wear one of those outfits out from the store. It was a beautiful sky blue pant set. Then Tray surprised me with a beautiful blue and beige medium size Gucci tote bag and we took the picture. The picture was taken in the summertime. I had to be about five or six months pregnant.

Also in the scrap book I had a picture of her foot prints that the hospital gave me when she was born, a piece of her' baby hair and the favorite songs she sang as a toddler. In the area of written words, I inputted her favorite television program she enjoyed watching. Now, I took a Polaroid picture of her first day going off to school.

Just for the record I was starting one with Brandon too but so far I just have his foot prints from the hospital.

By this time Thomas had taken to Champagne as if she was his' biological daughter but I kept the picture of me and Tray. I sometimes showed the picture to my daughter saying, "This is your father." She was so young. Anyway I had kept the picture to show her the picture of her' biological father someday, like when she older and can understand.

After a while, thing became a little disturbing with Adrianne. My little family, we were in the living room listening to a reggae tape I made from off the radio as I braid my daughter hair. We heard knocking sounds coming from the apartment door.

Knock, knock, knock, I turn to Thomas who laying down on the couch in his normal house attire......his boxer. I asked, "Thomas can you answer the door."

Thomas got up from the couch all of a sudden I heard Adrianne voice. She's in the living room asking, "Tami can I borrow a cup of sugar?" I look up from braiding my daughter hair, turn my face in the direction I heard her' voice just to see Adrianne standing in the living room with nothing but a tee- shirt on and a pair of flip flops.

Shock at seeing her almost naked I said "**Adrianne!** What you doing coming downstairs dress like that?" Even my daughter was looking her up and down. I said, "Don't you think that kind of short walking out like that in the hallway."

She said, "I have on shorts underneath." So I called Thomas because my hands were greasy from the hair grease. Adrianne turned her head behind her to see if Thomas was coming, but Thomas was nowhere in sight and he never answered me or came back inside the living room. So I got up to go to the bathroom but the door was lock.

So I had to come back into the living room to wash my hands in the kitchen sink and I said to Adrianne, "Can you not come knocking on my door dress like that again." She said, "Tami, I have on clothes." "Yeah you do, but I appreciate if you won't knock on my door like that again, because this is where I live, it's not where you live. The way you dress right now is how you dress in the comfort of your own home."

I walks her to the door with her cup of sugar.

Finally Thomas came back inside the living room. I asked him, "Why did you stay inside the bathroom with the door locked?" He didn't say anything. So I asked, "Did you see how she came down here?" Thomas still didn't say not one word.

Thomas is never so quiet. Then I asked, "Did she make you nervous or uncomfortable is that why you lock yourself up in the bathroom?" Thomas still didn't say a word instead he just stretch himself back out on the couch and closed his eyes listening to the music.

We occasionally attend small dinner parties held by Rude Boy and his live in girlfriend Natalie. They recently purchase their new home in the Brownsville area. With Jamaican, I notice there' house party are a little different than Americans. Soon the people will start arriving. Then the men would go to the kitchen and the women would stay inside the dining room. Or the women had went into the kitchen and the men stayed inside the dining room.

Which at 1st I thought was okay in a sense because it gave me time to mingle with the women from Thomas country but after a while the Caribbean females would slowly separate themselves from me, leaving me sitting in the area alone.

At first I just thought the small crowd of females wonder off into another room of the house and I just wasn't keeping up with them. So I follow them into the next room and I found myself by myself again. Then I realized it was being done on purpose. We were invited to the house party by Rude Boy and, I saw Thomas nor Rude Boy said anything about the issue.

So while attending the party I went up to Thomas and told him what was happening. He seemed concern but he didn't say anything. I wanted him to at least speak to Natalie, asking her if there seem to be a problem. Like, why am I being alienated? Or, maybe I just misunderstood, but nothing was said about it and I didn't like how I was being treated so I asked Thomas to take me home.

Because of that I stop going with Thomas to their small intimate dinner parties.

While picking up my daughter from school, I meet and became friends to a woman name Donna. She a Caribbean women and a home owner. One day walking from our kids' school I found out she lives down the block from me with her husband Bunchy. She too was like Shelby and I. Started out with our families, having young children and supporting the men in our lives. I visit and hung out with Donna and her' family. We became good friends over the year just like Shelby and I.

Stop........To the reader: I just want you to know if Thomas would have asked me to marrying him I would had said yes.......but he didn't. Back to the story.

While Champagne was in school Thomas came home early with Conroy he was ready to ship the barrel to Jamaica but then he gave me a big surprise.

Thomas and Conroy started moving the washing machine. I said, "What are you doing?" "I'm taking the washing machine to Jamaica," he said. I screamed, "You're what!" Thomas said "Mon me shipping the washing machine to Jamaica, Tami me buy you another one."

Putting my body in front of the machine I said, "You're not taking this machine. I thought you brought the washing machine for us now you telling me you taking the machine, o hell no you not!" Thomas started giggling while looking at Conroy saying "Mon what wrong with this girl?" Then Thomas said "Tami stop it, mon, me going to buy you another one." While standing in front of the machine I said, "You just did buy me one and you're not taking it!"

Thomas said to Conroy "Mon help me put the washing machine on the dolly," and both men proceed to move the machine. I had on my light cheap house coat that I purchase from one of those discount store on Main Street and I push Thomas away from the machine saying, "You're not taking this goddamn machine!"

Thomas looked at me cause he never seen me act so angrily toward him. He said "Tami, mon, your day soon come." "I'm tired of hearing my day soon come from you. When is my day going to come **Thomas? When?!** I don't give a **fuck** what you saying. You not taking my machine," firmly I said as I stood in front of the washing machine.

When Conroy saw me behaving in such a way and seen that I was really upset. Conroy tried to convince Thomas "Man, leave the machine with Tami. Come on let ship off the barrel."

Thomas said "No sir, me taking the washing machine. Help me load the machine on the dolly. Conroy, me going to buy Tami another washing machine mon."

I started pushing and shoving Thomas saying, "Leave the machine get off of it." Thomas laughed as he moved the machine on the dolly while I was hitting him yelling "Get off the fuckin machine!"

There was a rumble tumble, five minutes it lasted. I looked at Thomas and yelled "You dirty bastard."

He and Conroy got the washing machine out the house and I yelled in the hallway while they were struggling trying to get the barrel and the washing machine down the step with the dolly, "No more barrels coming in this got dam house!"

On Saturday mornings I played a lot of music as I clean and cook inside the apartment. Thomas was lying down on the couch in his boxer enjoying the tapes I was playing. We were interrupted by someone knocking on the door.

I went to the door it was Adrianne, "Tami can I borrow two eggs." I said "Sure come in." When she came in my apartment Adrianne notice the washing machine was gone she asked, "Tami what happen to your washing machine?" I said "Please don't even asks."

When we reached the living room I went into the kitchen. I heard Adrianne said, "Hello," to Thomas but he didn't say a word back. When I came out of the kitchen and handed her the two eggs. Again, I heard her say, "Hello Thomas." I looked at Thomas as he laid on the couch. He said nothing. I'm about to walk Adrianne to the door but it seemed Adrianne got stubborn, like she wanted Thomas to answer her. So, she said again but harshly, "Hello Thomas."

Quietly I question and I looked at Thomas to see *why he didn't speak back* but finally he said "Hello." I said "Come on Adrianne, let me walk you to the door because as you can see I'm busy right now."

One day, I went to visit Donna, (my Caribbean girlfriend) and she was downstairs working in her and her' husband small grocery store. I said, "You know what Donna, there's this girl who lives in my building and I'm having these feelings like something going on between her and Thomas."

Donna said in her St. Vincent accent, "Tami, once you have them feeling you can't tell me something not going on. Tami there got to be something going on or you wouldn't have those feeling Tami."

I said, "Donna, I could be a little paranoid." Donna said, "Noo Tami, these West Indian men can't fool me. I know them and they are no damn good." ....I heard what Donna said but I wanted to be sure and not go on gossip because this is my relationship I'm talking about. We said our goodbyes and I went home.

As usual, Thomas left and came home, and again, I notice Adrianne outside. She sure be outside a lot when Thomas coming home. So this time when Thomas came inside the house after taking a shower he went into the bedroom.

Our small bedroom is packed. Thomas and I still slept on the brass bed I supposedly had brought for Champagne. Inside the bedroom now, was my son crib, and Champagne still slept on her converted crib/captain bed.

As Thomas laid on the bed, standing by our bedroom door I said, "Thomas, I can't help but feel something going on between you and Adrianne." Thomas didn't say anything.

I said to Thomas, "I'm going to bring her down here and get to the bottom of this." Thomas said "Tami don't do that you only going to embarrass yourself."

"Embarrass myself? Now I'm really going to go get her," I told Thomas.

I knock on Adrianne door, "Who's there," she asked. "Tami," I said. She open the door and I said, "Can you come downstairs for a moment?" She said, "I'll be right down."

When I got back inside the house Thomas was still laying inside the bedroom in his normal attire, his red nylon boxer while his legs cross at the foot and his hand to his nostril.

Adrianne knocks at the door, I open it and said, "Come in," and I close the apt door.

Adrianne and I was standing together by the apartment' door and, at the entrance door to my and Thomas bedroom. We both can clearly see Thomas who was laying on the bed.

I said, "Adrianne. Lately I been feeling a little disturb about something." Adrianne looked at me densely. She wondering where this conversation going. She could clearly see Thomas laying on the bed in the bedroom.

I said, "Lately I feel there is something going on between you and Thomas. Is there anything going on that I should know?" Adrianne looked at Thomas who laying there as I described earlier not saying a word.

She said, "Going on, what do you mean?" She started acting densely again. I see this approach wasn't getting anywhere. So I asked her, "Do you find Thomas attractive, Adrianne?" She said, "Attractive like, Attractive! Or do you mean is he an attractive man?" Her word stumble then she said, "I see Thomas as a father figure."

I see I'm still not getting anywhere. So I asked, "Thomas. Do you find Adrianne attractive?" Now that's when it got quiet and now I believe I'm getting somewhere. Adrianne, she was actually waiting to hear what his' answer was to the question. Thomas just didn't say one word.................I repeated, "Thomas do you fine Adrianne attractive?"

This woman actually stood still wanting to hear his' answer until I saw the tears swelling up in her eyes. At this point Thomas was still quiet, then he closed his eyes. He laid on the bed, the same way like I described earlier, and like he said....he did embarrass me.

So I turn to Adrianne who seem like she wanted to cry and I said, "Do not ever knock on my door again. I want you to get out of my apartment **now**." I open up my door for her to leave. **Shocked**...seeing that some of the people who lived in my building was eavesdropping on our conversation.

I had open up the door so quickly they didn't have a chance to run away from my door. By now Adrianne had tears rolling down her face. She quietly looking at Thomas, and I guess still waiting to hear an answer to the question I asked Thomas.

I yelled at her, "**Get out!**"

I was so upset. I was piss the **fuckoff!** Thomas still lying in the bed with his legs cross and his' eyes shut. I started yelling at Thomas saying, "**I fuckin dare you**." I wanted to continue but I stop when I noticed Adrianne was still standing there like she didn't know what to do or, was she still waiting to hear the answer to my question of, "Thomas do you find her Attractive!

I yelled at Adrianne saying "Get the hell out I said!" Adrianne left.

The people who was eavesdropping left too as I began cursing the shit out of Thomas but one guy he'd stayed behind trying to talk to Thomas saying "Yo man you should have answer Tami."

I wanted to kick Thomas out right then and there but I thought he would run upstairs to live with her and I couldn't take that type of humiliation. **Oh gosh!** I just had his' baby for Christ sake! So instead I went inside the kitchen got a knife and ripped up **all this partying outfits** until he got dressed and he stop me from ripping his' clothes.

Now he wanted to talk to me and say something he thought I wanted to hear. **Too late** he should had man up in front of me and her and those people that were listening to our door. Setting the record straight proving it's me he love. It's my feelings he cares more about. For goodness sake I thought she was my friend. I just had his child. I slap Thomas **so hard in his face**.

Stop! To the reader: To me Thomas did embarrass me because when I ask the question, I wanted to hear him say "No Tami she not attractive in my eyes, I love you." Or he could have said "Yeah she attractive but not as attractive as you." **Anything** giving me the upper hand on the bitch but he couldn't please me in front of her cause it would had hurt Adrianne feeling? So he choose to not say anything and hurt mine. Well it put a melancholy in our relationship.

I really wanted Thomas to leave but I had my children to think about. I had such a hard time with one child now I have two. So I chump it in but I never forgot it.

The next day I goes to Shelby and Shelby tells me, "Tami, Adrianne was down here crying so hard talking about you and Thomas. That snots was running out from her nose as she cried. She was crying so hard. I and Wilbert didn't know what to do for her."

I didn't want to hear that bullshit because inside I was hurting but I just wasn't crying.

Then after a while Adrianne started dating the guy from the meat market, the butcher. I could tell he was wondering why I wasn't or wouldn't speak or even acknowledge Adrianne. I know he had to figure something bad had to have happened.

By now Thomas became the man to know in the construction business. He was working steady on a major construction sites and he finally gotten himself into the union, getting paid forty-two dollars an hour. No more riding the bus with the collision. Wow I was happy for Thomas, for us. Now I wanting Thomas to do more for us and for himself too for that matter, because everything he had was going to Jamaica.

I remember me wanting to move from the building. Wanting Thomas to buy us a house so the kids could have a backyard to run out and play in. I was thinking in this way; we would have become a real family turning our house into a home.

Not only did Thomas have his union day job. He had acquire jobs on the side too. Thomas started lucking out with job proposal and contacts whereas he was put in charge. Thomas had the privilege of hiring the men he wanted to work with on his team in order to help complete the job. The white man had paid Thomas an enormous amount of money to get the job done and at the end of the contact Thomas paid his' workers. He had his full time union job in the daytime. He came home, shower, ate, rush right back out to the next job that started in the evening.

Sometimes he didn't have time to shower. He would grab a machinery or tool that he needed and be gone. Not to mention he worked on Saturdays too wanting to complete the contract. So that the bosses would be well please with him therefore they would keep giving him work.

That Christmas holiday, Thomas went back to Jamaica again. He knew he was still in the dog house with me so he left me his mailbox key, asking me to drive and pickup his mail from the post office. I did and for the first time I started snooping into his' personal business.

When I came across a letter address Mr. and Mrs. Thomas Benton? I read the letter address again....to Mr. and Mrs. Thomas Benton. I open the letter.

"WHAATT!!!!!!!"

Just to find out Thomas was married to the lady who was banging on the pots and pans in the kitchen when I first meet him. Oh my, he's married!

He's married.......but it didn't add up?

I was at his' apartment with him occasionally before he had moved out coming into my apartment. Thomas goes out on Saturday........but every night he's here. Not one night Thomas stayed out all night since him and I been together.

The question played over and over inside my head, is he really married? I wanted answer but he's in Jamaica and he didn't even leave me a contact number. **Dam**! I got to wait till he come back.

In the mean time I had gotten a new neighbor. She lives directly across from me. Tina, she older, single with a couple of teenage school kids. She drives a yellow cab and her snort cocaine by the pound. Tina has an expensive coke habit.

After finding out this new information about Thomas. The disappointment with Adrianne. The constant going back and forward and shipping everything except the kitchen sink to Jamaica. I'm still on welfare. I'm still struggling. Now with a second child. Unmarried! I was getting feed up with Thomas. Kind of getting feed up with everything.

I knocked on Tina door just to hang out. Tina started telling me as she sat in front of her cocaine snorting up, "Tami you are such a beautiful women." Then she started snorting up again as she said, "Thomas should be buying you pearls. Girl, you should have a ring on your finger. You're not only beautiful, you smart."

I'm just looking at her as she takes another long hit of the cocaine.

She continue, "You faithful, you in that house day in and out making a home for a man who should be giving you the world. Your kids are gorgeous." Now she snorting again, then she finally said, "I wouldn't allow my daughter to settle for that kind of treatment," as she lean back on the couch.

Now she sitting up separating the cocaine with a blade. Now she snorting again.

I didn't say one word I just listen as I watch her snort because I was feeling kind of bad anyway. As I sat there listening, I'm watching her kids raid the kitchen cabinets bringing down boxes of various oddle of noodle soup. I guess the soup is their' dinner because I didn't see or smell any other kind of food on the stove.

Finally, she leaning her back up against the couch like she satisfied from her get high as her breath. Tina said, "Thomas make good money. He out every day working. Make that man do right by you."

Tina was just talking about Thomas and me, going on and on and on and on. I was just thinking, he's married, as she spoke. He's married! I didn't even tell Shelby. I definitely didn't tell Donna. I didn't say anything to nobody. I was just waiting for Thomas to bring his ass home.

Tina said, "You can't tell me he's not making good money Tami and he's way older then you too. You are young.......no Thomas will be doing me right. He be driving me in a Benz, shit."

I don't know who older Tina or Thomas anyway I said, "Tina let me get a ..." Tina shouted "Maymay make Tami a pack of oddle of noodle," as she started snorting the cocaine and continual talking about Thomas.

A shouting voice came out from the kitchen. Maymay asked, "Tami what favor do you want? Beef, chicken, spicy or seafood?"

Tina is so high. I said, "Noo, Tina let me get a hit." "A hint of what?" Tina asked. All of a sudden rapid knocking sounds had suddenly come upon her' apartment door. Knock Knock, knock knock knock knock knock knock knock ... Tina shouted as she took another hit, "Will somebody get the door!"

As Maymay ran and went towards the knocking door. Tina said to her, as she pass us in the living room, "Don't open that door while I got my shit on the table."

Maymay just stopped in her tracks and proceeded slowly towards the door, like she was paranoid and asked "who is it." "**Swiss**," a man voice said from behind the door.

Standing at the door, Maymay turns her head in our direction and said to Tina, "Its Swiss." "What **the fuck** you telling me for? Open the door," Tina said as she took another hit of the cocaine as Swiss came through the door. He's greeting the kids.

I had to yell because she so dam high. I said, "Tina!

"What!" she said.

I said, "Let me get a hit of the cocaine."

Stun at my request. Tina said ...."This is an expensive habit. You can't start something you can't support because you not going to be snorting up my shit for free." Swiss walked in the living room towards us lightening up a cigarette.

Tina said, "Swiss this is my neighbor Tami, and Tami this is my cousin Swiss."

Standing up while staring at me, he said "Nice meeting you." I said, "Like wise." When he sat down on the couch ready to engage in a conversation with Tina. I asked, "Swiss, can you spare a cigarette?" "Sure," he said as he lifted a cigarette half way out of the box while pointing the box of Newport in my direction.

While they talk and snort. I started making myself a stogy I rubbed out some of the tobacco from the cigarette. Inputted some of the powder cocaine then rubbed the cigarette mixing up the tobacco with the cocaine and I twist the end of the cigarette. Swiss held a lighter in front of me, for me to light it up.

As I sat there inhaling Tina said, "Hey take an easy, that some good shit."

The following day I went to the store and brought a box of Newport. It had always been my choice of cigarettes anyway. I haven't done any drugs or purchase a box of cigarettes since I became pregnant with Champagne but I'm getting bored now and a little disappointed in how my life is going. So later on that evening when Tina came in from work I made another cocaine cigarette.

When Thomas came back from Jamaica he was shock to see me smoking a cigarette.

He said "Tami what's that?" I said, "A cigarette." Thomas said "Only a man smokes cigarettes."

Thomas have such a caveman mentality, me man you women. Man do this, women do that.

"Please, I'm an American and women in this country do smoke cigarettes," I told him. I gave Thomas his' mail and his' mailbox key. I asked Thomas, "Are you married?" Thomas told me "It business." I asked "Thomas are you married yes or no to that woman?" Thomas said "Yes and no."

He said "I only married her to become a citizen." Then he went into a story about some of his paper getting lost. I said, "No matter what I had a right to know. You should had told me instead of me finding out this way."

Security Mac. Dan enter the dorm announced, "Bed check." After I signed for my bed. I laid down looking up at the ceiling inside the shelter. "You know what? I speak to yall tomorrow.

Goodnight."

Chapter Twelve

Yawwwwn! As I gave myself a nice arm stretch. I open my eyes to a bright room. Wow, I musta over slept, as I turn my head looking at the nearest person next to me. Looking at her, I'm thinking, that my neighbor she is as weird as weird can be. She laying perfectly still in her bed on her back with her face facing the ceiling; wearing a long dark skirt and dark tights. Her legs are crossed at the ankle and upon her face are those cheap black dark sun shades.

Next I looked at the red heart that she has now placed on top of her' locker. Then I look at the picture of the heart I drew, which I had a heart on my locker first. Now I'm turning to look at the clock which is hanging on the wall. The time now is eight clock. Wow, I had really over slept. I missed breakfast and all.

That one thing I like about Bridge Net, every dorm has a clock inside their room. Have you ever noticed a lot of homeless' people don't wear watches? There so much a homeless' person got to do when they get their' money, and the last thing on their mind is buying their self a watch. Even if a homeless person thinks about wanting to buy a watch, their own money always goes towards something else.

As I lay on my bed, while looking at all my roommates. I see the majority of the women are up and moving about. They getting their self-prepared to leave the dorm. Security Guard Marsha open up the dorm door. Holding it slightly ajar as she announce, "Ladies it soon be nine, you must leave and exit the dorm," as she removes her hand, allowing the door to slowly close.

Marsha the security guard is Dominican, I think. She doesn't look Puerto Rican. I see Country has lost her bed because it stripped from all of its linen, just the plain green plastic mattress is showing. I betcha she lost her' bed because of a guy. Lots of the ladies here, leave the shelter to live with their boyfriend, just to come back to the shelter system a couple of months later in need of a bed. Looking for a place to stay. When females do that, it set them back in line for their housing. Causing them to stay in the shelter system even longer.

You have to be in the shelter system at least a good nine months consecutively before your caseworker can submit your housing package.

Too many times here inside a shelter, I heard females say this, "I'm in a serious relationship with someone and he has his own apartment."

Personally I feel like this, if you're in a relationship and you're telling everybody he's your boyfriend or saying, "That's my man." My question is, if the relationship was so serious, why are you living here inside of a shelter? Lots of females that are in this kind of relationship, and who too, lives inside a shelter, when asked-that question they always say, "Because I just want my own place."

To me, you not in a serious relationship, you just in a booty call relationship, not a committed relationship. So to me, the female should be saying when she bragging, "I been with this same guy for years and he have his' own apt" and then we all know what that means.

I get up with my towel, soap and toothbrush and stand by the bathroom door. This is how roommates know you're next in line to use the rest room. I prefer taking my shower at night but sometimes a resident just can't for one reason or another. Then, while being homeless, you would have days like today, sometimes you would wake up late and you didn't take a shower the night before, therefore a resident got to wait in line to bathe.

When I first enter a women shelter, I was really surprised to see how shelter women had such good hygiene. They are really very clean. First time for me entering a women shelter-I was thinking all kinds of shits and one of them was the women would not have such a good hygiene but I was so wrong. Some of them take a shower at night and then another one in the morning. I used to be like that too, when I had lived at Sixty Eight Lexington. For years, I took two showers, but now I only shower before I go to bed.

When I came out from the bathroom Security Guard Marsha came back into the dorm. This time she walks down the middle of the dorm, slowly with both hands behind her back, as if she is inspector gadget who checking each bed area. She walks till she had reached the end of the dorm and with a pivot turn, she turns around walking back towards the dorm door. Just before her exit she says, "Ladies you've got to be out by nine am."

Thru our crack room door, I could hear the sounds of many voices from other residents who are in the hallway as they are talking and moving about. The Spanish girl in bed six is the only one in our dorm still asleep in her bed. I started making up my bed. Beside the shelter girls having good hygiene everyone makes their' bed up.

When I lived at Sixty-Eight Lexington (the dirty shelter) I always made my bed when others didn't. At 68 Lex, after a really busy day I came into that dirty shelter, shower downstairs and jump into a clean made up flatbed every night. One of the main reasons was, I didn't want mice jumping on my sheets and climbing into my bed. Back then, that was what was happening to the girls at Sixty Eight Lexington.

In order to help keep the mice from coming into my area. Every time I came in I swept my area with some soap dampen paper towels that I got out from the bathroom because there wasn't any mops or brooms around. Then I pick up the garbage and the dusks with two sheets of paper. Back then there were a few females who made up their' beds, but not many like nowadays. Not trying to pat myself on the back, but I do believe by me cleaning and making up my bed other residents followed seeing my method works because no one wanted the mice jumping in their bed. So in other words I'm the one who help started the trend with residents making up their beds every morning.

Sixty-Eight Lex, their maintenances weren't cleaning like how the maintenances are now cleaning up in shelters. As a matter of fact, back then, the city maintenances was two or three guys, taking care of this enormous shelter that was completely filthy. Back then anything and everything got overlooked meaning what dorm got clean and what area got mop and swept. The workers used to make all kind of reasons why they didn't clean. For example I heard "They in there having sex or the big lady she butts as naked and I'm not going in there!"

Also back then they seemed to have limited cleaning supplies as if the city didn't care how people lived inside the shelter. Residents didn't have to leave the dorm on time like the way they do now! It was terrible. That why back then people chose to sleep in the streets. Remember back in those days we saw way more homeless people sleeping on the train and on park benches. Well it was way safer doing that then sleeping inside the shelter. The shelter system was totally off the hook now it just slightly unorganized to a certain degree. I'm speaking from a women point of view who has lived inside women' shelters. All I can say now, is the shelter system has improved and came a very long way.

Anyway back then, at 68 Lex, the females that slept in my dorm and the ones who slept on the drill floor started noticing how exceptionally neat my area/bed looked. It was all due to me making up my bed and tucking my sheets underneath Sixty Eight Lex, cheap ass flat mattress. Not to mention keeping underneath my bed, NOTHING! And every day of every night when I came back for bed check, removing all dirt and garbage away from my area that the big dirty dusty industrial fan may have blown my way.

Now a days majority of female like to put a stuff animal on their pillow after they had made up their' bed. Or the stuff animal sit up on the bed in front of their' pillow. Depending on the shelter, few women liked to buy their' own personal bed sheets and blanket to make their' area look like their own. Some females had made crochet blankets that they had hand made themselves from yarn. Which I had done too. I have seen residents' beds-blankets, crochet-with the Granny stitch, single stitch, double stitch and the triple stitch technique styles of crocheting. Some residents crochet their bed blankets made from tiny colorful crochet squares. I had even seen a blanket which was sewn together from assorted squared fabric.

When I was living at Sixty-Eight Lexington, a Japanese girl named Sue, had hand sewed me a tote bag from plain fabric. She told me that I didn't look like the type of person that should be walking around with plastic bags. Therefore, she cut out two large squares of fabrics from these large rolls of fabrics that was donated to that shelter. Then she hands sewed the two pieces of fabric together with a needle and thread and, Sue even put on shoulder straps. Well let me tell you, that was a strong bag too. I used to put any and everything inside it as I walked all around in Manhattan. It sure was a durable bag and it was machine washable too. I loved it. Not to mention she and I did become very, very good friends to each other.

The bed sheets that the many shelter's use are like the hospital white sheets and blankets. Over the years, the shelter has changed their' bed sheets color to light beige. I even been to a shelter that had quilts for their' blankets. Moving, living from shelter to shelter I even seen various type of wool blankets. Like the ones they have in jail-unfortunately and sadly, but briefly-I had lived there too.

The only ladies that doesn't make their' beds nowadays, are the one who are nasty, mentally sick or mad young minded immature females. And they are easy to spot.

When you open up a dorm room door their complete area just looks dirty, wrinkle with just sheets thrown -balled up together on top of a plastic green mattress. Let me tell you too, it makes the whole room remind all of us where we are at...the city shelter!

"Exit the dorm ladies it nine o'clock," Security Guard Marsha said. Man time flies doesn't it. Now, what I'm about to speak on, is the side of the shelter I never knew existed, until I became unemployed.

Favoritism!

Now everybody in the Q dorm is leaving to go out except for Q six. I noticed she was still in her bed sleeping and Marsha the guard didn't even tap on her locker or try to wake her up. I said to myself "Um, now that's not fair." Why we all got to leave and she still sleeping in her bed? I don't even see a bed pass tape on her locker and I know she doesn't work.

Come to think of it, she was in the dorm yesterday too because I saw her. I see it like this, we are all residents and clients of department of homeless services (DHS). If one rule applies to me, it applies to you too. If I got to follow the rules, you do too; regardless of your race, color, gender, sex preference, age and personality. If security makes me leave the dorm every got dam day at nine o clock and a lot of days, I be tired and don't want to get up so earlier either. What make you think you so special?

When any security guard seen me still asleep in my bed and the time is around eight thirty, security would be tapping on my locker while saying, "Miss Jones, nine o'clock, you got to leave the dorm." Sounds of tap, tap and tap be coming off from my metal locker and the persistence guard standing over my bed will be saying, "Miss Jones...tap, tap and tap. "Miss Jones, tap, tap and tap-wake up........wake up Miss Jones."

One day when I refused to get up out from my bed pretending I was still asleep because I'm tired of getting up early everyday just to go nowhere. After the security guard repeatedly tapping on my locker and calling my name wanting me to get up so that I can be able to leave the dorm on time. When I didn't obey, you know, that security guard radio the Shift Supervisor on me. The guard actually stood over me waiting until Shift Supervisor Mrs. stink ass Vanessa Wilks, and the head Supervisor for Security, Miss Peterson came to my dorm shaking me and making me get out of the bed. When I finally opened up my eyes, Mrs. Wilks said, all nasty and mean, "Give her an infraction. I don't have time to be coming up here, getting grown women out of the bed. She knows what time she supposed to be out of the dorm."

I wasn't allowed to go on any trips, use the shelter computers, get late or weekend passes, all my privileges was revolt. Even though I don't use passes it's just the principal I'm pointing out here. One time, I pretended to be sick trying to get a little extra sleep. When the guard Fancy came to my bed. I said, "I'm not feeling well." Fancy radio Shift Supervisor and said, "Electra, in the Q dorm is still in bed. She said she not feeling well, copy" Shift Supervisor Wilks, responded back by saying, "If she doesn't need EMS have her get out of bed and see medical to get a bed pass. Copy" The guard said, "Copy."

Being forced to get out from the bed I went downstairs to the medical office. After waiting in line because so many girls were using the same excuse. The doctor only issue my bed pass till twelve in the afternoon. Don't you know security came into my dorm and made sure I was up and out of the dorm exactly at twelve's clock.

Security Guard Marsha came back inside the room pokes her head in the dorm and said, "Ladies you must leave the dorm. It's after nine." As I walked over to Security Guard Marsha, I ask, "Why is she still in the bed? I don't see a bed pass on her locker and she doesn't work."

Marsha said, "Oh! Is there somebody in that bed? I thought it was a bunch of blankets."

I'm thinking to myself yeah right.

Marsha walk over to the sleeping girl area and tap taps on the Spanish girl metal locker saying, "Hello ... hello. Hello do you have a bed pass?"

The Spanish girl jumps out from a deep sleep rubbing her eyes saying, "Que?" Which means "what?"

Her voice is now in a little more authority. Marsha asks sternly, "Do you have a bed pass?" The Spanish girl say, "No."

She couldn't lie because Marsha would have to ask, can she see it.

The guard said, "You have to leave the dorm. It's nine o'clock." The Spanish girl look around the dorm and see me in the dorm looking their way so she starts speaking in Spanish. Now both her and the guard holding a conversation in Spanish. I know she speak English cause I spoke to her yesterday and she understood everything I said. The only reason she speaking in Spanish is because she doesn't want me to hear what she saying; neither one of them for that matter. I notice when the Spanish girls don't want Americans to know what they're talking about-they speak in Spanish.

Have you ever tried to join in a conversation with Spanish people, by speaking Spanish along with them? And when you do, now they don't understand what you're saying in Spanish so they talk back to you in English. In other words, they don't want you to speak Spanish with them and why do you think that is? I tell you why, because they want to talk about you or to keep you from knowing what they talking about.

I walk out the room.

When I get to the dining room it was packed. So I exit the building and goes to the library to continue with my writing. When I get to the library I see quite a few of the girls from the shelter sitting in there reading a book, just to pass away the time. By the way, lots of homeless girl and guys' hangout in the library for extensive amount of time reading a book or holding a book pretending they reading.

I found a seat and start to write. *Back to the story.*

Thomas didn't like me smoking the cigarettes. He didn't know anything about me taking cocaine, when he was in Jamaica. I only smoked one cocaine cigarette two times with Tina.

Why did I do it?

Well I could have said cause there wasn't anyone I really felt that close to, to share my most intimate and personal secrets with. Or I could say I was so upset with Thomas, and overwhelm with his shit, that it started to blow my mind and stress me **the fuck out**. Maybe I could say I was having problems and I knew I wasn't being treated right by him including with my own family. Or maybe what I just found out (him being married) was the icing on the cake. Maybe I did the drugs because I didn't want to feel or think. I wanted to take a break from what was going on around me, like what I was feeling and thinking. For a brief moment I wanted to become numb just take a stop in time because all these thoughts with emotions and feelings are racing through my brain. I just wanted everything to stop. Thinking the drugs could help me not think about ANYTHING.

Anyway, it wasn't a cool thing to do because drugs alter your thinking and do damage your body. But I wasn't thinking about that. I wish back then they had commercials on TV saying don't do drug when you are face with a dilemma. Instead call the help save your life hotline number at 1800, etc, etc I forget the rest of the numbers, but back then-we didn't have all that good stuff, like, knowledge-what you kids have at your fingertips today. Plus when the high is over you still have the same problem. I went through a phrase and thank God eventually I did stop smoking cigarettes but yall will find out that it was at a hefty price.

Anyway I began getting restless staying in the house. Thomas told me he had to be married to that woman for a couple of years before he could divorce her. I was going to make sure I see the divorce papers.

Early in the morning, one day while having sex with Thomas, he did something he never done before. He wanted me to urinate while is penis was still inside of me. "Pee Tami, pee," he insisted.

It was so weird I thought, "Pee in my bed. On the sheets, what?"

"Pee Tami," he said as he laid on top of me while his penis was inside of me. I was thinking uugh! On top of the mattress? What kind of shit is this? But he wouldn't let up "Pee Tami, pee," as if my peeing would set him free.

I don't know but is this what people call kinky sex?

"Peeee!" He was so driven. So I peed. I remember how the warm pee felt as it went on top of the mattress and under my butt on the sheet. Thomas seemed relieved. But for me, it was a real turn Off.

The strange part of the whole thing was when Thomas was asking me to pee, he felt and sound like a pedophile. Just so you know, let's clear up the air. I wasn't high or hallucinating. The whole experience made me feel like he was talking to a child.

I don't know why I felt this way and I never thought of the word pedophile before but the touch of his hand, his voice... uugh! It made me think of a child molester? It was a complete turn off and it never happen again. This too was something I forgot about until I started writing.

After some time has passed since Thomas came back from Jamaica while I was shopping in the neighborhood I came across a sign that read sell Avon.

I went inside and came outside as an Avon representative.

When Thomas came in from work I was all excited. I said, "Guess what Thomas?" He asked "What is it Tami?" I blunted out, "I got a job!"

It was more like he asked a question when he said "Eehey?"

"Yep. I'm going to sell Avon and I'm going to start right now, by getting some orders from the people in the building. Watch the kids," I said.

I knocked on Shelby door.

"Who is it?" Wilbert asked. I said, "It's your Avon representative."

"Your, who?" Wilbert asked. I repeated, "Your Avon representative. Would you like to buy any Avon?" Wilbert creep open the door "Tami, that's you?"

"No, I'm you're Avon representative. Would you like to buy any Avon?" I asked.

Wilbert giggled as he turned his head from me calling his wife. He said loudly "Shelby, Tami here and she's selling Avon." Shelby came to the door and asked, "She doing what?" Wilbert hands her the door while giggling.

I said, "Hello. I'm your Avon representative for this area. Would you like to purchase any Avon?" Shelby said, "Sure I'll buy some Avon." I hands her a book and say, "Circle the items you want. I pick up your order next week."

Smiling I said to Shelby, "I like it. That sound like a good sales pitch. Hello. I'm your Avon representative for this area. Would you like buying some Avon?"

Shelby said, "You got me with it." I said, "So that it. I use that line to get myself inside stranger' home. Allowing them the opportunity to buy my Avon soooo I see you later because I got work to do.

I walked in my neighborhood while knocking on strangers doors using that line in order to get customers to buy Avon from me.

That's when I met AP and JP (the Gillmore family). AP she too were like Shelby, Donna and myself starting out with her' family. Raising small kids and help supporting the man in her life. I became good friends with the Gillmore family. Now I had another girlfriend to hang out with. AP she too is a Black American woman. She and I, we became buddies instantaneously.

Next to my mother, Shelby, Donna and AP they became my biggest supporters in helping me achieve my goals in selling Avon products. Then I had a fantastic idea. I'm going to go to Westbrook Projects to my old building to sell some Avon there!

This time when Thomas came home I left the kids with him and I went to work. I did well too. I didn't realize how much people enjoyed buying this kind of merchandise and the Avon-custom jewelry. The older ladies was loving this stuff. Everybody had their favorite and me too. I purchase all sorts of stuff for my kids. After a while it got hard because the orders had really picked up. I found myself walking back and forward just picking up promised money and customers' orders and then, dropping off their' orders.

I needed a car but I didn't have my driving license so I eventually had to stop and put it on pause. Tomas told me how to obtain my driving license. So I went downtown to the DMV to pick up my driver manual book. While I had stood in line, on the opposite side, I heard a guy say "Bambi?"

Wow it was Dove. I hadn't seen him in years. He too was in line but he got finish before I did. When I glance in his direction I saw him waiting for me. We walked out the building together and outside we talked briefly. He seemed like he still cared for me. He was complaining about his' daughter mother being such a bitch.

I said, "So you have two kids now?" Then I asked, "By the same woman?"

Dove replied "No. My daughter is by this Spanish **bitch!**" Then suddenly this picture came to my mind.......I remembered a long time ago, one day, when I was going to my father apartment which was across Eastern Parkway. I had bump into Dove and he was hugged up with his arm around this Spanish chick. But as we spoke briefly outside by the DMV I recalled being a little standoffish towards him that day. Anyway we went our separate ways.

One night after I put my kids to sleep I figure not too many people would be out driving late in the night so that when I took our car out, practicing-learning how to drive and imitating how Thomas drove. I was learning how to make turns. How to stop at a red light and how to park a car. When I took my road test for my driver license I passed and that how I obtain my driver license.

Then one day I met this lady who lived in New Jersey. How we met I forgot but she introduce me to Cameo lingerie LTD. It was just like selling Avon by me going to people' houses, but with a little twist-because now, I'm privately giving fashion shows for lingerie.

To become a representative for Cameo Lingerie LTD for starter, I had to purchase a kit which consisted of lingerie pieces, an ensemble metal rack that came with it on carrying canvas bag, Cameo lingerie LTD ordering books, Cameo lingerie LTD customer receipt ordering forms and an appointment book for booking lingerie parties. I'm not talking about sleazy lingerie either. Cameo sold elegant lounge wear, tasteful teddies, satin beautiful robes and an array of adults' pajamas. The lingerie was absolutely gorgeous. Then they had their pieces for getting your man in the mood as well.

To make my parties a success I always purchase cool adult games, selected nice give away and bought some of my homemade music tapes to rally up the crowd.

My first lingerie party was held in my apartment. My models were Shelby, and AP. I had them coming out from my bedroom into the living room like run way models as I introduce the piece of lingerie they were wearing to my guest as the music played in the background.

To keep the crowd interested I cook and served sumptuous finger food. I had Thomas drive and pick me up some beverages from the beer warehouse. By the company (Cameo) I was taught how to play games while hosting a partying, how to enhance my sales as well as how to book more parties. I bought really cool prizes for the Hostess and the customers who won the games. I wanted to incorporate bringing in Avon along to the party but my hands were already full.

From my own lingerie party I booked two or three more parties and that how I got started. Driving from one house to the next giving these fabulous lingerie parties. Whoever hosted a party was responsible for having their own models, food and drinks. My responsibility was bringing the sample lingerie, for the models to wear. The hostess gift and the Cameo Kit. Sometimes if someone wanted to host a party but didn't have models I occasionally asked Shelby and AP which they gladly helped me out. It was really fun and hard work, entertaining, and selling the products, being the life of the party and convincing other to throw lingerie house parties took skills.

Cameo, Avon and Mary Kay were similar in business with the same concept. It's your own business, and you got to go and get your customers and invite whomever, into the business. So at parties I also invited women to come into the business, which help me move up the ladder, as I help the lady from Jersey move up the ladder. My mother host a party and she even join the Cameo team. Due to my sales of lingerie in my area I won Cameo pins and other little awards from the company, which were a great inspiration for me to carry one. The biggest highlight for any Cameo employee with the highest regional turnouts in sells won the chance to go to Texas or Dallas-it's where Cameo headquarter was located, and there's no need to mention it, but you reader should know, I was going for it.

Around this time in my life, Brooklyn started building up the neighborhoods by building these lovely two and one family brick homes. He working. I'm hustling. The city is paying our rent for sure I knew that Thomas and I were going to purchase a home with a backyard. So lots of times I would park the car in front of these new one and two family homes that was popping up everywhere thinking it sure would be nice becoming a home owner. Owning one of these brick homes, eventually, Thomas and I will get married. Even one of Thomas best friends, Seymour purchase one of these homes for his' family. We sometimes went over to his home for backyard barbecue and good cook outs. Thomas was making good money with no worries about paying the rent, because the welfare system, the city paying my/our rent.

Now that I found not one but two jobs that was paying me tax free money off the book therefore it wouldn't interfere with my budget from welfare. I'm thinking, we should be able to save a lot of money to buy one of those houses.

Being that Thomas and I both love dancing and entertaining we thought it would be nice to throw parties for our friends and family. It could be a way for us to make extra cash as well as have some fun. We rented this small place from Thomas' friends. We invited friends and family members. Thomas went to the warehouse and purchase the bags of ice and plenty beverages for us to sell. While I cooked and prepared my American dishes and some Jamaican food too, with the help from Dennis Thomas Caribbean friend.

We hire a DJ and we hire light entertainment. Our parties was okay it just wasn't so successful we spent way more money than we got back.

One of my most memorable lingerie parties was held at Top of the Hill Two dance club /bar on West Avenue.

It was fun and exciting but it got to be a bit too much because... I'm pregnant again. It's not something I planned but nevertheless Brandon he is the cutest little boy so I couldn't abort the pregnancy. With my daughter in public school, having a one year old son, taking care of my man and the apartment, now, expecting another child sadly, so sadly, I had to say good bye.

The next day I goes over to Shelby. "Hi Tami," she said as I walked in. I said "Guess what?" She said "You're getting married." I said "I wish. But guess again." She said, "You engaged!" I said "No, I'm pregnant." Shelby said, "Well, you already have a child from each sex so at this point what do you want or does it matter?" I said, "I wouldn't mind having another boy." Shelby said, "Oh you like boy children. Well you can have one of mine."

She has three boys and one girl.

Shelby told me, "Last night Wilbert and me heard a lot of moving going on upstairs in the apartment above us. Early this morning, I saw the lady upstairs throwing out a chair. I asked her if she getting new furniture? She told me she will be leaving this building in a month or two because she just purchased a two family home."

"One of those lovely brick homes I was telling you about," I questioned. "I think so. She didn't really go into details but she did say it was brick," Shelby replied.

Changing the subject I asked, "Isn't that apartment above you a three bedroom just like your?" Shelby said "Yeah it is."

I said, "I like your apartment so I'm going downtown to see if I can get that apartment Shelby."

Later on, I went to Asbury Management and announce to the nice lady, "I'm expecting again. I just found out there going to be a three bedroom in my building that will be vacant soon. Can I have it? Now with two children and another one on the way I definitely will need more rooms."

The nice lady said, "I'm still looking in to it for you Miss. Jones. I haven't forgot I'm aware you need the extra rooms." "I appreciate that. Thank you," I told her.

These new brick homes started popping up, I mean everywhere. I wanted one so bad. I don't know how many times I drove and just sat in front of these homes, thinking it would be nice to own one of these. I used to always ask the construction guys if I can go inside to see how they look because they had different style and shapes.

When Thomas came home I said, "They building these one and two family houses all over in Brooklyn. It sure will be nice if we became home owners."

Thomas would just listen but he didn't put much inference into it.

So, late at night after Thomas came in from work I took the car scrolling up and down the blocks to where all these homes were being built. Remembering the area or what street I seen them on. Sometimes even while running my household errands I would park the car and sit for a half hour with the kids in the back seat. Just picturing me opening up the door, or imagine me watching the kids run out playing in their front yard. I then wondered-how would I decorate. If I have brushes or flowers. The home' owners they were remodeling the front of their homes all kinds of ways. Some had put up small porches. Others made a driveway.

I wanted Thomas to do more for me and my kids after that shit with Adrianne even though I never brought it up again. Watching him send down all that stuff to Jamaica. He work all the time, every chance he get and he makes good money. It not like he had so many household bills. I started wanting much more from him, for us. I wanted that brick home to raise our family in.

Asbury wrote me a letter asking me to come downtown. "Miss Jones have a seat," the nice lady requested. When I sat down she said, "We have a larger apartment for you in the same building."

I'm was so happy just thinking of the extra bathroom that's in the master bedroom just like Shelby apt.

I asked, "Is it the three bedroom on the second floor?" She said, "There is another Miss Jones in that same building. Miss Adrianne Jones, do you know her?" I said, "Yes."

"Sorry you didn't get that apt. Miss Jones have an elder boy with two school aged daughter. We decided to give her the three bedroom and you a two bedroom. The apartment we have for you is 3bd."

I said, "Miss Butt' apartment!?"

Smiling, the nice lady said, "Yes. Miss Butt' old apartment."

"That's the worst apartment in the building," I said.

The nice lady said, "That why we evicted her because of her wild parties. Not paying her rent on time and constant repairs. We been trying to get rid of her for the longest. When Miss Butt realized her lease had been terminated, she totally destroyed the apartment, and flooded the bathroom. We have to put in a complete new bathroom. Replace kitchen cabinets and we will give you a brand new refrigerator and stove."

Now all that new stuff sounds appealing even though I had my eye set on that three bedroom. I said, "Remember the time when I came down here and put in a request for my ceiling to be repaired. Could it be that's where the water damage came from?"

The nice lady said, "Yes. It came from her' apartment. Miss Jones, I would need a current budget letter to determine the rent. Bring it to me as soon as you can."

We didn't move in right away but when the apartment was ready. I wanted to add some of my own special touches to the place, like having Thomas shellac the wooden floors and have the place painted. With the extra money I'm now received from welfare such as my moving allowances, pregnancy allowances and furniture allowances I plan on buying the paint and some of the children bedroom furniture.

Someone at my door, "Who is it?" "It me," my mother said. I open the door. My mother was all excited saying, "I got something to tell you," as she walked inside of the apartment. I was curious to know what it was that bought my mother to my house. My mother said excitingly, "I just got approve as a foster mother."

I was thinking here it is she's going to help take care of a stranger child, and her' own grandkids from me, she doesn't even help.

Excitedly she said, "Yeah since I have an extra bedroom I could let the children stay in that room. The agency had given me a crib just in case if I get an infant. The agency told me I could have a babysitter **AND,** listen to this."

She said extra happy, "The person could be receiving Public Assistance and it won't interfere with their case."

I remember I just sat there looking at my mother with my babies next to me. She gave me a look of, where is your enthusiasm at? I said, "That's nice."

Looking around the apt my mother asked, "What's going on here?" I said, "We soon be moving upstairs to a larger apartment." Shocked at the information my mom said, "Isn't that nice. In the same building too?" I said, "Yep, right upstairs but management still working on it. They are just about finish because it was really damaged but I have the key now. Come, let me show you my new place."

When I open the door as my mother looked around she said, "This building has the cutest apartments. Electra I don't know which apartment I like better, this one, or the one downstairs. I see it a two bedroom which you really do need the extra room. Oh, I just love this cut out from the kitchen. You always find nice apartments for yourself." I said, "Yeah, it's going to look even better once Thomas shellac the wooden floors and I paint."

My mother said, "I could ask Dave to paint. He loves to paint. He have this place done in no time."

I said, "I want both bedrooms and kitchen to be a different color from the living room but the hallway got to be the same as the living room. Are you sure he wouldn't mind?"

"No he wouldn't mind," my mother said.

Looking around at my new empty apartment my mother said, "Well what do you think?" I replied, "What do I think about what?"

My mother said, "Babysitting? Electra do you want to make some extra cash for yourself?" I wasn't so thrill. I had always picture it would be the other way around; her babysitting for me. She said, "Obviously I rather would see you get the money then someone else. Look girl you could use this money to help get some furniture for yourself."

I asked my mother, "How do you know it won't interfere with my welfare case?" Disguisedly my mother said, "Because I already asked. Look do you want to make some money for yourself or don't you?!"

I say, "Okay." My mother say "Here." She hands me a form and say, "Fill it out. Then you have to take it to the agency with your ID. I'll write the address down for you."

I looked the form over. It asks for the hour and days that I would be babysitting. I ask my mother, "What should I put here?" She asked, "Where?" I said, "Where it asks for the hours and days." My mother said, "Put nine to four. Monday thru Friday."

All of this writing had made me become very hungry. It's lunchtime, so I left the library going back over to the shelter. When I got back to Bridge Net there was signs tape all over the building. House Meeting held in the dining room. Tomorrow at five thirty.

Right before lunch I ran upstairs to my dorm, just to see Q six coming out from taking a shower and her bed unmade as if she just got out of it. Before eating my lunch, I stopped by the intake office. I ask for a complaint form to fill it out.

Resident name: <u>Electra</u>. Indicate the type of complaint: I check <u>security</u>. Date of event that led to complaint: I <u>inserted today date</u>. Time: <u>nine o'clock am</u>. Location: <u>Q dorm</u>. Description of complaint: **Favoritism**. Before I left the Q dorm today, I noticed a client that was still sleeping in her bed without a bed pass attached to her locker. This client

306

does not work. I spoke with Security Guard Marsha and asked her why she get to stay in the bed. Everybody else have to leave the dorm on time. Security Guard Marsha goes to the resident area and wakes her up. The guard Marsha had found out that she doesn't have a bed pass, she unemployed and she not sick. They held a conversation in Spanish. Plenty times, Security Guard Marsha had come into the Q dorm asking residents to leave the dorm because it nine o'clock. At twelve o'clock in the afternoon I goes back into my dorm for a quick second. I was shock to find only Q six, the same resident that was sleeping shortly after nine, taking a shower. My question is how come security Marsha had allowed her to break the shelter rules but others got to follow the rules and how come she not threaten with receiving a fraction. What make her special or better than other clients that sleep inside of this shelter? Resident signature: <u>Electra Jones</u>. Form Accepted by: <u>Mrs. Wilks</u> Shift Supervisor signs the paper and I ask for my copy.

I goes to the dining room and have lunch. They served sandwiches and for desert small assorted cookie packs. I took the banana flavor cookies, sat on the side where the radio was playing. The radio station is on one o seven point five.

After eating my lunch I goes to Miss Taylor desk asking her can she put me in for carfare. I needed to have my ppd read. I goes back into the dining room, sit and start back writing.

Back to the story:

In a couple of days my mother came to my house knocking on the door. It was nine o'clock sharp. I open the door. Quickly my mother came walking in with four small children. Once we were in the living room my mother said, "Here the diaper bag and some money to buy them all lunch."

Dam, she didn't even bring lunch for them. I remember thinking shoot I had my own kids I had to cook for. Then my mom starts walking toward the door. Quickly I turn around walking behind her going towards the narrow hallway right before she hit the apartment door. Fast I asked, "what's their' names? Is there anything I should know?"

As she reaching for the doorknob my mother said, "The agency doesn't tell us anything about them. They know how to talk. Ask them they tell you their names," as she walked out the door. When I went back into the living room I saw four quiet Black Americans kids looking at me. Their name were Penny, Angie, James and Casper and they were extremely undernourished.

School was out for my daughter so every day I took all the kids to the park. Most of the times I went to St. Paul Park because the kids had more activities to play with. Plus the park had a small section for babies and toddlers. These foster girls were so timid they didn't even know what swings were. They were afraid to be push so I had to push their swing gently as they watch me while I pushed Brandon. Champagne loves the swing so I could push her hard. Then I went back to the foster girls swing and push gentle until they got use to the swing and started enjoying their selves.

The boys Casper and James went buck wild. I had to constant make sure they didn't hurt themselves by falling and reminding them, "To be careful and stop running while Champagne and others were swinging in the big swings cause a swing could hit you in your head." They were very hypo. I saw St. Paul Park was good for those hypo boys to burn up all that energy.

The boys acted like cave children like they never been in a park before. I just allowed them to enjoy their selves running and exploring like how little kids their age are supposed to act.

I just had to monitor them making sure they had time out, to calm their selves down when they got a little out of hand. Once they calm down I let them go play again. Burning up all that young energy. There ages were between seven and nine. Besides being hypo and couldn't stay still, they had a bad case of ringworms on their' scalp.

The boys took to me right away, maybe because I took them to the park every day. So whenever they spoke to me I constantly had to remind them to slow down and breathe because from their excitement trying to get out what they wanted to say to me, they stutter a lot in their speech.

The baby was two years old. Her name is Penny. She had a serious stomach infection. When she moved her bowel, which was constant the awful smell lit up the entire area. The smell alone made me want to gag. The light brown dodo it not only ran out from her pamper but also down her legs. When I laid the child down to remove the dirty pamper there was chucks of different color dodo mixed with diarrhea. It was just disgusting.

The first time I removed her pamper filled with diarrhea I was so astonished to see her private part front and back was raw and the area was extremely sensitive to touch. Oh my Gosh her parents or wherever she came from must had left the dirty pamper on her for so long that her private area was the color pink and she a dark skin child. When I got the baby wipes out of the bag to wipe the child, surely it had to be painful as I wiped that completely pink area. As a matter of fact I couldn't use the baby wipes. To make it less painful on Penny when I had to change her diapers I used a clean warm washcloth with no soap just warm water. I pressed the warm cloth on the swollen fleshy area just dabbing her' sensitive area. Removing all the light brown diarrhea from the raw part of her private area and her buttock. I felt so sorry for that poor little baby.

I remembered after a while when Penny got use to me. Even Penny herself didn't like the smell because whenever she moved her bowel she would come to me standing there looking at me to change her diaper. It's not that my mother didn't pack enough diapers for Penny. This child had a severe case of diarrhea so I use to use them all up.

309

She couldn't hold anything down not even water. It was a constant run of bad smelly diarrhea. Her hair was so knotty it was stuck to her head, short and dried.

As a matter of fact I felt sorry for all four of the children.

Angie the oldest girl, age four, she wouldn't talk. Besides being bonny she seem to be traumatize. It took her a while before she spoke to me and when she did she stutter and spoke in a whisper. When I asked, "What's your name?" She didn't answer. The boys told me "Her name is Angie." They said "She can talk." I ask them why she doesn't speak they shrug their shoulders.

These children clearly had signs of abuse, along with signs of neglect and bad health. So when my mother came at four I was tired. I said to my mother, "Penny must be dehydrated. She needs a bottle of pedialyte water and ointment for her raw backside. The next time you bring her over here she needs not a couple of pampers. I need a box."

The next day my mother show up again exactly at nine o'clock. She had everything I ask for. She brought ointment, the water, a pack of pampers and money for their' lunch. Due to Penny messed up stomach I had to watch her diet so I made her light food like toast, Jell-O, tea, and farina until her stomach was able to hold heavier food. After a while I noticed her bowel movement was still in diarrhea form, but tiny solid dodo here and there. It was so disgusting. It took a while before I got her hair to look descent and her looking like a pretty little girl.

I help Angie with her' shyness and stuttering by asking her to take her time when she spoke. Also encouraging her to holding small conversations with me. By the way my mom's paid me herself for doing the girl's hair. My mother never was a hair stylist.

James and Casper still were hypo but they weren't acting so out of control like the jumping off the wall boys that first came through my door. They came to respect me and they listen to me without giving me such a hard time. So when I said the words, "Time out. You go to that corner while you go to the other one," they oblige, but I couldn't stop them from hitting their self and giggling.

I hate to say it but my mother was in it just for the money because I was the one who took care of them. Just because on the babysitting form paper it said I babysat from nine to four. My mother brought them to my house every day at nine and left those sick kids on me, on my pregnant ass till four o'clock. **Everyday.**

By the time I got finish with them my mother received stars from the Foster Care Agency and a lot of respect. She along with Dave became the number one foster parent's at the agency. Whatever mommy wanted from the agency she got. Why I included Dave name simply is because him and my mother live inside the same apartment as boyfriend and girlfriend with me knowing surely my mother left those children on Dave too while she ran her errands on the weekends. The agency probably thought my mother healed and broke through barriers with those kids. It was me who did it, because she left those kids on me.

I took the responsibility of a parent and brought the best out of those kids in a short period of time. Teaching them manners. How to have confidence in their selves. Promoting their' exercise by taking them out every day and helping them find their' own inner self. Healing them and most importantly becoming a caring person showing them repeatedly I really do care.

My mother told me their' parents were drug addicts. Once a week she had to take those children to the agency for a visit with their' parents. My mother told me even their' crack headed parents didn't recognize their' own children. She use to tell me when their' parent came for a visit how they praised and thanked my mother for taking exceptionally good care of their' children. My mom may have brought them nice clothes keeping them clean but

I healed their body and their mind which helped brought out their' personalities and character.

I actually enjoyed the challenge and wanted to see how far I could have gotten with them but the children got moved. I was surprised to see they got moved so quickly, especially when they were coming along so well. I forgot the reason why they left so soon. Oh yeah, I remember, my mother for the agency is an emergency worker-meaning, she had to have her home ready for emergency drop off of kids until the agency found permanent homes for the children.

I help brought those children back to life. They were really damaged. Wherever those kids are I really hope they are alright. I put a lot of work into those four children in a short period of time while I took care of my own two kids and my baby inside that I'm carrying.

To tell you the truth I was a little disappointed when the agency remove them. I wanted to see how far I could go in making a different in their' life. When they left they weren't the same kids my mother brought through my front door. I was sad to see them leave.

Not to be funny, but after a while those kids were dressing better than my children. My kids didn't have much but they were happy, healthy and energized. They had a descent home and they had me. A mother who was there for them through thick and thin. Isn't that's how it supposed to be.

Stop! To the reader: I would just like to say that's why it so important who you leave your children with. While in the shelter a lady express how she left her infant with someone and someone rape the child in the butt and mouth causing the child to have seizures for the rest of its life. The city then removed this child from this women leaving her tormented and broken hearted longing for her only child. My question is how come the person who watched the child wasn't penalize? And if the story was true how come the mother didn't get another chance to be reunited with her' child?

Anyway back to the story:

Well my apartment is ready. We moved upstairs to apartment 3bd and I no longer babysit for my mother. I didn't feel like raising another group of sick kids. Not that I'm being disrespectful, it just that foster care kids need a lot of attention and I felt after I did such a good job in helping them while we all getting to know each other than the agency goes and move them. Then bring in another set of kids who need help to overcome whatever obstacle that has been inflicted. Well, I had my own small kids to raise and as a family we trying to get ourselves together.

The first check the agency paid me was a little over fourteen hundredth dollars and with the additional money I got from the welfare I had my children' room painted, in serenity blue. I purchase a dark blue metal framed bump bed for their bedroom, a circus chandelier and a tall chest. Inside their room I also had Brandon old crib for the baby.

My bedroom was painted in the color of a dusty rose. I had a telephone jack installed inside my bedroom as well as in the kitchen. Because I receive Medicaid I qualify for the life line program. It's the cheapest call price for making telephone calls. My kitchen I had it painted a light yellow and I brought décor stick-on brown bricks to cover the wall small section behind the stove. Also I purchase for the kitchen a small deep freezer and I bought a washing machine. I also bought a beautiful glass dining table set that came with four sleek black armless, grey pleated chairs. Behind the dining table, the wall where the cutout is at AP helped me put up a mural of a waterfall. It was beautiful.

For my living room I had it painted in eggshell white. I purchased beautiful off white multicolor sofa and matching love seat from Seamen Furniture store. The set came along with two glass end table and a glass center table. The second check, along with Thomas help I bought a white lacquer Italian platform queens' sized bedroom set and mattress. I carpet my bedroom with multi shades of pink and brown. Then I bought the most gorgeous drapes for my bedroom window and an AC. Then after all of that with the help of my check from welfare I got the living room set professionally cover in plastic.

My apartment had finally came together. Just those two large checks alone were a big help. Those foster kids, the moving, shopping and me decorating, everything, it all has tired me out.

Now since I have gotten the house phone, not only was Thomas family from Jamaica calling him collect, guys from Jamaica was calling Thomas too letting Thomas know they would be coming to New York since Thomas had a spot on the job waiting for them. Sometimes Thomas drove the car picking them up from the airport. Making sure they were ready to start work the next day.

Eventually I found out where to get an application for one of those new two family homes that were being built.

I saw Thomas helping so many of his' people one day I ask him, "Thomas why won't you ask the guys that always hanging out in front of the building if they want to work? You know, like Troy, Peanut or Divine if they would like to make some honest cash for their' selves."

Thomas didn't say a word. I said, "They always helping us with our grocery bags when we come in from shopping and they always help you with the car when it get stuck in the snow. It would be nice if you can help them make some money too. Especially you the one that's during all the hiring."

Thomas never asked not one American guy if they wanted to work. I was mad, and surprise to see Thomas acting like that. These boys helped us out from time to time. They always in front of the building. I'm started thinking, Thomas couldn't help out one American male bring home a little money for himself? Especially Thomas is the one who was getting those private contracts on the weekend and he's the one doing the hiring. Everyone he helps out had to be West Indian? I felt he could have at least offered one of the American guys a job.

He loaned his' brother money to open his own mechanical shop. Thomas' mother came to New York from Jamaica. She bought up with her from Jamaica one of Thomas nieces name Vivian. Thomas' mother she didn't even bring one gift for the kids acknowledging them as family. I took her shopping, treated her nice. Introduced her to my mother. We had a lot of people coming in our apartment, visiting from Jamaica and looking for Thomas to help them find work. When his family and friends went back home all I know is when I went to my linen closet all my towels were gone.

I started noticing how Thomas was driven to only helping out his' people. Even when his family or friends did come around us, it was always give me, give me, give me, or take, take, take. Dam, when you look at it they weren't even socializing with the Americans. Putting their' children in private schools, swearing they better than someone. No one asked "Thomas, Tami could we watch the kids so yall can go out." I never received or heard one thank you for helping ship all that stuff overseas. Not even Thomas said, thanks Tami for helping me support my family.

So with my PA check I put my daughter in private school wanting to show Thomas I want her to have a decent education too. This way it would allow him to do more for us with his money. Me putting and investing my money on my daughter is allowing Thomas to be more responsible for paying the light, gas and telephoned bill. Thomas could have even help put JB in private daycare if he wanted too. Allowing me to have quality time with myself while carrying my third child but nooo, the only thing he concentrated on is Jamaica.

That year I made a Thanksgiving feast. We invited Thomas Brother Rude Boy and his girlfriend Natalie. When they came through our apt door Thomas' niece was with

315

them. When I saw her I said, "Vivian I thought you went back home with Thomas' mother to Jamaica. Weren't both of you on the same ticket?" Vivian said, "Tami I'm not ready to go back home I want to stay in America." I asked, "So how you going to get a ticket and go back home? You told me you came up here to visit? You don't have a job and you don't work?" She said, "I'm not going back. I'm staying here in this Country. I'll make it somehow."

Anyway I asked, "Can I make yall a plate?" Everyone said "Yes." I notice Natalie didn't eat her food she started complaining, "Where the curry goat and rice and peas?" Asking me, "Tami what is this and what that is?" Natalie started saying, "Me don't eat this macaroni and cheese. Me eat macaroni pie. No oxtails Tami."

Oh gosh why is she was so disrespectful. I said, "Natalie this is what I made for Thanksgiving and you said you wanted a plate. When I gave you the plate, if you didn't want it why did you take it? So what I didn't make curry goat and I didn't make any Caribbean dishes, because I'm American and this is what I eat for Thanksgiving-turkey with cranberry sauce. If I was to go to Jamaica and all you served was curry goat, I eat it and be happy! So you came to my home and you know I'm American that I will serve American food. Why complain trying to put me down? I can't help it if I eat more meat then just curry goat!"

Stop! To the reader, this was a time when Jamaicans only cook their Caribbean dishes, which consists of curry goat, curry chicken or oxtail. They didn't know how to cook collard greens, fried chicken, barbecue chicken or a ham, pork chop and lots of other American dishes.

Reader: Let go back to the story.

Natalie threw the whole plate in the garbage and just because Vivian snuck in the country and was staying with Rude Boy and Natalie in their' new home, she threw my food in the garbage too and they left! I was so mad.

Thomas didn't say one word. That was the last time I had **anything** to do with Natalie.

Thomas family called the apartment collect regularly from Jamaica saying they needed this and they needed that. Wire down some money and for him to help pay this bill. Again Thomas went to Jamaica for the Christmas holiday. That was also the Christmas Tray came by to visit me and Champagne again. My son was sitting on the couch, drinking from his bottle and Tray said "Tami he ain't no good either. Why didn't he take you with him to Jamaica? It's Christmas. He should be here with yall." He handed Champagne another doll and he left.

You know, I hate to say it, but Tray was so fuckin right.

One day Thomas, I and the kids were going food shopping. When we got to our park car. We standing in front of our small four door white car, shock, we found someone had written on the top of the car; in a blue marker over the passenger side. That's above my head where I sit.

Shocked at the discovery. Thomas and I both stood by our car as we both read the message. The message seemed to be spiritual it was weird and disturbing. Thomas tried scrubbing it off the car but it wouldn't come off.

I saw Thomas glance towards Adrianne window.

I was upset I said, "Thomas why would someone write this on top of our car? It was right over my head, or the head of anyone who sat on the passenger side. I wanted this **shit** off the car!"

We couldn't get the blizzard message off the car.

Thomas said "Tami, don't pay attention to it. Me get it off soon."

We drove around with that message on top of our car and if anyone stood by our car they too can clearly see it to read it. Next, Adrianne just started reappearing in front of the building whenever Thomas and I would be coming back inside the building. She seemed upset and I heard her no longer seeing/dating the butcher anymore.

My only outlet from the house and kids was when I went downstairs to visit Shelby. After coming inside the house, from visiting Shelby I went to my bedroom. Thomas was lying down in our bedroom and JB was laying down next to him. I decided to change Brandon pamper and put him inside his' own bed. I got the most amazing discovery. Brandon little penis was stiff as if he had a hard on. I said, "Thomas I didn't know a baby boy could get a hard on so young?"

Once again, Thomas didn't say a word but I didn't like the thought that went through my head.

I couldn't help it now because the idea... the thought was already planted. Was Thomas playing with my son wee-wee? Cause how Brandon got a stiff little penis. I always change his pampers and I never once saw that. Hum.

Then something else weird started happening. When I took the car out and came back I notice Adrianne' mother would park her car in our normal parking space. Or when Thomas and us went food shopping Adrianne' mother will have her car park where we were parked before we left. I started thinking, is we being watch by Adrianne? Every time we leave she have her silly mother park her' car in the parking space we had before we left. Sometimes when I went outside, Adrianne mother would be sitting in her car and I could feel and see her watching me. Then, I started feeling Adrianne' presence, around me. I said, I know I'm not going crazy but what is this eerie annoying feeling. I started feeling like I was being watched by Adrianne and her' MOTHER! I never experienced something like this before. I didn't even know how to put it in words.

I remember when I first moved into this building. I had a nice mailman from Everyone COGIC Church (church of god in Christ). He always invited me to attend his' church as if he known spiritually something was wrong. *Or maybe he thought I needed prayer?* All I know he kept asking me to come to his' church.

I didn't want people to think I was losing my mind. Something so weird like this. Feeling her' presence around me while I was sitting alone in my living room waiting for Thomas to come thru the door so I said, there no one else I can speak to about this eeriness so I'm going to test out God. I'm thinking now, this gives me a chance to see if there's a God. Anyway I wanted to know the truth about something and I'm going to ask God for the answer. Talking and thinking about God' spirit I said, "Sooo, if you so real, and you exist, then tell me, show me a sign....Is Adrianne and Thomas fooling around?"

Then I had seen Adrianne face as clear as day! Her' face was in a round circle and she looked like a **witch!** The vision had scared me so bad that all the hairs on my body had stood up. Next, the door to my children bedroom, their' bedroom started moving all fast, opening and closing. I couldn't believe what was going on?! I actually stood there watching and listening to their' door open and close quickly. Watching and seeing and hearing the door opening and closing, well....I got to say it did frighten me but I had to find the courage cause all my babies were in there.

I went walking toward my kids' door. I put my hand on the doorknob in order to stop it from opening and closing. I looked into the room. I saw a dark shadow moving on the wall. I watched it go up on the wall. It going towards my oldest daughter. Champagne, she slept on the top bunk bed. It just disappeared.

When my mother came to visit me. I told her what happened, how I saw that girl' face! My mother got angry and she looked to be a little concern for me. She said, "It sounds like voodoo but we could do voodoo right here! People in this country can do it too and mess up people' lives."

I said, "Voodoo... What?"

My mother asked, "**Who is she!**" The first time I ever seen my mother act as if she wanted to fight for me. I know my mother and my Aunts they can get a little wild and crazy sometimes, but I'm trying to make sense of what I seen and hearing my mother talk crazy....... Voodoo. I told her I speak to her later.

You know what though, I got the strangest feeling that when I saw her face...she knows I saw her. It sound weird right? I told Shelby and Wilbert what I saw and how she looked like a **witch!** Shelby said, "Tami you know some people practice witchcraft." Wilbert said "Tami maybe she want Thomas and she's out to get you." I said, "Stop playing......for real yall. Listen, I really did see her face, and she knows I seen her in that form."

To tell you the truth that's when mysterious things started happening after I spoke to God in my living room. It gets weirder. More inexplicable things started happening like for instance when I saw Adrianne standing in front of the building. She was standing there glaring, as I came out from the car and I started saying to myself, "God be with me and protect me from this **witch**." I'm not lairing Adrianne started running. Not walking I mean I watch her run away from me.

Another unexplainable thing happen. One day when Adrianne' mother was coming out of the building going towards her' car. I started praying to God within myself and her mother moved out my way like she was scared. I don't understand it myself all I know is, it did happen.

Wow writing sure bought me back to a lot of memories about my past. Going down memory lane sure does bring back a lot of memories I disregarded. I gather my belongings' and heads to my dorm. After taking my shower I stretches out on my bed because what else is there to do in a place like this?

After a while security Mac. Dan open the Q dorm door and say, "Bed check ladies." As I looked around in my dorm I see my neighbor still has the red heart on top of her' locker. Then I looked at my picture of the heart I drew in art therapy and I thought-how good it look on top of my locker. It made my area looked lively so I plan on doing more art work.

Residential Aide (RA) knocks on the door. He say "Man on ladies. Are you dress?" Nobody said anything. He repeats **"Man on! Ladies** are **you dress**?"

"Come in," Lacy said.

Malcom the RA enters. He walks toward Country' bed and clips her' locker and starts bagging up all her' belongings. Then he left out with her stuff and the locker wide open waiting for the next occupant.

At 10:10 pm Shift Supervisor Lisa enter the dorm and gets everyone signatures.

Around eleven o'clock a new resident enter the dorm. She a dark skin women with long thin netted dreads. She goes to Country old bed put the sheets on the green mattress and lay down.

11:05 pm. Security Mac. Dan says, "Light out ladies," she clicks off the light. As we all laid in the dark room all quietly, all of a sudden in the dark, I heard a loud animal sound..... **"Grunt!"**

I say to myself, "What the fuck was that?" as I fell off to sleep.

Chapter Thirteen

"Good morning ladies it's six o'clock," security Abuja announce.

Opening my eyes to the sound of her voice. Uhmmm! Where is that pissy smell coming from? Oh my gosh...um! Who peed on their self? I walk to the bathroom and open up the door, man, no toilet tissue again. I'm going to start keeping a roll of toilet tissue inside my locker because this is ridiculous. I wonder who keep stealing the dam toilet tissue. Rushing back to my locker to get my toothbrush so I can brush my teeth and soap to wash my face. I see our new roommate... SHE STINK! She smells like pure pee or did she lay there and just piss on herself. I know it her cause this room never had a pissy smell odor until she came into this dorm. That's another thing us residents had to learned to overlook, because we have no other choice but to deal with another resident' mental illness or their bad hygiene because staff can't make a resident bathe. They can asks, but they can't make them.

I started checking my wallet that's inside my bag making sure I have my Medicaid card and my Fedelis Id card. Pulling out my clothes that I plan to wear today I goes downstairs to the intake office so I can iron.

As usual.......there not a guard on the fourth floor. When I get inside the intake office I see one girl whose ironing and a couple of other females sitting down in the seats. I ask, "Is anybody next in line to use the iron?" A female say "I'm waiting." "I'm waiting too," another girl said. Sunset said "And I'm behind her," "Then I'm next," Brenda said. "Okay, well then I'm behind you Brenda," I said.

Sabricka enter into the intake office. She ask Mr. Berry, "Can I get the TV book."

Mr. Berry replies "Where's the good morning? No good morning first. Just give me the TV book," as he sigh while shaking his head walking over to the area to pick up the TV book.

As I'm watching Mr. Berry, he's scanning the titles of the large notebooks. He's looking for the TV notebook. Watching Mr. Berry just ajar my memory. While I'm here waiting to iron I might as well pick up my metro cards. So I gets in the line behind Sabricka. Mr. Berry hands Sabricka the TV book. I watch Sabricka as her fingers goes down the columns in the TV book. She looking for her desire slot.

Disapprovingly Sabricka say, "Not again! Copper she always get the TV slot for 8 o'clock. I wanted to watch a program that's coming on TV tonight but Copper already signed for the 8 o'clock slot. She signed last night too for the same slot.....AND the night before that."

Mr. Berry suggest "Well sign for another slot." Upset Sabricka said, "The program I want to watch comes on at 8 o'clock tonight and it's only a quarter to seven in the morning. How early does Copper get up?"

Mr. Berry said "You know the rules. First come, first serve. The TV book opens up at 6 am." Sabricka said, "But **dam**, let somebody else get a chance to watch a program at 8 o'clock. Copper always getting the same slot. We only have up to 9:30 pm to watch the television."

Mr. Berry reply "Well, you know what you got to do. Get here before she does. Is there anything else I can help you with at this presence time Ms. Griffin?"

Sabricka is really upset.

She saying, "Come on now, you know Mr. Berry it's not fair she always get the same spot every day, for one hour." Mr. Berry replied "What do you want me to do? At six am Copper came down here and she asked for the TV book. I can't tell her no you can't sign for that slot if it's open. Don't get mad at me. I didn't make up these rules."

Sabricka leaves from the office complaining. Everyone inside the intake office can hear her telling other residents that's in the hallway, "Copper always get the gotdam 8 o'clock slot. She won't let anyone else have a chance to watch a program and Mr. Berry always allow her to do it."

Hearing Sabricka bitching, Mr. Berry sigh and shake his' head, because we all in the intake office can hear Sabricka mouthing off in the hallway to the other residents about Copper' behavior.

I walk up to Mr. Berry and say, "Good morning Mr. Berry. Can I get my metro cards?" Now Mr. Berry walking over to pick up the large metro card notebook. He brings the book in front of me while he's scanning the sheet looking for my name-I turns around looking to see what girl is using the ironing board. Making sure I won't lose my spot in line. I notice Dotti she taking her time because she still ironing the same sleeve on her white shirt.

Mr. Berry ask "Electra can you sign your name?" I look to where Mr. Berry has his finger pointed to on the page and next to my name I see the reason why Miss Taylor issued out the metro card. Its state medical and I sign. Mr. Berry then hands me two, two dollars metro cards. I goes back waiting to iron, and Dotti her still ironing the same white shirt, going over and over every inch of the sleeve making sure she got out every wrinkle.

More girls start to come inside the intake office asking for their' metro cards or they want their curling iron to curl their hair. Other walking over to the water cooler drinking water. Penelope enters the intake office with a pair of jeans and a shirt to iron. She asks, "Who last for the ironing board?" I raise my hand. Penelope comes over to me and says, "Good morning you going out early." I say, "I have a doctor appointment."

I'm thinking, Dotti her really holding up the line, ironing, she going over and over ironing the same white shirt. So I say, "Excuse me, but how many times are you going to iron that same shirt Dotti?" Dotti said, "Don't worry about my business. Worry about your own business." I ask again, "So, how long is it going to take you to iron one shirt?" Dotti told me, "If you wanted to iron you should have come down here much earlier. So now **you have to wait! So shut-up** and leave me alone."

Let me tell yall, occasionally in the shelter you will run across spiteful bitchy girls who get off making others late for their' jobs or schedule appointments. That's why I like to do my things at night; like shower, iron, because I came across some mean spirited shelter females that will deliberately try to fuck you up, in all areas of life. Something as simple as ironing. Dotti been ironing that one piece for a while. Just to put it on and sit herself down here inside the shelter. She quite aware of the long line of girls behind her, and she sees who's in the line waiting. The shelter girls who are here all day; the ones that doesn't work or have a life worth bragging about, they are the ones who mainly be doing that dumb shit. As a matter of fact, they don't want a life worth bragging about. They done sold their soul to the devil already and became mean, spirited, and miserable. They don't want to see you happy, so they sit here all day being noisy, hateful, stealing and destroying other females' belongings. Just because that girl who stuff they are destroying, may seem to have some type of joy in her' life. That female with some kind of joy, she still is holding on to some type of hope. She not completely ready to throw in the towel, giving up on her life, realizing, this homelessness is temporary. But other females like how Dotti and Copper is acting are just mean spirited. They do not care anymore about the good things that life has to offer. Girls like them became hardened and callous, wanting to breakdown a decent person' spirit anyway possible.

Now for the record, I'm not stereotyping all shelter females to having this type of characteristic. I'm just saying, a lot of them do and I just like to point it out cause you never know if you have to one day live inside a shelter, and you see this type of behavior, just beware. I'm speaking from the things I seen and witness in my time of homelessness. Like Copper, she do always get the TV at 8pm. We residents get a 1 hour slot to watch a program. The TV room doesn't open up till 6pm and the room closes every night at 9:30. This shelter provides their residents with the luxury of cable. I never knew how low a person would go just to destroy another one' dreams or joy, or any form of happiness until I came to live inside of a woman shelter.

Finally Dotti remove the crisp white shirt she ironed from the iron board and pick up a pair of blue jean from a stack of folded clothes.

"Wait a minute, you have to iron all that?" I ask. She has five pairs of pants and like several blouses. With an attitude, Dotti say, "Leave me alone! Let me iron in peace. Nobody else saying anything. Why should you?" Loudly I said, "I'm writing you up! You not going to make me late because you want to be selfish and inconsiderate knowing people have to go to work and keep their' appointments. You just being mean, taking forever ironing that cheap ass white shirt. Now you going to iron several more pieces."

"Hey, hey, hey, heyyy what going on here?" Mr. Berry asks. I said, "Look Mr. Berry how many pieces Dotti got to iron. She already took forever to iron her white blouse." Mr. Berry ask "Dotti how many pieces have you ironed already?" Dotti said, "Just this one shirt and she can't wait? Just bothering me and bothering me."

"I'm not bothering you. You taking forever with that white shirt. Now you want to iron all those pieces. While we got to sit here and wait till you iron all that?" I said. Mr. Berry said "Dotti you not supposed to be ironing more than one outfit. Those are way too many clothes to be ironing at this time." Dotti responded, "I like to iron my clothes for the whole week." Mr. Berry suggest "Can you iron one outfit for now and let others iron so they can get out of here. Later on you can come back when it not so busy."

Sheena just enter into the office while saying, "Good morning my beautiful sister of the world. May peace be with you all in everything you do and may every one of you carry the blessing of the Lord with you and have a beautiful, beautiful day."

I reach the clinic at 8:45. No matter how early I get here I'm never first. I stand in line to register. After the nurse check my arm where the ppd was implanted she put the result in my chart. I ask her if I could get a copy for my records. Then I stop by the receptionist area and pick up my four dollar metro card. Going back home I stop by Eastbrunwick trains station to sell off my metro cards but I can't because I see police officers are down there so I continue on home.

When I reached the block to the shelter I saw Billie, "Hey what going on Billie." "Good afternoon Electra. Would you like to join me for a cup of coffee?" she asked. I say, "Sure why not?" Billie said, "I like to go to the diner down the block." "No problem," I say. As we get closer to the diner I tells Billie "I have seen this diner in passing but I never been in there to eat. How's the food" "Same like any other Spanish restaurant," she said. We go to a table and take a seat. The waitress come over asking "What will you be having for lunch?" Billie say, "Two coffee please."

Billie start off by saying, "I've got a part time job in the ninety-nine cent store." "Really? That great," I tell her. Billie asked, "Have you been on any housing interview?" "Nope. Not yet. What about yourself," I asked. Billie said, "I've met with the housing specialist and she said she going to send me on some interviews very soon, being that my housing package is completed and now that I'm employed."

"That great Billie. I want you to keep me inform especially if you get acceptance anywhere. Don't leave without giving me your address Billie," I replied.

Billie said, "Electra that's a promise. Do you ever wonder how it's going to feel when you finally have your own place?" I said, "I can't wait to find out. I been living in the shelter system for a while. I can't wait to get out of here to have my own apt with a key." "Isn't that silly we both sitting here hoping for a key. A key! Doesn't that make you just want to laugh?" Billie said.

"Nope. Because I don't see anything funny. It's a shame that it's taking so long just to get a key. Who would have ever figure we as girlfriends would be drinking our coffee and our main topic is obtaining an apartment key," I said.

Billie starts giggling, "You just said the magic word again ....key. I told you it's the funniest thing." Then she raise her cup and say, "Here to mine key and your' key Electra."

Smiling we tap our coffee cups together in agreement. I'm thinking when she leave I'm really going to miss this chick.

Wondering what time is it. I say, "Billie thank you for the coffee but I have an appointment with my caseworker about my housing package. I have to submit my latest updated results of my ppd so hopefully I can get housed and get out of this place." Billie had smiled and said, "Go do what you've got to do my friend. We can always chit chat another day."

Once I had gotten back at Bridge Net, I goes to the second floor to Miss Taylor desk. I see Pepsi sitting at her desk so Miss Taylor say to me, "Electra just give me a minute. I soon be finish with Miss Edwards. I step out from the area and take a seat by the first empty cubical. Once I had seen Pepsi exit I goes to Miss Taylor desk and have a seat.

Miss Taylor say, "How can I help you Electra?" I hand her the copy of my ppd result. Miss Taylor take the paper and say, "Thank you. I put this in your file." I asks her, "What's going on with my housing package?" Miss Taylor said, "Your housing package is circling. It just that no one has pick it up yet and I can't tell you who or when a suitable housing for you would come through. Giving me this up dated ppd means your housing package is current and completed. Everything on my end is done. Electra, there is a housing meeting held today. I suggest you attend especially if you have any more questions concerning housing.

The sound of me sadly humming "uhmm," was all I did as I looked at Miss Taylor after taking in what she said.

Then I asked, "Miss Taylor is it possible you could put me in the book for carfare tomorrow because I have a dental appointment."

"Sure Electra. It be there for you to pick up in the morning," she told me.

I got up and walked away from her desk. The system is messed up! That's why I'm scheming now too on the system by making unnecessary appointments just to get metro cards so I can sell them off. It's not much, but it's my way of calling myself getting back some kind of revenge on this fuck up system for holding me down. Keeping me prison from getting an apartment. So I figure I can be slick too. If I could walk out of here knowing I have an apartment I do it in a heartbeat, but I can't afford the high rent therefore I got to stay in the system in order to get the help. I goes back this time into the dining room area and I had found myself a seat. The radio station on ninety seven point one. I start to write. Security guard Fancy comes into the dining room and announce, "Coffee talk is upstairs, now with Samantha ladies."

Coffee talk is cool. It's a class held in the shelter that discuss recent current events. In the room Samantha will have on the table newspapers of the Post and the Daily News. Each residents take the newspaper of her' choice. Read through it, then select an article to address to the group for discussion. All participating residents would take turns sharing their articles of interest; and it's done over sipping a hot cup of coffee. Anyway I'm skipping the class because I want to go back into the story. On that note reader lets go back *into the story.*

It Saturday and I get up wanting to hear some music as I cleaned up the apartment. I goes and look for my reggae tapes the ones that I made and I can't find them. Thomas he's in the back room so from the living room I project my voice, "Thomas do you know where my reggae tapes is because I can't find them." I get no answer so I walked into our bedroom asking the question, "Thomas did you see my reggae tapes?" Thomas tells me "Tami I forgot the tapes. I left them in Jamaica." I'm surprised and stunned to hear him say that....So with an attitude- I said, "Who told you to take my tapes to Jamaica.... and then you left them there? Thomas had nothing to say because he already said what he had to say.

So I said while huffy and puffy, "Thomas you know you had no right taking my shit to fuckin Jamaica without asking me!" As I stared at him. "Why did you do something like that? Thomas do you hear me asking you a question........... Listen. Call them right now and tell them to mail you back my reggae tapes Thomas!"

He didn't say nothing. I snapped "Thomas!! I want back my tapes. **Call them now** and have them mail back my reggae tapes." "Tami, its only music. You can make another tape why act like that girl," he replied. I snap as I yelled, "**That's not the Point**! Those were mine music tapes and you had no right taking my stuff. Especially without asking me or my knowledge. I want my shit back Thomas!"

Thomas came to me giggling and pulling me close to him "Tami you got to take tings light girl it was only music mon, people in Jamaica love hearing the music from New York. When I go back I bring them okay." I push him away from me. I was so mad. I loved those tapes I made. You know how long it took me to make those tapes. They were my partying tapes that made me and Thomas dance. So I went into the living room to play my music not wanting to think about Thomas, who is, by the way really getting on my last dam nerve. I sat Brandon on the couch. Then Thomas comes inside the living room goes into the kitchen bringing JB. a bottle.

I goes to Thomas and tell him, "Let me get some money I want to buy JB a training cup." Thomas said "Mon, it okay let him have his' bottle." After I saw my son with his little hard on or whatever that shit was I wasn't sleeping on Thomas. Once my antennas are up, they just up and now I'm paying more attention to my son and Thomas relationship for that matter.

Then Thomas and I went through this bottle on and off struggle with JB. I wanted JB to start drinking from a training cup and every time I turn around Thomas pushing a bottle in his mouth. JB he's like close to two. I felt it time he start to be weaned off from a bottle. What was wrong with him learning how to drink from a cup? Every time I threw out the bottle Thomas brought another one. I'm not playing this back and forward game anymore. I said to Thomas, "Whatz up with you and this bottle sucking? He is getting big why do you insist on JB keep drinking from a bottle rather a cup?" That was the end of our little battle. Brandon is learning how to drink from a cup now.

I gave birth to my last child, Moet and I have gotten my tubes tried not wanting no more babies! It too much of a constant struggle and sacrifice. I'm not married. I'm stuck in the house. I'm not living my life how I thought it should be. I wanted more for myself, much more. I already don't have shit meaning an education without a degree, no bank account and no money. I never traveled. I'm not living that dream life. You know, the one with cool friends and nice parties. Going out to different places, wearing nice clothes, jewelry and great smelling perfume. Probably driving a sport car or owning a home or in my case building one up with mementos and memories, for that matter. Now wait, I know I just said a lot of things like reasons why I don't want to have any more children but, I don't want anyone to get the wrong idea. I love my kids and each child I wanted but I just can't keep pushing out kid after kid after kid with nothing. Living on the system and always doing without. Not sometimes but all the time I'm sacrificing and struggling. I'm constantly finding myself struggling to make ends meet from a little bit of nothing. Well, I have my own family now. Champagne has a brother and a sister. Brandon he has two sisters. Moet has a brother and a sister. They would always have each other in case I'm not around so that's it. I'm finish, no more babies for me.

So, now, this is what happened:

I came home from the hospital with the baby, (Moet). I believe it had to be in the evening or at night because I don't remember a big family gathering. You know us making a fuse about the baby coming to her new home, but there is one thing I knew for sure. I was in tremendous pain after having my tubes tied.

Anyway Thomas and I were asleep on our brand new bedroom furniture. I heard the telephone ringing. It had woke me up-out from sleeping.

Both of us was awoken by the ringing telephone. Hearing the sounds of ring, ring, and ring.

Thomas had his arm around me and he turns over to answer the phone. I just barely open my eyes as he answered the ringing telephone. "Hello," I heard Thomas say. Thomas told me the bad news-His' father has died.

The next thing I know Thomas is out of the bed. I hear him saying "My father is dead. My father dead Tami." I'm trying to wake up and focus coming out from a deep sleep. I said, "Oh gosh! I'm so sorry to hear that Thomas." He started getting dress very quickly. Moving out from my sleeping position so that I can see Thomas.

He's moving so fast! It was a terrible thing to wake up to. Especially since I just came home from the hospital. Us bringing the baby to her new home for the first time but, I was in such pain after having tied my tubes-I couldn't move as fast as I wanted too. I found myself struggling just to sit up.

By the time I sat up in the bed. Thomas, he was fully dressed. I wanting to ask Thomas some questions like how did he die? Was he sickly? Or did his' death just come suddenly? Before a word proceed out of my mouth, Thomas said "Tami I need to buy a suitcase and some clothes. I'm going to Jamaica. I soon come."

He was.....Gone. He left the house that fast. What terrible news. The night I came home with Moet from the hospital, we received a telephone call early in the morning. Thomas father has died. What bad timing I'm thinking and I'm thinking, of this ordeal.... **the pain** I'm experiencing since I have given birth to Moet. The pain I'm in after tying my tubes! Scrabbling..... I had finally made it out from the bed but as I had stood up "oooo," I said from this agonizing pain I'm feeling. I can't believe I'm still having difficulties and still in severe pain after given birth to my daughter......Oh shit!... that when I realized I couldn't even stand up properly.

Let me tell you. I'm a very strong and healthy person and not sickly at all. I was hutch over, unable to stand up and walk normal-having much difficulties. I started thinking maybe I'm being punish by God. That I shouldn't had did it......the operation of getting my tubes tied. According to the bible scriptures I'm supposed to multiply and fulfill the earth. Then I started questioning myself. Does gas feels like this? Naw, no way. Something is wrong. That's why I am in so much pain.

In my bedroom I started to walk......Oh My God I couldn't even walk.

Painfully with tiny bitty steps, bit by bit, slowly, moving through my apartment I made it to the kitchen. I knew that the kids would be awakening and soon my newborn would want her' bottle. So in crucial pain I prepared the milk formula for the baby and put it inside the bottle so it would be ready for her when she wakes up. Since in the hospital I was in pain. I was counting on Thomas being there for me. Helping me with these kids when I had come home from the hospital. Right now I'm thinking what bad timing.

Thomas came back home carrying a large suitcase that he probably pick up from Bobby Department store or one of those small stores on Main Street. Immediately he started packing his' clothes then ironing an outfit to wear to Jamaica.

As I sat at the dining room table looking at Thomas iron his' outfit and the mess that he made as he had packed his suitcase in a hurry. I wanted to hold a conversation pertaining to his' father death but my oldest daughter and JB got up. So not in the mood to deal with them right now, I sent them downstairs to get the mail from out the mailbox.

I'm sitting at the table, looking at Thomas in his leaving mode. There was no conversation just him packing and hurrying to get the hell out of the house. Rushing to aid his' family in Jamaica. Me sitting at the table thinking, I'm in a fuck up situation right now. Out of all the years we've been together Thomas has never seen me sickly. The two kids came running back inside of the house and hands me the mail. I see I have a Con Edison bill and my telephone bill. I sent Champagne in the kitchen to make a bowl of cold cereal for herself and her' brother.

As I open the Con Edison bill it read that my lights would be turn off if they don't receive one hundred dollars by........ **Tomorrow!!** I don't have one hundred dollars.

So many times in the past when I first moved out on my own with Champagne I had received a notice of this manner and truly my lights were cut off. Freaking out and not wanting to be in the dark with three children and I can't barely move. I said, "Thomas the lights are getting cut off! I need one hundred dollars by tomorrow!"

Thomas was in such a rush mode and distraught about his' father death he didn't want to hear anything about nothing. His mind was only on going to Jamaica.

I said "Thomas do you hear me the lights are getting turned off. I need one hundred dollars."

He said upset, because I guess he was thinking about his father, "Tami go downtown and have the city to pay the bill for you." He means Public Assistance and I clearly wasn't in any fuckin condition to leave the house. So I said "No let me get the money."

Thomas said "Mon, the city will pay it for you. Me got to go," and he walked out the door leaving behind the bill and all the mess that he made. The iron board not put away. He just gone. Leaving me to be this superwoman.

Stop! To the reader: Nobody knows how they will react to a death. I don't know if Thomas father was ill or if the death came suddenly. All I'm saying is he didn't have to run out the house like that.

Anyway back to the story:

Freaking out! Thinking! So what else to do? Where else can I get the money from besides the welfare? ....I called my mother.

I'm freaking out and in mad pain. I said "Mom! Thomas father just died and he's going to Jamaica." I hear my mother in the background saying, "Oh no." Then she asked me, "Electra let me speak to him giving him my condolences." I said "He left already!" My mother was taken by surprise with that one............She said, "Hum. He already left?" She know I have just given birth and that I just came home with the baby from the hospital and I was in tremendous pain the last time she saw me in the hospital.

I said "Yeah! I have more bad news. I just received my light bill and it say my lights are going to be turned off by tomorrow if I didn't bring in a minimum of 100 dollars that I don't even have."

"**What!** Thomas didn't leave you the money?" she asked. "No. He needed his money to get him to Jamaica," I said. Sternly my mother asked, "Electra, how did you let your light bill get back up like that? A hundred dollars?"

"I don't know. Maybe with the holidays, moving, and decorating and all. I wanted to buy things for the kids and my new two bedroom apartment. The baby on its way, shoot, I don't know because things happen.....Can I borrow the 100 dollars mom?" I asked.

My mother told me, "I have received some more children and I do need a break from them. Let me bring the children over to your place and you can watch them for me and I give you the 100 dollars so you can pay your bill."

I wasn't in the mood to babysit but I had no other choice. Frantic I told my mother, "Mom! I need to be at the Con Edison building before five. This way I know the lights won't be turn off." "I'll be right over," she said.

Security Guard Cammy enters the dining room, "Ladies can I have your attention?" She go to the radio and turn down the volume announcing "Ladies we are about to have a House Meeting." I'm thinking the time sure do flies when I'm writing.

In walks the Director Mr. Ron Winlesky. Clinical Director, Kimberly Stewart. Housing Specialist, Nomi Scott, and both floors caseworkers' Supervisor, Mrs. Portner of the 3rd floor and Mrs. Santiago of the 2nd floor. They look around the room seeing who all is present for the meeting. The Resident Aides, (RA) opens up the other side of the kitchen exposing Hawaii Punch juices and several boxes of Dunkin Donuts.

Housing Specialist Miss Scott, starts out by saying, "Ladies, I will be passing a sheet around. I want you all to sign." She pass a sheet of paper on the left hand side of the room. Then passed another sheet on the right hand side of the room.

The sheet is title: <u>HOUSE Meeting Attendees for the month of November.</u>

Mr. Winlesky ask Security Guard Cammy, "Can you have the guards that are posted on the floors to check all dorms and the yard, having all residents attend this mandatory meeting."

Security guard Cammy gets on her walkie-talkie saying, "Security on the second floor pick up." "Go for security on the second floor," the guard said. Security Guard Cammy say, "Check all dorms on the second floor and have all residents attend a mandatory House Meeting in the dining room, copy." The guard for the second floor said "Copy." Security guard Cammy did the same for all other floors as well as the yard.

Clinical Director Kimberly Stewart said, "Quiet down please. Can someone open up the windows in the back? We will be starting in a moment. We are waiting for more clients to attend." The R.As' had started pouring juice in the foam cups and putting out the napkins.

Many more clients pours in finding a seat. Quite a few clients are saying, "This is bullshit." Some are questioning one another, "Why are we down here? The residents are frustrated because the shelter not moving fast enough in helping residents get housing. Some clients are saying, "I don't want to attend any meeting just let me get my housing and get the hell out of this shit." Other residents including myself are wondering what this is all about now- like, what the system is going to do with us now. Or what's going to be changed.

Some residents are tired, they coming in from a long day of work or frustrated with the City Back to Work Program known as (WEP). WEP, it's a requirement now, it's another program for all people who is receiving Public Assistance which inquire that the person now has to work a couple of hours a day in order to keep receiving their government allowances. Such as cash and food stamps.

Stop! to the reader: I just want you to know I was on the WEP program myself. In order for me to keep receiving my welfare money and food stamp for me and my family before I became homeless I had to help clean up the city park and work inside a nursing home, for about 6 or 7 hours a day or was it from 9-5?

Anyway.

Some females are exhausted from attending school. Then you have those females that had given up some hope and were just sitting there waiting to return back to their dorms to go back to sleep. Quite a few girls were high and intoxicated, not giving a damn to what's going on. Others were just plain inpatient wishing the meeting hurry up and be over with. More residents are coming inside the room now while some residents are standing waiting to have their' curiosity fulfill. One thing I know is a fact all us residents no matter the circumstances is hoping the meeting will have good news-like the system has found housing for us and that housing is on the way.

Housing Specialist Miss Scott said audibly, "Ladies! Ladies please sign the attendance sheets that circling around in the room. The sheet that is filled can it be passed back to me." Then she hands out another blank attendance sheet.

Residential aides are ready to hand out the light refreshments. So females are forming a line.

Mr. Winlesky started the meeting by saying "Good evening ladies. For those of you who don't know me, let me introduce myself. I'm Ron Winlesky, Director of Bridge Net Women Shelter. Are all of you aware who these people are standing with me? To my right is Clinical Director Kimberly Stewart." She bow her head. Mr. Winlesky said "Standing next to her is Housing Specialist Miss Scott." All the girls cheer and applauds Miss Scott. Mainly because we want housing. Mr. Winlesky waited for the cheering to die down. Then he said "On my left is Mrs. Portner-Supervisor for the caseworkers' that's on the third floor. Standing next to her is Mrs. Santiago-Supervisor for the caseworkers' that's on the second floor. Now the introduction has been acknowledge I like to lay down some ground rules before the meeting begins. #1. If you have a question raise your hand. We can all sing together but we can't all talk together. #2. All questions should be addressed after the person has spoken and remember, no question is a stupid question. #3. Save all personal questions you may have at the end of the meeting. The quicker we get started the faster everyone can go back to doing what it is they were doing."

More ladies starts piling inside the room as Miss Scott take the floor first-saying, "ladies I'm so glad to see that so many of you have showed up tonight. I can't express enough to you at how very important it is getting your housing package ready and circling. How do you do this? Well, you all need to take accountability for yourself by making sure that you are up to date with your ppd and your psy evaluation. Also by attending your schedule bi-weekly meeting with your caseworkers and in asking he or she is my housing package not only completed but making sure it's stay updated as well. I also like to express, for housing, times now are difficult with the many changes we are now faced with in this country. Programs are being drop from left to right. Placement for housing is constantly changing so now, with this knowledge, the curfew violator (CV) is not, I say again, is NOT the way to go. Because it only step you back. By constantly becoming a (CV) it wastes all the time you already established. By constantly becoming a (CV), now with these new changes, DHS is suggesting there a good possibility that you will not get housing, instead that you would only be transferred. I also want to let you all know every month I would conduct an open housing meeting in order to discuss opportunities. Keeping you informed of all upcoming changes including with any new projects DHS may share with me. Then in return, I will bring it to you."

Lots of sounds are coming from the residents of disappointment because there was no mention of available housing therefore Clinical Director Kimberly Stewart saying, "Ladies Quiet down please."

Miss Scott announce, "At my next housing meeting I will discuss what available, who qualifies and what has been eliminated. Are there any questions?"

Simone raised her' hand. Miss Scott say, "You have the floor right now." Simone asks, "I have been here for 11 months now. Shouldn't I have at least been on one housing interviews?"

Miss Scott said, "Like I just express the housing market is slim now, for single adults at this present moment. Section 8 is closed. We are offering single room occupancy, abbreviated (SRO.) The problem with that is there aren't enough SRO. Most people that we had already house in the SRO programs hasn't left their' unit of placement unless they had gotten a voucher of some sort and has moved on to more desirable housing. In helping the residents' who resides here, overtime, we have had several organizations-which has SRO or accommodating housing. They come here and invite the residents to tour their' facility, by the way, it has become a step up from Bridge Net, as a way of finding independent living-which the majority of you have turned down every time."

Shortstop the Spanish lady raise her' hand.

Miss Scott say, "Your question will be the last question I take because my co-workers have something they would like to express, and for any other questions pertaining to housing-it can be address to me by appointment. Go ahead with your question."

Shortstop said, "I been here for 1 year and 8 months and I haven't been on one housing interview. Do I have to go and find my own housing?"

Miss Scott said, "You are welcome to do that but in the meantime I have to check your package and see if it is circling. And I have to say, some of you had made it bad for others, because there are several clients I know, who are in this room right now, has been sent on a housing interview and have been turned down because they didn't show up! Or came on the interview intoxicated. There are more shelters than Bridge Net, who are applying and sending their housing packages to these buildings looking for permanent housing for their' clients as well. Any step up from here is a plus in my book, being you must be here at Bridge Net every night at ten pm. Now to let you know, we are not keeping anyone here nor stopping anyone from seeking housing opportunities on their own. Before I end my segment of this House Meeting I would like to express I fight very hard for all the residents here at Bridge Net and yes, it is challenging as well as competitive to find placement for so many people but I do my best every day. Clients, keep an open mind as well as keep your end of the bargain, such as performing well on any housing interview and together we shall overcome barriers. Thank you."

Mrs. Santiago and Mrs. Portner had both step forward together. Both ladies look at each other wondering who shall be the one that goes first. Mrs. Santiago starts out by saying, "Good evening, as you well know we are the Supervisors for the caseworkers-and there are going to be a couple of changes in our department. I want to touch on the issues dealing with metro cards. Sorry, but there will be no more issuing out metro cards to any residents without documentation proving of a scheduled appointment-Ladies starting as, of, tomorrow. Also all documents, given in, a copy will be made by your caseworker and placed inside your folder."

Mrs. Santiago continue, "Starting tomorrow all caseworkers will have a bi weekly mandatory meeting with their caseload. These meetings will be conducted in the morning, as well, as in the evening, so there is no reason a resident can't say she couldn't attend the meeting."

Mrs. Portner step up and said, "this is being done because we want our caseworkers to know how their' clients conduct their selves in a group setting. Because lots of times clients say they want housing, but like Miss Scott express, several clients fail their housing interview due to not showing signs of really wanting independency. Also many residents have return back to the shelter even after being housed for one reason or another and we like to address the problems. A few examples; not paying the rent, drug addiction and simply not wanting to be in the environment. We know and understands yall don't want a SRO but that's all we have at this time."

Mrs. Portner adds "Another reason for these group meetings is commitment. If you can't show us commitment in attending a group meeting, how can we be sure you will be dedicated in keeping and conducting a stabilized home, for yourself?" Mrs. Portner asks, "Does anyone has any questions?"

Shawna raised her hand.

"Go ahead with your question," Mrs. Portner said. Shawna said, "I go to school and I have a part time job, so how can I attend these meeting?" Mrs. Santiago said, "Bring in your school program, and your job schedule to your assign caseworker. Then your caseworker can determine if you can attend a morning group, or a night group. If so you may have to sit on another caseworker' group meeting."

Mrs. Portner said, "Notices of residents attending a group meetings will be handed out by the Shift Supervisor during head count." Mrs. Santiago ended by saying, "Thank you all for your cooperation."

Sternly, Kimberly Stewart says "Good evening I won't be before you long. I just like to address one very important fact. Under no circumstances will I tolerate any residents to disrespect any of the social service workers here at Bridge Net. I am their overseer for the Social Services Department, and I have heard from my staff of the enormous threats coming from residents. Whatz that phrase I hear yall like to say...don't let me caught you outside or a resident getting very loud and using profanity causing a caseworker to feel threaten. These are the complaints that I had been hearing from the social service department-from frustrated unhoused residents. I'm telling you right now! I won't stand for this type of behavior. I'm letting you know, and pass the word around to your buddies that aren't here to hear this. NYPD will automatically be called as well as EMS. Under no circumstance will I allow this street mannerism to be conducted. It is positively not acceptable and will not be tolerated inside this establishment. I will not allow any client to stop the progress of my team, simply, because you don't like what you hear. Therefore causing alarm towards any one of my staff, or myself, to be afraid to do what their' job entitle them to do. If a problem shall arise there are ways an individual go about handling a situation. Insisting on bodily threats isn't one of them, good night."

Mr. Winlesky said, "Ladies I have three topics on my agenda. #1. DHS has made some changes in the way we conduct things. There will be no more Weekend Passes, over nights or late Passes to issue."

From the crowd of women, all you could hear was, "**What!** That not fair! Who can stay up in this place, every day all day? We not children." Mr. Winlesky said, "Ladies please can you quiet down. I know it's a disappointment, but the passes has been revolted because DHS feels if you can stay out every weekend, from Thursday till Sunday night or from Friday till Monday night, bed check. You have a place to stay. Everyone must be in by ten o'clock unless you are working, then we have the proving documents just in case DHS surprise us with a unannounced nightly head count. We will have the documentation for saving **your** bed."

Mr. Winlesky said "#2. We are not in the storage business anymore ladies. Some of you ladies have bags on top of, bags. By the end of next week, there will only be allowed one bag under your bed. No exception! The reason, for this, is, first of all, it's a fire hazard. Another reason we have way too many curfew violator and the RAs has been reporting there are way too many heavy bags to bag and tag when clients loss their' bed. Plus, in actuality we simply don't have enough room to turn this place into a storage unit, plus it is a fire hazard reported from the fire department. I'm giving everyone a week to find another solution for your many belongings, because after the following week, when we conduct our dorm inspection all your personal belongings will be, thrown, out. The 3rd and finally on going dilemma, starting tomorrow all metro cards will only be given out from the Shift Supervisor in charged. No longer are security issuing out cards. Also the Shift Supervisor will record the serial numbers behind each issued out metro card because too many residents are complaining that the metro card that they received has no value on it. When you receive a metro card from Bridge Net and when you swipe the card, if it read insufficient fund. Bring the metro card back to the Shift Supervisor. No more would the Shift Supervisor just issue out you another metro card without checking its serial numbers that's on the back of the metro card, making sure that it is indeed, the card you received from our office. Before ending this community meeting are there any questions?"

One resident said, "The food around here is terrible." And I asked, "For breakfast, can we have boil eggs sometimes." Tatiana asked, "Can we have hot lunch from time to time because I'm tired of having those same old dried out sandwiches for lunch every day."

Lenore said, "I'm sick and tired of washing my clothes in a dirty laundry room. In the morning when the laundry room opens the floors are despicable and the machines are dirty. We're not allowed to bring in bleach. Lots of times machines be filled with dirty clothes and balled up tissue paper. Is there anyway maintenance or an RA can clean the laundry room nightly after the laundry room has closed? Then lock the door so that residents can enter into a clean laundry room for once, on the following day. Or that someone from staff could clean it in the morning, before the laundry room opens again. Anything that help keeping a clean laundry-room."

Mr. Winlesky said "All your comments, questions and suggestion will be taken in consideration, and discuss with the proper department. Have a good night ladies. The House Meeting is now over." After the meeting, majority of the ladies were discussing what they had just heard. Quite a few were gathering their' belonging and heading back upstairs. Others were waiting for dinner to be served. As for me, I'm going to my dorm, cause I been down here in this dining room for quite a while.

As I made it through the crowded hallway, girls were still talking briefly to each other about not having weekend passes. I stop by the intake office to check the mail list. I see I have two pieces of mail so I ask Mr. Jefferson if I can pick up my mail. He hands me the mail and I sign that I had received my mail. When I look at the envelopes it was the bill collectors calling my name.

I made it upstairs to my dorm. I open the door to an awful odor. Let's see who's all in the room? I saw Marcell, that new resident, Luting and the Spanish young girl. I sit on my bed turn to my locker and starts to unlock the combination code.

The Dominican girl who fascinated with scent comes out for the bathroom holding her nose looking like she wants to gag while walking and moving quickly going to her' area. The new resident starts making animalistic noises. With my locker now opened I looked over at the new resident, who was laying down in her blue jeans and orange short sleeve t shirt.

Pepsi enter into the dorm. She comes to my area. Turning my head seeing Pepsi standing there with one hand on her hip and her face has a twisted lip while saying, "Tat mess uPP we can't get noo moRe weekens pasSes," as she stood by my bed with her hand on her hip.

"Ou heard no mOre inkkens passes," she said looking like what else could she to. I said "I was at the meeting." Lacy walks in immediately put a frown on her face and say,

"**God Lee**, its stinks in here," as she continues to walk to her' area.

As Lacy get to her area and start taking off her coat I tell Pepsi quite a few girls was upset at the meeting. Pepsi still in shock with disbelief saying, "Nooo mOre pasSes," as the truth begin to settle in her mind with acceptance. I said, "The meeting was real big and a lot of people were there."

Lacy asked, "What happen at the meeting?" Pepsi quickly said as she walked to her own area "We can't get nooo mOre inkkens pasSes." I said, "And no more late passes either."

"No mOre inkkens pasSes and nooo mOre late pasSes goodnezz why they do someend ike tat," Pepsi said as she takes off all her clothes. The new resident made another loud animal sound.

I, Pepsi, Lacy, the Dominican girl even Marcell, we all looked her way. Pepsi said, "I'm going to really go cra zee in this pace. We need a bake from here ight! This like jail. Everybodee gOing to be fighting."

I say, "Yo, my head hurts. It really sinks in here. Lacy look at me and shake her head in agreement then grab her nose as she putting earplugs in her ears. Pepsi standing in her area butt ass naked saying, "Whear tat pissy smell coming from?" The Dominican girl starts pointing her finger at the new resident while quietly saying, "It stink mommy, right."

The security Guard Michal knocks on the door while standing in the hallway. He yells "Dinner time ladies." Pepsi yells back, "Doon't O-pen tat door I'm noT dress."

Then Pepsi say, "It really stinnk N here." The new resident, "grunted," out another loud animal sound.

Now while lying on her back, in her own bed with a book in her' hand-Lacy say, "It's going to be a long night." I get up and leave the dorm because I'm hungry. The shelter serving hamburger and French fries. RA asks, "Do you want a hamburger bun?" I shake my head and mumbles, "Hum um."

After I finish eating I get up to leave the dining area. I see Marcell, she standing on the dinner line. I'm exiting completely from the area as I overhear RA Houser say, "Ladies, hurry up and eat. The church's coming tonight and we have to clean this side of the dining room.

"Hi Michal," I say as I enter on the fourth floor. "Miss Jones," Michal said. As I walk pass him I seen two girls sitting down in the laundry room washing their' clothes. When I open up the room door I said out loud "Oh no this room **stinks!**" I knock on the bathroom door. Pepsi opens up the door butt naked while rubbing white perm which has completely covered her short hair saying, "I'll b ight out." Walking going back into my' own area I look at the picture of the heart I drawn.

Laying down with my head, at the foot of my bed I'm starring at the picture. I not thinking about anything. I'm just looking at the picture while lying there. Then I looks at my neighbor bed. I wonder where she's at and I see she still had the heart on top of her' locker too. I look around my dorm the Dominican girl now has tissue in both of her nostril as she cleans her area. I must had drifted off to sleep because I was awaken by the knocking sounds from Security Guard Michal. He's knocking on the door while announcing "Everlasting Faith Outreach Ministry on site."

When I open up my eyes, I see my neighbor. She was lying in her bed. I sit up. I open my locker get out my King James Bible and left the dorm. When I had enter into the dining room I see the sisters were pulling donated clothes on one of the tables. I had taken a seat waiting for the fellowship to start as I watched them set up. A couple of the older women who lived inside the shelter has enter the room. Miss. Noraine and Mrs. Pat both of them lives on the first floor, in the B dorm.

Miss Noraine she about sixty two and Mrs. Pat looks to be about fifty eight. Mrs. Pat is a dark skin, stocky, big boned women. I detect her from the deep part of the south because she has a southern demeanor about herself. She always worn a fashion wool hat on the top of her head. Sister Riley turns around and see me sitting down and she say, "Praise the Lord." I say back to her, "Praise the Lord." I watched the five ladies set up. They brought another sister whom I never seen before, with them.

About six more residents had shown up. There was no sight, of Billie so far. Once they had finished setting up the tables, they immediately, went into their ministry because they are allow only one hour, to fellowship with us.

They stood next to each other, as us females sat quietly in our seats watching and waiting. They sung slowly and sweet, "Wel_ come__, into this place_____. Welcome__, into this bro_ ken vessel you de sire__ to oblige__, in the present of your peo ple___ as we lift__ our hands, as we offer up, the praise_ to your name___." The missionary woman that always wear the black veil on top of her' head said, "Ladies please join in."

They sung, "Wel_ come__, into this place_____. Welcome__, into these o_pen vessels_ you de sire_ to oblige__, in the pre sent of your peo ple___, as we lift__ our hands_, as we offer up the praise_ to your name____." A lot of resident don't know the spiritual song, but they are really easy to catch on. Anyway I stands with them.

"Wel_ come__ into this place____. Welcome__, into these o_pen vessels_ you de sire_ to oblige__, in the pre sent of your peo ple___, as we lift__ our hands_, as we offer up the praises_ to your name____." Once the other residents see I'm so serious and the ministry is worshiping, they too starts to sing and imitate us, trying to be respectful of the spirit. Wanting to feel the holy one presence.

"Wel_ come__ into this place____. Welcome__, into these o_pen vessels_ you de sire_ to oblige__, in the pre sent of your peo ple____, as we lift__ our hands, as we offer up the praises_ to your name____."

"I don't know about you but I love the Lord," Sister Riley said. All of the women from the ministry had agreed by shaking their' heads in a yes head nod. "Just feel him and welcome him into your heart, and let's welcome him into this place where we are right now," she said. "Wel_ come__ into this place____. Welcome__, into this o_pen vessel_ you de sire_ to oblige__, in the pre sent of your peo ple___, as we lift__ our hands, as we offer up the praise_ to your name____."

Sister Riley say, "The Lord is good. We won't be before you long tonight but as faithful soldiers of the Lord, we tired, but we knew yall girls will be expecting us. So we push our way this evening to bring you're a word and the word is, love."

"Love. The word love is so small when you write it down on paper but the word love is strong and mighty. It is God first commandment. Let turn to St Matthew twenty-two, verse thirty-seven. Before we read God's words I want to pass out bibles. Raise your hand if anyone would like to read from the bible," Sister Riley asked. Some ladies did raised their' hand. The missionaries' walks quickly passing out bibles and helping them find the verse.

Sister Riley continue, "Thou shalt love the Lord thy God with all thy heart, and with all thy soul, and with all thy mind. This is the first and great commandment. And the word of the Lord is blessed. Do you know God is a jealous God? God he don't want you to love anything more than him. He don't want you to love your job. Your money. Your house. Your drugs more than him. If you put God first in your life, do you know what amazing power you could have simply just by loving our God? The word love can conquer all things. Something as simple as saying I love you, can make a difference in your loves one life. When was the last time anyone said to you I love you. When was the last time you told anyone that you love them. Better yet when was the last time you showed someone love?"

The ministry started singing, "I love you. I love you. I love you more today___ because you care for me__ in such a spe_ cial way. That why I praise you. I lift you up, and I mag-ni- fy your name___ that why my heart is fill with praise____. My heart. My mind. My soul be long to you____. You paid the price for me____ way back at Cal-va-ry. That why I love you. I lift you up, and I mag-ni- fy your name_____ that's why my heart is fill with praise____. My heart. My mind. My soul be-long to you____. You paid the price for me____ way back on Cal-va-ry. That why I love you. I lift you up, and I mag-ni- fy your name___ that's why my heart is fill with praise____. That why my heart is fill with praise. That why my heart is fill with praise.

Sister Riley said, "In St. John, three, verse sixteen for God so loved the world, that he gave is only begotten Son, that whosoever believeth in him should not perish, but have everlasting life. Do you know that how much our God love us that he sent his one and only son to die for us that we may be saved. That's how much he love us that he sent his son, to die so we can be saved. And Jesus had to love his' father to carry out the mission. Sometimes the word love can be look at as loyalty. The word love is something that is felt. It's shown. Is there anybody in your life that would go to the ends of the earth with you? Or better yet that you will go to the end of the earth for someone you love. That a powerful act. I love you so much that I would go to the end of the world with you. I love you so much that I gave my one and only son God said.

Sister Riley rejoiced as she continue, "I love you so much that I will die for you. Who else can you say love you that much? The word love is nothing to be taken for granted. Love it can make you or break you. It nothing to be played with. How? You might ask. Some of you has never really been loved. Shown love. Some of you don't even love yourself and that's sad."

Sister Riley said, "Love. The act of love require giving of one self. In love you have strength. I'm proud to know that someone took the time to love me so much that blood was shed not just for me, but for you, **and** me. Think about it, have you ever been in a situation and you called on the name of Jesus and you received amazing strength. That my dear is Love. I love you so much that I died for you. Jesus sledded his' blood so that we can have a connection to our heavenly father. That we may come to worship him. That we may call on his' name in time of trouble. In time of sickness. That we may call on his name when we need healing. In time of protection. That we may call on his name in the time of TRUTH. In time of victory.........God did all of this in the name of **LOVE**. He love us so much that we can be born again in his likeness. Where the old thing are passed away and new things are becoming new. Let's praises God for all he done and for what he is about to do. Praise ye the Lord! Praise the lord our God. Before I end ladies I want to remind you to talk to God when you need a friend. Talk and get to know God by reading his words in the bible. Did you know the bible can be look at as born instructions before leaving earth? Get to know God," Sister Riley repeated, "And it Amen, Amen and Amen. It is done saidth the Lord."

One of the other sister step forward and asked, "Do anyone in here know Jesus? Is anybody ready to give their' soul to Jesus? It's easy all you got to do is come, for all to see, and confess. I am a sinner. And say, I believe that Jesus did and perform all those miracles I read or heard about in the bible. When asked, you say, I want Jesus to be my Lord and Savior. Because we got to go through Jesus-to get to God. That is the first step. Then you must be born again, but right now let's concentrate on confessing Jesus Christ as Lord and Savior. Come the spirit is waiting."

... ...

Not one person got up.

I already confess Jesus Christ is my Lord and Savior. Why didn't any of the other girls get up? Were they ashamed or is it they don't believe or did they already confess like I did. There this a quote in the bible that speak on when people who are ashamed of God. Coming from St. Mark 8:38 in the Kings James version it reads: Whosoever therefore shall be ashamed of me and of my words in this adulterous and sinful generation; of him also shall the Son of man be ashamed, when he cometh in the glory of his Father with the holy angels.

Maybe the females here are like monkey see, monkey do. But that not good because getting to know God is personal. When they ready they will go. Or when, if you chosen and lucky. When your calling come from the spirit which is God hopefully they would come because every knee shall bow and confess-Jesus Christ is Lord and Savior.

The older sister from the ministry asked, "Does anyone need prayer? The time is now. You may come up." The other two missionaries was standing beside the table where they had put the donated clothes. When I walk to the donated table she said, "Take whatever you like. I saw on the table there was tops and small pocketbooks. I didn't see anything of interest so I said, "I had a good time. Good night."

I stood in line by the kitchen. I signed up in the laundry book for a slot to do my laundry tomorrow before I went upstairs. When I got to the fourth floor I heard hands clapping. The sounds are coming from the library. I peeped in and I heard the speaker Dan Diazlow say "We are strong and we can do it!" Again the clients started clapping their' hands. The guard ask me "Are you attending the sobriety support group?"

I closed the door quietly saying, "No. It's just I heard hands clapping and I was curious to find out what was going on? Before I continue to my dorm I saw a sign posted on the wall. Sobriety big award celebration party count down in two days. The Next Class will be starting in two weeks. Be strong. Fight back. Sign up. Walking the hallway before I reached my dorm I notice a lot of hair collectively together on the floor. It stood out because there wasn't any more trash on the ground. I continue walking and I saw those same two Caribbean ladies talking in the hallway. The ones I mention before whenever we have a church service going on how they would be standing in the hallway while holding their own conversation. This time I seen that both of them was watching me. I'm thinking why are they watching me? I walk pass them and the matted hair that's on the ground. Maybe it's my imagination they not watching me. They were just having a casual conversation. Before I turns the corner I looked back. Surprised, they are looking at me. So it wasn't just my imagination they were watching me. What's that all about? I question myself. Just before I reached my dorm door I saw more matted tangle looking hair on the ground. "Umm?" I mumble just before I went inside my dorm.

When I enter inside the Q dorm, the funk hit me smack dead in the face. The urine smell is so strong it almost smell like pure alcohol. I sit on the bed. I'm starting to get a headache because the smell is so awful and strong. I know it that new clients smelling up the dorm.

I'm not sure I can approach her because lots of female in the shelter take medication. Some of them, well a lot of us, is like a bomb, ready and waiting to explode! The shelter life is a stressful way of living. Instead of me dealing with a confrontation. I exit the dorm.

Wow, I wondered-where are those ladies that were just having their own conversation? I was in the dorm for a minute before I decided to come back out. Why aren't they in the hallway? I found that to be odd because they seem to be engage in a serious secret conversation.

I see Mr. Diazlow locking up the door to the library. I guess the sobriety group has finished. Taking the stairs. I going downstairs to the intake office.

When I reached the office I fill out a Resident' Complaint Form.

Resident name: <u>Electra.</u> Date, I put: <u>today date.</u> Indicate type of complaint: I goes to the Environment Column and input <u>smell.</u> Date of event that led to complaint: I insert <u>today date.</u> Time, <u>9:15 pm.</u> Location: <u>Q dorm.</u> Description of the complaint: <u>Resident' funk.</u>

The Q dorm has a terrible smell. Even others in the dorm notice the awful smell. It coming from the resident that make the animal sounds. She smells like pure pee. It not healthy for me or anybody to breath in her' funk. Right now I have a serious headache because of the smell from her urine on her body being it is so strong. I would appreciate if someone can speak to her about her bodily odor. Maybe a Resident Aide can help to assist her with her' hygiene. The client is Q 7 and since she has come inside the Q dorm, the odor has been in the room.

I hands the complaint form to Mr. Jefferson and he read the form over before he signed it. With a copy in my hand I re-enter my stinking room. I take my shower and lay on my bed. I hear Valerie say to whoever she speaking to on the phone, "If I had kids they be with me. Of course I got to get up and go to work tomorrow. I not going to just lay up inside the shelter all day doing nothing. I'll speak to you tomorrow."

Just to tune out my surroundings right now and Valerie malicious gossip and my stinking dorm. I thought about how did I get in this gotdam situation as I looked at Marcell pouring water to clean her wounded foot. My neighbor who doesn't say one word but now has a heart on top of her locker, only reminds me, she only did it after I put a picture of a heart on top of my own locker. The sound of a loud "grunted," just went off inside the room. Dam she just made another animal sound again.

Reader lets go back *to my story:*

Relived at knowing I would have the one hundred dollar and me and the kids won't be in the dark. It help me a hell of a lot in a sense but not completely. I still was in a lot of pain.

My mother got to my house quick. When I open the door she knew I have gotten my tubes tied because she visit me while I was in the hospital. Seeing me in that condition, hump over not walking properly she said, "Ughumed," as she shook her head.

I was hoping that she help me out especially seeing my condition, by giving me the one hundred dollars and let me babysit for her another time but my mother was in a hurry herself-wanting a break from the kids she was now taking care of. I remembered being mad that I had to take care of my mother' foster kids in order to pay my bill. I was in so much pain that I went to my kids' room got Moet and laid her on my bed. I asked all the kids to come inside my bedroom to watch TV so I can lay down.

On my bed was my newborn. My mother brought over this seven month old baby who I had laying on my bed too. JB my son soon to be two. My daughter Champagne age 7. At this time the kids my mother was taking care of, consist of two or three siblings who were all younger than my oldest daughter. I didn't do much with them. I made the foster kids and my kids all sit down at the bottom of my bed inside my bedroom watching the TV- all day.

I had Moet bottle and thal foster baby bottle in the room with me. I had my oldest daughter bring in my bedroom a loaf of bread, peanut butter and jelly. My intention was to make sandwiches for everyone even myself because I knew I had to keep those children for several hours.

I know I needed the one hundred dollars but I was kinda mad at my mother for making me watch them all those hours because I really was in pain. At one point I passed out leaving my oldest daughter in charged.

Anyway by the time she came to my apartment to pick up those children I believe Tonya was with her.

Stop! To the reader: My memory with my last daughter is so blurry. As I'm writing this book, I'm looking back into my past and I see my memory is wishy-washy. I guess it's because I had a lot of stressful dilemmas occurring back-to-back at this point, of time in my life; for example the delivery of a child, the procedure of tying my tubes, moving to a larger apartment, finally buying furniture for my apt, Thomas leaving household responsibilities on me again and my own anxiety, fearing my lights are about to be shut off.

I'm lying on the bed with all those kids sitting at the foot of the bed. As I laid at the top of the bed with two infants. Coming in with my mother I was surprise to see Tonya. It's the 1st time she ever came inside my apartment. She said she come over to see Moet hearing that I had another girl. I was too sick to move, but also, I got the feeling Tonya, she really came by to see the condition that I was in. Neither one of them stayed long nor can I remember who left 1st or if they both left out together. I do recall my mother, she had a new hair style and she said, "Yeah having these kids are too much. While they were with you I cook my dinner and got my hair done. Well let me hurry-up and get home because I got to feed them."

She left.

At this stressful time in my life it's blurry because did they both walk out the door together? Or did Tonya leave 1st. Anyway, mother did give me the one hundred dollar and I remember her rushing out the door. Before she left I know, I had to ask my mother, to watch my kids so I can drive Thomas' car and pay the bill or could she pay the bill for me. Whatever excuse she gave me, all I know, is she didn't help me because I had to call upon Shelby.

I called Shelby on the Phone. When she pick up the telephone I asked, "Shelby can you come upstairs to watch my kids so I can drive to pay my Con Edison bill because I received a notice saying that my lights' are going to be turned off."

Shelby says, "Give me a minute. I'll be right up."

"Bed check." The shift supervisor is making her rounds while collecting signatures. At eleven pm security say "Lights out."

Falling off to sleep after I had to sprayed perfume on my pajamas top and underneath my sheet while laying with the covers over my head- blocking out the funk as the new resident made these loud animal noises.

Chapter Fourteen

When I woke up the lights to the dorm were on. I just saw Rowena the African Security Guard take a glance at herself in the Q-dorm plexi-mirror right before she exited the dorm. Another loud animal sound came from, the stinky new roommate of ours. I don't know why she does that and I ain't trying to find out either because I have my **own** problems.

Today is the first of the month. I received my food stamps of one hundred and forty-five dollars along with my cash benefit of, twenty two dollars and fifty cents.

As I laid in the bed I thought about it again, really, why is it my memory a blank or wishy-washy when it comes to Moet?

I'm had trouble telling yall about her' delivery. I can't remember distinctly everything that happened when I brought her home from the hospital and like,...did Tonya appeared with my mother or not? And if she did, who left 1st? *Did Tonya leave 1st* or did they leave out together?

Reader, as you can see my life has not been easy but my memory is intact except around this time.............. Ummmm?

And that is so freaking weird to me. As I'm writing, it feel as if it's something more than having a memory block, simply because there nothing there. When it should be.

Even with Moet actual delivery is just a blank. But now I'm questioning could there be something else going on? Then again, I could have sworn Tonya came to my apartment with my mother that day. At this point as I'm writing I would really like to know why?

Why is it? Or how come, I can remember things so clearly with this particular point in my life. If I dig, and continue with my story maybe I'll find the answer to everything clearly from beginning to end...................Okay. Now, I clearly remember the phone call...........and Thomas rushing out. Also knowing the lights were about to be turned off. I know I had to watch a couple of children for my mother. I just can't remember the exact amount of children that I watched that day. Like, was there three or four children? And why can't I see their faces? Or remember their' age and genders.

Um......I do recall this set of foster kids my mom brought over for me to watch there was an infant. A baby boy. I know this for sure because I was laying on my bed in pain and there was two infants that needed to be bottle-fed. Mine and her'. Moet and her' four or was it five months old, baby boy? Anyway all I knew it was another baby and all I can see faintly is this dark skin baby boy laying with me and Moet at the top of my bed.

I do remember being anger how Thomas ran the fuck out the house. Then shock at my mom not loaning me the money but instead bringing me a few of her small batter kids again to watch. Then left on me in my condition. I remember being really upset.

Then again maybe the reason why I can't describe them is because I did only kept them just that one time. Anyway, I recall being upset with my mother too because she left them on me for **hours**. I know I needed the hundred dollars but damn, I just had surgery. I was hoping she would have just loan me the money. I didn't really think she was going to leave all those kids on me like that, and all day too. I remember the kids was getting restless being confide to one room. I kept telling the kids to, "Sit down! Don't touch and play with the knobs on my brand new bedroom set. Be quiet because my newborn and the other baby were sleeping." Once again I had my hands, full. Little did I know that was the beginning of me not getting any slept and also the end of Thomas and mine relationship. I couldn't rest with all those small children in the bedroom-touching this and wanting that as well as monitoring them, making sure no one get hurt. Making sure no one destroyed my brand new furniture. Then I had to feed everyone too.

When my mom came to pick up her children. I was so happy to get rid of those kids and relieved when she handed me the money and overwhelm with emotions at how my day had started out. Frustrated already and slightly disappointed as I watch my mother just pick-up her' kids and dotted out of my apartment without even helping me, to the point that I had to call on Shelby. Asking her to come watch my kids while I drove to pay the light bill.

Whew! My lights were saved, that was a close call.

Then another emergency had happened.

I had to call and ask Shelby again to come watch my children because the corner store ran out of the Enfamil milk, which Moet was on. Enfamil milk in the can comes in two colors, blue and pink. The color represent one can is for iron supplements and the other is regular. Well Moet couldn't drink from the blue can. She had to drink the milk from the pink can because it was determine from the hospital. So now I'm driving all around going from one store to the next, wanting to find the right color can of milk for my baby. When I did come across the correct milk formula that store didn't accept WIC voucher. That was another reason I was having difficulties. So here I am driving all around until I had found a store all the way on Nostrand Avenue. I remember I brought two cases because all the stores seem to be out of the pink can.

Security Guard Fancy is knocking on the Q-dorm door. There's rapid knocking sound of tat, tat, tat, tat, tat, tat, tat, tat, tat coming from off the Q dorm door. Then she opens the door and say in her Jamaican accent, "Ladies nine o'clock be ready to leave the dorm." I get out from my bed, start getting ready to leave the dorm. I'm thinking let me go pick up my metro cards that will be a little extra more money in my pocket especially once I hustle it off. Before I exit the dorm I check my pocketbook to make sure I have my Medicaid card so I can pick up my cash benefit.

Mrs. Wilks is the Shift Supervisor inside the intake office today. I stands in line as she hands out metro cards. When I'm next I say, "Good morning Mrs. Wilks can I get my metro card." She scans the book for my name. Then she pulls two packs of metro cards out from a bunch of metro cards that were wrapped up in a lot of rubber bands. In the book Mrs. Wilks write down both of the serial numbers that are behind the two dollar cards. Next she ask me to sign. Signing next to my name I see my caseworker state the reason for issuing is dentist appointment.

I leaves the shelter. First thing first, let me go pick up my little bit of money. Hopefully I won't be going to the cash checking place anymore to pick up my cash benefit of 22 dollars and 50 cents being now, the government is taking out a surcharge fee of 2 dollars and 50 cents. I found out through the grapevine meaning (word of mouth) Bank of America atm vestibule are now issuing out PA cash money. All you got to do is insert your Medicaid card into the slot, enter your pin number and the money comes out without paying the surcharge fee. So that where I'm going, to see if it's true.

There's a Bank of America right down the block from the shelter. I felt so weird inserting my Medicaid card into the bank' atm slot instead of a bank card. Surenough, the rumor was true because once I inserted my Medicaid card the machine ask for my pin number. Next a selection came up for me to choose. I select withdraw, which is only 20 dollars in my case. By doing it this way I got to keep the surcharge fee of 2 dollars and 50 cents. I know it sound lame but for me every little bit helps.

Now I'm heading to the subway station on the M line to hustle off the metro cards I accumulated. I prefer the Eastbrunwick trains station because it always so busy with people coming in and out but I just don't feel like taking the walk. So right now any train station would do.

Standing there by the token booth trying not to look suspicious as if I'm waiting for the train. I make my way by the vendor machine where I see lots of people who are now buying cards. Audibly enough so that only the people buying the cards could hear me. I asks, "Anyone need to buy a metro card?"

A guy standing in line, look like he's rushing to get to work say, "I need a card." I say, "I have a single ride and a four dollar metro card." The guy who's in a rush say, "Let me get the four dollar metro card." I give him the four dollar metro card and he hands me $4.00.

I watch him as he take the wrapping off the card. Assuring him that it was not a bogus card. It's my way of building up clientele proving my metro cards are good and making sure he doesn't switch the card on me-trying to scan me. He swipes and go through the turnstile.

Once he goes through I quickly go back to the small crowd by the vending machine and say to a lady whose about to put her' cash inside the machine to buy a $4.00 card. Quickly I say, "Excuse Miss, can you purchase the $4.00 card from me. I'd like to buy me a cup of coffee." She looks at me standing there with the two metro cards in my hand. I say, "The cards is good."

The lady say "I need a $4.00 metro card." I say, "I have two single rides. They good. Quickly I press the card information on the machine and inserted the card. The machine read $2.00. I did the same for the next card. The lady ask me, "You have change of a five dollar bill?" Realizing I got the sale. I quickly say, "Yes."

Going back to the machine and stand on the side awaiting for some more people to arrive in the train station. If I was at Eastbrunwick all the cards would had been already gone but this station isn't so bad. There's a lot of Spanish people on this side and a lot of them don't speak or understand English, or pretend not too. Anyway I receive more play from my own Black people. There were a group of people coming through the station doors. So quickly I ask, "Do anybody need to buy a single ride?"

I see one black guy goes over toward the machine. Walking up to him. I ask him, "Do you need to buy a single ride?" The guy say "No. I need a four dollar metro card." I said, "I have two, 2 dollars metro cards, and they good. Could you buy them from me? It's just that I'm trying to get something to eat. I could show you the cards are good." He said "That's alright. You don't have to do all that." He bought both cards. I sold all my cards, I'm outta here.

As I went down the subway stairs heading towards Sub-Subs delicious supermarket counting my cash money. I goes into the supermarket and order a sandwich from the deli. "Can I have Maple Glaze Honey Turkey with Swiss cheese, mayonnaise, lettuce and tomato, and with that I like a Mountain Dew soda." Then I pick up a large bag of Lays potatoes' chip, and the large pack of Vienna cookies. Heading back to the shelter I see True God standing in his same spot.

"Good morning True God," I would say. "Yo whatz up, Electra," True would answer back. I continue walking, turns the corner walk a couple more steps now tapping on the entrance door to the shelter. Security Guard Monique buzzes me in.

After watching my bags go through the scanner now she physically hand check all my bags. After I walk through the magnetometer device Monique hand wands me and announces on her' walkie-talkie, "Electra coming up with food copy." I heard a guard on the other end say "Copy."

I goes to the dining room passing the busy intake office. I had found a seat by the window. Just in case; if someone decide to take a shit in the dining room' bathroom, this time, at least I would be sitting by the window. I take out my food and start to eat and write. It's the beginning of the month so I should be able to eat in peace, because lots of girls receive their food stamps as well as their cash on the first of the month.

Back to the story.

Within days of Moet coming home I hadn't gotten any sleep. The pain from the operation along with my newborn was keeping me up at night. I kid you not, I did not sleep. At this time in my life, I had enrolled Champagne in this high notch private school. So in the morning I had to drive my oldest daughter to her school while I dealt with my son Brandon terrible two stage.... And all mothers knows what a struggle that can be. Not to mention at the same time Brandon was being weaned off his' bottle and going through potty training.

The majority of parents' know how newborns acts...... they have no sense of time. Moet slept in the day while I played and dealt with JB terrible two stage. When he finally fell asleep for a nap. Moet woke up needing to be fed and a diaper change. Before I knew it, it was time to go pick up Champagne from school. Her school was a twenty five minute drive away from the house.

When Champagne came home I had to assist her with her' homework. The homework, for her it was really intense because of the higher education coming from the private school. I call myself spending money on my daughter education, wanting the best for her so she could succeed. Copying off the West Indians, by not putting their' kids in our public school system. By doing this, I had a really good reason to say to Thomas, "I really don't have the money when a bill needed to be paid."

Fixing dinner for the kids, washing out Champagne uniform, ironing, doing her hair, keeping the apartment tidy, bathing everyone for the next day and putting them to bed I'm thinking finally, I'm going to get some sleep but nooo Moet keeps me up in the night. In week two of Moet coming home, I'm still in pain. During the same thing since I brought Moet home but now I'm driving keeping schedule appointments for my WIC checks. Picking up WIC vouchers, cashing in WIC checks, doing the food shopping and buying baby food. I found myself calling on Shelby a lot to watch my kids while I drove quickly around the neighborhood taking care of my personal business.

Still I haven't had no sleep. I kid you not, no sleep.

Shelby started becoming worried about me saying, "Tami you going to kill yourself. You carrying and doing way too much. I don't know how much longer you can keep it up."

Seeing me still limp over Shelby starting to worry.

I'm taking care of JB with his demanding terrible two stage. Driving Champagne back and forth to her school. Helping her with her' homework projects, preparing dinner, fixing bottles and driving to Toy's R US to pick up large boxes of pampers simply because it cheaper, and, by doing it this way I get more pampers for the buck/money. I'm washing and drying clothes, making breakfast and lunch-doing all this, as I had still found myself experiencing pain.

Plenty of times I had to call and relay on Shelby to watch my younger kids'. One reason why I couldn't take both younger children with me when I drove is because I had only one car seat. Plus it was faster to me, leaving out of the house preferably getting all of us dress and preparing a diaper bag plus I couldn't carry Moet. I was still very much in pain and unable to stand up properly. I felt it was easier just to leave and to come right back into the house so I called on Shelby- A Lot. Shelby was well aware of me not getting any sleep.

When I pick up my cash benefits I had to pay Champagne' school fees and the gas bill. My telephone bill was also high because Thomas' children and his' mother called the house often collect from Jamaica. I just put down enough money on the telephone bill so that it won't get turned off. Purchasing pampers for two children, and training diaper for junior, keeping food on the table, gas for the car-my cash was gone quickly.

I started getting really cranky wondering......... where Thomas was. His father should have been buried by now. I thought I should be seeing him walk through the door any moment now. I was leaning on Shelby so much even Shelby started asking, "Where is Thomas?" I said, "He still in Jamaica." Shelby asked, "Well how long is he staying Tami? You need his' help. Shouldn't he be on his way back by now? I never seen you so stressed and you don't look so good. Girl, you going to pass out. You can't keep going on this way. This doesn't look good Tami."

"I know. I haven't gotten any sleep," I said.

This is the first time Shelby ever showed any signs of me being a bother to her. Maybe because she too was expecting and she's in her last trimester. I found myself calling on Shelby to watch the kids while I ran and did this and that. Thomas he should be the one here helping me. Where the hell is he?

Becoming overwhelm, and thinking ... why Thomas isn't back from Jamaica? Well I did something for the very first time. I made a phone call to find out whatz going on with Thomas.

I called Rude Boy (Thomas brother).

"Hello," I said. Rude Boy said "Who speaking?" I said, "It's me Rude Boy, Tami." Shock at my call he said "Oh... hi, Tami."

I said, "Rude Boy I see you back already from Jamaica and I'm sorry to hear about your' father passing away." He said "Thank you Tami."

I asked him, "So when did you come back from Jamaica?" Rude Boy said "Tami I been back for a while." I said, "Really? So where is Thomas?" Rude Boy said "Eehey. He didn't come back from Jamaica." I said, "No."

There was a moment of silent then Rude Boy said "I thought he came home already. I'm surprises he haven't come back yet."

I ask Rude Boy, "Did yall bury your father okay? Did everything go well?" "Yeah mon," Rude Boy replied.

I asked Rude Boy, "Did your brother George attend the funeral? Is he back in New York already?" Rude Boy said "Yeah mon he went and he already back home."

George is Thomas oldest brother who also is married. He and his wife' both are West Indian and they are Correction Officers. They purchase one of those beautiful brick homes I was telling yall about for their family. Thomas brought me to their' home a couple of times.

I asked, "So why isn't Thomas back?" Rude Boy said "Tami mon me don't know. How's everything with you? Are the kids alright?"

I said, "Beside me being tired I guess everything is okay." Not having much more to talk about we said our "Goodbyes."

I was pissed off! You mean to tell me Thomas still in Jamaica knowing I just had his' baby and I wasn't even feeling well because of the surgery. He seen the condition I was in when he left. Rude Boy and George, both brothers been came back from Jamaica and Thomas nowhere around to be found. See, that's what I'm becoming to realize about Thomas, he's selfish, one minded and...and......and he really doesn't love me.

After I had given birth and we bought our daughter home from the hospital. I came home to this shit! This is not how it supposed to be when a women bring home her newborn from the hospital. Well, this is not how I wanted it to be or pictured it to be. I'm a beautiful woman who deserve to be treated like a lady-with some respect. I'm not a street walker. Thomas didn't pick me up from a street corner. Whereas he can treat me like shit! Nor am I this chicken head female; meaning a dumb woman that stupid, who allow anything and everything to go on inside her' home and she don't give a fuck what happens to her' children or her' self. Nor am I anyone second dish.....unless I want to be.

I'm handling a crying baby who wants to be fed. An energetic son who wants to go outside to play. He's burning up all his energy climbing and running around here in this apartment. I'm driving my oldest daughter back and forth to school while helping her with challenging homework for her' age. I'm doing dishes, maintaining my apt, keeping everything up and running like my telephone, the rent, my lights and gas, putting gas in the car, supplying food on the table and packing school lunches for my daughter. I'm washing and folding clothes, giving baths, braiding hair, changing pampers, potty training, mixing milk formulas and dealing with temper tantrums from this bad ass little boy in his terrible two stages. Handling all of this while I can't barely stand up straight to walk!

Because of the pain it hurts to breathe, it hurts to laugh. It hurt when I got to stand up from sitting down on the couch. I couldn't turn left or right without flinching. **I'm** fucking tired. My newborn keeps me up all night. My older kids keeping me up during the day. I'm running errands and keeping the house together becoming completely overwhelm. I have my hands completely full. What the FUCK!

I didn't get any sleep. Let me rephrase that, I CAN'T GET ANY SLEEP BECAUSE THE KIDS WON'T LET ME. I became furious because I haven't been asleep in weeks and Thomas Black Ass is hanging out some fuckin where.

I'm not lying. I haven't had a chance to get a good night rest since I brought the baby home from the hospital. Man fuck this! I'm tired of Thomas always going off leaving me penniless. Taking me for granted because I'm a welfare recipient, knowing damn well all I have to do is go to the government and have the system pay the bill.

So what if PA picks up the bill, what is he doing for me...........for the kids? For us! ....fuckin nothing! Everything is in my damn name. Even the kids is in my damn name. The apartment, the lights, the gas and the damn telephone is in my name..................What the FUCK is he doing?

Why Hell! The Black ass mother fucker doesn't even take care of his' own damn self!

Every time I turn around Jamaica need this. Jamaica needs that. Jamaica, Jamaica, JAMAICA! Give me a break already. My God, he's not even buying food for our' kids like that....cause **I am**! Wait let me back that up a bit, the city is, because our' children is on fuckin PA and they receives WIC vouchers for their' supply of milk, cereal and baby formulas. Not only that, my Medicaid card is paying for all their' shoots, medicine and doctor visits. My food stamps is buying the food for the house. The government pay our rent and when you look at it feed us too! So what the **Fuck** is Thomas doing?

He ain't doing fuckin **Shit!**

My food stamps is buying the food he eat to keep him healthy going back and forth looking for work. When he come home with money and when he don't come home with money he still ate a well cook meal, wash his ass and slept on clean sheets with a roof over his' fuckin head.

I watch this man ride a bicycle in the cold looking for work-coming home with nothing. I watch this man rode on strike buses and then paid dues to the collision, all in an attempt of looking for work and yet he had my support. I watch this man walk, I watch him car pool sitting in the back seat of his friends' vehicle looking for work and through it all, good and bad, paid checks and unpaid checks he had my support. Thomas came home to a home that didn't have any worries. I even watch him perform certain auxiliary duties with the precinct down the block from me, while only wanting to appear like a descent citizen. And now I fully understand why............ to add on to his' resume for citizenship because he married to stay into this county.

I had supported Thomas in all his many endeavors. Thomas doing more for his' people then he is for the family who helping him **help** his' people. Damn, everything going to Jamaica, **mother fuck those bitches**......what about us?! When is Thomas going to start caring **for us?**

I'm tried!!!

I know Thomas had no control of the situation that his' father has passed away. But give me a break already he could have at least left some money here with us, with me I mean. Whereas I didn't have to babysit all those children in my fuckin condition. Thomas went to Jamaica but he should have come right back when the funeral service was over. Not stay there like he's on vacation. This is not the time for a vacation! I'm the one who is in need of a vacation. When my turn going to come?

I'm beginning to **hate** Thomas.

His father' death was really bad timing, and I'm getting pretty upset with Thomas always leaving me high and dry every time he goes to Jamaica. I'm starting to have doubt about our relationship. I needed him here with me but he was already gone and I'm in all this pain, all alone to defend for myself while taking care of our children. I can't stand up for goodness sake and I can't even breathe normally.

.......Sitting there on the couch looking around angrily at the situation I'm in. I saw my telephone bill on the table. Struggling to get off of the couch trying to minimize the pain, walking over to the table. I open up the envelope. Dammm, my telephone bill so high.

Inside the envelope, beside the bill, I received a telephone statement with all the calls that were made from my telephone number, as well as, all the accepted collect telephone numbers', from Jamaica. I notice there was some numbers to Jamaica that were called more than once.

Then I got this magnificent idea.

As I sat at the table I decided to inquire about Thomas' where about. So I pick up the telephone and called the first number at the top of the statement page, to Jamaica.

Ring, ring, the telephone is ringing. A female Caribbean voice said, "Hello." I said, "Hello my name is Tami and I looking for Thomas Benton. May I speak to him?"

I could tell the woman was shocked to hear me ask to speak to Thomas because she paused and there was complete silence for a moment before she answer back, "He's not here." I said, "If you shall see him can you let him know Tami called. And ask for him to return my call." The Caribbean woman said, "If I see him I would tell him."

That was my beginning, because now, I was on a roll. I went to the next number and did the same thing. "Hello, my name is Tami and I'm looking for Thomas Benton. May I speak to him?" The person was shock too and said "He's not here." I said, "When you see him can you let him know Tami is looking for him. And ask him to give me a call."

Well to tell yall I called every number on the statement. It took some time calling all those numbers. I'm quite sure Thomas would get the message and also, he will be shock to here I call Jamaica looking for him all the way from New York, especially, without him leaving me not one contact number in case of an emergency. I'm quite sure Thomas is stun, and pretty amaze that I tried to reach him in Jamaica.

Shortly after I made the phone calls a day or two later, frankly I really can't pin point it. All I know sometime in the evening I get a knock at my apartment door. I looked out the peephole and see Thomas' face. I had Moet in my arms because it was her feeding time. I open the door. Thomas was standing there with this Caribbean male cabby. Who he said drove him from the airport talking about "Tami he help me carry some of my tings to the door." As I observed Thomas standing in the hallway with the cab driver......
.......A whole month done went by. One month! The kids came running to the door, wanting to see who it was I was

talking to. I said not one word. I just handed him his wrap up one month old daughter. Shove the baby bottle at him and went to my bed and I pass out, meaning I finally got me some sleep.

Security enter the dining room announcing, "Yoga is being held on the third floor." Not wanting to stop writing but I decided, I eat a couple of cookies before I head upstairs to the yoga class. Suddenly a couple of resident comes to the table asking me for some of my Vienna cookies. So I hand some out.

Leave the dining room. When I reach the third floor I saw Security Guard Marsha sitting on her post by the laundry room. When she notice me coming through the third floor exit door, she rolled her eyes at me. I question myself what did I do to her?........Ooh I know what that's all about, someone must had told her I wrote her up for playing favoritism with the clients.

So, as I got closer to her so that I can go inside the yoga class. I rolled my eyes right back at her ass because we are all residents of this shelter. There ain't no one resident better than the next.

When I open the door there were Bertha, Thomasina, the white girl named Carla and skinny Catrina-I think she Jewish. As I enter the room I heard Samantha say "as we inhale deep breathe opening and lifting the shoulder blades." Samantha turns in my direction and smiles at me, saying in a whisper "Glad to see you made it to the class. Sign in and stand on a mat." As the music played softly in the background. I quickly wrote my name.

To the class, Samantha continued by saying, "As we stand tall, ladies, let's begin to move our head slowly to the right. Turning your neck as far as it can go comfortably. Feeling the stretch in your neck from your left earlobes to the left shoulder. Holding the position, while inhale deeply through your nose. Hold it..... Now exhaling slowly through your mouth as you bring your neck back to the center. Great! Let do the same for the left side."

We ladies slowly moved our head going to the left. Then coming back towards the center. Sam said, "Feel the stretch alongside the neck ladies as we glide our head from left to right. Now the next thing we will be doing as we stand. With our shoulders-let's begin moving our shoulder blades up and down. With each movement we are releasing tension. Inhale through your nose as we move the shoulder blades up and exhale slowly as we release, all tensions. Focus ladies on bringing your shoulders as close to your earlobes as you possibly can. Letting your movement become slow and precise. Let's repeat this movement two more times."

"Good job," Sam said, "Now let try rotating the shoulders backward in a circling movement. Losing the joints by opening, bringing in life to the upper section of the back." As I looked around the room I notices more residents coming inside the room as Samantha quietly said, "Please sign in and stand on a mat."

Sam continue, "Ladies now let's rotate them forward in a circling motion." Everybody was noticing how their' shoulder bone was cracking with the movement. Catrina said, "Shit. I know I'm getting old but I didn't think I was that old hearing my bones snapping." Thomasina said, "Snap, crackle, pop, all they want too. This feel soooo good."

Samantha said, "Exercising and stretching is good for the body. With our busy day sometimes we forget to pay attention to the small thing. I encourage each and every one of you to practice these movements everyday showing your body that you love it and appreciate it."

Sam spoke, "Okay ladies, let's shake it off.......... Now let lift both arm towards the ceiling stretching each arm. First with our left arm-stretching those fingers. Reaching upward as if we reaching, now trying to grab each star, in the sky. Remember ladies! In yoga what we do for one side of the body, we also do for the other side. For creating balance and strength equally."

Samantha spoke with enthusiasm, "Now with our right arm-stretching our fingers as we reach upwards as if we are reaching and grabbing the stars...... Quickly now let switch back to the left-Grab! Grab, grab ladies! Stretch your fingers, lift those arms and pay attention to your breathing techniques. Quickly move and switch arm. Showing the same amount of energy to each side of the body. With your right fingers grabbing each star, bringing life into your arms."

Samantha shouted "Now bring both arms down to you side. Quickly now bringing both arms in the air. Twinkling your fingers for a job well done. Now inhale strongly through your nose.....while exhaling slowly through your mouth...... while bringing both arms to your side."

Samantha asked, "How do you feel because I feel great! I only hope you feel the same way ladies. Let lift the left arm, bending and gently messaging the back of your neck with your left fingers. While rotating your head concentrating on each finger working the neck muscle. As we release any stiffness. While pointing your elbow towards the ceiling as you look up for opening the ribcage to your heart. Concentrating on stretching the ribcage becoming tension free. Now let do the same for our right arm. Messaging the neck with a pointed elbow. Opening up the right side ribcage. Don't forget to breathe ladies. Inhale.....and Exhale....."

Sam spoke, "With both arms now at our side. Find a spot on the wall. I like for us to focus on that spot. Inhaling and exhaling concentrating now only on your breathing. Listening to your heart beat with each breath you take as you inhale, slowly and deeply allowing your chest to become full of oxygen. Now exhale long making your heart pump strong. Now with each slow inhale you take allow your chest to become full. Focusing on that one spot on the wall as we exhale release positive energy in the air. Let's repeat this two more times. Good job ladies."

Samantha said, "While standing let start to roll our head in a full circle. In a steady continuous motion going around and around. Notice how each movement feels as your head goes around and around. Okay ladies lets switch and rotate our' head in the opposite direction. Now stop."

Sam asked, "Do you think our eyeballs need a little attention?" Bertha said, "Now how we going to exercise our eyeball? I gotz to see this one."

Laughing Sam said, "Our body is our temple and everything need attention from time to time. So ladies knowing this please lets show love to this area on our body. As we are standing still, only moving your eyeballs look towards your left and hold it as we count to five. Now let's look up and hold it as we count to five. Now let's look to the right. Hold it as we count to five and lastly let's look down, hold it as we count to five. Holding your head up ladies with all eyes are now on me. Now let us blink those eyes ladies. Blink, blink, blink, blink and blink. Remember yoga is all about balance and strength for good health. So only moving your eyeball look to the right. Now let's look up. Look to the left and lastly let's look down. Great! Now facing me."

Samantha said, "Welcome to yoga, now that we did our beginning stretch. Lets' concentrate on working the body and losing and stretching the muscle for maintaining good health, flexibility and balance. Ladies please take a seat on the floor," as we all sat on our mat.

Sam spoke, "With both legs stretched out in front of you, and both arm resting at your side. Lets' lift and bend your left knee, while placing your left hand behind you. Now bring your right arm over to your left bended knee as comfortable as you can go. Lets' place the right elbow to the outer side of your bended left knee. Exhale as you turn your body while looking totally toward the left giving your spine a good twist, as you hold and breathe in the position. Concentrating solely on the stretch you feel in your upper and lower back." We did the same for our right side.

Sam said, "Lets' separate our legs as far as we can go comfortably. Wanting to concentrate on the stretch from your inner thigh. With your legs still separate let's take both hands, pressing forward between your inner thighs, bending as far as you can comfortably. To intensify the stretch, let's try walking your fingers in front of you. Hold it. Now lean into the position lift those arms pushing yourself to go a little farther by giving yourself small pulsing pushes. Push, push, push now inhale as you come up slowly. Exhale resting with both hands behind you."

Sam said, "With our last position sit up properly and fold your legs and if you can't fold the legs it alright too. With hands place firmly on the floor let's start to rock those hip bones. Lifting our butt check from the ground in steady movement. Fill how your side is opening and closing with each rock." We did that for a couple of minutes, rocking, feeling each side open and close.

Sam said, "Stop and feel the energy that you have put out into this room. With both eyes closed. Lifting your hands in the air, ladies start pulling whatever you need from the space around you. Pull in what you need to make yourself fill complete. Start pulling positive energy and putting it into yourself. Thinking only good thoughts of inspiration and good health."

Sam said, "Keeping your eyes closed as we go around the room tell us what is it that you pull from your space. Keep your eyes closed." Sam called out my name "Electra can you tell us what it is you pull into yourself from the space you in." I said "I pulled in a set of keys to my apt."

Everybody bust out laughing even me. Sam said with folding hand in a prayer position. "Namaste. Meaning honoring the grace in all living beings. Yoga is now over."

Leaving the class we had all felt alive and energetic. It's not quite 4 pm for the dorms to open so I went to Jose and brought a 16 oz. diet Pepsi, in the bottle. No cans or glass bottles are allowed inside any shelters. When I walked into my dorm it didn't smell like piss and I was surprised to see that Q one, Marcell was gone. Her' bed has been strip of linen and her' locker is open and has been cleared out of all her belongings'. Wow she didn't stay in the shelter long at all. I wonder where she went. I wonder if she got transfer to another dorm. Or did she simply just leave? Anyway I heads into the bathroom to take my shower. Sat on my bed to continue writing.

Back to the story.

Once I gotten my rest, when I woke up I wasn't interested in Thomas any more. My attitude towards him has change and he did notice it. I was upset with him and I'm really starting to analyze our relationship. I getting tired of Thomas and his' bullshit. He may have spent his nights and majority of holidays with me but his' heart was in Jamaica. To me, our relationship were already approaching towards shaky grounds because of Adrianne. I was still piss off at Thomas about that situation and I haven't forgotten it either. I believe they were having an affair but I couldn't prove it. Now this shit. I had to face fact that this man doesn't love me and I'm being used. Every time when Thomas came home from Jamaica he had to start building all over again, meaning there was a big telephone billed that needed to be paid from making and accepting collect calls from Jamaica. Thomas had to start looking for work all over again. I found out he empty out his saving account whenever he went back home to Jamaica. That's why he couldn't help me pay the light bill. He would have to buy himself a whole new wardrobe and Thomas' clothes are expensive. Some of his partying shirts cost one hundred dollars. Some outfits cost more! Even his' shoes he gave away. Oh man, I was getting so tired of this lopsided relationship. He never even brought me or the kids' one thing back from Jamaica out of all the times I had watch this man go over there. Not even a lousy cheap ass tee shirt.

I'm starting to realize all my sacrifices and hard work is getting me nowhere but tired and exhausted. I'm helping build up another country helping people I don't even know. Nobody telling me thank you or showing me any kind of appreciation for helping aiding them. Thomas mother did tell one of her' daughters that I treated her well when she visited New York. Thomas made me feel like his people were so poor that at first I wanted to help them but I'm not getting anywhere financially with Thomas. I don't see me, progressing in the relationship I have with Thomas. Every time he accumulate money, he spends it on Jamaica. Then he would leave, come back and start the process all over again.

I'm not getting anywhere! The relationship we have I'm making it, creating it and funding it. What is he putting inside this relationship? Nothing! Majority of the time, Thomas' kids and his' mother calls him collect from Jamaica. When the phone call is over or during the phone call I could hear him saying "Eehey, the water bill. Don't worry I send the money. Or there's a problem going on with the house?" I'm sick and tired of hearing him say "Tami me need to buy this and I'm shipping down that." The money was always going to Jamaica for one reason or another.

Since Thomas been back from Jamaica I was giving him the cold shoulder. Not speaking to him. Just not completely sure how to handle this delicate situation I was face with, thinking I want out.

Thomas think he can have his cake and eat it to. He started wanting to fool around with me, wanting us to have sex, but I wasn't interested. Just like a dumb ass man, he was thinking that all I wanted is a piece of his dick and I will quiet down and start acting right.

Once he realize, seriously, I wasn't interested. He got his ego hurt.

Thomas force me to have sex with him.

That was a very bad mistake. Thomas shouldn't have did that to me, because I had to actually go along with it! Unless it could has been seen as rape.

Then........... Oh no! He did something, so like a bullshit **nigger**, of a man. He came inside of me so hard on purpose hoping he can impregnated me. That disgusting mother fucker!

Oh no......I hope I'm not pregnant again. Having sperm go inside me less than two month after I have given birth. You know any woman would get pregnant fast. Even the doctors tell a woman "Abstained from having sex after you had given birth because your chances are so high in becoming pregnant again."

You know he's a dirty dog trying to get me pregnant on purpose. That all he want is to see me bare foot and pregnant. Making me become vulnerable so he can have his way. Thomas want to help me do what? Have more children out of wedlock? Stay on welfare and not do anything good worth talking about with my life? Stay here in this run down building with a bunch of desperate single females boosting his' ego, making him feel like he the best man on the planet. Pleasssse!

Oh gosh I had to wait a whole month to find out if my menstruation will come down. I was piss off! Once again he proves to me he isn't shit.

Please don't let me be pregnant...... please. Thomas knew I wouldn't have another abortion because early in our relationship I did became pregnant with his' child. That was when Thomas had just moved in with me. Thomas remember how I contemplated and express my feeling to him about not wanting any abortion. It was clearly due to not being ready to have another child, at that time, plus we have just moved in together and I felt it was way too soon.

We both waited in silence to see who won.

My period came down for that month and I was amaze at how fast the tubes tying work.

YES! What a relief knowing I wasn't pregnant. Thomas is dirtyyyy-trying his best to keep me bare foot and pregnant wishing that I stay down, while leaning on me, he's move up. I know a lot of women who like to trap a man with conceiving a child. In hoping by doing this, the man stays with her.

Not only girls/females do that type of trapping, men/boys do it too. Trying to tie you down. Well, Thomas it didn't work. I'm not pregnant! Tying my tubes even through it hurt like hell was the best thing for me cause if I had not tied my tubes, maybe I would have been giving birth to another child for this bull shit man who really doesn't love me or have my best interest at heart. Tying my tubes.......it work because I did not get pregnant. Aha!

So now I know that I was not pregnant. I wanted to have a serious talk with Thomas concerning our relationship. I wanted to know where our relationship was going. Would Thomas and I in the future take that type of commitment? Or am I just playing wifey? I came to a decision if Thomas not taking this relationship serious, well, neither am I.

Plain and simple what good for the goose is good for the gander. That just how I feel.

For some reason Thomas must have felt I wanted to have this type of discussion because he keep avoiding me. One night after I put the children to sleep. I finally got Thomas to sit and talk. He couldn't put it off any longer the moment was here. I said, "Thomas you can't keep living this way. One moment you here with me and the next moment you in Jamaica. You told me you were not with your' children mother but yet when your' father had passed, you stayed in Jamaica for a whole month and you can't tell me you were with your' mother."

Thomas was sitting on the couch listening, not saying a word.

I said, "Surely this got to be tiresome living two lives. It's not fair to me or to you. I want more from this relationship. I didn't have babies just to be having babies I thought we were going somewhere. You got to make a discussion. I understand if you not ready to make a commitment but you can't expect me to stay here being all faithful, playing wifey, while you live this double life. You don't even take care of your own self because you are so busy doing everything only for the people in Jamaica."

Thomas sat there on the couch leaning with his elbow on his knee listening. He didn't say one word.

So I said, "Thomas you work so hard and I don't see where you save even for yourself and you know I express to you about purchasing one of those two family brick homes. I even found out where and I got us the application." Thomas not saying a word. Then I said, "You have to make a decision."

Standing up from the couch Thomas said "Tami I'm like a fish out of water and where the water leads me, I go." What did he just say? •∗!⊗∗≅ Ω.

I said, "Thomas well if you can't make a decision and you going to leave this conversation to where the water leads you...............well you may not like where the water may lead you to!"

Thinking to myself for Thomas to be ten years older than me, he sure said something stupid, or, maybe......I'm just not the one for him and...... he just not the one for me.

That was the end of our conversation, as for me, all that matters, that was the end of our relationship. With an answer like that, to such a serious question. It's over. Man this is my life, and to me, it not some kind of a joke business. So on that note, I didn't want to be with Thomas any longer. He made his choice and I made mine.

Thomas saw I was serious and sometime after his disappearing act when he cash in his paycheck he started coming home with a bottle of Champagne; Asti Supmanti. I guess wanting to get back in my good grace. Or, I hate to think him trying to get me drunk wanting me to become an alcoholic so he can have his way.

Thomas disk me in front of Adrianne. And he disk me when I came home with our' daughter. He disk me always putting his' family needs and his' needs in front of mine. He disk me and the kids by never ever bringing us a souvenir back from Jamaica when he went there. He disk me by never leaving me any money behind when he left for Jamaica-taking me for granted feeling that my city can and will supply all of my financial needs. He disk me by never leaving a contact number in case of an emergency for me to reach him while he was in Jamaica. He disk me by not being honest why he putting all kind of merchandise in my apartment just to ship them overseas building up their apartments or homes. He disk me by forcing me to have sex when I said no and I had every right to be upset with him. He disk me by not putting our son in private daycare especially when he had the money to do it so in order that I can do something more productive with my life than just stay here inside the house. He disk me knowing he was marry and not allowing me to know the truth and of the reason why he married her. Thomas he disk me so many time that I no longer wanted to be with him sexually nor did I want to play house, anymore. I realize I deserves better. So I became somewhat distance from him and he notice it.

In my book, our relationship it is so fuckin over!

Every morning I got up not acknowledging him. I cook breakfast just for me and the kids. I was thinking what to do with this man who is living in my house, who is using me. So I gave him the silent treatment because it a hurting thing realizing I been play for a fool by someone I would had marry if he had asked me. I fuckin would had said **yes**. Even though he wasn't rocking my boots. Even though I wasn't madly in love with him. Even though he is a pig headed man not willing to compromise and always putting his' needs first. I would had marry him.

But why?

The question is why would I had married him? Plain and simple I would had just settle because he was a black man who have a job and worked hard on his job and, I saw in him that he was trying to always obtain a job. Thomas don't do drugs nor did he have a drinking problem or a background from our jail system. Compare to the black guys in my neighborhood and in my surroundings Thomas seemed to be a hardworking man. A good man. I did care deeply and to a certain degree, I loved Thomas. I just wasn't madly in love with him but I did loved and respected him enough that I would had said yes and been a faithful loving supported wife in every way. After a while he started grabbing on me saying "Tami come here girl, you know that mouth of yours is so small, but mon, a lot of words come out from it. One day I'm going to take you with me to Jamaica."

Oh now he wants to take me to Jamaica.

Thomas told me in his' country it is legal for a man to beat their' women because the man is the head and she must had did something wrong. That's why the man beats her because he loves her. He told me no cops interfere when they see this.

If what Thomas said is true. I truly feel sorry for the Jamaican women.

Shoot, he didn't care about the wellbeing of me and the kids all the times he went to Jamaica and he shipped everything while leaving us penniless and not helping to put anything inside of our empty apartment. All that money he made. He can kiss my black ass. It's fuckin over. I realize I could do badly all by myself. I didn't want to be like those women, like Tonya, who are just happy to say the sentence and to let people know.......... "I've got a man!"

Isn't it embarrassing to say that sentence and then the man doesn't have your best interest at heart. I should had asked Thomas, "Do I look like a chicken head to you? Like all I want in a relationship is a piece of your dick, a good fuck!

Stop! To the reader: I know yall are probably thinking yeah she just mad. She know he was good in bed. Yes he was okay but honestly he didn't have me screaming yes, yes, yes. Or even no, no, no. As a matter of fact sex does play a role in a relationship but a committed relationship isn't all about sex. Isn't there supposed to be much more to it? Well, Electra Tami Jones doesn't want to play that shit. Especially I thought we were in a committed relationship. Now my eyes are wide open. Shoot I'm tired of these bullshitting black men who call their self being in a serious relationship and all they really want to do is fuck and have a good time in the hay. Then a baby comes along, so what the problem. I tell you what the problem is, WHERE THE RING BITCH!

This girl like to know where she stands so I know how to act.

One day in the morning, as Thomas sat on the couch I started ranting and raving being disappointed in Thomas response to my question. I told Thomas "I want more for myself then this and you know you're not in love with me so why hang around? I know how it feels when someone love you."

I'm so upset thinking, he didn't even know how to romance me by not bringing me no mother fuckin flower or a piece of jewelry on Valentine Day. Showing me and the world on that special day, she is the one who makes my heart tick. Shoot I had a guy who treated me like the queen I am. Someone who spoiled me and bought me gifts just because he thought about me and wanted to put a smile on my face. Walking around the house and feeling stuck in a dead end situation. I walked into the kitchen still ranting and raving, saying, "I know how a guy makes you feel when he really cares about you." Then that when I saw the picture of him.

It was on the kitchen counter.

I had the picture in my hand, while walking towards Thomas, wanting to show him. I said while showing the picture to Thomas, "This is the guy who treated me so special and his name is Dove."

.........Wait a minute!

Stop! To the reader: Where did that picture come from? How did that picture of me and Dove suddenly appear? Quickly let go back *to the story.*

I had the picture in my hand of me and Dove, my very first boyfriend. We were so very much in love. I was so happy. We met in high school. He has a fantastic family. They loved me and treated me like I was a part of their family. Everybody just knew we were going to be married. I even thought, one day we were going to get married ....
Oooo. Wait! I had forgotten all about him-how I used to be and how it feel to be madly and wholeheartedly and passionately in love.

Then I got scared................Wait! What happen? How did I forget *this* this love?

Supposedly the love of my life. We were high school sweethearts. I fell madly in love with him from the very first time I laid eyes on him. It was love at first sight. The first guy I ever kissed. The 1st guy who ever held me in his arms and made me just want to melt. He was simply gorgeous. Dove, he had the most beautiful brown eyes and the sweetest lips. To me, he was simply breathtaking. He played baseball and we fell madly in love the very first time we laid eyes on each other. I guess, and I heard that what people they call love at first sight; puppy love. Whatever it called-we had it. And anybody who knew us, knew it too.

When Dove and I were together everybody called me by my first name, Electra but Dove called me Bambi. He was so handsome. He treated me so nice, kind and respectable like how a man treated a woman he truly cares about her. He would open and hold doors for me to pass. He bought me beautiful gifts just because. He took me out on dates all the time. Whereas, I had to get dress up, and so did he. And we always held each other hand as we walked down the street. Or he always had his arm wrapped around my shoulder. Dove he was slightly older than me. I met him late in the school year. I was in the ninth grade on my way going towards the tenth. We were inseparable. I was in love. I was truly wholeheartedly and joyfully madly over heel in love. He made me so very happy, but-my mother hated him. My sister adored him. My father respected him. Fran, my best friend she knew that I had found a gem. For the life of me I never understood why my mom had hated him so much. She gave me so much problems whenever I was around him. Looking at my track record with **these** dud spud sorry ass niggers I dated and had kids' for-Dove, he was way better by far. He was the best guy I ever dated. Immediately I started getting some feelings or flash backs of feelings-about how it feels when a man is in love with a woman and how Dove made me feel so much that it scared me.

Then I remember not wanting to fight anymore with Thomas-but at that moment, I wanted his' friendship because...... something was happening! Something was happening to me. I wanted to discuss and *disclosed something* with Thomas about someone-who I had forgotten-in my past. **Dove**! Precisely at that moment I needed Thomas to be my friend. I needed his friendship at least I thought I deserved that much from our relationship. I mean, a friend is supposed to be there in a time of need, right? Well I was there for Thomas when he needed a friend, when he didn't have a job, when he needed a place to stay and when he needed me to be in his' corner, in understanding with his driven need to support his family in Jamaica, when I thought, he had moved on with me. I'm was thinking, he needed to ease his' conscious because he met someone he wanted to be with and he is moving on. Even though, at the end of the day, I was and still am Thomas' friend.

The forgotten memory and feelings of Dove had scared me so much. It scared me because I forgotten all about someone who meant the world to me and who I truly cared about. I wanted to talk about it to Thomas. I thought to myself, how the fuck did I forget all of those good time of pure happiness. I wanted to tell Thomas but I remember he didn't want to hear about it. Vaguely, and it was lowly too Thomas mumbled "This life is better. If I leave I will regret it," and he walked out of the house.

He knew I wanted to confide something in him which was very important to me. He knew the picture meant so much to me but Thomas, he's gone. He done left the house. Thomas left me sitting there while I was thinking, how I could have forgotten someone whom I have fell so madly in love with...............**Wait**! Where did that picture come from? And how did it suddenly appear in the kitchen because I dam sure didn't put it there. Where did that old picture come from? I look around the living as I sat on the couch and I saw Thomas was gone.

So much was going on in my life around that time. I remember I put the picture up and I never saw it ....again.

Stop! To the reader. Maybe this is the first clue, to figuring out what had happened to me because I always felt there was something wrong and as I get deeper into the story, I forgot about finding this picture, and wanting to tell Thomas something but he didn't care anyway. I remembered being hurt, because after all Thomas and I been through, I always thought I had a genuine friend in him. But I see I was wrong so very wrong. At that point that's when I knew our relationship was really over. As I sat on that couch I felt so all alone and for some odd reason I felt like I was being **LIED TO**.

Security Mac. Dan knocked on the Q dorm, while announcing, "Jewelry making in the fourth floor library." Me not working anymore I came to appreciate these classes. I tried yoga and I enjoyed it so let me try jewelry making. Thinking, what female do you know who doesn't like to wear jewelry?

So I put on my jogging suit and head out the door just as Lacy and my weird next door neighbor enter the dorm. Being already on the fourth floor all I had to do is walk down the hallway.

Once I enter inside the classroom Samantha had a pot of coffee brewing as well as a pot of hot water for tea. "Hi Samantha," I said. "Hello Electra, please sign in, and have a seat at the table. I'm still bring out material for you girls to use," Samantha said.

As I found a seat Margret came inside the class. The radio was on one o three point five.

Shortstop came inside the room saying, "The coffee smell good. Can I get a cup?" Samantha said "Coffee only if you are participating in our' group." Shortstop said "Why do you think I'm here just for coffee? No I'm not like that. I want to learn how to make jewelry too." Samantha said, "Help yourself," as she goes to the closet to bring out more supplies. Shortstop asks, "Where the milk?" Samantha stop what she was doing and goes to the area where the coffee is brewing and said, "I forgot to bring up a couple containers of milk. Sorry guys. Let me see what I can do."

Going by the door she asks security Mac. Dan who is posted outside the door, "Can you supervisor this group briefly for me?"

Glad to help out. Security Mac. Dan said, "That's not a problem."

Talking to the guard Samantha said as she grab her key ring that filled with a bunch of keys. "I'll be right back. By the way, please don't allow the ladies to touch the supplies or enter inside the closet bringing out material. If anymore ladies come in, have them sign the attendance sheet on the table over there." Mac. Dan said, "Will do."

Samantha left the class as more girls had enter. Sabricka, Bertha, Vanessa, Sheena, Maria, Mendez, Marta, Carmen, Debra, Lenore and Thomasina.

The Spanish girls Maria, Shortstop, Marta and Mendez sat together talking in Spanish.

While waiting for Samantha to come back into the room Mariah Carey hit song came on the radio. We Belong Together.

Samantha comes rushing into the room saying, "Sorry guys I forgot the milk because of that I will give yall an extra fifteen minute to finish up your' project."

Mac. Dan leaves the room going back to her' post by the laundry room as Samantha say, "Thanks I appreciate that." Once again Mac Dan said, "It's not a problem."

While inside the room I could see other residents walking in the hallway. I'm looking at the other residents that are coming in from their busy day going to their' dorms'. Some notices our small crowd gather together in the library room they peeped their' head in and asked, "What's going on in here?"

Samantha said, "Jewelry making. You welcome to come in and join us if you like." A few of the passing by residents did enter the room. As a couple more residents drifted into the room. Samantha said, "We have coffee and hot water for tea if any resident is interested."

Samantha even brought up some assorted cookies from the kitchen for us girls to enjoy.

I never made jewelry before. This was my first time making jewelry. There were all kinds of beads in containers. Shinny ones, neon looking beads, beads that had letters on them, wooden beads, tiny beads in all kinds of colors and shapes. Samantha also had strings that stretches and thin metal that curved. In containers were silver posts that could go through your ear lobes, hooks for key chains and fastener that hold jewelry pieces together.

I choose the string that stretches for my base. Then I pick out beautiful pieces of turquoise beads that had designs imprinted on them. A couple of plain black beads and white pieces beads that had almost look gray along with beads that contain turquoise and black pieces together. Then I started creating my artwork.

When I got finish it came out simply beautiful. I made a choker with matching earrings and a matching ankle bracelet. I mean it's really pretty what I created. My jewelry was so nicely put together that all the girls adored it. They started grabbing for the pieces I selected but I already put up my jewelry so they wouldn't imitate the design.

I was equally impress and shock to see what I had created because I had never made jewelry before. I must say how lovely the pieces were. Not trying to be funny but if I wanted to I could have sold the set. The necklace was stunning, with three big gorgeous pieces of turquoise and black with just a hint of grey. Small like pearl going around distinctly in precise areas making the necklace more alluring than ever. The ankle bracelet is what I adore the most. I made the ankle bracelet pattern exactly like the earrings. When class was over going back to the dorm I felt really good about myself. I did three things that I never experience, sewing, yoga and I handmade really nice jewelry. I plan on wearing it tomorrow. Living inside the shelter as you can see I manage to find the positive side from this negative situation. I'm learning a lot about myself and people. The time now nine forty pm.

Goodnight.

Chapter Fifteen

It semi-dark in the room. The only light that's coming in, is from our dorm' cracked room door. I wake up in the middle of the night needing to use the bathroom. I jump out of bed goes to the bathroom door, turn the doorknob... and it's locked?

Looking quickly around the dorm to figure out who's in the bathroom? Seeing everybody sleeping in their' bed, so I knock back on the bathroom door. .....Oh wait. Behind the wall from the bathroom I seen that a new resident is in bed number one cause there is clean white sheets on the bed and a coat on top of the open locker.

I had fallen asleep before seeing the new resident who came inside our dorm. Samantha did say after during yoga sometime the body gets tired. I actually slept through bed check and when security turned out the light.

I knock back on the bathroom door once again. Knocking sounds of (knock, knock, and knock). "Un a minto," I heard a voice say.

Oh she Spanish, and she's in the bathroom this time of night? What time is it anyway? I walk quietly to crack open the room door a little wider so I can see what time it is, from the clock hanging on the wall.

Two am, dam, it's early in the morning. Walking back by the bathroom door hoping she hurry up because I gotta pee. After waiting, standing by the bathroom door wondering what she could be doing in there. So I started listening at the door. I don't hear any water running. Maybe she shitting but I don't smell an odor. So I waited for a few more minutes than I knock back on the door. "Un a minto como," she said.

Then I heard a clicking sound of unlocking the door. Out come this short stubby woman with jet black hair reading a bible. She didn't even look at me. She looks Mexican. I rush inside the bathroom and quickly started peeing instantly. Feeling oh what a relief. Just to let yall know, I never sit on the toilet seat. I always swat even when I do number two. It just way to many girls running in and out of this joint for me to be sitting on the toilet seat. To me the shelter bathroom almost like a public bathroom you use outside in the street. As I'm peeing I'm looking around the bathroom to see if I see anything out from the norm but everything look normal. I'm wondering, what was she doing lock up inside the bathroom? Once I finish, I flushes the toilet, check behind me before I exit making sure I didn't leave anything behind unclean. I open the door. **Shocked** to see the stubby woman was standing next to the bathroom door reading her bible. She was waiting to go back inside. When I came out, she walked in reading her' bible.

I heard the door click as it closed. Then I heard a harsh gurgle and a loud split. Hum, that was gross. "I hope she spitted inside the commode," I thought to myself.

Not falling back to sleep right away. I ponder about my past. So reader *let go back to the story.*

Wowww.

I forgot all about finding that old picture of Dove and I...............and showing it to Thomas.

I guess from going through constant turmoil of struggling just to survive. Plus facing and hearing the realization of Thomas true feeling about our relationship. Me handling three very small children and finally, my body finally healing. Then me wanting to find my independency from the house and explore the world. I guess......I guess I simply forgot about the picture. Then, wowww... I don't remember ever seeing it again.

Uhm..... Like, where did it go? Thomas had to remove that picture from the house. Me desperately wanting to live a normal life more abundantly. So me forgetting about the picture so quickly after I saw it. I think, I left the picture alone because, maybe, I know I had put it up. Around this time in my life there was so much chaos going on around me but I'm wondering, where the picture is? And.... why I never saw it again?

Thinking back on it now, I did went looking for that picture, realizing I couldn't find it. I did ask Thomas, "What happened to the picture?" Thomas asked me "What picture?"

With a puzzle expression on my face knowing I did put that picture up. I said, "The picture I had of me and Dove showing you when I was a young teenager in love." Thomas said "You had it. I don't know what you did with it."

Yeah right! I'm the type of person that cherish things. I don't lose things but I simply don't know what happen to that picture. Right now as I'm writing I'm wondering how come I didn't question Thomas...... Asking him where did this picture come from? And how did the picture get on the kitchen counter because I dam sure didn't put it there! You see what I mean, with this last pregnancy I see things, and then I let it go after I had asked a questioned, or talked about it-then it like I forget about it. Why is that? Maybe it because I became distracted with being tremendously busy. My memories are so cloudy around this time in my life. I'm not seeing everything so clear. It my life. I went through it, meaning my up and downs. My good times along with my bad times. I lived it. So why can't I remember EVERYTHING!

I should because my children they are the love of my life especially since I loss the close ties with my family not being around me at this stage in my life. And... not to mention my close friends of longtime companionship whom I grew accustom to having around me, sharing my life with friends. It was like my children had fulfilled that void inside of me; where my family and close friends used to be.

My oldest child she like seven years older than the baby, but with my oldest child I can see everything so clearly. I can remember lots of things about her. Like how she was conceived, how she looked as a baby and some of the outfits she wore. ......Wowww! But come to think of it, with the last two kids, some of my memories about them are cloudy or just blank. Like I got to really force myself to concentrate.

Man I hate this because Thomas can lie and say I'm making it all up that why I can't remember it. But now that I'm looking back on it, Thomas he's lying and he got that picture from...whom, and....from where?

Anyway around this time after I had my last child and when Thomas finally came back from Jamaica I remember wanting to gain some kind of independency for myself. Wanting to get out from the house and I'm, doubting the relationship that I had with Thomas. Me not knowing how to go about getting Thomas out from my apt, and he clearly showing signs he didn't want to leave. But, I'm stuck in poverty and with very small children playing house with this man and I'm not going anywhere financially or progressing while I'm with him. How many times I'm going to keep saying it but the truth is just the truth. I have no kind of real family support from them-just isolation. On top of that, I am young minded with no guidance dealing with life tough situations.

I'm learning first hand from my own experiences of the do's and don'ts about life and its problems. At the same time I want to handle my own business like the responsible adult I know I am but it's becoming completely overwhelming. Then this constant struggle with poverty I'm facing and being all alone. Sadly I'm in this mess all by myself and I had no other choice but to handle what in front of me.

I realized I did a lot for myself despite the negative odd of being with Thomas.

I finally have an apartment with furniture, nice furniture. And I must say it a gorgeous decorated two bedroom apartment that I created for myself. Just to think it was the worst apartment in the building. Now it the best decorated apartment in the building, simply gorgeous. How I know this, because lots of the tenants knocked on my door wanting to see how I had fix up Miss Butts mess up old apartment. Some of the female tenants were flabbergasted seeing how beautiful my place has turned out. Especially with them knowing how the old apartment use to look. Everyone who had seen it said, "You decorated the place so well." Then (men and women) most of them wanted to know where I purchased the furniture from. Some of the female tenants started saying to me, "I should have gotten this apartment because I been had my name on the list for a two bedroom."

I felt like this, that's just too bad isn't it. I felt, I struggle and came a long way to get what I had acquire. I had accomplish something. I turned a negative situation into a positive outcome. My children have siblings to play with and even though it did take a long time and a lot of hard work, by my own sacrificing, I manage to make my little family a home.

Anyway, around this time in my life, I wanted to explore some of life other pleasures like working and bringing home a paycheck. Getting out of the house and going to real parties, like clubs and disco. Purchasing things for myself that represent me. You know, moving forward, turning my apartment more into a real home by hanging up pictures of my family on the wall and buying flowers and plants.

Me knowing when Thomas didn't have to work I got up and I went job hunting. Leaving him with the responsibility of taking care of the kids he helped me create. Giving me the chance to tackle something more worthwhile achieving. So I walked out of the house.

Back then it wasn't even a concept of anyone giving out free business clothes to an individual to wear so that he/she could seek work at professional companies. At this time not having any business attire. No resume on hand, just a High School Diploma. I didn't really know where to go look for a job. During this time in New York City there wasn't any back to work programs like (WEP) that helped a person like myself who been in the house for quite some time get back on their feet and enter into the work force. No programs directing you towards possible job leads or sponsors, hosting job fairs. The only thing that I had heard available was joining the service, going away to job core or applying for a city job.

Another thing that we had plenty of back then, if a person had wanted to upgrade their' employment skills, there was Business Trades Schools. Which require you to take out a loan and a lot of those schools at that time were rip-offs.

I tried to upgrade my marketable skills once when Champagne was like eight months. I join a business school which offer me the opportunity to take out a loan. The advisor at the school explained to me how the school is free because of a grant but the grant doesn't cover the school books. The advisor knew I was receiving PA and I was so eager to improve my life financially that the advisor pointed out, if I take out a loan, I will have enough money to cover for my school books. Also I would have extra money on hand for whatever I needed.

So I had found a babysitter who lived in my building when I lived in Westbrook Projects. The only thing was that the babysitter wanted her money upfront and I was having trouble getting the babysitting money put on my budget from welfare. That why it was so easy for the advisor to convince me to take out the loan. I felt until my babysitting money came through from PA I could use the money from the loan to pay off the babysitter and have carfare and lunch money. The loan would help me financially take care of my daughter until I got a job and paid it back. The school offer and promise job placement.

I received one small check that help me purchase the books. Then all kinds of problems had started happening with the Welfare in order to issuing out the babysitting money. To make a long story short the school turned out to be bogus. The business school had scan me by using my signature in order to get the loan money. Then it closed down while taking the largest check of the loan, leaving me stuck to pay back the full loan-I never got. The government then added interest to it over the years. Fucking up my credit whereas I couldn't apply for anything because I'm in default with higher education until I pay back the loan which now has become enormous due to the added interest.

I got to pay back way more than the original loan itself.

We didn't have any computers or the internet back then. All there was for a person like me was family support, which I didn't have, and college which I couldn't afford because I had bad credit due to going to one of those bogus business school.

THE WELFARE OFFICE. Back then. For many years, people who received Public Assistance/welfare all they was require to do was just stay at home and wait for their' PA pick-up date. For me, this time was in the mid-Eighties.

Everybody just sat home in the project waiting for their' pick up date in order to go to the cash checking place to pick-up the money that the government had issued out. That how it was back then. So when I became pregnant with my first child since I had no real family support or a husband. I did what all of the other mothers in the Projects done. I applied for welfare. I stayed home while waiting for the date I go to the cash checking place to pick-up my money and pay my bills.

For the record not just women in the project behaved this way. Lots of Black American unmarried women with children did the same thing. Waiting in that long line like so many others were doing and has done before me. All we were require to do is hand the teller our welfare photo id card and the teller gave us our cash benefit which included our small allowance, monthly rent and our monthly food stamps-that came in coupons. Our food-stamps coupons in a way was similar to monopoly money. Anyway, unmarried women with children picking up their' benefits. The lines were long and lots of time you heard of someone getting rob when they came out from the cash checking place. Back then everybody knew, if you needed money that was the place to be because EVERYONE was on the line.

There was way too many Black American mothers receiving their' income this way in order to pay their' bills and to put food on the table. Everybody received their monthly share of food stamps coupons depending on their family size. Depending on how many kids' you had on your' budget it had determined your cash allowance and food stamps allowance. Maybe that explain why single woman were having so many kids, not trying to be funny but especially the Puerto Ricans. For years, I can even say decades it was a way of life because I know people mother and their' mothers that was on the welfare line. This was a way of living for lots of Black Americans and the non-working Puerto Ricans. All I did was waited inside the house, just like so many before me to pick up my money.

If the younger generation of today is reading this book and say to their self....... that how welfare used to be? Well, when I was a young teenager I watched that movie called Claudine. I know yall remembered that Black American movie named Claudine. Well look how welfare used to be in my mother time when I was a baby. Just watch that old time movie named Claudine.

Times are different now but back then it was common in the black community to see unemployed females/mother sitting at home waiting for their Public Assistance money and food stamps coupons. Everybody sitting home watching the soap opera. That's my era. Watching All My Children, One Life to Live and then General Hospital. Those was the biggest highlights of our day seeing what Erica Kane did on "All My Children."

Everybody. Even in Manhattan including Nana. In all projects. Every borough in Brooklyn, Bed-Stuy, Crown Height, East New York and Brownsville, who all received welfare, lots of us watched All My Children. Everybody I know watched the soaps. Except one or two individuals. Majority of all Black American people watch the soaps. It became so talked about in the black community that even the people who work and had jobs program their' VCR to tape their' favorite soaps. There were some people who watched the Young and the Restless which is on a different channel. That soap had their fair share of fans too but the most talk about soap in my area was All My Children, Susan Lucci. I can't understand why she didn't win way more awards for the role she played. Do you detect (jealousy) someone just didn't want to see her have it all? She clearly was the star in All My children next to Adam. We didn't even call her by her real name. When any type of discussion came up about her. It was like, "Did you see what Erica did today? Or the outfit she wore?" She was the one everybody loved, and everybody hated or envy.

I remember when Erica was young on the show as a spoil little brat, being mean to her loving mother, Monica. I watch her tackle the modeling business, becoming successful and watch Erica turn into this sleek, savvy business woman she is today. Her many marriages to some of the most gorgeous, smart and wealthy men. Erica moving up the ladder of success while wearing the most stylish clothes. She living such a beautiful, full exciting life which she had created for herself. The show was greatly written and the actors and actresses were so believable.

Erica Kane, I liked her style, she so full of life, such a beautiful white woman. I like her because she was a fighter, a go getter, outspoken, so full of robust and fire. Let's not forget intelligent, she has such a free spirit for wanting to live her life to the fullest, surrounded by power and luxury. To me, there was nothing boring about her. Besides the mundane task of taking care of my oldest daughter and housework she gave me something else more to wake up for in the morning.

I never had a role model; someone I wanted to be like or a person whom I admire. In a way I guess she was mine. I adore everything about her. How she wanted much out from life and not to mention she wasn't anybody fool. Even when so many people I know who watch her, hated her guts. I figure they were like that towards her because of her beauty and of her ability to triumph and become successful at whatever she tackle and all those magnetic gorgeous wealthy smart men she dated. She a winner, full of personality and determination.

Lots of people in my neighborhood hated her for that but I see they watched the show faithfully too maybe, hoping to see her fall so they can say "ha, ha see what happen to her." Or say "That good for her she deserves that." But Erica never gave those people the benefit to say that. She made triumph after triumph until she became the bitch to watch on day time TV.

My two favorite things outside of taking care of the kids. Watching All My Children and shopping at Pathmark. I would had gladly wore a tee-shirt saying I love All My Children or Pathmark is the store to shop.

If there was anybody I wanted to be like I would say it would be her. Believe it or not a couple of my closet family member and friends secretly back then view me as the black Erica Kane. Now they probably see me as a complete loser saying, thinking, what happen to her? I was beautiful once, a total knock out. I seem to have had a promising bright future once.

Wait. At this time of night, the light to my dorm just turned on.

It's Lowene, the African Security Guard. I said to her, "Aren't you supposed to use a flashlight?" She didn't even answer me back. All she did was stop in front the dorm' full plexi-glass mirror to look at her hair style. Then she went to open up the bathroom door but seen it was locked. Lowene asked in her African accent while knocking on the bathroom door, "Is everything okay in there?"

I heard the Mexican woman say something in Spanish. I wondering what the hell she still doing inside that bathroom? Lowene looked at her' hair one more time in the mirror then turn out the light and exit the dorm. Lowene is the only guard at Bridge Net that does this when making her nightly rounds. She knows she supposed to use a flashlight while checking the dorms at this time of night. She always turning on the light looking admiring her new hairstyle. I bet her hair dresser just love her.

Going back to the story.

So here I was wanting to get out of the house after being inside raising my children and Watching All My Children while shopping at Pathmark since the age of 21. Now I soon be 30. Anyway, as I was saying, I wanted to exercise my independent. So I started leaving the kids on Thomas showing him I want more out of life then what he is giving me. So I went downtown to Young World Department Store. Thinking, I could easily get a job there. All I have to do is stand up on my feet and put the cash inside of the register. Then bag up the customer' store brought items. They should hire me easily because nobody really wanted to do a job like that I thought. Most people wanted a job in the city getting benefits and making that good money.

When I got downtown I saw a help wanted sign in a couple of the stores' windows. So when I enter the store I ask the first person I saw on the floor. "Hi, I see yall hiring. Where can I get an application?" The girl said, "Go by the register and ask to speak to the manager." So that's what I did.

When I got to the register I asked, "Can I speak to a manger?" A girl called for a manager to come to her. When the manger came he asked the girl "What seems to be the problem?" The young lady pointed towards me. The manger asks me "How can I help you?"

I said, "I see the hiring sign in the window. Are you still accepting applications?" The manger reach under the counter and pull out a pack of applications. He tore an application from off the pack and he hands it over to me then he walked away.

I started filling it out right then and there.

Once I finish with the application I ask the cashier, "Can you call for the manager again?" He walks over to me and I gave him the application. He takes my application and say nothing. So me always being curious and excited I asked, "What happens next?"

The Manger looks at my application and say to me "The application will get review and someone would get in contact with you; depending on your availability."

As I walked away I notice another woman who came up asking him if she can have an application. As I walk around the store seeing what's on sale, I notice the woman filling out the application. I figured while I was downtown I would hit a couple more of the small department stores.

So I goes into another children store and I ask the security, "Where can I find the manager of the store?" The security guard said "Go ask her." I went to the Spanish girl who was folding tee shirts and asks, "Who the manager of the store?" She points the manager out to me. I goes to the manager and asked, "Are you hiring?" The manger says "Yes, follow me." He hands me an application and I fill it out and give it back to him. He said "Someone will be in contact."

When I had gone to a couple of more stores downtown, I had gotten the same response. "Someone will be in contact."

Going home I was thinking, it sure was hard trying to get a small job like that. I imagine it must be really difficult getting a job with the bigger corporations. When I got home Thomas was dressed and couldn't wait to leave the house. Even though I didn't get a job right away I was hopeful thinking that some manager would give me a call and ask for me to come in for an interview.

After waiting for a couple of weeks I got no returned calls. So I decided to go back downtown again to find out the status of my applications. When I got inside Young World and asked for the manager. I noticed that it was a different manager and that both manger's were West Indian people because I heard their' accents.

"Good morning," I said "my name is Electra and I filled out an application a couple of weeks ago and I was wondering if the store could use my help." The male manager asked me, "Who did you give the application to?" Not knowing the person name. So I described him. The manager said, "Just a minute."

While standing there I was shocked to see the girl who ask for the application, behind me, now working on the floor. She was standing on the floor folding tee shirts by the table, and she was wearing a red smock, that read Young World.

When the manager came back to me he said "I don't see your application. What day did you hand it in? Or will you like to fill out another one?" Shocked that he wasn't able to find it, I filled out another application.

Once I finish, I had walk up to the girl, who I seen asking for work on the same day that I filled out and had handed in my first application.

I said, "Hello." She gave me a shy smile as a way of saying hello, as she slowly continued folding. I said, "I remember you. You came here a couple of weeks ago filling out a job application right?" She didn't say anything she just showed a shy smile. She was very quiet, maybe because she didn't know me.

So I said, "We both came into the store the same day requesting a job. You didn't see me because I already filled out my application by the time you came in." She moved over a little and started folding the tee shirts in that pile. So I walked over with her and asked, "When did you start working?" She didn't say a word as if though she didn't want to talk to me. Being persistent I asked again "When did you start working?"

She finally answer. She said, "A week ago." I ask her, "How is it? Do you like working at the store?" She smiled again and said quietly "It's alright." I said, "Alright have a nice day, bye."

As I walked away from her...wait a minute, I'm starting to see a pattern. Both of the manger of Young World were of Caribbean descent. The girl who just got hire, had an accent, also, of Caribbean descent.

I wanted to see if my theory was correct so I played it off acting like I wanted to check out the hair accessories by the register just to listen to the black female voices behind the register. It was stunning, when I realize that all cashiers are Caribbean and Spanish.

Wait, I couldn't believe what I was seeing I went up to the security guard and ask him, "Do you have the time?" He too was of Caribbean descent. Hanging around Thomas, I could detect the simplest of accents.

Wait a minute.........why is everybody working in the store, Caribbean? Oh, that is discrimination! I went to the manager and asked him "What is the qualification for obtaining a job here?" He looked at me and said "You have to be willing to work." I said, "I'm willing to work and I had filled out my application which you can't find. So I want to know why haven't anyone called me to come in to work for a couple of hours?" The manager said "You just gave me your application. I have to go over your qualification and see if this job is suitable for you."

I said, "Well you just told me I have to be willing to work. Isn't that enough for you to give me a chance to get a job working inside of this store?" The manager said "Don't worry. If I have a position for you I will give you a call."

I said to the manager, "That all I keep hearing. I'll call you. I want to know why everyone in the store that working is from another country. Everybody working here has an accent?" The manger didn't have anything to say behind that and he seem shock that I had pick up on it. As we spoke I notice some of the other employees there were listening to my conversation, and looking around at each other.

I told him, "That discrimination and I'm going to tell people to boycott your store if I don't see any Americans working."

The manager told me, "Let me go over your application and I'll see if I could give you, a day or two."

I know he wasn't going to call me because I remembered when Thomas got that contact. He never once gave anyone of the American guys who hung out in front of our building, an opportunity to work and to earn some money for their selves. Thomas didn't even give them a chance to say "No. I don't want to work but good looking out and thank you."

Even when he saw them every day standing in front of the building when he came home. Not all of them smoke weed but so what if some of them do? Lots of Caribbean men smoke weed and they work. The American boys were all so nice to Thomas. Besides helping us out with our groceries bags, after we came home from shopping at Pathmark. They helped Thomas with his' car when he needed it to be push out of the snow. Or to help in flagging down someone they knew, when Thomas had needed a car boost.

All I'm saying is Thomas could have given at least one of them a chance to make an honest paycheck for their self. Lots of them had criminal records for dumb shit. Thomas was just being greedy and selfish, just like the managers of Young World Department store, only hiring their' own kind.

I never got a call back and I wasn't surprised but I did call and I told my mother, "Mom you know Young World, and a lot of the small clothing store downtown Brooklyn have a lot of Caribbean and Spanish workers."

My mother said, "Electra yeah you know those people look out for each other."

I said, "There's nothing wrong with looking out for each other, but to take all of the positions and not give an American a chance; now that's not right."

My mother laugh and said, "No, now that's not true." But she didn't know what Thomas did. I said, "Maybe you never looked at it before."

My mother said, "Well if that is happening, it not right, but I've got to go and deal with these children. How the kids?" I said, "They alright." My mother said "I'll speak with you later."

Well, to the reader-It's really getting late and I got to get up in the morning. By now, you know that I have to be out the dorm by nine am but before I go I just want to let it be known she is still inside that bathroom. I really wonder what is it she doing in there? I should go by the door and listen but I don't feel like getting out of bed.

Anyway speak to yall later.

Goodnight.

"Miss Jones." I hear taping sounds coming from someone hitting upon a metal object. "Miss Jones." Taping sounds of, Tap, Tap, Tap, tap, tap, tap and tap. "Miss Jones do you have a bed pass?" I open my eyes to see security guard Monique. She standing by my locker still taping on it wanting to wake me up. Coming out from my deep sleep I moved the cover from off of me and sat up in my bed.

Monique asked, "Do you have a bed pass?"

"No I don't. And can you stop tapping upon my locker because I'm up," I replied. She walks away from my bed, exiting out the dorm. When I came into focus and looked around my room oh wow, the Mexican women have a ton of bags in her' area. Between her and Lacy the room looks chop.

My neighbor is gone. Lacy gone. Pepsi gone. Valerie gone. The zoo lady gone and Luting is gone. The only ones in the dorm besides me is the Dominican girl who is about to leave because she tying up her' sneakers. The new girl, and sleeping beauty, the Spanish chick.

The new girl, the Mexican chick, her area looks disguising. She over there looking through her papers. Sleeping beauty, the Spanish chick, who use to sleep without having a bed pass is slowly moving getting herself ready to leave out just like the rest of us.

Being that I already took my shower all I have to do is wash my face and brush my teeth. I'm a quick dresser. The majority of my clothes doesn't need to be iron because I always fold them immediately after washing and drying. I came out from the bathroom, got dress, and I'm out.

I told you I move fast.

I went to Jose and order bacon eggs and cheese on a roll, with a cup of coffee, light with three sugars. Then I pick-up one pack of vanilla cake finger. Going back towards the shelter I bumped into Billie. She's going off to work as well as lots of other shelter females who is heading off going about their' merrily business. I remember when I use to be like that, working.

When I got by the door to the shelter I looked into the yard I saw Nomi Scott talking to Langston as he sat in the driver seat of one of Bridge Net' vans. I haven't seen a trip posted so somebody must be going on a housing interview or, someone had gotten housing. Then I saw Celeste coming out from the building and she sat inside the van.

Security Marsha was scanning the girls as we enter inside the building. "Luz Medina is coming up with her camera phone, copy," Security Marsha said on her' radio. I heard another guard radio back, "Copy." As I waited for my stuff to go through the scanner I saw Luting come downstairs. She had started to exit the building. When she saw me she stop in front of me and said, "Bye." I said, "Bye? Where are you going?" Luting said, "I got housing." Shocked I said, **"You did**? Where you moving to and why didn't you say something earlier?" Luting said, "I'm moving to the Bronx. I just found out."

Miss Nomi Scott came into the entrance vestibule interrupting our conversation by saying "I was just about to have security radio for you. The van is waiting. Let's go." Luting looked happy she turn towards me and said, "Bye." I said to her, "Good luck."

As I put my stuff on the scanner. Waiting my turn to move up in the line, as the guard searches everyone. I thought-that's how it is in the shelter one minute you here, the next you're gone. You be like what happen to this person. I haven't seen her in a while until someone tells you, she moved or she just left or maybe she got transfer to another shelter.

My belonging went through the scanner while Security Marsha hand check my grocery bag. Security Marsha radio on her walkie-talkie, "Electra coming up with food, copy." I heard the guard on the other end of the radio say, "Copy."

The 2nd door buzzes for me to go up.

Once I got to the second floor pass the intake office, going to the dining room. I found a seat at one of the tables. I sat next to this woman named Gail. She was sitting there reading a book. Before I sat down I said, "Hi, how are you doing." "Hi Electra, I see you going to eat your breakfast," Gail said. I replied, "Yeah I went to Jose," and I pull out my sandwich and show it to Gail asking, "Would you like to have a piece?" "Oh thank you," she said as she took half of the sandwich.

There not to many black people that will turn down a bacon egg and cheese sandwich only unless they don't eat pork. I sat down took out my coffee and started back writing. *Back to the story*:

Upset I didn't get call for a job. After all the small stores I hand put in an application. Not one manager called me for an interview.

Shortly after, Thomas came home saying "Tami mon me going to buy a van." I said, "We already have a car." He said "No mon, a van so that I could start to do dollar van." "Dollar what?" I said. Thomas repeated "Dollar van, mon." I asked, "What is dollar van? I don't understand. What is that?" Thomas said "Me and some people getting together. We all going to buy a van to help people get from one place to another. People sit in the seat. I drive them down the road and I would charge them a dollar for the ride."

I didn't see what sound so good about that, just one more thing Thomas had to do for his self. He still here. We still sharing my apartment. Maybe I could get him to help me buy one of those nice two family home. I even had an application hoping we could apply for one. I wanted a backyard so the kids could go out and play.

I said, "A dollar van. Where you supposed to be doing this?" Thomas said "Up the road mon, me going to buy a van so when I'm not working construction I would be hustling doing dollar van. Keeping money coming in."

The carfare at this time was one dollar and twenty five cent. I'm so tired of his' schemes and my constant struggling I wanted a piece of the American pie. I said, "I don't know about this Thomas. It sound similar to a taxi-cab driver."

Thomas said "Tami it good mon you see, don't worry me soon come." Thomas left the house because somebody had a van for him to purchase rather it was Rude Boy or someone else who had wanting to sell their van. He wanted to go check it out.

Sometime after this dollar van discussion Thomas had this man and a woman visit our apartment. They came up from Jamaica. I can't remember if they were a couple or not. Anyway after they had gone. I went inside my bathroom, sat on the toilet, as I was peeing something inside of me told me to look up.

I looked up and said "What the Fuck is that?! I was still peeing couldn't wait till I finish so I could get the fuck out from the bathroom. The pee was just coming down and I was just looking up trying to figure out what the hell I was looking at.

I remember me looking up not wanting whatever it was to fall down on me. What I was looking at I couldn't make it out. It was tape to the ceiling over the commode in the corner. It was black. It was taped so neatly, and carefully, as if someone had taken their time but who could have done that and when did it happen? How long had it been there I had wonder? Whatever it was, it wasn't moving...... what is that?

After I finish peeing I stood up from the toilet staring at it. Squinting my eyes, as if I was trying to zoom in on it, taking a closer look. I couldn't make out what it was that I was looking at....."Thomas." I started calling, "Thomas!" I hurried out from the bathroom calling "Thomas. Thomas come here."

Thomas came towards me and I grabbed his' hand, taking him to the bathroom, moving quickly while saying "Look whatz in the bathroom!" When we got inside the bathroom I said, "Look!" I had my finger pointing towards the object tape on the ceiling.

Thomas followed my finger looking to where I was pointing. We both stared at it in silence until I asked cautiously... "What is that?" Thomas said "Eehey," as he stared, looking at it too. Both of us stood, silently, looking up.

I asked again, "What is that?" He said "Eehey.......... mon, it looks ....it look like a dead bat."

I said, "A dead bat! As I looked at Thomas.

Then I looked back up towards the ceiling and I asked, "How did that shit get there and I wonder who put that there ....and how you know it's a dead bat?"

Thomas was just looking at it in puzzlement.

We both were until I said, "I wonder how long that shit been there and how the fuck you know that a dead bat!" Both of us just looking at it. Then I said, "Take it down!" Thomas said "No mon. I didn't put it there," as he just looked at it puzzled. I said, "I didn't put that shit there and I want it down, right now Thomas." He said "No mon I didn't put that there. I'm not moving it."

I yelled, "**Thomas**, I'm not touching no fuckin dead bat. Take That Down!" Thomas still looking at it while lean to the side with one hand under his nostril and said "No sir... me didn't put it there and me not taking it down." I said, "This is where we live and where our children sleep what do you mean you're not taking it **Down**!"

I was furious with Thomas.

I said, "Thomas you just had those people visiting you from Jamaica, that man and that women with the dead eye. I didn't have any company. How did that shit get taped neatly up to the corner of our ceiling over the toilet?" Thomas was adamant that he wasn't taking it down.

Thinking, as I watched whatz taped on our bathroom ceiling I said, "Well since neither one of us, did it. Those people who had came over to visit you from Jamaica, **they did it**!"

Thomas said "Eehey." Then thinking-he said suspiciously "Your mother was over here too." Yelling I said "My mother wouldn't had did no shit like that!

I had already condemned the couple that was in the house so I said, "Let's go find the people that were staying here at the apartment. Let's find out why they would want to do something like this?"

I wanted answer because I felt that we were being nice to allow them to stay in our apartment treating them like descent human beings, offering them food and making them comfortable. I was helping with answering all their' questions and telling them how to get around in New York City. To me this was a violation of my home and I wanted to kick somebody in the ass for this shit. I dare you come into my home, and disrespect us like this. I found it to be so ugly and distasteful. I was bloody mad. I said, "Let go and find them Thomas."

Thomas had seen that I was very angry. Thomas said "No mon," because he know I wasn't about to ask them any questions. I just wanted to start hitting that cock eyed bitch, pull her by her hair and stomp the shit out of her, while Thomas dealt with the man.

Thomas didn't want to have a confrontation. So I had wanted to **fuck Thomas up**!

I remember wanting to fight Thomas. I so sick of him putting me and my kids' on the side, in the back burner. He was not standing up for us or helping us. I was so mad at Thomas for not sticking up for us. He **gotz** to **go**. Thomas got to leave! I didn't like having that thing, whatever it was, inside of the apartment. I'm over going to my dad. And I'm going to get him to remove it.

I got to my dad' house so fast. I said all upset "**DAD**! Thomas had company; this man and woman were at the house. Now all of a sudden I goes into the bathroom look up and I see an object tape to the ceiling. Thomas said **it's a dead bat** and he's not moving **it** because he didn't put it there. **Dad**, you have got to come with me to my place. **I want that crap remove off the bathroom ceiling**!"

When my father and I got back to my place, Thomas was sitting in the living room with the kids. My dad and I went immediately inside the bathroom. When my dad saw it, he asked "Who put that there Thomas?" Thomas acted as if he was scared or stubborn and he still didn't want to take it down as he sat upon the couch with the kids.

My dad said "Well if you didn't put it there, then, who did?" As Thomas got up walking towards my dad who standing by the bathroom. They standing side by side. My dad said "Surely you can see that Electra didn't do it."

By now I done took off my shoes and I was sitting on the couch, lacing up my sneakers, saying "it going to come down one way or another!" I was riled up and I was ready to fight. I'm just going to start swinging on Thomas. He supposed to be the man of the house. He always put me and the kids on the back burner while bringing all of these bitches inside of our home and allowing his people to disrespect me. He never could stand up when a confrontation arose or he just wouldn't stand up when he known I was being disrespected by his' people.

Thomas knew that he was about to get jumped because I was getting to the point of becoming uncontrollable and my dad wasn't going to stand there and watch Thomas hurt me and I knew that so I'm just going to start swinging.

When Thomas realized a fight was about to break out between us.

He said "I'll take it down." I started to calm down and become rational but still very upset with Thomas. Thomas went inside the kitchen. Got the broom and he walked into the bathroom and started to jab at the object until it had fallen inside of the toilet and he flushed it.

To tell yall the truth, was it a bat? I really couldn't tell you because I had never seen a bat in real life. Plus the way that it was taped it was hard to figure out. I didn't see any eyes looking at me. It was tape by the legs but I didn't see nails or claws. I couldn't make out, what it was. When it fell inside the toilet I don't remember hearing a loud splash and I know I didn't say, "Oh that nothing but black paper."

My father left. This was the last straw. I want Thomas out of my house.

Whenever Thomas couldn't stand up for us to help find out who had violated us in this gruesome way, plus on top of the many other shit I endure with him already. I was really starting to think I could do badly all by myself and I don't need him. I'm still young and still attractive maybe I could find someone who really loves me; someone who is just right for me because I can see, it, is, not, Thomas. He's not the one for ME. He don't love me, nor the kids, or himself for that matter. The only thing I see Thomas love is Jamaica, uplifting his country and uplifting his' people. He gotz to get the fuck out of my apartment.

And that exactly what happen. I eventually kick Thomas out of my apartment.

I threw this intimate party with some of Thomas closest friends and brother. Just before the party was over I went inside my bedroom threw some of his' clothes inside his' suitcase, came out from the bedroom saying, "When yall leave can you take Thomas with you."

Samantha came into the dining room and made an announcement, "Open studio is now going on, in the library on fourth floor. Ladies, I'll be looking forward to seeing you attend the class. Meet you there," as she exit the dining room. That's it for me.

I did a lot of writing today and I need a break. Time flew. I didn't even stop to eat lunch but that what happen when homeless people get their' food stamps we eat when we get ready. I pack up my stuff, heading to open studio on the fourth floor.

Walking up the stairs. When I came out from the staircase. The first person I saw was Fancy, the Jamaican security guard. I can't stand her. She is so bossy and always talks to me with such an ugly attitude. There she is sitting on post by the laundry room with her low cut hairstyle that has touches of the color pink at the ends. Soon as she saw me walking her way while coming out from the exit, she said, "Electra. I hope you have a bed pass. You know no one is allowed on the fourth floor."

As I'm walking closer towards her. I said "I'm not going to my dorm. I'm going to open studio."

As I got even closer about to make that turn. Fancy gets up from her' seat extends one hand showing all five of her fingertips that she had done at the nail salon, as a meaning for me to stop walking as she says to me, "Wait right here." She casually walk, goes to the library where open studio is being held and open up the door.

I could hear her asking Samantha, "Are you about to have a class because I'm not aware of any class happening at this time on the fourth floor.

As I walked closer while eavesdropping. I heard Samantha say, "The guard that was here before you, I asked her to announce on the floors that open studio is now in progress." Once I heard that I proceed to enter inside the room. Guarding the door with her body so that I couldn't get inside the room. Fancy said "No guard reported it over the radio."

Then Fancy pull her radio to her mouth and said on her' radio, "Security pick up." I heard another guard over the radio say, "Go for security."

Fancy said, "Please be advise clients could come upstairs. Open studio is in progress, copy." I heard a guard say, "Copy." Then Fancy said, "It would have been nice if the guard posted before me, on the fourth floor would have made the announcement so that all guards be made aware of the activities going on, copy." Leisurely Fancy moved away from the door so that I can pass and enter into the room.

She such a control freak.

I walks inside the class and ask Samantha, "Could I put the radio on?" "Sure go head Electra," Samantha said. I put it on, ninety eight point seven, kiss. The station is playing

Keisha Cole, Heaven Sent. Besides brewing coffee and hot water for us girls Samantha brought snacks for us too. She had out a large bag of Potato Chips and pretzels also a large pack of assorted crème cookies.

As I took a seat, I grabbed a couple of cookies and put them inside of a foam bowl. Others started coming inside the room. "Sign in ladies," Samantha said.

While I sat waiting to decide what is it I'm going to do this time in open studio? It was fun because me along with others girls we started singing the lyric to Keisha Cole hit single, Heaven Sent. Which took Samantha by surprise. Samantha not realizing how much we all loved that song and knew all the lyrics so well that she just stopped what she was doing listening and looking at us residents in amazement. As we sung. Samantha feeling the energy that coming from the room as she now listen to the lyrics of Heaven Sent.

Impressed. When the song had finished, Samantha asked, "And who the artist?" We all said like where you been, "Keisha Coles!" More girls came pouring into the room wanting to be part of the action. I guessed they heard use singing as they were on the fourth floor.

Sam asked everyone to take a seat. Some residents were signing up for the computer to check their' email. I decide to finish my collage. I asked Samantha for my folder that contain my cut out pieces. In the meantime I collected more magazines, cutting out more pieces so that my collage will be full of energy. I cut out various pictures of guys I thought were sexy. Then I got a huge white cardboard.

I had title this piece of art work.

Beauty is in the   of the beholder

Underneath the title I had sexy pictures of guys in blue jeans with no shirt. Some guys were sitting in a chair. I had pictures of sexy men, in suits. Men with long hair, blonde hair, black hair, short hair, no hair. Sexy guys with blue eyes. Gorgeous men with beautiful smiles. Men with sexy, slim, muscular, toned bodies. Men that are medium built, with a six pack stomach. Guys with kissable lips. Some guys looked dreamy, some looked seductive. I had various pictures of guys with their' tongue sticking out of their mouth. Guys licking their' lips and blinking their' eyes. Some guys showing their hairy chest.

There were guys lying down. Guys with muscle, leaning up against walls. Guys with tattoos. Men in uniforms. There were so many guys, doing normal activities, while looking simply irresistible. I thought they were sexy and adorable. When my artwork was completed lots of the ladies that were in open studio was amazed at what I had created. It was a work of art I must do say.

The only thing, was that I didn't think I would get so much controversy from the ladies who lived in the shelter about my poster. I created it because I had got tired of looking at women all day and every night. The first thing in the morning and the last thing I see before I gone to bed. I wanted something else to look at. So I created it.

It took a while putting the many pictures of guys in the right spot making the collage look full of energy and lust. I was very pleased with what I created. Class is over and the dorms are open. When I got inside of my dorm I looked toward Luting bed. Everything was stripped and her' locker was open waiting for the next person to occupy the space.

I took the picture of the heart off my locker and I put up the poster collage of men, entitle: Beauty Is in the Eye of the Beholder.

I sat on my bed then I bent down to open my locker so I could put inside my heart drawing. While doing that I notice a bunch of ants in my area on the floor. I looked around and I notice the dorm hasn't been swept or mopped again. This was the second day in a row my dorm hasn't been properly clean. The only thing I seen maintenance did was put toilet tissue inside the bathroom. There are way too many girls coming and going, for maintenance not to have clean the dorm. All types of women come through this place clean and unclean, sick and healthy. Occasionally you may even catch females who don't belong inside your dorm, sneaking in to use the bathroom. Germs we don't need it. So I went downstairs to fill out a complaint form.

I goes inside the intake office ask Shift Supervisor, Jefferson if I could have a resident's complaint form. As you already know the form consist of several parts. Resident Name, it's optional. I input my name. It ask for today date, I input the date. Then there a large box that contains five columns, indicating for a person to check what applies to their situation. I check Maintenance.

Date of event that led to the complaint. I insert today date. Then there is the time. I insert the time. The form asks for the location, I input the Q dorm.

Description of complaint:

I write: The Q dorm haven't been mop or swept in two days. Can someone please make sure the Q dorm get cleaned? I found by my bed a bunch of crawling ants. There was not any food underneath or besides my bed. Where and why the ants are there I don't know. It seem like a nest of ants has formed by my bed. Thank you.

I submitted the form to Jefferson. It's always good to practice paper trail in a joint like this. You never know when you need facts to present your case. Anyway I ask for a copy of my complaint.

Going back upstairs I thought about when I first arrived at Bridge Net. I clean so much while moving from bed to bed that it wasn't funny. Before I laid in my bed I had cleaned the mattress, then the bed railing and the locker. I even wiped the wall area behind my bed and wiped the corners on the floor that surrounding my bed picking up all kinds of left behind dirt.

At Bridge Net lots of times the bathroom was so dingy looking and dreary, not to mention the stale smell that came out from it when you open up the bathroom door. I would clean and bless the entire bathroom. I would go downstairs to the intake office, and take a couple of plastic gloves from out the box and get busy.

I would make my announcement asking the ladies in my dorm, "Do anybody got to use the bathroom because I'm about to clean it." I get a bottle of tilex with bleach and the spray for mildew from maintenance. Then clean the entire bathroom.

I will wipe all the bathroom walls, the bathroom door and the bathroom' doorknob as well as the doorknob to our dorm' door. The entire basin cabinet inside and out. Lots of times I found in the cabinet, left possessions from the old clients of their accumulated corroded dirty items. I knew that this junk didn't belong to anyone in the dorm but before I threw out anything. First I would ask my roommates just to make sure, "Does these items belong to anyone before I throw it out?"

Nine times out of ten the dirty items belong to no one who lived inside the dorm. Girls had come and gone so fast things get left behind and for some reason maintenance never look and clean out the bathroom cabinet decayed items. They get left until a person like I decide to clean house.

I cleaned the tub, inside and outside, all the faucets inside the bathroom and wipe the mirror with Windex. Every cleaning product I use, I had to go and get it from maintenance as well as assuring him I bring it right back. The most disguising, nasty part of the bathroom that maintenance always seem to forget. Is wiping the back and sides of the commode/toilet. There you will find dried up urine, dirt, dusk and sometime harden feces.

Then I clean our tall garbage can that inside the bathroom, lid and all. Throw out the used black plastic garbage bag and get a new one. If our shower curtain look to stain and dirty at the bottom, I will ask maintenance for a new one.

After a while girls in Bridge Net got to know me for cleaning in such manner and the maintenance too that's why whatever I asked of them, I got.

I think sometimes because I clean so professional and thorough and you know how it is when others want to rain on your parade or try to down size you when you doing something well. Anyway when I was in the L dorm, I had a Caribbean women name Ruthie who seen me cleaning so well. Once I got finish cleaning the bathroom and the last thing I had to clean was the shower curtain. It was so stain and had some many black spots at the bottom. I figure why try and clean the tarnished curtain. I'm just going to throw it out. So I made an announcement in my dorm, "Whoever wants to take a shower, give me a minute to get a new shower curtain from maintenance."

After all that cleaning and scrubbing I did. Ruthie, the Caribbean women said trying to make me look like I just wanted everything new, "Mon you don't need to get a new shower curtain. Just soak it and scrub it clean."

I said, "I'm not scrubbing all that black stuff and I shouldn't have too. The shelter has lots of shower curtain. This one is destroyed. I don't see anything that's so flamboyant about me asking maintenance for one of their' cheap dull looking new shower curtain. Why not get a new one?" Ruthie said, "All you got to do is scrub it mon."

I said, "That's the problem. I don't want to scrub that old nasty looking shower curtain. It's destroyed. Why do all that work for that dingy dirty cheap curtain when you can simply just go get a new cheap curtain from maintenance? That's clean, smell fresh and doesn't look so used. It's a waste to scrub it and I'm not scrubbing it."

Giving off her' body language as if I'm acting like a princess wanting new shit Ruthie said while sucking her teeth, "I'll do it," and she did.

She wanted to make herself look good in front of the other roommates who lives inside our dorm.

I said, "First of all, I'm not trying to make myself look good. It about hygiene. You were the one living in this dorm all these freaking months, like a nasty, human being. Taking showers in a sinking dull half cleaned-up bathroom."

Anyway, she soaked and scrubbed the crap out of that cheap dirty shower curtain removing most of the black spots at the bottom but the shower curtain was so damaged that when she had finished the black spots were still there just a little lighter.

I feel like this; the shelter has tons of cheap shower curtains why waste the energy on that cheap curtain. What's the staff saving it for. To take home to their' apartment or give out to friends like Ruthie who probably want to ship it over to her country anyway.

It good to be clean but I found myself cleaning so much, that I had to realize I didn't work at Bridge Net. Bridge Net has employee that receive a paycheck for this. At one point they were moving me from room to room and I found myself constantly cleaning bathroom walls and blessing the bathroom. Cleaning my new bed areas and lockers. After a while I started thinking they weren't getting me an apartment but just moving me around from dorm to dorm just to clean and bless the bathroom. Then I started writing maintenance up cause I shouldn't have to clean up like this.

I'm living in the system dealing with all the madness that goes on everyday then when I have to go and take a shower I felt the bathroom wasn't clean properly. The bathroom looks dull and doesn't have a fresh scent. So I will clean it like every Saturday or every other Saturday.

Lots of times I be tired when I walk into my dorm after a long boring day. So if the bathroom is mess-up. I can't shower like that, now I have to go up and down the stairs getting supplies to clean the bathroom that the shelter pays a paycheck for someone to clean.

Now, for the record, if it was stated we had to clean our' own dorms, that's different. I wouldn't have a problem doing it but so far it was not stated. Therefore I shouldn't have to clean like I work here. I had to check myself and stop doing it so now I just write them up.

Chapter Sixteen

It's the weekend. Thank goodness, no announcing guard at 6am and no lights. It's strange seeing so many girls here since DHS has taken away weekend passes. You know, I'm in a mood for some, grits. Do everybody know what grits is? Well, it like farina, a hot cereal. Not everybody could cook a good pot of grits. In this area we have a couple of Spanish restaurants who make American food but, there's this one restaurant up the block-the cook in there makes a darn good pot of grits. As I'm walking to the restaurant I'm thinking, I sure do miss my own cooking. Due to homelessness, I eat out so much which is something I rarely did. Lots of times, I do get the taste for my own cooking which is something I prefer. The Spanish restaurant up the block is the only place I know that I could honestly say, make grits the way I like it.

The Spanish restaurant I'm about to go to has two cooks. One is Spanish and the other cook is a Black American-who make what I'm about to order taste as good as if I cooked it myself. He makes his grits just the way I like it.

Once I'm inside the restaurant I find a table for myself and take a seat. The waitress comes to me and asks, "What will you be having?" I tell her, "I would like to have an order of home fries, some grits, beef sausages, scrambles eggs with two side order of toast and a cup of tea. I like my butter on the side please." Money goes so fast this way, constantly eating out because I'm homeless. If I had my own apartment I could have bought a dozen of eggs, a box of grits, a bag of potatoes and a box of sausages, which would had last me at least two week, and cost me just about the same amount of money I'm about to spend. If I have a taste for the same breakfast later on in the month, sadly, I would have to spend another twelve dollars. Being

Homeless isn't glamorous and it keeps you broke. Mmmm, that was so good. It hit the spot, I really enjoyed it.

On my way going home I decide to stop by Sub-Subs delicious supermarket to pick up my snacks for the day. Like I expressed before, I want to finish this book so I plan on staying in until I get the job done. I pick up a box of Ginger Snaps cookies, a bag of jelly beans, a cold sixteen ounce sprite soda and a large bag of Cheetos. I have my bag of munchies so, it's off to work I go. I'm going back to the shelter to start writing. On Saturday morning it kinda quiet around here in this neighborhood. Not that many people are walking around in the streets. I guess lots of them are in their' house sleeping late because it is a non-workday and a non-school day.

By now, you readers should know the deal. I got to get scan by security. Then the guard radio up that I have food. Then I got to play it off by going to the dining room pretending I ate up all my snacks. Then hide my goodies, of goodies, inside my tote bag underneath my jacket.

After I done all that, I'm leave the dining room.

Once I reach to the fourth floor, I see security guard Johnson is on post-sitting down next to the laundry room. "Good morning Officer Goodboy," I say. She turns her face in my direction while sitting stern in her seat and say, "Good morning Electra." I like messing with her, by calling her Officer Goodboy. Her real name is Bonnet Johnson.

Once I get by my dorm, I quietly open the door. Knowing everyone who still inside the dorm will be sleeping. Once I'm in the room I hear a loud animal noise. I don't know why she does that. Just as I was getting ready to take my goodies out from my tote bag, to hide my snacks inside the locker, I hear knocking sounds coming from the Q dorm' entrance door.

Knock, knock, knock and knock, leaving my snacks hiding inside my tote bag. I turn looking towards the door. It's Security Johnson. She slightly open up the door saying,

"Man on ladies. Is everyone dressed?" Security Johnson looked around the Q dorm checking to see if all the ladies in the dorm is clothed.

Security Johnson then open up the door wider saying, "Shack you can come in."

Oh that's maintenance. Shack have a pest control bottle in his hand walking towards me asking "Where did you see the nest of ants?" I moved away from my bed while saying, "What up Shack?" I pointed saying, "I saw them over there."

Shack moves my bed to find some ants that were crawling in a bunch. Some ants also were crawling alongside the wall and down by the wall-black panel strip. He turns towards me enigmatically asking "Electric, these little bit of ants you afraid of?" Then, humorously Shack asked "And what do you mean that I didn't clean up this room yesterday?"

I said, "Yeah right, you know you did not clean this room properly yesterday. Cause if you did how come you didn't discover all those ants yesterday. Especially when there were so much more ants then this little bit."

Shack, he sounding more convincingly pleading his innocent by saying "I did too clean and mop this room and don't you be writing me up no more."

I didn't know it was Shack I complain about. I like Shack, but the dorm was a little messy as if no one really clean so I said, "Shack, you see over there that same piece of paper was on the floor next to the bathroom for two days. Besides I didn't know I was writing you up. I didn't know who the maintenance was for the dorm yesterday. I hate that I had to write you up but the room wasn't clean."

He said jokingly "I did too clean this room woman," as he sprayed some liquid on the ants and squirted liquid inside the small crack open black panel from the wall. Then Shack looked at me and said "I'm going to write you up for pulling up this panel." Immediately I said, "Seriously. I didn't do that."

Looking at the sprayed ants I said, "There was much more ants then that and I hope none of those ants had gotten inside my locker."

Shack said "I hope they did." Then he started laughing saying "Let me stop playing with you before you go and write that up too."

Once he finished in my area. Shack looked for Goodboy. I mean security Johnson who is standing guard holding open slightly the Q dorm door. Shack had Goodboy to knock on the Q dorm bathroom' door, wanting to make sure there was no resident inside there. Then he puts inside the bathroom a new roll of toilet tissue and paper towel. He change the garbage bag that was in the waste basket. After Shack had finished inside the bathroom, both of them left the dorm moving on to the next dorm.

The maintenances crew never cleans the dorms on the weekends in any shelters. All they do for the dorms is put a new roll of toilet tissue and paper towels inside the bathroom. Also they change the garbage can plastic bag and input a new one. On the weekend the maintenance crew does other things for the shelter, like clean the offices, clean out the garbage cans heavy containers that's in the yard, assist with the cleaning for the shelter' special holiday celebrations, assist in, driving us girls on schedule trips also on the weekends they are taking accounts of the maintenances inventories and cleaning out the shelter vans.

When I open my locker to hide my snacks, wow, I seen my dirty clothes laundry bag it is getting full. It's still very early in the morning. Maybe the laundry list will have a slot open so hopefully I can squeeze in a wash. After I had locked up my little bit of goodies, I left the dorm. Going downstairs to the kitchen. At this time it is where I would find the shelter laundry list. The shelter rule for doing laundry is that residents have to sign up the night before in order to use a washing machine. If all the slots weren't taken, you can probably catch an open slot early in the morning. When I reached the kitchen I asked the RA (residential aide) for the laundry list. I scan the laundry sheet, hoping I can get in at least one wash but every slot was accounted for.

As I proceed going back to my dorm; I get on the fourth floor, look inside the washing machine room, no one was in there using the machines. I ask Officer Goodboy who sitting on her post by the laundry room, "Is someone washing now?" She stands up and look at the posted laundry list that's on the door and say, "Yes a client has signed, for this time."

I asked, "Where the person at?" "Don't worry about that Electric the person will be coming soon," she said. I said, "Goodboy. You know lots of times residents sign up for the machine and they aren't even in the building." Officer Goodboy listen but she didn't respond back. I asked, "Can you check to see if the person is here inside the building, because if not, I'd like to use the machine to wash my clothes?"

Officer Goodboy said, "Miss Jones the person should be coming soon. If you need to wash, you have to sign up like everybody else."

That is another problem I discovered. Is that a few clients always sign up for the machine but lots of times they not using them. By some residents doing this it keeps others residents, like me who may need to wash from washing. I said to Goodboy, "I went downstairs to sign the laundry list but it was full. Now I'm looking at two empty machines that I could be using. Maybe the person who had signed up for it, is not going to use il. She signed, but she not going to wash, probably just to be mean and stopping others from using the washing machine."

Miss Jones didn't you understand what I had just told you. The person should be coming to wash," she said. "But the time now is nine forty-five. The person signed the nine thirty slot and you can't even tell who she is because she didn't write her name legible so you could read it. I feel Bridge Net should have a grace period for doing laundry," I replied.

Security Johnson said, "Um. You have to take that up with the RA." I said "That's not right. Residents sign for a particular time and then she comes very late to wash. You know Johnson this is a perfect example how and why the laundry schedule be getting backed up. Could you radio and inquire to find out who the person is, being you see its empty and I like to use the machines so that I can wash." Getting annoyed at me, Security Johnson said while moving her hands through the air, "There's nothing that I can do Miss Jones. If your name is not on the list I can't let you use the machine."

As I stood there looking at the empty machines I was thinking I really need to wash a load. I should have signed up last night but today is Saturday. I was hoping there would be at least one open slot for me to use since everybody like to sleep in late. For goodness sake it's still early in the morning. I was thinking I should go to the third floor trying to sneak in a wash, but I bet the guard posted there will give me the same response.

I decide to go take the matter up with the RA. As I walk back downstairs going towards the kitchen I notice a small line. There were girls waiting in front of me to be served. Lots of residents were picking up toiletry' bags. The Residential Aide now has to follow the shelter procedures after issuing out any toiletry bags, the next step would be for the RA is to get the toiletry' book, look up the client' name, then check off what that client took. Next insert the date. Now the client has to sign. Reason is the shelter only hands out certain items to us residents once a month.

The next resident in line was waiting for sanitary napkins. Now the RA had to go get and pick up the allow amount of pads a resident is entitled to, look up her name, check off what she took and date it. Then that resident have to sign her signature in the book. Reason is because the shelter only hands sanitary napkins once a month.

Finally I reached the RA. I asked, "Do you know who the resident is that sign for both washing machines on the fourth floor-at this time?" RA Houser gave me a stupid look and said "No."

I asked, "Can you get the laundry book and check?" RA Houser she giving me attitude because I guess what I ask is not written in her job description therefore she doesn't want to do the work. She stress out or, she feel I'm just not important enough for her to want to help out. Therefore she asks me, "Why?"

I said, "Because someone signed for the machine and the person whoever she is, well, she not using it. Since her not using the washer machine I have a load I like to wash." Impatiently and giving me attitude Houser replied, "Look. Just sign the book." "I can't because every slot is taken," I express. Houser ask sarcastically, "So what do you want me to do?" as she paused, while looking me in my face with her insulting attitude. Then she said harshly, "Just wash tomorrow." Frustrated because I know there is an empty machine that I can used. I said, "That's why I'm asking can you,"…Houser, had, cut, me, off! She said all disrespectfully while her head shaking, "I can't stay here with you with this nonsense. I'm not trying to feel it! Go let someone else help you," as she walks away from me leaving me standing there feeling stupid and helpless because there was no other RA around to help me.

You see that why sometimes I be breaking on people because they have these jobs and they seem not to really care. When they should. Where did all the good people go? When I was working with the public I performed good customer service. **And** I had money to go to the Laundromat. I just used to sign up for my two small boxes of Wisk detergent that this shelter gave out weekly. I didn't have to deal with this crazy shit.

Going back to the fourth floor I was stop by Security Johnson, "Electra you have to wait here. EMS is inside your dorm." Being I was standing by the laundry room I happen to glance in, just to find the unused washing machines. So I said to Johnson, "You see, I could have used the machine." Officer Johnson looks at me and rolled her eyes.

I heard the pushing of machinery and guys talking. I looked down the hallway, it EMS. They have the lady that makes the animal sound sitting in a chair with an oxygen mask on her face. I knew something was wrong with her. Anyway that's the last time I saw her. I never even got to know her name. I watched her as they had rolled her pass me and they got into the elevator.

At the same time coming out from the elevator and moving out of their way was Samantha. She said to me, "Good morning Electra." "Good morning Samantha," I had replied back.

Samantha asks me, "Will you be coming to pamper yourself?" "What time does it start," I asked? Samantha said, "Right now." So I follow Samantha inside the room and took a seat. She hands me the sign in sheet. As I'm signing my name Samantha busy getting out all the containers for the group. One container had nothing but fingernail polishes. Another container consisted of, cotton balls, emery boards and a couple of different fingernail polish removers; lemon scented and non-scented.

Then Samantha goes to the library' entrance door and had stuck her' head outside of the door asking security Johnson, "Could you make the announcement to the other guards as well as to the ladies on this fourth floor that pamper yourself is in progress."

I heard Officer Johnson announce on her radio, "Attention to all security posted on floors. Please be advised pamper yourself is now on the fourth floor. Tell clients thank you," as she get up going to the dorms to make the announcement to the ladies on the fourth floor.

I'm watching Samantha as she was just moving. In another container she had various facial scrubs like honey almond, apricot, cucumber, mint jelly and a bunch of other facial peels. There were various body creams and lotions. Then she had brought out a couple of plastic mirrors for applying the facial products.

While listening to music I painted my nails light pink. Then I applied the hot pink nail polish-making poker dots. Once my nails has completely dried I put some cucumber facial scrub inside of a foam cup. I planned on taking it back with me, to my dorm, so when I take my shower later on I would use it. Once the class finished I headed back to my dorm. Normally, I would do endless walking around, outdoors.

Opening my dorm door, my eyes automatically go to my area, looking at my poster, Beauty Is in the Eye of the Beholder. I'm thinking of that song-it's raining man by the weather girls but, it's raining man on top of my locker. What a difference a picture of a poster upon my locker makes and, it so artsy looking too. I really like it.

Oh **sweat!**........I see my neighbor removed her' red heart, and had put up a picture of an white ugly old man' face, with his tongue sticking out of his' mouth, ew!

I walked completely into my area, sat on my bed just looking at her. She lying perfectly still in her' bed. She knows I'm in the room and yet she say nothing. I can't even see her eyes because she always wearing those dark sun shades. You should see her lying there-straight with both arms at her side, her' face, facing the ceiling. I'm thinking, she can't be that much of a loony tune liking art... right? Maybe this would be a good time to strike up a conversation. So I said, "Hello." She didn't say anything back. Maybe she didn't realize I was speaking to her. So I said, "Q 9. Hello... how are you?" I got no response she just laid there looking towards the ceiling.

I'm thinking for her maybe today is not a good day. So sitting on my bed I started thinking what happen after I kicked Thomas out of my apt.

Reader: Let go back *into the story.*

Yelp. I asked him to leave. He made his decision or did he forget, he like a fish in the water. So the water rode his ass right out of my house. Naturally he didn't want to leave and he was angry or maybe even a little embarrass. AND shocked. Now he know how I feel all the times he embarrass me in front of others. Don't act surprise now because it over. Thomas knew, he seen it coming. I wanted more than a live in boyfriend with more kids and...he knew it. I wanted marriage and commitment. All I got to say is hit the road Jack.

I called and told my mother the news, "Mom me and Thomas broke up." She said, "Oh no!"

Sucking her teeth, making sounds of disappointment. "What happen? What you mean yall broke up! When?" she asked. "We broke up mom! We not together anymore. I kick his' ass out last night," I said.

"YOU DID WHAT! Oh no, why"....then her sounds of disappointment by sucking her' teeth.

I said, "It had to happen." "E lec tra think about the kids. They're so young," my mother said. "He's gone already mom," I said.

My mother yelled, "Why would you go and do something like this!" I said. "**Mom**! I wasn't happy!" Again my mother made sounds of disappointment by sucking her teeth then saying "um, um, um, um, umm."

My mother said, "The kids are so young. Why won't you stay with him until the kids get bigger?" Then she said, "I and Eddie had our problems but we stayed together till yall was teenagers."

Immediately I said "Mom! You mean to tell me you weren't happy with daddy and that yall stayed together for me and Tonya benefit? **Yeah right**, mom!"

"**We did**. We stayed together for yall," my mother said. "I don't believe you," I said. "We did," my mother insisted.

"Well I'm not you. I'm not going to stay in a relationship where I'm not happy. Pretending for who? Thomas was too busy supporting everyone in Jamaica. He don't even love me cause if he did me and the kids would have come first in his life."

My mother asked "Girl how are you going to make it?" I told her, "You act as if Thomas was doing so much for me. It's my apartment. Everything is in my name. The rent, the light, the gas! The telephone and even the DAM kids are in my name mom. Shoot."

"Um, um, um, um, umm," that all I hear my mother saying on the other end of the phone.

I continue, and told my mother, "At least daddy married YOU, and was the provider for our' family. I put in most of the furniture in this apartment by watching and taking care of your' foster care kids. All the time I'm sacrificing and doing without! Thomas don't care about my needs and whatz important to me. Just recently Thomas had some of his' friends over from Jamaica staying here. After they left. Something told me to look up, just to see someone had taped a dead bat to the bathroom ceiling!"

"A dead bat!" my mother said. "Yeah mom a dead bat! At least that's what Thomas said it was. **He didn't want to take it down either.** So I had to **go and get daddy** to make Thomas **take it down**," I told her.

Sad sounds of "um, um, umm" were all that my mother at that point could say. "Look it just didn't work out mom," I said.

I also shared this news with my grandparents. My mother' parents. Unfortunately they were the only grandparents that I had left at this time. By this time in my life Grandmamma was already confined to a wheelchair and Granddaddy, is completely blind. When I broke the news to them. I told Grandmamma first.

I said, "Grandmamma Thomas and I aren't together anymore. I ask him to leave the apartment." Sadden by the news Grandmamma said "Electra how are you going to make it with those babies?" I said, "One day at a time, Grandmamma."

Grandmamma asked me, "Could you stay with him until your kids get bigger?" I said, "I see lots of women raise their' children on their own. The relationship wasn't how I expected it to be. I could do badly by myself. Plus everything is on me anyway."

I got the feeling Grandmamma didn't want to see or hear again of the struggle I endured with my first daughter Champagne. Even though she wasn't up front and center watching what all I endured. She knew I had, a very, hard time.

When I told Granddaddy, he too was deeply sadden to hear the news but he said softly and slow "Well. If you're not happy. You shouldn't stay with no one that doesn't make you happy."

At least Granddaddy understood how I felt but I could see in his' face he hated to hear that I am on my own raising three small children.

To me, no one should have to stay with someone for the children' sake. If both of you are not happy, the children wouldn't be happy either. An unhappy home is just not a happy home with one parent or two-that's just how I see it.

When I got home my telephone was ringing. Ring, ring I pick up the phone "Hello," I answered.

A woman with a Caribbean accent said, "Hello, I would like to speak to Thomas."

I said, "Thomas doesn't live here anymore."

Shock at the news, she paused before she said another word. Within those few seconds of silence I knew it wasn't Thomas' mother on the other end of the phone because Thomas mother' voice is very loud and old sounding. The woman on the other end said, "I'm the mother of his three children and I would like to know where Thomas can be reached?"

Stun. I said, "I don't know where Thomas is at." The Jamaican woman said, "Didn't you know he had children" and......I stop her right **then and there.** I said, "First of all let just get one thing straight. When I first met Thomas he told me that you and he no longer had a relationship."

The woman said, "He have a family in Jamaica so why did you go ahead and give him a son knowing"....**I** interrupted her, and said, "He denied being in a relationship with you because if **I,** would have **known** he was still in a relationship with **you,** I would have **ne ver** took the relationship this seriously. **Definitely!** I wouldn't have had any children by him. All he ever said to me the very few times he spoke about his family was he wanted to take care of his' teenaged daughters.

The laughing woman said, "Who do you tink he was with when he visited Jamaica?"

I said, "I didn't think he was with anyone because he wasn't gone that long but, you see me, I'm not going to be like you. To teach my teenaged daughters to degrade their' self and to accept this kind of treatment from a man! When he's in Jamaica, Thomas is with you and when he's in New York, he is with me and that's not okay in my book." The woman said, "Excuse me."

"For what?" I questioned. Then I said, "I have far more respect for myself. I didn't have any idea that Thomas was with you. Only when Thomas didn't come right back after burying his father I knew he was lying to me and that I didn't come first in his life. That why this number is where he **used** to be. This is no longer Thomas address! You see, I didn't know about you still being in a relationship with him. Because he told me yall were threw (slang word for over,) but I see you knew about me. And **you**...still **slept with him!** He was with me in New York all...this time and you **knew,** and you were still sleeping with him when he goes to Jamaica. And now you are calling my apartment wanting to know where Thomas **is**? Why did you wait so long?!.... To come and inquire about your so called man! Oh, and by the way **yes**, we do have a son and **now a daughter together.** But that's the difference between me and you. I'm going to teach my son not to have children all around the world because he's **fuckin!** Instead to have children by a woman he loves and wants to marry. As far as my daughters goes, I'm going to teach them by examples. I don't lay down while **supporting** spreading my legs knowingly I'm taking turns sharing my man! Like I SAID, he don't live here anymore and *please,* I'm asking, do not call here ever again." I hung the phone up while she was still talking.

Kicking Thomas out I had moved so fast. I didn't plan on how I was going to do things after he was gone. I just wanted him out. No more barrels in my fuckin living room. No more hearing those words your day soon come Tami. No more sacrificing trying to make ends meet to support another family. All of the sacrificing I had done for a better tomorrow, got me tired and nowhere just for what?! To send everything to Jamaica! No more playing house and no more playing wifey!

Dam!......................I didn't think about how I was going to get Champagne back and forth to her' school. Oh man- her' school payments. She in the second grade and she had about a month and a half to go before school had let out.

I don't have to tell you reader, because you should know due to the breakup it was a real struggle for me. Now all of us have to leave the house early in the morning in order to take Champagne back and forth to school. Paying my household bills and the school fee from my PA check, well, it was a struggle. If Thomas wanted to he could have helped out but he was mad at me for kicking him out of the house. He could have left me the car or even came by in the morning taking Champagne to school. He left me high and dry while taking care of his share of the responsibilities again-with our kids.

St. Mark's Academy private school was ahead of the game. All the school payments had to be in ahead of time. By the school doing it this way the school knew exactly how many kids would be attending for the fall semester. Plus how many seats would be open for each class. There were plenty of parents on the waiting list trying to get their' child or siblings into this school. The school also had a reduction fee plan for siblings that attends the school from the same family. The more siblings from the same family attending the school, the more dollars deductions that were taken away from the school's fee cost.

This private school started enrolling children from pre-k and it went all the way up to the eighth grade, which was just another factor I found appealing. Before we broke up I express to Thomas, "Look at how much the school fee will be when Brandon starts. Then, look how much it would be when the baby starts."

Right now I was paying an arm and a leg for one child attending the school but her education is worth it. Champagne' school fee was mine solely and always been my responsibility to fund.

I didn't/couldn't make the payment as of yet for Champagne September school enrollment, ensuring her and the school that she had a seat for the third grade. St. Mark's Academy only have like three third grade classes. Now because of this I had to meet with the school' principal concerning Champagne attendance for the fall.

The principal was courteous and give me a dead line date to have the money in. Along with her generosity came a late charged fee. It was the school way of penalizing parents when the school payment wasn't on time. I'm only receiving but so much on my welfare allowance. With Thomas supposing to pay the light and gas I had a chance of paying Champagne' school fee. Now that he has disappear without a trace, light, gas and his' collect telephone bill is now on me. Now, our carfare too, riding back and forth on the bus. I was finding it hard to squeeze the money out from my welfare budget to pay her' school payment. Now on top of that I'm face with the school late fee too.

Every day I got up early. Loading the stroller making sure all of us were dressed and ready to go on the bus. Making sure Champagne reaches school on time. In the middle of my busy day stopping whatever I was doing, just so I and the kids can hop on the bus, running, rushing to pick her up on time. A couple of times I was late picking her up. The bus was way too crowded for the bus driver to stop at the bus stop where I was standing. Champagne didn't like being left behind looking at her classmates who has already left the school. So I had to leave extra early making sure I reach to the school on time.

Since I asked Thomas to leave. I haven't seen or heard from him. He didn't come by or call. Even though our relationship was finish he still had children he had to support and see. Dam, that nigger stuck me with his' enormous telephone bill of collect calls he accepted from Jamaica.

I see the game Thomas is playing.

He knew everything about me and the challenges I face. He wanted me to suffer and to struggle knowing what all I had to do with a newborn and a two-year-old would be difficult. By disappearing he thought that when he come knocking back at my door I gladly take him back saying, "Thomas I need you. Watch the kids while I go pick up Champagne from school. Thomas can I get your car' keys to pick Champagne up from school? Thomas do you have the money for the telephone bill because the money I have is for Champagne' school fee. Thomas, you have money for pampers because the children don't have any. Thomas I need a break can you watch the kids because

I'm tired. I need to take a nap. Thomas can you feed the baby while I clean up the apartment?"

Instead his actions of disappearing made me hate him even more. He knew I had to take Champagne back and forth to school. He knew her school wasn't right around the corner. He knew how much money I received on my check. He knew her school fee had to be in ahead of time. He knew the light and the gas and the telephone had to stay on. He knew I had to go food shopping to keep food on the table. Thomas know our' children were young and they needed pampers. He knew everything about me. We only been together for the last 5 ½ years.

So we not together anymore. He still have responsibilities and children he have to support and see. He didn't leave the mother and his kids in Jamaica penniless. Nor, is his' family back home caring about supporting our wellbeing. So, we not together therefore he just walk away from his responsibilities' he have with me?

Come on! He wasn't serious about the relationship because if he was he would have put us first in his life. Why is he so mad, because I'm the one who said, "Were threw?" The point is, Thomas he know he didn't love me because if he did, he would have shown me while we were together. The only thing I heard was his promises after promises of him saying "Your day soon come Tami." Well I got tired of seeing him up build another family and himself. When **is** my day coming? My day will never come with Thomas and that is something he and I had to admit. What does it matter who say it's over first? Especially knowing that's not the person you really want to be with. Give me a break already. Why do black men do this? They say "I like you. Let me get to know you and be with you." Nine times out of ten they would move into your apartment. Create a baby. Then he cheats, having all kind of affairs on you. Some men not helping out with the bills. Some men are helping out with the bills, but the bottom line is that females get tired of men bullshit after constant bullshit of showing non-commitment to the relationship. A female be like WHERE'S THE RING BITCH! So, she finds the nerve and the strength to say, "Alright we've threw. It over. Get out."

Then he acts like a fuckin fool and disappear completely. Knowing kids involve, that we both created. Knowing the children were going to wake up hungry. Kids wanting to go outside and play. Knowing the kids, they need to keep a roof over their head with running water and soap. He knows they need clothes to wear and knowing it takes money to take care of them and support them! I could just her my mother now, "I told you, you shoulda stay with him until those kids got big."

It's a dam shame to know or to even hear women are staying in a miserable relationship for the sake of their children. But to me, I didn't see those women staying in the relationship for their children sake. I see the women that are staying in these type of relationship because they don't want to be financially burden while raising their children; like me who is always struggling to make my ends meet. Also some women may look at it like, he the father, is free as a bird to do what he please, like sleep or hangout or be in peace without hearing and dealing with supervising energize nagging children. Because being a parent is a full time underpaid responsibility. So, I guess some women may feel that we are going to go thru this together!

Going through what I had experience with Thomas and what I'm experiencing now, honestly do I want to stay with him for my children sake? The answer is .... no! I did the right thing by kicking his ass out even if it means I'm only eating grits for dinner, and at the moment, I won't be buying myself nice clothes or going out to parties anytime soon. I made my bed and I got to lay in it. I just had babies by immature men-by someone who didn't really love me. I should have been more responsible in choosing who I have a baby by. I was young minded and I made a very big mistake. Like a fuckin chicken head female..........Damn I don't believe I just called myself a chicken head.

But.....I'm not a chicken head female because I thought Thomas and I had something real, a relationship that was going somewhere but I was wrong. That's why **he's out.** I do love myself therefore I am no chicken head because a chicken head female puts everything and everyone before her own needs. That's why I'm no chicken head because I can look at myself in the mirror and breathe knowing, I did the right thing for myself by taking a stand to make Thomas respect me and to show him that I do love myself more than I love him. That I do respect myself and without a doubt, he knows I'm crazy in love with my kids.

I never forget that comment Desmond made on my sister Tonya. It was a crowd of us gather inside our apartment in the project. Loudly in front of everybody Desmond said "Tonya love me so much that she will run through fire with gasoline draws on." Look how he aided in the destruction of our family. To me Tonya is the true example of a chicken female.

Knocking sounds coming from the apt door. When I went to the door it was Thomas.

Thomas was like "Tami let me speak to you." I open the door. He came inside the apartment and sat down on the couch in the living room. It was night time because I already put the kids to bed. I just got finish washing dishes now I was sweeping the living room floor. I had on my cheap thin house coat and true I was a little weak and exhausted. I was carrying a big load. Moet was like three month. Brandon just made two. Getting all of us up early every day, taking that bus ride back and forth to Champagne' school. I already put a deposit on the telephone bill Thomas left behind. I paid my light, gas and rent. Did my food shopping already while running around pushing my children in the stroller taking care of personal business while Champagne in school, like keeping all the children doctors' appointments, picking up and cashing in WIC vouchers, cleaning the apartment, giving baths, cooking dinner, you know the small things mothers/housewife's do.

Thomas sat on the couch while I was sweeping. He said "Tami me couldn't leave my children mother with nothing; she was good to me. I figure by me helping her start her' own business, she be able to stand on her' own two feet. Wouldn't need any financial support from me. She be able to take care of herself."

I was sweeping and listening as he was talking. I stop and said "You help her start her own business?"

Thomas said "Yeah mon she has no income in Jamaica. By having a business for herself she be able to take care of herself and I wouldn't have to worry about her.".................. Not only was Thomas shipping down barrels. That night I found out he was wiring money to her through Western Union to help her start a business too. Everything he was saying went through my head so fast. Maybe because I was blown away from what my ears were hearing.

Now let me get this straight.

First he made me feel sorry for Jamaicans thinking they live in a hut so poorly that he had to redo his house for his kids but in reality, first, he had to buy the land. Then I found out he built the house from the ground up and in order to build this house I watch him shipped down expensive machinery and tools. After he done brought and placed these large barrels in my apartment. I watched him fill those enormous barrel up with merchandises, not one time, not two times, but so many times! I watch this man send down everything but the kitchen sink. Then Thomas had to pay to ship the barrels to Jamaica. Then pay Jamaica for those barrels to come into that country. We struggling. He works. We struggling, then he get paid. He cleans out his saving account-he go to Jamaica, he's back from Jamaica. We still struggling. He works. We struggling, then he get another paid check once he's back in New York. We struggling just to save money so he can repeat the process all over again. Me doing without. I found out for him to become a citizen, he is married to the woman that was banging on the pots and pans in the kitchen. Could he be a child molester? Because I'm thinking about my son hard on? I'm **not marry**! Then there was a dead bat hanging up in our bathroom! I'm always doing without, and not counting all the DAM money he wirer down behind my back. He just told me he help start a business for another **woman** then he have to pay for his plane fare ticket too!! Heaven only knows what else!!! Here I am struggling, killing myself for **WHAT!!!!!!!!**

Momentarily insanity just sat in. I said "YOU STARTED A BUSINESS FOR HER!!!!"

All of a sudden the broom in my hand became a baseball bat and Thomas as he sat on the couch talking with his head tilted to the side, his head/face became a ball. Before I **knew it!** I took that broom and Ba BOOM!!! I hit Thomas so hard in his head that my cheap boom had broken in half!! When I saw the lopsided point from the broken broom I CHARGE him!! Wanting to stab him!! Thomas jump up so fast from the couch as I was jabbing trying/wanting to stab him!

Momentarily insanity had occurred!

I think I was trying to kill Thomas because I was jabbing at him. Thomas was moving swinging as he hitting trying to knock the pointed broom out from my hand. When he got the broom out from my hand. He grab me! Because I was swinging wildly with both fists but I was so fuckin weak and tired my hit wasn't shit. Thomas pick me up and held me in his arms. He had me in such a tight grip I couldn't swing my arms. I was out of control. Knowing I couldn't move my arms so I started acting animalistic, swarming and moving, biting at his fingers, hands and wrist trying to free myself because they were the closest objects to my neck and mouth.

Quickly moving his' fingers and hand away from near my face, Thomas, he held me down in a tight bear grip.

Getting buck wild I started to kick him while stomping on his feet wanting freedom from his tight grip but Thomas held on to me he wouldn't let go until I got tired and my angry slowly started disappearing.

Once he saw I was calm he let me go and tried explaining how he felt. Saying, it was the only way out for him. At this point I didn't want to hear anything else from Thomas or about the people in Jamaica. I asked Thomas to "Leave the apartment **now!** I yelled, "Just get away from me." He left.

Stop......To the reader: First of all, I just like to say I'm really glad Thomas didn't get hurt when I swung that broom against his head because I really tried to hit a mother fuckin home run and then I was trying to stab him too. He's not worth me spending time in jail doing a bid, for him and his greedy family in Jamaica. Second of all, I am glad that God had an angel looking over me for not really hurting him and for Thomas being a man and not really hurting me after I knock the **shit** out of him and stab him a couple of times with the broom.

Back to the story.

After that I realized Thomas he bringing out the worst in me. I lost my cool and control and that wasn't good. Anytime any one can make so much anger come inside of me to the point of me losing control like that. I can't be around that person. I know sometimes couples may argue but to fight with this much loathing and animosity it's not good. Taking me to that point that I flip out and went blank and swung like that! Anyone who was driving me to the point of insanity while wanting me to do him bodily harm. Naw...he gotz to go, because I can see if we stay together, somebody was going to go to jail and it's not good for our kids.

My mother and Grandmamma talking about say with him for the children sake. I can't even look at him. Less fuck him. All the time I did without just for him to help her jump start a business and for him to build a home from the ground up so he can say I have a home in Jamaica. I hope they be very fuckin happy together.

Thomas knock back on the door but this time I didn't let him inside the house. I just open the door hoping to hear Thomas say something like, I want to see the kids. Or let me take them out. Instead he stood there, standing inside the hallway looking at me. Breaking the silence I said from inside my apartment door, "The kids' need some things. Can I get some money?" Thomas asked "Need tings like what Tami?" I resented that he wanted me to go into details with him. I said, "Champagne' school fees are due and I need money for things like pampers and whatever else I feel they need."

Thomas asks "What do they need? Pampers? I'll buy it for them." I said, "Oh, you can't give me the money to purchase the things the children need?" Thomas said "I'm not giving you none of my hard earn work money." **Oh no**! He didn't just say that after all I helped him with. Like shipping things to Jamaica. Supporting him when he didn't have any money now because were not together he leaving me high and dry. Treating me like I'm not capable of taking care of the kids with the money he gives me. "Fuck you Thomas! I don't need any of your money. You going to say something like that after all I help you do for your fuckin tribe in Jamaica. Oh... it's alright for you to wire down money and barrels helping your' teenage daughters and their' broke ass mother but for me and my kids you treat like shit. You don't want to give me any of your hard earn money, Fine! YOU BLACK BITCH! I will never ask you again for nothing," I said.

I slam my damn door.

I say what I mean and I mean what I say. I will never asked Thomas for a mother fuckin dime! Well....... I don't even have to say it..........yes it was a struggle. Him leaving me without any support but I was so pigheaded that I was determined to make it on my own. **Fuck him!** That's just what I mean.......Fuck that Black Bitch.

A couple of days later, someone was at my door. Knock, knock, and knock. I goes to the door look out the peephole I see Thomas' face. I'm mad at how he's not helping me with our children and stubborn, sticking to my grounds not taking him back or asking him for any of his hard earned money. Even through I'm catching hell dealing with my hardship and being hurt, because at the end of the day I always thought no matter what, I had a friend in Thomas.

I had lost some much weight.

I open the door "What do you want?" He had some groceries bags in his hand. Thomas sounding voice of uncertainty saying...... *"Electra?"* Did he just call me by my first name Electra? What happen to him calling me Tami? Oooh... so now he wants to act paranoid like I'm flipping a script. You know what..... I'm not going to even feed into this shit. That's my name too. I still said, "What do you want Thomas!" Sounding uncertain he said.... *"Electra*... I bought some groceries for the kids." I open the door allowing him to bring in his' groceries.

When we got inside of the kitchen he pulls out from the brown paper bag, a gallon of milk, a loaf of white Wonder Bread and a small pack of cheap baby pamper; even though he just played me, again. He also just played himself.

I said, "Thomas I could have gotten this grocery off of their' WIC vouchers."

From my experiences already with Champagne, in buying cheap pamper, well they are good for only one piss. After the cheap diaper has been spoiled it start to crumble, making the child look like it is carrying around a pound of shit inside it's pamper. Anyway for me it was hard with the small kids; it was like I'm robbing Peter to pay Paul in order to sacrifice the money for Champagne' school fees. She really did like her school. I figure it was just a matter of adjusting.

Getting used to my new routine of doing things.......again by myself.

Things have gotten worse with me. I had lost a lot of weight. The situation was draining me. I didn't want to but I had to have a talk with my oldest daughter. "Champagne come here." Listen mommy can't take you to school anymore I can't afford your carfare and mine and still pay your school dues. I'm so sorry sweetie but you are going to have to ride the bus by yourself when you go to school, but I will pick you up though," I told her.

Before I had actually done it we had practiced, until she was comfortable riding the bus all by herself. Every morning, at the same time, we all walked her to the bus stop. We had watched her get on the bus. I made sure she sat in the front by the bus driver and that the driver knew exactly what stop she had to get off at. I hated that I had to do it, but I had no other choice

Now this was when the shit hit the fan.

Champagne school was close for the summer vacation. Private schools closes a week earlier before public schools. Thomas started coming by the house with small groceries items. Like a box of Corn Flake cereal. Again the smallest bag of white wonder bread and a gallon of milk. Real trivia stuff. The kids made their way to the kitchen because they heard Thomas' voice. Moet was either on the couch drinking her bottle or sleeping inside her' crib. When Thomas saw the kids he started saying "Mon the kids look so poor." That Jamaican slang for skinny/undernourished.

Thomas asked "Electra you not feeding the kids? Why they look so skinny?" He pick Brandon up with one hand while saying "Look at this mon. the boy needs weight on him." This sounding voice of uncertainty again. Thomas said....."*Electra*?" Ok, now he getting on my nerve with saying my name.....*Electra*. Like he scared or is it really me, Tami? Ignoring him. I said, "JB the same weight he was when you were here. He eating the same amount of food he been eating off **my** food stamps."

Thomas said "No mon, listen. Me want to take him to Jamaica. I want him to go to school in Jamaica. Let the boy get some porridge and go inside the sea water making him body look pretty and nice." Just humoring him. I asked, "And who is he going to be staying with while he's in Jamaica?" Thomas said "Don't worry about that Electra. The boy will be alright. I want him to grow up like a Jamaican mon." I was looking at Thomas to see, is he really serious about what he saying to me? Oh shit....... he's serious! Not sounding alarm I said harshly, "Hell no you ain't taking my baby, my son to Jamaica."

Sounding voice of uncertainty.

He said..... "*Electra*? Listen to me it will be best for the boy. He needs to be with his father." Sharply I said "He need his mother too! What are you talking about? Do you know how you sound talking about sending JB to Jamaica to stay.... and with whom?! You here in New York! I'm here in New York."

"Look Electra he my only son. I tried so hard to have a boy but I got three daughters. Everything I have and own will be his," Thomas said with a gleam in his eyes.

I gasp! I'm thought And what about Moet? He not even recognizing her. I can't believe Thomas is saying this. I'm thinking to myself as Thomas continue speaking. Oh shit he wants to take my son. Maybe that was the plan all along, to impregnate me. Someone who look helpless and alone. Then take my son to be raised by his' children' mother in Jamaica.....as their own child?

Coming back out from my own thoughts, again listening to what he was talking about. Thomas said "You have a boy for me and a girl for you." As he continue speaking. Quietly in my mind, I had tried to understand his concept. This is not the first time I heard Thomas say that. I remember

faintly he said that same phrase after I've given birth..........
but which child was it?

I was so frustrated! See what I mean; why isn't my memory
intact? It had to be while I was pregnant with Moet...or was
it sometime after I conceived Brandon? Anyway I know
I heard him say that same sentence before. AS I replay
the sentence in my head. The boy is for me and the girl is
for you. It had to be after I had Moet. Anyway I looked at
him and said very firmly and very believably, "My son ain't
going nowhere without me. Now, I'm glad that we are
having this little conversation Thomas, because Brandon,
won't EVEN be VISITING Jamaica without me. You can just
get that stupid thought out of your mind," as I pick up my
son moving him away from Thomas. Now I'm holding JB, on
one side of my hip assuring him and myself saying, "Right JB
you not going anywhere without your mommy," as I kissed
him on his' cheek. I said to my son, "Your mommy loves you
so much, right. Xoxoxo. (These are kisses.) You're my only
son. I always wanted a son too. Xoxoxoxo."

I love my son. He better get the **fuck** outta here. I love
my daughters too and Thomas seen it and he knew it. If he
pretend like he didn't knew it, well, he dam sure knows it
now. I held JB in my arms till he left the apartment, which
wasn't fast enough for me.

When Thomas came around never once did he mention
Champagne or Moet? He never talked about wanting to
see the girls. Or asked about how they were. It was always
just about JB. As a matter of fact he never even ask about
JB well-being. All he talked about was wanting to take JB
sending him off to Jamaica.

I was quite sure that Champagne misses him. She 7 ½
and I'm quite sure that she had questions or was a little
confuse as to why Thomas wasn't in the house. Maybe
in her' eyes she thinks that Thomas is her' real father. I
didn't have time to dwell on Thomas' favoritism. I couldn't
because there was so much I had to take care of already.

One thing that I should have done was taken out the time and sat Champagne down having a talk with her, but so much shit was going on I didn't think about it at the time.

After a while Thomas became out right ridiculous about JB.

He became outrageous!

I would be walking down the street, right, minding my own business. Walking on my block going to my apartment building. Pushing my daughter Moet in her' stroller, while Champagne be walking along the side of me. Around this time I had brought JB a basketball for two reasons. One, to become a dam good basketball player. Two, hoping he become a professional basketball player. Out of nowhere this fourteen seat, big, white and burgundy van pulls up alongside of us. Thomas jumps out the van from the passenger seat. Charging towards us saying "Give me my son!" He reaches for Brandon, to snatch him away, but my reflexes were quick.

I'm Shock!

Surprised! Scared! Unbelieving this was happening but I'm finding myself in this tug of war.

The tug of war is with Brandon. Us both yanking on our son. While I was screaming, "What you doing! Get off of him!" Scared to let go of JB arm/hand. In fear of Thomas taking him inside the van and driving away and I never ever see his face again. Not knowing where Thomas lived. Or how to get in touch with him. I'm holding on to my son for dear life.

Thomas has one of JB hand and I had the other. And both of us pulling to take the child. Frantically and stun at whatz going on, at some point the mother instinct kick in and came out of me. I found myself fuckin fist fighting for my son. Outside in broad daylight. On the block I live on for all who was out there to watch and see. I was swinging on his **ass.** While this tug of war match was going on. I held a tight grip on Brandon with one hand while swinging exchange blows with my other fist shouting angrily, "Get off my son mother fucker! Get off him!"

At this point I didn't know what my girls were doing at this time. Surely it had to be disturbing for them to watch. And poor JB, outside having a good time playing bouncing his' basketball and out of the blue just being snatch violently up in the air, by both parents that pulling him in different directions. Stretching his' little arms while listening to his' screaming mother curse as his determine father tries to put him inside the van and drive off. Both of us just pulling, yanking on the child. You know that was **fuck up** but it did happen.

Thomas did this type of shit plenty times to us out in the street.

Coming home from the park.

Jumping out from different kind of vehicles.

Laying... waiting to see us, or him sitting park-inside his' big white and burgundy van with the engine running. Waiting for us to walk up on the block, or walking towards the block. His stupidity embarrassing me in front of my neighbors with us outside fighting like that. It gotten to the point whenever I saw a burgundy and white van I would walk in the other direction.

So I see this van is his dollar van he was talking about purchasing. That's way he not helping me support our kids because he bought it after all. So, for my son sake I found myself going down streets where the cars was going in the opposite direction I'm walking. Then also strapping JB inside the stroller with Moet as I got closer to my building. There was no need for Thomas to behave this way. I never denied Thomas his' rights to having a relationship with his children. He going about it the wrong way. He the one who stop coming by to see them. He the one who not supporting them. Then he started with this talk about taking JB to Jamaica to live, causing me to believe I will never see him or my son ever again.

Now it had come down to this, us fighting and grabbing at our son outside.

Let me say, not only was this scary and embarrassing. It was also so... real. If I allowed Thomas to take JB to Jamaica I would had never seen Brandon again. I just knew it. I had no information on nothing besides the old phone numbers which were listed on my telephone statement. I wasn't about to take a chance on letting that happen. What happen to a normal conversation? Like Thomas saying "Tami/Electra (whatever name he chose to use) I would be coming by to pick up the children and have them home at such and such of time, but Thomas wasn't behaving like a normal person. His actions and talk was causing me to become alarm.

I mean, I just be walking down the street and zoom, out jump from a car, a van, this man grabbing at my two year old son. Trying to put him inside of the vehicle to drive off. I never seen no shit like this before! I never heard of anything like this happening with people I know. Thomas he became ruthless and callous. You see I was young I didn't know what I was getting myself into with dealing with this Jamaican man.

Stop! To the reader: Maybe some of you are thinking "Yeah if that man wanted the child he could have snatch him and drove off. Or some of you may be saying "Thomas pretending to take the child." Fact number one, the precinct is on my block. Therefore lots of police cars rode up and down the block. Thomas didn't want any trouble with the law. Trying to become a citizen or, just newly becoming a citizen. Trouble with the law he didn't want. I just wanted to clear it up and **state** it was real. I fought for my son not to go into the vehicle.

Back to the story.

When Tray and I broke up or fought, never once did Tray try and take Champagne away from me. Never once! As a matter of fact all the Black American men in the neighborhood when their' relationship was over they left their responsibility and children with the mother. That's why so many women were on PA. The biological fathers wasn't around taking care of their obligations. They were living with someone else or in jail. Never once, did I ever see or hear of any shit like this. A father, is trying to take the child away from it mother? And it was only JB that Thomas wanted. He didn't even look at Moet nor did he acknowledge her as his' daughter. He said he have three daughters' and a son when he really has four daughters. Champagne made five and a son.

When my mom and dad had separated. I never forgot that day. Tonya and I were inside our apartment in Westbrook Project with our mom. Daddy wasn't inside of the apartment with us. I thought maybe he was at work or he went out for a drive. Anyway he shown up at the apartment door. While standing in the hallway Daddy said "Come here Electra and Tonya. I've got something to say to yall."

My dad led us into the staircase that was directly in front of our apartment' door. I was in the sixth or the seven grade. Once we got inside the staircase, we all was standing on the steps. My father said "I'm leaving your Mama."

I remember me being shocked at hearing the news. Just like that, no warning signs. I didn't even see it coming. Then my dad said "I want yall to know, yall are not the blame why I'm leaving." After hearing the shocking news I asked, "Why you just going to leave us like that?" My father said "I'm not leaving yall. I'm leaving your Mama."

That news fucked my head up. I was so surprised and disappointed at my' dad for walking out on us, breaking up our nice family. Just out the blue, no kind of warning sign, no tears, and no hugs or kisses, just a finale .... bye. I didn't see any suitcases or packed luggage for him. It was just the conversation. Shocked, puzzled, mad and disappointed the way my dad had done it.

There were a couple of questions that got tossed around like "Where will you live? How can we get in contact with you?" The conversation wasn't long at all then he sent us into the house where my mother was at. At this time my mother wasn't even working for the telephone company anymore. She was unemployed. My father wasn't an EMS driver anymore either. He became a school bus driver. When we both went inside our' apartment my mother didn't say anything. There was no discussion, nothing.

For some reason I felt I had to be strong for my mother, maybe because I'm the oldest. I felt sorry for her. I felt, she didn't deserve that type of humiliation in front of all her' family and friends and those who secretly were jealous of her and their' relationship. My parents they seemed to love each other. My father was gone.... but I love my father and I loved my mother. They good people.

As a child growing up in the projects, back then there were a lot of marry folks raising their' children-Husbands and Wives were a union. I couldn't believe my parents had split up. As I had aged, I started noticing that relationships between a man and a women had started changing. In my teens I noticed that people were starting to shack up with no kind of tradition of the American Black family values. Then there started becoming a trend of single mother raising her children alone. Somehow I got caught up in that trend as well. Anyway my father didn't try to take us away from my mother. None of the Black American men did this kind of shit and if they did I didn't know it, or heard about it or even seen it. If it did happen, it had to be like in West bubble fuck somewhere, cause where I lived, in my area, in my neighborhood this type of shit just wasn't happening.

You know how many people gossip in the projects and yet I never heard of such nonsense. The man wanting to take a child away from it mother. The shit wasn't even on TV. Where I come from the rule of thumb was the children always had remain with their' mother but I had to realize that I wasn't dealing with an American. I dealing with a Jamaican.

Wait a minute, there was a segment on All My Children when Erica was in a custody fight because the man at the time she was married too they separated. I think Erica fell in love with another man and her extremely rich powerful husband was mad so he wanted to hurt her. So he had Erica' first born baby, her' only child at that time removed out from her custody which did hurt Erica deeply, very deeply. But THAT'S TV. In real life like I said what Thomas was doing to me, just was happening in my part of town.

Stop! To the Reader: Let me stop right here because what I'm about to say is so very important. Take it as a word of wisdom from someone else experience. When you decide to have children with someone and the father/mother is from another country get to know what their' custom is, when it comes to raising children and with married. Besides understanding their' own custom dealing in relationships, also get to know what they worship, and what their' own beliefs are.

Back to the story.

In my eyes Thomas was just another black man. I didn't know Jamaican Black men were so very different from Black American men. My parents never talk about people from different countries and to examine their' customs. Maybe because when I was growing up we were surrounded only around our own kind, American Blacks.

Before my parents split my neighborhood was dominantly American Blacks, just like myself. In the projects we had a very small handful of Puerto Ricans. Around the earlier eighties or was it around the late 70's that's when I notices that there were lots of Caribbean people who were coming over to America. They had migrated and had filled up the neighborhood, especially over there where my dad has recently moved too, across Eastern Parkway after he left my mom. That's when I noticed that the communities were changing and we had started to have those Labor Day Parades. But to tell you the truth, I really never paid attention to the Caribbean or the Spanish or any people outside of my culture. Honestly, I didn't even pay attention to my own culture because as a young teenager I was just living my life which consist of being around my family and friends. We didn't discuss cultures or looked at different cultures. It was simply treat people like how you would want to be treated.

Anyway I do recall and notices, that the cops were arresting lots of our Black American brothers for stupid reason and there was some valid reasons too. I remember thinking, wow, a lot of our boys /men are going off to jail but I was a young teenager just starting to explore life, thinking about having fun and wanting to hang out. Even though with me being young minded, I did noticed, that many of our Black American men/boys were going off to jail or they were getting hook on drugs and becoming addicts. Also I remember it was hard for us-meaning people of color, in the Black American culture to obtain good jobs. It seem to be White Americans holding a lot of the jobs position that were really good jobs and us Black Americans really didn't have a chance of getting. That's the era I was growing up in.

Then lots of the black American kids had only started being raised by single mothers who were on welfare. We stop saying and hearing of the words, Mr. and Mrs. I had grown up like that because that was how it was back then, in the projects. Mr. and Mrs. had children named.... and they lived on this floor. Even though I lived to see these changes in families, never once did I see or hear any gossip of the child' biological father wanting to take the child from its own mother! That's what Thomas was doing to me. I really wish that **anyone** would have told me about acknowledging cultures and that dating outside of your culture and bringing kids in it can become a big problem.

Security Johnson by the door. She just announced "lights out ladies."

Goodnight reader. I'll speak to you tomorrow.

Chapter Seventeen

"Six o'clock ladies. Breakfast will be served downstairs," Security Guard Abuja announced. Bright lights shines on my face "Oh boy," I immediately thrown the covers over my face. Before I knew it I fell right back to sleep. When I woke up the dorm was nearly cleared out of my roommates.

Getting out of the bed. I notice a memo was placed on top of my locker. It read.

Attention Residents of Bridge Net Women Shelter:

Excessive bags are no more. There will be no more excessive bags permitted underneath a client's bed or on top of the locker. As prior to the last House Meeting, residents were told only one personal bag would be permitted on top of your' mattress. **This week** is the last week for all **Residents** to make their arrangement of removing any of your extra belongings from the building. Starting the following week the Residential Aides of Bridge Net will be making their' **1st rounds**, to all dorms to confiscate **all** extra bags. Once an RA has removed any clients bags' that client would have exactly **seven days** to collect their' property and to remove their bags off of the premises. Or they will be **thrown out** by staff. As expressed and order from the Department of Homeless Services excessive bags is a **fire hazards** and are of no more. Bridge Net Shelter is about providing safekeeping for all residents as well as for our staff who work here.

Thank you all for your cooperation.

Well that's one thing I don't have to worry about. Everything I own fits inside my locker. I took a look around my room and I see Lacy and that Mexican chick has a serious problem. They both have a lot of bags to get rid of.

When I speak of bags I'm not speaking about small plastic individual bags or the plastic bags you receive when you go food shopping. The shelter, upon entering make a resident take all her belonging' out from her' suitcase and scans everything. Then security has to hand check everything. Once that is done the client put all clothes, toiletries, belts, shoe, sneakers, pocketbook, miscellaneous such as papers and makeup in these large clear see through thick plastic bags. Suitcases aren't allow inside any shelters. Depending on the shelter, maybe one luggage carrier might be permitted if it can fit inside your locker or neatly underneath your bed.

Me personally, I'm glad they passed this rule. I remember when I was at 68 Lexington before coming to Bridge Net. 68 Lex, also had us girls remove the majority of our bags because when the fire department came, 68 Lexington always got fined. They had always said us girls had way too many bags.

Over the years I had seen and lived with females with so many bags, which had completely cluttered up their area. Piles of piled up plastic bags of clothing, piled up, on top of lockers. Multiple piles, of clothes in these large plastic bags. Piled up underneath and around a bed, or beds, making her or their area look like a pig slop. These large piles of clothes inside clear plastic bags, lots of times would be blocking another resident space-causing that person, who sleep next to them having to step/walk over their' multiple bags of clothes just to get to their own space. Keeping that client uncomfortable and miserable-causing serious big arguments, that always leads up to fists fights. In another dorm even once I had gotten into a fight in the middle of the night because my bed was in the middle between two other beds and while I was sleeping the woman who slept next to me on the right, one of her piled up bags, has fallen off from her locker and had landed on top of my head. That's just another reason why I prefer a corner bed. Anyway, anyone who lives inside a shelter, we all are living out from our locker, but there are some girls that live out from their locker **and** their multiple piles of large clear plastic bags.

It disgusting when you see large clear plastic bags all piled up around and on top of each other. Showing clients multiple colors of wrinkled clothing. Not everyone so clean either, because many bags be smelling. Some bags has strong unpleasant odors. Then, seeing and looking at another resident or residents piles of clear plastics bags that contain their junk papers, toiletries, clothes and dirty shoes. That's your view soon as you enter inside the dorm-until you go to bed. Just imagine sitting on your bed and this is your scenery across from you or right next to you. Then when you lay down there piles of large clear plastic bags crowded over your head from the girl locker next to you. All these bags of clothes on top of your neighbor locker. In a dorm, I felt sorry for those clients who slept in the middle of two beds **And Sometimes** that client would have both neighbors with mad accumulated plastic bags.

When I lived at 68 Lexington I use to sleep on the drill floor before I got a bed inside a dorm. On the drill floor there is something like 40 or more beds, and clients with these big bags. In this shelter there are ten girls to a dorm. Imagine seeing residents with all of those large clear bags of personal possessions' in one room every time you open up the door. It just makes you get more depress because it's where you spend most of your time after 4 pm. Once the dorm opens up, you're up in that dorm or coming back and forth, until the lights get turned off. It's bad enough you got to live inside the shelter, dealing with a sinking system of changing rules and constant confusing, mainly, it be coming from the staff, as well as DHS-that seems to be holding a person down, leading a resident to nowhere, anytime soon.

Then when you sit down or lay down on your cot which is and supposed to be your private space while living inside the shelter, plenty of times you will want to get a break from all the madness of just being homelessness-so, you are in your private space, in your own world surrounded by lots of excessive bags from the resident who sleep next to you or across from you and her bags may leaks with odor besides, simply looking like a clutter of junk. Then this always happens, when a person who has so many bags causing her and her roommate too encounter with so many arguments, an imaginary line goes up.

This imaginary line is supposed to represent boundaries and respect; meaning, not one bag better not touch over this line unless there will be a problem. Which usually mean a heated argument or now a fist fight. After boundaries are establish between roommates' eventually, residents, even I, had learn or adapt and tune out the girl or girls, who sleep next to you with all those large clear plastic bags.

I mean, you have girls coming from all over the world. Some of the girls which are really women are just plain nasty! Especially if she an addicted. Or has any sort/form of mental illness-her bags would be all opened, unorganized and just sloppy looking. Anyway these bags bring in roaches, spiders and centipedes, plus it just looks so disguising because you already living inside this dreary room that's half way clean. Residents with all these bags make the entire dorm look gloomy and dirtier especially being that the majority of shelters are already halfway gloomy and dirty. Some shelter more than others. As a residents walking in the shelter hallways the residents can't help but to look in others' dorms because the dorm door is open and all you see is rooms with females lying or sitting on clots/beds with these large clear plastics bags well, it is just a pure reminder of where you at-the city shelter.

Me personally, I welcome this new change. It's something that should have been in place a long time ago for all shelters, since day one. Anyway, I turn to my poster. Beauty is in the Eyes of the Beholder and say, "Good morning boys." I just laid back on my bed placing both my legs up leaning them against the wall while my feet are crossed at the foot. My head is at the foot of my bed as I'm facing towards my locker. I'm looking at all the different sexy men in the poster. I'm trying to figure out which one was the cutest. I tried picturing each one personality. I day dream about what outfit I would wear if I was with this one on a date. What outfit I would wear with that one if I went out on a date. As I laid there admiring the poster, I occasionally turned my head towards the busy hallway of passing females being that the door to the Q dorm is wide open anyone whom passed the dorm can see my beautiful poster sitting on top of my locker.

While looking back at the poster, and then hearing the sounds of the security walkie-talkie getting louder I got up and got dress. It's Monday morning. The weekend is over, let me get out of here before I get an infraction.

Going to Jose, I order a BLT; bacon, lettuces and tomatoes with mayonnaise. A cup of hot coffee with milk and three sugar. I pick up a large bag of Doritos and a snicker candy bar. Heading back towards the building to finish writing the book.

Before I lost my job, on the weekends, I had money to take the kids out. Since I lost my job and before I started writing my time would normally be occupying with these long walks of sightseeing, window shopping and visiting my kids for brief moments. That if any visit did occur, by the way which is another story by itself so, let's see how I can tell the story about my life so far in this book. On that note reader let go back *into the story*.

Anyway like I said lots of brothers in Westbrook Project were going to jail. During this time there were lots of talk about three women to one man. In my neighborhood we were having a man shortage because majority of Black American men were incarcerated. Lots of the Black brothers were being arrested for one thing or another leaving us

Black American female to fend for ourselves and to raise the children alone.

Gradually I notice Black Caribbean people / West Indians / Jamaican started migrating to our neighborhoods, especially over Eastern Parkway where my dad now lived. There was nothing but Caribbean people. I remember this cause as a mid-aged teenager I spent a lot of time over at my dad one bedroom apartment after he left my mom.

We were having difficulties (my mother, Tonya and I) after daddy left. Meaning we fell off our high horse. What I mean by that, was we stop eating certain food we became accustom to eating when daddy was around. Falling from our high horse meant no more great Christmas presents. No more long drives. No longer did our parents buy us nice clothes. Sometime for dinner we ate peanut butter and jelly sandwich. Mom she wasn't working at all. She eventually had to apply for welfare herself to pay the rent for our apartment. What a step down that had to be for her, especially, since she was the daughter who seemed to have it all. Employment and a supervisor at that, a supportive well liked and easy to get along with husband. Mother, she had a paying job as a supervisor, going off to work every day, dressed up, to a high rise building in Manhattan.

She has a fabulous apartment with appliances and back then, you could tell how a family was financially just by the appliances in their apartment. My mother had the admiration and big time respect from both her' parents as the daughter who had married and was not financially depended upon them for anything. Also, if she needed it, my mother has the supported from both of her in-laws. There was in addition two beautiful daughters. My mother was the envy of a lot of her' friends and even some family members. Now, she just like a regular project chick, applying for welfare to make her ends meet. My mother never discuss with me or Tonya about when she had applied for welfare. Back then parents weren't open like how they are today telling their children all their personal business and including children in their affairs.

Back then, they were just the parents who had provided for the household. We kids in the Black American community were taught to respect our own parents and the elders. As children we couldn't ask any questions. We just had to do what we were told and we couldn't even talk back either. We had to hold the doors for our elders and address the adults by Mr. or Mrs. Most differently we as children had to stay in a child place by not engaging in adults' conversations. We were kids that were brought up as having morals and values along with the proper respect, for the family traditions.

Nor did I ever see my mother stand in line at the cash checking place to pick up her food stamps. Then one day the surprised telephone call came. Daddy announced to Tonya and me that he have a son and his name is Ed Jr. Daddy said "I want yall to treat him as if he is your brother from your mom."

We love our father, so daddy said he had a son. I'm excited cause I now have a brother but sad because the baby wasn't by my mom. I accidentally walk in on my mom crying inside the kitchen to the newly found news. She's looking out the kitchen window with tears rolling down her cheeks, crying softly while standing next to the washing machine that was inside the kitchen. Quietly I just turned and walk away never letting my mother know I saw her in the kitchen crying that day.

I remember hearing my mother conversation saying to somebody, "She need a job off the books." This way the extra money off the books wouldn't interfere with her' government monthly allowances. Eventually she became a barmaid in the neighborhood local bar. Then I guess my mom couldn't handle the struggle or should I say her' hardship alone. She gone way beyond the life style she once had-hitting rock bottom in a way and getting on welfare.

Finding out the devastating news on daddy becoming a father with another woman. Realizing her marriage must be really over. I really felt sorry for my mother even though I never told her so; and I was a little upset with my dad for leaving us too.

After daddy left it took a little adjusting because we really did have this great family, meaning (mom, dad myself and my little sister Tonya). Just when I was getting used to living alone with us girls, meaning just my mom and my sister. I thought my mom was going to do the girl thing with us. Like teaching us how to put on makeup, cooking and dressing up. I was like in my early teens around this time with no introduction, no warning, me and my sister woke up, and went into the living room and mom said, "This is Dave."

At first I thought well she do need a boyfriend to share her life with but I didn't think he was moving in. I was hoping that my mom and dad would get back together. Mother just brought this stranger into our home, to live with us, and him sleeping in my parents' bedroom! Uugh!

Dave enter a nice home with three beautiful females residing there. Personally I thought my mom should had held out. She moved to quickly to include this man into our home....... And to live with us? Again I'm thinking, ... matters of the heart. Daddy had a son. Maybe that's why she did it?

Being that we, meaning Tonya and I, were brought up to respect our elders. Those mannerism were embedded in me so I looked at Dave as an adult black man. Then he spoke. He didn't sound like the black people that I was used to hearing. He has somewhat of an accent. He's Caribbean. I didn't know much about these kind of people. To tell you the truth I didn't even know they existed. I only hung around Americans, Black Americans. I only eat American food occasionally as a child, Chinese. I played with the American Black children except for a handful of Puerto Ricans who also lived in the neighborhood. I listen to only

Black American Music. Not that I have anything against Caribbean. I'm just so American cause that all I know. All I cared about was I wanted my parents to be happy. Both of them and all I knew was, he not replacing my dad!

Just because my mom appeared to be so thankful cause we weren't eating peanut butter and jelly sandwiches anymore. It seem like she wanted us to worship Dave. She kept saying things like, "If it wasn't for him we wouldn't have this or that. Dave help made this dinner possible. Thank God for Dave. Respect Dave. He taking care of this.... and if it wasn't for Dave. Dave. Dave. Dave. Dave. Dave. Dave."

Oh my! I just enter into the ninth grade by the time this man had enter into our home. My parents already made our home for us and already raised us too for that matter. We already had our traditional Christmas and celebrations and our family gatherings included with love and laughter with our mother and our father. Dave could sense he came into a well establish home. To me, Dave was there for her, not us, speaking on me and Tonya. All Dave was doing was picking up where my dad left off, and my dad left us pretty damn well off, even materialistic wise.

If my mother shall ever read this book. She needs to hear this and have a wakeup call. That Dave came into an already made family home. He didn't make us because our family had already existed way before he was even thought about!

I didn't give a **fuck** if Dave bought us gold plates to eat off of. He wasn't replacing my dad! Plus we weren't children. We were already raised by our parents. Dave sat on the side as if he had wanted Tonya and I to praise him as if he was better than our real father which I **couldn't understand**. My dad on the other hand was stupid for walking out the door and never returning back to the apartment. Instead, my dad had gotten hook up with drugs. He was a functional addict. He wasn't the kind of drug addict that you would normally see who had lost everything and was currently living out on the street. He had a good job with the school bus company but he constantly got high with his pay check.

Again, I was thinking again ....matters of the heart. Dave moved in. Maybe that's why he did it? Meaning he got hook-up on the drugs. Anyway back to the original topic of me and Thomas. My dad, he never tried to take us away from my mom.

When Thomas and I were together around this time the hairstyle to have was called a dobee. It was another word for a wrap. It consist of wrapping your hair around your head. The hairdresser would do a roller set and have the clients sit underneath the dryer. Once the hair is dry the hairdresser would comb out the curls, blow-dry then pin the hair sparingly with bobby pins to keep the wrap up hair in place. After wrapping the hair around your head with bobby pins, your hair kinda resemble a bee hive. The next day you take out the bobby pins and comb down your hair. The wrap gave the perm hair so much body and bounce. I just had to have this hairstyle.

So one day Thomas he drove me to this Dominican hairdresser in the Bronx. Maybe there are some black girls that are reading this book who are saying, you can get a wrap down the block. Around this time the Dominican weren't so well know like they are now for doing this type of a hair style. When it first came out, us Black girls was traveling to get this hairstyle done, especially if you wanted a really nice wrap.

This black American girl who lived on my block, I admiral her hair. It looks so healthy and lively. She recommended me to her' hairdresser. The hairdresser was in the Bronx.

That's one thing about black American girls when it come to our hair we will travel to get that look. As well as pay that money because we love hair. And I love hair and style. Anyway, Thomas drove me and the kids to this Dominican hairstylist in the Bronx. I'll never forget what this Spanish hairdresser said to me. I never seen her before in my life. She asked me in a whisper, "Is that your man?" I said, "Yeah."

She asked next in my ear while Thomas sat in the car with the children. "Does he drive you to places you need to go all the time?" I just thought she was being noisy or wanted to make some small talk. So I said, "Sometimes." She asked, "Is he Jamaican?" I said, "Yes," while thinking to myself she sure is asking me a lot of personal questions.

The hairdresser said, "I want you to hear me good. My sister dated a Jamaican and girl, she had a hard time getting rid of him. I'm not trying to scare you but when it's over they won't leave. They are very possessive type of men."

I said, "He's not like that." She said "Good. I'm not trying to tell you what to do but be careful."

After we broke up here this man is jumping out from cars. Us fighting over our son outside in the street with him saying "Give me my son! Give Brandon to me so he could have an accent mon and get a job. I want him to live in Jamaica. Without an accent he won't get a job."

Ha, **ha**!

Thomas just proved my theory. I told yall when I went job hunting that the mangers downtown were being discriminating by only hiring foreigners. They were hiring anybody with an accent but a true blue American. Making it seem like us Black Americans don't want to work. Holding us down incognito, in order to help keep us in poverty while the foreigners move up. All along they throwing our applications in the trash can. That all Thomas was saying "Mon he need an accent. He need an accent. JB need to go to Jamaica."

Let's look at it. Why else was Thomas saying that because he knew the West Indian people came to America for one thing only. To work and to build up only their selves! And fuck the American people because remember all of the myths I told you Thomas had about us American people.

That we are lazy and that we don't want to work. Well, they were making sure we didn't work by dominating the work force!

They were making sure to it by them going to work every day just to become the managers. Then hire their own kind. Anybody with an accent or who came over here to America, and when you look at it that's being prejudiced and discriminating. They are employed in all of the nursing homes, the Hospitals, home attendants and construction workers. In the school they are teachers and daycare providers but yet the majority of their children are in private school. They made sure our kids had stayed on the waiting list keeping American mothers at home. While they became managers and supervisors. They came here for one thing, one purpose only, on their' calculated evil little minds and that is to take us Americans OUT! Impregnating us so they can become citizens knowing our Black American men aren't around. Then stepping off out the relationship just to bring more mother fuckers from their country over here.

After being with Thomas I started analyzing and realizing a lot about cultures. Our American Black men were too busy going back and forth to jail. Hustling, always calling there self-trying to support their family because they couldn't get decent paying jobs. Remember I told you, back then it was like white Americans holding all the good jobs. So our Black American men most of them became hustler and drug dealers wanting or trying to make that fast good money in a means of supporting their families, or their selves, but it only destroyed our American men and our Black American families.

Another thing our Black American men were getting too fuckin high. Which foreigners love to see that because drug do alter your thinking you become depress and laid back not wanting to work. Looking all skinny and undernourished, possession a lack of energy or enthusiasm, or you may seem carefree like.......... "I don't give a fuck!"

You don't give a fuck about nothing, not even your own self. Once a person gets hook on drugs then suddenly you are now a drug addict that make you steal and do anything, even kill, to get that drug. I know this because I had seen drugs destroy Champagne' father, Tray. Whatz that word us Blacks used to express a person hooked on crack- "he's a crack head and he's on a mission." Tray he did anything to get that shit. It fuck up his' life. Leaving and making me become the sole responsibility for our child.

Anyway, after I removed Thomas from my apartment now he want to take my son away from me to live in Jamaica! Thomas didn't even live in Jamaica. Thomas is going about it the wrong way. I don't know those people in Jamaica. I just can't give up my son! What he wants is impossible.

I wanted JB to be a true American just like me, playing music on Friday nights and laughing and joking around with the family and his close friends. You know the things us Americans do. Cuddling and dressing up when we going out on dates. Playing house games like cards and board games. Being around family and most importantly respecting the family. Helping in cooking our family recipes. That what made us so special besides us wanting to make money in order to pamper ourselves.

I didn't want JB to be like him, a fake ass Jamaican who just want to use people and take everything that matters in life for granted. I didn't like their' custom or their beliefs. I don't want JB to grow up being a punk and not defend his home and think only about work, work, work, work and not enjoy what life have to offer; like the Christmas spirit and celebrating the small moments. Being romantic when he falls in love and differently caring about himself. And caring about his sisters and me.

Thomas was worst then a punk he is evil and conniving. He wants to take my son for what! My son love his' sisters and his' sisters love him. We a good family, and I hate the drama Thomas is causing. It disrupting all our wellbeing even JB. Thomas jumping out from vehicles trying to snatch our son and acting like a dam fool, and making me act like one too, because he **not taking my son, anywhere!** I'm not going to let him just take my son out from my life! I love my bad ass spoil son.

Everybody who knew us was stun at Thomas behavior, even Adrianne. We were the couple people respected. Now, all Shelby kept saying, "Just when you think you know somebody. I'm so sorry to see you going through this Tami." I said to Shelby, "I prefer to be called Electra now."

Shaking her head Shelby said, "Electra /Tami? You sure going through some shit now aren't you?" We both started laughing. I guess it kept me from crying and I could see tears swelling up in Shelby eyes cause what I was experiencing wasn't funny at all.

Shelby could see that I was stress. I wasn't acting like my normal, bubbly, energetic self. I was way down into thoughts, thinking about my problems and how to solve them. So, breaking the silence after the laughter Shelby said, "Electra sounds so funny, I still like the name Tami." Then in her squeaky high pitch voice she said, "I'm used to it." "Okay since you so use to it you could keep calling me Tami if you want," I said. Shelby said "Tami I never thought Thomas would behave this way. Even Wilbert shocked at the way he is carrying on."

When Donna found out how Thomas was acting. We were in her kitchen while she was setting up cook food to sell in her store. As she cut up the onions and peppers Donna said, "Tami that's how those Caribbean men are. They very selfish Tami but me, I'm not a fool. I told Bunchy I want half of every ting. I heard he brought land back home and I heard some young girl he seeing behind my back."

I said Donna, "This the first I'm hearing of this. You never mentioned to me you buying a home in your' country."

Donna said, "No Tami! I heard Bunchy bought the home but he didn't tell me he brought the home. All the time he was going down there, I found out just recently his purchase of a piece of property. He doesn't know I found out about it. You see I'm no fool Tami. I know Bunchy was up to something when he started taking trips back and forth and his family coming over here picking up money."

"Ooh," I said.

Donna keep on talking "Before Bunchy tink I work hard for nothting. He got another ting coming. I'm going to get a lawyer and I want half of the store, half of all his' properties in New York and half of the property he just purchased quietly in Grenada. The young girl tink Bunchy all **that**. Well. Let's see how she like him **broke** Tami, cause me going to take his ass to the bank, girl." Then she suck her teeth so long and hard saying, "Tami don't let Thomas get away without helping you with your kids. Even if he did take the kid to Jamaica to live he still will have to provide Tami. Make him pay you," she said.

Did I tell yall that Donna was slightly older than me and another thing I forgot to mention to yall around this time too Donna and Bunchy was going through marital problem.

Donna said to me, "You got to have a plan with these Caribbean men cause they slick mon but Tami, me a Caribbean women and I'm not going to let you out slick me. I want me money too." Donna suck her teeth long and hard.

I'm sitting down in her kitchen, with my left elbow that's on the table, supporting my head, listening and hanging on to Donna every word. When she get mad her' accent become deeper.

She said in her Grenadian lingo "Me didn't give him no picknee for him to walk out leaving us with nothting. Bunchy not going to make me look like no fool. My kids need to go to college. I work damn hard supporting this family. Building up this store. Bunchy going to give me half of every damn ting." She suck her teeth hard and long again.

While listening, I thought I had relationship problems? Well she do too. I love her and her kids and Bunchy too. I think they are a great family. On the down low, I always tried to keep them together but it look like a lost cause because I see they really fighting too. Anyway…she was going on and on and on and on about her relationship, until I said "**Well.** I'm about to go home now Donna. I got to get dinner started for my kids. So I speak with you later." As I was getting myself and the kids ready to leave Donna home, she said, "Tami don't let Thomas make no fool of you. You were too good to him. He owes you. You helped him so much."

When she spoke that sentence her words just took me from listening to her problems right back to thinking about my own problems. Now I'm back sad again overwhelm and angry at the situation Thomas is creating. I said, "Alright Donna."

Heading towards the door I remembered something. Quickly I turned around. I said, "Donna. Can you show me how to make Maubi and Sorrel?"

Those are Caribbean homemade drinks that taste so good to me. She also make homemade Ginger beer, which is an acquiring taste but it taste good to me too.

Donna said, "It's so easy. No problem Tami."

Happily I said, "I'll be back by next week and you can let me know all the ingredients to pick up from the store when I go food shopping……….Thanks!" I shouted as I walk out the door.

"Bye Tami," Donna said as I closed her' apartment door.

When I got home after putting the kids to sleep. I started thinking why do Thomas want to take JB away from me? That's so cruel and harsh. I'm such a good mother and Thomas not saying he want both the kids. Why just only JB?

I know JB is his only son but Moet is his' child too. Shouldn't he want her to learn his Jamaican custom as well and have their accent? What is he saying? That he only loved JB and his' teenage daughters in Jamaica? These daughters of his I watched him support over the years. What, he don't love Moet? And what about Champagne? I thought Thomas loved Champagne. Why does Thomas want to break up my family? Yo, Thomas is a total loser and he has shown me so many signs he don't love neither one of us, (meaning me or the kids.) Well I'm not about to allow JB to become split from his two sisters or Thomas breaking up my family. Then I went to my children bedroom. They were asleep in their own bed. I bent down and I kiss each one of them on top of their forehead as I whisper, "I love you. And I love you. And I love you."

Going back to my bedroom I was thinking that's so true what Donna said earlier if Brandon did go to live in Jamaica, Thomas would still have to provide for him but he not providing for him now or Moet. **Shit**! What's wrong with Thomas as I laid in my bed a vision came to me. The vision was of the time when I came upstairs from Shelby house. That night, and JB was lying down on the bed in our bedroom with Thomas.......remember I told yall JB had a little hard on.......Um? Then there's something else I forgotten about.

What I'm about to say occurred sometime after Thomas came back from Jamaica, after burying his father. Thomas he slept on the outer part of our bed which is facing towards our bedroom door. Just before I fell asleep that night, Thomas he rolled over putting his arms around me as I laid on my side which is facing towards our bedroom windows.

I fell asleep. I was lying on my side and all of a sudden both of my eyes had just popped open as if someone or something just separated and pulled open both of my eyes lids. It was in the middle of the night...surprised, I'm staring looking at the curtains in my bedroom. I didn't move or say a word as I just laid there still. I'm watching the bedroom curtains wondering wasn't I asleep? How did that happen? I'm sleeping, then out from the blue my eyes just opened up like that.

When unexplainable things like this happens. I immediately think, is someone or something trying to tell me something? Like whatz the subliminal messages to what had just taken place.

So...as I laid there and I'm listening to Thomas movement because he walking, and I'm shock that my eyes just open up like that. My back is towards him so Thomas didn't know I was awake. I felt him as he crawl into the bed and I immediately got up. Not saying a word to him I went into the bathroom. The bathroom is between both bedrooms. Walking out from my bedroom looking straight ahead I could see the kids' bedroom.

JB was lying down on the bottom bulk bed...He's awake?

I saw my son face because he peeped up at me when I came out from my bedroom. Going back to my bedroom I insisted Thomas to show me what it was he did with JB to make him quiet without his bottle at night but Thomas refuse to have a conversation. He just turned over and went to sleep. I'm saying this man is so fuckin stubborn and selfish you can't get him to do shit when he don't want to. That's one of the main reason we ain't together now. He could never compromise with me. It takes two people to be in any kind of relationship and it take two people to make the relationship work. Anyway Thomas and I got into a little argument because I really wanted to know how he got JB to lay there without his' bottle. Without me hearing him cry. Then I started receiving sickened thought because of Thomas stubbornness.

Brandon stiff little wee-wee came into my mind. Then I reminisced the time when Thomas wanted me to pee on his dick when we were having sex and the way he made me feel that day. Like he was a child molester. Then I'm thinking about the struggle I had to go through with Thomas about allowing JB to start learning how to drink from a training cup.

I really hated to think this...... but was this man fondling with my son?

I can't believe that thought just went through my head again and I'm actually saying it again.

Okay, **what**, am, I supposed to do? Just ignore it......... my intuition.

It's an old saying, I heard lots of people repeat; if your intuition is telling you something, well then it must be true. But what's funny is that I couldn't knock the thought out from my head that night..........is that why he wants to take Brandon...Ooh sweat! I remember when Thomas mother came up from Jamaica. She was saying how, "When Thomas was young everybody thought he was a girl." Um?! And what about the time when I went into labor with Brandon. I signed those papers with the nurse when she asked me the question, "If the baby is a boy, would you want him to be circumcised?" I signed for the child to be circumcised. Thomas and I both were inside the room when the nurse had asked me all those questions. I was shock when I saw the circumcision wasn't done. Unaware and not knowing, secretly behind my back, that Thomas asked the Doctor not to do it.

We were packed up and ready to walk out of the hospital room. But thanks be to God for putting the thought in my head to check on Brandon pamper. Confused. I ask the nurse, "Can you get the Doctor?" She ask me, "Is anything wrong?" I told the nurse "I'm not going anywhere because I signed the paper for my son to be circumcised. I done already signed the hospital discharge papers and as you can see I'm just about to walk out from the hospital with Brandon but I'm not going anywhere. Why isn't he circumcised?"

The nurse asked "He isn't circumcised?" I said, "No. What happen because I sign the paper?" The nurse said, "Let me go find the Doctor."

While the nurse went to look for the doctor. I went looking thru my hospital policy forms and all of the other papers I sign before I was admitted. Thank God I saved all of my paperwork. I had found the paper that I signed-if the child is a boy I will want him to be circumcised before I left the hospital.

When my Doctor came into the room, I asked, "What happened? Why you didn't perform the circumcision for my son?" The White Doctor before answering he looked at Thomas and then at me. The doctor said "The father came to me asking not to circumcise the boy."

Shocked! When I heard the news. Completely unaware how low Thomas can go behind my back. That's the first time I witness Thomas deceitfulness because he was in the room with me when the nurse asked me all those questions. He heard my answers. Why didn't he say how he felt when the conversation was taking place? Right then and there that should have been a warning sign for me to be careful in my dealing with this man but I was young, inexperience, so trusting and upright thinking we are all good people. I didn't even imagine how low a person can go or shall I say will go.

I said to the Doctor "Here the form I signed and it's dated before I gave birth." Once the Doctor saw I had the authentic form. His apology was to me and said "I'll perform it right now." I replied, "We're already sign out to leave the hospital."

The Doctor said "Everything will be alright. He could still have it done right now because if you wait till he's older it will be much more painful for him." That's how Brandon have gotten circumcised.

Now here we are fighting over Brandon. Well if JB going to be gay it would be his' choice and his' choice alone. Not because some sick old bastard decided to impose his adult act on my son, when he is a toddler, still a child, and not fully understanding the sexual act and the sexual role of a man.

Now you see this shit is now going through my head.

Mind you, I already have so much on my plate already. Gayness/rape/child molesting was the least of my thought but now I have to consider it. Maybe I didn't put too much emphasis in it because I'm straight and to me it was so far fetch, plus I knew, Thomas wasn't going to take my son. Anyway that is how I spent that summer that year with Thomas. We fighting and he wanting to take JB.

It really got ugly.

Once he saw snatching JB from me wasn't going to be that easy. He thought by persuading me it will stop me from acting like a fool in the street. In order words, like Mike Tyson, because I was ready to bite his mother fuckin ear off if it took saving my son. If it's a fight Thomas wanted then it going to be a fight he's going to **Get**! Word to my mother fuckin mother! "Ladies art therapy on the fourth floor in the library," security guard Fancy announced to us girls sitting in the dining room.

The sound of her voice bringing me back to my present reality. I looked up, as I watched the guard exit the room saying on her walkie-talkie, "Attention to all guards, announcement was made in the dining room. Copy."

Packing up my belonging, heading to the class, "Excuse me." I said to Doris, as she sat there crocheting her blanket. When I got to the fourth floor Samantha had color pencils and assorted colors of paints on the center of the table. Turning toward me she said, "Hello Electra take a seat."

I walk by the radio and put on WBLS. Then I poured a cup of coffee and got a chocolate donuts from the box of Entenmanns. Sitting down I watch more girls enter the room doing the same thing, getting their' snacks. Once we had a nice size group Samantha went to the guard on the fourth floor saying "I'm about to close the door. No more clients are allowed." I watch Samantha close the door.

Going towards the center of the room Samantha said, "Hi ladies, this is art therapy and to get the most out from the group I will not allow anymore clients in. This is one rule for the group what is said here, stay here. Once yall have finish with your art work I will come around to collect it. Then I will hang it up on the wall. After that, each artist can tell us all about their' painting if you choose too. Let me know what material you would like to work with."

I got up and I ask Samantha for the color pencils. I discover I really enjoyed creating collages. I also enjoy art. When I went to grammar school and high school we didn't do any form of art work. I wonder why? It relaxing and it take you away by allowing you to be silly, creative, expressional, inspirational and wishful. In art you get to express yourself in so many different ways. Going back to my seat I had a terrific idea. I got a couple of magazines and I started cutting out pictures of various cars. Two seated sport cars, like mustang, Saabs, convertibles. Jeeps like wrangler, Hummers, Navigators and Escalades. Truck like Yukon and Expedition; cars that had moon roofs and lots of convertibles and stylish cars like Lexus, Ferrari and Porsche.

Samantha started collecting the pictures taping them to the wall. Then she turned off the radio and asked, "Who'd like to go first?"

Ellen said "The picture with the flowers is mines."

"Tell us about your artwork. Why you decided to draw pictures of flowers?" Sam questioned. "Ellen said in her' country she had a backyard and her mother kept a garden." Samantha asked Ellen, "Were you and your mother closed?" Ellen said, "Yes I'm an only child and I love and miss my mother very much."

Samantha said, "I can tell. Your pictures are always relating to your mother. She must have been a very nice woman. Thanks for sharing." We all clapped our hands.

"Who would like to go next Samantha asked?" Sophia said as she stand, "The picture of the book is mines." Samantha said, "Tell us about your artwork."

Sophia is a Spanish woman. She said, "The book is the bible. I love God so much I wanted to draw a bible to let the group know Jesus love us."

Samantha said, "That would have been a great title for your portrait. What denomination are you?" Sophia said, "I have no denomination. Jesus love us for who we are and I want everybody to know Jesus loves you." Samantha ask, "In the bible is there a favorite scripture that inspires you?"

Sophia said, "St John the third chapter verse sixteen. It say for God so loved the world, that he gave his only begotten son, that we may have life more abundantly and whosoever believes on him should not perish but have everlasting life." Samantha said, "That's a lovely scripture and thank you for sharing." We all clapped our hands but Sophia didn't sit down instead she remain standing saying, "I love talking about God. I can talk about him all day and night. That how much I love him. God woke me up this morning and started me on my way"... Samantha said, "Sophia." But Sophia kept talking. Samantha intervened and said "Sophia! You had your chance already. Please take a seat let have respect and allow others to share their art work."

Sophia said, "It just that when I speak about God I don't know how to stop. I love him so much." Samantha said, "I see and we totally acknowledge that and respect that but please lets give everyone a chance to express their' artwork."

Now, smiling Samantha said "Again Sophia, thank you for sharing." We all immediately started clapping our hands hoping Sophia get the message to shut up and sit down.

Samantha takes a deep breathe. "Is there anyone who would like to go next?" Samantha asked. Since no one volunteer. Samantha asked, "Shirley why won't you share your painting?" Shirley said, "I didn't paint a picture. Samantha asked "Well what did you do?" Shirley said, "I didn't do anything."

Samantha said, "I'm sorry. How I missed not collecting your painting? Well unfortunately you have to leave because everyone hear participate in some form of art. It's not mandatory that you share but it is required that you use your imagination to create a drawing. So I'm going to have to ask you to leave."

We all became very quiet.

"Just because I didn't draw? Oh come on. I can't sit here," Shirley asked. "No it not fair to others who applied their drawing as well as shared their art work. Rules are rules I'm so sorry but I'm going to have to ask you to leave the class. And if you don't leave I'm going to have to call in security, which I don't want to do that either. Next time, you come to class maybe you can display your artwork and we all would be glad to hear what you have to say about it," Samantha said.

Shirley said "I can't believe I have to leave. This is bullshit."

We all sat quietly as we watch her take out a couple of donuts before Samantha said, "You already have one donut. What left over you can have but those snacks are for the ladies participating in the group. I would let you take the ones you already have in your hands but no more, please. I see you at the next art therapy group." Samantha walk to the door and had opened it for Shirley to leave.

When Samantha came back to the class she asked, "Ladies how yall feel with Shirley not participating and listening to you express the painting you did?"

Ellen said, "I didn't see anything wrong with it." I said, "Well it would be nice if we all had the chance to share our pictures. That why we here right. I would have like to hear why Shirley didn't do nothing then maybe we could had view her picture as a blank. That it just abstract. Probably then she would have got to stay being that she didn't want to leave."

Samantha said "Why didn't I think of that? I like that this class is bringing out levels of talent in expression because that what art is about. It's about the artist reflections on ultimate levels. I appreciate that thought and the next time I see Shirley I let her know I was wrong because all artist work should be shared. Thank you Electra."

Kenya said, "Samantha you did the right thing. Why should she stay and listen to what we're doing. She knew this was art therapy. It only right that she participated in a form of displaying or she would have to leave."

Samantha said, "Well thank you for your input as well. Class our time here is a wasting. Let get back to what we came here for. Who picture is title I like to dream in the fast lane?"

I raised my hand saying, "That's my painting. One day I would like to have a car. I just don't know which one. So what I did was cut out pictures from the magazines of the cars that I like and subtitle colorful eye popping words throughout my collage. My artwork is title: We all can dreamed, can't we?"

Samantha asks, "Electra which car really sticks out to you?" Before I could answer Tony jumped in and said "That Porsche looks real nice." Others started pointing out their favorite cars. Laughing. Samantha said, "Electra I also see you enjoy your artwork to have passionate debates."

I asked, "Why you say that?" Samantha said, "So far everyone have an opinion when you display your artwork. They actually come in it and I think that's so cool. You never know where your creativity can take you."

"All I'm doing is putting on paper what is inside me," I answered. Samantha giggle again and said, "I like it. Keep up the good work. As a matter of fact I enjoy everyone work. Yall girls are very detail in expressing yourselves. I think that I will leave all of the pictures hanging up on the wall for everyone who enters the room to see your displays until the next class. How do yall feel about that?"

I said, "I don't have a problem with that." "Neither do me," Thomasina replied. Ellen said "I don't care." Kenya said, "It doesn't bother me either." Sophia said, "I love telling people about the Lord. It's a blessing and I like to say the Lord is our Shepherd and we shall not want. He lay us down in green pastures" ...Tony stops Sophia.

Tony she's a lesbian. She the aggressor in the relationship. Tony said in her Spanish accent, "Sophia, enough already mommy, we get the picture. Samantha do what you got to do because I don't have a problem in displaying my artwork."

Samantha said "Good! I think yall girls are doing such marvelous work. Being Shirley had wanted to hang around I think that the other clients will be interested too. Maybe your artwork will inspire more residents to participate. Now, back to you Electra.... I like to know which car really sticks out to you."

I said, "Well if I had to pick just one. It so hard since all of them are so nice. Well, I would enjoy the convertible Lexus." Samantha said "Good choice. Thank you for sharing." Everyone clapped their' hands.

Samantha asked, "Kenya would you like to tell us about your art work? Kenya said, "Blue is my favorite color. So my picture is the one color blue. Blue is for Kenya. Every day I try to wear something blue. When I get my apartment I'm going to paint the walls in shades of blue."

Samantha asked, "At what age did this color fascination start?" Kenya said, "You know, I don'l know. I never thought about when it started. Probably all my life because I have always liked the color blue." We all clapped our hands at her remark. Samantha said "Thanks for sharing this information with us."

Pointing to the picture of colors. Samantha said, "I think I know who painting this one is. Jessica is this your art work?" Jessica said, "Yes." "Could you tell us about your art work?" Samantha suggested. Jessica said, "I don't feel like sharing." Samantha said, "Thank you for your art work." We all clapped our hands. Jessica' painting contains colors of purple, black and brown. To me it's intangible no definition.

Tony jumps in and say, "It's the last picture and it mine." Samantha say, "Tell us about your artwork Tony."

Tony said, "I'm a Puerto Rican and it is the flag for Puerto Rico." Samantha said, "Obviously I can tell you are very proud of your heritage. Is there anything else you can tell us Puerto Ricans are very proud of?" Tony said, "We make good pastelis. For Christmas we make pastelis for our family and friends."

I said, "I never ate pastelis before." Tony asked, "You never ate pastelis? Oh they're so good. You can go to any Spanish restaurant and ask for pastelis."

Samantha said, "Tony thanks for sharing." We all clapped our hands.

Time now is four o'clock. The class was over and I'm heading to my dorm. The hallway is busy with females carrying and lugging bags. Walking to my dorm I glanced in the dorms that had their' door open, just to see large clear plastic bags in the center of the floor. Girls going through their' lockers trying to make space because the big sweep is in a couple of days. No more extra bags. Finally I had reached my dorm and open up the door.

My neighbor lying down on her bed in her usual attire. The Mexican chick sitting on her bed going thru her bags deciding what goes and what stays. It a mess over there in her' area.

Once I put up my bag I decide to go to Jose to buy a hero for dinner. As I pass through the hallways I seen Billy. "Hey Billy what's up?" I say.

"Hi Electra. Can't chat because I'm off to work. We speak later," she says while rushing. "Okay later," I said.

Once I'm inside of the store, I see lots of girl from the shelter buying food. Some were cashing in their food stamps for cash. When my turn comes I say to Jose, "Can I have maple glazed turkey, Swiss cheese with mayonnaise, lettuce and tomatoes on a roll. Jose asked "Do you want oil and vinegar?" I say, "Naw that's alright." Jose ask me "What about salt and pepper?" I say, "I take a little bit of black pepper but no salt." I pick up a pineapple soda, a bag of plain Lays potato chip and a bag of pretzels.

Security Michal he buzzes the shelter door in order for me to enter. I put my jacket through the machine as he hand checked my bag of food. Michal announce on his radio "Miss Jones is coming up with food. Copy." On the other end I heard a guard say "Copy."

I goes inside the dining room. After eating my sandwich, I sneak my chips and pretzels upstairs. Sitting on my bed I reminisced on my past.

Back *into the story.*

Lots of times I would be standing in front of my building allowing my children to run and play outside. Then Thomas started bringing his' brother Rude Boy and some of his other Jamaican male friends occasionally to the building. While sitting in his car with his window rolled down- smiling. Smirking, he would be insulting me in front of them, pointing me out and saying "Look at how fat and nice I made her. She never had anyting. She was so poor. She had noting. I mean no ting."

Then he gloated to some of his' Jamaican friends how he help build up these poor building for Americans to live in. He started spreading rumors to everyone he had met about me and pointing me out whenever he saw me walking down the street. Whenever he seen me talking to anyone, he would tell the person how much he did for me. Letting individual know I never had nothing just embarrassing me. Then he started telling people he was a peace maker.

Now let me stop talking about my story to ask a question. Why is it with a man when the relationship he was in is finish he get mad? Especially when he's the one who cheats and is the one who wasn't faithful. When we was together Thomas wasn't even the main provider, I was. Thomas put everyone and everything in front of my needs. When a man loves a woman, everybody knows that man loves that woman. I really don't understand this man thinking concept. Am I supposed to stay with him, making Thomas feel that I love him more than I love myself? So why be mad when the relationship is over? **Why is he mad**? What **the fuck** is his problem? He want me to go through all of his expectations and tolerate all of his bullshit and we haven't even walked down the aisle? I don't even have a ring on my finger.

I just like to take this time out to talk about Black men.

Why did I say Black Men?

Maybe because I'm black and I date black men. I had my babies by Black men. I could hear some of the brothers saying "Oh here she goes." I don't even want to hear that from yall (referring to any black man) the words from that same old cliché "Just because he wasn't a good man. Don't blame or hate all black men for that one brother mistake."

Now wait a minute my brothers. There's a whole lot of sisters out here un-fuckin wed with children. I understand not every woman wants to get married. To clear the record I'm not talking about those type of women. I'm talking about those women who are in love with their man and do want to get married.

Lesson number one. Clearly guys, when you find that special someone, you are supposed to go that extra step and put a ring on her' finger. Don't let money be the reason why you didn't make her your wife. Stop thinking that you need to be rich just to be someone husband. If you have a good thing you should want to keep it. If you love her why doesn't he show her?

Lesson number two. Females really want commitment to know that you love them and how do she really know....... By putting a ring on her finger. In the relationship the man is supposed to lead. Especially yall have 2 or 3 kids maybe even going on 4. Come on grow up guys you can't stay little boys forever. What wrong with getting marry? What's wrong with growing old with someone and looking back on what both of you had accomplish together? Watching your kids grow and go off into the world as they start their family. What's so wrong with being grandparents who share the same home? Black Men- why do you always want to grow old alone?

Then don't get mad and vindictive when she says, "It over." You didn't love her because you would have put the ring on her finger. So, why stay around and chase after someone who you really didn't want to be with? Making her life uncomfortable? Wish her the best and move on.

The question I am asking my Black men is why, not, let, her, go?

Could it be that our black men don't have respect for the black woman? And why is that? Really have yall guys ever really given it any thought. Do I hate the Black women? And why?

Let's take a look at Kerchief. I never took or asked the guy for any money. He wasn't my man but he came to my house everyday uninvited. When I asked him not to show up at my door every day like he's the one who paying my rent. What happened! He beats me up! Not only did he savagely punch and beat the shit out of me with both fists, he tries to rape me too!

What am I supposed to do just chuck it up? Say was he just sick? No I think there more going on that's not being tackle with. Like do our Black men hate the black women?

I'm sorry but I got to ask do the Black Men Have a Problem with the Black Women?

All I could say at this point I'm so glad Thomas didn't ask me to marry him. Knowing what I now see about him, plus over the years how he had treated me and now he wants to take my son and destroy my family. I don't think it because he loves our son because he not the one providing and supporting him. How do you beat up somebody you claim to love whether it be physical, verbally or emotional? No matter how you look at it Thomas is hurting me. This Black woman. Don't even say he a Jamaican, he's not black. Please lets not play stupid.

Well, even though I'm kind of sad, no, I was more disappointed in him at this point. I never thought I would have three children by two different Black men and not be married. This didn't seem like my life. It's so weird. How can I say this? It like everything I thought I never do, I did. Everything I was totally against, was right in front of me. The harder I try to improve my life, the deeper I fall inside of a pit where I can't succeed. It's like the more I try, the more I fail. Like what I picture for my life outcome turns out to be my total opposite?

…..Um…

I never had the time to sit back to analyze things. I had sure been through some struggles for sure. Thomas didn't move on with his life and he didn't do the right thing by me and the kids. Instead he became very threatening. Causing me to become alarm because of his' behavior. I couldn't run away from my problems this time. I couldn't just get up and leave. I had three small kids, who would take us in. I don't have no money. Thomas is turning into a person I don't recognize. I couldn't turn to my family because so much shit has already happened to me and I never had the family support. I always was on my own.

I had to get a dog for protection. It was either a gun but no one would ever give me a gun because I tried getting one for Kerchief. Getting a gun wasn't that easy for me. When I went looking for the machete we had in the house.

Dam! I see Thomas had taken that too. Then I thought if somebody was to give me a gun, it could have been a dirty gun and if the cops had ever caught me with it I probably go to jail for a crime that I didn't do.

So the best dam thing to get was a dog.

A Pit bull.

Security knocks on the door saying "Bed check." I put my notes up, laid on my bed being quiet.

Chapter Eighteen

Wow I needed protection. Yep Thomas done changed into this different person. His instigating and stalking really started getting out of hand. I don't know when and how but, somehow Thomas befriended Karl, this young troublesome teenage boy who live inside my building. As a matter of fact, my family had beef with this boy family a very, very, very long time ago.

Remember when I told yall about my missing in action Uncle _____? Remember how I spoke about him coming over to see my Aunt Melody and us as children how we acted. Well before he left the family and went missing. As I said, we were really small kids at this time. I, Tonya, Sheryl and Lee Keisha we were outside playing games with other children on the block in Brownsville. I told yall we were a really close net family, always spending the nights at my cousins' house, hanging out with each other. While outside playing hiding games, this really, really bad boy name Chokeman hurt my sister Tonya. All I know is, us kids were outside playing in Brownsville at my grandparent' house. Tonya came running up to us crying, saying, "Chokeman tried to put his wee-wee in my butt!" She was sobbing. We brought her inside the house.

It was in the night time when this had occurred. We couldn't stop my sister from crying. Tonya told all of us the same sentence over and over while she sobbed, "Chokeman tried to put his wee-wee in my butt. Chokeman put his wee-wee in my butt."

That all we could get out from her, to tell us about what happened. She suffered from asthma really bad as a child. Lots of times she had to stay in the hospital and because of her wanting to tell us where it happened all Tonya was able to say was the sentence above. It was very upsetting to her therefore we didn't really push her to tell us more because we didn't want to bring on an asthma attack.

I never forget that shit, but I did. You guys know by now I have time on my hands to reflect back on my life. Anyway, we all, I mean my whole family went looking for this guy. We heard that he lived somewhere down the block because we never played with him to know exactly where he lived.

Boy it was something to see all of us marching, walking in Brownsville, trying, wanting to located this boy. I remember it was me and my cousins, Sheryl, Lee Keisha and Coon. My Aunt Melody and Uncle _____. My dad, Aunt Lynette and Granddaddy. I know my mother wasn't there cause back in those days my mother used to fight a lot. She use to act a fool. So I know she wasn't there because I would had saw my mother fist fighting. I think Daddy came to pick us up to take us home.

Anyway.

I remember hugging my sister as we walked down the block telling her "Don't cry. We going to find him and make him pay." We all was hugging her meaning my cousins and me; as she sobbed. I was very protected over my sister. I guess, because she was always sickly plus, I'm the oldest and the strongest between us two. Not to mention, I love her. We all was protected over her. So here we all are walking down the street. Everybody know us, so other kids in the neighborhood that we had played with, tag along too, asking "What happened?" Wanting to see a fight. We found out where he lived and knocked on his' door.

When his mother saw this angry crowd asking for her' son and she saw my sister crying. She asked, "What happened!? Why are yall looking for him?" My dad or was it Uncle _____ who told her what her son had done. She asked my sister, "Is that true?" Still crying, Tonya nodded her head up and down indicating yes that is what he did as she weeps.

This woman knew her son was going to get a serious beat down. So to prevent his' faith the mother called him to the door and when he came she took off her shoes and started wailing on him. I mean she was hitting him all upside his head. Then she told one of her other children to bring her a belt. She beat him with a belt in front of all of us. Back then that how we got punished, you did something really wrong, your parents beat you with a belt!

She beat the shit out of that boy. She beat him so bad that Tonya had finally stop crying as she watched the mother wail on him. He was crying and begging his mother to stop but she didn't. She beat him as she yelled at him for what he had done. With every word out from her' mouth came a devastated blow, while we all watched. She beat him until she got tied then she made him apologizes to my sister in front of all of us.

I tell you, he got beat so bad by his mother! I have never seen any child get a beating like that by their' own parent. I guess Chokeman was so embarrassed that we never seen him again. He wasn't a child that we played with anyway. He saw a group of kids outside playing having fun and he join in. Anyway he's the oldest boy in his family and my sister is the youngest in my family. Shoot, come to think of it Chokeman was even a little older than me.

Now get this. I never seen Chokeman again until one day I seen him inside my building. He remembers me from a kid. I guess from that kind of a beating he never forgot anyone face. He approaches me and said, "Don't I know you?" I couldn't believe I was standing face to face with Chokeman! Come to find out, Karl is Chokeman' baby brother. Who would have ever known?! What a small world. Anyway Karl has a reputation of being derange, disorderly and very disrespectful to everyone, especially females. Karl have no respect for the elderly, women, animals or children. He's a disgusting human being, a troublesome kid. I knew of him and seen Karl for a while since living in the building but I never knew he was related to Chokeman! I thought he was just somebody who lived in the same building I lived in. Even though I didn't have any dealing with Karl, from my window or when standing in front of the building I seen him do bad and naughty things. I also was too shocked, to find out Chokeman-mother lives in my building as well!

Anyway I had gotten a dog, like I said.

After seeing Dove downtown that day when I went to the DMV and with me going thru these ups and downs with Thomas, I called him.

Surprisingly I remember his' house phone number, but I shouldn't have been but so surprise being that I spoke to him each day and every day on the telephone. Why after all, he was only my first love and his home telephone number was embedded in my heart as well as in my mind. How can I forget his number? I can never forget his telephone number. I called it every day, all day. If I wasn't calling him, he was calling me. Mainly he was the pursuer in our relationship. He really liked me and I really liked him. After a while my mother started to have a problem with our relationship. He was always calling me and we held long endless conversations on the phone with each other. Until my mother started yelling telling me to get off the phone. I hang up but then Dove will call me back later on in the night while he was at work. Or he came by to see me. We were inseparable.

When I called him his' mother answered the telephone. She was surprise but very happy to hear my voice on the other end. It been such a long time since I have been around this family. She told me Dove wasn't home and ask for me to leave a return number.

When we finally gotten in contact with one another we talked briefly on the phone while playing catch up, in a way. Dove questioned me about my family. He was so intense and inquisitive. He wanted to know why wasn't my family in my life and why wasn't they helping me for that matter. He still seemed to be angry towards my mom. Dove said "If they didn't want you, why wouldn't they let you go with me?" It was too deep, because obliviously this man still had feelings for me. I was going thought this aggravation bullshit with Thomas concerning my kids. My mind was already preoccupied and overwhelmed with my personal issue.

Then I had realized, that I had a memory loss on someone I loved very dearly. How could I have forgotten someone who I thought I was going to marry? Now here he is on the telephone pushing me to talk to him about my family and, about me. He wanted to know where I been and where I'm living at. For me the answers to his questions was so embarrassing. Mainly knowing that I'm out here struggling in the worst kind of way I could had ever imagined.

When I was with Dove I had all this family and friends around me. I'm the same girl that he knows but I changed and it's not for the better. When he knew me I was ready to conquer the world, fill with enthusiasm for life. I was happy. And beautiful. This fashion diva. The oldest child in my family with lots of family who was very much in my life but something terrible happened. We broke up.........I got kicked out.......... I'm not the fly girl anymore who he remembers as the girl who stood out. The girl, who other girls wanted to be like. The girl who was supposed to have it all-handsome husband. Great career. Family and best friends by her side. Back then I was a role model with charisma, well respected and aspire for greatness compared to the people in my circle of friends and family. I had this young man who adore me who brought me the most wonderful surprising gifts and clothes. It was just because he thought about me, and he's in love.

I'm damn sure not that fashion diva I use to be. I changed, because I been fighting. I'm no longer pure. I had a rude awakening. My heart hurt because I taste bitterness topped with evil. I was no longer this pure innocent person that he had known. I been toss out to live among the wild.

His questions seem to be endless. He was so pushy. Now, Dove wanted me to meet up with him. I told him "I'm here alone with my kids." He wanted to know how many kids I had. If I remember when we use to go out on dates? *I'm thinking* boy, that was such a long time ago. He wanted me to answer him but his questions are coming so fast. He asking me, questioning me, about when we use to date. Questioning me and asking me, do I remember how we used to cuddle? He wanted to hear and know my answer to all his questions then quickly he asked "Why your mother not helping you?" Then he asked "Do you remember when we use to go out to the movies and how I use to kiss you while cuddling?" I was at a loss of words because I respected him so much and I didn't want to lose his respect because my life is so different now. He saying "Bambi, Bambi, hello. Are you there? Hello." Quickly I responded "Uhmm... yes I'm here. But can you give me a minute? Look I have to check on my kids for a moment. I be right back."

I'm lairing.

Because I needed a moment to get my thoughts together. I was thinking, Dove seems like he's pushing me and it way too much going on in my life to talk my personal private affairs over the telephone. It not like I can say it all in a couple of sentences either. How can I tell this man I once was so in love with-the truth? The truth, that was revealed to me that I didn't realize my family would treat me like the black sheep of the family and that I got kick out of the house. And if I would had known they were going to treat me this way, I would had run away with him. But I can't talk about that right now because I needed a dog for protection, my life, and my children, who is my family I felt that we were at stake. I'm having problems and he can't help me. Our time has gone.

So when I came back to the phone I said, "Dove I need a dog." He was the first person I ever seen with a pit-bull. He said a white man gave the dog to him. Dove was the first person in Bed-Stuy/Crown Heights ever to walk down the street with a Pit-bull. Back then, to me, the best dogs that were out was German shepherds. Then there were dogs like Collies; like the one I use to watch and cry off of the television show as a child. The program named was Lassie. You know, back in those days we just had regular dogs in the hood, no fancy dogs. Oh yeah, wait a minute there was my next door neighbor dog. She had a toy poodle named Daisy. I loved that dog. Whenever she allowed me, I used to take Daisy out all the time as a young child, maybe, even up until my early teens.

So I asked Dove, "Can you get me a dog?" Knowing the only dogs, he deals with are Pits. He knows everything about them. I remembered when he first brought his' Pit to the projects. When I open the door I was a little uncomfortable because I never seen a dog with such a big head like that. Dove will grab me saying "Bambi that dog ain't going to bother you," as he kisses on my neck caressing me to his body. We kissed all the time.

Over the phone he pleaded "Bambi I want to see you. Come to my job I'll pay for the cab fare." I wanted to see him too. Me, wanting to recall my past life when I had my mom and dad and my sister and close friends by my side, wanting to feel like the person I use to be. So I hop in a cab only after asking my new next door neighbor can he watch my kids briefly. Rondu, the man I always gave dinners to, had got shot causing him to live out the rest of his life in a wheelchair. I figure all the dinners I gave him over the years he could help me out this one time.

In a cab I pulled up to the location. Dove was waiting outside. Wow, I wasn't love struck by his' appearance, like I use to be. He still doing security work. I was there briefly, anticipating to meet with an old dear friend. Dove took me into a room where the guards hung out at. I guess but no one was there but just him and myself. Dove said to me, "Have a seat Bambi." I looked over at the seating area thinking to myself that love seat sure looked dirty. Dove know me, he said "Bambi go ahead and take a seat. It's not dirty." It was the only seating area in the small room anyway. So I walk over there and sat down. He still sweet though, because he offers to buy me whatever I wanted from the store but I didn't want anything. He insisted. So I said, "I take a soda."

knowing I can't stay long. I had to hurry and get back to my children. His mannerism reminded me of the good old days whenever he brought me anything to drink. Opening my drink, and how he took the wrapper half way off of the straw for me, and had placed it into the beverage. I asked him, "How many kids do you have now?" He told me "Three." Wow, just like me. I asked him, "Do you have any pictures?" He did. He pulled them out from his' wallet. His kids they looked well provided for. Like he been a good man and father towards them, which quickly sadden me. Thinking about how it would have been if I woulda had a child by him.

Dove was quiet as he watches me look at his children school pictures. Maybe he was thinking the same thing too or maybe he was thinking about when we went wrong. Anyway dismaying our past giving him back the picture of his' children. Bringing me into my reality how I need to get back to my own children. He was sitting beside me and I said to him, "I really need to go," which he looked a little sad watching me with his dreamy brown eyes but then he realized that he was at work.

I asked, "Dove so can you help me get a dog?" He said "Yeah. I know someone who needs to get rid of a puppy." Immediately I said "Dove I have small children and I don't want a vicious dog like Terror, the red nose Pit you gave me when my family' apt got rob in Westbrook Projects."

Remembering that time as well, Dove said "Yeah that was a good dog, Bambi. It's a shame you couldn't keep her." Looking at Dove I suck my teeth and said, "Shoot, my mother wasn't going to let me keep that dog after she saw how vicious that dog was." Mad. Dove leaned forward sliding both elbows along his leg as he rested. Thinking and remembering Terror, he turned his head towards me, looking at me deeply with those brown eyes and said "Bambi she wasn't going to bite you." Me shaking off the thought of Terror.

Then he laughed and said "If anything she was going to bite someone **ass** if they **fucked** with you."

Stop! To the Reader. Let me tell yall briefly about Terror. Then I bring us back to this point where I left off. While living in the project this was after my father left and Dave done moved in, both Tonya and I was in our early teens. I was working at Burger king, downtown Brooklyn. Our apartment got robbed. I was mad. All the years my family we lived inside of the projects, how the fuck somebody going to rob us? Who did some shit like that? Anyway, I remembered wanting to protect my family. I wanted revenge on whoever rob us. Dave was new to the family so I wasn't looking at him as our protector. In my mind at that time he was just my mother new boyfriend who soon will be gone.

Being the oldest daughter, I don't know why I felt it was my job to protect my family. Maybe because that how it is handled in the hood. We protect what ours. I had that same demeanor. You violate me, I'm going to violate you back! So to teach these mother fuckers a lesson that had robbed us, I asked Dove for a dog so that it won't happen again. Letting whomever know, that I didn't like what went down. I didn't like it so by getting the dog to protect the house while we were at work and school I felt was a good solution.

Dove said "Bambi I got this **dog** for you. The next **motherfucker** that come up in there going to get his ass bit the fuck up! You don't even **gotz to train this mother fucker** because he already trained." I said, "Word!" He said "I'll bring the dog to your house tomorrow. All you got to do is leave him by the mother fuckin door. That's all you got to do."

Out of curiosity I asked, "Well how old is the dog?" Dove said "Bambi, she six months. She still a puppy." "Alright see you then." I said.

The next day before Dove went to work he brought this light brown, gray eyed dog to me. He said "Her name is Terror." Looking at the dog I said, "Dove this damn dog is big. You told me she was a puppy." Dove said "Bambi she is a puppy." He gave me the leash.

In my book Dove is the original king of pit-bulls. He's the one who got it all started in our neighborhood. In Brooklyn with the dog fighting and being seen walking in the neighborhood with a Pit. Lots of Black American guys liked being seen walking with a Pit but they started taking it out of text. Always wanting to see a dog fight. They started challenging Pit-bull to fight German shepherds and the Pit-bull **wax** ass, then Rock wilder and again Pit-bull waxed ass. After a while it started getting out of hand. The Black guys especially the young ones became blood thirsty always wanting to see a dog rip, tear and lock on to anything, cornering stray dogs, killing cats, after a while it became abusive to me. You know like, animal abuse I couldn't stand to watch or hear the animals fight.

The only reason the Pit-bull were wining was because, beside them being flexible and quick, these type of dog lock their jaw on another animal; even a human being. When a pit-bull lock, the owner need to prey their mouth open with a stick or something. **Everybody** started getting a Pit because they wanted to walk down the street with a dog that protects. When it was a known fact, Pit-bull can beat ordinary dogs **AND** protect. Dove allow his' dog to fight but not much. Dove' dog was older and already had a reputation of being a good fighter. Dove really loved his' dog and he became Dove' pet, as well it seemed, also his' best friend. As a matter of fact, the dog became a part of Dove' family. They all loved that dog. I cared for him too. He was a good dog. Anyway Dove told me while standing outside in Westbrook parking lot "Bambi Terror, this dog mother is a champion and the father is the best dam dog fighter. He won fight after fight. The father is a Grand Master Pit. So you're dealing with a pure breed the best of the best."

I stood watching and listening to Dove as he talked about the dog parents' glory like I had a prize dog. Then Dove said "This dog will teach them mother fuckers." I said, "Dam Dove, I just wanted a dog to protect the house. So you telling me this dog is from the best of the best." Dove said "She top of the line, Bambi." I then look at the light beige dog that had her' head down as we both spoke.

I said, "Well she doesn't look like the top of the line." Dove said "Bambi," as he bent down to lift the dog' head up. He said "You see her nose? It red, meaning it a red nosed Pit the meanest it could come." I asked, "Then how I know it ain't going to bite me?" Dove said "Bambi this damn dog not going to bite you. She going to protect you." Dove started to leave because he had to get ready for work. I said, "Hey wait a minute. Can you stay with me a little while letting me get the feel of the dog?"

So we walked around the projects grounds and Dove shown me the dog grip while the dog was in midair, locked on a piece of rope. Dove said "The dog' adult teeth are coming in now so that mean she's starting to lock. All you've got to do is feed the dog cook chicken backs, with cook white rice. After a while the dog will know who all belongs inside the house. Walk him before you leave out and tie her up by the door. I got to go Bambi," he said.

"Thanks," I said. Watching Dove walk away I looked at the dog thinking to myself she doesn't look like a champion with her head down like that. So I started walking with the dog. Everybody who saw me with the dog was looking at me as Terror and I walked around the project grounds.

At this particular time in my life the streets had a lot of stray dogs. I was a little hesitant having a Pit bull of my own because I saw the damage these dogs can do. They weren't like ordinary dogs. They were fighting dogs and Dove was breeding them. So I figured the dog was good for two reason. First reason, a protector for the house. Second reason, just in case if another stray dog ran up on Terror, I was confident that she can handle herself because of her' family history.

After walking my dog getting to know her I took her upstairs to my apartment. I did what Dove told me to do. I tied her to the apartment doorknob. I was inside my bedroom, the back room Tonya and I shared. The first person to come home was Dave. I heard the house keys jingling by the door so I peeped my head out quietly looking at the dog seeing how she would react. The quiet dog heard someone at the door. I watched this dog get up and quietly move away from the door and sat facing the door waiting for the person to come in. Tip toeing, I moved up to the living room wandering what the dog was going to do. I thought she was going to start barking but she didn't. As soon as the door got ajar, the dog leap into the air attacking the door viciously, growling and barking casing Dave to rapidly close the door.

I didn't expect that! "Oh shit," I like it! Terror was going ballistic, growling and barking viciously. Quickly I ran to the door yelling, "Dave! It alright just don't come in right now! I got a dog. Wait! Don't open the door." Going to Terror and calming her down, I said, "Good dog." I stood in front of Terror blocking her view as I open the door for Dave. I tell you Dave didn't like that. When he came inside the apartment I said, "Dave just keep on walking."

Dave stop when he was far away from the door. He turned around mid-way in the living room. When he saw Terror he gasps! He turned around and went into the bedroom and closed the door. That something he always did anyway, the only thing that was different was, he gasped.

Once I had seen how Terror reacted when someone was coming inside the house. I decide to stay inside of the living room waiting for my mother and sister to come home. When I heard the keys jingling by the door I did the same thing I had done with Dave. I yelled by saying, "Wait! Don't open the door!"

I walk over to the door and open it. It was Tonya. She was looking at me puzzle. I said, "I got a dog. Just walk normal into the house," and she did. She walked in, she did the same thing like Dave. She stopped and looked at the dog from inside the living room. I said, "This is Terror."

She asked me, "Where did you get the dog from?" I told her, "Dove give it to me for protection being that the robbers rob our house and stole my personal shit too. Like my jewelry and some clothes. They took all our TVs and the electronics like our stereo system, and our portable radios." Then when my mother came home I did the same thing.

Three times in a day I took Terror outside, and quickly, her' mean personality started surfacing. I took her to a park and I sat down on the bench. While holding the leash the dog got up and moved away from me but was still sitting. As I sat on the bench I looked at Terror trying to figure out why she moved away from me. Oh well, I stop wandering and just sat enjoying the summer breeze. While sitting there I saw a man walking towards our direction. The stranger was far away from us but still coming down the walk path where we were at. Terror was sitting tall and strong. The man was getting closer to us, just walking minding his' own business. Terror stood on all four paws, moving her paws then planting them strongly in the ground, as she sat down strong and tall.

Me looking at the dog holding her leash wandering what the dog doing now. Anyway. Then I heard a low growl. I wondered, if it's Terror who made that noise? I notice her head was up. I didn't see her teeth but I know I just heard a growling sound. So I stop just to listen but I didn't hear anything. As the man came closer I heard the growling sound again. This time it was a little louder and I thought to myself, oh, that is Terror growling.

The dog was so cool. She was just sitting there not even looking in the man direction or mine. As the man got closer I really heard Terror' growling. It was long and sounded like she was giving out a warning, like, come any closer I'm ready to attack! So I held the leash a little tighter as I watch the man come closer. I said, "Terror?" The growl got so loud and long that the man stops and looked at Terror. Even I looked at Terror. Oh sweat, it like was she sitting away from me but **guarding me**. The man looked at me and then at Terror who was still at a constant growl. He nodded his' head and moved over not walking to close to either one of us as he continue on his way. The dog looked at the man as he walked passed us then turns his head looking straight enjoying the sun. The growling had stopped. Never once did the dog look back at me. I said to myself, oh yeah this dog is really bad, and I liked her even more.

I remember there was kids in that park and the dog didn't behave like that, only just to that man she did it to. I figure he must have been a bad person because dogs can sense it. Even mommy started liking her. Never once did the dog bark inside the house. I figure the dog was good too because we really didn't know Dave. For some reason I sense Dave really didn't want the dog inside of the house. He seemed to be very irritable. The dog was a good protector for the house but I had sensed anger coming from Dave, about something else. I still was a little cautious of Terror though.

The next day I took the dog outside. Then Terror did something that startled the shit out of me as we walked around the projects. The dog started jumping in front of me, going left, right. Then left, right, and before I knew it she done jumped up and grabbed a hold to the sleeve of my unbutton dungaree jacket. Oh my God. I couldn't believe it. That big head dog notices the unbutton sleeve on my dungaree jacket. That little bit of material hanging from underneath my wrist and had grabbed a hold of it. Thank God she didn't grab or nip my wrist because I was wearing that denim jacket. By the way which it one of my favorite things to wear. I love the denim outfit. I had a blue denim jacket that I paid a guy to do graffiti artwork on the back section of the jacket. I had my name embedded in artwork on the jacket, it was so fly. Anyway. Terror done leap up and had a piece of the fabric tightly secure in her' mouth cause me to hang down slightly. So when I had stood up which made the sleeve from the denim pull upward from the dog mouth the dog growled, pulling it back which made me bend back down again. If anyone was looking it making us appear as if we were in a tug a war over the jacket.

Now, I didn't like that shit. I wanted to scream for help but I don't think anyone would had help me because this dog was new to the area and it was a Pit, known for fighting, not too many people was brave enough to come closely near us. Then she let go. Thank God I said to myself. We started back walking and Terror done leap and did it again. Oh no I had to wait until she let it go. Why didn't Dove tell me she would do this?

While us standing in front of my building with me showing off. Letting whomever rob my mother' apartment, see this dog, saying to myself come rob us **now!** The damn dog done leap up on me and did it again attaching his' mouth to my jacket sleeve.

I started saying, "Get off my sleeve," trying to look like I'm the one in control as people in my building walking pass me shaking their' head knowing what kind of dog I had. I, realizing not to pull back cause the dog think I was playing. As the dog held the fabric in its mouth I was thinking this dog has good eye sight, and accurate timing leaping towards me, and grabbing that little piece of fabric, which was underneath my wrist-without nipping me.

Once that was over the dog started to do something else. As I told yall already before, I lived on the twelfth floor in the projects. I got inside the elevator and so did two other people I knew very well. When they came inside the elevator, and the elevator door closed. Without warning Terror leaped up at them violently, aggressively growling and barking. Terror was so fierce that she causes me to quickly wrap the entire leash around my wrist trying to hold her back from attacking them as we all rode up silently inside the elevator. By now, because I had to wrap the leash quickly around my wrist, she standing up on both her' hind legs, savagely wanting to tear them apart as we all rode up in the closed elevator. Because of the dog strength I had to lean my body back while planting both of my feet securely on the ground with the chain wrapped completely around my wrist as her thrust towards the people made my body rock hitting back and forth against the elevator wall as her big head growling, barking savagely showing all her teeth trying to get at the two people that were with me in the closed elevator.

The two people inside the closed elevator where pin together standing by the elevator buttons looking stunned or I guess shocked and probably hoping they won't get bit. We all was amazed at the dog actions as we all rode up silently in the elevator as my body was hitting up against the elevator wall from the dog impact. Neither one of the two elderly people dared moved.

Terror big head showing all teeth growling, barking viciously and savagely while standing on both her hind legs. Well, I can tell you they didn't like that **at all** and neither did **Terror**. Thank God my reflex was quick in wrapping the leash around my wrist. I held her powerful ass **down!** The way Terror acted I didn't even think to ask anyone of the two scared people, to "**Press for a lower floor!**" Terror action stun the crap out of me too and all I was thinking about was **hold on** to the wrap around leash that was holding her ass **down** so that she wouldn't bite the **cramp** out of those two people that was inside the elevator with me.

When I got inside the house I put the dog by the door like I always did. I called Dove telling him what the dog did. He laughed and said "Good. Now they know not to **fuck with you**! Then I realize I'm going to have to ride in the elevator by myself until I teach the dog not to behave in such manner.

In my room while getting ready for work the dog done got a loose inside the house. To tell you the truth I was scared, because I used the leash as a clutch, in controlling the dog. When I looked out from my bedroom the leash was on the floor and the dog was jumping up and down inside the living room. The dog jumped and jumped when she came down from jumping one of her front leg hit on the table causing the front leg to stick outwards. The dog was crying! Quickly I called Dove again telling him what happen to the dog. Dove said "Bambi, just go to the dog and push the leg down." To tell yall the truth I was scared to put my face so close to the dog mouth in fear she might bite and lock on me.

The dog was crying walking only on three legs so I had no other choice but to do it. I did it and Terror licked me in my face and I rub her without the leash being on her. That was when I realized I had a pet and not to worry because the dog wasn't going to bite me.

Well I went to work. At work my manger came to me saying I have a phone call. Surprised. What? Who could be calling me at work? I thought. I never received a phone call at work. I get to the telephone and it's my mother speaking in a frantic manner. Telling me to, "Come home now!" Yelling with shakiness in her' voice. My mother said, "Come home. Come home now! I want this dog out of my house. Electra I took Terror out for a walk." .... Shocked, and I think I yelled a little at my mother because, she was yelling at me.

I asked my mother, "**Why did you do that**? I walked her before I left." Her voice sound shaky as if something scared her. My mother was talking very fast. She said, "Because I wanted to take her for a walk but this dog was walking with her head down and every time someone walk pass us she snapped at them. At first, I thought she didn't do it because she did it so fast. So when the next person walked by I watched! And I saw Terror snap trying to bite the person."

Yelling louder my mother said, "**Then the dam dog Terror went crazy!** She was growling trying to bite everybody as I was walking towards the building. People were coming home from work, and I had to tell the people get out of my way! This is not my dog! It my daughter dog and I don't want to see anybody get bit!"

My mother said, "All of the people had moved out of my way but when I got inside the elevator the **damn dog leap! I screamed!** And told everybody "Don't get inside the elevator, please this is my daughter dog. **Everybody was mad at me** because they wanted to go upstairs. **Girl** after I seen that when I got inside the apartment I was shaky so bad. I called **the police department. The fire department!** Come get this dog out from here Terror is too vicious and **wild**! I don't want no vicious animal like this in my house. How do we know it not **going to bite us**! I want the dog, out, of, the, house. Even Dave mad because **we both locked up inside** the bedroom." While she talking, I'm thinking, I just connected with the dog. It ashamed.

Sadly, I asked, "So where's the dog at now? My mother said, "I put her in **your room** and **closed the door**." I asked, "Is she tied to the doorknob?" My mother said, "Girl I'm shaking so bad I just took her to the room and closed the door!"

I went to my manger and told him, "I have an emergency and I needed to go home." Going home I was thinking if

I would have known my mother was going to walk the dog, I would have told her what to expect. My mother she doesn't know anything about Pit-bull and how they fight and lock, so I know it must have been terrible, she thinking she walking just an ordinary dog. I'm happy Terror didn't lock on anybody because if my mom would had seen that I believe she would have scream and fainted. And when she woke up and saw me standing there she would had FUCK me up! Hurrying home in the night thinking the worst. I reach home it was quiet. My mother was in her bedroom with Dave. She told me again how the dog performed and that Terror was inside my bedroom. I open my bedroom door not knowing what to find. My mother over exaggerated. She made me leave work to come home and remove the dog. The dam dog was in my room unleashed by my bed, not Tonya, chewing up my shoes.

To make a long story short Dove didn't want to take the dog back. You know what I hate the constant fights that I have to go through, between Dove and my mom. They both get me sick. Eventually Dove took the dog back after I punched the glass out where he worked which left a scar on my finger for a long time. So, reader, now that I told yall about Terror, let's go back to the story.

I said, "Dove so can you help me get a dog." He said "Yeah. I know someone who need to get rid of a puppy." Immediately I said "Dove I have small children in the house and I don't want a vicious dog like Terror."

Dove said "Bambi the dog is four months. He's a pup. Do you want the dog or not?" "Four months mean the dog up to my knee already," I said jokingly, but really wanted to know.

Dove said "The kids going to love him. They can grow up together; he's a mutt." I asked "Oh, he's mixed with what?" "Bambi the dog is a full blooded pit-just a baby. The kids will love him and you have a boy too. Trust me your son is going to love the dog." I said "I gotta go." Dove told me "I'm going to call you soon."

Security guard Mia Dowser came inside the dining room announcing, "Sewing class ladies on four." I look up from my pen and paper. I needed a break. So I got my stuff together heading to the sewing class. I'm passing the medical office. Just pass the Social Service office, now I just passed the Intake office. I turn the corner walking toward the stair case. Just before I reach the door, looking on my left the elevator was there. "Hold the door Dowser," I said.

When I got inside of the elevator. I asked Mia D the Security Guard, "Is the elevator going up or down?" Dowser said "It's going down." As the door closed I press four. Breaking the silence Mia Dowser said, "Lately I noticed you've been writing a lot." Not seeming so enthuse I said, "Yeah, believe it or not I'm trying to write a book." "A book. Wow that's nice," M. Dowser said wanting to show me encouragement. "Well I been writing on and off for a while," I said. Dowser asked, "What's the book about?" I told her, "It's about life ups and downs."

The elevator door open and Mia Dowser starts to walk out. Before M. Dowser had left completely from the elevator she said, "Well I see you putting a lot of time into this book." I say "Writing a book isn't easy." Mia Dowser said "I bet. Knowing you Electra you'll get it done and I wouldn't mind reading it." "Thanks Dowser," I said as the elevator door closed.

The elevator stopped back on the second floor and more girls gets in. Then the elevator stop on the third floor and Miss Taylor walks in the elevator. More residents came in as other residents had gotten out. "Hello Miss Taylor," I said. "Hello Electra, how's everything," she asked. I replied, "It's alright." But really reader, it's not because I hate how I'm living. I got out on the fourth floor and said, "Have a good day Miss Taylor."

When I got into the sewing class the residents were already inside of the room. No one at the sewing machines everybody getting yarn and crocheting, so I put my bag and jacket on the good sewing machine seat. Then I went to sign my name on the attendance sheet. The radio was playing as normal. I didn't see Simone. I sit down and started to relearn the component of the machine. I removed the bop pin and thread. Then reloaded it back properly. I practiced threading the needle, and I practice re-threading the machine. I reacquainting myself with some of the sewing machine features.

Looking back over my shoulders I wanted to see if Simone would be entering the class. No sight of Simone. So I got two pieces of square fabrics to learned how it feel to sew them together on the machine while using the machine foot pedal. It felt awkward at first. The sewing machine kept cutting the tread causing the bon pin to become tangle. Having me to reset the thing over and over, it stops breaking once I learn how to sew the fabric in a steady pace. I had to learn how to press the pedal correctly with my feet. It took a little while before I got the hang of it.

After that I started to practice how to sew in a straight line. All I did was imitate how I seen Simone hold her hands while gliding the fabric and listening to the rhythm of the machine. Simone, she never made it to class but my time spent there wasn't in vain. I did more on the sewing machine this time then what I did the last time I was there. So, it a good thing and it had taken my mind off the book, and my troubles.

I saw some of the young girls they had made a pillow for their' bed. Me personally I don't care for a pillow. It not that I don't like pillows it just that in the shelter when someone doesn't like you they do all sorts of disgusting things to your personal belongings. Someone always sat on my pillow making it smell like pure ass. It happened a lot to me at Sixty -Eight Lexington Shelter. Or sometime when I laid my head down at night, my pillow, it smelled like there a light scent of vomit. Then there were the times when it seems like someone rub dodo but only in one spot and whenever I toss and turned while sleeping, I smelled it from time to time. Until I got fed up tossing the pillow to the floor-saying no more.

To tell you the truth I don't know why someone would do that to me because I never bother anyone or stole anyone shit or instigated in any fights. All I did was try to do the right thing and follow the rules hoping I get housing. I mind my business. I often stay to myself but yet someone constantly did this. They did it so much that I don't sleep with a pillow at all.

It didn't bother me because I wasn't trying to get comfortable but what did bother me was the trouble makers never seem to have a problem with their shit missing or being tamper with. Their beds had two pillows and they sleep on their pillows comfortably every night. At first when I came to the shelter all I thought about was doing the right thing. For instance, like waiting my turn in line to get housing, coming in every night on time and never becoming a curfew violator. Following the shelter rules and leaving the dorm on time. It like the more I did the right thing, the system or should I say the staff or maybe it's a little of both. No matter how you look at it I just got fuck and eventually; I got lost in the system.

Being stuck inside the system for so long girls started getting vicious doing petty things; childish things. For example, like with my pillow and putting neat hair remover inside my shampoo or rubbing my toothbrush in their asshole or something that stink causing me to say Uugh! As I'm am about to brush my teeth. That why till this very day I keep my toothbrush with me. Then fucking up my clothes while inside the laundry dryer. These are grown ass women; what the fuck are they acting like little children for? Anyway I'm moving a little ahead of myself. As I listen to the music and looked around the class I saw what some of the clients had created. Other starting, or continued crocheting their blanket as usual. I used to crochet and I had made lots of nice pretty blankets but I don't do it much anymore. I miss being with my kids and I just want housing at this point.

Reader just to let you know, eventually all by myself I made myself an outfit, a skirt set on the shelter sewing machine. I was so pleased that I gladly wore it with the jewelry I made.

Anyway, when the class was over, it wasn't quit time for us residents to go back to the dorm. We still had a half an hour before we are allowed to enter inside our dorms. Well, I'm not that goody two shoe resident anymore after being stuck here inside the system for way too long. Being miss perfect, wanting to play by the books and do whatz right. I see other girls sneak into their dorm so I began to do it too. I saw Security Watts sitting on post speaking on her cellphone. I whisper to her, "I'm going to my dorm to drop off my fabric. I'll be right out." She nodded her head indicating go head as she engages in her' telephone conversation. Once I got inside my dorm I see maintenance sweep and mop the floor. The Mexican lady still hadn't organized to removed her bags. Neither did Lacy. We still had a couple of empty beds in our dorm, which I like, because less girls means less drama and not so much smells of farts and the bathroom should have toilet tissue in the morning which I don't understand, why we still don't.

"Hey handsome," I say to the poster. While sitting on my bed I open my locker just in case Pamela decide to come by. I'm so tired living like this. Living out from my locker. Sitting/sleeping now on a much improved cot. No social life. No boyfriend. No dates. No sex. What the fuck did I do to deserve this life? Shit! I got to be in the bed every night at ten o'clock like I'm a child. This is not my life. It feels like someone else. You couldn't tell me at Sixty- Eight Lexington someone wanted me to become baldheaded. Every time

I wash my hair glob of hair would fall out. Some girls were trying to tell me I'm stress out. That's bullshit I been stressed out a lot of times before I became homeless and my hair never fell out. Plus, my hair texture feels different. But, I notices whenever I open up a new bottle of shampoo, my hair wasn't falling out when I wash it. Only after I leave the shampoo inside my locker then reuse it, I noticed that I was having these problems. I believe someone tampering with my products. When I used to work someone use to damage my clothes and take some of my perfume body lotion. I couldn't understand how that was happening. I never told anyone my combination for my lock even through the shelter provide a resident with the combination lock and the staff log the number in their record book. Which I don't understand why they do that because when a resident loses her' bed the RA clips the lock. I always cover-up my combination lock when opening it. Making sure no one see the combination code. Then after a while I started even purchasing my own locks that had to be open up with a key.

Still my lock-up belongings were being tamper with. Then I found myself just buying a new lock from time to time constantly changing my lock in order to prevent theft. It not my imagination either. You know when someone is tampering with your stuff.

Now I don't work and I don't have shit, motherfuckers, still fuckin with my shit. It has gotten to the point that I had to speak about it because being silent and constantly replacing locks, all it did was make me feel abused and have no fuckin money. Realizing I had an unknown enemy or enemies, because why is it happening? So to stop the madness I started writing complaints about it. After being in the shelter for so long writing up complaints, it had turned into a way of learning how to survive. It was known as cover your ass with a paper trail and not wanting to become a victim, anymore. I started to wear extensions in my hair while keeping a paper trail of complaints wanting to see if there was a pattern. I wrote so much I eventually had a meeting with Mr. Ron Winlesky, the Director.

Breaking from the silence of me bitching to yall about the negativity side of shelter living, because I'm going thru the motions of being angry and feeling stuck. With her loud mouth, quickly I turn around because I didn't even realize Miss Peterson **had entered** into the room. Miss Peterson asks **"Miss Jones!** What are you doing in here?" **"Shit!"** I mumble.

She the Director of Security, *reader.*

Quick I said, "Miss Peterson. Oh, I already told the guard I just wanted to put up my project I did from the sewing class." **"Well hurry up!** And get out of here because it's not four o'clock yet. And by the way **you** got to removed that poster off the top of your locker," she said. "Why," I asked. **"Because I said so that why**! Nothing belong on the top of the locker," she said hastily.

Right now, I'm looking around the room at all the other stuff the other residents have on top of their' locker. Then I said, "Since when does nothing belong on the top of the lockers? Everybody inside the room has something on top of their locker."

Exerting her authority as the director of security she said, "I'm not talking to them. I'm talking to you." While Watts the security guard looked at me smiling, moving her head from left to right, indicating, you know how she is. All in one breath Miss Peterson asked, "Watts who bed is this?" Security Watts said, "You know the Mexican lady with the black hair."

Miss Peterson put a look on her face like who? Then she said, "No, I don't." Watts said, "You know her Debra. She's short, always has a bible in her hand." Miss Peterson still look like she's trying to picture who Watts describing. Then Watts said, "She's new."

"I don't have no time for this! I don't know who she is and I don't CARE who she is. All I know these bags have got to go. Her area is a mess! Look ask an RA to come up here to clean up this mess. I want all of these bags removed NOW." Security got on her walkie-talkie paging, "Debra want an RA to come up to the Q dorm immediately." Miss Peterson look my way still wanting to yell, she says, "Miss Jones what are you still doing up here? It not four o'clock can you leave the dorm please."

I said, "I'm leaving I just had to close and lock up my locker before someone else steal my shit."

"I going to pretend that I didn't hear that," Miss Peterson said. I looked at the clock time on the wall, it read 3:42 pm. I started walking toward the door. I heard Miss Peterson **yell** when she saw Lacy bed as the door to the dorm closed behind me. I'm walking real slow down the corridors hallway. This time I'm thinking I'm going to wait for the slow elevator hoping by the time it come, it be time for me to turn right back around to go back to the dorm. While walking down the corridor I seen some of the bigmouth girls and Spanish girls inside their dorm-like they don't have a care in the world. I guess by the time Miss Peterson reach their' dorm it will be 4:00. Out from the elevator came RA Gloria rushing while talking on her' cell phone. I over-heard her say, "It about 4:00 pm and my shift is over. I don't know what Debra expect for me to do at this time." As she walked away, I look behind me before I entered the elevator. I saw a bunch of plastic gloves hanging out from her' back pocket.

I went inside the dining room and it fuckin smell like shit. Someone shitted inside the dining room bathroom again. Thank goodness the scent was half way fading away by the time I got there. Everybody laying with their head down on the table. Some females are glazing out of the dining room window. Other were sitting there just waiting for the time to go upstairs. Some females are sneaking upstairs, and the radio was on listening to the gossip of Wendy Williams.

Valerie came inside the dining room with a box of Popeye chicken while talking on her' cell phone saying,

"Dam it stinks in here! I don't even want to open my food but I'm so hungry and nobody better not ask me for shit!"

Valarie she still had the cell phone by her ear- now she having a conversation with the person on the other end of the cell phone. I heard Valarie say, "Yeah they be asking for food. No I'm not giving out a damn thing! I work hard for my money. What I look like feeding another bitch!"

The time now is five to four and most of the girls are packing up their' belongings about to head up to their' dorms. Shoot I just sat down, now I'm about to get up and go back upstairs. I'll tell you living this way, it mentally drains you and absorb a tremendous amount of wasteful energy on bullshit. Once I got upstairs I didn't feel like just sitting on my bed and looking around the room. I just wanted to write and be in my own little world tuning out everything and everyone around me.

Stop! To the reader, I just like to say please excuse me because sometimes I get like this bitching and ranting because I guess this is how I let out my stress. It starts to get to a person after years of being lock up in this shelter system and especially you're not going anywhere anytime soon. Other residents fight. Some drink and get intoxicated. I have noticed that some girls just sleep and can't find the energy to do simple things like wash their ass. Lots become curfew violators and that's a really easy way for the system to find the excuse why a person is still here living inside a shelter. Once in a while I got to let out my anguish and frustrations, one way or another, after all, I'm only human too.

Back to the story.

Dove came by my place. He brought me the dog. It was a puppy; jet black about four/five month old. Just like Dove said, a dog that can grow up with my kids. I named him Joe-Joe. Around this time in my life I had accumulated so many animals after Thomas left. The first pet was a cat. In the beginning of the summer while in the hallway a kitten had just walked and went into the bottom of Moet' stroller and had curled up on her blanket. I took her home with us and I renamed her Pebbles. Then I purchase two baby snapping turtles and we named them Lilly and Speed Bob. How the turtles got their names is because I allow the kids to take the turtles out from the tank and we call ourselves letting them race. Speed Bob won every time. I wanted my kids to have pets in their home. I guess this was stemming from filling in a void by not having my American dream. You know-the house, the husband, and the kids with the picket white fence, besides, I'm an animal lover. I knew after the house; a dog would be purchased. I mean too me you can't have the American dream without a dog/ animals being in the picture. Well what I have isn't how I imagine it or thought, but I kind of have it. The kids, a nice apartment, animals and now Joe-Joe. It a little off, my American dream, and I really didn't expect my dog to really be my protector but, it is what it is.

Out of all the kids Joe-Joe took to JB the most. For some odd reason Joe-Joe he used to chase JB down the apt hallway. JB used to run fast and hop on the couch before Joe-Joe had a chance to nip him on his' butt. They use to play that game for hours. Even Pebbles our cat who didn't like Joe-Joe used to watch him and JB run up and down our long hallway playing that game for hours. I see Joe-Joe wasn't a violent dog with the kids or the cat. We all were happy and it seem like Joe-Joe was please too. The dog was very smart because after he watch me bathe and put the kids to sleep. When I finally retire for the night Joe-Joe would follow me and sleep on the floor right underneath me. Then Pebbles I guess got jealous and fell asleep at the foot of my bed. Pebbles knew I didn't allow her to sleep on my bed so her sneaky ass waited till I feel asleep then she jump on the bed and went to sleep. Pebbles was smart too because she knew if I would have felt her by my foot I would had awaken and push her off my bed. So she always knew not to touch me if she wanted to stay on the bed. In my mind she belongs in the kitchen keeping away the mice but I understood Pebbles, she just wanted the extra attention because Joe-Joe was in the house now. So when I woke up and seen Pebbles at the bottom of the bed I allow her to stay. We were all close and adjusting to our new living arrangements.

Before I got the dog I use to quietly tiptoe out of the house while going to the card games in acquaintances' apartment while the kids slept. I did it like four or five times in the summer. It was a hustle for me; a way of making extra money for Champagne school fees. I'm kind of lucky at gambling, playing cards, especially pity-pat. So when I got my welfare allowance I used to cash in some of the food stamps in order to obtain $50 dollars in cash to gamble with. People, came to the card game with their pay checks from their jobs and I always did well. Not to mention I had fun. I even had a couple of drinks and brought a dinner. Just so you know whenever I planned on going to a card game. I used to tire the kids completely out by keeping them outside all day. Letting them run and play out in the park. Play in the sprinklers, getting wet. Then I would take them on these long walks while JB bounce his' basketball. To make sure that they sleep for a couple of hours I then gave them a little Robintusin cough medicine just before they fell asleep. Assuring that no one will wake up for at least the next four hours.

School started back up. I had my hands full and a job that was cut out for me. Every morning all of us walked Champagne to the bus stop with Moet in her stroller. By now JB wouldn't leave the house without his basketball. I had Joe-Joe with us too. So here we all went walking down the street, taking turns walking Joe-Joe, heading to the bus stop. Every time we get to a garbage can, I say, "Throw the ball in the hoop JB." For JB to be small he was getting really good at handling a basketball. After Champagne got on the bus. I'm thinking her' school fee soon be coming around and it getting harder and harder for me to continue this way. Me and my two younger kids, walked around allowing Joe-Joe to use the bathroom.

The next day sometime in the afternoon I get a knock at the door. Knock, knock, "Who there?" I asked as I'm walking down the hallway. I looked out the peephole and see Thomas standing there. The dog was right behind me. I open the door while blocking the dog from running out into the hallway. Thomas wanted me to take him back. He hoping that my hardship would take him back. Instead he saw I was stronger then what he thought. Thomas was insulting me, saying "Look at you Tami, you look terrible." As he spoke his' voice was low so that Rondu my next door neighbor couldn't hear him. Me, not wanting to hear what Thomas was talking about I told him, "If this is what you came to my door for, you mightiest well leave." Before I could say another word or did anything. Thomas cut me off, lowly and bossy in a demanding voice he saying "Girl, listen to me hey." Abruptly I said, "No I don't want to listen to you. Thomas I don't want you knocking on my door if this is how it got to be."

Low growling sounds appeared.

Both of us got quiet because we both heard the noise and for a brief second we had stopped with our heated argument but we continue back when we didn't hear anything. Thomas started back putting me down. "Your clothes are dirty. Look at you girl." With attitude I said, "Don't be knocking on my door Thomas cause you..." **Suddenly** growling sounds that's becoming louder and stronger causing Thomas to shut up and wonder, *what that?*

Shocked. I said to myself, that can't be little Joe-Joe acting like that. I turned around Joe-Joe was behind me standing boldly with his tail straight in the air. His growling turned into loud audible snarling growls that made me block and close the door even more so he couldn't even see Thomas. Thomas realized I had a dog. Surprised he look stunned. Joe-Joe growling was really intimating. Thomas couldn't tell if the dog was a pup or a grown dog. Caught off guard Thomas was taken back by surprise, as he had walked away because the dog was getting a little agitated. I close the door.

Then one day, very early in the morning I had gotten up walking Joe-Joe outside. I'm trying to get us a routine develop. While outside, a block down from the building, inside this small section of the park, I went inside and closed the gate. Allowing Joe-Joe to run around and to use the bathroom quickly.

Standing there while waiting for Joe-Joe to finish I was startled when I had seen this brown skin woman standing there just looking at us. From far away she said something to me. She said something to me as she stood watching me from the outside of the fence. I couldn't make out what she was saying. I do remember she startled me because of her sudden appearance. I don't know how long she was standing there watching me. She was behind the fence watching us until I had turned around and she had caught my attention. She was weird looking due to her wearing funny clothes. I think she had a strange hat upon her head. Maybe I recall her being so strange because the weather was warm and here it is she had on all of these clothes.

I walk to her because she called to me from behind the fence. I figure Joe-Joe will bark if he thought she was a threat but he didn't. Her conversation was nice and there was something intriguing about her. She told me about a warning/a premonition? But then she walked away. I remember in wanting to finish the conversation or to ask her something, because of her conversation. I quickly got Joe-Joe, attaching his leash to his collar in order for us to leave the park. I wanted to speak with the women but this is where it had gotten weirder. I couldn't find her. Like, where did she go?

I'm so serious I couldn't find her. I didn't see her walking down the street. I remember I quickly left from the park wanting to say something to her. I saw the direction she walked off but I didn't see her walking down the block. As I walked down the street I looked inside every park car before I got to the end of the block. In the park, I wasn't far from the corner. I should have at least caught a glimpse of her turning the corner, or something.

At the end of the block there was a crossing guard. I even asked the crossing guard which direction she saw the lady go. The crossing guard looked at me strangely and told me I was the only person she seen coming down the block.

There was not a car coming down the street. It like the lady vanish into thin air. For some odd reason I thought, could she had been an angel indisguised? Was she my angel? Don't even ask me why I would say something like that, but I remembered I questioned that shit. Where did even a thought like that come from? The thought came from because she vanished. Angels are not something I talk about or even think about. Due to her sudden appearance as well as her quick vanishing, was she my angel sent on earth to warn me about something or to protect me. I remember thinking like that.

I haven't seen Thomas in a while. One night I went into the hallway to empty out the trash. When I crack open the door I was shocked to hear Thomas' voice. I became really good in opening the door quietly not wanting the kids to follow me or anyone of my neighbors to catch me half dress in the hallway while emptying out the garbage. So, I'm tip toeing out the house to see who it was Thomas is speaking to. I couldn't make out what was being said because my heart was pumping so fast cause I didn't want to get caught eavesdropping while partially dressed. I'm shocked to see Thomas holding a conversation with Chokeman and Karl? I never knew of him holding conversations with anyone of them. The only guy in the building I ever heard him speak to was Wilbert which those conversations weren't long at all.

Thomas back was turned to me. Chokeman had gone inside the elevator. Then it was just Thomas and Karl who were talking. I couldn't make out what they were saying because my heart was bumping so loud because anybody could have opened up their apt door on my side of the building and had caught me eavesdropping. Which I didn't want that to happen. Anyway they looked real cozy together. **Oh shit!** I heard Chokeman voice. He's up on the upper floor. Not wanting to get caught, thinking all Chokeman has to do is run down the steps so I took another look at Thomas and Karl before tiptoeing quickly back inside my apartment. Quickly putting on more clothes, I waiting for Thomas to knock on the door but he didn't. So, playing it off, I went back out into the hallway to empty out the trash. Stunned to see no one was there. The hallway- it was empty.

Normally I take all of us outside in order to walk Joe-Joe out before turning in for the evening. Thomas was making accusations of me being an unfit mother. Spreading more vicious rumors about me to the people in the community. This one night I didn't want to go thru the hassle of preparing all of us for the walk and taking the stroller out. I recall being extremely tired and I told the kids, "I'm going to walk Joe-Joe by myself."

By now Joe-Joe was getting used to going outside and using the bathroom. Knowing, I was going to leave the children in the house. I went quickly to the park down the block. I was inside the smallest section of the park. It's the same section where I saw that lady before she vanished.

Outside, it was slightly darker than normal because one of the street lights were out, causing the small block to appear even darker. I went inside the park took off the chain as I normally do. Joe-Joe peed a couple of times and when he finally moved his bowels I called to him putting back on his leash. I open up the gate. I'm walking back home towards the building.

On my way in-coming back from the park. I noticed how my lilted bedroom window stood out on the block due to one of the street lights being out. I could clearly see all three of my children on the window ledge in my bedroom. They were all sitting on the wide window pane. Champagne had Moet holding her up on one hip as she points towards me. Moet looking in my direction. JB was on the other side of Champagne waving at me and being active as usual. My children they were all watching me and Joe-Joe walking, coming back towards the building.

Turning my head off of them, as I walked on the opposite side of the street from the building. I'm looking straight ahead. As I approach closer to the building passing all the parked cars I took a glance at the entrance of the building. I gasped when I saw Karl with his' adult Pit-bull standing in the building entrance way. They standing underneath the building light. They look like they were **shining!** Walking closer towards the building passing all the parked cars on the semi-dark block I see Karl, he's outside in front of the building with his' adult pit-bull dog, and............and the dog was unleashed! Soon as I finished the sentence it seems like his dog **smelled us** because the dog headed pointed in my direction quickly like I was a target. Before I could blink an eye I saw this huge dog come **Charging!** I stopped. Immediately I started **screaming** from across the street, "**Get your dog Karl**! Karl your dog!"

Not knowing which direction the dog is coming from due to the parked cars that were in front of me I started franticly looking around. Quickly I looked towards my bedroom window and I could tell not only me but my kids saw it too because I saw the' frighten look in their' eyes. I'm standing across the street by a large van wondering which direction is the dog coming from. I'm wondering is the dog coming from the front of the large dark blue van or is the dog coming from the back? I turned only my head anticipating to seen but from my side view I saw my kids' their hands go up against my bedroom window with open mouths. They screaming! I'm so scared and everything is happening so fast! Champagne was pointing but I couldn't hear what she was saying because the window is closed.

Quickly I looked back in front of me to see which direction the dog is coming from, because the van parked in front of me it's blocking my view. I decided to walk quickly, wanting to move where the light was at by Karl. I couldn't see the dog but I knew the dog had to come from the front or the back of the van. I panicked not knowing which way the dog coming so I started screaming again. "**Get your dog**! Karl the dog is running towards me! Get your dog!"

I caught a glimpse of Karl from the side of the van he seemed to run behind the dog. He called the dog but the dog didn't listen. Oh my God, seeing with my eyes the unleashed running dog is now in front of me the dog had done cross the street. The dog is on my side of the street. One of the young boys saw the charging dog and he tried to grab the dog in order to stop the charging animal but the dog was too fast. The adult pit was running near the corner so fast that it had leaped through his open arms, jumping pass him aggressively as the young boy hit the ground. Everything was happening so fast as I saw this dog running towards me I yelled out "Call your dog Karl!" The dog is charging running at top speed clearly towards me, in the dark so I completely froze. I stood there watching his front legs and paws stretch outwards then inwardly as all the paws touch the ground quickly, bouncing running at top speed. Paws stretching outwards then flexing inwardly quickly bouncing tapping the ground softly but charging like a bull. Jaws wide open, coming clearly in my direction.

At this point I didn't scream out anymore. I just helplessly watch this dog get closer and closer. I just stood still. I picture the dog leaping on me with his' front paws on my chest taking me down from the impact of his enormous speed. Then jumping on my body while savagely attacking me. I thought I was going to die, this is it. I froze as I watch my faith come upon me but............ *something happened.* The dam dog ran right pass me! Unbelievable.

The dog aim was slightly off. As I now watch in the semi-dark only with my eyes while standing completely still as my head turning watching the dam dog run pass me!

Hypnotize... Shocked and un-believed at this dam dog, running so fast, that he **ran**, right pass me. Being mesmerizes by this huge charging angry dog the only thing that moved was my head and neck as my eyes is following this dog. Unable to move because I'm in shocked that the dog ran right pass me and **I'm still alive!** My head was already turned to the side as I watched this dog now abruptly, trying to stop, while pivoting his' body from his speed.... pivoting, trying to make a U-turn. I'm seeing and watching this dog turn his complete side-as his muscle legs bending, breaking his speed by pounding on the pavement, turning -to go for the kill.

I had to blink, because, before I knew it-the dog had **Joe-Joe**. My pup looked like a flag being waved up violently toss and turn in the air. I started screaming uncontrollably.

The young boys suddenly should there to watch this dog fight until I started screaming at them **"Get your fuckin dog off my dog!"** They were laughing as if it was a joke. I was screaming and watching helplessly. Joe-Joe was getting devoured by this adult Pit. Without thinking as well as feeling I was being picked on. I'm watching my pet get killed. I'm going thru the drama so I leaped on Karl. I charged him swinging.

I flipped! When Karl' friends saw that they quickly grabbed me telling me "Tami, calm down!" As the others boys now started punching on the adult dog in order to free my dog from his grip. Karl said **"Bitch!** If you would have touched me, **I would had killed you!**

My crazy ass was in a **zone.** I had gone beyond all thinking. I yell back "**I'm right here bitch!** Come On! **Come on!** That's what you want to do! **Kill me!** I'm right here!" The group of boys and Karl were shocked in seeing me behave that way because after all I'm just a mother who always stayed inside the house, behaving like a Betty Crocker Mommy feeding whoever asked me for a plate of food.

Seeing my dog looking like a flag being waved in the air, I flipped out and **charged** Karl again wanting to fight but by this time someone just gotten the dog off of my dog and by now Karl had his angry growling dog standing up on his two feet in front of him saying "Bitch I'll make him bite you. **You think that I won't bitch?! You think I won't!**" His friends stared telling him "**Nooo! No Karl.** Don't do that. *Karl*, no, don't do it." I held my keys so tightly in my hand thinking I'm going to jab his' dog eyes **out** and bite his' **fuckin head off.** I was railed up. The boys started to push on Karl who was holding his dog-while the dog was standing on it two paws. They were saying "No. Come on Karl. Nooo!" But Karl was mad because I charged him wanting to fight **him.** The young boys started pushing towards him like wanting him to go in the building. They were pushing on him till they made Karl go inside the building.

Karl was being push to start walking but his head was turn looking back at me saying "**You lucky bitch**! You're lucky. You fuckin lucky!" He was so mad.

Once Karl was gone, inside the building. The reminded boys then told me to "go get your dog." Sadly, I said, "He's dead." The boys said "He's alive but he won't let anyone touch him. You're the only one he would respond to."

I was scared to go by my dog not knowing what state of mind he was in. I took the dog upstairs. My crying children met me and Joe-Joe by the door saying "We saw everything from the window." JB asked "Did the dog bite you?" I'm shaken up but I smile wanting to assure my son as I reached out and touch him. I said, "No the dog didn't bite me. I'm ok."

Champagne said, "I was so scared. Is Joe-Joe dead?" "No." Quickly I responded while moving the kids away from the door so I can come into the house as I tied Joe-Joe to the doorknob.

I said "No Joe-Joe not dead. Someone go get a blanket for Joe-Joe." Once I put the blanket down for Joe-Joe I told the kids, "Come I'm fine. Come leave Joe-Joe." I wasn't sure how Joe-Joe would behave around the kids for fear that he might have snapped at them.

This happened on a Sunday night because I remember me trying to call any kind of dog hospital or dog shelter for help. I was pretty dam angry and I wanted Karl to face consequences for what he had done. I told my kid, "I'm going to the precinct to file out a report and don't go by Joe-Joe. Stay in my bedroom. I be right back."

Shaken up and angry I went to the precinct down the block.

When I had gotten inside of the precinct I told the white cops what happened and how I wanted to press charges. The cops laughed at me saying "There's no law in the books they can give me for a dog attacking another dog."

I expressed, "But the dog was off the leash and the owner was unable to control his' dog." *Stopping me from writing and remembering my past security came in the dorm and announce* "Bed check ladies."

I started putting away my notes. I heard Lacy cough. Then the Dominican girl started coughing. Then I heard a harsh gurgle and a loud split. Ugh I bet you that's that Mexican chick. I notice she does that a lot. I'm waiting for the Shift Supervisor to enter into the dorm so I can sign for my bed.

Speak with you tomorrow.

Good night.

Chapter Nineteen

This morning I was awaken by the Residential Aide voice. When I opened up my eyes the lights were on and I heard Gloria the RA say to someone, "You're got to move your bags. All these bags got to go. You know these bag supposed to leave."

I over slept. Turning over focusing I looked at the clock. The time read 8:15am. I'm listening hearing the commotion going on between the RA and the Mexican chick. RA Gloria telling her she needs to remove her bags and she speaking confuse in Spanish.

I sat up. Sitting on my bed while rubbing my eyes and listening to RA Gloria argue with my Mexican roommate while I shuffle my feet still halfway sleep slipping on my flip flop. I got up walking towards the bathroom. Walking around the trolley cart the RA brought with them to remove all bags from the dorm. I knocked on the bathroom door and I got no answer. So I open up the door. The first thing I did was look to see if there was any toilet tissue and there was none. So I turned back around walking to my locker as I glanced around the room seeing other roommates preparing their selves to leave the dorm to. Except for the Spanish girl in bed Q6. She still sleeping.

I bent down while covering my combination code. I unlocked my locker. Opening up the locker I'm on the bottom shelve digging down toward the back of the locker. I pulls out a ½ of roll of toilet tissue that I had saved for moments like this.

I figure since I'm inside my locker I mightiest well take out my toothbrush and soap to wash my face and brush my teeth. As I search for my personal items I could hear RA Gloria getting annoyed with the Mexican Chick. Gloria speaking annoyed in English while the Mexican chick speaking annoyed in Spanish. The Mexican chick she very feisty. I think she want them to go away from her and leave her alone.

When I turned around I see the short stubby Mexican woman pacing in her area while speaking loud in Spanish. It seems like she knows what they want but I think the Mexican lady has nowhere to put her' belongings.

Frustrated RA Gloria saying to her co-worker, "You see, that's why I suggested to Debra why not leave 3 trolleys with the guards on the floor. I don't want to deal with this. I don't have the time Houser trying to raise up my blood pressure."

RA Houser said, "Then don't!" She looked at Lacy saying, "Yo! What you standing there looking for? You got to remove your bags too!" Lacy responds back, "I know already. **God**! Don't you see me moving?"

Tweeter shook her head like if I can just punch her in the face and get away with it. I would. Frustrated Gloria said, "It too early in the morning. I calling Debra and let her come handle this."

As I'm walking back towards the bathroom-now Gloria, is standing in front of the bathroom door, pulling her walkie-talkie towards her mouth saying, "Debra pickup."

I say to Gloria, "Excuse me." She sees me clearly walking towards the bathroom and that I have my towel and personal toiletries' in my hand. Gloria snaps at me saying, "Where I'm supposed to go with all these bags in front of me and a trolley kart?" I'm just standing there because I need to use the bathroom......................Slowly then she moves out the way while saying, "Some people so inconsiderate."

I'm just waking up and getting out of bed to all this confusion so I say, "Don't take it out on me because you got to work. How can I get out of here on time if I can't get inside the bathroom?"

Standing there, I understand RA Gloria-she frustrated because the Mexican chick being stubborn not respecting the shelter rules or what Gloria is asking her to do, but don't take it out on me. I go into the bathroom. From behind the bathroom door I could hear RA Houser saying, "**You** put your own bags on the cart. I'm not **carrying nothing**! Move them Lacy. Why give us a hard time?"

As I'm peeing and now, washing my face I can't help but hear what was going on inside the dorm. Lacy and the Mexican chick both of their beds are by the bathroom door. When I finish, I came out carefully, opening the door, not wanting to bump into anything. Pepsi, she standing near the bathroom door asking me, "Is there issue in the bathOOm?" I said, "Nope."

"Can I get sOme issue please?" Pepsi asked. I unroll some of the tissue off of the roll and hands it to Pepsi. As I walk back to my area I notice my next door neighbor has removed her picture of the man face. I'm thinking what the fuck is going on with her? It like, she wants my attention or something. Well I tell you, she got it but I'm trying to figure out what is her game. Like, why she was doing this, but yet, never says a mumbling word to me.

Miss Peterson come busting in the door with her' side kick Black, but when Black notice all of the women weren't quite dressed and ready to exit the dorm he stood outside the door allowing the room door to close in his face as Debra proceeded inside the room yelling "**Why isn't everybody up!**" Oh my gosh she yelling with an attitude. I guess Miss Peterson was really furious now, because her side kick Black, had to wait in the hallway, while she handles her business by herself.

All loud she said, "**Excuse me!** I want to know why everybody not up, ready to leave the dorm." I sat on my bed getting my clothes out from my locker. Then I used my locker doors as a shield to cover me, as I got dressed watching Miss Peterson in action. She marches right over to sleeping beauty (The Spanish girl) tapping loudly on her' locker saying, "I don't see a bed pass on your locker so why are you still in bed!" The Spanish girl open up her eyes fast because she was startled out of her sleep.

Once Miss Peterson seen her eyes open, she asked the Spanish girl with an attitude, and out loud, "**Why are you still in the bed sleeping?**" The Spanish girl didn't know what to say because she was busted by Miss Peterson.

Marsha the security guard had come walking casually inside the room. Wanting Miss Peterson to see her doing her job-getting us females up and out. My naked body is half way shield behind my locker door. I had my top on, thinking to myself, oh that's why sleeping beauty was still in the bed because Marsha patrolling the floor.

I caught the Spanish girl making eye contact with Marsha. I'm thinking, bitch, she can't help you in front of Miss Peterson. Now I'm putting on my jeans watching Miss Peterson yell at the top of her voice saying, "All of those bags got to go now!"

In the meantime, RA Gloria had suck her teeth saying "This is unbelievable," as she shakes her head in disappointment while looking at all of the bags that Lacy and the Mexican chick had.

RA Houser said, "Yo, I'm not trying to get myself stressed out for nobody. My back is already hurting from moving all those bag on the 3rd floor yesterday. **Put your bags on the trolley.**" Marsha walking around in the room making sure us all up. Before Marsha reach where Miss Peterson was standing at. Her boss yelled, "Can you ask her why she was still in the bed?"

Immediately Marsha started speaking in Spanish to sleeping beauty. The Spanish girl got up rolling her eyes because she being made to get out of the bed as I'm thinking **yes**, you have to leave and get out like everybody else as I watched her tired ass go off to the bathroom.

Miss Peterson said, "Black come in." That's all she wants is have her side kick Black, standing by her side. When Black didn't immediately come in. Debra yelled "Black, Black you can come in now." Here he comes like her puppet on the string.

Now that she has her crew standing by her side she really shows off her authority. As she spoke she clapped her hands to every word, while saying, "Ladies what is the pro blem? The time now is 8:45am. Dorm close at nine so be ready to get out."

RA Houser lean against the wall acting like her job is so hard. By now I'm fully dressed. I closed my locker and sit on my bed cause it not nine o'clock yet so I sat on my bed tying up my sneakers. Then I'm going to make up my bed.

Miss Peterson goes over to the Mexican chick while saying, and pointing her finger-at the bags', like she knows her is the top dog who's in authority, "All of these bags are going today. Why are you giving my RAs a difficult time?"

RA Gloria was looking at the Mexican chick with a twisted lip, like yeah, why?'

Immediately the Mexican chick started talking in Spanish all fast as if she had a long story to tell. Not having patient, Miss Peterson ask Marsha "What is she saying?"

Marsha speak to the Mexican lady in Spanish and tells her boss, "She doesn't have anywhere to put all her things." Miss Peterson said loudly looking at the Mexican chick as she clapped her hand to every syllable, "That is not my pro blem."

Immediately RA Gloria threw her hands up like, told you."

Miss Peterson said loudly to Marsha, "Tell her right now the bags got to go." Immediately Marsha replied. The Mexican chick seen there was no way around the situation.

Miss Peterson replied and shouted, "She had ample time to figure out what to do with her belongings. This is not a storage place. The most I can give her is 3 days. Sorry!" Marsha started telling her quickly what Miss Peterson said in Spanish, making her aware what's going on."

She understands very well her just pretending. She understood when I had told her ass to get out of the bathroom. She moved especially, when I said by the bathroom door, "I'm going to write you up!"

Miss Peterson turned towards RA Houser and RA Gloria saying "Make sure all these bags are out this room today!" Then Debra walks over to Lacy' bed, with Black tagging along and say "You too, I want everything out. Understand?"

Lacy said, "Gosh you don't have to yell."

Debra said, "I wouldn't have to be in here if you comply with the rules." Then she looked at the Mexican chick who looks like she was struggling with the pressure of clearly out her disgusting area. Black not saying a word, but was standing by her side. RA Gloria walks over to Lacy and asked, "How many plastic bags do you think you would need to pack up all that stuff under your mattress?"

Before Miss Peterson leaves the room she tells Pepsi as her voice still speaking all loud, "As, for you. I received numerous complaints about you being constantly nude. Nobody want to see all of that, no more prancing around the room butt naked, can you have respect for your roommates and show your naked body inside the privacy of your own presence? Like when you get your apt."

Miss Peterson head towards the door before exiting. She takes another look around the dorm turn towards the RA saying, "If there is any more problems, call me." She walks out the room with Black following right behind her. I went to Willy. I brought a large cup of coffee and two butter roll. When I got inside the dining room. I found a seat by the window and had started writing because they not trying to get me housing. I want out from this mad house.

Back to the story.

Yeah so when I went to the cops they told me a crime wasn't committed. Then the very next day Joe-Joe started vomiting all kinds of green stuff; so much I had to take him to the vet. The only thing was I didn't have any money. I didn't want to see the dog die in the house. Champagne didn't have to attend school today so I got us all dressed to go to the vet. Joe-Joe was sick. I put the blanket underneath the stroller and had laid him there. We all were ready to walk out the door. Then the most amazing thing happen, pebbles our cat, jumped on top of the stroller. I thought she didn't like Joe-Joe. So here we all was, walking to the vet. The only one vet place I know, is this run down looking place on Nostrand Ave. All the pets that I ever owned I had taken to this vet. Except for Terror and that because I didn't have her long enough.

Stop! To the reader: You should have seen us, Moet in the stroller; Joe-Joe, underneath the stroller lying in the pouch; Pebbles our cat sitting on top of the stroller; Champagne holding on to the right of the stroller; JB bouncing his basketball not too far away, from the stroller; and I was pushing the stroller. We may not have money or fancy clothes but I tell you one thing, we were a loving family, even down to our pets.

Anyway back to the story.

When we finally got to the vet, I seen that Joe-Joe was really sick because he kept vomiting and occasionally I had to stop to let the green stuff out from the stroller. When the veterinarian seen me with the kids, the dog and the cat, he seemed astonish. I explain what happen and told him my financial status. His heart went out to us and he took care of Joe-Joe. He even gave us the medicine, free.

The veterinarian told me "Joe-Joe' chest bone in the front was ripped and to stop it from going deeper the medicine would help with that." Then the vet open Joe-Joe' mouth and the vet made sounds of laughter or should I say like sounds of approval of being impressed. He said "Your pup was fighting back. He broken a couple of his baby teeth on him." The total cost was way over a hundred dollars.

When I got home I rode the elevator to my floor. When the elevator door open Karl and his cronies were sitting in front of the elevator. Now, that I am writing and thinking about the past. Karl was sitting in the same spot when I was eavesdropping and saw him talking to Thomas. I don't know why I didn't see that before. Maybe because it was too much I was going thru and I never would have thought that Thomas would have gone this far or stoop this low but now that I'm writing, I see that Thomas did go that far. That explain why he never came to my defense when he heard of the trouble I was having with this troublesome teenager.

Anyway as I was about to get out from the elevator I immediately pulled the veterinarian receipt out from my hand and had lifted it up to Karl saying, "I'll see you in a small claim court." I wanted him to pay for what he did.

Karl said "I don't care what you got in your hand. I'm not paying for shit bitch." I said, "We'll see about that."

I remember my two oldest kids looked at him, then at me out of concern because they never heard anyone speak to me in that tone of manner. Struggling to turn the stroller properly coming out from the elevator, I could feel Karl watching me as I and the kids are going to our apartment. When I got inside after unloading everything and everyone. I couldn't get the picture out my mind about how that adult dog had turned in my direction, as if he smelled his' target.

I remember after Dove had brought me the dog. How the young boys in my building were impressed that a girl had a pit? I remember them saying "Tami got a pit." Then some of them asked me "Where you got your dog from because they wanted one." Come to think of it, I was the first girl with her own pit in the project too. These dogs around this time was rare and when anyone did see a person walking the street with a pit, nine times out of ten it was males walking them. Then I recalled when one of Karl' hang out buddies started knocking on my door. When I first got Joe-Joe the young boy asked me "Tami can I take your dog out for a walk." I hesitated at first but the young boy, James pleaded with me and said "How he going to ask his mother to buy him a pit. I promise I won't let anything happen to your dog."

Having my hands full with my housework and the kids I thought it would be a big help to me. Being an animal lover myself I understood him wanting to walk a dog. Especially a pit too. Then I remember when I was like that, as a youngster wanting to walk my neighbor dog. Begging my next door neighbor, to walk her' toy poodle, name Daisy. I thought what harm could there be, plus I had my hand so busy with the kid, the housework I haven't yet scheduled in when and where I would be walking the dog. So I got Joe-Joe prepared to go out. Before there was dog's clothes I allow Joe-Joe to wear JB out grown T- shirts and shirts. Beagle Boy with the two initials BB on the shirt was one of my favorite shirts from JB I gave to Joe-Joe to wear. He looked so cute walking outside with a shirt on. Lots of people stop and admire the dog when he had on JB shirt. JB old Beagle Boy shirt fitted the dog, so cute. I used to always put a shirt on Joe-Joe when I and the kids walked him outside. When the boy, named James brought Joe-Joe back in, his' Beagle Boy shirt was missing.

I questioned James asking, "What happen to Joe-Joe shirt and where is it?" Honestly I don't remember what line or excuse he told me. All I know is I told the boy, "I want the shirt back and you had no right to remove his' clothing, James. Bring his shirt back or I will not allow you to walk Joe-Joe again."

James did bring the shirt back two days or three days later. I opened my door and here James was handing me back Joe-Joe Beagle Boy shirt. Then he asked "Can I take Joe-Joe out for a walk?" I told him, "No," and closed my door. I just wanted back the shirt and I didn't appreciate him removing it in the first place and then for him to take so long in bringing it back.

Reader, just for the record, that night when the attack had taken place, Joe-Joe wasn't wearing a shirt.

There no need to tell yall what's coming next. Just when I thought things couldn't get any worst. I thought Chokeman was bad but his' psycho baby brother, this monstrous young man, Karl, started harassing me.

Dam! Then I found out, all these years, Chokeman had been in jail. When he got out, he came home to live with his' mother, who lived in my fuckin building. The funny thing about it was when we bumped into each other, we both, after all those years known immediately, who the other one was. Now, here, it is, many years later and I'm the oldest in my family who now is having problems, with the youngest person, in Chokeman family. Ain't that a blimp!

And what a complete turnaround because now the only difference is my family not around me to have my back. I'm force to deal with this lunatic nut by myself and what's even sadder is **Chokeman knew**.

This boy, Karl, started coming on my floor doing all kinds of crazy shit. Like kicking on my door; waiting in front of the building when I came home; saying disgusting things to me in front of my kids. One day I asked Champagne to take Joe-Joe outside. She came upstairs running and panting saying "Karl' dog tried to attack Joe-Joe again." I couldn't believe that! Dam, I couldn't even let my daughter walk and bond with her own pet.

I took the dog out and again; Karl dog was vicious wanting to attack Joe-Joe. The dog keeps charging but this time Karl held on to the angry dog while picking him up and going inside the building' elevator. It was only a matter of time before something ugly happened. I just knew it!

So to make a long story short I had to call Dove and ask him to come and get the dog because at this rate I felt the dog was in grave danger. I had myself and my kids to think about too. I got attacked already. Then my daughter could have gotten hurt in this mix up shit too.

At some point I decide to go to church.

I remember when I first moved to this building and how the mailman had always invited me to his church. I didn't know much about church. Maybe it was everything I was going thru but on and off I had always felt that something was terribly wrong. It not that I was having suicidal thoughts because of all of the pressure. I felt I needed help and I had nobody to talk to, or turn to. To disclose my inner most feelings. I remembered when I ask God about Adrianna and Thomas, and how her face appeared in a form of a witch, inside of a circle. I'm remembering the kind mailman who had always invite me to come to his church.

I got up and I and the kids went to church. Not knowing if the church was open while feeling low in spirited I walked on Southern Street, to Everyone Baptist Church of cogic. I saw some people going in. I looked at the church bulletin board and it had read-that tonight was Prayer Night and I walked in.

They were singing this song that I didn't know at the time but I know it now. They sung-in the name of Je sus. We have the vic tory_. Oh oh oh in the name of Je sus. In the name of Je sus. Satin will have to flee__. Oh oh oh tell me, who can, stand be, for us, when we, call on, that great name____. Jesus Jesus pre cious Jesus we have the vic tory_. Oh oh oh in the name of Je sus. In the name of Je sus we have the victory_ oh oh oh in the name of Jesus. In the name of Jesus. Satin will have to flee__. Oh oh oh tell me............I found myself saying, "help me." as they sung. "Who can, stand be, for us, when we, call on, that great name____. "Help me Jesus," I said. They continue to sing Je sus Je sus pre cious Jesus we have the vic tory.

I found myself starting to say softly and quietly, "I need you Jesus help me cause something wrong with me." They continue singing Jesus Jesus precious Jesus we have the victory. I was feeling low in spirit. I can't call on Thomas because he's not here. No matter what, we share this family. We have two kids together. So what, if our relationship is finished. So what if it's over. He supposed to be here for me. I thought he was my friend. I was there for him so many times. I was such a fool to have loved him. To see how he has betrayed me like this. I hate him. I hate him so much right now. I'm so very disappointed in him. My life with him has been a lie. Just a big fat lie.

As I sat there in that church all those thoughts about our relationship and more was going on thru my head, as well as feelings of being alone and scared in the inside. They finished the song Jesus Jesus precious Jesus we have the victory. I sat there listening to people announce what all God has done for them in their life.

I started wondering could God help me because I had nowhere else to go and there was no one there I could turn to. The leader inside the church made an offer "Who needs prayer to come to the front." I felt I needed prayer.

The music started playing. He said "Come fast because the spirit is moving." The people in the pew pit started swaying and humming. He said "Come now. Come now."

I had not known much about God, demons, bad sprits the devil or Jesus; just plain and simple, the spiritual world. I forced myself to go up because I knew something was wrong. I just didn't know what it was. When I went up the man came to me. He asks me, what do I need. Unable to put all of my anxiety, the disappointment and hurt into words I said nothing. Then he had immediately summoned the pray committee to form a circle around me.

There I stood in the circle among the saints while allowing them to pray for me because I knew something was wrong. I forgot about my shame of humiliation. I see the mailman who had always invited me to come to his' church holding hands with his spiritual brothers and sisters just praying for me. I just saw him praying not paying any attention to me. They all had their eyes closed while holding hands and praying for me.

Then something happen. I can't explain it but it felt like I could **see**. My eyes were open and I felt like I saw everything and everyone so clear. It was overpowering and magical. That was my second experiences of anything religious.

When it was over I went back to my seat. I had tears rolling down my face. A lady came over to me and she asked me, "Do you belong to a church?" And I replied, "No." She invited me to come to the church on Sunday, which I and the kids did attend.

When the woman saw that I came to the church she encourages me to attend an eight step course about Christianity. I received a medium size loose leaf notebook which were filled with steps on becoming a Christian, which was all new to me. No one in my family went to church, talk about Jesus or God or Christianity or about the power of prayer. Anyway I don't remember why, but I just stop going to that church. Then, I got a new next door neighbor. She a female. Her face looked slightly familiar. I remembered she was shocked to see me as her neighbor and that the people in the neighborhood had called me Tami instead of Electra. She wanted me to remember her in attending the same high school I went to. She remembered when Dove and I were this popular sweetheart couple. She younger than me and Connie had two darling little children. Now I have not one but two neighbors that I welcomed. There was an instant connection with her' son Denzel and my children.

I remember around this time in my life, at one point being anger at my mother. Mainly due because recently I thought of Dove. When I had spoken to Dove. I wanted answers from her; like why she didn't approve of him. When I was so happy and head over heels in love. I spoke on how nice and well taking his children looked in the picture that he had showed me. How it seems like he still cared for me **after all these years**. I wanted to know why she preferred and supported my relationships with guys like Tray and Thomas but hated and didn't support and helped to destroy the union between me and Dove?

After complete silence my mother said, "I didn't want to see you with anybody who did drugs." I said, "Drugs! What are you talking about? Dove didn't do drugs! All he did was work and brought me nice things. He took me out on dates. Tray was the one who did drugs and look how Thomas is treating me? You mean you prefer to see me with guys like this?"

I said to my mother, "I did the right thing. I picked the right guy. Maybe you should have minded your own business. I feel like my children should be yours and you should take care of them. Dove on drugs? What about Desmond, he's the one smoking weed and drinking? Why didn't you break up Tonya and Desmond then! I never saw you give Tonya a hard time about Desmond, and we all know he do drugs." My mother had nothing to say. I remembered being very mad at her, more than I could ever, ever express.

One day I met up with another girlfriend of mine. Her name was Deidra. She was another young mother like myself. All of my girlfriends we live in the same area. Anyway Deidra heard about all the trouble I was having with Thomas. She heard I also been going to church, too, which neither one of us did when we first met. She told me there was this crusade tent on Main Street and she wanted me to go with her because number one, she didn't like what was going on with me. Number two, she was telling me about these new homes being built in the Poconos. They had rentals and that she did applied for an apt. She wanted me to apply as well. I was thinking to myself, I just finally got my place fix up with furniture and moving wasn't even on my agenda.

She wanted me to think about it saying the people in our area weren't going anywhere and that they were nothing but troublemakers.

By this time Thomas became more ridiculous. Now he was spreading rumors that I'm an unfit mother and pointing me out to everyone, telling them, what all he wanted them to know about me, exaggerating facts and just pure lies and talking about my financial history to anyone and everyone, constantly! His gossip about me, it was getting so fuckin annoying.

When I got to my building and came off the elevator stun I saw Thomas and Connie together on my floor and by the look on Connie face, I figured Thomas had been talking to her about me or inquiring something about me.

No matter what, how I see it. I could tell it was negative with seeing how Connie had gone inside her apartment as if I have a problem, while saying, "Hi Tami. Alright yall have a good one. See you later."

When little Denzel saw me immediately he asked "Tami can I come to your house?" Before a word came from my lips Connie had shoved him inside the house saying, "No Denzel not now," and she closed her' apt door.

I saw the devilish grin on Thomas face. I was wondering what it was I just stumbled upon realizing that he causing such stress in my life by putting our business all out in the street. What else makes it so bad, he didn't have anything constructive to talk about when he had seen me. He didn't even have anything for the kids. I went right inside the apartment and close my door. When I got inside my apartment I believed Thomas had wanted me to beg him for some money.

One day I was riding with my mother in her car. I was still mad at her about Dove. I started venting then she said something to me that brought me back to my past. She said while driving, "If I had wanted to that I only could have killed you."

Stop! To my reader. At that very moment after my mom just said that sentence above. These thoughts went thru my head. Around this time in my life after I broke up with Thomas

542

there was drama, after drama, after drama. I'm only one person, who raising three small children and paying the bills, dealing with an anger vindictive man, handling tiny flashbacks of memories of a forgotten love and trying to rationalize unexplainable dreams and encounters. Simply just not acknowledging but now wondering.... uhm and out from the blue, **how did** I become the black sheep of the family? And for what reason? I just got disown and kicked out. I feel like, there was a part of me fighting for my son man hood. Not to mention I wanted answers because something seemed to be a little off? Now, to top it all off, my mother just told me that she could have **killed me**. As you can see it was a lot to absorb.

Reader, let go back to the story.

When my mother told me she could have killed me. That was such a terrible and evil thing to say to your own daughter. I have never done anything harmful or totally disrespectful to my mother for her to want to kill me and how can she had killed me or when did she have the opportunity to kill me? Since my relationship with Thomas is over, something with me just didn't feel right. When my mother said that malice sentence. I responded back by saying, "Only if God allowed you too because you don't have the power to take my life. Only he does," and she look at me. So I left my mother alone because I was hurting. I was mad because my life was very stressful and to me it's **fuckin abnormal**.

Later on in the night time I get a knock, knock, knock at the door. I go to the door looking out from the peephole and seen strangers standing in front of my door. I opened up the door and two black women asked, "May we come in." They had briefcases and I allowed them to enter into apartment. I was wondering what this was all about? I thought they were undercover cops at first. They looked so professional. When the two ladies got inside the living room, then they pulled out their' badges and said, "We are from B.C.W." Abbreviation for Bureau of child welfare and we would like to see your kids." With authority, they asked, "Where are the children?"

They asked as if they felt my kids were in harm. My heart was pumping. I was confused so I questioned, "Why are you here?" One of the ladies said, "We received a telephone call of possible neglect." With authority, the dark skinned fat woman had repeated, "Where's are the children?"

Quickly dismaying the alarm in her voice I said, "They here. In their' room sleeping." The dark skinned fat one said, "We would like to see them." I walk them to their' bedroom and there they were my kids, sleeping. Everyone laying in their own bed. Champagne was on the top bunk. Brandon was on the bottom bunk and Moet was inside her' crib.

Both of the ladies had looked at each other as if to say where the signs of danger is?

Walking away from the kids' bedroom, the other lady looked around my apartment seeing it was well kept. The apartment was quiet with no smell of smoking of cigarettes or drugs. Both of the ladies started looking around my place because it really was a nice decorating place for a person on my budget. Since I noticed them looking around I took them on a tour. I said, "This is **my** bedroom," indicating this is where I sleep. I had showed them my bathroom with toiletries. I open my linen closet showing them that my children use their own wash cloths and towels. I even pulled out Champagne' scrapbook. The other lady could tell clearly a mistake was made. She said, "We received a phone call."

She asked, "Can we see your kitchen cabinets?" Now that was one thing I don't have a problem with. I always kept food. The problem is, I just never had any money. The lady asked, "What did the kids have for dinner tonight?" I said, "Hamburger helper," after checking all the kitchen cabinets and the refrigerator. Going back inside the living room the dark skinned fat lady said, "Can you go get the kids? We like to see them and speak to them."

I went to Champagne first saying, "Champagne, Champagne wake up." "Um," she said coming out of her deep sleep. I said, "I'm sorry but we have an emergency. I need you to go inside the living room." I helped her off from the top bunk bed.

Then I went to JB. I tapped him, "JB. Brandon, wake up. JB, wake up." He opens his eyes I said, "Come on get up." I picked him up and brought him into the living room. I sat him on the couch next to Champagne. Then I went and got the baby.

The ladies wanted to check their' skin for body marks. I asked Champagne to take off her' pajamas. Then I had to help her since she was cranky at being woken up from out her sleep. The fat lady held her arms turning them over to see if she had seen any marks. Then she looked on her back and she asked me, "What is that?"

I said, "I guess it's a beauty mark because she was born with that on her skin." Then the fat lady asked Champagne, "Is that true?" Champagne nod her head in a non-verbal yes.

She did the same for the two smaller children. They wanted to see the children immunizations booklets, birth certificates and my identification. They asked, "Are you up to date with your rent? Who goes to school?" They asked to see Champagne' report card for grades and attendances.

The dark skinned lady had really wanted to take my kids away from me. She had the nerve to ask, "Champagne does your mommy beat you? Do you want to live with your mother?" Champagne was just looking like she didn't understand the question. The dark skinned lady asked "Would you like to come to live with me? Are you afraid of your mother?" Now you know I really resented her, in talking to my young daughter, like that. It seems like she just wanted to take them away. Until I said, "There's nothing wrong with any of my children. Someone did this to me to be cruel and I'd like to know why would anyone stoop this low to have my descent kids removed out from their home?"

I sent the kids back into their room and put them back inside their bed because they were tired anyway. I'm thinking people are dirty! I never thought that someone would stoop that low and call BCW on me. Now who could had done it?! Just to think of all the children I see who are really being neglected and abused. Those kids are running around here unnoticed but a malicious person might see a struggling mother and do the unimaginable, like call BCW. I see I really got to watch my back. I got to watch what I do and say. Someone hated me that much that they would lie and cause not just me but my own children such misery and heartache in breaking up our home.......and our family by having them removed. What monster would do something like that? I'm a dam good mother.

That fat ugly bitch couldn't find any reason to have the kids removed. It like she got mad. Her ugly ass really wanted my kids to be remove. I remembered her appearance, she was dark skinned, short and stocky. She had dreads that were pinned up. She wore tan pants. I remembered her not looking very feminine and attractive either.

The other lady had finally said, "Thank you for your cooperation. She said to her partner, "Let's go." The fat lady turned around saying before she reached the door, "If we feel for any reason not to close the case you may get another visit from the bureau."

I remembered being upset and I had insisted on knowing who called and did something like that. **I wanted a name.** Both ladies told me, "We are not at lodge to give you a name or any names." So I questioned the B.C.W policies and procedures asking, "What if someone just didn't like me for whatever their reasons might have been and called making fake allegations. Shouldn't that person be convicted for perjury, brought in, and then explain why he or she did what they did?"

I recall that the fat one was surprise at my questions. Then that was the first time that I see her not really insisting on more investigators coming out to my house. They told me that they were going to close the case. I was really upset behind this ordeal and really wanted to know who the person was that had done it.

Anyway.

At this time in my life, it's just that I was totally unaware I'm living among wolves, who are people. Totally unaware of how they think and how they act.

Back then I remembered hearing a lot of talk around that time. People were calling BCW and their children were being removed from their home. I remember questioning to myself, all these Black mother are abusing their kids? Then also I was thinking and looking at how all these Black families' homes was just breaking up and being destroyed. Thinking that maybe the parents were all on drugs and then feeling sorry for the innocent mothers and their children's, especially if they were false. These times, were the early nineties, when people were making these calls without leaving their names. A lot of children got into the system this way and a lot of Black American family traditions went out the window. It seems like every time you turn around someone was calling BCW and a black child was being removed from their home.

I been writing since this morning. I'm hungry now. I put down my pen from writing to stop thinking about my past. Looking up I see lots of ladies forming a line. Lunch, in the shelter is about to be served. I'm sat in the dining room waiting just to see what was on the ladies' tray, before I decide what I was going to have for lunch.

One girl has finally come over to my side in the dining room with her' tray. I ask, "What's for lunch?" The lady reply, "Salami sandwiches and chicken noodle soup."

Lacy enters into the dining room area with her' tray and had taken a seat by the window. She been out walking all day. I get up and walk where Lacy was sitting. I ask her, "Lacy, can you do me a favor? Can you watch my bag for me so I could go to the store?"

Lacy turns around look at me and say, "Could you leave me alone?" Then she turned back around-start to eat her food. I'm not mad at her; because living in this type of environment, you can't be that sensitive. Everybody.... meaning us residents, well, we do all have our moments. So I turned around looking to see who else was in the dining room I could ask to hold my seat, while I go get something to eat.

I see Doris, now I walk over to Doris and I say, "How're you doing?" "I'm fine Electra. How are you?" She asks. I responded "I'm fine. Doris I want to go around the corner to the pizza parlor to buy a slice. Can you watch my bag because I don't feel like going thru the hassle of lugging my bag and I don't want to lose my seat?"

Doris say, "Look Electra. I'm not going to be down here all day. Right after lunch, I'm leaving." I say, "Seriously, I'll be right back. Please. You know how crowded it gets around lunch time especially since the weather change and it getting cold out."

"Electra hurry up, cause I'm not going to be down here fighting over no seats now," she said. "Thanks," I said as I quickly walked over to my area, grabbing my jacket.

The pizza parlor is around the corner. I see lots of females outside making it back to the shelter for lunch. You know whatz funny; we don't speak to each other when we're outside. It like an unspoken code. You would never think her, and, her over there, coming up the block lives in a shelter. It was like us residents', don't want yall (meaning people that lived in the neighborhood or work in the neighborhood) to know, that we live in the shelter, around the corner, or up the block.

Even our caseworkers or the shelter' other staff members, when we bump outside, we don't speak to each other, unless we're really cool with that individual and it would just be like, "Hi." You can never tell who live in a shelter and who don't, because not all shelter people stink, look raggedy, and beg for money or food. Some women dress really nice. Some have jobs, or go to school, and look normal, like any other person walking down the street. The only way an individual can tell who lives inside of a shelter is by standing nearby a shelter, and watching who all comes in and out.

I walked inside the pizza parlor. He asked "How can I help you?" "Can I have two slices; one with sausages and the other one plain," I order.

For us residents, even us, like I said, we all would never knew who all lives inside the shelter until you see the female who you know who lives in a shelter talking to another female. Then the next time when you see that person you know, who lives in the shelter. You would be like, "Does she live in the shelter too?" The person you know would be like, "Yeah." Then a resident would say, "What. I didn't know that she lived, in the shelter too. Or I hear residents say, "She lives in a shelter too?" I had seen and heard that sentence happen all the time. The only way that you would be able to tell who all lived in the shelter, was well, first of all, you needed to know that the shelter is there. Then maybe you would see them going in or out of the shelter. Or you might have noticed that the person was in that particular area a lot-maybe see their face as they sit in places for long extensive time like a library, coffee shop, terminal and soup kitchens or standing on the corner.

Once I got my slices I ordered a fruit punch drink. The church would be coming over tonight so instead of buying my own snacks, I wait to eat up their snacks. I made it upstairs just as Doris had finished her lunch. "Thank you so much," I say. I had gone over to my seat in order to eat my own food.

Then I had started back with my writing. Let's go back *into the story.*

By this time in my life I was in contact with Yolanda; my new found hangout cousin, and telephone buddy. We had recently found out, down in our own family tree, that were cousins and we began getting to know one another. She told me about a home attendant program. Me wanting to get off the welfare system and needing money to help pay for Champagne' school fee. Therefore, I enrolled in the school and was given a specific starting date. In the meantime, I had to purchase a white uniform with white nurse like shoes.

After a long day and the kids done ate and bathe. I needed a little space from the kids and from the house, and my situation. I told my oldest daughter, "I'm going to take a plate of food to my dad' house. I want yall all to stay inside the bedroom and watch TV. If anybody knocks on the door do not answer it. Don't even leave the room."

I looked at my son and said "You hear me JB," because sometimes when I step out the house while leaving Champagne in charge he had a habit of showing his ass when I wasn't around.

I repeated, "JB do you hear me talking to you? I mean what I say, I don't want you to be running around in the house and you better not go by that door."

When I got to my father' building he buzzed me up. When I gave him his plate of food. I remember my father being very abrupt with me that night. I was having some problems and he knew but there was no need to cry on his' shoulder because he couldn't help his own self.

He's a coke head. Someone who was constantly getting high. His drug of choice was cocaine. So how can he help me? I was always cleaning his house taking care of him. Anyway after I gave him his plate of food, he said "Electra go home to your kids."

Normally I check his fridge throwing out spoil food. Tidy up a little and taking out the trash.

This particular night daddy had told me to leave. Maybe because he known that someone had already called BCW on me. My father apt going to and coming from total only a five-minute walk away from my house. Once I got inside my building. Rode up in the elevator. Coming out from the elevator I heard a familiar voice by my door. As I walk quietly. Remember, I can tiptoe really well. I was listening to the conversations and I couldn't believe what I was hearing.

I heard my mother voice. She was at my door saying, "Baby are you okay?" There was knocking sounds hitting upon my apartment door. My mother said, "Champagne are you in the house again by yourself? Open up the door Champagne, it's me, Nana."

As I had stood there listening, I wanted to see if my daughter or my son would have disobeyed me and opened up the door to a familiar voice......but they didn't. So I continue listening. I heard my mother say, "I don't know where my daughter is? Something told me to come over here to check-up on my grandkids." As I'm listening to my mother chat. I'm wandering who the person she had brought with her over to my apartment. From what I'm hearing by eavesdropping on the conversation, and what I pick up from the sound of my mother' voice, she was making me seem unfit in front of whomever it was she had brought with her.

I heard the person say, "hum, hum, hum." Those are sounds of disappointment as if the person is feeling sorry for my kids because my mother was painting a picture of me being unfit. My mother was also painting a picture of herself as a grandmother who is concern about their (my children) welfare and fears the worst that her daughter (me) was not worthy or capable of taking care of her own children.

My mother began knocking back on the door again. Almost like banging, saying, "Champagne, JB I know yall are in there. Now my mother she talking. She said, "I told you Pat I'm so concerned."

Ooh I know who the other person is. I couldn't take it anymore I walk right behind them and said "Mom what are you doing? Mrs. Miles looked like she almost jumped out of her' skin. She turns around and said, *"Hi Electra,"* while given me this half hearty smile.

I said, "Hello Mrs. Miles." As I pulled out my keys and had start to unlock my door. I said "Mom what you doing telling Mrs. Miles I'm not a good mother? And making it seem like I'm constantly abandoning my kid and hanging out with what money?" Mrs. Miles immediately said, "Electra it nice seeing you again. Take care of those kids. Bye. Sylvia, I wait for you downstairs."

So now, I and my kids are standing by our door. Champagne has Moet on her hip. JB next to her and I ask my mother, "Why were you trying to make it seem like in front of Mrs. Miles, I'm neglecting my kids?"

My mother said, "They had looked so skinny. Are you feeding them properly?" Then she started waving at the kids saying, "Hi, how yall doing? Thomas came by my house. He said he was concerned about them. He was saying that you were not taking care of them."

I shouted, "And you believed him! My mother said "Electra why would he want to lie?" I said, "Mom I can't believe you listening to Thomas especially since we had broken up. He hasn't helped me financially with these kids since he been gone. He come over to your house telling you a bunch of lies and you believed him and bring Mrs. Miles over here with you as you try and make me look bad in front of her?"

My mother didn't know what the fuck to say. I said, "**Mom I heard you**!" Then all of a sudden my sister Tonya voice appeared. She by the staircase and Tonya immediately jumped in and had said all loud and nasty, "So what if mommy came over here! She concerned about the kids!

552

Thomas had told her that you were not taking care of the kids."

I'm shocked to see Tonya and I can't believe her tone of voice while she speaks. Then at what she is implying. I say, "And how do you know if that's true? If you're so concerned, just don't come over here making accusations. What happen to knocking on my door, coming in, and seeing for yourself how I'm doing? Then if you see something wrong what about asking me? What can you do to help? Don't just come over to my place embarrass me then to bring Mrs. Miles with yall, trying to incriminate me too."

Looking at my mother I asked, "And since when you and Thomas became so close? That you can come over here bringing his name out from your mouth! And defended him too."

Some people in my building had started to come out from their' apartment doors wondering what the commotion was about with me. Shelby oldest son came on the floor with some of his friends when they heard my voice loudly talking, echoing, in the building. Even Karl had sat on the steps with his friends actually listening to me argue with my family.

When Tonya seen the crowd forming she had not known that there were a lot of people in my building that knew me and cared about me. Some of them had probably even felt sorry for me when they saw me struggling after Thomas and I had broken up. Tonya said, "You know you're not doing a good job in taking care of these children. You're leaving them alone in the house all the time."

Stunned! I can't believe Tonya was standing there, telling me what I was doing and she never comes to my house. I said "You got some nerves, being you never came inside my apartment. Where did you get that information from? I don't be leaving my kids in the house by their own selves all the time. Stop lying."

"Yes you do, and you can't tell me you don't. I know you Electra," Tonya said.

I said "You don't know shit! How you going to tell me what I do when you don't even come anywhere around me! So stop talking about things you don't even know anything about."

First of all, I couldn't even believe that Tonya came over to my house, even though she standing is in the hallway. Then for her to say I was not a good mother! While coming over here and popping shit about what she thinks she knows about me, in front of my kids and neighbors too.

Then the boys and other neighbors had started whispering "Who are these people bothering Tami? Shelby oldest son asked me "Tami who are these people?" Not wanting the boy to worry I said, "That's my mother and my sister."

Sounds had started echoing in the hallway from the crowd. "We never saw them before. That's her family. I never knew that she had a mother...or a sister."

Some of the young boys came to my defense saying loudly in the background "She's a good mother. Who are yall? Go back where you came from."

Shelby' oldest son had run down the steps. Apparently he ran down the steps to go get Shelby. Before I knew it Shelby was upstairs too. When Tonya seen the small crowd she wanted to impress them. She said, "You can't take care of your kids. I'm going to call BCW on you because I care for my nieces and nephew. You are leaving them all the time in the house. They look hungry like you are not feeding them. This is a case for BCW. You need help! I'm not going to let you abuse the kids anymore. You need to have your kids taken away from you. I'm going to make that call for their own sake."

I couldn't believe my ears so I walk up to Tonya angrily and said, "What do you mean; you are going to call BCW. I dare you come over here popping shit about me and my kids." I went to hit her because she had made me so mad.........and before I knew it my mother jumped on me from behind. She had me in a head lock twirling me around and punching me in my head. Shelby started screaming and so did Champagne.

My mother jumped on me to stop me from getting to Tonya. I'm shock, my mother on me like that and was hitting me too! I was scuffling with my mother trying to get her arms from around my neck from choking me, as I watch Tonya run down the steps-she saying, "I'm going to the precinct to tell them these kids need to be removed right now."

My mother holding me down in this kind of neck choke as I'm trying to free myself from her grip. It may have looked like we were fighting but honestly I was trying to get her off of my fucking neck!

I could have punched my mother in her face for jumping on me like that. I wanted too but my kids were watching and besides I'm a decent person.

The bible scripture read "Honor thy mother and father that your days may be long on earth." I had always hold the upmost total respect for my parents. That just how I'm made even though I wanted to punch her in her face so bad. I finally gotten my mother arms off from around my neck. I shouted "**mom what's wrong with you!**"

Rubbing my neck, I moved to the left, while wanting to contain my balance. Directly in front of me my mother, she had stepped to the left, while huffing and puffing like she wanted to fight. She had both fist balled up, maybe she had probably thought that she had deserved a fight. Then again, maybe she wanted me to fight her because it was part of the plan, in having my kids removed, as Tonya went to bring in the po-po.

In those quick seconds I saw my mother railed up like she wanted to fight me. As I came more into focus breathing in the air from her choke hold, looking behind my mother I saw Shelby who was crying. She standing next to my kids in shock, crying saying, "That's your mother fighting you like that?" Then the horrible look on my kids face. They were waiting to see what was about to happen next.

I'm all they have, and I really see that now. At that time, the picture was much bigger than fighting. It was so, so much bigger. So I walked around away from my mother to my kids who was looking at me with horror in their' eyes, and with, total disbelief, at what they just seen. I'm standing by the door where my crying girlfriend was. Someone had to be the bigger person. I told my kids to "Come inside the house."

My kids were at stake. Their emotions, and their removal from our home, due to my reaction could have been devastating. This moment could had interrupt their own picture of family, trust, love, honor, respect and my family traditions. I didn't want to see those things damage because I believe in those things. I didn't think that was cool my children seeing me beating up on my mother. Or my mother beating me up. She my mother for **Christ sake** and that's not how I roll, even if she does deserve to get **punch in her face**!

How can I teach my kids to respect me and believe in our family traditions if they see me fist fighting with my own mother? Also most importantly those feeling of safeness, by a nurturing parent that's responsible and in control. It important to me, that they could also depend on me, to come thru for them. So on that note I walked away from my stupid mother with my kids and I lock my door.

When we all got inside the house. I rewash their' face, hand and feet because I hate grimy dirty stuff on clean sheets. That was a little too much excitement for them.... and for me too. It late, they should be in bed sleeping. My oldest daughter that night when I was preparing her for bed, was so upset. Champagne said, "I don't like Nana anymore. I hate her."

That's the first time she ever express hatred to me towards anyone. I just looked at my daughter not having anything positive to say. She asked me, "Why did she do that mommy?" From that night on, that when I noticed I seen a change in Champagne, whenever my mother came around us.

Shelby sat in the living room quietly crying because I saw tears rolling down her face as I'm putting my children to bed. When I was finish I went inside the living room where Shelby was at.

"Tami that was your mother behaving like that?" She had asked as she were wiping the rolling tears from her' eyes looking at me wanting an answer. "Tami is that your mother!" She had asked me again because I wasn't saying anything.

"Well she didn't look like a mother to me! All I saw was two horns sticking up from her head. All that was missing was the tail. I can't believe your mother treated you that way," she said.

I was speechless, and embarrass myself. I didn't want to discuss my mother ugly behavior because I was hurt and couldn't justify her actions myself. All this is so surreal. I called AP on the telephone.

I said, "Hello. AP you won't believe it! I just got jumped by my mother and my sister for Thomas. My sister is trying to get my kids taken away from me. I don't know who all they have with them at the precinct so could you come with me down there? Just in case they try to jump me again."

I heard AP say on the phone to her husband, "JP Tami need my help. We may have to kick ass. I'll be back."

I told Shelby, "AP is on her way over here."

"Get the fuck out of here. You mean to tell me all this happen because of Thomas? No way! Tami your mother just jumped you, and you're telling me, she did this because Thomas told her something to the effect, that you not taking care of the **dam** kids?!" Shelby questioned.

Shelby started shaking her head in unbelief saying, "But that **YOUR** mother. Why would she take Thomas side over yours? This is some shit! I don't understand this shit," she said as she shook her head from left to right.

I asked Shelby, "What made you come upstairs?" Shelby replied "My son told me you having problems with some people, but I didn't know it was with **your family**! And that your sister?"

I was so embarrassed.

I didn't know what to say to Shelby. She seeing me go thru all this bullshit. I just didn't know how to respond because I'm so angry. Wanting to calm down and see what my no good family was up too I said, "Well I just called AP. She should be here soon. I want to go to the precinct to see if a child abuse complaint had been filed by my sister; like she said she was going to do. Shelby with all of this going on, I'm really scared to leave the kids alone. Please can you stay here while I and AP go down there to the precinct?"

"Your mother. Thomas, **and your sister**; you'd better take someone with you, because from what I just saw... you need someone on your side," Shelby said, as she sat there. Then she said, again "That was your MOTHER?"

The reason Shelby keep saying that is because she is very close to her own mother and she close to her sisters too. Shelby knows I'm a decent person and she is a witness to everything that's going so wrong in my life. Or has went wrong so far in the time Shelby has been in my life.

I looked up from writing.

Just to see that we, have a new female guard. I see the shift had changed. The time is 4:00. The dorms were opened. I started packing up my belongings. Samantha enters into the dining room her stapling a notice up on our small dining room bulletin board. Before I gone upstairs. I stop to read the notice plastered on the board.

It read:

Come one. Come all to Holy Divine Thanksgiving feast.

Located 3506 Rutland Blvd. Brownsville section of Brooklyn.

Dinners will be served promptly 12 noon.

Menu consist of Turkey, cranberry sauce, String beans and mash potatoes.

Wow Thanksgiving came so quickly. I wonder if any of the residents be going to this celebration? Because I'm thinking maybe I go, and we can all go together.

When I got close to the new female guard I said, "Hello. What is your name?" She said Nookie. She looks black but her grade of hair and her skin tone make her look mix with Spanish. When I got inside my dorm I notice my neighbor had nothing on top of her locker, just like me.

The dorm looks so much better with all those bags gone. Maintenance has sweep and mopped the floor. I knocked on the bathroom door and Pepsi answered. So I walk back to my area. I take off my clothes wrap the towel around my body. From out my locker I get out the Tilex bottle and the sponge to wipeout the tub, my soap... oh, I see I need more soap. My soap bar is so small.

See what I mean about living inside a shelter. I already walked up the step, have off my clothes, preparing myself to take a shower. I don't even feel like putting back on my clothes. Then, putting everything back inside my locker just to run downstairs to get a care kit **and**......I'm next to go in the bathroom too.

Shoot! I start searching through my locker to see what I can substitute with. I look inside my care kit package and take out the small bottle of shampoo. When Pepsi come out, I'll next. So I'm sitting on my bed with one plastic glove on, waiting for Pepsi to come out the bathroom. Clearly, whoever comes inside the room can see that I'm next in line for the bathroom.

When Pepsi came out. I went in. After I bathe. I laid a crossed my bed thinking, I forgot I went through all that stuff. I took out my pen to continue writing.

Back to the story. The sound, of knocking sounds are now coming from the Q dorm door. It stops me from continuing to write about my past. The door opens, "Ladies there will be no church service tonight," the security guard had announced.

Once I heard that I pick back up my pen.

AP knocked on the door and we left. When we got to the precinct, I saw a black lady sitting behind a shielded window. I asked the woman, "Did a woman come in here? She had on a red bubble jacket, wanting to make a child abuse complaint."

The black women who sat behind the shielded window said, "Yes she did, but we threw her out, because she wasn't making any sense and we had smelled alcohol on her breath."

I'm looking at AP. Shock my sister really tried to get my children removed. While looking at AP I said, "Maybe I should take out an order of protection on them. Since after all they were the ones who started the fight with me over my kids?" AP said, "Whatever you want. I told JP I was with you."

When I went back to the window I asked, "How do I go about filing a complaint and obtaining an order of protection because someone just jumped me in front of my kids?"

That was when this white man had intervened, and said "You shouldn't do that because if any report is filed and there are children involved, that an automatic open case for Child Welfare to get involved." I'm looking at this man, like who is he and where did he come from? He walked over to me from behind the blocked area and extended out his' hand saying "Hi I'm Salvatore Finaoni. Detective of the 56th precinct. Talk to me. Tell me what's going on." Reader, Goodnight.

Chapter Twenty

I open my eyes to a stream of light coming in from the hallway gleaming into the dorm. I see someone has cracked open the door wanting ventilation because our room' door was ajar. It's being held open by a bunch of rolled up newspapers, which has been placed in between the door hinges and the door frame. Roommates that live inside the dorm, do have the right to crack open the dorm door when the person chooses. Most likely you will find it happening after bed check when girls are in their beds sleeping or reading with a flash light.

Even if another resident from another dorm, see a dorm door open, or close, the rule of thumb is, if you don't live inside of that dorm, you can't come in. If someone, who doesn't live inside the dorm wants to enter, she must first get the permission from a female that does live, in that dorm.

Say that female who allowed an outsider to enter into the dorm, does it quite often, then her roommates' will detest it verbally in order to put a stop in doing it. By limiting the flow of people coming in and out of a dorm, it helps to stop theft and uncleanliness in the bathroom. It's bad enough having 10 people share one bathroom and there's only just one toilet. In addition, these 10 people you already got to compromise in dealing with, hopefully, their cleanliness or dirtiness or their sloppiness of leaving personal items left behind in the bathroom. It's just a no-no for outside residents to really enter into others' dorms, because bad enough in your dorm there is already, 10 faces you got to see and 10 personalities you have got to deal with. This is a rule of thumb for all dorm living, inside all shelters, and this rule is taken very seriously.

If there is a roommate who keeps allowing outsiders into the dorm after her' roommates or roommate had spoken to her about it. That roommate who doesn't like it do have an option to go to the staff and report it, also, by writing up an incident report. For security this is another one of their job descriptions, knowing which client, belongs in what dorm.

Getting out from my bed I walk to the bathroom door. I automatically turn the door knob because around this time of the night everyone is usually sleeping. The door didn't open. Looking around my dorm I notice bed # 1, the Mexican chick is the one in the bathroom because due to the fact, her bed is the only one that's empty. Immediately I said to myself...she's in the bathroom again! I tapped lightly on the door not wanting to wake up my roommates.

"Un a minto etc, etc, etc, etc." What is she saying? I don't understand Spanish so I knocked again on the door. I heard a loud gurgle and then the sound of a loud split, while not understanding why she always in the bathroom late in the night. I sat on my bed waiting for her to come out but she didn't come out right away. As a matter of fact, she didn't come out all. So I waited a little while longer then got up and lightly tap on the door again. She didn't answer. I looked over at the time and it was 1:10 am and I see, she not coming out. So I put on my flip flops and go inside of the hallway. I'm turning the corner, down a distance, a couple of feet ahead, I see security Guard Nelson sitting on his post by the laundry mat. He's Caribbean too.

As he had sat there, looking down the hall watching me because he is wondering where I'm going this time of night? I walked straight to him and stop in front of him to say, "Nelson. I need to use the bathroom but that Mexican chick has locked herself up inside the bathroom." He asked "How long she been in there?" I said, "I been waiting for fifteen minutes."

Security guard Nelson said "There's nothing I can do. Wait, she'll be out soon." I told him "I really need to use the bathroom through." "Well use the bathroom in the dining room," he suggested.

I take the stairs to the second floor. I go inside of the intake office. I see Mr. Berry and I go over to him and tell him "Mr. Berry, that Mexican girl locked herself up in the bathroom again. She won't come out and I need to pee."

Mr. Berry replies "I didn't hear anything from the guard on the floor like there's a problem. Did you ever think her using the bathroom?" I said, "I notice her always in there late at night though." "That's not a crime Electra. You can go use the bathroom in the dining room," he suggested.

After using the bathroom in the dining room. I go back inside the intake office and ask for a care kit. RA Alfre pulls out a care kit package from underneath the desk and hands it to me. As she gets up getting the care kit book for me to sign I open the care kit packing up, checking that I have all the supplies like soap, a soap holder, toothpaste, toothbrush, and the small container of baby powder, a small container of shampoo/body wash, a small package of Kleenex facial tissue and the thin tube of Vaseline.

After signing my name and the date when I received the care kit package. I filled out a resident complaint form.

Resident: Electra. Time: 1:15 am. Location: Q dorm bathroom. Description of complaint: It not fair I have to use the bathroom in the dinner room because Q1 is in the bathroom spitting, gagging and coughing. She in there all the time late at night reading her bible and she doesn't even attend church or come to the church services which are held here inside the shelter. Please get her out of the bathroom. The time now 1:41 am.

When I had reached my floor coming out from the exit, Nelson gave me a smile. When I got to my dorm I look to see if I saw that Mexican chick in her bed. And she wasn't. Not falling asleep right away I remembered the first time I met Detective Salvatore Finaoni.

Reader, let go back *into the story.*

Surprise by his gesture of wanting me to talk to him about my problems, and overwhelm with all the wrong issues going on in my life. I look at him like I didn't know where to start. He said "Wait a minute is she with you?"

He pointing to AP. He asked "Who is she?" I said, "She's a friend who came down here with me for support."

He asked AP "What's your name?" AP walked over to us and said, "My name is Angela Penn Gillmore." The detective said "Alright."

He looked at me and said "Follow me." As we walked he had pointed his' finger for me to say my name. I said, "Electra Tami Jones."

He opens up the wooden gate for me to walk through. I'm looking back at the receptionist. She smiles at me, encouraging me to speak to him. Like, I'm in good hands as if he a good cop because she could see I was troubled and weigh down with a dilemma.

When we got to his' office there was a vendor machine on the floor. He brought me a can soda. He opens it for me. He said "Here take this." After handing me the soda he sat behind a desk. He asked me to have a seat. Then he said "Talk to me."

I started telling this detective, "I was with my children' father for over 5years. After a while I became unhappy with the relationship. I'm trying to be a good mother and wanting to see him contribute more to the house, but he wasn't. Because all of his money was going to Jamaica. All the bills are in my name.... because it's my apt. So with my money, I put my daughter in private school while wanting to see him spend more of his money, towards benefiting me and our kids. But the only thing on his mind is supporting the people in Jamaica. When we came home from the hospital with our last child. His father unexpectedly died, causing him to return to Jamaica again-where he stayed about a month. Leaving me to struggle all alone paying the bills with an infant and two small kids while I was in pain after my surgery of getting my tubes tied. I thought he cared about me and hopefully we would get married, and buy a house. But I found out... I was being used. So I kicked him out. Now I fell behind in my daughter school fee and now I got to pay the late charges. He mad because I kicked him out! Now, he started spreading rumors about me and tried snatching my son from me wanting to send him off to Jamaica. Because he wants him to have an accent. I have a light bill that needs to be paid. I just enrolled into a training school for myself. All I wanted was a good steady home to raise my kids up in. Eventually, hopefully get marry. Tonight my sister threaten to call, BCW and my mother just jumped me because he's telling my mother, I'm an unfit parent" ......then before another word came out from my mouth I had broken completely down and started crying. I couldn't stop. I cried. And I cried. And I cried. And I cried. And I cried and cried for a while. I never cried in front of anybody before, not even my own parents or family members ever seen me cry the way I was crying in front of this perfect stranger.

Here I am crying. I cried for a while. I don't know for how long I was crying for while my head was in both hands lying on my lap, just weeping. At some point I suddenly realized I'm crying......and, I guess I got it all out. I had to get it out one way, all my frustration of what I been experiencing lately. All I know I was just crying. Finally, when I had gotten myself together. Now wanting to compose myself because I can't believe I just cried like that ....and in front of a total stranger. So I found myself listening to the silence in the air while my head was in my hands, laying on my lap because I was crying. I guess I just lost it.

I'm listening to the silence in the room with my hands covering my face as I laid there with my head on my lap......... I'm wondering.......... where he at?

Feeling completely embarrass because I just lost it-as I laid with my head down on my lap, again, I'm wondering where he was? So I spread my fingers apart to see if I saw his feet standing anywhere near me or around me. I'm sniffling as I'm still listening to the silence in the room. Sniffling up the liquid that ran out from my nose. Through my fingers all I saw was my long braids that were dangling down in front of me. So I lift up my head as I wiped the tears away from my face.

Salvatore, he's sitting behind the desk with a box of Kleenex tissue in his hand pointing the box of tissue in my direction waiting for me to take a few. I did take some tissues to blow my nose and to wipe the remaining tears off my face as I looked straight ahead while slumping back in the chair feeling embarrassed......I'm tired, and I felt slightly relived.

He asked me "Do you feel better?" I didn't say anything. Immediately he said "Apparently your mother is taking his' side in things." While shaking his head, he said "I don't understand why your' sister will do something like that. After listening to what you told me the first thing you got to do is take your daughter out from the private school."

I suck my teeth cause DAM! I didn't want to do that because she loved her school. I'm sitting there thinking all this happen within seven and a half months after I had given birth to my daughter. Then the unspeakable happened, we broke up. It just kept going on downhill and getting worst.

Wanting to rationalize with me, Detective Salvatore said "Public school not that bad. I went to public school and I turned out alright. Did you go to public school?" Upset I nodded my head and said, "Yeah. I did," while resting my elbow on the desk with my hand upon my face thinking, what all I did to make a good relationship with this man and to give my kid a piece of the good life, what a waste.

He said "Well you turned out alright."

He could see the disappointment of failure which was written all over my face. I guess bringing me back to the matter at hand, Salvatore said "Clearly your mother is taking his side. Maybe she doesn't want to see her beautiful daughter, struggle by herself. You don't know what he could be telling her about you. I'm a man and obviously he upset he allow someone, like you to get away." I looked at him cause what a kind thing to say.

Looking directly at me he said "From what you are telling me." He smiled and continued "You sound like you are a good person, not to mention, **you are beautiful**."

I'm thinking, "What a great compliment coming from this establish man because, he is really a handsome man. Jet Black hair. Stocky, well maintained in his physic. Mouth full of teeth. He wasn't a bad looking man at all.

He said "You know; you are a beautiful looking black woman." "Thanks," I said, realizing that cry kind of made me feel a little bit better.

Then he had gotten up from his chair and said "You did mention something about going back to school." I said, "Yeah. I will be starting soon." "That's good. You should do something personal for yourself now," he agreed.

He asked "How many kids you said you have again?" I said, "Three." He asked "Who's with your kids now?" I said, "A girlfriend who lives in my building." Looking towards the door Detective Salvatore said "Come on. You'd better get back home to your kids."

Walking down the steps he said, "Electra everything going to be okay."

Then he called my name again. When I looked back he said "Here." I reached out my hand and underneath his hand I'm surprise it was money. When I saw the money in my hand automatically I got upset "Oh man." I thought he was thinking that I was a trick about to make a proposition. Upset and not with the program I said, "Take it back. I don't need your money."

Detective Salvatore said "It's not for you, it's for the kids. I don't want to see them in the dark." I got quiet for just a moment because I didn't expect to hear him say that. Salvatore said "I been on my job for 17 years. I have a home. I travel and at this point, I have no regrets in my life. I could do a good deed for someone who clearly deserves it."

Not in no mood to argue I put the money in my pocket and said "When I get my job I will pay you back." "Don't worry about it," he said.

As we walked in silence down the steps he said "Listen go home take a bath and get some rest."

When we reach downstairs by the woman who sitting behind the shielded window, Detective Salvatore he walked both AP and I to the exit door of the precinct. Then he said "Electra here." This time when I looked it was his' business card. "Take it. Call me when you reach home."

When I got home I told both my girlfriends, "Thank for being here. I really appreciate your help." They both wanted to stay. I assured them both I'm fine just exhausted. AP went to her home and Shelby went to hers. Feeling exhausted, I went inside my bedroom reached in my pocket and when I saw the money I took it out. The money was rolled up. I counted the money and it was 100 dollars! Is he aware that he had given me 100 dollars? I called the number on the card. He picked up immediately "Detective Finaoni."

I said, "Hi." Immediately he said "Electra. So you made it home." "Yes I did," I said. He asked "So this is your number?" I'm thinking, he has caller id.

I ask, "Are you aware you gave me 100 dollars?" Quickly he said "So what? I have no complaints in my life. Take a bath and get some rest. I call you tomorrow to see how your day turns out."

I stopped writing and reminiscing about Detective Finaoni. I turn around in my bed at the shelter to read the clock that's hanging on the wall. Time now is 2:28am. I speak to yall when I get up in the morning.......... You know that Mexican chick is still inside of that bathroom. Getting out from my bed I creep tip-toe like to open up my locker, putting up my notes. The bathroom door opens. So I turn my head, I looked at her holding on to the closed bible. She mumbling something to herself as she walks to her bed.

Watching her, as she walks to her bed, I'm thinking I don't care what nobody say, something not right. So I go inside of the bathroom to see what she could have been doing in there. I close the bathroom door and then lock it. Quietly, I open up the basin doors looking for anything usual. I didn't smell anything out of the ordinary. I didn't see anything left behind. The bathroom garbage can is full but I'm not going through that without my plastic gloves. So I open up the bathroom door and goes to bed. I immediately fall asleep.

"Good morning ladies, its six o'clock. Breakfast will be served downstairs." As I turn over I caught a glimpse of Abuja who was just about to leave the dorm. While coughing, "Good morning Abuja," I said. She turns her face in my direction and said, "Good morning Miss Jones," right before exiting the room to continue her rounds.

Yawning as I give myself a good arm stretch. I'm surprise I'm up early. I was not that tried after going to bed so late last night. Sitting up on my bed I see we had gotten two new roommates. One in bed 7 and the other is in bed 8. Wow, they must have come in, in the wee hour of the night, because I went to bed late last night. Anyway our dorm is completely full again. I'm going to Dunkin donuts to buy me a cup of hot coffee. I want to get a good start with writing today. Later on, I plan on going to Jose, to see if I could cash in some of mine food stamps. After tying up my sneakers, I grab my tooth brush and the small bar of soap to wash my face and hands. I get inside the bathroom before anyone else jumps out of bed and run in there.

After washing my face, I'm about to brush my teeth. "Urrrnnn.... Urrnnnnnnn." I said "Get out of here!" Repeated loud sounds of Urrrnnn.... Urrnnnnnnn. Oh shit us having another fire drill. Dam! This early in the morning, again?

I'm so glad they didn't catch me off guard this time. Urrrnnn.... Urrnnnnnnn. Urrrnnn.... Urrnnnnnnn. Abuja the security guard **buss** through the Q dorm door motivationally announcing "Fire drill! Fire drill! Everyone get up, fire drill!"

I walk out the bathroom. "It's a fire drill Miss Jones. You got to leave the building," Abuja shouted. "Calm down," I said "Yeah I hear the alarm."

"Get up fire drill. Everyone get up," the guard said as she hurries to the next door doing the same thing. I looked at my roommates ain't nobody budging, they all still in the bed sleeping.

I grab my Jacket and put away my toothpaste and soap. Take another look at my roommates. Lots of girls are still sleeping in their bed. I'm thinking Abuja going to have a hard time getting them out the bed so early in the morning because after a while residents get tired of the shelter fake fire drills and they do it constantly too-early in the morning or late at night, they don't care. Time now is 6:25 am.

Quickly, wanting to beat the crowd that will be coming down the steps. A resident is allowed to leave the building, at 6 am, without being consider a curfew violator. If I would have walked out of the building before 6 am, the staff would had taken my bed away saying I'm a curfew violator. Since I know 6 am is safe for me to leave the building when I got downstairs I had walked right out the building going around the corner to Dunkin Donuts.

I ordered a cup of hot coffee and a toasted bagel. Sitting down I watched the alarming fire trucks race down the street to the building. You know Dunkin Donuts has a TV inside their establishment. I remember how I used to order a cup of coffee just to watch the soaps. With nothing else to do I use to sit there sipping my coffee slowly while watching people, police officers, students come in and out of Dunkin Donuts during commercials.

After sitting there for a while I got up heading back to the shelter. I didn't even make my bed due to the fire drill. The time is now 8:00 am. Bridge Net' staff shift has changed. When I walk up to the shelter I saw RA Alfre who serve out the breakfast. She's outside waiting for the bus to take her home.

When I reached the Shelter, security guard Watts was at the door. She performed her' job procedures then allow me to go inside the shelter. This time I waited for the elevator. Moving out of the way as girls piled out from the elevator. The majority of them are going out into the yard. I rode the elevator up to the fourth floor.

I see security guard Monique is now patrolling the fourth floor.

When I got to my dorm, the majority of my roommates were there but I didn't see Valerie or Pepsi. Looking at my new roommates, one was a much older lady. She had a small frame and was black, but I couldn't tell what her' nationality was. She had looked to be into her late fifties.

The other new girl is black too. She a little heavy set. She taking her' belongings out of the large clear plastic bags and arranging her stuff inside the locker. After I finished making my bed, I walk out of the dorm with my tote bag and my jacket.

Earlier when I went out for coffee, the weather was a little nippy out there. That meant the dining room was going to be crowded. Thank goodness, I happen to find my seat at a table by the window. I pulled out blank sheets of paper to write.

Back to the story.

Detective Salvatore he calls me the next day around five. "Hello Electra how are you?" "Good," I said. I told him, "Thanks for the advice. I took my daughter out from the private school and had registered her in the public school down the block from me."

He said "Very good. I know you meanl well by your daughter but sometimes, things just happen. How did she take the change?"

I told him, "Well, I explained it to her this morning. That today it will be her last day at St Marks Academy because I can't afford the school payments anymore. Being, I'm **always** trying to find something positive from a negative situation.... so... I told her, the best thing about her new school was.... it's down the block and that she would no longer need to ride the bus by herself. Or have to get up so early. Point blank, she wasn't too happy about changing schools."

Then he asked me "Did you buy yourself anything out from the money?" I replied "No. I brought Champagne, her new school uniform. You know school uniforms aren't cheap. I spent good money on her private school uniforms. I had brought her blouses, skirts, sweaters and 2 pair of burgundy pants. Her old school colors were burgundy and white but the uniform she wore she no longer needs because her new school uniform is a different color. Now her school colors are blue and yellow."

Salvatore asked me "So what you doing now?" I said, "I'm about to cook dinner and feed the kids." "Alright good. I call you later. Bye for now," he said.

Sure enough, he's a man of his word. He did call me back. He asked me "What's going on? You sound relax." I said, "I know. It's quiet. We had a busy day between yesterday and today. I'm sitting up watching TV with the kids." He said "Could you come to the precinct." I said, "Alright."

When I reached the precinct he gave me a **box** of hair products. The good stuff to. Nexus shampoos and the conditioners and Nexus gloss for shine. He has great taste and he smelled so good. I asked him, "So what time are you getting off tonight?" He said "Around midnight. .... Electra." "Yes Salvatore," I said.

"Enjoy your shampoo. I think your children are waiting for their' mother to put them to sleep. Good night Miss Jones," he said.

Went I had got home, my telephone rung. "Hello," I said. "Hi Electra it me Yolanda." I said, "Oh whatz up." Yolanda ask me, "You ready for school?" I said, "Yeah I got my uniform and everything."

"That's real good. Why it so quiet in your house?" Yolanda asked. I said, "I just put the kids to bed. **Yo**, I met this cop." "You met a cop? When did you meet a cop?" Yolanda asked. I said, "That night when my mother and sister jumped me." "Yeah, I heard about that shit," Yolanda said. "Who told you?" I asked.

Yolanda said, "Girl you know Tonya tell my sister Cheryl everything." "No I didn't know that," I said.

"Well now you do. I and Cheryl felt that was wrong though. I don't understand it. Your mother always helping out Tonya with her kids," Yolanda said.

I asked, "How do you know." Yolanda said, "Electra. I just told you Tonya tells Cheryl everything. Plus, since Cheryl just moved to the project. You do know my sister lives in your sister' building right?" I said knowingly, "Yeah I heard Cheryl lives in the projects now." "Cheryl be at Tonya' house all the time," Yolanda told me. "Oh," I replied.

I asked, "So how you doing so far in the school." "I'm doing good. The only thing I got to tell you is stay on top of the lessons and you'll be fine. I see you in school. I gotta go get the kids ready for tomorrow. Bye." Yolanda said. "Have a good night. I see you in class," I told her.

The next day right before I was about to get Champagne from school, I get a knock at the door. "Who is it?" I asked. "Andy." That's the building new security guard because the building has been getting a little wild lately. Anyway he's Jamaican too.

Rushing to get Champagne, I just open the door and Andy hands me a piece of paper. When I had taken it. He said "You been served." I open my door wider and see Thomas grinning and he and Andy tap each other on the knuckles.

I questioned myself as I closed my apartment door reading the paper. I been served? The letterhead read family court......What he talking about? Nobody in my circle ever been to family court. I'm the 1st to experience this.

I read the letter. I couldn't believe **this shit!** Thomas served me with court papers. It read he didn't believe Moet is his' daughter. That he wanted proof. So he was asking for a maternity test. You know he is a son of a bitch, Moet and JB are both his' kids. Imagine, of all the years we shared living together. Thomas should have never moved in with me. He and I making babies with me believing my relationship with him had some kind of significant. I was totally faithful when I was with Thomas.

Only one time I ever had sexual intercourse with another guy and it was sometime after I have gotten my rest when Thomas had finally come back after burying his' father. He had cheated on me so I cheated back on him. There's an old saying that goes what's good for the goose, is good for the gander. Whatever that saying means, anyway it was pure revenge meaningless sex, and it was when I realize he wasn't loyal; **besides** Moet looks just like him.

You know looking back on it now maybe he was hoping that I had cheat. Me turning into a hoe. Hoping that I lose my values and morals and become a dog like him. Therefore, never taking any relationship seriously. Fucking all over the place, never wanting to settle down until I become numb inside, like him. Being unable to sustain in a healthy relationship not knowing how to love with my heart and soul.

I got caught up in the moment of being hurt so I cheated on him. Realizing his' unfaithfulness. I thought stupidly and I had wanted to hurt him. I had wanted to get him back for hurting me. I hate to say it but sometimes Black men can make you act that way, with their constantly cheating ways of seeming never wanting to settle down to make a commitment. All they want to do is just fuck and who behave that way... animals!

I'm not an animal fucking only when it's mating season. I'm a human being who would have love having children by a man who's totally committed to me. Us building a home together with pictures of our family on the wall, showing our celebration after celebrations. Sharing our memories of yesterday that are now cherish as we grow old together and seeing our children go off to live their own independently lives. I don't see anything wrong with that concept. What's wrong with sharing your life with someone and knowing that you have something more significant? I think that's beautiful, too bad our Black men don't see it like that. Anyway I know better now. Black men ain't shit and they want to stay like little boys who never grows-up.

For the record, I'm not talking about my dad or grand pop or granddaddy. Their marriages may had had their shares of up and downs and they maybe even had cheated, but at least as men, they grew up, wanting to settle down and got marry with someone at one point in their life. Another factor, is, it's how you grow up too that it does or probably will play a major role in your adult life, maybe that's why I feel this way. Seeing that my parents and grandparents were Mr. and Mrs.

Detective Salvatore called me later in the evening. He asked me "How was my day?" I told him "I got served with papers today for a maternity test because Thomas doesn't believe that the baby, our daughter is his."

Salvatore asked me "Is she?" Immediately I said "Yes!" He said "Then you don't have anything to worry about. Hey you never know maybe this can work out in your favor. Did you put the kids to bed early? So you can relax and enjoy some quiet time for yourself?"

Still piss off because I been served! I said, "They went to bed at their regular time. Tomorrow I try to put them to bed a little earlier so I can make more time for myself to unwind... So how was your day?" He told me he had done a double shift; that he didn't go home last night and that he's tired.

Then Detective Salvatore replied "Thank you for asking Miss Jones. Listen, your court date, I wouldn't advise you miss, so don't. Go get your beauty rest." "Goodnight," I said.

Then I started to notice a disturbance with Moet. Her eyes were becoming cross and she wasn't making sounds of trying to talk. I notice whenever I sat Moet in her walker all she did was sit. She didn't try to stand up on her legs. Becoming alarmed, I had taken her to the doctor. From there, I was set up with appointments to take her in for a series of therapy sessions. One was for voice and speech and the other was for learning-practicing excise for her limbs for walking. So lots of time I went back and forward to the clinic on her behalf.

Eventually the doctor gave my little pretty bald headed baby girl, glasses.

He had said that the eye glasses, it should help her eye muscles to develop stronger. Then I was taught how to practice various leg exercises, by pulling each leg forward and stretching the leg out as far as possible then bending the leg back, allowing the knee to become bent. Then, pull the leg completely out again. Also I had to flex each foot turning it left then right. Moving the toes back and forth as well as the foot for rotating her ankles.

My baby, I held and carrying her around a lot. I was glad she was born a girl because it gave me the opportunity to spoil her by holding her and kissing her a lot on her cheeks, because I knew, I wasn't having any more children. Knowing she would be the last baby of mine to hold so I wanted to embraces my mommy moment and really enjoy it -of holding my last child.

Plus, she was such a cut little bald headed baby girl. She had a little piece of hair sticking out from the middle of her head. I knew that she was going to have a lot of hair when she had gotten older and, out from all my children as babies, she favors me a little.

Today is my first day in court. When our case got called, the judge had asked "A petition filed for maternity by whom?" Why the judge asked that was because after re reading the paper Thomas had served me, it was conflicting, because it appeared like I wanted a maternity test, as if I'm the one who asking Thomas to appear in court. The judge held his head up from the court papers asking "Who making this petition?"

I looked at Thomas for him to say something. Finally, Thomas said "I want a test proving that she is truly my child." The judge took one look at Moet who was sitting on my lap. Then he looks back at Thomas. The Judge said to Thomas "Do you want to waste tax payer money this way?"

Because Moet look just like him. Even though I could see me in Moet. The truth is both my girls, favor and resemble their' father way more than they resembles me. After the judge made that comment, Thomas looked at Moet who has the same shape head just like him and that same droopy expression both of them can make with their eyes. He's looking at Moet and Moet looking at him; both of them with that same droopy look on their face. It was almost like looking in a mirror.

The judge asked Thomas "Do you have any doubt that this child I am looking at is your daughter?" Thomas looked stupid. He said "No your honor." Making fun of Thomas the Judge said "If you have any doubts we can perform the test, which I could say one hundred percent this child I'm looking at, is yours." Thomas looked so stupid.

Looking back on this now I guess the Judge viewed Thomas as a crappy irresponsible human being of a man because Thomas did such a stupid thing by bringing **ME** to court questioning maternity, when Moet look just like him. Then on the other hand in the court house I appeared like this young attractive but struggling descent mother, who looked financially poor. The Judge probably didn't take it as a joke. Seeing a struggling mother and wasting the court time for such foolishness and, I did not have a clue to the formalities of a court house. The judge is probably tired, of seeing time after time, the same old bull cramp from black men, making children, then leaving the women to struggle alone while running away from their share of responsibilities. Then leaving the Government to pick up the bill.

The Judge asked me "How many children do you have?' I said, "Three." He asked "Are they all by this man?" I said, "Him and I share two children together. We also have a son together. His name is Brandon." The judge asked me "Are you receiving any child support for your son from this man?" I said, "No."

The judge spoke to Thomas saying "You came down here saying you didn't think the baby girl was your child; but we just established that she is. I could see why at first you didn't want to support her but why are you not supporting your son? The child you know is yours."

Thomas said something so stupid!

Thomas said, "I didn't come down here for that." What a dumb thing to say. I was thinking, but, that's Thomas for you. He always never wants to compromise. It always got to be Thomas' way and what all he wants.

The judge response was "Well maybe you didn't come down here for that, but how are you helping support your children?" Thomas said "Whatever they need I buy."

The judge asked Thomas "Do you have any receipts proving you have been supporting these children?" Again Thomas looked so stupid because he didn't have anything to show and you know why, because he **wasn't** supporting his' children that's by me.

The judge asks me "Is there anyone helping you to support your children?" I said, "Yes." The judge asked "Who?" I said, "The city, because my children and I are on welfare. The city gives us our food stamps, pay my rent and our doctor fees too."

The judge just looked at me and so did Thomas.

The judge turned to Thomas and asked him "Do you work?" I looked at Thomas and I could tell that Thomas didn't like these questions. He started getting upset. Thomas knew he couldn't lie because he's not that stupid, he knew what the next question would be. Can I have your social security number?

The judge asked Thomas "How much money do you have in your pocket?" Thomas pull out a little over fifty dollars. The judge order Thomas to give me fifty dollars. Now I was Shocked!

Thomas was mad. The judge adjourned our court date and told Thomas next time to bring in his pay stubs to determine child support. That's what Thomas get, he tries to fuck me, but he fucked his self. What was he thinking, bringing me to court?

When I got home I started to practice various legs and foot exercises for Moet.

Salvatore called me on the phone "How did your day go?" I told him, "As far as the court goes the case had gotten adjourned. And at the moment I'm practicing various leg therapy right now, with Moet."

Then excitedly I said, "The judge made Thomas give me $50.00 right on the spot."

Detective Salvatore said "Just to think you were worried. It sounds like you had a good day, being that you're busy right now. I'll call you later on when you put the kids to sleep." And he did. Just like he been doing from day one when I first met him. He would call and then would ask "Tell me, what you did for yourself today?"

Anyway I also told him, "My big day is tomorrow. I'm going for home attendant training."

Today I put my nursing uniform on and went to class. The school was located in Flatbush. Nothing but a classroom filled with Caribbean students and even their instructors were Caribbean, who were the teachers. Yolanda and I were the only two African American Blacks in the class.

I took a picture for my ID badge and received a lot of medical papers in various subjects dealing with the elderly, home care, the human body, signs of problems such as bed sores, Alzheimer and methods for rotating the body. The school had dummy dolls for practicing CPR. A bed, for students learning properly how to make a bed and tips on how to make a bed while a patient lay in it.

The classes were design in cycles for the students. Every day a complete lesson was given **And** every day we had a test from the prior class lesson, that was taught. What the school was actually doing was cramming a year work of teaching, into a six months' program. So a person had to be very committed in order to complete and graduate.

I had to take off from school one day to take Moet to her scheduled appointment. When I took Moet to speech therapy. The therapist lady told me, "You should put her in movies. She could be a great actress one day, pretending that she can't speak when she really can."

It was time for Champagne to come home from school. As I stood waiting outside for her, approaching the building, Thomas had pulled up. He was driving in our old white car. He was really angry just because the judge had made him give me fifty dollars. He came out from the car and he had pick JB up. I wasn't worried about him running off with our son because I knew we had to go back to the court house.

He was saying "This is my son," showing the men in the car, JB. Then he put JB down and he started with his insults towards me again, saying loudly as he had laughed to the guys in the car, "Yeah the white man wants to give her my money. You see in Jamaica we don't have no white man telling us how to run our business. This is an American ting."

All the men were shaking their' heads up and down like in agreement.

"Me a man, eehey" then Thomas made a fist and he started tapping his fist to all the other men fist that were sitting in the car. I'm standing there looking and thinking, dam them mother fuckers hate Americans so much that they want to even change how we give five to each other. Remember back in the days when we Americans agreed upon something how we would slap each other hand, with a high five.

I recalled one day, when Peanut the Black American young boy who always hanging out in front of the building said "Yo, what up?" to Thomas and he went for a high five. I never forget what Thomas said and did. He said "No mon, like this." Thomas took Peanut hand, made a fist then with his' hand, he made a fist and Thomas tap his' fist to Peanut fist. That when I first saw this new way of black men greeting one another from Thomas, the Jamaican.

With Thomas. This Jamaican, I mean I was going to all of their' parties and eating their' food which I got to say, some of it is really **delicious**. I was even dressing like them with rip up tee-shirts and jeans, wearing **prum -prum** shorts, listening and dancing to reggae. I remember Thomas brought me a pair of earring but they were Caribbean style. A big gold leaf with a red stone smack in the middle. Couldn't tell me I wasn't Caribbean living with barrels in my house. Constantly shipping and having West Indian seasoning all up in my kitchen cabinets. I was doing so much of his lifestyle until I forgot who the fuck I was, An American. Thomas didn't want to do **ANYTHING** American.

So Im standing there watching him with his friends in our old car gloat, and the joke was on me. While watching Thomas walk back to the car to tap fist with each of his' corny friends through the car open windows. He forgot, **he's** the stupid motherfucker, because he's the one who took me to court in the first place. Trying to make the petition, look as if, I took him into court begging for his money.

Thomas saying "Only in America the white man tells you what to do but no sir, they not going to tell me nuting. I is a man not a boy, eehey. Me don't need nooobodtee telling me how to handle my business you understand that Tami?"

I told him, "Of course you do……. you uncivilized motherfucker. I be HELL, if you think, you going to come over here to my country and make a monkey out of me. Well you have another got damn thing coming! You the one who took me to court asshole! Now you're, coming over here, trying to embarrass me, in front of your friends. Acting like I'm begging **you** for **your** MONEY. You weren't supporting these children anyway. That's why I kicked your black ass out! That's why in America we do have a system for bum ass niggers like you. If you were supporting them, doing right by me for them we wouldn't be where we at right now **Thomas**!"

Thomas giggle while going back to the driver side of the car. As he walked to the driver side. Thomas said "I think Tami taking drugs but, you see me, I'm going to be the peace maker." He got in his' car and drove off.

When we got inside the apt, Champagne telling me that she was going on a school trip. After fixing dinner and checking on Champagne' homework, which is something I always did. I ran the water inside the bathtub. To me, it so much easier in letting children take a bath then a shower. This way they learn how to wash their' own bodies. I was also giving them some time to soak their' body inside the sudsy water. Then all I had to do was quickly rewash and then rinse. So easy.

At this stage of the game each child had taken their own bath separately too. Champagne had her' brother by a good couple of years in age and besides, JB being a boy, he's older than Moet. To make sure anyone didn't drown, their bath water level was small but enough water that each of my older children could enjoy their' bath. I came to realize children sleeps all night when they clean. I don't know, maybe it because I'm the one who enjoy taking a bath compare to a shower. The telephone rang so I picked it up "Hello." "Can you speak right now?" detective

Salvatore asked. I told him, "Let me call you right back. I'm taking the last kid out of the tub."

Time now is 9 pm. "Good night," I kiss that one. Kiss this one and kiss the last one. What a day I had. Walking to my bedroom I thought about Salvatore. So I called him.

"Hey how're you doing?" He asked all cheerful like he's happy that I return his' call. Next he asked "Where the kids?" "Finally in bed," I said. "Did you go to school today?" he asked. I said, "Nope, I had a medical appointment for Moet." "Can you come down here to the precinct for a second," he asked. "Sure no problem," I said.

Quickly I got to the precinct. I walked up to the shielded window and I said to the black receptionist "I'm here to see Detective Salvatore." She called him on the telephone. He came downstairs and asked me to follow him. Going up the steps he asked "Is everything alright with your daughter?" I said, "mum hum." We stop by a different office this time. He went in and I followed him as I was telling him how Thomas is a nuisance and how Karl is starting back up with his' harassment. Then how I hate seeing Adrianna see me struggle. How I wish my section eight voucher hurry up and come through."

Salvatore said "This is the second time I heard you mention section eight voucher. What is it?"

I explain, "A section eight voucher is a program for low income people. Geared purposely for giving money allotment going toward their rent. For example, say I find a three-bedroom apartment and the rent is $850.00 a month. You know I can't afford to pay that type of money. If the landlord accepts the section eight voucher through the section eight program, I will be able to pay the $850 dollars. The section 8 program will determine how much from my income I will have to contribute towards the rent of $850.00 dollars. Being I have a voucher and I'm on the program, I'm only expect to pay 30% of the rent according to my budget and the program will pay the rest."

"For how long," he asked. I told him, "As long as I qualify. Every year a person has to go thru recert... "Who's Karl?" he abruptly asked. "O," I said, "He's this young punk who lately target me because he doesn't have anything else to do."

Then he asked "Who Adrianna?" I said, "A female who use to be my girlfriend but I think her and Thomas had somewhat of an affair. Which this older man who lives on my block, told me, it my fault because I should had never allow her to come inside my house, but me personally, I feel the guy who said that to me, he wrong, because I feel I shouldn't be alone and not entertain inside my apartment because I have a man? Thomas should had said something to me if the girl I brought inside the apartment, as my friend, was coming on to him."

Salvatore said "You really got your hands full don't you."

Thinking to myself, now he understands a little more why I wanted my section 8 voucher.

He asked me "Do you want out from there? Because I have a friend who is the director of Human Resource. I bet she could help move up your application besides, she owe me a favor anyway. I help her on a case once and in return I have her permission of a favor owed. I'm going to call her up right now." And he did. Unfortunately, the friend has retired and no longer had anything to do with Section 8. He got so upset and at that moment I was so touch by his attempt to help, I was speechless. That's when Salvatore gently put his hands on my face and he gently gave me a kiss on my lips. It was the kindest act of human kindness that I had felt in an extremely long time. It touched me so much that I must had blank out because the next thing I knew; he was tapping me on my back for me to open up my eyes.

When I open my eyes, my face was still up in a position for a kiss. He said "Your children need you," and he gave me fifty dollars, telling me to treat myself nice; like to go to the salon and get a manicure and a pedicure.

Stop! To the reader: Just to let you know, reader, at that time 50 dollars was a hell of a lot of money for a manicure and pedicure. The going rate around that time was 20 bucks. Anyway its lunch time. I stop writing to get something to eat. Putting up my notes all of a sudden I started coughing.

I went to Jose and cashed in some of my food stamps. I brought food out from the Chinese restaurant. I order chicken wings, french-fries and an egg roll. This time I'm going to eat my food inside the neighborhood Chinese restaurant. I didn't feel like sharing my food with the women inside the shelter and I didn't want to tell anybody "No, you can't have any." So to prevent all that I ate inside the restaurant.

While I was eating my food. A man came in begging for change wanting to buy something to eat, "Hello my name is Troy and I'm hungry and homeless. Can anyone spare some change or can you buy me something to eat?"

I watch the man work the small restaurant making his way to each of the tables with his hand out, looking for any kind of donation. As I took a bite of my chicken wing. He came standing in front of me, "Could you spare some change or something to eat, Miss?" I shook my head indicating, no. He asked the people who just walked inside the restaurant to, just as they were about to place their order. I watch him head out the door panhandling the people as they walked up and down the street. As I'm sitting there eating my food looking at him. I started thinking; just when I thought I could eat my food in peace, that I came outside to get away from the beggars inside the shelter, just to come outside, and niggers, still asking, can they have some of my food to eat. Sometimes I feel like I'm in a no win situation.

Back upstairs at the ranch I grab a chair to continue writing. Security Cammy enter the dining room to announce "Open studio on four, ladies." I going to skip the class cause I'm just about finish with this chapter so on that note. *Back to the story.*

Moet was getting stronger every day due to the routine exercise I was doing with her. She had more strength in both legs now that she was able to stand. The doctor told me she was like this because sometimes the muscle doesn't quite develop. Then another factor could be her not realizing she out the womb, and needed a little help for her to know she has different body parts, that function in different ways.

She had gain more strength in her arms and fingers to, now she holding her own bottle and picking up things. The therapy with her limbs I see had worked, except for her speech. She still wasn't speaking much.

Exactly 4 pm Salvatore called me. He asked me if I could come to the precinct. He also wanted to see a picture of my children. It funny because we just took our first family portrait. I got the portrait taken at Kings Plaza. I asked him to give me a moment.

I knocked on Rondu' door and I asked him if the girls could stay at his place for a minute because of the bitterness from Thomas, the commotion with BCW, then that crap with my mom caused me to ask Rondu who is my next door neighbor being I gave him quite a few meals. Lately he has occasionally watched my children for me to, in order for me to do my emergency quick seconds runs to the corner store.

This time going to the precinct I took JB with me because sometimes he just didn't listen to Champagne when I'm not around. I had our family portrait in one hand while holding JB hand with my other hand. When I got to the precinct, this time Detective Salvatore was standing outside. He asked "Who's this?"

I said, "My son Bandon but we call him JB." "Hey there," he said. I said, "JB this is Detective Finaoni. He's a cop." They both smiled at each other. I showed him the picture. He said, "You have a nice looking family." Looking at the picture smiling I said "Yeah we all look happy don't we? I think the picture came out great too."

Salvatore asked me "What's going on?" I told him, "Same o same o. I have to go back to court.... remember the child support issue?" Anyway, I said "I wish I could stay a little longer but I can't. I need to hurry back home because I got to pick up some groceries at the corner store. Soo, later."

When we returned back to court, Thomas started to tell the judge how he didn't have a problem in supporting his children and how, he wants his son. The judge didn't understand why Thomas only insisted on having JB, not both of his' kids meaning Moet too. While I was trying to explain to the judge, my fears of Thomas wanting to take my son away from me to send him off to live in Jamaica. Without me having no real contact address of where my son would be staying at and with who and for how long.

Well it turned out to become a **Big Mess** that Thomas done started with this family court. We stood in that court house **all day**! The judge made Thomas supply our lunch. Because in Manhattan, where was I going to get something to eat off of from my food stamp card? You see all this took place in the early nineties. There weren't any stores in Manhattan accepting the food stamp benefit card from welfare.

Our court case got adjourned, again! This time not for one court, but now, for two. Why? Reason #1, Thomas still didn't provide the necessary amount of pay stubs. He didn't supply the accurate data of his work place either. Due to Thomas not supplying his correct documentation the judge set a temporarily child support amount of $25.00 a week for each child in effective **immediately and,** a return court date but I didn't receive any of that money from Thomas.

The 2ⁿᵈ reason was the judge sense a lot of tension in the air regarding parental visitation rights. Because when anyone deals with family court matters, after child support next in line is visitation rights for both parents'. Being the judge sense tension he order that our children receive a lawyer for their best interests concerning visitations. Due to this court jurisdiction, in Manhattan, we being sent to the family court in Brooklyn where we reside in order to deal with visitation rights and to determine how it should best be set, being that I feared abduction.

Another thing that came out **from those long** court hearings held in Manhattan, was that Brandon and Moet had gotten their' last name changed. Because now Thomas was stating that he had wanted his son to bear his last name. The judge asked me how I felt about that. At 1st I didn't want it because I wanted my children to remain Jones but the judge help points out Thomas reason, circling around JB his son. My argument was Thomas he could had been said this to me since day one JB was born. Why wait to come to court to express his wishes. Anyway, well, that's exactly what the judge did but for both of them.

Finally, Thomas and I are finish with the child support court in Manhattan.

Oh, let me tell you how it turned out. When we came back to court, for child support the 3rd or 4th time. When the judge asks Thomas for his' current pay stub. Thomas stood up and said proudly "I don't work with the union anymore. Your honor I no longer have a job."

I was so **shock!** He quit his construction job so he didn't have to pay child support. I was so mad because we use to stay inside that hot tacky court house **all day.** Just for it to end "Your honor, I'm no longer working. I'm unemployed." Thomas is a real piece of shit even the judge thought what kind of man are you? The judge still made Thomas contribute $50 dollars a week for both kids.

Thomas said "Your honor how can I give $50 a week and I don't have a job?"

That white man told Thomas "$50 dollars a week for your two children is nothing. It not my problem. Case dismiss."

I was **piss!** All this sitting down here in this court house for him to quit his dam union job because he didn't want to give me (which I wasn't getting anyway) any of his money after I struggle with this man helping him get a dam union job. Anyway Thomas, **he lied**. He wasn't unemployed he became a full time dollar van driver. The only thing was at that time, dollar vans were off the books. The city or I couldn't collect any child support from that.

As for the temporally child support money that Thomas was ordered to pay, well, I never received one **dime** of that money because all the money went over to the child support unit, of the welfare department. **What a fuckin waste!** The only thing Thomas had to do, was to be an **adult!** Be a responsible man and provide for his' kids! Because too me, Thomas not only **fuck** himself by having the government tell him how much money to give up for our kids he also **FUCKED** me too, because I'm still receiving the same government grant I pick up every two weeks in order to support **4 people!** Which is myself and my three kids! I don't see how I or my kids have benefited from this experience. I have no extra cash in my hand from Thomas to help support the kids we created, because all Thomas money, now, goes to the welfare office. **Dam!** To top it all off what else make it so bad, is the judge order that Thomas, pay the city or welfare, **retroactive** money. Meaning, since our kids were born. **DAM!!**

Stop! To the reader: Looking back on my life, I don't see where I and my kids benefited from going to court because I was still **struggling!** The money Thomas dishing out, or will be dishing out-now, to support our children, that he could have been giving to me for our kids, it's all going to the **CITY!**

THOMAS to me is so fuckin stupid! And to me he fucked our kids too because who buying them anything they may want-like an ice cream cone or wish to have, like a toy or a pair of shoes? Anyway when I went to bed that night, I had another unexplainable dream. This time I had a dream about, Miss Perking?! Wow it been a long time because I haven't seen her face since I left the Projects. I woke up thinking, even though we were neighbors, the last actual time I saw her was when my oldest daughter was about 9 months old. I recalled, she became very distant towards me, after a while. She would only say "Hi and bye," if that much. Anyway in my dream it showed me, I needed medication and she was the key.

I started falling behind in my studies with the home health aide training program. I found myself cramming way too much information. I wanted a job so badly but I was dealing with too much personal affairs which was bringing a lot of stress in my life. Even though I was passing my tests I was touchy, agitated and impatient. Around 8 pm my cousin Yolanda called "What's going on Electra? You've been missing from class."

I said, "I know. I gave the instructors proof showing where I've been. I had court cases and I've been taking Moet back and forth to the doctor." "Humm," Yolanda said. Then she asked, "Is the instructor going to allow you to make up the tests?"

I said, "She should. I see all of those other people in there taking more than two tests a day trying to catch up. Sometimes I see they have their notes open, cheating too." Yolanda said, "That's why I study. I come home, study, and when I go to class, I take two tests. She should allow you to take more tests in a day. She allowed me. We did lesson 21 today, and I passed in 19 & 20. I'm finished now I received my hospital badge. I be doing my internship tomorrow."

"What! Wow Yolanda thatz good," I said. "Other than going back and forth taking care of business what else is going on?" she asked. Smiling I said, "Nothing much but remember that detective I told you I met? Yo, he so sweet."

Yolanda shouted "a **DETECTIVE!?** I though you told me he's a cop?" I said all happy, feeling warm inside, "I did but he's a detective. Yo, he brought me a box of Nexus hair products. Yolanda said "He did all that?" "Yep. He calls me on the telephone to check up on me AND the kids," I said. Yolanda asked, *"Is he black?"* I said, "No, he's white."

Yolanda said with caution, "Girl you'd better be careful because some white men are psycho and he's a detective too. Girl he can take you anywhere, and kill you, AND get away with it."

"**Shut up Yolanda**!" Quickly I said "Yo hold on I got another call coming in," as I clicked to pick up the incoming call. "Hello," I said. "Hello Electra," Salvatore said.

"Hi. Could you hold on please I'm on the other line?" I clicked before he had a chance to said anything. "Yolanda that him," I said. "That's who? That cop? I mean that detective?" Yolanda asked.

I said "Yeah. Listen Yolanda I" She just cuts me off! **Yolanda** had said frantically, "I don't want to talk to you while he's on the other end. He could be recording us right now." Hysterically I burst out with a laugh I said "Yolanda you're so funny." She said, "No I'm not! I'm hanging up and don't call me from this number anymore." Click.

Out loud I said, "Oh, damn! What the fuck wrong with her. Naw I can't believe she so paranoid like that." Click, "Hi Salvatore," I said. "Electra can you come to the precinct? It won't take long," he asked. "Um…well the kids are in the bed," I said. He said "It will only take a moment."

I had reached the beginning entrance to the precinct' parking lot. Surprised Salvatore, he came out from behind the parking lot wall. "Hello Electra," he said. Immediately he asked me "Close your eyes." And I did. While blindfolded, he walked me a few steps. Now he asks me "Open your eyes."

I was standing in front of the most beautiful sport car, which had my initial on its license plate. He told me I'm a beautiful person and that he's married. He said he love his wife and his' children. That he won't be calling me anymore. I was stronger to go on now. That he didn't have to worry about me anymore **AND**, as mysteriously he came, mysteriously, he left. I felt like he was a knight and shining armor who helped me to get through a very dark place, maybe he even helped saved my life, in coaching me to hold on that things would get better.

STOP! To the reader: You know I have tears in my eyes right now even though I didn't have tears back then. He was a very nice person and sensitive not to mention he seemed to be a caring human being.

When I got home I called Yolanda back but she never really did picks back up the phone. I'm thinking what the fuck is wrong with her? Why she had to act like that? Dam!

Anyway, the next day, I was speaking to my father on the telephone. I said, "Dad guess what!? You won't believe who I had a dream about?" Daddy asked "Who?" "I said, "Miss Perking." Daddy said "Get out of here. You know, she's a pastor now?"

"What!" I was surprise to find that little bit of information out. Daddy said "Her church is right on David Avenue." I asked for the address because I been church shopping and I haven't found the right church I felt to join. After hanging up the telephone, I knew that I had to go to that church and to see her, especially after me seeing her in my dream, as her being like medicine to me.

That Sunday the kids and I went to her' church. I remembered I took a cab. Miss Perking was renting out a space in a building that she had turned into a sanctuary-A house of prayer. When we walked inside the church the first person I seen was, my father? Wow and he's an usher. Shocked, to find out that he was also a member, and a very big supporter financially. I found a seat for me and the kids. It was towards the back because I wanted to have enough space to allow Moet to remain seated in her' stroller. While me and the other two kids sat in the church' folding chairs. Well I already been having strange occurrences that were unexplainable this is when it really took clarity. I knew, I had personal issues. I was looking at Miss Perking and I was impressed to see this new, Godly look. She had on a robe and wore a white collar around her neck. Come to think of it, I do recall seeing that white collar in my dream on her too. I just didn't expect it for a biblical thing.

Pastor Perking had started singing a gospel song. I don't recall which song she was singing. All I know is that the service has started. Daddy was sitting down. My kids and I were sitting down but then something happens to me. Like I said, they were singing a gospel song. It sounds very nice that it moved me, so I stood up from my seat, clapping my hands. All of a sudden I couldn't stop my legs from dancing. I'm serious. I couldn't stop. I remembered that my legs were going up and down. Up and down fast with joy. I felt so much joy. That my children started watching me. They never saw me jump up and down like that in church. I never thought of myself doing that either. It wasn't a leg dancing movement like you see in a club. Anyway I was stunned, but it felt so good. My action amazed me so much because I couldn't stop my legs from dancing.

Fast up and down, up and down my legs were going and I felt so good, that I took my happy dancing legs down the aisle over to where my dad was sitting. He was sitting on the outside of the aisle looking straight ahead. I went up to him and I couldn't stop my legs from moving. I couldn't stop moving. I said, "Dad!" While he sat down in his seat, with his arm folded across his chest looking ahead, my father turned his' head to the right to look at me. He said "Yeah."

While my legs were still moving up and down like I was dancing, I asked, "Dad don't you feel like dancing?" Looking at me. Casually, he said "No I don't." I'm still jumping up and down. I said, "Well I do." Daddy said "Go ahead," and I was gone. Jumping up and down to the beat of the gospel so much, I was truly amazed that I couldn't stop my legs from dancing. When I finally stop, I felt so, good! So accelerating! Refresh and brand new. It was wonderful!

Only after attending many church services later, I found out, that called having a Holy Ghost party. In other words, being filled with the Holy Ghost or some say the Holy Spirit. Another amazing thing happen to me on that day; immediately after the sermon, Pastor Perking encourage those that needed prayer to come forward. Okay I needed prayer. I have secret issues only God knows, what all I'm going thru. Nobody knows, what all I'm enduring. My kids were the closest people to me and they probably sense something but them so young. And when I go to sleep, I have all of those strange dreams. If anybody needs prayer, I really did.

I started to wonder about the power of prayer and think on those intangible gruesome ideas of witches and spells and demons and angels, the devil and hell, and heaven and earth. These thoughts were seeking into my existence and I know it sound crazy. Also totally unbelievable, but sorry to say, it happening and it's happening to me and secretly, I'm afraid.

I'm afraid because it the unknown. I could feel inside of me something not right and I got to do something. I'm in trouble and can't no doctor help what going on inside my head. In my heart. Something is so wrong. I being lied too, and my family, my friends, my boyfriend aren't in my corner to convey something to me which is so deep, that going on in my life. Anyway I got to be here for my kids so I'm going to take a leap of faith and go up for prayer.

This is new to me, this church thing and spiritual awareness. Voodoo workers, witches, dead bats. ..... Jesus. Just the mentioning sound of Jesus, to me is strong and powerful. Thinking back how Adrianna' mother ran when I mumble Jesus underneath my breath. You know what she reminded me of that night Van Heisler. I hope I got the right movie about the vampires' women sucking the blood from that young man. Remember the scene how the women glided across the wall all fast when they felt threatening.

Well, that what she looked like guiding across the building wall. Come to think of it I haven't even seen that movie when all this were happening. I'm recalling that night when I called on God and questioning his' powers. Demanding for him to prove his' existence and Adrianna appear to me in a circle as a witch. So I already knew at the sound of mentioning Jesus and God there is power but I just wasn't aware of the depth of the whole thing.

When I got up there to the altar not knowing what to expect beside she going to pray for me. I watch quietly as Pastor Perking went to the person who was before me as she prayed. We all was watching because it a very small church and a tiny congregation. The lady fell out on the ground. "Oh sweat," I said within myself as I watch the lady on the ground. Someone put a sheet of some sort covering her from the waist down.

Pastor Perking coming to me. I'm thinking, I really got some problems and I'm not up here playing around. I'm really seeking prayer. I'm not going to be a hypocrite that going to fall to the ground. So when Pastor Perking got in front of me. She asks me to raise my hands. Then she dabs her finger with the oil. She puts her hand on my forehead. At this point I can't really hear what she saying because I'm wishing within myself, "please God please help me." Then I start too audibly hear her' shout, saying, "Lose it!" At this point now for me, her voice is clearly audible. Loudly she said "**Lose it.**" My head is going back and forward as she shouts lose it! I saying to myself I'm not falling. Then the most unbelievable thing happens! I drop like a hot pancake unable to get up right away. Whoever pulling the sheet on me told me "Stop trying to get up." The person said "Not to fight it, because God is working something out for me in my life."

Amazed and shocked, I'm on the ground. Feeling this invisible weight all over me, as I tried to get up from the ground. Realizing this is really happening. I'm not faking.

From the ground, I was looking up at the people who are standing up. That was in my view, so I closed my eyes while feeling totally relaxed and weak. I laid there feeling vulnerable, which was a little awkward for me. The feeling of vulnerability of letting go, and not fighting anymore. Quite a few times I did go back to the church not fully becoming a regularly member because of financial burdens and personal issue, but, that's when I began learning the words to gospel songs and how to pray, and worship God. After a while, I even started listening to the gospel on the radio station. I even, had purchase a few gospel tapes for the apt because I liked the feeling and the vibes that I received while listening to the gospel songs.

Wow, I appreciate I did a lot of writing today. Looking at the clock on the wall time now is 5:00. My back hurt because I was clutch over while writing. Samantha enters the dining room "Hi Electra," she said as she walks toward the bulletin board and staple yet another notice.

Before she leaves, she says to me, "Hope to see you for open mic tomorrow." "I plum forgot Samantha. Thank you for reminding me," I told her as I watch her happily exit the room. Goodnight Reader.

Chapter Twenty-One

I woke up it was 7 am. I jump out of bed so I can catch breakfast. As I sign my name on the clipboard I see they serving corn beef hash with those powder cheese eggs omelet. So I lean my face against the plexi-glass to see what kind of cereal they have. If a resident doesn't want the hot food, now on the menu from our house meeting, this shelter gives out cold breakfast in a form of two tiny boxes of cereal.

Miss Alfre said, "Good morning." "Good morning Miss Alfre," I said. She asks, "Would you like corn beef hash?" I say, "No. Not this time. Instead I take two boxes of cereal please." She asked "Which box of cereal would you like?" I replied "Applejacks and frosted flakes."

Miss Alfre asked, "Do you want a cheese egg omelet?" I said, "Yeah that sound good." "How many," she asks. I said, "Two will be fine, thank you and two slices of white bread please."

Walking down the line to pick up some sugar for my coffee. I stop in front of Abuja. She asks, "How many sugar do you want Miss Jones?" I say, "Four regular sugars." Walking down the line to pick up my carton of milk I'm thinking, that why we never have a security guard on the fourth floor. They always down stairs in the kitchen helping to serve our food, and the guard belongs upstairs sitting on post.

Sitting down eating my breakfast. I was stun to see clients come in eating with their' pajamas on. Didn't staff say we not supposed to enter the dining room in our pajamas anymore? That one thing you learn about the shelter; their rules changes every shift. The employees on one shift tell us residents to behave this way. Then when the next shift comes in, the employees on that shift tell us to behave,

597

that a way. This is a prime example when you hear me talk about us residents becoming stress out over the shelter and their madness of constant changing rules. I'm telling you, it can literally drive you crazy due too so much confusions. Sometimes a staff employee yells at a resident when she not following the rules. Which to me is embarrassing and insulting for an adult to be yelled at, AND loud too in front of others. Then another resident does the same shit on a different shift and not one employee say a word. The shelter staff their employees really need to be consistence with their rules and every employee, regarding, what shift they work should be on the same accord.

Reader-Did I tell you I lost everything I had and that the only clothes on my back was the clothes I was wearing. Did anyone ever think they can lose everything they ever own. I don't think anybody will think they could lose everything including every article of clothing they own. Some people take for granted the small things –in life.

It was Lacy, another homeless person who came up to me and told me after she notice I wore the same outfit every day, where to get free clothes from. I am a native born American and yes I should know these things but it just that I never been so down on my luck to the degree of losing everything I own. I guess when so much hardship and struggling falls upon a person it become over whelming and they, or I can say, me, I wasn't thinking. Especially when a person carries the burden of hardship all alone with no family or friends support. It's a lot that goes on living out in the streets.

At one point I left the shelter temporary which again it didn't work out. When I came back surprisingly I was placed back inside the Q-dorm this time I received bed Q10. Every night I hand wash my only blouse, pants, and underclothes. Until Lacy approach me one day and told me, "You know they give free clothes out at the church every Wednesday.

At 8 am sharp three boxes of clothes are put out and you can take whatever you want."

When she told me that I was like, why didn't I think of that because in my life time I had donated my children good outgrown clothes to churches. Maybe I didn't think about seeking donated clothes for myself because no one in my circle of family/friends ever discuss what organization is giving out free clothes. Growing up in my parents' house my parents never donated. My mom just threw our clothes out. We always brought our clothing from retail stores and as I aged I threw out what clothes I didn't want any more just like all the other people in the projects. It's not till I had children of my own churches started asking for donation of clothing. Us Black Americans, we were the ones who occasionally helped with clothes donations by being kind wanting to help support our churches in the community. It never occurs to me what happen or where the small selection of clothing I did donate go. I never wonder how the donated clothes were issue out. Maybe I didn't think about it either because I never been so down in life to this degree. Anyway, I can't believe I did it. But I did. I got up early and I had hand pick through boxes in the street looking for free clothes to wear.

Then I found out from other people, who did this kind of shopping which other churches gave out free clothes. And that's how I got clothes for myself by getting up early in the morning, standing outside, waiting for whichever church or soup kitchen to put out a box, or, open up their doors for people like myself to stand in line to get free clothes.

But not everybody in line was homeless. Lot were Caribbean, foreigners/immigrants, lots from the Spanish race who didn't or did have jobs but, to me they use this method for saving money by getting free clothes especially for their young kids like infants and toddlers. Or, I think to ship overseas. That's just one dam reason why I had to get up so early in the morning with some churches because these people got up early in the morning and they came with shopping karts every time, because in some places a person can take as much free clothes as he/she can carry. There wasn't a limitation.

I use to be angry because these places didn't open up their doors till 10 or 10:30am. The same people with a shopping kart came early therefore, now a line is forming. A line waiting for the doors to open. So if I wanted to find anything good before all the so called good stuff was taken I had to leave the shelter 6 in the morning so I can be at least at the front of the line because these people were coming with shopping karts racking up. Even when I left the shelter early to shop for free clothes I was never 1st in line. The same people was always at the front of the line. I would found myself like the 8th person to go in.

I used to always state my frustration verbally out loud saying "This a dam shame there a line 7am and the doors don't open till ten."

When I was struggling with my young kids on welfare I wish I would had known about these places because I sure could have saved a lot of money in getting free clothes for my kids. The money I spent purchasing on their clothing I could have put that money elsewhere like towards the house or on myself.

The clothes at these places are nice all you got to do is wash them. I mean all the buttons and snaps were in place. I literally mean when your kids are from infant to about 4 years old you can get everything for that child or your children to wear. Lots of sleeper, pajamas, T-shirts, jeans, tops, bibs, jackets, coats, and blankets. For adults they had everything you can think of raincoats, pocketbook, blouses, dresses, pants, dress clothes and shirts for men, belts, hats and neck ties. I mean they have everything even shoes. It just like shopping in a department store. The only difference is in the adult section you got to look through the kind of damage tacky clothes to find good clothes anything that can fit. And it's all free. At places like these a person would find clothes for all seasons and ages even adults housecoats/slips, pajamas you name it, I mean they have everything. Now I see where Lacy had gotten all her jackets from for every weather condition but I just don't wear other people shoes. Once I wore other shoes donated in Manhattan and I received a bunion.

People in Brooklyn use to laugh at me when they saw me walking with clothes I got out from a box on the street or off a table until I started dressing better than the people who worked inside the shelter. Get this, off from other people thrown out clothes. **Shit,** I started dressing better than people in my own family. Then some residents started copying me but none of the American girls because I think they were too proud to let people know they stood in line at a soup kitchen going thru clothes that were donated laying on a table. I got a lot of my nice coat and clothing free but it took time accumulating the stuff because sometimes I found a nice sweater but I had to wait till the winter come to wear it. Or sometimes I had a nice blouse but I had to wait for the spring to put it on.

When anyone does this kind of shopping the person has to be aggressive like greedy, or like you hungry because this type of shopping you snatch and grab quickly moving through clothes looking for anything descent. Depending on the church, you will find a lot of elbow bumping and shoveling taking place while you shop, not to mention a person hogging an area.

Then the shelter started posting up signs about bedbugs. So now, but not before, but now it's official all clothes brought inside a shelter upon arrival has to be wash or at least dried to kill bedbugs that may be on clothing. Some shelters are really serious about bedbugs' manifestations more than others. At Samuel shelter located in the Bronx no matter what time you arrived even if it was 2 in the morning that resident wasn't going to her bed till all her clothes and bed linen was at least dried killing off any signs of bedbugs.

Talking about bedbugs, as an American I never knew bedbugs existed. Remember the prayer we use to quote as children. "Lord lay me down to sleep. I pray to the lord my soul to keep. If I die before I wake, I pray to the lord my soul to take. Amen. God bless mommy. God bless daddy." Then you God bless every one you love but at the end we always said, "and don't let the bedbugs bite." I never knew bedbugs were real until the foreigners started coming to America. Why I say that is because we never had or seen a bedbug before until they started coming over here. In some shelters us residents were getting all bit up.

Being homeless I learn to appreciate and respect everything. Like my privacy, a roof over my head, cooking, a refrigerator, my freedom, taking a bath, having a complete apartment meaning with a kitchen and a bathroom or, just having an apartment. Also being homeless made me look at the word support. Who really support the individual when a person is down and out? If you are homeless who is the person or individual, or people, can the homeless person say support him or her in their time of need?

Well, I better get up from here and get to my dorm because the dorms will be closing soon. It's almost 9 am. I don't feel like staying inside the shelter today writing so when I leave out from the shelter I'm walking over to the library to continue writing there.

Once I reach inside the library I found a cozy seat in the corner. Around this time in my life now Thomas and I got finish with one court but now we in another court. Family court. I thought the court in Manhattan was bad but this court house here in Brooklyn is plain outright ridiculous because to my surprise all we do is go back and forth to court. I'mma tell you it's really turning ugly between Thomas and I in this court house. We have to appear adjourning date after date after date with this family court house with all these people in our business, and Thomas foolishness.

Oh yeah!!! At the shelter tonight reader, it's open Mic Night! I don't want to miss that so Reader: Let go back *into the story.*

I went back to class and I had crammed a lot of medical material. A part of the curriculum for the school, in order to receive the certificate every student had to perform X amount of volunteer hours at Downstate Hospital.

After not hearing from Detective Salvatore in a couple of days. I went back to the precinct. I asked the black receptionist who sat behind the shielded area, "Can I speak with Detective Finaoni." She told me, "He no longer work at this precinct."

Wow that really took me by surprise. I asked, "Where did he go? Did he get transfer?" The black lady shrugged her' shoulders. Then she gave me a smiling face because she remembers the condition and state of mind I was in when I first enter the precinct. Anyway, he's gone. I'm mean completely gone. He no longer works at the 56th precinct.

In school I'm moving on now, going towards the 2nd stage with the school. The patient I received at Downstate Hospital was Miss Collins. She is a Black West Indian, age late eighties or early nineties. The instructor of the school to me made sure I received the worst patient. I felt she didn't want to see me succeed after watching me cram so much material.

The nurses in that hospital has neglect this senior citizen so much. That I couldn't barely touch her due to her' bedsores. I had to change Miss Collins hospital bed sheet. I couldn't because I couldn't even touch her. She would start to flinch and moan every time I put, tried to put my hand near her. I went out the room to get one of the nurses to help me. The nurse came in there saying, "Miss Collins you know you got to get your bed linen change." Miss Collins was shaking her head whispering, "no, no, no, no."

That West Indian nurse had no kind of gentleness what so forever. She lifts up one side of the mattress. That old lady scream so loud as she bumps her head up against the bed rail. I actually had to hold my ears.

I spoke up saying, "Be gentle with her!" The nurse told me, "She was going to yell no matter what. That she was already given a special mattress because of her' bedsores."

I literally felt sorry for her. I don't think those nurses was rotating this patient. Something I learned attending the school. Someone should had come allowing her to sit up in a chair before her body had gotten rotten into this condition. Miss Collins saw I was moved by her and how upset I was with those nurses who seem to care more about their' paycheck then her care.

The only comb I had was the hospital tiny black teeth comb. Gently with water I comb the knots out of this elderly woman hair. I ran the water making the water become nice and warm while I did her hair so that later with the warm water I can bathe her body. I had to walk back and forward to the nursing station asking for items I needed. After I took the knots out of her hair I gently massage and rub her scalp with a little soap and warm water that I put on a clean wash cloth. Miss Collins really appreciated me doing that for her cause I saw her' head nodding, like, go head child. It seems no one never really bathed her properly, because shit I never in my life saw came out from her ears, that I almost gag. While doing this I sung gospel hymns because it always helps me to relax and think of a higher power. While I sang, secretly I asked God, "To help me, help her."

Gently I message lotion on her thin dry crack skin. Miss Collins seemed much appreciated of me taking care of her. I think I had to be there from 10 till 3. Anyway, that's how long it took me to do her hair and bath and oil her skin. With her help, I manage to change her dirty hospital grown all by myself as she moved extremely slow while shaken, because of the pain she was in. I tidy up her room.

I open up the window for fresh air. I was exhausted when I got finish working with Miss Collins but to see her lying there with a smile on her face was worth it.

From what I gather she had no visitors, no family, so I held her hand and she held mine the best she could and I prayed again with her and for her. When my work day was over I knew I gained her trust and a friend. Miss Collins knew in me she had one too.

I was so excited to see her the next day. I went to her' room door. I open the door and the bed was……. empty? The room was the same way how I had left it, with the window cracked open. So, I went to the nursing station and I asked, "Where Miss Collins?" The nurse looked up from her' paper work and told me "She died." Tears swelled up in my eyes and I said to myself "no more pain Miss Collins. No more pain."

The nurse from Downstate Hospital told me, "Have a good day." Because my patient has pass I was sent back to the school. When I got back to the school the instructor told me, "I see and heard you did well with the patient in the hospital. Unfortunately, I cannot give you your' certificate. I been watching you. You seem to be distracted and seem to have a lot of anxiety." I asked, "What does that have to do with me not receiving my certificate? I pass all your requirements."

The instructor said, "Everything. I cannot sign my name and send you into an elderly home at this time. Who knows you may go off and hurt the person because you seem to be under a lot of pressure. Why won't you take some time to take care of issues that going on around you in your life I'm sorry."

WHAT! I was so mad at her. I really wanted a job. I needed the money. I passed my testes. I did well in the hospital. All this cramming I did for **nothing!** Another fuckin failure. The more I try the more I fail. She just didn't want to see a smart descent American like me hold a job. Probably afraid I do well and make lots of promotions. I was so mad at her. My personal life drama I did not bring to my patient and I will not bring to my patient. Nor did I bring all the issues I'm facing to my class. Looking back on it now I believe she was too much into my personal business when I gave her proof of my absentee documentations. I believe she held it against me, not to succeed.

It was a bit too much but I was handling it. I guess from the stress of still living like this, feeling stuck or from the boredom of not going anywhere exciting. I started back smoking cigarettes. My life wasn't going anywhere worth talking about. There was nothing exciting in my world besides taking care of my kids that I love. I love being a mom I really did. But I wanted more for my life other than the kids and keeping a clean apartment but, I keep waking up every morning doing the same repetitious thing like cooking, cleaning and staying inside the house. Being broke, sometime I'm just looking out the window. Lots of times I'm just listening to the music on the radio.

I have another court date coming up. It dealing with visitation rights again and it downtown Brooklyn.

I stood up for a stretch. I looked around and saw people reading a book but most of them waiting to use the library' computers. Anyway, reader, how can I make a person understand that I have been in the shelter system for so long that one day-My mother said to me, "Electra. There's good money as a live in."

Well, I just like to put it out there that a couple of times while living at 68 Lexington and in the earlier years of me staying at Bridge Net that I did try to live in my mother parent' house with my cousins in Brownsville. And the only reason I knocked upon my grandparents' door looking for help was due to me seeing I'm not getting housed, nor section eight, nor the project, nor any low income apt, or lottery apartment. Not even the SRO I was sent to has worked out for me, as a way for obtaining residency. Therefore, after many years of being homeless, trying to be independent in seeking my own housing from the system, and point blank, I saw-it just wasn't working out for me. Therefore, one-day, I knocked upon my grandparents' door-seeking if I can live in one of the rooms in their house. Because I found myself still living inside the shelter system year after year after year.

Unfortunately, by the time I had come knocking upon the door for help I only had one grandparent living....... Grandmamma! And she was bound to a wheel chair. I don't recall which one of my cousin had open up the door to the house for me to enter. Anyway I went to the back room and I spoke with grandmamma and explain to her my hardship in finding housing. As a matter of fact, I made a video tape on homeless when I lived in Manhattan at 68 Lexington. I had showed it to her, and my cousin Tie he was present too. Anyway I asked her if I can live in one of the rooms in her 2 family house that came with an unfinished basement.

Grandmamma said to me. "Everybody got to die some day and that I can come inside the house."

I heard what she said but I didn't know what she meant by that saying. I was just so happy to hear her say "Take the room in the front". I wanted to spend time with my kids who I truly miss. I wanted to have a normal life. I wanted to get on with my life because I felt I was being held back from enjoying my life. The shelter system seems to have put my life on hold for a very long time. It felt like my life it had just stopped. And after a while of being homeless, I felt as if mentally and physically a small piece of me was dying every day. Due to my hardship with homelessness, I became desperate with feeling like I want to LIVE and not die. Don't get me wrong I had lots of good moment and I was grateful while living outside in the shelter but it was the **worst days** of my LIFE.

So when Grandmamma said I can come in I was so thankful cause I been living in the streets for such a very long time trying to find a place call home. And not to mention my children, all three of them they needed me because I'm their mother and I see they were dying too in a way. Due to my homelessness there was nothing I can do to help them, so I had always felt so bad within. And knowing they are dying slowly from my tradition and how I picture their life to be was killing me too. It hurts so bad to watch them go thru life issues knowing there's only but so much I can do to help because my hands are tied.

I felt bad for myself but I felt worst for them and every day it added more secret pain in my life that I never told anyone until now. It's a shame to watch your kids disappear from their roots and there was nothing I can do to stop it. It bothers me every day, it kind of like, destroying me. Because they so young at least as a child growing up I had a steady foundation and family all around me which helped mold my character but I see in my kids they didn't even have that which ate at me a little everyday knowing only if I had an apartment somewhere I can stay that I can make a different on their-my children outlook on life. So when Grandmamma said, "Electra everybody got to die come in," and I finally had a roof over my head a place I can say was mines. I felt me-breathe like I had my chance to survive even though, I was so very tired. For such a beautiful pretty, pretty girl who lived out in the street for so, so very long.

I just wanted it to be known to the reader that I did go to family quite a few times seeking help.

It lunches time now in the shelter. So I put down my pen and paper to go get something to eat. The RA, are passing out bologna sandwiches. When I unwrapped my sandwich to put mayonnaise on the bread the bologna meat seems too had been old because I saw the poke holes' mark left in the bread. We had green pears for desert. Two 4 oz. frozen juices.

I'm walking away from the dining room. In the hallway I bumps into Miss Taylor my case worker. She calls to me and say, "Electra I'm so glad I see you. I was about to leave your message from me with the shift supervisor." I asked, "Why? What happen?" She hands me a letter and say, "This is what I written for you. You and I have to meet with Mr. Ron Winlesky." "**For what**?" I question. "He didn't say. The time is in the memo. Bye," she said.

After lunch I went back to the library. This time I found a seat by the window. I pull out my papers to finish writing. Reader let go back *into the story*:

I called my father, "Hey dad how you doing?" "So, so," he said. I asked him, "Is Pastor Perking church still located on David Avenue?" Daddy said "No she been left that place she on Pearl Street now." I asked him, "What bus will take me over there?"

This church on Pearl Street was also rented space but it was much bigger. Pastor did a wonderful job in turning it into a sanctuary. The church still had a very small congregation. All that was missing was a choir. So she formed one.

She remembers when we all were next door neighbors. Me as a young teenager how I sounded when I sang gospel. I had always loved music, between my parents, they had so much music in the house. My sister and I was playing records. We were having a sing off contest. So looking for my choice of the next song to sing, I came across an unusual album. It wasn't R and B. I think the name of the album was called, Getting in the Sprit. …. So like I said, I came across a gospel album and I played it.

I recall how quickly I learn the lyric. I was surprised that I really enjoyed this type of music-it moved me. What Pastor heard that day was my sister and I singing-having a sing off. The music was loud, but when I, even my sister Tonya, when we having fun we always playing loud music.

Pastor asked me to join the church choir. She said, "I remember you sung that gospel song so well." I join the choir and surprisingly I fell in love with gospel music but what I remember most, is I feel in love **with God**.

I was so amazed to see Pastor Perking so religious and that she knew so much about the bible. I mean we (meaning her family and my family) didn't grow up like this. She uses to party with my parents. I use to hang out with her' kids. Paris and her' brother, Superman. We always teased him saying, "Look who wanna be Superman." So we named him Superman, his nick name of course. Our families weren't gospel playing, godly feared people. As a matter of fact, for my family that was the only gospel album in the house and God wasn't even spoken about. In pastor defense now that I'm writing I do remember in my late teens Pastor Perking did become very distant, maybe that when the spirit of God came upon her, changing her like how it beginning to change me. Changing in a way, spiritually, like me, is starting to know God.

Anyway attending church, I see even my dad has changed. He wasn't getting high anymore. He was sober. At this time in my life I was so touch by hearing the sermons preached by Pastor. I couldn't wait to hear, what was the word God wanted to send to his' people, on those Sunday? I also became so engross with gospel singing about and for the Lord. I wanted to know more about him. I started falling so in love seeing and hearing and believing how he and Jesus helped all those people. I asked Pastor how she became so knowledgeable about God and the bible.

Pastor told me to start reading from the book of John.

Then I sing:

I love_ you lord ___ and I_ lift__ my voice__ to wor ship you on my soul___ dear lord. Take joy my king__ in __what you hear__ and let it be a sweet, sweet sound to your ear. Let it be a sweet, sweet sound to your ear.

I felt madly, deeply in love with God. I came to believe the scriptures. Especially I love the psalms. I started learning how to pray. I stared talking to God. I didn't know nothing about gospel singing so Pastor wrote down the lyric to the song for me to sing along. I LOVED singing for the lord. The spirit of God came faithfully every Sunday and I was touch and I use to find myself crying taking my burden in pray to the lord.

I was changing spiritually but I was unaware. What's old is now becoming new like being born again............. The choir will sing:

I'm___ gonna walk. I'm gonna walk. I'm___ gonna talk. I'm gonna talk. Well_ I'm_ gonna sing. I'm gonna sing. For my hea ven ly king. For the heavenly king....... I'm gonna be there. When they march around the wall. I'm gonna be there. When the general roll is called. They tell me that **half** has never been told____ but the Holy Ghost took control. I gonna walk, for the father, **sing,** for the son, shout for the Holy Ghost three in one, I'm on. I'm one my way to heaven. I'm on my way__ I'm on my way to heaven. I'm__ on my way__. I'm on my way to heaven, to meet the king -ing-ing. Whoop, you just listen. Listen let me tell you. You just listen how I view the promise land. You just listen. So many had been tested and tried **but** you must be born again. Your way and my way would not get told__ until we get to heaven on one accord. I'm on, I'm on my way to heaven. To meet the king-ing-ing.

I would cry tears of joy when the sprit came through the sanctuary. I mean I got so holy. The sprit was around me so bad that I could have become a nun. I had pure joy in the midst of all my misery on Sundays. By me writing this now I understand what took place when I was put in the circle over at Everyone Baptist Church. Remember I told you I said "I could see everything so clearly." Well it was the beginning of me coming into this new world. The spirit world. I was saved by grace. Which is God grace. This was the new world that was coming into my existence. I'm beginning to understand the scripture of the meaning, leave it on Calvary.

Now I do see. God saved me! I was blind but now I see. I use to cry so much because I was hurting so bad so when I kneel down telling God in secret all I'm going through. I was really seeking wisdom and I didn't understand what was wrong with me. Or what did I do to have such an abnormal life. Questioning why was I'm suffering so badly as if I had committed a crime and was being punish. In the church Pastor always had the entire church to concentrate on God and speech to him. "Pray to the spirit," she would say. So on my knee I cried my soul out to him because I knew something was wrong but I just couldn't put my hand on it.

Around that time, I was still smoking cigarettes. The first miracle God did for me was to help me stop smoking cigarettes. I asked him in prayer. It took a little time to manifest but eventually the taste was removed from my mouth. It was my first testimony proving what God had done for me.

Only on Sunday did my life seem to be normal. I found something other than raising my kids that I enjoyed doing. Even though everyone in the church could tell I was dirt poor. Our clothes (referring to me and the kids) were clean and iron. Our hygiene was very well taken care of. I never beg or asked anybody in the church for anything. My tithes were a dollar.

I was shining on Sunday so much, it seems like everybody in my neighborhood and family started going to church. Superman join his' mother church and he became the drummer. I saw my father being impress by me. Especially when he saw me began to get filled with the Holy Ghost as I sing gospel with the choir. I got so spiritual, and enjoyed singing the gospel that even my mother came to Pastor church and at that time she didn't go to church. She brought her' foster kids with her. Then Paris had visit the church. She done went and got married. Then lots of my cousins started going and joining a church.

One night I went to bed and I had a dream. The dream was about people knocking on my door. They wolves but in like sheep clothing coming for my kids. Which I didn't understand it. My dreams, these weird dreams are starting to scare me. When I woke up it felt so real. I recall not paying much attention because after all it nothing but a dream plus I had so much to take care of. Maybe within the next two days or even the next day or was it later on that night. I can't remember how many hours, or days has pass since I had that dream because this was so very long ago but the dream CAME TRUE.

I and the kids were inside the house. What caught my attention and made me think of the dream was because I heard the same exact knock that was in my dream but is now knocking at my apartment door. There was people voices talking behind my apartment door just like how I heard in the dream, but in my dream, I open up the door for them and something terrible happen. Leading up to my kids getting removed from the home, violently.

Due to the dream I did the opposite-there was people voices talking behind my apartment door just like how I heard in the dream. Quickly I had put my index finger to my lips. Especially looking toward JB, because he was such a bad ass little boy. "Shhhhh," telling the kid don't say a word." My children started to laugh thinking I'm was playing some sort of game. I made them listen to me, "Shhhhh," and then I started pointing my other hand for them to hear the knocking sounds that coming from off our apartment door.

The people started knocking obsessively wanting me to open the door because they knew I was in the house. I remember I keep telling the kids, "Please. Shhhhh be, quiet." I begged my children to be quiet cause in my dream when I open the door, something very bad had happen in my dream. Whoever it was they knocked on the door for a while until they went away. Then I heard Tonya yell from outside. "Champagne! Don't worry we coming for you." I remember I looked at my daughter she was like 8 or 9.

I distinctly remember even Champagne heard her name being called. She was looking at me as I was looking at her wandering what the hell do she want with my daughter?

Even though I'm in the church. I still am a babe in Christ. Meaning I have more to learn. I started to pray and bless my apartment. I started praying over my kids and my situation. One thing I realize was my dreams were helping me. Warning me about things to come or what to watch out for. Like I have a guarding Angel or maybe it just God. There wasn't anyone in my corner who I felt I could trust to tell about these dreams. They were unexplainable so how can I tell anyone anything when I'm not fully understanding everything myself. Then again, I didn't want to mention my dreams to my family. I felt I was being lied to anyway....... or......or I'm living a lie. Something is so wrong.

I was praying. While attending the church, Pastor will have me to stand and give a testimony. Announcing out loud what all God had did for me in the past to inspire others and to give the power of the Lord all his' glory so that other may come and get to know him.

After a while, Karl started back with his harassment. Well actually he went away for a while because I haven't seen him. You would think Karl stopped after the dog was gone............no he hasn't. Sometimes he be waiting on my floor when I came in the building taunting and teasing me or giggling as my children and I walk to our apartment door.

With nothing else for me to do besides go back and forward to family court, my kids needed to go out and play. I decided to take my children to that park that sit on Murray Street. The park that has those big trees. Great for sitting under for shade. I passed it lots of times when I went grocery shopping. As I sat in the park unmotivated, I happily held Moet in my arms while watching my other two children run and play. I thought on these things............. I was selling Avon and lingerie but had to wand up quitting that because my responsibilities for my family became too much to bear with expecting another child. I'm sitting there thinking, boy, I can't wait till these kids of mines get big. Then I tried getting a job downtown that didn't work out. Took a home health aide course that was consisting of cramming enormous amount of medical information. Then when I got my first intern patient, she died on me. I even tried a couple of times working at Macy Department store for the Christmas help. I didn't get that because of discrimination! Recruiters were West Indians and only was hiring the West Indians or Spanish, **Anybody,** but a true blue American. After repeatedly seeking employment with Macy dept. stores for the Christmas help when I finally got thru I had to quit because I had problems with babysitting. I even attempt going back to college which was all the way up in the Bronx but the furthest I got was seven credit-applied towards my remedial courses. I also tried 2 different computer business schools when I only had one child and that to have not worked out. I sigh, as I sat there thinking I've knocked on so many doors wanting to improve my life. I went to so many school that even Grand pop once called me an educated dummy. On the outside, I made to look like such a loser but in the inside I don't feel like a loser.

You know as a youngster I never picture my life like this. I thought I had a prominent future. I just knew I was going somewhere. I was a fly girl with a hot ass boyfriend. How did I get here? Raising three children by myself and they aren't even from the same man! One father a street hustler that turned into a crack-head. The other one is much older than me who running me thru the mud with family court. I'm now thinking he could be gay or even a child molester. He wants to take my son away from me and break up my happy little home-who's telling anyone and everyone who listen to him how much of a bum I am. How I don't have shit and pointing me out humiliating me constantly in front of others every time he sees me. I'm lost so much weight.

My clothes are dirt cheap. I feel like I been through the gate of hell, **twice already**. There so much more to me than being a good mommy. I feel like my life is being held back. I never thought I be sitting here alone with no family or my old friends. I hate my life.

After I thought about all that, with nothing else to do I brought one of my college book outside with me. I'm thinking, I mightiest well open it and read something out from it. Even though I may look like a loser I don't have to act like one. So, I open up the book to camouflage my falling success. Not quite ready to give in the towel-of not wanting success...........................I couldn't read a paragraph. Not even a sentence because my mind is so far away with so many consuming thoughts, dam! He asked "Excuse me is this your bicycle?" Wallowing in my own thought of self-pity I heard his voice but I didn't even look his way because I know, he just wasn't talking to me.

"I'm sorry to brother you but is this your bike?" As I just sat there wallowing. Just watching Champagne and JB run all around the park as I listen to the sound of his voice. Tapping me on the shoulder "Miss I'm speaking to you." I turn to my left and it this man pointing to a child dirty bicycle asking me, "Does that bike belong to you?"

I looked at the bike leaning against the park small maintenance work unit unamused and said "No." The husky guy said "Sorry to have bother you and he walked away." Wallowing again.........Wait a minute I've seen that guy before. So I turn around to see where and what direction he walking too.

As I watch him go across the street. I retracted and recounted in my mind, the times that I have seen him. Once when I was standing by the bus stop. Another time cutting through the park rushing to get Champagne off to school. Another time when it was raining and my umbrella blew away while carrying groceries.

Oh yeah! I even saw him one day when I was going to family court. Every time I saw him he waved at me. I found myself making a joke about him. Saying there goes that news van again. Because each time he waved I always had way too many issues going on maybe that why I never paid him much attention plus anyway I was with Thomas. Anyway, he walked inside that company across the street.

Dam. I'm going thru so much, I never really noticed that small gated company over there. I wonder what he does over there? What kind of company is that? Um.... I wander if they hiring.

Oh shit there he goes again. He walking to another small opening/entrance of the company. When I was selling Avon why I never noticed that company before?

Oh he's coming out again. He walking going back to the other entrance he first came out of. I wander what kind of business he does over there? Um, let me put on my sunshades' so I won't look so obvious while I check things out.

Oh sweat! He came out with his' sun shades on too. Now he's sitting outside on top of a large empty garbage can? Oh he thinks he is so funny. Is he over there watching me? By George I think he is! Oh! Oh, oh he coming back across the street. He coming towards the park. He coming right over here to me.

Standing in front of me he asks "Are you checking me out sitting over here?" "No, why would you ask me something like that," I said.

"Maybe because I saw you looking my way. It didn't bother me if you were checking me out because I'm someone worth checking out," he said.

He has a big ego don't he," I thought.

He asked "Is everything alright because I couldn't help but notice you look so sad when I came over here before?"

Man, for a couple of seconds my mind wasn't on my problems because I'm thinking about his ego when he said he worth checking out. Then when he asked me, if everything alright, the answer it reminded me of all the problems I'm having. It sent me right back into this depressing state. I must had started staring blankly into space thinking about the many issues I'm facing because I didn't even see his' hand reach to touch my face.

His finger gently, smoothly guided across my cheek towards my lips. The tip of his finger started circling in motion around my lips as I rotated my head to the gentleness of his' touch. Snapping out from his soft sensations. I question, "How did you do that!" Surprise at how his' touch made me correspond to the movement of his' finger.

"I got the motion in the potion," he said. I laughed. Thinking maybe he does. Anyway I thought it was a good comeback. "Hi my name is Diamond. What's yours?" he asked.

"Electra," I said. Diamond asked "Do you live around here?"

I said, "Yes, I live in this area. Just a couple blocks down the street with my children."

As I sitting there wondering-really how did he make me act like that from just one touch? Knocking the thought out from my head checking out the man who standing in front of me. I asked Diamond a dump question because I didn't know what else to ask. I said "Is that where you work?"

He said "Yeah that's my company." "Oh!" I said, now that information was impressive. I question, "So what kind of work do you do over there?"

Smiling Diamond said "I'm the man you call when those little bitty bugs crawl on your skin and bite you late in the night. When you want any rats and mice to scram, call me because I be that man. I am your neighborhood pest control, and that's just, who, I, am."

.... Breaking from the silence. I said, "Oh. Thanks nice," as I looked across the street I saw people haul in a large package. Looking back at Diamond I said, "I pass this block so many times and I never notice your' business."

Diamond told me "Because I'm new to the area. That store was boarded up. I just recently bought it."

"Ooh," I responded. Diamond said "I notice you a couple of times but you always seem busy? I tried to get your attention but you never paid me any attention."

A black guy came out from one of the entrance and call "Diamond, you needed in the inside." He said "I be right there," but before he left he turned to me asking "Are you sure that not your bike?" Looking back at the kid dirty bike. I said, "I'm positively sure that not my dirty bike."

Walking going toward his company Diamond said "Why won't you take it home and give it to your kids." Who were now standing by me wondering who the strange man mommy speaking too?

I said, "Naw, they good, that's all right. They have enough toys but thanks though."

Diamond said "Duty calls. Are you going to be sitting here for a while?" I said, "I don't know. Maybe," as I watch him walk away going back across the street to a group of guys by the large package.

As I sat there I started back wondering how did he make me act like that and how did he know I was sad. I wonder, did I have my lip poke out showing signs of distress. Then I also though dam, he's good because he the first person who got me to laugh when I was feeling really sad. I contemplated maybe he do have the motion in the potion.

I sat there for a little while longer because now my kids running around again. Then I got up calling to my kids, "Come on yall lets go. Time to go home." I stood up to starts preparing myself to walk away as I look across the street to see if I saw any signs of Diamond but I didn't. As I walked away, JB ran to catch up to us.

I just like to say my son is really a good little boy. I think he's so happy and a little spoil which makes him overly active knowing he is highly loved. Anyway, once everyone was in bed I thought about that park thinking it wasn't bad at all. I don't know why I never went over there sooner.

Wow. That's all I can say at this point as I look around to see who all still inside the library from Bridge Net. I got up to ask the librarian what time is it. "It 4:00," she answered. The dorms are open. I went back to the table where I was working, pack up my belongings and went back home to the shelter.

When I got upstairs. I quickly jumped into the shower. That felt so good.

As I organize my locker deciding what stays and what goes because the locker can only hold but so much I hear her say, "Hi my name is Shrill." I look to my left it's one of the new residents. Um, I see she seems to be sociable. And I see she is a lot older than me too, and she is American like me. Introducing myself I said, "How you doing my name is Electra."

Shrill said to me "I didn't want to come to a shelter but so far it not so bad as I thought."

I said, "Yeah this dorm isn't so bad compare to other dorms. The girls in this rom don't fight as much and you right, the shelter not that bad anymore. We laying on new improve mattress now, and thank goodness they just made everybody get rid of all those extra bags cause before, girl, the dorms use to be a **mess.**"

"For real. I glad I wasn't living here then but looking around the room, it doesn't look bad at all. It really better then what I thought," Shrill said.

"Of course it is but it wasn't always like this because people like myself made a difference in how we live inside a shelter by writing up complaints and speaking up at the house meeting on issues that affect us residents. You coming inside a halfway clean up room. Like I said, for the shelter, **now it is.**" I replied.

Shrill asked me "How long you be in the shelter?" I told her "In this shelter a little over 5 years." Shrill said "I hope I won't be here that long." I said "I understand how you feel," as I got out my notes to continue writing.

Shrill said, "My kids were worry for me. They didn't want me coming to a shelter. I'm going to call them to let them know it's not bad at all. Well nice talking to you."

Before I started to write I told her, "By the way, this shelter has churches that come here for inspiration. And there a calendar posted with activities that goes on here throughout the day. You can get a copy of the monthly activities downstairs in the intake office. To me it helps pass the time."

Shrill said, "Thanks. I'll think I do that because I'm not going to be sitting around here doing nothing."

"I don't blame you," then I told her "Like tonight we having open mic night after dinner." Shrill asked me "What that?" "It like karaoke," I told her. Then I said "You should come. I think it's fun."

Shrill said "It sound like fun. I know it got to be better than sitting up here on this bed all day." We both laughed because it so true.

Shrill left the room. I thought on what I wrote about earlier and thinking how nice it was to see Paris after all these years when she came to visit the church. So sitting on my bed I went back *into the story.*

Paris and I shared the same classrooms in public school and because of our' immaculate reading and math score we both were bus out to a junior high, in a good neighborhood. Really it was a white neighborhood. Back in those days us children who was talent in achieving remarkable scores in education scoring highly and above average got bus out our neighborhood.

Well at least I did. Back then we didn't have many choices of luxury schools, like how yall kids have it today. Luxury schools meaning different charter schools, Academies, private schools or schools-for the gifted and talent. So when my public school teacher made the suggestion to my parents and Paris mother that was something new for a kid coming from my hood out of our stomping grounds. It's not like we going to a different school from out our neighborhood just because. For my grade I was really highly intelligent and always scored exceptionally well. I guess that why the teacher made the recommendation. Thinking about it now in my area I was the 1st kid that travel to a better neighborhood for my education. Back then I never heard of any students traveling out their communities for a better education. It wasn't how the kids or parents of today behave thinking let attend a school in Manhattan to be around kids who family is richer than mine thinking their education level is higher than the educational level in your community. The recommendation for me and Paris were made due solely on our test average.

Now that I'm thinking about Paris. I really do miss her. I wish she was still in my life because we were really great friends to one another. I wonder how is she doing and I really do hope she's happy.

Anyway, while growing up in the projects I did have one best friend who I hung out with every day, Fran, but Paris was my next door neighbor up till I was a teenager and classmate as a child. Occasionally I will go next door and hang out with her and us teasing her brother, Superman. I really started liking Paris beginning to view her as another girl on the top of my list consider for my best friend. Back then as a child coming into teenager stage I had 2 best friends that were totally awesome but Paris never got to know how I really felt. As a matter of fact, this is my first time saying it out loud realizing to myself how much she really meant to me... and Superman. So in reality I had three great girlfriends Paris, Patricia and Fran I consider them as my best friends.

Also back then to me it seems my father was never impress by anything I did. When I ask Dad, "Do you love me?" He would tell me "You know I love you." For many years especially as a young teenager I felt I always tried so hard wanting my parent's approval. Especially my father to be proud of me and to show it. I gave and gave so much to my dad because I felt I wanted to be accepted by him-his' approval and for him to treat me like the daughter that he cares about. Showing others that he loved me not by words but by his' action too. Not by simply saying "Oh that my daughter." Like that all I am to him are those words. I found myself wanting to be accepted by him by doing things for him. Showing, this is how much I love you by never forgetting to give him a gift for father day. By coming by to see him and check up on him or calling him on the telephone. By bringing him a plate of food. By cooking his' dinners. Supporting ideas for his weight loss. By cleaning his' house. I did so fuckin much cleaning when he was on drugs before I had any kids. All daddy friends knew me. If they didn't see me in person I was the daughter who always answer his' house phone. His' neighbors knew me. I went to the store for him. I wash his clothes and mind you he was not the neatness person either. Frankly at that time he was a slob. I don't know what went wrong with my father. Maybe he became depressing and felt guilty after leaving us? Or he could have still been grieving the passing away of his' lovely mother, or, just maybe it could have been the drugs too. Maybe he was just spoil and highly loved because everybody else always cleaned his place trying to take care of him. Me, Aunt Bee and Grandma-Grace was always cooking and cleaning up his' place because we all loved him, but I did the most work, just ask them.

Tonya never came over to clean up or help daddy out. Everybody in the neighborhood probably thought he had only one daughter. Me. I mean I loved my father so much but yet I felt something was missing. I think I loved him way more than he loved me. You know why because love is also shown. It not just words.

When my mom started kicking me out the house as a very young teenager-where the fuck was I supposed to go? It was night time. I had no money because I had no job. Where the fuck was I'm going at that time of night? With nowhere else to turn I went to my dad' junky apt. He always had open the door for me to come in no matter what the hour or the weather condition was. Or if he had company. Or if he was in there getting high and lots of time he and his buddies were. My father had never kick me out of his house like how my mother use to do. I was always welcome and for that reason I develop a special bond towards my father. At that time, not knowing God had his hands on me back then because I could have been rape/ killed/ abducted/ got hook up on some serious drugs, anything could have happened but God had my back and that why it didn't.

When your mother and father for sake you. God will step in because he knows I'm a good person and I did not deserve that fuckin shit! Getting kick out the house by my mother. You know why God step in because my heart is Pure! I hear right now, as I'm writing....... the song:

Way_ in the water. Way_ in the wa ter children. Way_ in the water. God gonna trouble the water.

One day coming back from the corner store I bump into my cousin Coon. He said "Dam you look like you been through hell!" I asked, "What you doing over here?" He was visiting someone in the area. Even though he lives in Brownsville. Coon enjoyed hanging out in Bedford Stuyvesant.

Anyway, enough writing. It's dinner time and my food stamps are gone. Back to the old drawing board. I got up taking my pocketbook with me as I stood in the dinner line at the shelter. I could had left my pocketbook on a chair for holding me a seat. Even through there's cameras around I'm not stupid, this still is a shelter. I rather a resident takes my seat then my id because to me it such a hassle to get all my id back.

Waiting for the kitchen to open up. I like number six on line. The first person in line is Pepsi then Thomasina, a Spanish girl, the quiet Trinidadian women who knits but she mean. Whenever she notices you looking at her while her knitting she turn her back on you. Block her entire area so you can't see how she moves her hands just in case if you wanted to learn how to knit. Next in line is this light skin girl with the big tits. She been in the shelter system too for a while just like me, she American. Then there me. At dining time there always a guard posted cause lots of big mouth bitches like to come downstairs jumping the line. So the guard is there preventing this from happening. I'm not going to lie but sometimes I had jump the line too but not much like other girls.

The kitchen door has open. There a clipboard by the door waiting for us residents who are about to eat- sign. We have to first, flip the pages until we find our dorm then look for our name, next put our signature on the dotted line.

For dinner we had rolled up pot-roast, mashed potatoes and carrots. Two 4 ounces' juices, bread and butter. For desert we had apples. I sat on the other side, in the kitchen where there is no music this time. Only time when their music on this side is when RA Miss Alfre is serving breakfast. For the record I rarely cash in my stamps. I can't take eating this slop but it's better than starving. As I'm sitting down eating, occasionally glancing up seeing all the women passing by with their tray. You know who I haven't seen for a while, Sunsel.

I just want to point out we residents all know most of us in here. Rather we speak to each other or not. I'm an old timer I been here for a while. I know a new girl immediately by the way she acts. Which resident has return and who left? Like I said, after I stop working I begin seeing a different side to this shelter life.

With a wet rag in her' hand RA Houser yells, "Ladies this side is close. You got to go to the other side." She referring to the dining room side where the radio and bathroom is at. So I get up to empty my tray. Walking out from the kitchen. I see the other RA pulls the enormous cake out from the refrigerator. Time for cutting the birthday cake. I got a glance of the cake its Pink and white.

I like open Mic night. Bridge Net does this kind of party once a month for us girls. It a birthday celebration honoring all residents' birthdays that born in that month with a large birthday cake. The event always take place in the dining room from 7:30 pm - 8:45 pm. Samantha she orders the enormous cake from selected bakeries. To change up, sometimes she orders a sheet cake from major well known markets like BJ or Costco. Then she purchases a variety of home style baked cookies. After many years of partying this way at one of our house meeting some residents brought up concern for more nutritionists' snacks. So besides our original snacks Samantha now orders packs of plantain peanuts and raisins. The only thing with those so call healthy snacks everybody grabs those snacks first including staff, pocketing extras for later.

The long table will be set with juices to drink which staff use as a form of blocking/separating the dining room area from the kitchen area. The RA's that on shift start to slice the cake putting cake in foam paper bowls before open Mic starts. Also several cups of juices will be poured in foams cups too, waiting for residents to pick up. This type of party at the shelter is self-served.

There will be napkins and plastics forks on the table to take. The only things that are handed out to a resident when she walks over to the table will be the cookies of her choice and whatever other individual goodies they may have. The best thing about it is while others are performing residents can come back and forth for seconds or thirds until everything is all gone.

The long tables that usually are in the dining room where the radio at will become folded and place on the other side. The sitting chairs will be placed facing the windows because the karaoke machine is always by the window near the outlets. Beside a signing sheet Samantha passes out several songs booklets that contain the artist and their' title song.

Then on the table where the karaoke machine is at is tiny pencils and post note paper so us residents can put our' name on it with our song of choice. Open Mic mean a resident can do her' performances of choice. You don't have to sing. You can dance, do comedy or recite poetry the choice is yours.

I have a ½ hour before the show begin. I'm almost finish writing the book so I decide to take a walk.

I went to my mother' house who lives about eight blocks away from this shelter. By now the foster care business has helped her tremendously. I open the gate to the front yard of her 2 family house. I walk up to the door and rang her doorbell.

"Who is it," she said. "It's me," mom. She came outside while closing both doors. One door includes the house screen door. Standing outside in front of her door, "Yeah want you want Electra," she asked. "Nothing I just came by to see how you doing," I replied. "I'm fine," she said.

I ask, "What did you have for dinner." "Girl you know I don't cook that much. It just me and Dave inside the house. Let me go back inside the house One Life to Live Is On," she said.

Stop! To the reader: My mother was never a soap watcher. She recently develops the soap crave after seeing me watch it and she videotapes, therefore she watched her soaps at night.

Back to the story.

"You know mom that's too is one of mine favorite soaps as well as, All My Children. What going on with All My Children," I asked. My mother said, "Greenlee left the show."

"Wow she did! What about One Life to Live," I asked. She said, "Oh that stupid Jessica broke that cop heart to be with Nash." I said, "Oh I like Nash." "My story on. I'll speak to you later." She went inside her house.

I'm walking back to the shelter.

Stop! To the reader: I just like to say my mother has always lived a couple of blocks away from this shelter Bridge Net where I lived, also that will be the last time I will knock on her door. What happen is....... well like me approach it this way. Now my mother she attends church on a regular basis now and she, no longer take care of foster care kids. One day an outside church gave a function-the theme was about family. This same outside church, has left flyers in the shelter inviting us residents to attend. Well I attended and surprisingly I bump into my mother. She too attended this event. Everyone who lives in this borough of Brooklyn knows that I'm homeless because they have seen me sitting on benches, eating in soup kitchen, standing in line for free clothes from various churches who giving out free clothes though donations, walking endlessly though out the day carrying bags till 4 pm, hanging out all day in libraries, every day mainly eating from Sub-Subs delicious supermarket buffet bar or Jose corner store ordering a sandwich. Riding buses all the time wanting to visiting my children which always is for brief moments outside and that's if I got the chance to speak to them. Not to mention, this part of Brooklyn is where I was raised up at-therefore lots of people do know me and my family. People seen me attended various churches while also praying for an apartment. I had gone to the altar so many times seeking prayer so when this church congregation realized she is my mother and them knowing she supposed to be this women of God because every Sunday in Brooklyn, she wears all white which represent-she is an usher in someone church.

I forgot to mention by the way when I lived at sixty-eight Lex I was an usher too. Anyway. After this church had just gave a sermon on family and when I bump into my mother. I know my mother lives in a duplex that she owns and that her duplex comes along with an attach 2-bedroom rental apartment. I been expressed, over the years to my mother how the shelter is not a 5-star hotel. So, when I saw my mother that day I express to my mother the shelter still hasn't found me an apt and I question her, "Why can't I live in one of your houses?"

Why I said one of your houses is, besides my mother owing her 2 family house- she is also the co-owner of her parents already paid for, two family house in Brownsville.

I guess my mother didn't want to look bad in front of the church people who lots were looking at both of us wanting to hear her responds. So my mother said I can come and say with her. So I went back to the shelter telling the staff, **"I'm leaving!"** And I started clearing out my locker.

I been there so long that the administration staff came to my dorm wanting to know where I was going. They were stun to hear I was going to my family. So stun that they wanted to meet my mother because I told them she coming to pick me up in her' car. So when she pulled up. Employees from the administration office, the shift supervisor on duty, I even saw other staff members from the maintenance department come downstairs outside to witness my big event which was something I never seen them do **for any client.**

I collected all my artwork from Samantha and finally from staff I received my going home care kit package and their blessings as they send me on my way. Unfortunately, things for me with my mother didn't go as planned.

I just turned the corner going towards the shelter. After leaving, knowing my mother, she enjoys the same soaps that I do. I get in front of the glass door and security guard Watts buzz me in. I take the stairs going to the dining room. You know why?

It time now for Open Mic Night! Which is something I enjoy.

You know lots of residents are shy they enjoy being the audience. I feel like this, I only have One Life to Live, so I make the most out of mines. It beats staying in the dorm just sitting on the bed anyway which to me is so negative.

Therefore, I got to turn a negative situation into a positive. So to me, it's a form of partying and it starts at 7:30. Hey, I never dreamt I will have to party inside a women shelter all these many years. I would have loved to spend my young adulthood partying in clubs or at some discotheques whatever it is normal people do for an outlet.

You should know my slogan by now. Behind every negative situation. I got to find the positive. That the only way I was able to endure all this shit! If I didn't flip it over, so that when I woke up the next day, still living inside this shit of a hell hole. After all the injustice, to me I received from my family, the government, the court houses and all the many loop holes I fail thought dealing with New York City **FUCK UP** system. I could have flip the fuck out! Killing someone. Because after all, no matter what, taking my life, it was not at all-an option.

STOP! Reader, I like to say I appreciate you taking this journey with me. Sorry but the story has to end. Who knows maybe I write a sequel telling you all the juicy details in how I summed up these last three chapters. And remember, it not over until you read those two beautiful word, THE END.

Back to the story.

Through the years I have sung songs like Car wash, Mr. Big stuff, Killing me softly, Celine Deon, Slush splash, little Richard: good golly miss molly and a whole lot more. Any way the song I choose tonight is by Whitney Houston:

The Greatest Love:

And I sing I believe the children are our future. Teach them well and let them lead the way. Show them all the beau ty they pos sess inside__. Give them a sense_ of pride_ to make it easier. Let the chil dren laught er remind us how_ we use_ to be. Everybo dy search ing for a hero, people need someone to look up to. I never found anyone to fulfill my needs. A lonely place__ to be. So I learn to depend_ on me. I decided long_ a go never to walk in anyone shadow, if I fail, if I succeed. At least I live as I believe no matter what they take from me they can't take away my dig ni ty be cause the greatest love of all, is happening to me. I found the great est love of all inside of me. The greatest love__ of all is easy to achieve. Learning to love yourself is the greatest love_ of all and if by chance that special place that you been dreaming of. Leads you to a lone ly place find your strength in Love____.

Hands clapping and the audience said, "ruff, ruff, ruff, ruff." By the way.... that's something I taught them.

Good night.

Chapter Twenty-Two

While sitting at the breakfast table Shrill said, "I had a good time last night at open mic. By the way I think you sung that song well. Whitney Houston she is one of my favorite artist."

I said, "Thanks. I had fun too. That song was the theme song for my eight grade graduation. ..... Shrill, let me tell you something." While eating her food she asks "Yeah...what's up Electra?" Quietly I whisper, "I never knew Spanish girls were so prejudice."

Shrill said, "They are? Why would you say this?" I said, "Because lately I been noticing they only sit at the table among each other. It seems like they don't want to sit with us Black American girls. They always sitting together, among themselves."

Shrill said, "You know they stick together. And I really don't give a damn where they sit."

Quickly I said "Me either, but... I'm picking up different vibes like, separation, hatred, jealousy, envy and that's not good. Shrill it one thing to stick together but it another thing to cause segregation. I mean, what our ancestors and some religion groups of today protest and saying about the white people. For instance, like the Israelites... you know who they are right?"

Shrill just eating her food.

So I said, "Those guys you see preaching on the street holding the Quran/bible, and they be dressed in dresses like outfits or robes. One man would read a scripture from the Quran, while the other man tells the crowd in human words what the scripture is saying."

Shrill said, "Segregation? As long as they aren't fuckin with me." I said, "But I think they are. After the relationship with my kids' father I got to see a side of West Indians/Caribbean

632

people that open my eyes to this rude awakening. But I'm **shock** and applaud to see the Spanish behave with such ugliness. Let look at it, all the bodegas in the area not one of our' Black American men working inside their store. Everyone is Spanish. Then when you do see a black person, well he came from another country. I never notice that before until I become homeless and I started analyzing shit. Maybe before I didn't notice or paid any attention to it because I was inside the house so much, or working or going to school, or just being broke and upset that I never took the time to smell the roses per say. You know, sit back and check things out."

Shrill said, "You know you should be an activist for the community if issues like that passion you."

I told her, "I never was this way before, but in my relationship and after, my relationship was over with this Jamaican man. I notice a lot of people from other countries praising where they came from. From their actions, it made me like who I am and recognize Americans we too have our style and ways about ourselves and that I'm proud I have a flag to wave and acknowledge too. I see people from other countries always want us Americans to acknowledge their' flags. As they upheld and cherish their' country flag indicating how much they love their country. I guess all those years when I was with my children' father, seeing how he supported his' country, hearing West Indians bragging all the time about their' country and where they came from, made me look at my country and where I come from......Um.... Do you understand what I'm saying Shrill?"

Shrill said, "I never paid any attention to it. I don't like them anyway." "Shrill, who you talking about? Who do you don't like," I asked? Shrill said, "Whoever don't like me."

"Um" .... I told her, "It not about that. This world will be messed up. United we stand, divide we fall. It about **respect**. Okay, we are all different, but when your hatred taking you out of character to the point of alienations, discrimination,

633

scheming and plotting to destroy innocent blood, **now**, that a problem that needs to be address."

Shrill asked, "Have you ever met Al Sharpton?" "Yeah I meet him," I said. "Well you need to give him a call," she said.

Changing the subject.

I said "Look, look. Here come sleeping beauty."

Shrill asked "Who that?"

I said, "You sleep right next to her. I just call her sleeping beauty because she always gets to stay in the bed sleeping without a bed pass. Let see if she sits with us? After all, we all, are roomette."

As she walks pass. I said, "Hi, here an extra seat over here. Would you like to come sit over here and eat your breakfast?" She shook her head indicating "No," as she joins the table where now a group of Spanish females are forming.

"**See** I think that ugly. You can't come to our country take our jobs and our food stamps. Fuck our men. Then we support them by going to their' beauty parlor like every other week. That's why I stop going to their' salons so much, and the Africans too. I'm going to start financially supporting people like myself. Example, my Black American' hair dressers. Cause nobody supposed to think they are better than anyone else," I told Shrill.

Shrill said, "I'm going to tell my daughter about you. She has a Spanish neighbor and she never once invited my daughter over her' house when she entertains. I understand what you mean. We can all be a little kind to one another by hanging out with each other from time to time."

"Exactly. Why do people always have to separate their selves? The only time they want to be around you when it's something they want to get out of you. Shrill I hate to say it but, I'm glad you here homeless here with me because I have someone that I can relate too. I find that sometimes

Black Americans can be kind to everyone else. And lots of times they forget to be kind to their' own kind," I told her.

Shrill said "I'm here for you." "Like I'm here for you," I said.

After leaving the shelter I decided to return back to the library. I'm so excited because I'm almost finish the book. I found a seat and pull out my pen and paper.

Back *to the story.*

The next day on my block I heard a lot of commotion going on outside. I looked out my window and I saw a big crowd shouting down by the park area. I told my kids, "Something happen outside. I be right back!" Quickly I ran outside to see why was there such a big crowd standing down by the park.

As I approach the area with caution cause we are in the hood and sometimes, gun shoot just break out before you know it. Walking slowly ahead. I saw James-he's crying. Reader-you remember James right? Remember he's one of the young boys that hangs out with Karl. He also is the boy who knocked on my door, remember-asking to take Joe-Joe out for a walk. Well he's sobbing. I wonder what happen to him? I see the boys standing with him are looking down at something.

When one of James' friends look up and saw me approaching. I caught him elbowing (James) as I'm walking up towards them. James look up, and when he saw me, he tried to compose himself-in order to stop crying. He started sniffling-up the water that's running out from his' nose, quickly wiping the tears that were already on his' face. And trying to stop more tears from flowing down his' cheeks but he couldn't, because he was crying so badly. Quietly....... *now all the young boys* are watching me as I'm walking pass them all.

I'm walking. I wondering-why are they looking at me like that, as I continue walking towards the larger crowd. As I approach the crowd I gasped! Uggh!

James mother had finally brought him a pit bull dog. James took exceptional good care of that puppy. His' dog had everything and more than any animal could every want. What I saw was, James nice pup head bit completely off from its body. The head was there and its body over there!

Apparently, it was a very sad day not just for James, but also for the other dog' owner.

This older man he was crying too, as the police already had removed his' long time pet. His pet was placed inside the cop van. I had seen this man around the neighborhood with his' older dog for a long time.

Confused and upset, I overheard this older man saying, "I don't know what happen? My unleashed trained dog, just got up-walk away from me and bite the 4/5-month old pup head off. Then walk back and sat down next to me," as he seemed to be looking for anyone to give an answer of why the dog did it.

But what was even more amazing to me. The dead animal was exactly by the FENCE! Remember I told yall about the sudden appearance of that lady that I said vanished. Well, the dog head was right **there!** In the same fuckin spot but in the inside of the fence where Joe-Joe and I stood.........*Unbelievable!*

One day while sitting in the park allowing my children to play. I look across the street and I saw Diamond. I waved at him. To Diamond I said, "Hiii." He gives me a smile as he walked into the other entrance of his' shop. While sitting in the park, strangely then another one of Karl hang out buddies came up to me. He appeared to be so sad and he apologies to me. And he said he needed the telephone number for the animal hospital.

I'm thinking....... for an animal hospital?

Apparently his' long time Shepherd had babies. Heartbroken the boy said for no reason his' Shepherd bit the head off all and it was just that pup he had, that was barely still alive. Anyway he had the pup in the box wanting to save its life. He was asking **ME** for help. Unbelievable!

Some people on the block started looking at me as if I did voodoo or some form of witchcraft. I didn't. The only thing I did was went to church. I hate to say it, but, what goes around comes back around. In this case it came back quickly to James.

I and the kids went back to the park quite often and I became friends with Diamond. After a while I got baptized in a lake-in the name of the father, the spirit, and the Holy Ghost. It was totally awesome.

Then one day while sitting in the park Diamond ask me out on a date. He asked "Do you want to go with me to see a show?" Out the blue, he just asks me just like that. I was so stun. I haven't been out in such a long time, not knowing what else to say, I asked, "What kind a show? And where is it?" He said "The Pointer Sisters and other artists are performing at the Westbury."

Immediately I thought about **Yolanda!**

Remember she said that detective can take me in his car and **Me** going somewhere far to a place I never been. Like Westbury! He could kill ME! And get away with it! It's a shame but I haven't been on a date in a long time. I never left Brooklyn. So I said, *"I don't know."*

Diamond said "Come on it be fun. Let me know because the tickets cost $75.00 dollars each." He smiles at me before he walks away going back across the street to work.

I'm thinking, I always wanted to go out. Also I thought well this is my birthday weekend and I haven't been out anywhere descenl with a man I find appealing in a very long time. Thomas he never took me anywhere, not even Tray.

The kids saw me talking to Diamond as he walked off. My children came by me and was sitting right next to me. I looked at them and I said to my kids, "He ask to take me out on a date." I remember how all three of the kid was looking at him over there across the street. Champagne asked, "Are you going to go?" All three of them were waiting to hear my answers. So I said, "I haven't decided yet."

Walking home, and until I went to bed, I thought about it, and I thought about it and I thought about it and I thought about it. I thought about Yolanda. And then I thought about it and I thought about it and I thought about it. And still Yolanda has not return or pick up any of my calls since I been calling her.

When I went back to the park. I said, "You know what Diamond, why not. It sounds like fun." I remember I went home so happy because **I had a date!** I'm so excited that when I got home, I went to my next door neighbor bragging, "Guess what!? I got a date! I'm going out this weekend," I said while gloating.

Because Brenda she was always party! She always saying, "Bye Tami. See you later." First I'm smiling while gloating because I have a date. And I'm the one who's going out. Then I remember! Now I'm begging, "Brenda pleassse come on Brenda say you watch my kids?"

"I'm going out that day," she said. "Oh come on! You always going out. Please Brenda could you stay home just this once so I can go out on this date. Pleassse," I asked. "I'm sorry girl. I really can't," Brenda said.

So I remember asking one of the old ladies on the block who always saw me struggling with my children. I told her my good news and asked her would she babysit for me that day. She said, "She will."

Looking out my window now I'm all dress up. Diamond pulls up in a kind of nice but old blue 2 door sport car. He steps out from the car with the same sun shades he had on when I first saw him staring at me, while I was staring him.

In the house excitedly I said, "He here!" I told the kids, "Quickly come on." Champagne ran to the window to see for herself. JB he was jumping around so I grab him by his hand. While I told Champagne, "Here's the food I pack for yall. Only you change Moet Pamper and when JB has to use the bathroom go with him. Don't sit on anybody toilet and **don't** give the lady a hard time, please."

When I got outside I walk up to him with the children. Moet in one arm, dragging JB with the other hand as Champagne held the food. I said, "Hiii."

Diamond said "Hello Electra." I said, "I'm going to need some money for pamper and the babysitter." When Diamond went inside his pants pocket. I looked across the street. I saw BRENDA. She watching us with her' mouth wide open as she seems to be talking on the pay phone.

I smile thinking and kind of gloating like, I told you I had a date.

Diamond gave me the money I hurry across the street dropping the children at the sitter. Came back and sat down inside the sport car and the music lyric was singing "I found what this world is searching for." Diamond and I, we drove off listening to Barry White sing his song: never ever going to give you up, that playing on the car radio station. As we turn the corner I saw Brenda still looking with a drop lip.

Then I put my sun shades on, matching his. Diamond reach for my hand and held it. I thought that was cool and kind of romantic. Why after all, we both are just Black Americans.

Once the show was over. Diamond was the perfect gentlemen. I remember I kiss him on his' cheek and nibbler at his' ear because it was the best birthday gift I had in a very long time. Afterwards we went to a Motel with a Jacuzzi. Every time Diamond went inside the bathroom he removed an article of clothing until finally he came out with nothing on but his silk boxer shorts.

Together we laid on the bed as he massages my scalp gently with his' fingers. I told him, "I remember this." Diamonds said "You remember what?" I sat up saying, "I remember this feeling." Diamond ask me "What feeling?"

I didn't tell Diamond anything. I brushed it off asking him, "What day is your birthday?"

When he told me, **I gasped!** His birthday was the same day as Dove.

The feeling I remember was when I 1st fell in love and how it felt so warm inside. It was a lovely birthday. God gave my heart a second chance to love. Anyway Diamond got me home before midnight and we kind of became real cozy in a way after that.

As for Karl, well he got worst. He started following me to my door. The more I spoke up for myself, like to stop the harassments. It made him angrier towards me. It seems like he wanted to treat me how he wanted to treat me-with me saying nothing about it.

I never told Diamond the issues I was facing because we weren't like a committed couple. We weren't even in a relationship and he was so busy wanting to jump start his' business. He had hung up his logo over the front part of the store. He had his hand full ordering equipment, with workers and keeping everything up and running. Plus, it's so early in our new friendship. I didn't know if it was going to mount up to anything more. He wasn't calling me on the telephone like the detective was and he wasn't pushing to come over to my apartment, or inviting me to come over to his place either.

Eventually. Karl got a gun. Approaching that winter he started shooting bullets from the backyard. My bedroom windows face the front of the building and my children bedroom window faced the backyard.

That spring due to a lot of nonsense with Thomas and visitation and repeatedly family court issues-along with Karl stupidity of harassment. After the cops came repeatedly to my home finally, the cops at the 56th made the suggestion of me and the kids going into a shelter. The cops from the domestic violence unit told me I'm living in a dangerous situation. Because of their constant foolishness, then again, by the police, I was asked to go to a shelter. I remember literally I had to ask the officer, "What is a shelter?"

I work so hard and sacrifice so much to build this place I can finally call my home. Even through, something was still off....... which was weird because I couldn't put my hands on it. Anyway, my home it was a steady foundation for my kids and for myself. It was built from love and using my creativity to make something out from nothing. It took planning, sacrificing and hard work. A place I can call home which was something I haven't had in a very long time. A place where I can close my apt door and be at peace, and in comfort, in the privacy of my own surroundings-my steady foundation. That's why it was so hard for me to leave when the cops made the suggestion the 1st time wanting me to leave and go off to a shelter.

BANG! BANG! BANG-those are gun shots!

Karl shooting bullets in the backyard again. I felt it was just a matter of time before he goes to the next level. Anyway I wasn't waiting around to take that chance. Beside myself, I had my kids to think about, as you can see I always will have them to think about. I ran before from Kerchief. I fought with Tray. I went and lived thought hell with Desmond. I'm in family court all the time now, with Thomas. I wouldn't mind seeing or wondering what a relationship will feel like with Diamond, but not like this. Now I have this young man Karl that comes from a family who has little or no respect for women and mankind.

Today is Christmas and he shooting out from the backyard. It around 10 or 11 o'clock at night. I took one good look at the 2-bedroom apartment I created for myself. All the beautiful toys my children had underneath and around their Christmas tree. I told my children to take one toy that they really like. I tell you what ... **it was the sadist day of my life**. December 25 1995 it the first time I became homeless that is the day my journey began. It also was a day of great courage. The day I decided to leave my safety net and step out into a world of the unknown. It took guts because it wasn't only me going to this unknown never heard of place before. I'm also traveling with my three very small children. I went to the 56th precinct and I asked for the domestic violence unit. I told them, "I'm ready to go to a shelter now."

I was sent to a domestic violence family shelter. While living inside different family shelters, me and the kids, I still keep up with the constant demanding draining schedule dates for family court. Due to my fears of abduction and unknown of Thomas living address, now suspicion of child molestation. Therefore, the appointed visitations for Thomas was schedule supervised, order and stamped by the family court system.

At first the supervised visitation was held at my mother, in her old two-bedroom apt where we had our 1st and last Thanksgiving dinner. Then it became unbearable, because Thomas was coming back late or not showing up for the visit. Again, Thomas was constantly bad mouthing me to my mother, till my mother couldn't take anymore. So family court has now sent our supervised visitation to the 56th precinct which came with much drama, along with made-filed accusations reports which Thomas and I both took back and forth to Brooklyn family court, arguing.

I was so stressed. Me dealing with this visitation from hell, while the domestic violence unit, is now court order to monitor our visits. This lasted for a very, long, time.

Just to think I never wanted Thomas to break up my family. **Well he did**.

On the very first visit at the precinct in Brooklyn when I reached there from Queen or Manhattan depending on which family shelter I was staying at-Thomas took only his' two biological kids. Thomas, he kisses Champagne on her' cheek and said, "Blame your' mother for this Champagne." As she watched her' younger brother and sister drive off in the van with Thomas. While Champagne and I walked endlessly around in Brooklyn because I'm broke and I had to pick up the children from the visit on time that's being taken place in Brooklyn.

Deep down inside I know Champagne was hurt, I saw it in her face. Thomas is the only father she ever known. All my children probably thought they had the same father. I didn't want my children to find out in this crazy way. Later on that night inside the shelter I had to explain to my children because they all had questions wondering "Why Champagne didn't go on the visit? And Moet wondering why she couldn't stay with me."

In the shelter, inside that one room in Queens I told them, "Even though yall have different fathers, because Champagne has a different dad, but he was never around and I don't know where he's at. Yall all came from me, so in my book yall are very much brother and sisters." It was sad, but a true rude awakening for them all to find out that way. Quietly as they looked at each absorbing in that bit of information. **I hate Thomas**.

Every Saturday I had to travel to Brooklyn with these children no matter which shelter I was at to meet Thomas for court order visitations at the 56th. It got to the point I hated seeing motherfuckin cops. I'm a descent parent why in the hell I was made to look like a piece of shit and a spectator for all when it came to raising my kids. Then I had to keep commuting to Brooklyn with no dam money. I didn't understand the stupid family court system that's putting me through hell. Thomas the man with the car and the van, the court should had made Thomas come to the borough I was living at. I'm so fuckin humiliated! Especially when I knew there are so many other fuck up parents out here raising their children! Thomas can late for every fuckin visit. Causing me to have to sit inside the precinct with my children and wait. If he didn't pick the children up late. He came back late causing me and Champagne to spend hours waiting for him just to come back with the 2 **kids!**

Sometimes but not much the cops from the domestic violence unit asked for me and Champagne to wait at my mom 2 bedrooms apt for a call, letting me know when Thomas came back and that I should come and pick up my 2 younger kids. I just like for it to be known-never once, whenever I was at my mother apartment did she every drive me and my daughter Champagne in her car to the precinct while these crazy visits from hell was taking place. Not all the time around this time, were there foster kids in her 2-bedroom apartment. Champagne and I always walked back to the precinct as well as walk from the precinct to her apt. Both my parents were very much aware what I was going through. Yet neither one of them showed me or my kids any kind of support.

The first shelter I went to was located in the Bronx. It was an assessment center. After one weeks of me and my children sleeping in chairs and on the floor. The assessment center places us inside a Domestic violence family shelter in Manhattan. After staying there over 1 year and some months, we got transfer to that disgusting shelter in China town-the one I told you about with the large rats, on Catherine Street. Then from there we relocated to a family shelter in Queens-inside the room in that shelter, that had this serious roach problem but thanks to my sloppy dad I became a professional at cleaning my surrounding and finally, because my dad had a bad roach problem too back in the days, I finally found the best remedy for getting rid of roaches.

At this family shelter in Queens those dreams had started back resurfacing, I started having really frightening dreams concerning my entire family-my mother, cousins and my grandmamma. In my dream my cousins all looked like demons and Grandmamma looked like an experience witch.

Grandmamma was making a potion cooking it in a large cast-iron round pot, and the fire underneath it was on the ground. The dream it was really scary. Then it was something about the house, it's like I was on the outside looking in. One time in my dream my mother blows up so big that she **popped!** Sometimes I was afraid to go to sleep. One time I asked Champagne before I napped if I tossed and turn in my sleep wake me up.

I was floating from shelter to shelter with me having these crazy dreams. Whenever I can, I catch a church service here and there. I forgot which family shelter I was in but by this time my grandfather, Granddaddy started getting sick. He was in the hospital. Columbia hospital, anyway it wasn't good. When I got to the hospital he had a tube fasten to his throat. His lungs had clasped and it's the machine what was keeping him live.

Granddaddy always said he never wanted to live on a machine.

He was already piss off that he went blind. Then for some reason it like he was being mistreated by love ones. Why I say this is because when I came by to visit him, our loving family not only changed on me, but it seems like they changed on him too. Granddaddy skin got so dried it look white ashy. He was smoking so many cigarettes-like a chimney smoker one after another. I got the impression he was alone but he never spoke on it. Back then with only one child at the time, I was going thru so much probably that why Granddaddy didn't mention anything to me like he may had needed some help. But now, I already had so much again on my plate with family court and the visitation from hell with Thomas, that I wasn't able to visit my (mother parents) the only grandparents I had left-as much as I would have like too. They knew I had problems going back and forth to family court. Now my entire family knowing me and my kids are living inside a family shelter. I'm the first in my family, and circle of friends to ever go to this unknown word of.......... a shelter.

Anyway there he was in the hospital blind and couldn't talk. On my 2nd hospital visit I wanting to pull the plug so bad and he must had known what I was thinking because I saw him lay his head straight back on the bed. I saw his chest going up and down rapidly, ready, like he is anticipating, that I was about to pull the cord attach to the machine right out from the socket. So I looked behind me because he's in the intensive care unit and by now his' bed got moved right in front of the nurses and doctor station-they were so close that I couldn't pull the plug. Then I didn't want to hear the machine make that long line sound when his' heart has stop beating.

He was so agitated lying on the bed then he started saying something. He was trying to tell me something. I said, "What?" He was saying something but I couldn't hear what he was saying. He raises his body off the bed trying to say something. I still was unable to hear. I think they had straps on him. So I told him, "Write it on paper."

I got a pen out but he got frustrated realizing he couldn't write it down because he couldn't see. I think I made him try but it was unsuccessful. His chest was pounding it was going up and down that I started to get scare for him. I wanted Granddaddy to calm down. He was so frustrated. I even saw tiny tears running from his' eyes. I never saw granddaddy cry he been through so much after he lost his sight. At this point I felt it was out of my control. I needed him to calm down and he needed to tell me something. So I said, "**Stop**," because he's breaking my heart.

I had to be strong for him now because he was uncomfortable and under so much stress.

He never asks me for nothing but he needed me and he had something to say. I got real close to his mouth hoping his' voice could come through the tube that was down his' throat but it didn't. So at that moment I asked Granddaddy, "Do you believe Jesus Christ walked the earth?"

He got so upset like **dammit!** What the hell you talking about? Laying his' head back resting on the bed, frustrated but it like he got kind of calm. I notice his chest breathe normal as he shook his head meaning yes. I asked him, "Do you believe all the miracle we heard in the bible." He shook his head meaning yes.

I told him how wonderful God is. I gave him testimonies what God had deliver me from and how God has protected me over the years. I told him "God is real and that he loves all his' children and Granddaddy he will tell me what it is that you are trying to say." I assured him my faith is so strong. I told him, "You have to have faith too, it can be small as a muster seed. Have faith that what you are saying will come to pass."

He was lying there listening to me speak as Granddaddy wasn't no longer breathing that hard but I could tell he was still uncomfortable. I ask, "Do you confess Jesus Christ as your Lord and savior?" He shook his head meaning yes. I asked, "Do you confess that you are a sinner and through Jesus Christ you will be saved?" Hearing my voice, he shook his' head again for yes. Then in faith believing I grab his hand as we held each other hands as I prayed then saying, in Jesus name. Amen. Sometime quickly after that he died.

Another weird inexpiable dream.

This time it was about me, Tonya and Desmond. We were running through the forest playing and as I ran I caught a glimpse of God face on a cut down tree trunk. As I looked at the face on the trunk the next thing you know I'm way up in the sky. As if I'm on top of a peak from a mountain. This mountain was so far up in the sky. It was the most gorgeous serenity blue sky I had ever seen. As I was walking its only path, barefoot, the path became so narrowed that I started holding alongside the mountain for balance because the drop down look like it could have been almost infinity. I knew I was up pretty high. Then I came to an opening and the path slowly as I walked became wider.

Then I saw the most **amazing thing!** I don't know if it was God or Jesus their self, because I heard no one ever saw God face before. Anyway it looks like God and Jesus, they were covered in all white, almost like, not a see through-white, just pure bright white clothes-like robes. They were up in the air. I asked them, "How yall walking up in the air like that?"

They weren't walking, they were standing looking at me like discussing me? I can't remember exactly how many men there were. I know there was two for sure. I think it was more but it was so long ago. I remember I'm looking up at them and I asked, "How yall walking/standing up in the sky like that?" They were gather together looking down at me, discussing something among their selves. They wanted me to do something. I remember feeling so bad because I fail or I didn't want to fail.

Now that I'm writing this book I wonder did I fail because sometimes dreams are backward. I didn't mention before to yall that some of my family are superstition that how I know some of these things. Anyway, I found myself walking bare foot looking at my toes as I walked on the concrete ground. Like I'm back on earth. I'm walking in the middle of the street. I hear my favorite type of hip hop music. I figure "**Yeah,** I'm going to the party." I get inside the house, people were there. Tonya was there too. Then all of a sudden Grandma-Grace appeared. Grandma-Grace didn't want me dancing to the hip hop. I recall being so mad because I love that kind of hip hop. Then Grandma-Grace took Tonya with her and they were gone.

...............Something is really going on with me.

Anyway. We stayed in the family shelter system approximately 3 or 4 years before I received my section eight voucher.

I found an apartment.

A-three-bedroom apartment back in Brooklyn not too far from the old building Thomas and I once shared. Then

SURPRISE! I found out my beautiful girlfriends, -not one, -**but all 3** of my girlfriends (Shelby, Donna and AP) along with their' husbands, had split-up as well.........Unbelievable!

Next. I found out my mother has gotten married to Dave. **Get the fuck outta here!** And I wasn't even invited or made known of their ceremony. **Dam!**

Ooooh, remember those brick homes I told yall about. The ones I use to sit and watch for hours when Thomas and I were together. Well, I finally had gotten an application. I figure Thomas is gone and I didn't need it. I remember I showed my mother the print layout of the new home and I give her my application that I had for those brick homes. Surprise when I came out from the shelter and back to Brooklyn not only was she marry but she and Dave are now home owners of one of those 2 family brick homes. They actually live like 3 blocks down the street from me. .... Unbelievable!

Unbelievable now the welfare finally changed!

The city no longer wanted people staying home doing nothing, just collecting a PA check. By now, the law or should I say the government has changed the welfare program. In order to become eligible now for welfare, the city started making welfare applicants also meet the requirements of the WEP program.

It was mandatory.

WEP, it's abbreviated for the work experience program for trying to help build resumes for unemployed people who been on welfare, like myself for a lengthy amount of time. If any applicant who receiving any form of help from the city from the welfare system, if you didn't meet and oblige with the new WEP program your case got automatically cut off.

After sitting home on the welfare all these years I know a lot of girls who cases got cut off because they didn't want to work all those free hours for the WEP program. I don't blame them who wants to work just to keep receiving their welfare check when that is no real money in your hands after paying your bills. The welfare started sending out letters to applicants to come meet their new reform back to work program, (WEP). When the welfare applicant didn't oblige with the new laws of the welfare the applicant case got cut off immediately. Meaning the government will not pay the ex-applicant rent. Meaning the ex-applicant, no longer eligible for food stamp or medical coverage. Meaning whoever all on the ex-applicant budget received nothing from the city. Including your kids.

When an applicant gets cut off from welfare or another way of saying it, is when the applicant case got close. The applicant had to re-apply **all over**. In order to become eligible now for welfare, the city change the laws, making the new applicant wait under this pending allotment status-meaning, the applicant receives nothing while allowing the welfare system to check out all documents submitted and nothing takes place until after 45 days of a completed application.

After I saw what happen to the other girls who didn't apply with the new reform back to work program (WEP). I knew when I receive my letter I was going to oblige with the Work Experience Program because I didn't want to get caught out there like that because my rent needed to be paid and we had to eat. I had to keep food on my table.

Thomas and I spend so many years in family court fighting and arguing. I was so stress from living inside a family shelter, Thomas harassment, stressed from the family court keeping us in court and dealing with Thomas not obeying court order visitation stipulation, causing me to constantly modify the order. Not to mention the struggle with the sole responsibility of raising and funding 3 kids by myself, that when, I finally got my 3 bedroom apt I gain some weight. Thomas told everybody "Tami on dope."

Then having so much stress and aggravation I started back smoking cigarettes, then I just lost the weight. Now Thomas telling everybody "Tami on crack." Consecutively still with family court cases behind one behind another. Then now from Thomas constants lies of my drug use, now-ACS (agency for child services) got involved. The agency no longer went under the name BCW.

We were in court so much and so often until I loss count how many **YEARS** we wasted in that court house. I mean our case was so bad everyone in the court house know, all of us! Then the judge did the most unspeakable thing. Thomas he had way more money than me. The judge, she did the most amazing thing.

I didn't even see it coming!

Like I said, I found us a three-bedroom apartment and it was time for the children to come out from school. We were in court and Thomas and I always spent long hours downtown in family court. This time while inside the court house my kids would soon be coming home from school. By now all three of my children are in public school. Moet was in pre-k, JB was in the 1st or 2nd grade and Champagne was in 6th or 7th. So from court I was allowed to go pick them up from school. She awards Thomas custody of our two children. "Thomas you are the custodian parent for Brandon and Moet Benton," the white judge said.

I couldn't believe what the **fuck** I just heard!

Actually I repeat her' words over and over in my head because I didn't see that coming. Nor did I understand what she said. I can't begin to describe how painful that was for me. When the judge gave Thomas custody of my 2 kids. The entire court room went silent....... You know why? Thomas was crying.

It was so unreal. I **know** she just didn't take my children **away from me**? I repeat the words as I saw me **joking the shit! Out of her white ass**-then I heard the...... sounds. The sound of a grown man crying.

.... Thomas was crying, no let me rephrase that he was sobbing.

We all had lawyers. I had a legal aid lawyer. The children had a lawyer. Thomas paid for his' own lawyer.

Overwhelm!

Because I just can't believe what happed. It like I space out from becoming overwhelming with disbelief. Stun and without words I simply turned to my right. Just to see Thomas outburst of emotions. He's crying. No, let me rephrase that, he sobbing with tears rolling down his' face snots coming out from his' nose! .... And that's what stop me from jumping over the desk wanting to choke the **SHIT** out of that white lady not to mention, the court guards they were standing nearby, especially by me, with guns at their waist but in my space out mind I was already on top of that desk choking the **shit** out of that white **BITCH**!

I saw the guards standing by me with their hands by their guns. Quickly I question within myself as Thomas sob, "Why did she do that? I wanted to kill her. Why did **she do that?**" Then the sounds of Thomas crying keep snapping me back into reality as I sat inside the court room. I'm thinking....

I can't believe they took my kids.

They took my kids!

It was so surreal, as I turned back to the right looking at Thomas who still crying inside the room because his voice that is crying-is the only sound in the courtroom. I looked at this man because it's the first time I ever saw this man cry. I was thinking.... I'm supposed to be the one who crying...... but I was so numb and shock with disbelief I couldn't cry. As I sat there numb and speechless I'm wondering, what the **fuck!** is he crying for? He over there sobbing.

He cried so hard and for so long that everything stops.

All eyes were on him, even mines. Waiting for him to shut the **fuck up**. It so quiet the only sounds are of a crying man and it's coming from Thomas.

I was so very shock to see Thomas crying as I sat there looking at him. The judge she **fucked my head up!** That I was speechless and in a way I felt so helpless. I was piss at my lawyer, as I just watch Thomas cry. For a minute again, the sounds of him crying it took my mind off of choking the fuckin judge. After he kind of gotten himself together. The white judge asks very firm and slow, "Mr. Benton why are you crying?"

Everybody in the entire room been quiet but now everybody waiting to hear the words that's proceeding out from Thomas' mouth. I wanted to know the answer for that too. While sniffling up his' nose a couple more times, finally, Thomas said while still crying "me and her mother tried to help her."

Then he ball-out and cried.

I can't recall who because my mind in shock as a person came to me and told me the judge order immediately that I attend an outpatient drug rehabilitation for 1 year because drug was found in my urine. If I do this, I can get my kids back. Unfuckinbelievable! As I watch him immediately walk out the court house with my two children carrying their school backpacks on their backs while leaving me and Champagne behind. My 2 smaller children had no idea that they wouldn't be sleeping in their bed room tonight, or that they wouldn't see me in a week or so.

That's the day I quit smoking cigarettes. It was a hefty price to pay.

When I got home not one family member called me. Not one!

From family court I was the one who got weekend visits. In my neighborhood people was profound to see this happen because no one ever saw me do drugs and **besides**, the children always stayed with the mother. But then some mother thought I had it better than them by being free and that my 2 small children responsibility is on their' father. Which was so not true. I loved my kids and I was and still is missing my children. I loved being their mother. I had so many plans for them. I inputted a lot of my love into my children even thought I had a hard time financially but I enjoyed raising them every moment. They're my family and the word family means a lot to me.

The separation I nor the kids had any warning of this. I was totally speechless. The court employees (meaning the judge and the lawyers) doing our cases/trail was using all these big fancy words all the time. They kept adjoining our family court cases for one reason or another making us come back and forward to court all the time. The family court house played me very well because if I had imagined the outcome to turn out this way. I would **have never** kept showing up for this kind of bullshit. In my neighborhood the children have always stayed with their mother who's on welfare. The family court house knew I wasn't familiar with their court lingo. Truly if I had any knowledge of this fuck-up system I probably would had tried talking some sense into Thomas.

Raising my head up from the library table and putting my pen down I'm thinking, I didn't like how that went down and that it still hurts and I'm very angry about it. In more words then I can ever express. I guess, I can't express my feelings on paper right now because I'm still numb believe it or not, I'm still totally upset till this very day. Anyway, reader I got a lot of writing done. When I'm writing the time flies. Its lunch time and I got that big meeting today so I left the library heading back towards the shelter.

Chapter Twenty-Three

After lunch I got ready for my meeting with Mr. Winlesky and Miss Taylor. On the fourth floor I knocked on the Administration office door. "Come in," Mr. Winlesky said.

When I walked into the office Miss Taylor and Clinical Director Kimberley Stewart were sitting down in chairs too, waiting upon my arrival.

"Have a seat Miss Jones," Mr. Winlesky offer. "This look so formal," I said as I sat down. Kimberley Stewart said, "There's no need to become alarm. We conducting this meeting because we made some observations about you and we like to bring it to your attention."

I'm thinking, *observations*. About me? Oh this is formal, as I look at Miss Taylor sitting upright with her hands folding in her lap, as she put on a negotiating business smile upon her' face when I looked her way. With caution I ask, "*What is this about*?"

Mr. Winlesky had a binder that has my name on it in his hand, which is completely big and full because I been living here for so long. Mr. Winlesky asked Miss Taylor "This is her' correct HA # 8045866?"

Miss Taylor bent over looking at the binder Mr. Winlesky had in his' hands while comparing her' notes from her folder she said, "HA # 8045866 Miss Electra T Jones yes that is correct." Then Miss Taylor kind of smiled and told me, "It just a matter of time before I have to get you a new binder. Then you will have two binders."

Kimberly Stewart asked Miss Taylor, "How is her housing coming along?"

Miss Taylor responded by saying "Miss Jones was sent and has obtain housing at Temple Horizon in the Bronx, where she was placed in a SRO. She has return back unhoused to Bridge Net less than a year. Miss Jones was also sent to

Times Square Union Hall, location 42nd and 8th for possible residency. But she wasn't chosen as a candidate, and since to the present no other housing has been in place."

Kimberly Stewart asked, "And why haven't she been on any other housing interviews?"

Miss Taylor replied, "Her housing package is circling. Being Miss Jones only receives Public Assistance we waiting for suitable housing placement. At this time from what it appears Miss Jones will be sent to another SRO, or some kind of shared residency."

I interrupted and said, "Which I can't understand? Why is it taking so long for me to obtain housing? I would really like to know the answer to that question. I'm here every night at ten o'clock to sign for my bed. I thought by now I should had had something."

Mr. Winlesky said "Miss Jones we not keeping you here and we don't want to keep you here. Our resources are limited. DHS receives all the housing packages and the packages are being sent to various housing units, programs and developments not just for this shelter but for all shelters."

Even though I didn't express it out verbally, I still felt like that's not my problem. Ain't no way, all these many years I should still be in the shelter system seeking housing.

Looking at me sternly with those blue eyes of his, Mr. Winlesky said "Well Miss Jones after my staff and I evaluated your' chart. We notice that since you been here, you have never had a weekend pass nor a late pass. Not even an overnight pass. Even through those privileges aren't permitted anymore, I like to point out, you have been here for every holiday, Christmas, mother day, New-year eve and Thanksgiving. You have attended all the fourth of July barbecues as well, as, the Memorial ones too." ....Now all eyes are looking at me and it's quiet.

At this point I'm sitting in the chair taking in what I just heard him say, while wondering, so? Like where is this going? Then I looked back at them all and said, "That is correct."

Quietly they all looking at each other as if I didn't give the right answer.

Finally, Mrs. Kimberly Stewart said, "Do you find that to be a little alarming?" At this point it's quiet and all eyes are on me again.

Looking at them all. I said, "I don't understand where this is going?"

Mrs. Kimberly Stewart crossed her leg. She sat back in her' chair and open up a folder that she had. She said, "According to my records you do have a mother and a father who are both alive and you have children. Miss Taylor, in Miss Jones personal file how many children is written down for her?"

Miss Taylor looked quickly at her' notes; gave an assuring shook of her head and said, "She has three children."

Looking back at me Mrs. Kimberly Stewart said, "You came to Bridge Net from another shelter. No. I'm sorry, you were transfer here from 68 Lexington. I am aware 68 Lexington was a shelter that didn't allow their residents passes. We are concern about you Miss Jones. Do you have any siblings?"

I started wondering and feeling a little concern about myself too with these questions. Quietly not knowing where this is going. I said, "Yes. I have one sister and a brother but he has a different mother even though he has a different mother he is still very much my brother in my book."

Mr. Winlesky said "Miss Jones we think you're becoming institutionalize. As you are aware Thanksgiving is right around the corner. Miss Jones, I'm asking; do you think it possible you can spend this holiday with any of your relatives?"

I told them, "My children' father has always made it very difficult for me to visit my children since he been awarded the custodian parent. Somehow he has planted a picture of homelessness in their young minds as being unworthiness and it's a disgrace especially being, I been homeless for such a long time. Therefore, he shows me no respect and causes situation with me when I like to see my kids. He uses and plant my unemployment and homelessness as a clutch in order for my young kids to give him their totally respect of everything he does is right and that I was wrong. That I don't deserve to be respected. Because he's the adult showing them he's the parent who is responsible and that they have to listen to him being that they live underneath his' roof. It's like, he uses my situation as a clutch to gain their total control and reasons for me to be disrespected as a mother. I heard him say to my kids quite a few times when either one of them try to stand up to him and defend me "You can go and live in the street like her." Which my kids don't want to do so therefore they listen to whatever he says. He outwardly show and tells our children that I'm a disgrace by his actions of how he treats and talk to me and about me all the time. Its plants in their young minds I'm not worthy of their respect as a mother therefore they listen to any other adult more than me. Or he's hoping that's how they feel. He won't even allow me to speak to them on this house telephone. If I'm on the telephone and, is in the middle of a sentence especially, with my youngest daughter who is now in special Ed from his lack of supervisions. When he hears my voice on the other end or sees she on the phone, he always will abruptly interrupt our conversation by snatching the phone away from her, and say to me in front of her "You know you not supposed to call this house," and hang the phone up on me which, that is not true. There is no court order in effect for him to say or behave in that way. Due to his actions I can't even tell you how many cellphones I brought my young children since I have been homeless. He just took my parental rights away, by dis-including me with the knowledge of their personal records such as, their health records, their educational status and sometimes their whereabouts. So with an attitude like his, I cannot spend the holiday in his' home-with my children. Even though he is a homeowner I'm not even allow inside.

Since the family court gave him my kids I have always had a hard time just seeing them."

Then I said, "Remember when my mother took me out from the shelter that day-to her' home. Dave who is my mother' husband started to express how he wanted me out from their home. His expressing turned into him arguing how he doesn't want me there. By me, the cops got called a couple of times because by Dave wanting me to leave, but my mother insisting she wants me to stay, therefore, Dave became abusive and started doing stupid things to me, like locking my clothes in the backyard shed and removing the bedroom door where I slept-from off its hinges. The cops told him if they get another call from me about him harassing me that he's going to get arrested because I was invited into the home by his wife. If he wanted me out! He was told he would have to go to the housing court, which he did, but being I was already there for exactly 30 days it wasn't so easy for him by the court to just kick me out into the street. Then one day out from the blue he violently attacked me without saying a word as I was coming down the house staircase, from the bedroom where I slept-that's located on the second floor in their duplex home. Dave, he was standing at the bottom of the steps. I thought he was waiting from me to come down the steps so he came then proceed and go up the steps. As I got closer towards the bottom of the steps, surprised, he violently swung and I got poked in my forehead with an object by him. From the impact of his swing and whatever he poked me with cause me to fall quickly backward onto the steps as I let out a scream. It was an automatic reflect for me to grab my forehead from the sudden blow. I felt something warm coming down my face. So when I moved my hand out in front of me I saw the blood and it's dripping from my forehead now onto my hand. Dave, he was standing there by me at close range as I sat on the steps in shock and total disbelief that he hit me as I'm now watching the dripping blood drip into my hand. When I stood up, that when I saw a large video camcorder go up in the air that was in his hand, and before I knew it! He was swinging hitting me repeatedly all upside my head. Banging me with the hand that held the video camcorder before I could get from off the steps. I tried to move away from the narrow staircase but I was blocked in a way by his body as he was just swinging hitting me repeatedly with his video camcorder. Hitting me, slamming me all upside my head with this video camcorder. Somehow I moved away from the steps while he was still purposely hitting me wildly slamming that video camcorder all in the back of my head, and on the side by my ear as well as on top of my head." As I was remembering this whole ordeal by speaking about it -they all sat quietly listening.

Continuing I said, "When I got away from the steps he was hitting me so fast repeatedly and when I came out of the shock of what he was doing to me because it happens so fast and, he was hitting me so fast. He was holding me with the grip of one hand while viciously swinging his other long arm in the air coming down on my head hitting me so much and so hard with his large light grey video camcorder. Until he broke the got dam video camcorder in pieces **and** he was still hitting me with the piece that were in his hand breaking it all up, upside on my head like a mad man. Like hitting me all upside my head from the back and the sides, my first instinct was, fuck that, I had to fight back. Which I did but he kept banging me so fast while grabbing hold to my long braids in the back of my head holding on to me while with this video camcorder viciously banging me until it smashes all into pieces and there was nothing left. Then he grabs my long extension braids and started bashing my head up against the wall. Somehow we both fell on the floor. I figure to get him to stop hitting on me I tried to play like I was unconscious. Hoping he stop hitting me but, he **didn't**."

I told them "While I was lying down on the floor pretending to be unconscious he fell down on me like they do in wrestling. He kept falling down on top of my body with his pointed elbow, exactly like how they do on a wrestling match. Then he stood over me. Watching me as I laid there. Then he bends down took one of my hands and bend my fingers all the way back. I lay on the floor stun at what he was doing. Then he started kicking me with his foot in my chest and stomping me until I couldn't take it anymore. I jump up **fighting back!**"

Mr. Winlesky stop me from talking. He asked me "And where was your mother while all this was going on?"

I said, "The last I saw and heard from my mother just before I came down the steps she was in her bedroom on the telephone talking to my father. I was wondering why my mother didn't come downstairs knowing this man is beating on me like this. When she finally did come down the steps. She started hitting on me too like her jump in but then, she left quickly. For me this was totally unbelievable............By now Dave and I are fighting were at the tip of the stairs that leads towards their front door just fighting. He trying to push me down the step to kick me out of the front door but I switch my body around trying to throw him down the steps. Both of us were at the tip of the steps leading toward the front door trying to throw each other down the steps, but somehow we both fell into the other part of the house while violently fist fighting. While on the floor I grab a hold of his penis and both balls and I tried to twist **it off!**"

They still listening, as I'm telling whatz happening while shaking my head as I remember what took place that awful night....... **And,** truly feeling embarrass because this is **my mother** and **her' husband** I'm talking about. The man my mother brought into our home telling my sister and I to give him much respect -doing all this shit too me.

I told them, "He had to have it plan because from underneath the couch he pulled out a **hammer** from

nowhere! When I saw the silver hammer head go up in the air as he violently swung. He was swinging but he missed every time, because **God had to be** with me. To make a long story short. Dave went into **a rage**. To get away from him and not wanting to get hit with the hammer I ran upstairs into the bedroom where I was staying at. He was swinging that hammer trying to hit me in my head. In all honesty I should had ran out of the house but I was in the shelter for so long I just wanted to stay in the house. When I ran up the step. I didn't see my mother. **AND** her' bedroom door was close. I immediately ran into the open door which was the bedroom where I slept. Quickly closing the door and putting my body up against the now close bedroom door looking for something, **anything** to protect myself with. I really thought I was going to die. Frantically! With my eyes I'm searching the bedroom for anything to protect myself with because I knew he wanted to kill me. But then my mother she finally did something. Thank God because my mother she saved my life that night, by screaming so loud **"DAVEEEEEEEEE you going to kill HERR!** And that what she **WANTS! THINK** man **think!"**

I continue speaking telling them, "I was still searching the bedroom. Looking with my eyes while my body was up against the close door for something, anything to protect myself with. I saw the window but I wouldn't jump out the window because I was on the second floor. I guess my mother screamed so loud because she was hoping her' neighbors or anyone will call the cops. Then he ran after her, in a rage because I heard my mother loud voice saying, "Man what you going to do **kill me now!"**

"While he ran toward my mother. Quickly from my cell phone I called the cops telling them I was assaulted. That he tried to hit me in the head with a hammer. When I knew the cops were on their way I fuck up their house by destroying the 1st thing I saw which was the bathroom. Because I was mad at Dave for hitting on me like that while they were inside their bedroom with the door closed. I guess he was coming back to his senses. I don't know but I was mad at my mother too because I originally asked her to let me stay at her parents' home in Brownsville especially when I saw Dave getting mad because I was there. I kept telling my mother "Let me stay at the house in Brownsville," I told this group of people.

"When the many cops finally came. They asked "Where is the weapon?" I told them, "I don't know where he put it but I describe how it looked. The cops found the hammer downstairs in the closet and Pete got arrested. Ems took me to the hospital which I didn't stay long because I left. When I got back to my mother house she wasn't home so I waited in her front yard where she parks her car. I'm thinking her at the precinct with her' husband. Late in the night when she finally reached home and saw me sitting inside the gate outside on the step in front of her house. She took one look and drove away. All my id cards is in her house. My clothes-everything. She just left. I was so fucking mad. I know I didn't want to come back to the shelter but she should have just talked to me. Maybe she was scared because she never saw me fight like that. Or knowing she allowed her husband to beat the cramp out of me without her helping me or stopping it or jumping in on him. I don't know what she was thinking, all I know she was wrong to just leave me outside like that. Especially knowing that all of this could had been prevented. I believe all this could have been prevented because my mother is also a co-owner of another piece of property. The other piece of property is her parents' home-a 2 family house with an unfurnished basement that's fully paid for. By now sadly both her parents had passed away. Originally, that where I asked where I can live at in the first beginning-my grandfather house. It's where most of my cousins are living **rent free**. Instead my mother brought me from the shelter to live there with her and her' husband in their duplex home. I'm thinking she set me up because within a couple of weeks after me living with her and Dave, he started doing things to get me out of their duplex home. So I keep telling my mother let me live in granddaddy house because he's your father, and both your parents are dead. My cousins they been living in that house since 1960 something. My grandparents brought the house in the early 1960 I believe. The house is run down and is in need of repairs. Only thing my mom had to do was let me live there, but she didn't because the family, my family want to sell it once they found out I needed a place to live. So that where the problem stemming from with my mother other piece of property and my mom probably don't want to see me go over there because me and my cousins already been fist fighting too lately. Especially when Grandmamma allowed me to come and live inside the house. We been fighting because I wanted in, and my cousins they wanted me out. My cousins didn't want to see me live there therefore my cousins were finding all kinds of reasons to keep me **out**. My cousin Lee Keisha who is the other co-owner of this house said, "I sell it before I see you move in," I told this group of people.

As they listen I told them, "My cousin Lee Keisha who has always been living upstairs she keeps saying out loud that she pays all the bills for granddaddy house. Lee Keisha is lairing because I heard she only have to pay for the house taxes at the end of the year. Grandmamma pays for the oil for the house and her bills downstairs. So what kind of bills is Lee Keisha paying? Briefly when I did stay there I offered Lee Keisha to help her pay the bills for the house, but she never wanted to show me an expense that she had to pay. My other grown cousin I know don't pay for **shit**, because he never had a job. He don't work! I can't understand why my 2 cousins didn't want to see me living there, when they been living there all their lives, knowing I been living inside these shelter and neither one of them **brought that house. Granddaddy brought that house.** It's his' house! I know for years' no one paid the light bill for the house because the lights for the house got somehow hook up to the street light pole outside. After staying in shelters, so long, when my cousins wouldn't let me in I threaten to tell Con Edison when they were fighting with me and wouldn't let me in, but those bitches went and got the light put on legally for the house. But what piss me off about the family so called house-is granddaddy left several thousands of dollar in the bank after his death for it maintaining and up keep but the house is torn down from the floor up! So in reality my cousins who are living there **aren't paying shit!** While living there briefly I found out that my mother took the money my grandfather put away for the house maintenance that she used the money, to pay for re-wiring the electricity for the house also fixing the concrete in front of the house **AND** their hefty water bill. They all can stay, party, have cook outs and live up in the house when anyone of them get good and ready! For the life of me, I can't understand how my cousin Lee Keisha, who is the baby in her family have just the same amount of privileges' and rights as my mother as in who gets to stay in her parents' home. All my mom kept saying when it comes to her parents' home is her hands are tied. So now, the story with the house is, it's in process of being sold. Before my mother brought me into her duplex home I asked my mother can I at least stay there until the house in Brownsville get sold pointing out there is plenty room there for me to stay. I pointed out to her at least I would have my own privacy with a key to any one of the house large rooms downstairs where her parents lived before they died. I explained to her I can come and go as I please and have a place where I can allow my kids to stay the night. I told her anyway when you look at it after all, that's all the shelter is offering me anyway, is an SRO, a shared room. So I'm pretty dam mad at my mom right now, especially knowing I could had stayed at my grandfather house where she paying the majority of the house bills with the money granddaddy left behind for her niece and nephew. So I wanted to hurt her like how she been hurting me, so on purpose I slept in front of her house on the ground for all her' neighbors to see, this is how she treat her flesh and blood as she walks around here like she this Godly woman, wearing a white usher uniform every Sunday going off to church and paying her tithes. I slept on the ground in front of her door while blocking her tenant entrance to their' front door, in the cold for three days," I told them.

As I spoke the people in the room seemed to be speechless because everyone is so quiet. So I said "After 3 or 4 days of me sleeping outside the cops told me I had to get off the property because my mother has obtained and got an order of protection against me saying that I beat her 71-year-old husband up. By the cops I was told that I'm no longer allow on the premises and to get what I can carrying. For me to leave or I will get arrested. Then sometime after that I'm told by a shelter employee my mother has something for me downstairs. I didn't even want to go but the shelter employee made me go downstairs. She shows up with paper wanting me to know and understand the judge made the order to be in effect for 5 years! I was so hurt when I saw my mother show up at the shelter that I didn't even want to even see the sight of my mother, and for the 1st time in my life, I'm started thinking **she sick**. So for the holiday I can't go inside my mother house," I finally told this group of people.

Mr. Ron Winlesky said "This is the holidays what about your father? I said, "I just recently found out he re-married and I wasn't even invited to his ceremony either or made aware of it."

He asked "Do you know your father telephone number?" "Yes I do," I replied.

Miss Taylor asked, "Would you mind if I speak with him." I told her, "I don't mine."

"Electra in order for me to speak to your father you must fill out this permission slip allowing me to speak to him," she said. Miss Taylor she passes me the form. After reading it I signed it.

While Miss Taylor dialed the number. Mrs. Stewart put her hand on my knee saying, "I'm so sorry to hear what had happen when you left out the shelter with your mother. She seems to be such a nice woman when I place the set up kit in the trunk of her' car we give our residents when they move out. I know....Electra, you didn't want to come back here but thank God in America we are here for people like yourself."

Mr. Ron Winlesky asked "How long where you gone for." I said, "About 1 month and 3 days."

"Hello I'm Miss Taylor a case worker at Bridge Net women shelter. I would like to speak to a Mr. Ed Jones. Oh, hello Mr. Jones I'm calling on behalf of your daughter Electra. As you are aware your daughter has been in Bridge Net for the last 5 years and counting. Overall she had been in the shelter system over 9 years. And still counting. I'm calling to ask you would it be possible for your' daughter to visit you in your home to spend Thanksgiving with you and your family. We are willing to give her a metro card in hope of her spending quality time with a family member," Miss Taylor asked.

Then suddenly!

Miss Taylor looked at Ron Winlesky as she cover the receiver. She whispers, "He said no!"

Mr. Winlesky, uncrossed his' leg and moved my binder off his' lap putting it on the table. He was astound to hear what Miss Taylor whisper to him. He immediately said "Pass me the phone."

"Hello. I'm Mr. Ron Winlesky Director of Bridge Net women shelter. Mr. Jones your daughter has been in the shelter system over 9 years and according to my records she had not had a late pass. An overnight or a weekend pass. I'm concern about her mental health of becoming institutionalize. From what I could tell she a lovely young lady. Could you find it possible in your' heart to allow your daughter at least a couple of hour in your presence for the holiday giving her the chance to leave this place," he pleaded.

Oh man I felt so bad watching and hearing them go to bat for me with my father. Then bringing up those personal fuck up secret memories about me and my family situations. Especially being he's a white man too! I was so humiliated because honestly......I am a decent person-who just waiting for my housing to come though.

Well. I spend another Thanksgiving inside the shelter. Mr. Winlesky was so stun to hear and witness for his self what just took place, because he know, I'm good people. He is quite aware of the women personality and character in this shelter. He and his' staff has monthly meetings about us who lives here in this place. He knows if we lose our bed and why. He knows who work and who don't. In this shelter he as a director made it his' business to know everything. Including how many times we left the dorm late.

Anyway Mr. Winlesky asked me "Is there any concerns you have, Miss Jones?"

I told him, "Yes. I have a neighbor who don't speak to anyone in the dorm. She always imitating what I do as far as my living arrangement. For instance, if I put up a green picture on top of my locker. She buy a green object and place it on top of her' locker. If I put a wooden frame up on the locker. She bring in wooden branches from the street and place it on top of her' locker."

Mr. Winlesky said "It sound like the highest form of flattery."

I said, "Well someone told me her practicing voodoo. That she was caught praying in a strange way and counting beads early in the morning before the guard turns on the light. Having someone copy off what I do is flattery, but too me, it becomes a bit too much and offensive when it's becoming EVERYTING I do. It makes me feel uncomfortable like I'm being watch under a microscope by her and she won't even speak to me. If it's so much flattery why won't see speak to me? Anyway I caught her early in the morning doing that weird praying and it did look awkward. Now that I know about, I'm up early in the morning, peeping, watching her like around 4am. And **I'm** surprise to see she does this every morning. I feel like her religion and her flattery is a threat to me. I just don't like it and I want it to stop."

Stop! To the reader: Sum it up her was deported back to her' country and the dorm always had toilet tissue after her' departure. I went downstairs to finish writing what had happened after the court had gave Thomas custody of our 2 kids.

I have one question, if drugs were found in my urine why wasn't all my children removed that day. I tell you why....because it was a big fat lie. I don't know how drugs was found because I never did drugs to that extent for my children to have been remove out of my care but I did do that outpatient rehabilitation. My urine was tested weekly. I was told my result were negative from every test. **From one dirty urine test** of positive finding, my kids was permanently removed. Your court system is **fuck up** from the floor up. For all I care Thomas planted it on me because he the person spreading this gossip to everyone who listen.

Continuing with church, I still had faith on the inside in the mist of all my misery that I will regain my parental custody back. I wasn't giving in to losing my kids. My kids they are my family, my diamonds and my pearls. They mean everything to me plus after all I gave of myself to raise them. I was determine to get them back! I was doing all the things the family court/ACS wanted and ask of me to do. People/especially my family couldn't understand my behavior. I was really mad with the way things had turned out. When the test came back positive for drugs why wasn't

Champagne removed too......that day in the court house? My mind was confused and my heart hurt but God said to the devil "You can't have her."

Like Mary, Mary said in her song: But what they don't know is when I get home and get behind close door then I hit the floor and what you can't see is I'm on my knee so the next time you ask I say it the God in me.

Meaning I'm a praying mother because that's all I had.

I received my letter from the government asking me to meet the requirements of the new reform back to work program. Under the WEP program I got a job as a security guard. For over a year working at different locations which this was new to in my community because this type of job was held by men not women, but the times, had changed. Then the security company put me on a permanent location at JFK airport.

I kept my end of the bargain with the family court, with my parental visitations rights. I pick up my young kids every Friday and had them back to Thomas by Sunday. By me wanting to fight Thomas and the family court system for them to redo what they did. I submitted a petition with family court requesting that my 2 children be return back into my care as their custodian parent. Which, after submitting any petition is a process with the family court house. In a couple of months, by the time the family court sent out their investigator to my home I had lost the job with JFK airport because TSA has taken over the security position for the airport. I didn't pass TSA test to remain on as a security guard therefore I was fired.

After I had gotten a paying job with the security company, my potion of rent from section eight got increased therefore I could no longer pay that amount, nor did I get another paying job right away either. I still had to pay that require amount of rent until section eight changed how much I now needed to pay which cause me to get back up in my rent.

Being I got fired, now I had to re- applied for Welfare to pay the rent, and I was facing eviction. Now as a new applicant applying for welfare and showing I no longer work, and I needed their assistance in paying my rent, as well as my back rent owe, also I need help with my financial needs of supplying food for the house while I'm in this transition stage of my life.

Once I showed the welfare caseworker my proof of where I live by submitting a copy of my lease. Supplied the amount of back rent I owed and the address to whom the money need to go to as well as my proof of being on the section eight program, showing my rent now need to be adjusted, submitted my personal id of who I am, my bank account statement showing I have no saving account, birth certificates and social security cards of who lives inside the apartment with me. Once the caseworker received all that information I was told by the welfare caseworker that I have to complied now with the welfare new reform program by submitting her a work schedule from WEP.

When I re-applied I had to work immediately with the WEP program in order to keep my welfare case active with supplying me and my family with their food stamps the government through the welfare system was giving me and in order for the system to pay my rent as well as the back rent I owed. My application applying for welfare was completed. All I had to do now is comply with the WEP program and wait 45 days to pick up my government allowance. I was told from the social service of welfare that my rent, as well as the back rent owed will be paid.

The WEP program told people like mothers who been in the house for a long length of time to use what we did in the house for skills. So along with the security job duties I performed I also put down skills for filing, answering the telephone and cleaning. From the WEP program I was placed to start working inside the office of a nursing home.

By the time the court investigator came out to my home what she found was empty cabinets in my kitchen due to me recently just becoming unemployed and my welfare hasn't come in yet due to me being in the pending allotment status waiting period of 45 days. Therefore, I had no money and no food by the time the court investigator came to my apartment. So the investigator took me and Champagne food shopping as some of my neighbors in my neighborhood watched. Now the family court investigator wanted to know if my daughter can stay with a family member being I had no food in the house until 45 days.

At that point I knew I lost the fight of getting back my other 2 children with the court. For some reason my mother wouldn't take in my daughter Champagne in her new 2 family duplex home. I think Dave didn't want my daughter staying there.

Once Dave got married to my mom and they became home owners he **changed**, meaning he didn't want family members staying in their home. We never knew who Dave family was. So in other words what Dave is really saying, my mother can take care of foster kids who is other people kids but Dave didn't want my mother family coming in and staying inside their home. Which means, Dave really meant-me and Tonya and our kids. But in reality and not knowing back then, really, it something about **ME** who Dave didn't want to see inside their home. Being my mother wouldn't take my daughter in her home she told me she would speak to Tonya my sister who I haven't been close too since I left the projects. My mother told me she will ask her if she could help me out with Champagne. The next day, surprisingly Tonya calling my name loudly outside by my bedroom window. When I go down stairs she tells me mommy told her whatz going on with me and Champagne. That until I get this resolved Champagne can come live with her and her family. I had no other choice because I had to tell the family court investigator, I had placement for

Champagne, or the family court investigator was sending her off to a group home!

That Friday when Champagne went with my sister so I panicked thinking now I'm going to lose my 3-bedroom apartment with section eight because I don't have all of my kids on my budget anymore. So I figure if I go to a shelter I can turn my 3-bedroom voucher into a 2-bedroom voucher from section eight, because at this time section eight didn't have an address.

When I went to the shelter that night. I was surprise to find out I have to go to a women shelter because after all it was just me. So I was told where I can find a women shelter. I was sent to Franklin Shelter in the Bronx. I came back to Brooklyn checking my mail that Saturday. But Monday morning, I found a letter attach to my door that my oldest daughter got place in foster care reason why......... I abandon her. When I called the foster care agency I was told she in the system and there nothing at this point I can do because I wasn't reachable. I went to the shelter that Friday by the following Monday when I got to my apartment door Champagne was already placed inside the foster care system. **Unfuckinbelievable!**

How the hell that shit happen when I left her temporary with **Tonya!** Therefore, my sister she had to have set me up. I see that dream or vision I had-wolves in sheep clothing did take away my children. I couldn't even reach the family court investigator who asked me in the 1st place can my daughter stay with family. Even though this time I rush out to the shelter I still had an apartment. Maybe I shouldn't had done it, but a person does stupid or not thought out things when under such pressure, young and alone and unknowledgeable. And my children are just being taken away from me I'm upset and so I panicked. Or, maybe did I sense what was about to come?

Well when it rains-it pours. Once I seen what happen to Champagne I left that shelter because I still had my apartment. The weekend is approaching therefore I was getting ready for my scheduled weekend visited with my 2 younger kids. It too was on a Friday. I think it was that 3rd Friday after Champagne was removed. I just went groceries shopping as I walked up the steps in my building, I saw not familiar faces of guys coming down the step with apartment' stuff. As I walked up I figure someone must be moving in because outside in the front of the building was a medium size truck.

As I was walking going upstairs to my 3-bedroom apt. I'm looking at the guys carrying apt stuff down the steps and I'm thinking out loud, "Wow someone has the same exercise equipment just like me and it even have the same dirty spot just like mines." When I reach my apartment door, it was ajar? What this all about? I opened the door wider and saw the Caribbean super of the building standing with his' hand out asking for the key. I got evicted and my apartment was completely **clean out!**

This is crazy!

I'm confused because I kept my end of the bargain with the welfare. I submitted my application and gave in all documentations. I did my required WEP hours in that nursing home and I did my required WEP hours by cleaning that huge Park.

I was told by my mgmt. that they never received the check from welfare. Unbelievable!

My first adult female shelter was 68 Lexington. It was filthy. The beds were horrible and the flies use to stick to your body from the hot heat. At this time there was no air condition inside shelters. All we had was a large dusty dirty fan that blew dust in the air. At 68 Lex, the director over there wasn't so informed to who all lived there and who is employed, and who is not employed because he didn't care. That's one of the reasons the shelter that he ran was so dirty and filthy. He could have spoken up to the city about our living conditions. Oh! By the way did I tell you he was

Haitian. From another country with a high power position like that. At 68 Lex we girls were mainly all Americans just like at Bridge Net.

Anyway, that the first time I ever knew so many women were gay. I never knew there were so many gay girls in this world. Then the aggressive girls who looked and acted like boys.......... and regular girls, I knew in the shelter that were gay-lots pop up pregnant. Unbelievable!

So I came to realize not only are there gay girls but also bisexual girls. That's when the shelter system was raw and maintenance didn't clean and anything goes -I had got into a lot of heated arguments and some had turn into fights. I see girls/people, do a lot of dirty shit to others that I never imagine another human being doing towards another person. I'm speaking from things I seen and witness in my time of homelessness and again I'm speaking from my own experiences.

68 Lexington had this church ministry that visit that shelter. I attended. When asked to sing, which to start out their ministry, my favorite song to sing was Blessed Assurance which I requested for us to sing all the time. This outreach ministry wanted us resident to think about our future saying this shelter is not the end of our life. They were inspiring us to do more like learn a trade or go back to school. My spirit and mind was in no way willing to go back into any form of educational classes, courses, or schools, because I been to some many schools, training programs so much already. I was just school out!

It was only through a lady from this church outreach that came to bring personal growth and awareness exercises to us girls at 68 Lexington who constant talk-of where do we see our self in the future and by pushing me, because I was really low in spirit. She got me to check out this computer training course. I was totally reluctant not wanting anything more to do with education. I think the only reason she got me interest in checking it out was because she pointed out computers is our future everything would be run by a computer. That I needed to understand and learn how to operate a computer. Which too was a **New Thing** for everyone -**Computers**.

She keeps talking to me and pushing me to want to do more with my life. But I was so low in spirit but eventually, I check out the program. I enroll myself in this computer program course that was being offered by the Bowery Mission and that when I found out. **I was a home owner!**

I found my name attach to an already paid for 2 family house. A legal document of some sort saying ownership of survivor *between myself*....... and my cousin Coon? Wow! Apparently it was left to us by our blind Grandfather. **Granddaddy!** My name has been on the deed since I was the age of eighteen. I almost fell out my seat. **Unbelievable!**

What so dam funny about it was when I found out I owned a 2 family house. I also found out, I sold that 2 family house. To my MOTHER and my cousin LEE KEISHA! **Unbelievable!**

According to the deed in the municipal building, Granddaddy at some point had left the house to me and my cousin Coon. That explain when Grandmamma allowed me to live there briefly how I stumble upon an envelope with my name appeared on the house insurance. When I question my family and my mother whatz this about? No one told me the truth. In the municipal building it shows I and Coon had gone to a lawyer along with my mother and Lee Keisha and that the transaction of trading ownership among us 4 took place. Legal documents showing me and Coon with signed signatures sold the house to my mother and his' sister.... Lee Keisha. Unbelievable!

At one point after being homeless for so long, and living and working at 68 Lex when this uncovered bit of information of (inheriting) was acknowledge too me I did try to stay at my Grandparent's house. Then, **especially** after finding out this bit of information of (inheriting) and without their knowledge of me knowing about this uncovered bit of information I knocked on the door repeatedly, again and again needing a place to stay and wanting to reunite with my children.

Grandmamma she was the only grandparent living to see me go through all that I went though. I couldn't understand why my cousins were fighting me so much when my disabled grandmother allowed me to come live inside the house. And only **then** that's when I realized Grandmamma was being abused by my cousin who never **WORKED!** Even thought my family said she wasn't I didn't see it like that! Because I was the one who lived with her downstairs briefly. My family they all have been lying to me and maybe that's one of the reason I became the black sheep in the family because of their greed and jealousy. The house is all fuck up from the floor up! At 1st I didn't understand how Lee Keisha (my cousins, my **mother' niece**) had the same or more privileges in the say so of my mother' parent home, but now I do. Eventually I found out the answer to my always asked question.

But what really got me too, was how the fuck did they sell that house with fake signatures. I never went with them to a lawyer with the knowledge that this house is mines. And I am selling this inherit property to these people-my mother and Lee Keisha. In the year 2011 or 2012 my mother and Lee Keisha did sell granddaddy house. **Unbelievable!**

Majority of my family goes to some form of church now. Some are members and attend service every Sunday but they aren't true believers of God because the God I know is good and kind, supported, trustworthy, loyal and have enough love for us all that he sent his one and only son to die for us that we may have everlasting life. God is love and my family dam sure didn't show me love or tell me the truth to something I should had knowledge of. So therefore God still have a lot of work to do in their' life. Just for me to find out the way how I did was a lot to absorb. And to think once

I had owned that house that I loved so much because of all the memories it held in my heart of time spent with my family. Well my cousins, my mother, sister and aunt Melody could just go to hell now and take their jealousy with **them!** Then on top of that my cousins wanted to stand in my shoes with my sister children playing like they are their so call aunt, while my sister just sat back and allowed this masquerade to go on. All along me and my kids just got disowned now separated and **Destroyed!** Well, all I got to say I never knew I was so hated by the people I claimed to love. You know how the saying goes! If it don't come out in the wash. It got to come out in the dryer. I'm just glad that now I know the truth. I never knew how low a person will go just to destroy another one dreams or joy, any form of happiness or wealth until I came to live inside a **gotdam** woman shelter. To me it so utterly **Unbelievable!**

I lost my kids, things I cherish, my family pictures, Grandma-Grace coat and her photo album, my beauty, my smile, no kind of a sociable life, my freedom, my youth and vitality for living. I have changed unbelievably from that person I use to be. I never got raise my children because all 3 of them was taken from me. Thomas never give me one school picture or informed me when my kids were taking their school pictures. I never got to teach my kids all the wonderful things I wanted them to know and feel about life, about love and family, all of this because of a fucking house. Instead any and everybody thought they could do a better job than me in raising my kids especially those **foreigners people who come from other countries!**

Anyway to me this is so sad and I'm bloody mad and every day I wake up alone.

Reader, remember Lacy? Well she finally got housing. I heard she been homeless for a very long time too. Anyway the day she was going to her apt/SRO to finally get her' keys, she sat in the dining room which is something she never did. So excited with just the thought of her leaving this place she looking out the window waiting to hear her caseworker say "**Come on** Lacy, the van is here to take you to your designation." By the time the caseworker calls her name and she didn't respond. The case worker tap her on her' shoulder because the caseworker through she was just glazing looking out from the window like so many of us residents do all the time. Anyway the caseworker made the gruesome discovery and some girls like me screamed, "**NOOO!**"

So excited and thrill she finally leaving the shelter well sadly she had a heart attack and died. Unbelievable!

Reader, remember Vivian? Thomas niece who didn't go back to Jamaica when she was supposed to. Well she got marry to a Black American like myself. Now she can legally stay in America. Unbelievable.

As for Karl well I found out someone shoot him in the head. Isn't it weird-they all had head injuries meaning Karl and the young boys' dogs getting their' heads bite off? Sometimes as I write, I wonder - that lady who vanishes-was...... or could *she* had been my guarding angel who was with me and granted me my wish. Remember what I said that night when I held my keys tightly in my hand ready so I can jab Karl' dog eyes out. I said, "I'll going bite his **fuckin head off!**" I mean, it's kind of twisted, but nevertheless, it is something to think about. Still I find it totally Unbelievable.

I see how the welfare system changed. I see how housing had changed. I see how families changed. I see how men and woman relationships has changed. I see how the government changed towards single mother raising children on the system. I see how the system invented the name deadbeat dad and inputted mandatory child support and shared parents' visitations rights. It's either pay-up guys or jail. I see how NYCHA, New York City Housing Authority, known as the projects, **has changed**. Now I see how the shelter system has changed in a lot of ways. I remember when there was nothing but despair. When young girls as young as 18 came to live inside a dirty shelter. I see women as old as 71 come to live in a shelter. Last I seen now men-living inside a women shelter. Transgender they call their' self. Now there's talk…. for men to live inside the women shelter-they have to go through the procedure of clip-clip, because lots of females feel they are not women with their male parts still attach………. Un-be-lievable!

As for me now I receive SSI and SSD. How this came about was over a laundry slot of being 3 minutes late. The Spanish security guard Dumez had denied my privilege and gave my laundry slot to someone else. Upset I went to the West Indian shift supervisor Mrs stink ass Wilks to report what happen. When the Caribbean shift supervisor came to the laundry room. The guard told her I was late and that another resident needed to wash and she saw an open machine and the guard gave it to her.

Then all nasty, shift supervisor Wilks yelled at me told me to "Wash tomorrow!"

Which made me angry. I was pretty dam upset especially all my clothes was dirty and I followed the procedures in order to wash my clothes. So I express how I felt by telling them, "Yall constantly changing rules! I think yall so stupid. How you going to deny my wash and my name in the fucking book and I'm here ready to wash assholes!"

By the shift supervisor I was told to exit the building and that I can't come back inside the building till 8pm. Once my wash was unfairly revolted. Then I see I'm not getting housed. I haven't had sex. I don't see my kids. My family living in my so-call fuckin house. I got to leave the dorm every day at 9 am when others residents not doing the same because security playing favoritism. I got to be sitting on my clot every night by ten pm. I don't have any privacy. I don't have any girlfriends. I'm not living the life I thought I'm supposed to be, so I just got fed-up with the bullshit, and I refuse to leave the building, especially, I have to do…. **What?** Walk around till 8pm. So I told them all, "When yall dumb ass people go outside I hope you get hit by a fuckin bus!"

I thought they were calling the cops to have me removed from the shelter because I wasn't leaving instead Ems got call saying they wanted me to go to the hospital to get check out. So I got confide in the L dorm because it was the closest dorm to the laundry-room. Surprisingly I was sent to the psyche ward. After telling the psychiatrist my side of the story. The Indian male psychiatrist told me "It sound like you need a break from the shelter."

So he committed me. With me not knowing what the word committed means so when I got into the psych ward I had to take meds and I just couldn't walk out. So when I tried, I realize the **doors was locked**. I see I was being held against my will so I cursed out the fucking West Indian nurse. I said what I had to say and then quietly I sat in my room piss **the fuck off**. Then the next thing I know the hospital police showed up at my room door. They jump me, held me down while the nurse pulls down my pants as the nurse jab me in my big ass with a needle.

I didn't know they can do that to an individual, but they can and **they did**, because it happened to me. And some of the things I witness while being force to take their medication because I was told it's the only way out. Was totally unbelievable and I was totally speechless.

Then the ultimate thing happens to me. **I turned against God**. I was mad because I believed in the spirit and worship it. I gave up some much in his' name. Sex, doing the right thing by going to church faithfully, ushering every Sunday, joining the choir and leaving my troubles at the altar-like on Calvary. Praying for the things I want. Treat those the way I want to be treated and forgiveness to those who I really don't feel should have my forgiveness but because in the bible, God said he is the avenger. All I got was misery after embarrassment and more misery. I lost **everything I owed**. I found myself saying and asking him, "why! Why! **Why!**"

I got kick out from Bridge Net. I got transfer to Next Step. Now I don't care anymore because the shelter not getting me an apartment anyway. With my SSI check I still can't afford to pay the high rent. What the sense in being in bed by ten and sleep by 11pm. I started going back and forth to Atlantic City. Riding the shelter bus being transfer from one shelter to the next.

I lived at 68 Lexington, Bridge Net, Samuel House, Madison Place, Tillers, Salvation, Franklin and Catherine Street. Not to forget umpteen late bus rides as an overnighter when a shelter didn't have a bed for me to sleep. From shelter to shelters. Dorm to dorms and bed to beds **"Fuck Yall!"**

Since being homeless I don't feel pretty anymore. My hair not sandy brown anymore nor do I have a nice texture of hair. My heart is black. My hair now is kinky and I feel totally unattractive. Hate can change a person features without even knowing. Now living inside the shelter I'm placed in a different category. I'm no more under general population. My new category is MICA. I finally got housing after having to take psyche meds. A studio. I'm in the Bronx living in this brand new building. With nothing but Spanish people. Everybody else is Spanish or from some other country. Even though I got mad at God and I may don't go to church like I use to. My journey it wasn't in vain because what I learn was a lot. I learned a lot about my family and the world. Not to mention the words.... homelessness, a shelter, SRO, abuse, being committed, jealousy, envy, secrets, greed, prejudice, straight, bi, transgender, child molestation, different in cultures, my culture, love, corruption, religion, the power of prayer, family, deception, spirits, and....... Truth.

For such a beautiful pretty girl who has lived out in the street for so very, very long who has lost EVERYTHING that she has ever own. My oldest daughter once told me, "Mommy you my role model." My son said "I'm his hero." As for my youngest daughter well, I'm just her' Mommy. Then **the hate** has step in. I just like to say if I find out my children were abuse, and I will find out. I will find you and if anything is wrong I will kill **YOU!** I will find you and I will kill you! As you can see, I will always have them to think about.

P.S.Granddaddy I figure out what you were saying "I love you." "I love you too Granddaddy rest in peace."

This paragraph it for me, you know why, because today is my birthday and this book is my birthday present I'm gave to myself. You should know my slogan by now: behind every negative situation you got to find something positive. Writing this book show me I was never a loser. I was always a winner. I realize thru writing I just had a lot of haters and I was naïve and too trusting in a world with people who are so cruel.

Detective Salvatore asked me once, "What did you do for yourself today?"

I answered, "You won't believe this, but, I wrote a book."

Life is bitch but pay back is a mother**fucker**!

THE GREAT I AM. God spirit saying to me. It sings: He a way mak-er yes he is____. He a way mak-er yes he is____. He may not come when you want him but he be there__ on time. Cause he's a way mak er yes he is____. He on time. My God is on time. He on time. My God is right on time. He on time. My God is on time. He on time. My God is right on time. Cause he a way maker yes he is____.

Laying down I said, "What?"

The End.

About the Author

Tina Bridges was born and raised in Brooklyn, New York. My expectation about life was so simple. One thing on my agenda was to work hard for the things I wanted and needed. Another thing was I would get marry and eventually raise a family under my black heritage.

Proudly sitting in the seat as the oldest daughter of my parents, by the way, who are both born black Americans. I can say it loud. "I'm black and proud." Because of the hardship I endured, it made me become aware of cultures. That was something I never did pay any attention to growing up in an all-black American neighborhoods. Nor was I taught by my parents any kind of acknowledgement of various cultures or even my own.

About the Book

This book is about a black woman who is highly intelligent that felled upon problems that lead to much hardship. In her quest of wanting to figure out, how did this beautiful, attractive, upright woman suddenly become homeless and unloved. Electra's journey takes her as well as her readers into her past, digging for answers, while she lives in the present. Then towards her future just to discover the truth of her existence.